THE AGENCY OF THE ANCIENT LOST & FOUND OMNIBUS 1-3

JANE THORNLEY

RIVERFLOW PRESS

THE CARPET CIPHER

THE AGENCY OF THE ANCIENT LOST AND FOUND,
BOOK 1. A PHOEBE MCCABE MYSTERY THRILLER

A Phoebe McCabe Mystery Thriller

Book One

THE
CARPET
CYPHER

JANE THORNLEY

PROLOGUE

Venice, February 2019

*H*ow long had it been since she had last ventured into the Venetian streets at night—five years, ten? Too long ago, in any event, and to do so tonight of all nights, when the carnival finale was in full swing and the revelry would reach a raucous pitch, seemed foolish even for her. How she detested the noise, the crowds, even the fierce and gilded costumes that would press against her in the dark like fevered dreams. To stay home by the fire with a book and a glass of wine seemed far preferable. Still, it must be done. After tonight she would lay one matter to rest and possibly see the conclusion of another, much older mystery.

She opened the front door, hesitating briefly before leaving the safety of her palazzo and plunging into the throng, her velvet coat wrapped tightly around her to ward away the spring chill. As expected, the young people were outdoing each other with fantastic finery. Gone were the days when only the time traveler mode of long gowns and medieval costumes ruled, though plenty of those still roamed the streets. Now creative interlopers had arrived with glittery fairy wings, and was that a chicken? Yes, a chicken, complete with an enormous egg tucked under one false wing! She stifled a laugh.

Her own mask, on the other hand, was demure by comparison, a lovely sun/moon creation she had had especially made for another carnival long ago when she had been a young woman, her whole life stretching ahead. Then, the duality of light and dark had been no more than a playful game. As on that evening, she also wore the cape worked in deep blue velvet stenciled in gold stars with Mariano Fortuny's distinctive flair. Now, that subtle silken loveliness seemed to sink like a poor cousin against the surrounding sequins and gaudy trappings.

Never mind, she told herself, the man she was to meet would appreciate it for what it was: a testament to artisan beauty in a world that had long lost sight of what does not scream for attention. That she would reunite with the one with whom she had first worn the ensemble was a fitting end to their long torturous relationship. Though they had not seen one another for many decades, she prayed that he had finally forgiven her long enough to help her now. He of all people would know the significance of what she had discovered.

But first, she must resolve the other matter. There was to be no meeting at her family's weaving studio, on that point she was firm. The call had come just moments before she left the villa and her first response had been to refuse the request, but then she reconsidered. The matter could not be avoided forever and perhaps could be dealt with fairly. Her counteroffer was generous. She would make the meeting brief, citing her other appointment to excuse her haste, and hopefully the ugly matter would be laid to rest at last.

The chosen rendezvous was tucked away from the street in a corner she had reason to believe would be suitably private, close to the canal but not in the midst of the celebrations. She slipped through the press of merrymakers. At least they were good-natured and she could only hope that the person she was to meet would be in a similar mood, or at least open to compromise.

She passed a market stall now caged for the night and turned a corner to where the winter storms had damaged the street so that temporary planking now bridged the narrow side canal. Behind the repair works, tucked against the side door of an ancient church with steps leading to the canal, the meeting place offered privacy.

It was surprisingly dark, much darker than she had anticipated. Fool. Why hadn't she thought this out more carefully? Two, maybe three shapes detached themselves from the dark clot of shadows against the church door, one of them immediately recognizable, and at once she knew she had miscalculated. There would be no easy resolution, after all.

1

───────

*T*he man staring at me had been dead for over two thousand years yet still made a better companion than some of the men I'd known.

"Phoebe?"

I tore myself away from the bust to see Serena, my gallery manager and friend, arriving on my stair landing office carrying a mug of tea. The shop was closed for renovation but she had been busy storing our rare textiles while workmen banged away downstairs. Baker and Mermaid was in the midst of a metamorphosis from textile gallery to undercover art retrieval and repatriation center that we jokingly referred to as the Agency of the Ancient Lost and Found.

"So, this is what I've discovered so far," I began. "Our Roman here is a probable mid-first century A.D. funerary piece discerned because of the dark earthen encrustation on the back of the head. Dr. Rudolph confirms that assessment but has no idea where the piece might have come from. We ran it through Interpol's database but nothing." My specialty was actually textiles but no one can afford to be too narrowly focused in the art and artifact retrieval business. "Anyway, there's no trace of anything matching this description missing from any of the museums so I'm guessing it's from a looted grave."

"Phoebe."

I stopped and stared at her. "Serena?"

"You sit up here all day and many hours in the evening and work, work,

work. It is not healthy." She passed the boxes of books and personal belongings ready for storage and scanned the piles for a place to set the tea. "We thought you could use some cheering up." It took a moment to clear a spot on my desk. "There, see? Chocolate helps." A small wafer of very expensive Swiss chocolate was slid in beside the piled papers.

"Help what?" I could always use chocolate and tea, of course. That was a given. "Okay, so I'll take a break."

I pushed away from the desk and reached for the tea.

"Phoebe."

I looked up.

"You must snap out of this. You seem depressed, in the doldrums—is that the right word? Max agrees." Serena's English had much improved over the years but the Italian roots still tangled with her syntax.

"I'm not in the doldrums, I'm working—a considerably more productive state of mind altogether. Besides, there's so much to do."

Everybody had plunged into a fury of activity readying Baker and Mermaid for its dual existence. We had recently acquired a haul including three paintings, the Roman sculpture, and an assortment of other museum-quality artifacts as yet unclaimed or even identified, and that was only the beginning. Our colleague, Nicolina Vanvitelli, had a similar cache housed in Rome.

And in case you thought, as I once did, that there are well-financed government departments in the world with the sole purpose of handling the retrieval and return of stolen art and artifacts, forget it. What exists remains underfinanced, overworked, and shackled with cross-border red tape. Interpol's divisions on the theft and illicit traffic in works of art, cultural property, and antiquities accept all the help they can get, providing we work closely with the multiple affiliated organizations involved.

"You do not have to work all the time," Serena was saying. "We think you are depressed."

"Depressed—are you kidding me?"

"You have much to be depressed about, I understand this. There is no shame in admitting it." Serena was squeezing my shoulder as if testing a grapefruit for ripeness.

In summary, I had just sent my brother and only living relative to prison, ended a romance (actually, I sent Interpol after him, which is probably the same thing), and outmaneuvered a friend to the point where we were no longer speaking. I didn't blame myself for any of this, you understand. I had simply experienced a three-incident pileup at the moral crossroads of life and finally taken the high road amid the wreckage. For the record, the high road has to be the loneliest damn path on the planet.

"I would never feel ashamed admitting that I had any kind of mental health issue had I one but, in fact, my mood is more on the triumphant side."

It's true that for months all I did was work, primarily categorizing and classifying the art and artifacts and working closely with Britain's Interpol Works of Art Unit coordinator, Sam Walker. By hiding deep inside the minutiae of classification and research, I didn't have to examine too closely the yawning hollows in my life. That was not what I term depression but recalibration.

I stared at my desk and frowned. "I'm not sure I like the idea of you and Max discussing me behind my back."

"Then we'll carry on the conversation in front of you, darlin'," my godfather boomed as he marched up the stairs.

I sighed. A delegation. Max Baker had gifted me half of the rare textile gallery, Baker and Mermaid, but it was I who mostly bore responsibility for branching off into this new initiative.

Standing over me now, he was as debonaire and handsome as ever at seventy-five. "You really do need to snap out of this."

"I don't require snapping out of anything." I gazed up at him. We'd had this conversation before, multiple times.

"Really? You've barely left the building in weeks. Besides, you can't continue to sit here while they tear up the stairs."

That was true, especially since my open-plan Perplex office landing was essentially *on* the stairs. Soon we would have three levels, including a high-tech work space in the basement plus an enhanced gallery area on the main floor with my flat above caught up in the transformation. The basement art repatriation center was something entirely new. In two days or less, I literally would have no place to sleep.

"Are you going to come stay with me or not?"

A month spent under the same roof as Max wouldn't be unbearable but it didn't strike me as the best scenario, either. I had yet to make a decision. For some reason, decisions had become so monumental that I preferred to wait until they went away.

"Maybe," I said, gazing through the transparent stairs at the chaos below. Stacks of lumber littered the ground floor and none of our extraordinary carpets remained visible—all in storage. Part of me quavered at losing the view of those rare textiles on a daily basis, since each of them had comforted my beleaguered heart on more than one occasion.

"Nicolina says that you've barely communicated since she returned to Rome. She's sent messages and says you text only a few words back," Max continued.

I blinked at him, realizing I'd missed part of the conversation. "Pardon?"

"Nicolina, she says you are incommunicado," Serena added.

A little self-defense was in order. "Texting is hardly the safest way to communicate in our line of work. Who trusts encryption these days? By the way, is 'incommunicado' Italian or Spanish?" I lifted my head. "I often wondered."

"*Phoebe,*" Max said, tapping the desk. "I, too, am wrestling with the loss of Noel. I finally reconnected with my son only to lose him again, but I'm confident that he'll eventually find us. He always does."

"He can find you, if he wants, but he can leave me out if it. It's over," I said with more asperity than I'd intended.

"I don't believe that for a moment," Max said.

Why did people keep saying that as if I didn't know my own mind? "Believe it. Either we're together or we're not and he chose not, at least not any time before I turn sixty-five."

"He chose not to go to jail. Surely you can understand that?" Max was shoving his thick gray mane away from his forehead, a sure sign of agitation. It made my heart ache to think that he'd once dreamed of the three of us as some kind of weird semi-criminal family.

"It's totally his right to remain a hunted criminal all his life and equally my right not to join him. The moment he made his choice, it was over and, frankly, sending Interpol after him probably tipped the scales." I stared into space. "As for Toby, I sent my dear brother to prison to save his life. Maybe someday he'll even forgive me in time."

"You think three years a long time, then presto—" Serena snapped her fingers "—it is gone."

"Do you know what you really want in life, darlin'?" Max asked. He had to be watching *Oprah* reruns again.

"Yes," I said with enough assurance to surprise even me. "I want to retrieve stolen art and antiquities and return them to their original owners, thus preserving as much of history as possible for future generations." Okay, so that sounded stilted but I loved history and art with enough passion, to make everything else bearable.

A sadness gathered like clouds in Max's blue eyes. "Anyway, you need to take a break. While the shop is closed and renovations under way, it's a prime time for you to get out of Dodge."

"I have a feeling you already have a suggested location."

"Go to Italy to visit Nicolina," said Serena, jumping in with a flourish to land the trump card. "You always love Italy and Italians, yes?"

I nodded. "But who goes to Italy in February?" I caught the exchange of glances and knew the significance: *she's really in a bad way.* People of sound mind knew that any time was the perfect time for visiting Italy apparently.

"Nicolina, she needs you in Rome now. So much work to do, she says, but there are other matters that need your attention," Serena said. "She would not share the details on the phone but it all seems very urgent."

"She has Seraphina to help her," I pointed out. Seraphina was Nicolina's über assistant. Everybody in this line of work had talented, armed assistants seconding as bodyguards and I had just recently acquired one of my own.

"But she says she needs *you*, Phoebe."

"I suppose she needs my help in sorting through all the loot we brought back." After all, we brought home about fifteen crates from my brother's hoard—all that we could carry to the plane actually—leaving the remains for Noel to steal.

So far, we hadn't seen Nicolina's share and the topic was hardly safe for electronic communication of any kind. I did need to visit and soon.

Max was looming over me, hands on my shoulders doing the papa-bear thing, which I detested but totally lacked the energy to protest. "You must go to her, Phoebe."

"Yes, all right," I said flatly, talking to the top button of the vintage velvet waistcoat. Serena had given it to him for Christmas one year and I'd never seen him wear it until now. What else had I been missing? "I'll join her in a few weeks."

"Now, before your apartment is out of bounds," Max said.

"I suppose."

"She needs you, Phoebe, as in immediately," Serena added. "She made that clear."

I shrugged.

"There's been a death in her circle apparently," Max added.

I gazed up him. "What does that have to do with me?"

"A good friend, Maria Contini, passed and Nicolina says she needs your moral support and expertise."

* * *

Countess Nicolina Vanvitelli needing my support, moral or otherwise, was hard to get my head around. Needing my expertise was something else again. I didn't consider myself an expert so much as possessing good instincts with occasional jolts of pure intuition. My undergraduate degree in art history combined with a passion for textiles didn't hurt, but more than anything, I had a good eye and good instincts.

"Apparently Maria Contini has passed away suddenly," I said, standing in the downstairs demolition zone talking to Penelope Williams known as Peaches who happened to be my new bodyguard.

"Nicolina mentioned her to me once," I told her. "She has—or *had*—a fabulous textile collection of Fortuny and Renaissance textiles. Maybe she needs me to help with those?" Technically, Nicolina, Peaches, Max, and I were partners in this ancient lost and found initiative.

"That makes sense, doesn't it? I mean you're the expert in that fabric stuff." Peaches was definitely more hardware than soft wear. A curvy, toned, six-foot-one-inch-tall engineer by training, commando by inclination, she never could see the value in anything soft. Her current construction supervisor role with us was as close as she'd come to gainful employment in her field of study.

I gazed up, way up. "Textiles, not 'fabric,' Peaches. Anyway, I'm going."

"Whatever. I get that people collect all kinds of weird shit that would never float my boat. When are you leaving?"

"Tonight."

"Need a bodyguard?"

"Why would I? Anyway, you have to keep the construction team on track."

"Well, hell, sure. I'll keep these dudes whipped into shape."

"I know you will. Just remember that we can't afford to lose more construction guys."

"Right, Phoebe. Don't worry about a ting." And sometimes she slipped into what I called Jamaicanese. She stood studying me, outfitted in black spandex topped by a leather jacket, an ensemble which would have reduced most women to an ill-packaged mess of athlete-meets-biker-momma. On her, it was simply Amazonian. "Anyway, I'm glad you're getting away. Probably the sooner, the better." She shook her cornrows and picked up a piece of marble tile from a pile. "See this? You hardly pay attention to any of the renovations."

I mumbled: "I've been busy."

"Translation: uninterested—I get it. So listen up: we're laying this on the lower level, which will have a modern vibe—clean and antiseptic like a time laboratory instead of this whisper-rich thing you got going on up here. You're going to miss your colors, I know, and I totally sympathize with you, girl, but you're going to love it. You'll see. When you get back, we'll be that much closer to spectacular."

"I believe it." But I didn't really. Too much change in too short a time. I gazed around the gallery, or what was left of it. I'd seen the drawings for the new space but it was challenging to imagine this gutted shell as anything but what it wasn't—my beloved carpet and rare textile gallery.

"I know that everyone has the renos in hand." I turned toward her. "Are you all right here?"

Peaches looked at me hard. "Of course I'm all right here. Like you said, I have work to do. I told Mom and Dad that I'd come see them in Jamaica in a few weeks, anyway—have to get my work visa straightened out."

I smiled. "Fabulous. I'm so glad you're part of the team."

She frowned. "Did you really just say that?"

"Forget I ever uttered the phrase. I think I'm in worse shape than I thought."

"That's what I've been trying to tell you."

And then the doorbell rang.

"Who's that? We're not even open." Peaches strode though the debris to our paper-covered glass storefront and unlocked the door to Agent Sam Walker, who nodded a greeting and stepped in.

"Sam, what a surprise. We haven't seen you in, what, two days?" I said.

"I think actually that it was more like one," Peaches said.

Sam grinned in that lopsided way of his that sent his scar chasing his eyebrow halfway up his hairline. It was a singularly arresting face in a bald man that I'd grown to like but not in any romantic sense. "I just dropped in to have a word."

I stepped forward. "About?"

Peaches swung away to yell at one of the drywallers as Sam led me over to the far corner. "I was talking this morning to my Italian colleague who informs me that a very valuable painting has been stolen from a palazzo in Venice under mysterious circumstances."

"Are you putting me on the case or something?" The *or something* bit was critical since so far Interpol had happily allowed us to do the cataloging and database checking of the pieces we'd retrieved but had yet to assign us to a proper case. We were, after all, not trained police officers or even detectives.

"Not exactly," he said.

"I knew it: always the bridesmaid, never the bride."

He quirked a smile. "We appreciate your efforts in all respects, Phoebe, but our reason for approaching you now is because you may have an inside lead that could prove valuable. The painting in question belonged to a very good friend of Nicolina Vanvitelli, a friend who died that same night as the theft."

"It wouldn't happen to be Maria Contini, would it?"

"How do you know that?"

At that moment my cell vibrated. I pulled the phone from my pocket and read the text from Nicolina:

Phoebe, we must change plans. Meet me at the airport in Roma. We must proceed to Venice at once. I have arranged the flight. Nicolina

"Ah," said Sam, peering over my shoulder. "Ah, so her majesty speaks. Excellent. Go and snoop around but keep me informed this time."

2

I should have asked *where* exactly in the Rome airport I was to meet Nicolina. Why did I think I could just arrive in a metropolitan hub and suddenly the obvious meeting spot would appear like a mirage?

Apparently I was not supposed to do the finding but wait to be found. Once I got that into my head, it took less than five minutes.

"Phoebe!"

I turned to see Nicolina's assistant, Seraphina, shoving a man aside in order to commandeer my arm. *"Scusa,"* she said without giving him a second glance while to me she added: "We must hurry."

She attempted to take control of both my roller suitcase and my tapestry bag but I refused to relinquish the latter despite its weight. After a moment of tugging, she shot me an irritated look and gripped the roller while jerking her head to follow her. "The plane, it takes off in twenty minutes."

Small and fierce, Seraphina was not easy to warm up to. In fact, at times I found her unnerving the way one might a bad-tempered terrier that perpetually bares its teeth.

I followed along, expecting to endure yet another laborious security screening. Instead, we were whisked off to an alternative corridor and through a more streamlined system, emerging several moments later in a private waiting room. I knew without asking that Countess Vanvitelli, aka Nicolina, had pulled the gilded strings again and that we were likely taking her friend's private plane.

I looked around the small lounge with only time enough to see Nicolina sweeping down to embrace me.

"Phoebe! I missed you, and you would not properly answer my texts. How I worried, but things will be better between us now, yes?" Air kisses followed along with a gracious Italian hug, which I liken to halfway between a bow and a benediction.

I stepped back, admiring her sleek merlot-toned leather pantsuit and the flawless everything of my tall Italian friend. The fact that her reddened eyes almost matched the hue of her ensemble hardly spoiled the effect. "I hope so. I'm sorry for being incommunicado, Nicolina, but I've been preoccupied."

"There is nothing to forgive," she said with a wave of her hand. "You are here now and that is all that matters. What's going on?"

"Oh, Phoebe, such a difficult matter. Maria Contini has died suddenly. We were childhood friends, our families very close. It was only the day before yesterday when we spoke and now she is gone, and robbed, too." She dabbed her eyes with a handkerchief. "I cannot believe it. Something is wrong, very wrong. There are too many odd occurrences that I do not think I can wade through by myself—too emotional. I need your support."

Since when? I wondered. "And you have it. Was she killed during a robbery?"

"Yes and no. Both events happened on the same night, the last night of Carnevale."

I planned to wait until she told me about the painting. "How and where exactly did it happen?"

"Nothing makes sense. She was a quiet woman—a recluse, you say in English—and no longer even attended the festivities, and yet she left the villa by herself that night and ended up dead the same time that her prized painting was stolen."

"Really? I'm so sorry, Nicolina," I said, grasping her hands. "This is horrible. To lose a friend under such traumatic circumstances."

Her eyes might be swollen but they held such a glint of determination that only a fool would think it was due to grief alone. "Whoever did this will pay. No one harms my friend and gets away with it, no one."

I nodded. "We'll find out the truth."

"Poor Maria, she did not deserve to die like this!" She tugged her hands from mine and began to sob.

"Died in what fashion exactly?"

"I don't know!"

"Was the painting stolen from her villa?"

Nicolina shook her head and turned away. "We must talk more of this later. For now I must pull myself together." Then she turned back to me and smiled sadly. "I wish you had known her. You would have loved her. She adored textiles as you do and had gathered many fine pieces over the years, including her late grandmama's Fortunies."

"Look, I hate to grill you but could you tell me if the police believe Maria's death was accidental or if there were signs of violence? Where was she found and who found her?" I never bought into the one-question-at-a-time school of thought and, not surprisingly, my law background was already kicking in.

A loudspeaker announced that boarding would begin immediately.

"Maybe just answer the first question," I called over the announcement.

"Later. We must board now," she called back. "We go." She linked arms with mine as we followed Seraphina, who now carried four carry-on bags plus a grudge that I wouldn't let her make it five. Together we marched up to passport control. "We will speak later on the plane," Nicolina assured me.

But later was late coming, considering that I was enveloped in an effusive welcome by Fabio, our steward, followed by a hearty handshake from Otty, the pilot. This was the private plane owned by Nicolina's mysterious friend and we had all been together before.

Naturally, there was much to catch up on plus many treats to sample along with nonstop service of strong Italian coffee equivalent to jet fuel. I sank back in the plush leather seats and attempted to enjoy the short flight but I was getting very caffeinated very fast.

"So, do we have another priceless artwork to return to its rightful owner?" Fabio asked as he offered us a tray of biscotti. A touch of turbulence caused him to take a step back, pirouette, and quickly regroup. The man had acrobatic grace partnered with an equally showstopping sense of style, today in his uniform of a pale blue vest and matching pants. Apparently he had tried to dress his partner, Otty, in something similar but the captain preferred a more traditional look.

"Another?" I asked, turning to Nicolina.

"Well, there was Naples—" Fabio said before catching Nicolina's expression.

"We are coming to Venice to discover who murdered my friend," Nicolina said in her contessa tone.

"Oh, dear. How dreadful. So sorry for your loss," Fabio said, shooting me a quick look and promptly pivoting around to head back to the galley.

I kept my attention fixed on Nicolina. "Have you returned a painting already, Nicolina, without the necessary arrangements through Interpol?" The question was hardly irrelevant but maybe a tad insensitive given the gravitas of the moment.

She waved her hand. "Just one. This I told Max. It was a private matter, a piece stolen from a friend and returned to him in Naples. The provenance trail was clear. I did explain this to Max."

"You did?" I knew that I'd been distracted lately but I couldn't believe that I'd missed something so important. "And does Interpol know?"

"Interpol!" she scoffed. "They are every day in my villa, asking questions, poking around. They will not leave me alone. Forget Interpol. I am more concerned about you, dear friend." She leaned over to touch my hand. "I have spoken to Max many times while, Phoebe, you have been—" she fished for the perfect word "—unavailable. Yes, you have been unavailable. Did he not say?"

"Perhaps he did."

"You have not been yourself," she hurried on. "This I understand. Noel and your brother—all very difficult. I know this after my problems with my family. Do you remember?"

How could I forget? A grandfather who locked her grandmother away, parents killed by the Camorra, a husband who tried to steal her fortune, the overbearing brother who believed being male made him automatically head of the family, possibly the universe… "I remember very well."

"So, you know that I understand how one must heal by being strong and busy with purpose," she continued. "You have had two big blows and have been very, very busy."

"Actually, I counted three," I said, "not that losing Rupert's friendship is considered a blow by most."

"Rupert," Nicolina said with another note of impatience. "He or his manservant are never far away but stay out of sight like rodents, yes? Back to you: work helps much better than thinking too hard on our losses. I will help you move on, as they say, and you will help me. Now I have a loss of my dearest friend and I must discover what really happened to heal my grief. Keeping occupied is the only way. Together we help each other. I know you do not shrink from such things. Strong women help each other."

I sat back. It struck me as odd that she wanted my help in solving Maria's murder and odder still that Sam Walker had requested that I become involved. Clearly the police didn't trust Nicolina any more than I did. "I will do what I can, of course."

She nodded and smiled sadly. "We will solve this together now. Dear Maria, I cannot believe that she is gone."

I took another gulp of coffee. "I'm sorry, Nicolina. Losing a friend is so difficult. Where exactly in Venice we are staying?"

Nicolina gazed out the window, now nothing but a scud of dark as we began to descend. "I had thought at first of the Danieli but then knew that it would be best if we stayed at Maria's, as much as I will find it unbearable. She would want this and I have much work to do there, though the police will be coming and going. I always stayed with her when I visit Venice so why not now when I have business to attend and the police wish to speak with me? Maria's housekeeper, Zara, is distraught—she has worked for Maria for decades—but she has readied the rooms at my request."

"Did Maria have children, maybe a husband or siblings?" I asked.

"No family. Maria was an only child and never married, though she was engaged long ago. I was like her sister. She often called me her *sorellina*, her little sister." Nicolina subsided into her thoughts while I tried to muster mine.

I had so many questions but, once again, I was diving blindly into a situation and needed to figure things out on my feet. You'd think I'd get used to this by now but somehow I never could.

Fabio darted into the cabin to remove our cups and check that all the safety boxes where ticked before landing. "Just sit back now and relax," he said. "Otty says that we are in a holding pattern for a few minutes but as soon as we get clearance we'll be landing pronto."

I peered out the window, gazing far down at ribbons of light followed by dark expanses. I had never flown into Venice before, my string of one-day visits occurring back in my twenties while doing the budget thing around Europe. Venice had always been a day-long bus tour, the most recent out of Bologna, and remembered as a flash of mental postcards—St. Mark's Square, the Doge's Palace—along with tourist-infested streets and watery byways. I'd loved every moment and always left hungry for more.

And this visit was supposed to in some way help my own dark night of the soul? Venice as the site of sudden death did not a happy pill make. But this wasn't about me. This was about helping Nicolina. Still, an intense sense of foreboding had overtaken me and I was one of those people who took these things seriously.

As we flew over the black lagoon on our descent, the uneasy sense of about to land on water intensified as I strained to see the runway lights. I had a sudden thought and looked across the aisle. "Nicolina, what did you mean by having business to attend to and that the police wanted to speak to you?"

She pulled herself out of her thoughts and sighed. "Did I not mention that I am the executor of Maria's will as well as her main beneficiary?"

3

_____

I had flown into many airports but never one that required waiting for a boat on a dark rainy night. Naturally Seraphina had everything in hand and soon we were ushered to a private speedboat for a brief zip across the lagoon.

Lagoons should be turquoise, tropical, and warm, not inky dark, layered in mystery, and scented like the breath of time. That was Venice for you, always a mystery, no matter how often you approached her. She had once grown rich and gilded from trade centuries ago, and though that luster still glowed beneath layers of age, it now felt tenuous. Venice: you could never say you'd been there no matter how many times you had. She would always be the most unknowable city on earth.

As if the city had already cast a pall, my companions remained sober and disinclined to talk, not that conversation was even possible over the roar of the boat engine. There were so many things I needed to know. Of course, Nicolina had just suffered a loss and here I was about to intrude upon a house of mourning and as what—a detective, a purveyor of moral support, an observer? The whole thing made me edgy.

After a few minutes, I escaped the noisy silence to duck outside where I could feel the wind and rain in my face. I pulled up my rain jacket's hood and hunched down to watch Venice approach. I needed time with my thoughts. That Nicolina was Maria Contini's executor was a relationship I hadn't anticipated. What else about this situation had I yet to learn? Again, my own fault for not doing due diligence and insisting on answers before taking the leap.

Ahead, Venice appeared as a mirage—lights strung out over a reflective darkness whipped by rain. I held my breath as the boat skimmed past tall shuttered villas looming down over the water, and glimpsed the golden domes of St. Mark's Basilica just seconds before we sped into one of the main arteries—the Grand Canal, I realized—awash with light from the multitude of lamps and windows like some kind of ancient, dignified playground.

Stands of gondolas rocked at their moorings, a tour boat churned the wake beside us, and I glimpsed people dashing somewhere with their umbrellas popped on either side of the canal. When we sped under the Rialto Bridge, I could only gaze up as if I was seeing Venice for the very first time, overwhelmed by the impact of history and the city's unique kind of magic.

I wanted to call to Nicolina to share this moment, to see Venice as I did at that very instant, but how pointless was that? My friend struggled with grief while I tried to emerge from my own losses. A veil of loneliness came over me that set my mood adrift. If only I could visit Venice with somebody I loved— with Noel, maybe—as if that would ever happen. I had cast away the man of my heart, and if that heart was broken as a result, that, too, was my own damn fault for falling for a man like him. Color my mood self-recrimination.

The boat darted into a smaller tributary and the driver immediately throttled the engine back to a sedate putter. Now the slosh of water against stone accompanied the sounds of the boat as we snaked our way deeper into the city's heart. We passed under many bridges and slipped past multiple tiny *campi*, their rain-washed cobbles deserted. Once I looked up to see a man on a balcony gazing down as he smoked a cigarette. He lifted his hand to acknowledge me but the boat had turned into another artery before I could wave back.

Traveling anywhere in Venice with its watery streets and myriad *porti* felt like a journey of mythic proportions and always delivered you to some place unexpected even if it was your intended destination. Whatever I was expecting of Maria Contini's doorstep, it wasn't a narrow ledge tucked around a corner of a tiny canal with only a battered and algae-scummed hunk of timber for a door. No knob, no latch, not even a bell to ring. At least there was a light blazing blearily down on us from a motion lamp fixed to the wall above.

The driver grappled for one of the steel docking rings to secure the prow while I clambered to the stern to tie the rope around the other. He was calling something to me in Italian that I couldn't grasp—maybe *thanks for not being merely decorative* or *you know boats,* sì? I didn't require a translator to do the obvious. I'd been around boats most of my life.

Soon Seraphina appeared and the Italian truly grew intense as she began dispensing instructions, I'm guessing, while the driver argued back. That gave me time to look way up to where the dark wall of the villa loomed overhead. This was not my first experience with a looming Italian villa, but I had to admit, Venice did them best. If structures were faces, this one was totally inscrutable with closed eyes under long arched lids and a dark countenance. The arched windows indicated Islamic influences, meaning the building must date from at least the 1500s.

And then suddenly one lid flew open as a woman unlatched a shutter and called down. Seraphina responded and more debating ensued. Then Nicolina appeared, the hood of her coat flung over her head. "Zara wishes us to use the front door but the driver, he says that is not possible tonight," she told me. "There is construction in the front of the canal. We must enter through the cantina."

Cantina, I knew, did not translate into *café* in Italian but *cellar,* which meant we were to enter through Venice's idea of a basement, something which would horrify most hosts and certainly Zara, judging from her tone. In the case of Venice, a cellar was likely the villa's first-floor back door.

The moldy wooden door creaked open and the driver began to unload the luggage and try to help the ladies, though both Seraphina and I refused his proffered hand. I leaped over the stoop on my own steam whereas Seraphina insisted on helping with the bags. Nicolina, however, waited for assistance with her usual grace.

That left me standing alone in a damp cavernous space peering into the darkness lit by a single overhead bulb. A small motorboat sat on tracks pointed toward the now-open door, ready to be pushed into the canal when needed. These bottom floors also seconded as boathouses. This one had to be at the bottom of a very large footprint, by the looks of the capacious space.

I detected two more narrow boats propped on stilts way back in the shadows—very old by the glimpse of an ornate lantern peeking out from under one tarp. The area was also a repository for things stored for centuries with odd shapes clustered on stands in the shadows or hung from hooks on the damp walls. Repeated floods had those hooks positioned five or six feet above floor level to escape the jagged green line that seemed to chase the objects up the walls. The scent of motor oil, diesel, and damp was overpowering but brought me back to my childhood.

I had just caught the gaze of an elaborate mask covered in clear plastic when Nicolina came up and touched my arm. "Phoebe, come. Zara awaits upstairs."

I traipsed up behind her, Seraphina bringing up the rear. Masks on the walls watched our progress like a row of bizarre spectators frozen in shock. It was a relief to step into the villa proper where a small, dark-skinned woman with graying hair scraped into a bun waited for us in the shadows. Nicolina made the introductions and the woman shook my hand and shot me a perfunctory smile.

"I'm so sorry for your loss," I said.

She turned to Seraphina for a translation and nodded when it came but soon forgot about me the moment she enveloped Seraphina in an expansive embrace amid a battery of Italian. We were then ushered down a dark hall into a large high-ceilinged room and asked to sit.

The salon was like the reception rooms of all Italian villas I had known and yet different. This one had the same high-ceiling grandeur of Nicolina's residences and yet a pervading sense of loss clung to the walls along with the richest array of disintegrating textiles I had ever seen. Though the clear outline of a missing frame was visible over the fireplace, I was too distracted by the surroundings to focus there.

Threadbare brocades and velvets covered every shabby chair and settee, their deep Prussian blues and golds still rich in the lamp and firelight. It was as if the entire room was paved in fabric and jeweled colors. My eyes traveled around the space touching every glossy inch, marveling at the silk-covered walls, the kilim cushions, and magnificent patterned Persian carpets spread underfoot.

Nicolina spoke softly. "It is as I told you, Phoebe. Maria celebrated textiles as if they were dear friends, much like you do. It was in her blood, you understand. I will explain later. Please be patient for Zara speaks no English and I will translate when I am able."

I nodded, relieved not to be expected to speak, especially since my gaze had focused on a framed piece of damask on the far wall—very old, I guessed. Fabric treated with as much veneration as art met with my approval, though conservation didn't seem to be a consideration here.

While I studied every detail within my range of vision, Seraphina sat beside Zara while Nicolina and I sat on the opposite side on a flaking velvet and gilt wood settee. The Italian flowed, intense and emotional. I gathered that Nicolina and Seraphina were asking questions of Zara until, at one point, the housekeeper disappeared and returned with a tray of wine.

Forgoing the wine, I continued sipping water, absorbed in studying the edge of a rare carpet when suddenly I caught the change in Zara's tone. I pulled my attention back to my companions and noted that Maria's assistant now appeared to be answering Nicolina and Seraphina's questions as if every word had to be pried out of her. Her replies escaped her slight frame in bursts, one moment sitting silent with her lips pursed and the next responding with an artillery of short, terse sentences.

Nicolina asked her something that caused Zara to jump up from her chair with a cry and dash from the room, Seraphina following after.

"What was that about?" I asked, turning to Nicolina.

She sighed. "Maria's death has been very traumatic for her. She does not wish to speak of it to me any longer."

"But surely she must?"

"Yes, I agree she must, but not tonight. Today the police have questioned her over and over again and she is weary. This I understand. Seraphina will take care of her while we talk and enjoy our vin Santo. They have been friends since I first began bringing Seraphina here years ago."

Nicolina attempted to pour me a glass of her beloved sweet wine but I shook my head. Her eyebrows rose. "Phoebe, I hope you do not refuse the wine because of what happened in Amalfi? I only drugged you because of the need to keep you safe and—"

I waved away the notion. "It's not because of that, Nicolina, though it's true that I'll never look at Santo quite the same way again. It's just that I don't do well with wine in general and I have had too much coffee tonight already."

"Then you need the wine to help you relax, yes? Here, I will pour you a glass and you will drink or not, as you wish." She poured a goblet of the deep maroon drink and set it beside my water glass before sipping deeply of her own.

"Zara must have told you something about what happened?" I pressed.

"But of course. She said that Maria, for whom she has worked for nearly thirty years, had seemed troubled over these many weeks. She does not know why as Maria would not confide—they were not as close as I am to Seraphina, not as a confidantes, you understand. Their relationship was more formal."

As if I could ever understand the relationship between an employer and a long-serving employee/servant. Serena was more my friend than gallery manager so that didn't count.

Nicolina continued. "It had something to do with money, she believed. Over the years, the household has become increasingly poor and Maria had been worried. I noticed an edge in her tone when we spoke on the phone days ago but I thought it because she was feeling—how do you say?—under the

weather. She never mentioned an illness to me or to Zara. She was very energetic, very spry, as the English say. Zara thinks she was very worried about
something."

"How old was she?"

"Sixty-two."

"Oh, young, then."

"Exactly. Yet the police suggested that Maria may have tripped and fallen
into the canal that evening as if she was clumsy or drunk. That was not
Maria."

"Maria was found in the canal?" I almost choked on my water.

"She was found in the Cannaregio, yes. Apparently there were no signs of
struggle."

I followed her gaze to the ceiling-high brocade drapes I had been admiring
earlier, which I now realized must shield equally tall shutters that looked out
over the main canal. "They think she drowned?"

"The autopsy is not yet complete. There are many events during that last
night of Carnevale—the grand finale, the water parades, the revelry," Nicolina
said, pouring herself more wine. "Maria did not feel up to taking part, Zara
says. She said she would stay home and watch the water parade from her
balcony and yet she did go out. Nobody knows why. Perhaps she stepped out
to a café or restaurant, though they would be very busy that night, and Maria
did not take big meals in the evening anymore. Or perhaps she decided not to
miss the excitement, after all."

"But didn't she say where she was going to anyone?"

"There was no one here to tell, only Zara, who always spends Carnevale
with her niece in Mestra. All the other staff had been let go years ago,
including Zara's brother. Had Maria wanted her to stay, she would have but
she insisted that Zara go. In the old days, there would be parties that Maria
would host or attend but not for many years. She now lived a quiet life and
yet..." She gazed down at her glass, deep in thought.

"And yet...?"

"And yet she went out."

"But maybe she decided to join the festivities, after all?" I offered.

"Perhaps, but this does not fit with how anxious she had been lately. Zara
says that she suddenly became very concerned about the painting one day last
week. The painting had hung in the same place for centuries—in her
bedroom, and there had once been one over there, which is the one she sold
months ago." She glanced toward the vacant spot over the fireplace. "But last
week she received a phone call. She would not say who from but immediately

insisted that they crate up the last painting and store it down the street in the family vault."

There was a family vault. I fixed on the rectangle of lighter peachy silk wall covering over the mantel. "So, the remaining painting was stolen from this vault and not from here?"

"Yes. Did I not say? I apologize. Yes, the painting was stolen from the vault down the canal on the same night that Maria was found dead. The vault had been breached by explosives. The police say that the thieves must have used the fireworks and all the noise outside to hide the sounds. All very clever, really—the excitement, the masks, everyone running in costumes—how easy it made it for them to steal."

"But who knew that the painting was even there?"

Nicolina turned her red-rimmed eyes to me. "Zara, Seraphina, me, possibly one other."

"That's all?"

"I do not think she widely announced that she was the owner of such valuable art but many knew about the warehouse. It was once the establishment for her family's weaving business, now closed, and some of the ancestors once lived on the top floors. Maria resisted pressure to sell the building and planned to turn it into a museum to the weavers one day. It was a dream she clung to, though she had no idea how to finance it." She paused, gazing to the empty space above the fireplace. "She loved it there. She felt in touch with her ancestors as her family has had a weaving studio in that location since the fifteenth century. I will take you there soon."

"And the vault?"

"She called it the *banca*. It was there that one of the earliest Continis built a large vault that has served as the family bank for centuries. The Continis have jokingly called it the *banca* since then, though I suppose in the fifteenth century it truly was their bank. That is the way things were done in those days, yes? It has always been very safe. Maria had tried to keep the security features updated as did her father and his father before him down through time—cameras, sensors, everything—but it is difficult. So expensive. I offered to help her fund an update once but she wouldn't hear of it. That is where she had the painting taken just days before the robbery. It seemed so safe to her but Seraphina had checked it out on our last visit and thought the security full of holes, as they say."

"So it wasn't secure?"

"No, it was not and, in the end, neither was Maria. Zara says that it is almost as if Maria had a premonition—is that the correct word?—that the painting was in danger. There have been other times when she has stored her art there—when she traveled, when there were floods—it was not so strange. What was strange is that she would make the request after this phone call and that she would die on the same night that the painting was stolen."

"I don't believe in coincidences," I said, still gazing at the empty wall.

"I do not, either."

"If we find the thieves we may also find out Maria's killer or, at the very least, discover why she died."

"Yes."

I sighed, suddenly needing a swig of vino but still resisting. "Who discovered Maria was missing?"

"Zara arrived home late the next morning and found her gone. She called the police and the search began. She was found early yesterday morning... floating...in the canal."

Nicolina lowered her glass and quietly wept while I sat imagining the scene. How awful it must have been to arrive home and discover that someone you presumably cared for or looked after was gone—all the searching, the fear, the sense of pending loss...

And yet what if Zara wasn't as devoted as she appeared? "Did the police check Zara's alibi?" I whispered.

"I'm sure they would but it will not be so hard to prove that she was with her family." She sniffed. "I do not believe that she would do this thing. Why now when she'd have worked for her for years?"

"In any case, we need to find out who Maria was speaking to when she suddenly decided to hide that painting."

"Yes, I have already put Seraphina on the task. We will know very soon."

"And what about Maria's will? Are there other beneficiaries?"

She turned to me then, fixing me with her beautiful swollen eyes. "Of course. I know every detail and now it is time you did, too."

I gazed back, waiting. "Why are you hesitating, Nicolina? Is it complicated?"

She sighed and looked away. "Everything is complicated, is it not true? Parts of the will are not so difficult: Maria has left a sizable bequest to Zara, which she discussed with me. She will not have to work ever again."

"That makes sense," I agreed.

She nodded. "Other than that, I have been left the villa and the weaving studio and all of the contents, including the painting."

"Is this why you're hesitating? To me, that makes sense, too. Didn't you say that she had no family?"

"No immediate family, no, certainly no one who she would trust. I refused at first but she pressed me to agree. She wanted to entrust the studio to someone she knew would renovate it as she would and not just sell it to the highest bidder, as her cousin wished to do. And then there is this villa. Villas in Venice are—" she tossed her hands upward "—worth a fortune. This cousin once remarked that Maria should sell up and retire someplace less difficult. She would, if it were hers, but Maria would never leave. She said that Venice's canals were like blood in her veins."

"All right, so you are the major beneficiary and Maria was right to trust you with the largess."

"She also made me promise to follow through with establishing her weaving museum. I will do all these things, of course. The cousin will not contest the will." She shrugged. "I have spoken to her and she has no interest."

"Well, that's good. I know that you will honor Maria's wishes and your friendship." I studied her for a moment. "But why do I get the feeling that there's something else you're not telling me, something you don't want to tell me?"

She turned to me again. "You will not like this, Phoebe."

"Not like what—why would any of this be something that I would dislike in any way?"

"Because there was once another beneficiary in the will whom Maria had removed years ago. To him she had originally bequeathed both paintings because he loved them when she loved him. Love can make a strong woman weak."

"Don't I know it. And she removed this man from her will long ago, you say, and now the last painting has been stolen? That makes him a possible suspect. Is this what you want to tell me?"

"Yes. The man is her former fiancé but she did not tell him that she had removed him from the will, or at least, not that I know of. I believe he found out recently."

I sat back against the cushions and clasped my hands as if to fortify myself. "And I know him, don't I? That's why you're hesitating. All right, out with it, Nicolina. Who is our prime suspect?"

"Rupert Fox."

4

Sir Rupert Fox and I had been friends for years starting from when he and his driver/bodyguard, Evan Barrows rescued me from a spot of trouble. That he was a probable top-drawer pilferer of ancient artifacts was something I had long suspected but couldn't prove. Somehow he managed to fly under Interpol's radar. His London antiquities shop, Carpe Diem, appeared to do a thriving business in rare and arcane artifacts. In any case, for all the years I'd known him he'd only ever mentioned one love, that of his late wife, Mabel.

"Maria Contini and Rupert Fox were engaged?" We were standing on the stairs as Nicolina took me on a flash tour of the villa. I couldn't quite process any of it. In fact, I could hardly focus on the all the treasures she was showing me, for that matter.

"Yes, I said this before, Phoebe. They were secretly engaged almost forty years ago—long before he'd met Mabel and when they were both very young. This is how I first met him, too."

"But how, where?"

"He was in Italy with his father to purchase antiques."

"You mean that his father was an antiques dealer, too?"

"Yes. He owned the same shop Rupert has today."

"But I always thought Rupert acquired Carpe Diem as a front for his art-foraging ways. I had no idea he had inherited it. He's always had that to-the-manor-born thing going on so I thought he was a blue blood."

"Blue blood?" Nicolina gazed at me uncomprehendingly. "Oh, yes, I see: you think he was always wealthy, but before he married Mabel, he was not rich."

"And 'collecting'—" I put the word in air quotes "—art and artifacts has clearly contributed to making him richer even after marrying into money. Okay, so he and his father came here to the villa…"

"And I was there visiting Maria with my grandpapa at the time. Now I will continue my tour *and* my story also, so do be patient, Phoebe. Come."

I followed her up the next two flights. "I'm trying to be patient but you've delivered a couple of info bombs here. I never knew any of this about Rupert."

On the top floor, I paused to gaze through a round window that looked down onto a wide canal blurring with rain and lights—the Cannaregio. So, the way we came in was the back alley, so to speak.

"Why would you? A man does not tell everyone that he was jilted. Do come." I glanced up and hastily joined her.

"He was left standing at the altar?"

"Not exactly but almost," she continued. "It was all very painful for them both. I was never to speak of it to either Maria or Rupert again and, for a time, I never did."

She stopped by a glossy wooden door and slowly turned the brass knob. "We are here," she whispered. Touching my arm, she led me inside and closed the door softly before flicking on a switch. The room suddenly bloomed into a rich tapestry of color.

If a bedroom could be a museum of extraordinary textiles, this was it. At the foot of a four-poster bed swathed with deep blue velvet brocade stood a mannequin in a Fortuny evening ensemble. I'd recognize that style anywhere —the elegant gold-stenciled black silk velvet coat hanging in deep lustrous folds over a pleated silk Delphos gown. Those gowns were Fortuny's signature creation, a masterpiece of pleating designed to drape the female form in a way that enhanced both woman and textile. Even in modern times, no one had quite been able to duplicate the sublime sinuous fusion of color, handiwork, pleating, and design that composed those wonders.

"Oh!" I took a step forward, stopped, and pressed my hands to my mouth. "Oh."

"She could not part with any of them. The Fortunies she rotated from her closet to these stands. Some were her grandmother's, others she collected. There are more there and there."

I wrenched my gaze away from the black-and-gold to fasten it on the deep pomegranate, gold-embossed gown with the transparent pleated overtunic, which stood on another mannequin directly under an orb of light. From there, my gaze went traveling across the room to another illuminated design, this one a deep apricot pleated velvet seemingly etched in gold vining tendrils with one sleeve parted along the seam to reveal the pleated peach silk gown beneath.

The effect was mesmerizing, akin to fairy tale loosened upon a pre-Raphael dreamscape. "This is one of my favorite decorative periods. The organic flow of color and design, the dynamic movement of shapes and forms. But they should be in a conservation room away from the damp."

"Yes, I know. Come." Nicolina led me across the room and through another door where an enormous glass-enclosed closet opened up on either side. I recognized temperature and moisture-controlled storage shelves and hangers of the most sophisticated nature holding length upon length of fabric as well as boxes and trunks. "This had been her greatest expense—the careful conservation of these treasures so important to her. She would keep her gowns here but would bring a few into her room 'to breathe,' she called it. They were like her friends, her loves. She imagined them one day displayed in similar storage areas in her dream museum down the street along with samples of all the textiles her family made across the centuries. She loved them all. How she loved them!" Her voice caught.

"I'm so sorry, Nicolina."

A pair of slipper chairs sat companionably against one wall beside a low marble table holding a stack of books and a decanter of wine. A single painted crystal glass—I guessed early seventeenth century—sat nearby where I imagined Maria sipping vino while admiring her treasures. A halogen light shone down onto an empty rectangle of silk on the wall over a low marble table. Nicolina indicated for me to take a seat.

"And this was where the last painting originally hung?" I asked.

"Yes, her favorite, and it was once willed to Rupert also. I have photographs. They have never been published or shown in any gallery despite general knowledge that the Continis owned them." She picked up a large leather folder from the table and passed it to me. "The one on the left is the one she sold two months ago."

I opened the portfolio to find a rendering of the artwork on each side of the book-like holder. Once again my breath caught; yet again I succumbed to the glory of brilliant color but something else besides.

Not surprisingly considering the period, one painting was ecclesiastical, an annunciation rendering of incredible detail depicting an angel dressed in velvet trimmed with silk arriving at an open door to witness Mary receiving the seed of God, which appeared like a lightning bolt from the sky. But it was not the Immaculate Conception that interested me so much as the rich textiles revealed through the open portal. A carpet, definitely Anatolian from the late fifteenth century, blew in the breeze from a balcony above in a rich pattern of ochre and reds rendered with such precision that I could attribute it to the region without difficulty. A second textile covered a mantel behind the Virgin. That one I recognized as an Anatolian animal carpet. My mouth went dry. I looked up. "She sold a Crivelli?"

"Yes, Carlo Crivelli painted it in 1487. It broke her heart to let it go but for financial reasons she had no choice."

My gaze swept over to the second painting, which showed a gathering of richly dressed citizens wearing varying shades of silks and velvets celebrating what I assumed to be an engagement or a wedding in a church. An unusual prayer rug warmed the marble under the bride's feet while the family members stood on a carpet design I did not recognize but which almost looked Berber. That, too, was painted in such detail that I could almost feel the nap enough to know it was probably silk. "A Bartolo—seriously?"

"Of course you know your art. Yes, that is Domenico di Bartolo's *Marriage of the Merchant's Daughter* painted in 1441, the one that was stolen. Maria loved both paintings so, as much because of the textiles as the subject matter. She said that those very robes in the Bartolo—you see how the bride's gown features that feathered scroll design?—came from her family's very own fifteenth century silk looms. They sent their textiles far and wide as Venice had an active trade in luxury textiles at the time and that design was unique to the house."

I stared at her. "She believed that this painting illustrates her family's own fabrics?"

"Yes. They may have been painted from life."

"That's incredible provenance."

"Yes, it is."

"Bartolo's known for his frescoes, of course, but he painted other mediums. And the carpets? It can't be a coincidence that both paintings feature carpets prominently, or prominently to me. There are only a few Renaissance artists known for using carpets in such exquisite detail and these two are among them. But I don't recognize the design of this larger version where the wedding party is standing."

"Yes, it has always been an enigma."

My gaze returned to the photo. "The Bartolo carpets are an odd mix of symbology. It's very unusual for Renaissance painters to use Berber carpets in their work. They were usually purely Anatolian or Chinese. There isn't anything purely one thing or another in any of the symbols here."

"I knew you would notice. That painting was very special, as you can see, not just by a renowned Renaissance artist but perhaps linked to her family by the bride's gown. Imagine the value? Imagine how disappointed Rupert was at having them both slip away from his fingers again and again?" That steely look had returned, chasing away the vulnerability of sorrow I had witnessed seconds before.

I cleared my throat, fixing for a moment on the shy look the bride was casting her fiancé and his ardent gaze in return. That, too, was odd. "I can see how Rupert and Maria would have had lots in common but I'm sure the loss of his love hit him far stronger than the loss of these paintings, despite their value. Why did they break up?"

"I was still a young girl and watched the affair from the wall, as they say. Maria and he were very much in love, or so I thought." She sat with her hands clasped in her lap, staring straight ahead.

"But not enough to keep them together?"

"That is a romantic view, one that we Italians have celebrated in art since the being of time, but there are so many other kinds of love that tear at us, is that not so? I am no longer convinced that love conquers all—or, at least, not the romantic kind." Her gaze found my face again. "Do you believe that Noel did not love you enough to go to prison so you could be together?"

Where'd that come from? I met her eyes. "I believe he loves his freedom more," I replied carefully, "and I, in turn, love myself enough not to choose to continue living in a way that makes me unhappy."

I must have passed some kind of test because she rewarded me with a sad smile. "This is good that you stand up for yourself when it is all so difficult. That is what we women must do."

Were we speaking of me or Nicolina? "Back to Maria and Rupert," I said gently. "Did Maria choose another love over what she may have felt for Rupert, is this what you're saying?"

She nodded. "Maria's father was much like my grandpapa—very overbearing. His rule was the law and he believed family and bloodlines sacred. When he discovered the secret engagement, he went wild, threatening to have Rupert shot and Maria cast off from the family."

"A bit extreme, wasn't it?"

Nicolina regarded me sternly. "This is Italy."

"Of course. Sorry."

"Her father would not permit her to marry a penniless antiques dealer, you understand, or to sully the bloodline. Rupert begged her to elope with him but she refused. In the end, she chose the love of family over romance. It is equally powerful, is it not? To give up one for the other, so difficult. I have tried it and did not fare well."

"Poor Rupert."

"Poor Rupert? Well, yes, perhaps poor Rupert. Maria made her choice to remain a Contini and Papa Contini chased him out of town. In Venice, such things were easy in those days. It is a very small place still. Rupert never forgave Maria and Maria never forgave herself."

"That's tragic." I sighed. "So, Maria gave him up for money."

"Not money," Nicolina said, fiercely shaking her head, "but *family*. It was not being penniless that tortured her so much as it was being separated from her mama and papa, from her inheritance here in Venice, and the history that flowed in her veins—her blood, you know? To never live in this house again, to never touch and breathe among these velvets, to perhaps never again walk these halls—that she could not bear."

"So in refusing to marry him, she kept all this."

"Yes, these paintings that she promised to give Rupert as a wedding gift at first she decided to give him still—a very big sacrifice, you understand."

I really didn't like where this was going. "So obviously something happened to change her mind again."

Nicolina nodded. "This time, her mother. Though the paintings were Maria's by right—willed to her by her maternal grandmother—her mother raged against her for taking them from the family. She said that to rip them from the Continis was like cutting off her limbs and letting her very own mother bleed to death—chop, chop! Her mama was very dramatic. How they argued! And then Signora Contini had a heart attack right in the middle of their argument and died that very night."

"No, that's terrible!" Like a bad soap opera made worse by reality. Sometimes life is more bizarre than fiction, I swear.

"Yes, horrendous. These rooms have known so much sorrow. Maria blamed herself for her mother's death as well as for her father's heartbreak, and for hurting Rupert also. I told her over and over that she was not to blame, that she tried only to do the right thing by all, but sometimes there is no way we can please everyone, yes?"

"Yes, I mean, no: sometimes there is no one right way and you can't please everyone. So poor Maria rescinded her promise to Rupert once again because she believed she had no choice? How awful for her and for Rupert, too. I'm sure he didn't take any of this well."

"No." She said the word with short, bullet-like emphasis. "At first, he left the country—was chased from Italy, in truth. I did not reconnect with him until many years later, but when I did, I asked him about the broken promises. He was still very bitter."

"About losing his love, you mean, or losing the paintings?"

She turned to face me and I was struck by the rigidity of her jaw, how her mouth formed one hard line.

"Nicolina?"

"With Rupert, how would you know? I did not. I still do not. I only know that when he wants something, he goes after it."

"He would feel very wronged—who wouldn't?" I looked away—my turn to stare at the wall. Maybe Rupert would have felt very hurt and angry at first but I'd never known him to hold a grudge. Or at least I hoped not, since I had yet to mend the rift between us.

We sat in silence for a moment, deep in our own thoughts, and then I couldn't take it any longer. My mouth opened and I uttered the one thing neither one of us wanted to say: "And now the painting is missing and Maria is dead under mysterious circumstances and you think that Rupert may be responsible."

"Yes."

"Nicolina, no. Rupert may be a conniving little low-life weasel in Saville Row tailoring but he's a good man—sometimes—and no murderer."

Nicolina was on her feet in an instant towering over me with that hard light in her eyes. "You do not know him, Phoebe. I have known him off and on all my life and believe he is capable of anything. What he will not do himself, he makes his ex-MI6 man do for him. You know this. You know he is very dangerous—both of them are very dangerous."

"I know him, too, but differently from you. We have been friends for years. To kill a former love just to acquire a painting? No, never!" The words hung before me as if solidifying midair.

"People have killed for less."

She held my gaze.

"Yes, they have," I said after a moment. "Well, okay, I do know that people have killed for much less and that Rupert never fails to miss a trick." And how well I knew it. Hadn't I been there for the attempted Raphael heist, the Etruscan debacle, the Goddess hunt? "But murder, no. That I can't accept."

"Accept what you will, Phoebe, but I will tell you this: we have learned that a phone call was made to the house the night Maria left the villa and met her death. Should we discover evidence that places Rupert on or near the site of Maria's death on that day, I swear he is a dead man. I will kill him myself."

5

$\mathcal{N}$icolina was definitely capable of killing somebody. Hadn't I witnessed her impressive markswomanship when she gunned down a hit man on the streets of Rome? Still, killing an assassin was one thing, executing a friend something else again. Could she do it, *would* she do it?

I stood in the center of my room after Nicolina had taken me there, oblivious to the carvings, the inlaid furniture, the silken brocades, the tiny perfect Venetian canal landscape in greens and blues on the wall, even the folder of paintings on the table. For a moment I even forgot to breathe. Rupert could be a swine—that I knew too well—yet he had also saved my life upon occasion, even though it was often he who had put me in danger in the first place. And Evan, his "driver," that powerful and talented right-hand man, had I ever seen him kill? Never.

Nobody was black or white. Rupert was a man capable of great generosity while simultaneously attempting to steal something from under my nose. He'd saved my life at least once. Our relationship was complex. We'd become close even though I wanted to throttle him more times than I could remember. He lied, he cheated, and he stole, but I believed his heart was still bigger than his greed. I cared about him and for Nicolina, too. Where did that leave me?

True, Rupert wasn't speaking to me at the moment but only because I had outwitted him for once. At some point he was bound to get over his pique, providing he lived that long. Yes, he had the formidable and enigmatic Evan to protect him, but I was convinced that Seraphina might be equally dangerous in her own way and Italy was her territory, after all.

I strode to the window and opened the shutters a crack. Down below on Venice's liquid street, the rain had stopped and the canal had taken on a shimmery glow. Rupert was out there somewhere. For once, I wished I still had the special phone Evan had rigged for our private communications, even if those calls tended to come with an array of special features like detonating devices and tracking chips. Evan was a techno-wiz and endlessly inventive with app creation. Now I just wanted to find out their side of the Maria story, warn them, perhaps. And would that betray Nicolina's confidence? Maybe that didn't matter. What really mattered was the truth.

I took the folder of paintings and opened them under a lamp, studying every detail until my eyes hurt. So many elements that didn't add up, especially in the Bartolo, which was atypical for this artist of the Sienese School. In all my years of art and textile study, never had I seen a painting like this. I had once studied Domenico di Bartolo with interest because his use of textiles had been extraordinary. Though he had worked primarily in Siena, he was also believed to have traveled to Florence, and now apparently to Venice also. This was a commission, as they all were. His *Marriage of the Foundlings* drew striking similarities to the Contini piece and I wondered if he had been commissioned to do this one based on his fame there. I pulled away and rubbed my eyes. Nothing to do now but let it brew in my subconscious for a while.

I scanned the room, my eyes landing on my suitcase. Along with my battered carpetbag, which traveled with me everywhere, I had brought an equally beat-up roller. That's all. I tended to travel light and yet somehow a smaller Vuitton carry-on now sat beside them like an interloper. Not my bag or my style but by now I knew Nicolina's tendency to give me things I didn't know I needed or necessarily want. Whatever lay inside that bag was probably way above my budget, or deadly, or both.

Reluctantly, I lifted the bag onto the inlaid bench—mosaic, probably late fifteenth century—popped the lock, and stared down at mounds of folded tissue paper. A familiar tingle hit my spine. Anything of a textile nature did that to me and I recognized carefully tended fabric when I saw it. Unwrapping the contents revealed a long black silk dress, a velvet hooded cloak, black stockings, tall leather boots, and a short black leather jacket in the biker style, all from an Italian couture house I didn't recognize. I stared. Was I to masquerade as Little Black Riding Hood now? Maybe a Jane Eyre dominatrix? Baffled, I let the silken folds drop to the bed. Since I was wearing jeans, black trainers, and a green turtleneck to pick up the colors in my kelp garden wrap, presumably I was not dressed for elegance, whatever the occasion.

The jacket, however, was something else again. Nicolina knew my history with outerwear, considering I had stuffed a bloody postcard inside my last leather jacket and then dunked the thing in Jamaica's Rio Grande. Perhaps she offered this one as a replacement gift?

I left the clothes strewn across the bed and turned away. Then I had a thought. Returning to the carry-on, I reached inside, felt along the lower edges, and found what I sought. My fingers sprung what I knew to be the mechanism that hid an X-ray-shielded false bottom and soon I was pulling out a handy little Magnum pistol and several rounds of ammunition, the perfect accessory for a woman who travels apparently. Pack it right below your toothbrush, yes, ma'am.

Well, damn. I stared at the thing. Nicolina and her guns. She always carried them and expected me to, too, as much as I rebelled against the idea on principle. However, principle had taken a bit of a hit in the past few years to the point where I had taken firearm lessons with a former policewoman along with a side of martial arts training. Though I objected to violence, that didn't mean I planned on being a victim anytime soon. I took the thing and carefully set it down beside me on the bed. I'd leave the extra ammunition where it was for now.

Next, I whipped off a text in code to Max: *Here in Venice. Weather mixed. Nicolina says hi.* Max would get the point: something was going down in Venice and it wasn't the weather. Besides, Nicolina would never say hi.

I checked the time: 10:15 in the UK. Max would either be watching the news or tucked into bed, his phone left downstairs on the kitchen counter as usual. He never took to sleeping with his devices. No one I knew seemed to have quite the same relationship in bed with their phone as I did. That said a lot about my lack of sleeping companions. In any case, I wouldn't hear from him tonight.

Sighing, I gazed around. Obviously I needed to knit, my sleeping pill of choice and as soothing to me as hot chocolate and a lullaby. I was far too buzzed to sleep and yet the villa had gone quiet as if everyone had retired early. Now I wished I'd taken Nicolina up on her nighttime vino offer since wine inevitably made me sleepy, but no decanter and glasses had been made available. Apparently I was lucky to have access to water, which presumably I could fetch from the en suite bathroom.

So it was to my sedative of choice that I turned. I took my carpetbag and pulled out my beloved Melancholy wrap with its comforting lengths of green and mahogany silk that I had added only the night before. Oh, how lovely. Yes, this would do.

For a few moments the feel of the yarn in my fingers soothed me and I was ready to happily dive into those stitches until sleep tugged away. Or so I thought. The moment I thrust my hand in my bag to retrieve the second needle, my comfort was replaced by a stab of panic: I could not locate that familiar stick of polished wood! Alarmed, I emptied the bag onto the bed and pawed through the balls and skeins, my overnight kit, the change of undies and extra sweater, but came up empty. Absolutely no second needle. Somehow it had slipped from my bag and was gone.

My sense of loss was as powerful as it was ridiculous. I felt agitated the way one might when they realize a critical prescription had run out and some dreadful symptom was about to inflict itself. I stood up and began pacing the room, seized by the knowledge that, without knitting, I would probably obsess over Rupert and Nicolina until my body collapsed in a shaking heap. I needed vino, badly needed vino. I could honestly say that, without knitting, I could be driven to drink.

Pushing the door open a crack, I peered into the hall. Everything was dark and quiet. Presumably Nicolina had retired to mourn in private while Seraphina was either comforting her friend or asleep. Or something. What did it matter? I wasn't doing anything clandestine, unless locating a glass of nighttime vino was considered socially unacceptable in an Italian household, which I strongly doubted.

Still, no lights were left on downstairs, which meant I must use my phone light for navigation purposes. I padded downstairs as quietly as I could with the intention of heading straight for the salon where I had last seen the decanter. The place was much larger than I thought—room after room branched out on either side of the long hall but most rooms appeared to be locked. Working from memory, I proceeded down the long dark hall trying doors until I reached a room on the right-hand side where I was certain Zara had delivered us hours before. The door opened easily and I beamed my light toward the low table. Empty. Someone, presumably Zara, had tidied up after we'd gone upstairs.

Now what? I wasn't an ordinary guest in a hotel but an interloper in a house of mourning. I'd go straight for the kitchen and pour my own wine. I headed toward where I assumed a kitchen would be in a Venetian villa— somewhere at the back of the house—and I was right. As soon as I shoved open the tall wooden door, my phone light caught the gleam of chrome and porcelain. I was about to flick on the light switch when I caught a sound coming from below.

For a moment, I just stood listening. There was no way in hell anyone should be down in the cantina this time of night when the residents had retired for the evening and the place was dark. No, this was not right.

Retracing my steps, I bounded upstairs to my bedroom and knocked on all three of the doors. "Nicolina, Seraphina, Zara, get up! There's someone down-stairs in the cantina!"

I expected a flurry of doors to fly open or, at the very least, a cry of alarm. Nothing. "Hello?" I tried again.

Finally, a door squeaked open at the end of the hall followed by a light switching on, and there was Zara wrapped in a long mauve robe stomping toward me as if she wanted to shake out my molars.

I took a step back. "Where's Nicolina and Seraphina?"

Stopping a foot away, she asked me something in Italian to which I shrugged. Turning, she marched up to one of the doors and knocked on the oak imperiously. "Contessa Vanvitelli?" No answer.

In a moment, she was storming inside the room, me at her heels. Not only was there no Nicolina, but her bed hadn't been slept in.

Zara swung around and pushed past me out the hall across to another door where she repeated the process. No Seraphina, either. Standing in the middle of the elegant room, Zara peppered me with a battery of Italian.

"*Excusi*, me no speak Italian." The things we say when stressed. "But there's someone down in the basement—the cantina. *Comprendo?* Maybe Nicolina and Seraphina? We must look!"

She stared at me. *"Cantina?"*

"Downstairs!" I pointed downward and stamped my foot for effect.

Realization dawned. Zara straightened her bony shoulders and hurried off down the stairs without another word. I hesitated only long enough to return to my room and grab the gun.

I was shoving my feet into my sneakers as I climbed down the stairs, my phone in one pocket, the gun in the other. In seconds, I was at the top of the kitchen steps.

"Zara?" I called down. The light was on and I heard something like a grunt below. Holding the gun, I followed her down. Zara was standing beneath the overhead light, hands on her hips, glaring straight at the closed canal door.

Seeing me, she pointed at the tracks leading from inside the door straight through toward the canal. I got the picture: someone had taken the small speedboat, that someone probably being Seraphina and Nicolina.

Zara glared balefully at the gun, which I hastily lowered, at which point she assaulted me with angry Italian. *"Hanno preso il motoscafo!"*

"Well, don't blame me," I shot back. "I'm as in the dark as you. Is there another *motoscafo*? I'll even take a regular *scafo*."

Zara shook her head furiously. *"No motoscafo e non stai prendendo la gondola!"*

I wasn't certain exactly what she was saying but I got the gist: no boat for me, not even a gondola. I pocketed the gun and dashed back up the stairs all the way to my room to grab the new jacket, suddenly fuming. Nicolina and Seraphina had taken off on some midnight assignation and left me behind stranded like an extra overnight bag?

What was worse is that I knew it had something to do with Rupert. I had defended him to Nicolina, clearly didn't believe that he had anything to do with Maria's death, and now my deadly countess would do what she felt necessary with or without me. That was just all wrong, grief or no.

I bounded back downstairs and straight down the hall to slide the bolts on the grand front door while Zara scurried behind me, barking in Italian. A beeping had begun as a little red light flashed from the panel on the wall.

"I'm going out one way or the other," I told her. "You'd best deactivate the alarm unless you want the Venetian *polizia* here in a nanosecond."

Zara tapped the code onto the panel and the beeping promptly stopped. I swung open the door. *"Dove credit di andare?"* she asked as I stepped out.

Of course I didn't know what she said but I took a guess. "I'm not sure when I'll be back. Don't wait up."

6

I had no idea where I was going, only that I had to move. Remaining locked in that villa of sorrows while my friends went off on some dubious excursion without me stuck felt so wrong. At the very least, a walk might burn off enough caffeine-fueled energy to allow me to sleep. Maybe, if I was extraordinarily lucky, I might even glimpse Seraphina and Nicolina zipping by in the *motoscafo*.

Despite the lateness of the hour, Venice was not sleeping. Though the villas along the Cannaregio were shuttered for the night, the restaurants and bars still percolated with activity. In fact, after I had navigated the barricaded edge of the canal that had apparently been damaged in a recent storm, I found myself striding along a wide brightly lit cement walkway that was clearly still open for business.

On the left, gondolas could be seen resting among a forest of mooring poles while a handful of diners lingered inside their plastic-screened restaurant patios huddled up to outdoor gas heaters. I envied them their cozy company, the laughter rising up over the tinkling glasses. In truth, I also envied them their pastas and grilled fish, dishes I could only imagine by their scent. I was starving.

Nicolina had said that the warehouse lay farther down the street, but without a number or any other identifying features, I couldn't determine which was which at first. That is until I saw an armed carabiniere, an officer of the national guard, a kind of militarized police force that co-policed Italy with two other organizations, standing outside a nondescript door. Above loomed a large terra-cotta-painted building featuring rows of pointed arched windows reminiscent of Eastern influences. The building looked simultaneously welcoming and imposing and the uniformed officer did not look friendly. In fact, he looked quite out of sorts. I strolled by slowly, studying the warehouse.

"Move along, miss. This is a crime site," the officer barked in English. It was goading to be recognized as a tourist so easily. Picking up my pace, I strode quickly past.

It had stopped raining and, though still chilly, the air smelled fresh and watery. With a sudden ping of excitement, it occurred to me that I was actually in Venice, *Venice*. And that I was alone, which was exhilarating because it meant that no compromise was necessary, that I could go where I wanted, walk anywhere I pleased—be a random voyager, in other words. As my younger self, I had been leashed by a tour group and had never felt prepared enough to stroll a city alone at night.

Now I had a suite of skills at my disposal including martial arts and firearm skills. How I resented all those years when I'd felt restricted because cities were presumed unsafe for women in a way that didn't hold true for men. Considering what I had been through in the past five years and that I was armed and probably dangerous, fearing the ordinary criminal wasn't in the picture. I could defend myself against pickpockets, rapists, robbers, and the like, so cities at night no longer frightened me. In fact, I almost dared anyone to try anything.

Besides, the stalkers who had once dodged my heels had presumably lost interest now that Toby was locked up and I had broken up with Noel, not that we had ever really been together. It was as if the underground communication channels had informed the black market that I was no longer a person of interest. How long would it take for everyone to figure out that my friends and I sat on a fortune of rescued art? Until then, I flew under the radar, or so I hoped. I may as well enjoy it while it lasted.

The lively canal boulevard retreated into the distance the farther I walked. Enticing little alleyways beckoned me on and I took the path less traveled every time. Long dimly lit passageways hemmed in by looming buildings hundreds of years old suited my mood. I loved the mysterious atmosphere, the sense of treading in the footfalls of thousands of souls that had gone before me combined with that haunted hush that descends upon very old places at night. It was almost like walking among ghosts, a sense one rarely experiences when in the company of others.

Shop windows illuminated old bookstores, souvenir shops, and mask vendors, all closed for the night. The city still bore the tawdry remains of revelry as if Venice was just too exhausted after the Carnevale to wash off her face paint. I'd see streamers floating in puddles, a glittery mask hanging on a doorknob, and everywhere the sense of festive aftermath, from the ragged paper signs announcing past events, to the streamers and iridescent confetti plastered onto the damp cobbles.

Occasional groups of four or five pedestrians passed by me in full medieval regalia complete with sparkly masks as if nobody had told them that the Carnevale was over. Lost in time like Venice herself. One man dressed like a fifteenth century courtier poked his face into mine and said something in winy Italian while his companion pulled him away laughing.

Strollers of the more sedate variety squeezed past me in the alleyways, too —lovers arm in arm, a young man marching purposefully with his hands in his pockets, head down. I'd turn a corner and find myself sweeping over a tiny bridge, picture-postcard views of a sleeping canal on either side that left me enchanted, totally in the moment. I felt I could walk forever, stepping over and around this ancient city with its twinkling lights and watery byways while its foundations of ancient logs moldered away deep in the lagoon beneath my feet.

Of course, history always kept me company, a ponderous but fascinating companion. I knew how Venice was built as a refuge against invading marauders and constructed in the lagoon by logs plunged deep into the cold mud, wooden foundations that remained preserved for centuries. Amazing to think that this miraculous floating city was actually sinking by the minute and not because of rotting foundations, though there were signs of that, too, but because the rising sea levels threatened to swamp the ancient streets.

Lulled by the up and down of bridges, the twisting alleys and tiny *campi*, my mind traveled along its own windy path. After a bit, I left thoughts of history behind and focused on my own small universe. Look how far I'd come from the days when I wanted so desperately to please everyone that I could be lured unwittingly into danger time and time again. *If you don't know what you stand for, you'll fall for anything.* That saying certainly applied to me.

These days, I dove into trouble with eyes wide open. What I had to gain far exceeded what I had to lose, to my way of thinking—my life and those I cared about aside. Now I knew what I stood for and was willing to fight for it: protect the world's art legacy for future generations and prevent the priceless from slipping into the hands of the criminal few. And spread the love for textiles while I was at it. Yes, I'd protect my friends and loved ones, too—yes, I would—even if they didn't want me to. Toby came to mind since he hardly wanted to be incarcerated in order to get clean.

I crossed another bridge and caught sight of lovers kissing deeply in the shadows and an ambush of dismay hit me so hard I almost gasped aloud. I carried on across a deserted little *campo* toward a medieval well, and sat down on a stone bench, suddenly heartsick. So much for bravado. Bravado was a rogue wave of emotion at the best of times. Look at me now: I'd given up love in lieu of principle. Wasn't I grand? This new kick-ass Phoebe had handed over her brother and cut the heartstrings to the man she loved. I felt the hole in my heart as deep as the grave and it didn't matter that a moral choice influenced both acts.

What would I do if Noel were to appear over that little bridge right then? He had ambushed me at unexpected moments before. How I longed to see him and how I didn't—the conundrum of heartbreak.

I stood up. Yes, I sent my brother to prison for a reason, and if Noel seriously wanted to turn his life around and spend some good years with me, he could have taken a stand that night in Jamaica. But he didn't. He didn't want to turn his life around, not in the legal sense. Instead, he ran. That's not what I wanted in a man. I wanted a partner, a lover, a companion, not to mention somebody I could see more often than once or twice a year. I was tired of runners. Enough.

My backbone fortified, I continued my walk more resolved with every step but still oblivious to where I was going. Rupert and Evan were somewhere in this ancient city and by now they'd know I was here, too. Maybe they were even following me.

I swung around to gaze as another twisting alleyway disappeared into the shadows. Footsteps echoed behind me, stopping when I stopped, pausing when I paused. I had been so lost in thought I hadn't noticed until now. Who knew how long I'd been followed? Noel, maybe? My breath caught and I waited. And waited.

Not Noel. He'd approach. My spine tingled. Well, hell. Just when I thought no one cared what I was up to...but then again, maybe the mute stone walls, the narrow alleyways, the shadows, ghosts, and mists were wearing on me. Maybe my true stalker was my own conscience. I checked my watch: 11:05.

Turning away, I carried on down another alley, around and over and into and out, listening to the footsteps echoing out of sight behind walls and on the other side of bridges. Now I knew the stalker was real and it wasn't Noel. Maybe whoever it was had been keeping me company the whole time. The Accademia Bridge came and went in a burst of bright lights, bars, and clusters of people in masks. I turned, hoping to catch a glimpse of my stalker in the crowd but it was impossible.

Fog began wafting in from the lagoon, thick and atmospheric, and now I had arrived on the other side of Venice. All the mysteries set in the city rose into my imagination unbidden: *Don't Look Now*, every single Donna Leon book...

Hell. Stop that, Phoebe. I kept on walking and listening, thinking that I would find a dead end and wait for my stalker to arrive. That's what children were advised to do with monsters chasing them in their dreams—face them— and that's what I'd do, too. Only I was prepared to tackle my monster if necessary. I released the safety catch on the pistol in my pocket and kept on walking.

Two more small bridges came and went, each of which looked exactly like the other. I reached a dark body of water where the fog was so thick that lights across the canal could barely penetrate the gloom, where overhead streetlights pushed damp halos through the mist. Behind me stood the imposing domed church illuminated by spotlights that I recognized as the church of Santa Maria della Salute, consecrated in 1681 as a votive from the people of Venice following the devastation of the plague. Why did I have to recall all this historical minutiae at times like this? The plague church. Like I needed that. I turned and waited.

Before me lay the Grand Canal and across the water St. Mark's Square shrouded in fog, which may as well be a million miles away. I had walked across the whole of Venice, which also meant I'd have to walk the whole way back. I stepped onto the pier toward the deserted platform of a vaporetto depot. This late at night, I could be waiting for the next ride for a long time. Forget that. And what was worse, my pursuer did not step out of the alleyway to introduce himself.

I waited and waited and so, apparently, did he or she. Okay, so if my stalker wouldn't come to me, I'd just meet them en route.

Thus began a frustrating interlude of me trying to retrace my steps over these same two little bridges to get back toward the Accademia Bridge from whence I'd come. Somehow I'd end up right back at the foot of the Salute having gone in one big circle. I rubbed my eyes, obviously far more tired than I thought. I tried again with exactly the same result and still those echoing footsteps on my heels.

What was I doing, taking a left when I should have gone right? Was my stalker hanging back in the shadows laughing at me while I lost myself over and over again? I felt a presence standing deep in the shadows somewhere.

Once more I turned the corner following the side of the church until I reached the first bridge, and once again the second bridge led me to a passage between two buildings and straight back to the Salute.

"Who are you and what do you want?" I called out. Of course no one answered.

The fog was thickening, I was tiring of the game, and at last I pulled out my cell phone. My plan was to activate the GPS and find my way out of the maze but instead I found myself reading a text from Nicolina:

Phoebe, where are you?

I typed back: *At Salute pier. Where are you?*

We are at the villa, of course. Stay there. We will come get you. It will take at least fifteen minutes.

Great, fifteen more minutes of fog, shadow, and my unseen companion. Why not? I strode across the concrete to wait by the edge of the pier, looking down into the dark water. "If you're still watching me, the least you could do is step out and hold a conversation." Nothing.

Five minutes longer, I looked up to the sound of a speedboat approaching. Nicolina already? I stepped closer to the edge and waited.

A single figure manning a small speedboat approached, throttling the engine as the craft put-putted up to the wharf. It took me a moment to realize that the man wore a cape and a black mask, *Phantom of the Opera*–style. I was so not in the mood for this.

Fingering the gun in my pocket, I stepped forward. "Ahoy. Who goes there?"

7

"Good evening, madam," the figure called up with a grin that I found both encouraging and unsettling, under the circumstances. "I have come to offer you a lift, rather like an Uber Vaporetto."

My breath caught. I recognized that deep voice. "An Uberetto? Well, this is a surprise. A lift to where, may I ask?" I called down.

"Wherever you wish, madam. I am at your service."

"At my service, really—in a mask and a cape?"

The man shrugged and smiled. "When in Venice…"

It didn't matter, since I was extraordinarily glad to see this man no matter what his get-up.

"Were you just stalking me?" I asked. But being in two places at once was impossible even for him.

"Absolutely not. Was someone following you?" he asked, alarm in his voice.

"Someone was but refused to reveal himself in order to be properly introduced."

"How rude."

"I thought so." I accepted his gloved hand and allowed him to guide me into the craft as if I couldn't get my own self into a boat and drive the thing, too. He knew it, I knew it, but I took a seat in the prow facing my driver with my hands clasped between my knees. "Seriously, Evan, what's up with the mask?"

"Venice is a city of subterfuge, madam, especially now. Where would you like me to deliver you?"

"Away from here as fast as this *motoscafo* can take us. Nicolina and Seraphina are gunning their way toward me now and I'm sure you don't want that encounter. Take me to Rupert."

"Sir Rupert?" he called over the engine noise as we churned away from the pier. "Sir Rupert does not expect you this evening, madam. He's indisposed. We only wished to ensure your safety."

Bizarre that something that once drove me to distraction—being tailed by Rupert Fox and his multitalented right-hand man—should now cause me so much relief. "My convenience was more the issue here than my safety but thanks, anyway. Rupert is indisposed, really? Does he require his pajamas pressed or something? Well, you can take me to see him, anyway. Please call him to say I'm coming over and that's that. This can't wait."

"As you wish, madam."

"And stop with the 'madam' stuff, will you? You know my name." I'd lost count of the number of times I'd made that request but it never made a whit of difference. Apparently Evan was hardwired to call me "madam." If James Bond had been pressed into active service as a dogsbody following his stint with Her Majesty's Secret Service, it would be Evan.

While he spoke rapidly into his cell phone and steered with his other hand, I pulled out my phone and texted Nicolina: *Ride not needed. I have another lift. Will be back in a couple of hours. Sorry for the inconvenience. Don't wait up.*

When I looked again, I realized that Evan had darted the boat into one of the smaller canals on this side of the Accademia and for the first time I wondered exactly where Rupert was staying—not at one of the luxe hotels along the Grand Canal, as I had expected. No, we were winding deeper into this side of Venice's watery maze, the boat slowing down to a sedate putter after several twists and turns as we threaded between mostly residential buildings.

Soon Evan cut the engine and we floated for a few moments on the watery darkness. Had I not known him better, I would have thought he planned to slit my throat and toss my body into the canal—the perfect setting—but I'd always trusted this man with my life. Around us, Renaissance buildings with tall shuttered windows loomed down like long dark faces with their eyes closed. See no evil…

I was about to ask him what was up when he said: "Madam, what have you brought with you from the villa?"

I looked down at my new jacket and patted the pocket to indicate the gun.

He nodded at me and held out his hand.

Without a word, I shrugged off the jacket and passed it over, watching as he ran his phone up and down every seam until the device beeped. In a flash, he pulled a pocket knife from his jacket, slit the jacket's lining, and tugged out a shiny coin-like object, which he promptly tossed in the canal. Next, he studied my phone, turned it off, and returned it to the jacket pocket and proceeded to investigate the gun. That, too, had some kind of tracking device secreted on its barrel. Once it was dropped into the water, the jacket was returned and he held out his hand again.

I passed over my carpetbag this time and watched as he performed the same test over each seam, finding another device tucked into the lining.

"Well, damn. Seraphina. I've got to get better at looking for those things." I sighed. "They probably already know where I am."

"No matter." Then he pointed to what I thought was a black blanket folded beside another bundle at my feet. "There is a rain cape in that package, which you may find useful. Please put it on."

Though it wasn't raining, the mist was thick enough to dampen everything. I opened the package and unfolded a plastic rain cape, which I donned, pulling the hood up so as to give my hair less excuse to frizz.

"You will also find a mask in the other bag. Please put that on, too."

"Seriously? Carnevale is over, Evan. Am I going to a masquerade or something? I know Rupert loves his balls but this hardly seemed the time, though admittedly the place couldn't be more perfect."

I was rewarded by a small smile. "Not quite, madam. The mask is for your protection. Should you be interrogated as to Sir Rupert's location, you will truthfully be unable to provide directions."

"So it's not a mask so much as a blindfold?" I pulled something stiff and cumbersome from the bag. Holding it up to the meager light, I stared aghast at a hood to which was affixed empty eye sockets and a long beak-like extension like a grisly comic-book bird. I recognized it immediately. This kind of bizarre mask was once worn by physicians in the Middle Ages who stuffed the beak with potpourri in the hope that the herbs would protect them against pestilence. "The plague doctor? Are you kidding me?"

"I assure you I am not," he said. "This is the only thing I had on hand, and though not technically a blindfold, there's a very slim chance that you will be able to identify our route while wearing it. Sir Rupert feels that even though you might swear not to reveal our hideout, you are, he says, 'an abysmal liar.'"

"His fault for raising the bar so high. Is he hiding out, then?"

"The mask, please, madam."

Rupert was in hiding. Did I blame him? Thoughts of Nicolina and the stalwart Seraphina peppering me with questions I might not want to answer clinched it. I dropped the thing over my head and stared out into the muffled silence. True enough, I could barely see more than misty shadows through the eyeholes. "I just want to say that floating through the Venetian canals dressed as a plague doctor with a masked bandito at the helm of a *motoscafo* is not how I thought tonight would end." There was a mouth hole under the beak so presumably he caught the gist but he said nothing in return, or at least nothing I could hear.

In moments the boat lurched forward and we were on our way again, me caught in some kind of strange, sense-deprived limbo as we zipped along. With nothing left to do but think, it occurred to me that I knew the man at the helm only by his first name until recently. Though I'd spent many hours in his company, mostly in heightened situations, he remained a total enigma. That he had once been an MI6 agent was common knowledge, how he ended up as Sir Rupert Fox's right-hand man was not. He was amazingly skilled at multiple things, from cooking to finagling technological devices to performing improbable feats at short notice. Yet he appeared to live a solitary life attached to Rupert's side. Why would a man with Evan's talents be content to work for another, except for the obvious—money and adventure? And yet, there was something about him that made me think that there had to be more to the story. There always was.

I felt a tap on my beak. "Hold on, madam," he called.

All thoughts were jolted away when I heard the engine throttle to full as the boat hit open water. I stared ahead at nothing as we zoomed through the chop toward some undisclosed destination. I managed to catch glimpses of lights stacked off to the right. Skyscrapers? No, cruise ships! We had to be following the cruise pier on the right-hand side, which meant that we must be on the broad Giudecca Canal. Hell, did I want to know even that much?

Not that it mattered. Soon we were turning back into the canals, I guessed, judging by the multiple abrupt turns and the occasional echoes of the boat's engine under bridges. After only a minute of that, I was totally disorientated. Once I caught a whiff of blossoms—cherry or maybe apple—leaving me with the impression that we had passed a garden, but otherwise I may as well be a million miles elsewhere. Eventually and at last, the engine was abruptly cut and the boat coasted a few yards forward.

"Are we here yet?" I whispered

"Yes, madam. Directly. Best to be silent."

So silent I was. I kept quiet as the boat bumped against a mooring, sat patiently as Evan leaped out to secure the craft, and waited until his strong hand guided me up until I stood on a dock. He steered me forward with his arm around my shoulders—not an unpleasant sensation, though probably unnecessary—until I heard a door scrape open and a bolt shove home behind us. A security something beeped softly.

"May I take this thing off now?"

"In a moment, madam."

I was being led down a dark passageway, right into one room, left into another.

"Now?"

"Not yet."

We walked for about another ten yards and then I heard a voice. "My word!" it croaked. "Have you delivered death to my doorstop yet again, Evan?"

I whipped off the mask and stood staring into the candlelit face of Sir Rupert Fox. He stood before me wrapped in a blanket in the center of what looked to be an empty ballroom—marble floors, mirrored walls, slender pillars, a dark fireplace at one end—all of it lit by electric lanterns as well as candlelight. Though the light seemed inadequate for such an expanse, it didn't take a spotlight to see he was sick. "Rupert! What's wrong with you?"

"Phoebe! Imagine seeing you here...after all... Wasn't the last time just after you...sent us to Tahiti?" He began to cough racking heaves that shook his frame so hard I thought he'd topple over.

Evan and I raced to his side. "You must lie down, sir. To bed with you immediately. You were not supposed to get up while I was away."

"Yes, back to bed now," I seconded, looking around. So where was the bed in this marble wasteland? Surely not that foldout steel-legged mattressy thing set up in the center of the room beside a pillar and a single unlit Tiffany lamp?

But with Evan on one side and me on the other, that's exactly where we steered Rupert, while the whole time I glimpsed the ghost-like reflection of our movements in the wall-to-ceiling mirrors at the far end of the room.

"Where is this place?" I whispered.

"That must remain undisclosed at all costs," Evan answered as he tucked his employer under the covers, made him swallow two ibuprofens with gulps of water, and wiped his forehead with a cloth from a bowl of melting ice. "It is imperative that no one discover our hiding place." And then in a louder voice, he asked: "Have you taken your antibiotics, sir?"

"You gave them to me...before you left...old chap."

"Indeed I did. Just testing. Now, it is absolutely critical that you rest. Ms. Phoebe will only stay a short while—" he shot me a quick glance "—and then I shall deliver her to her accommodation, as planned. What can I get you in the meantime?"

"A doctor, surely?" I said, looking up at Evan.

His green eyes met mine—worried eyes, I realized. "He was seen by a physician earlier today—"

"At an exorbitant price—highway robbery…" Rupert wheezed.

"He charged a reasonable fee considering that we swore him to secrecy," Evan said. "At knifepoint, if I recall." Turning to me, he added: "Sir Rupert was diagnosed as having a probable case of pneumonia following a bad cold that he was fighting in London. We won't know for certain until the test results come back."

"The doctor bled me, Phoebe, *bled* me," Rupert rasped.

"He drew blood for the tests," Evan clarified, almost but not quite rolling his eyes. "You were in no danger of expiring during the procedure."

"Nonsense. For all we know he was a black market quack." Rupert coughed.

"I checked him out thoroughly, I assure you. The good doctor is a very legitimate practitioner, just one inclined to line his pockets with extra money."

"The Italian way," Rupert remarked in his alarming voice.

"Nevertheless, we were grateful for his services." Evan had the patience of a saint—an armed saint, maybe, but nobody's perfect.

"Valid doctor or not, Rupert should be in a hospital," I said.

"Impossible under the circumstances," Evan remarked while Rupert gazed up at me with feverish eyes.

"What circumstances?"

"They would have me…killed," Rupert rasped.

"Who would have you killed?"

"Unfortunately, we may have more than one candidate with possible murderous intentions in this city," Evan responded mildly.

I knew of at least two.

"I am not popular in…Venice," Rupert said.

"Then why did you come?" I looked up toward the tall ceiling with its ornate wooden timbers shrouded in shadows and suppressed a shiver. "And why here?"

"Long story…" Rupert closed his eyes. "No energy left to tell it. Evan, my boy, do fetch us…some tea…if you please. We may be camped out…in this haunted villa…but we needn't live like specters."

"Haunted?" It did feel haunted but then so did most of Venice.

"Tea, Evan," Rupert murmured.

"Tea coming up." Evan caught my eye as if to say *don't tire him* and was gone in an instant, dashing across the vacant room on his long legs and disappearing through an arched door on the far end.

"What is going on?" I pulled up a folding chair and positioned it by the camp bed. His face shined with sweat, his eyes feverish. "Tell me. This...this —" I gazed around, grappling for adjectives "—this moldering heap looks unhealthy, if not dangerous. I can smell mold if not ghosts."

"Ghosts don't smell, Phoebe—" he paused as if considering his words "— well, maybe they do. This...this is truly a lovely...building but I admit...to never wanting to stay in it...like this. Two murders took place here...and unaccountable misfortunes to the owners. I am here as a...last resort."

"Some resort," I muttered. Obviously it had been a large palazzo of some sort, a once dignified and ornate Renaissance establishment that had, for whatever reason, been left to ruin. "You should be recuperating in a hospital or at one of those luxurious hotels you favor. Really, I never saw you as much of a glamper."

He emitted something like a snort. "A glamper indeed. It makes a perfect... hiding place. The locals...think it's haunted and...avoid it at all costs. It has been...deserted for years." Though he labored with every breath he seemed intent to talk.

"I gathered that but from whom are you hiding exactly and why here?"

He waved a hand at the shadows before letting it drop back to the bed. "At least I own this and so can...stay with some impunity. I bought it decades ago...an investment. I planned to restore it as...my Venetian bolt-hole."

I looked around. "A bolt-hole the size of a palace?"

He took a moment to catch his breath. "But I am persona non grata...in this city, always have been. They have a long memory here...never forgetting so much as...an imagined infraction." He spent a few minutes recovering before continuing. "And I couldn't get workmen...to restore it...quickly."

"All right—" I nodded "—so you shafted someone, probably cheated them out of some priceless piece of art for which they'll never forgive you, plus you tried to marry some man's daughter, which didn't exactly work out—got it— but what brought you to Venice this time? Tell the truth." I just needed him to say it.

"Oh," he rasped, "a fine one to speak of truth, Phoebe...after you sent...us on a wild...goose chase."

I patted his hand. "And how did that feel, Rupert, after the multiple times you've tricked me over the years? I've been on so many wild-goose chases these days, I try to fly in a flock."

He looked at me aghast, almost like he was seeing me for the first time. Then he closed his eyes and emitted a sound like sandpaper against a chalkboard. "What happened…to you, Phoebe? You used to be…so sweet."

"Gullible, you mean. I've grown wiser. You lost nothing by taking a detour to Tahiti except maybe upping your sunburn quotient."

"Nonsense. I'm diligent…with my SPF." At least the old humor was there. "But you are wrong about losing something. I shall explain all as soon as I am able."

"The Rembrandts were all forgeries, compliments of my brother's consummate skill," I continued. "But that's all beside the point now. Let's put it behind us. We have more pressing matters to deal with. Besides, I've missed you and you missed me. Don't deny it."

"I don't…deny it."

"Good—" I squeezed his hand "—so let's get back to being friends and try a dose of honesty while we're at it—honesty as in full disclosure, not your shifty half-truth variety. Why are you really here, Rupert?"

He fixed me with his bleary eyes. "For the sake of Maria Contini."

I pulled my hand away. "I knew it. Damn it, Rupert. You know that Nicolina believes you may be responsible for Maria's death." I wasn't thinking. That was one bomb I shouldn't have dropped in Rupert's weakened state.

"That's preposterous!" He propped himself on his elbows and fumed at me. "Me kill Maria? I loved her once! She always has a place…in my heart!" And then he began to cough and cough.

"Calm down. It's all right, everything is all right." I dashed over to the little foldout table, retrieved what I hoped to be cough medicine, and spooned some down his throat followed by water. "Evan!" I called, but suddenly Evan was speeding into the room while Rupert's face reddened to the point of combustion. For a hideous moment I was afraid he'd expire on my watch.

Evan, wearing an apron and bearing a tray of tea things that he set down with a clatter, rushed to my side. "What happened?"

"I can't get him to stop coughing."

"Sir Rupert, calm yourself at once!" Evan ordered, laying a hand on his forehead. "You are not to get upset. Ms. Phoebe will leave you to rest immediately."

Rupert shook his head and clasped Evan's arm, his eyes nearly bulging from their sockets. "Tell her," he gasped. "Every…thing. Within…reason."

"I don't think that's wise, sir, for her sake or yours."

"Tell her!" Then he took a deep heaving breath and fell back against the pillows, eyes closed, one hand flapping in the air as if waving us away.

Evan caught my eye, lips stern in that chiseled chin. "You have exhausted him, madam."

"He has exhausted himself." I met his gaze steadily, trying to block how devastatingly attractive a muscled man looks wearing an apron and scowling. As if this was the time for such thoughts.

We watched Rupert carefully until the patient appeared to be resting and his face had lost its explosive flush. When I was certain he was dozing, my eyes met Evan's again and I pointed toward the door at the far end of the ballroom and mouthed, *Let's talk.* He nodded and I followed him across the marble floor.

Carrying a battery-operated lantern, he led me through another huge empty room with tall shuttered windows and damp-stained brown wallpaper that might have once been gold silk, down a dark hall, and into a back room lit with various portable lights. One spotlight blazed onto a microwave, hot plate, and a two-burner radiant-heat cooking surface.

I looked around at what appeared to be a kitchen/office space furnished with old-fashioned counters, a central butcher's block commandeered as a desk, and an assortment of blinking lights that may have been battery packs. A stack of books sat neatly on one of the counters, another bookmarked and sitting on the floor beside a chair.

"So not a crack of natural light is allowed in this fortress, right?" I asked, trying to read the book's title in the pocket of gloom.

"I have secured this building with the necessary features, including cameras, remote surveillance, and alarms. However, from the outside, it must still look like an abandoned building, which is admittedly a challenge. Please take a seat." He turned and offered me a chair at a folding table. "The book is on Renaissance art, by the way, history being a bit of a hobby." So he'd caught my curious glance. Well, of course he did: nothing escaped Evan.

In a moment, he whisked away a pile of electronic circuitry and clutter that occupied the surface. Evan was a technical genius but working under these conditions must tax even his abilities. A technical genius who read history and poetry? I caught another title on the spine of a book sitting on the counter at my back: *A Dedication to the Stars: The Universe in Poetry.*

I scraped over the metal chair and settled in, dropping my carpetbag at my feet, and waited for him to join me, which he did with his usual quick efficiency. This would be the first time ever that Evan and I had license to discuss a situation one-to-one without Rupert taking the lead. It was unsettling. Do we now behave as colleagues, friends, what? I knew Evan's deference to be only a veneer that locked down a fascinating and dangerous combination of skills and attributes but the man still unnerved me, especially like this. And I thought the feeling could be mutual.

"Is the Renaissance the historical period that interests you most?" I asked.

"All centuries interest me but I try to soak up as much detail as possible if the period is relevant to my mission."

"So the Renaissance is relevant to this mission?"

"Possibly."

Why was he feeding me these details? Really, I needed to take the lead here and the best defense is a strong offense, as they say. "Okay, Evan," I began, "so tell me what's going on and skip the 'within reason' condition Rupert added. The situation is critical, you must see that, and we have to work together. I know I can help. Nicolina believes Rupert—and you by default—may be in some way involved in Maria Contini's death."

"That's completely untrue," he said, looking mildly annoyed at the thought that he would ever participate in such an act. I waited but that's all he said. Getting information from this man would be like prying barnacles from rocks with a toenail clipper. Presumably he'd been trained to keep his cards plastered to his brawny chest during his MI6 days but still...

"What part's completely untrue—the part about us working together or the bit about you two being involved in Maria's murder?"

"The latter. The former is something we will continue to do, I trust."

And he was always so formal, which was disconcerting in itself. I leaned forward, watching him carefully. He had a little tick by his left eye that twitched almost imperceptibly when he was reining himself in. Maybe Her Majesty's Secret Service ousted him on that fact alone since it gave him away every single time. "Nicolina says that should she learn that Rupert was anywhere near Maria on the night she died, she'll kill him herself." I paused, waiting for a reaction. Something flickered across his chiseled features. "That worries me because she's fully capable of it. Well?"

"Well, what, madam?"

Hell. He was back to the "madam" bit. "Was Rupert—or you, for that matter—anywhere near Maria Contini on the last night of Carnevale?"

Evan fixed me with his gray-green gaze but said nothing. His twitch started twitching and, in this case, a twitch is worth a thousand words.

I flattened my palms against the table and stared at him—hard. He stared back in stony silence. He was a much better starer than I—didn't even blink. "Oh, hell, Evan. I was afraid of that, but why? Tell me there's an explanation."

"Madam—"

"Stop it, just stop it. Call me Miss Phoebe like I'm some character out of *Gone with the Wind* if you must, but stop with the 'madam' bit. It makes me feel like ancient history. Why did Rupert come to see Maria? Tell me."

He sighed, and glanced away before returning his gaze. "I admit that I disagree with Sir Rupert's insistence that you be brought into this situation. It is exceedingly dangerous. You would be far safer if you were to excuse yourself from the countess's company and return home."

I squeezed my eyes shut. "I'm just going to forget you said that. Try speaking to me like I'm an adult and not a child needing protection. Let's begin again: Why did Rupert come to see Maria?"

He kept his eyes fixed on my face. "In London, Sir Rupert received a phone call from Ms. Contini insisting that he visit her in Venice immediately. She said that it was urgent and that she had found something of great interest to them both. Naturally, Sir Rupert caught the next plane and we arrived in Venice on the final day of the festivities."

I waited. "And?"

"He called Ms. Contini upon arrival and arranged to meet the lady at a designated location of her choosing."

"Let me guess: the designated location was somewhere near where Maria's body was found."

He leaped to his feet and, in one swift motion, fetched something from the counter and returned to spread a large sheet of paper across the table. A map of Venice, marked in various places with red circles and perfect hand-labeling here and there, wound its sinuous blue canals before my eyes. "Ms. Contini was to meet Sir Rupert here." He placed a finger over one of the circles hovering beside a ribbon of blue. "He waited for nearly an hour but she failed to appear."

I leaned over to read *C de Cannaregio* typed over the blue. "She was to meet him not far from her own villa?"

"At her family's former weaving facility down the canal, yes. Her body was found here—" he tapped another circle "—floating in the canal."

My eyes met his. "That was the night the painting was stolen from the weaving studio—the Bartolo. There's no way Nicolina will believe Rupert isn't behind this. He looks as guilty as sin."

"We are aware of that. Furthermore, I have just been informed that Ms. Contini's phone records were hacked at 10:25 this evening and, should the hacker be Seraphina Tosci, which I have no doubt to be the case, she now knows that Sir Rupert made the last call that the lady received."

"And the one that drew her outside to her death. This is terrible. We have to convince Nicolina that Rupert isn't behind this." I stared hard at him. "Because he isn't, of course, is he?"

"Of course he isn't. Sir Rupert would never kill anyone and has never instructed me to do so on his behalf. I wouldn't, unless in self-defense. That's not who I am."

It was more information than he had ever previously disclosed about himself and it left me momentarily speechless. I flashed back to Noel killing a Camorra dude in Orvieto when it could have been avoided. "But you are former MI6. Surely killing was part of your job?"

"In self-defense. I was not and have never been an assassin."

Clearly he was a bit touchy on the subject. I let it drop. "I believe you," I said finally. And I did. "Besides, I have never thought Rupert a murderer—a scoundrel, yes, but a murderer, no. I don't know why I'm so convinced about that, considering the nefarious episodes he's involved me in, but there you have it. Nicolina, on the other hand, thinks he's quite capable of murdering her friend."

"Perhaps she judges Sir Rupert by her own proclivities." He tapped the table with one long finger. "Both the countess and her handmaiden are capable of violence with little provocation." Those gray-green eyes never left my face—steady, reliable, true. "We have never trusted the contessa, despite our long association with the lady. Furthermore, we are concerned about the partnership you have developed with her over this last year, an arrangement for which Sir Rupert holds himself responsible since he first introduced you two. However we believe—"

I held up my hand. "Stop right there. If you're about to make some inane statement about poor little Phoebe falling in with the wrong crowd, spare me. I fell in with the wrong crowd the day I was born and have been tangled in the roots of my gnarly family tree ever since. You two are also a result, I remind you, so anything you say that reeks of patriarchy is just going to piss me off."

He pulled back, a little smile playing on his lips. "I certainly wouldn't want to piss you off."

"Damn right you wouldn't, and discussing my relations with the countess is strictly out of bounds. I know what she's capable of. Moreover, I know what you two are capable of, murder excluded." I paused and studied him for a moment as he sat there holding himself in check from something—mirth, perhaps?

Did he really believe that little Phoebe was the same naive woman he had rescued in Turkey, or forgotten that I, in turn, had rescued him on at least one occasion? How quickly the male cranium forgets. Blame fossilized conditioning brewed in testosterone that seems to gum the brain cells together like solidifying tree resin.

More importantly, I wondered how much he and Rupert knew about our art repatriation plan. It wasn't exactly a secret since we were operating in conjunction with Interpol but our enterprise certainly must prick the interests of Sir Rupert Fox and anyone else who operated on the fringes of the law. Maybe my spell of anonymity had ended sooner than expected. "What do you know about 'my relations' with the countess, anyway?" I ventured.

"You just told me that discussing your relations was strictly out-of-bounds."

"It is unless I request it. Consider this a request."

"We know just enough to be concerned," he replied.

"A cautious answer if ever I heard one."

"Let me clarify. We know that you are forming an art repatriation agency—"

"Tentatively called the Agency of the Ancient Lost and Found."

The eyebrows arched as he continued with a little smile. "The Agency of the Ancient Lost and Found in cooperation with Interpol, but we are concerned that the countess may not be operating from the same good intentions as you and Max Baker. We have information that certain artifacts that probably originated from your brother's Jamaican repository have been passing through the black market."

"And you know that how?"

"The black market network is surprisingly tight in some respects and information has a way of getting around if you know where to look. At the very least, it usually has the means to identify which artifacts go missing and correctly identify the perpetrators. Your brother and Mr. Halloran were not discreet and, may I say, even haphazard in the end. Which pieces fell into their hands is more or less common knowledge. The only information that is not widely known now is which pieces are now in the hands of Interpol, which fell to Halloren, and which items are in the keeping of you and the countess."

"And which pieces Rupert missed out on."

"My employer came out of the debacle rather empty-handed, much to his chagrin."

"How that must have rankled."

He smiled. "True. In fact, it may have even compromised his immune system."

I couldn't resist a grin. Still, the only way to identify who has what was to cross-reference the contents of our vault and Nicolina's against Interpol's and thus determine which pieces were outstanding. As if that was going to happen anytime soon. We were still in the organization phase. "You must know that there is no way I'll ever disclose our holdings to you."

He nodded. "At the moment, yes. Perhaps at some point you may be persuaded differently. For now consider this: What if the countess is selling pieces from her repository without your knowledge? Keep that in mind."

"As if I haven't." I'd had my own niggling doubts about Nicolina from the beginning but trouble was literally my friend these days so I regularly walked the line between trust and suspicion.

"May I add that informants have alerted us to the fact that Halloren may be also selling pieces from his haul to fund his operation."

"What operation?" I asked quickly.

"His criminal operation as art thief. He has managed to regroup rather well following the Jamaican debacle."

I sat back, thunderstruck. "But I thought…"

"That perhaps he had mended his criminal ways? On the contrary, it appears that he's only intensified them." Then, after several moments of him watching me and me not speaking, he added: "I'm sorry to drop this on you, seeing that you and Halloren are—"

That did it. "Are what? We are nothing. Let's stay focused on the matter at hand, shall we? Nicolina and Seraphina may attempt to assassinate Rupert while the real perpetuator runs free. That's the issue at the moment. What are *we* going to do about it?"

Something snapped behind his eyes—satisfaction, what? "For the moment *I* intend to do everything in my power to assure that Sir Rupert stays safe. He is my prime concern. Sir Rupert's butler is arriving on an early flight tomorrow morning thus relieving me of nursing duties. As soon as he arrives, I will be free to investigate further."

"Sloane?" For some reason I couldn't imagine Rupert's fastidious butler clanking around this grand hovel.

"Sloane. I will then be free to work more directly on the matter at hand and with you, if you will agree. Meanwhile, Ms. Phoebe, you are in the best position to do the necessary groundwork since you are staying at Ms. Contini's villa and possibly surrounded by suspects or, at the very least, by those who may have pertinent information. I urge you to convince the countess that Sir Rupert was not involved in Ms. Contini's demise and would never harm her."

Just once I wanted to hear him talk like he didn't have half the British

Empire stuffed into his mouth. I sat back and crossed my arms. "Oh, that will be a piece of cake. You do realize that I will need to tell her that I've been in contact with you and that she will probably trust me that much less as a result?"

"Unavoidable."

"And since Nicolina is more than willing to believe Rupert is behind Maria's death and the robbery, too, she may not be moved by anything I say. She told me all about the broken engagement and the promised paintings and how Maria crumpled to family pressure on both points. To her, that gives Rupert motive."

Evan leaned forward. "If that alone was motive for both a theft and a murder, it would have happened long ago. Sir Rupert hasn't seen Ms. Contini for over two decades. Why did she suddenly call him and request that he meet her in Venice? That is the question."

I leaned toward him. "How do you know the call was even from Maria? There's another question."

"It was placed from her private line in the villa. The lady did not possess a cell phone. There was a second call that night, which thus far remains untraceable."

"But if Rupert hadn't spoken to Maria for decades, he might not recognize her voice. In other words—"

"Perhaps he's being framed."

"That's not what I was going to say."

"Nevertheless, it could be true."

"Whatever the case, that stolen painting must be behind this somehow."

"So I believe."

"She needed the money, Nicolina says, which the state of her house supports, which is probably why she sold the Crivelli. Maybe she was about to sell the Bartolo, too."

"I thought the same thing."

We stared at one another for a moment. I imagined his thoughts flickering across his features, the strong jaw clamping hard on determination. I pitied anyone who got in this man's path, but if it ever happened to be me, I hoped he'd be wearing that apron. *Crud, Phoebe, stop it.* I had yet to disentangle my heart from one man; I didn't need to be attracted to another.

"Either way," he said finally. "There is something else behind this, something bigger and potentially more deadly."

"Like what?"

"That's what we need to discover."

"*You* must have some idea. I only just dropped into this mess."

"There are possibilities too convoluted to get into now." He checked his watch. "It's 12:15 and best that I deliver you back to the villa immediately. We can resume this as soon as I can manage. In the meantime, I have something for you."

He reached into his pocket and pulled out an iPhone that looked suspiciously like mine, right down to the Anatolian kilim wallpaper.

"Oh, great—you and your phones. What does this one do besides monitor my every move—explode random articles, unfold into an instant gondola, play Vivaldi's *Spring*?"

His brief grin was heart-stopping. I made a mental note to provoke one just like it at the first opportunity. "Something much better. When used correctly, it will enable you to gather information from the surrounding environment. It—"

"We plebes call that spying."

"Spying, yes, but it's more than that. Among other things, it has some handy weaponized features that I'll instruct you on when next we meet. And you'll have me on call. Briefly, if you hold down the lower volume button and walk around a room, it will detect surveillance devices and even pinpoint their exact locations. It can also act as a metal detector with a bar graph illustrating the percentage of metals found when you activate the X-ray app by pushing the eye button. I'm rather pleased with the new X-ray features, but admittedly it's still very much at the development stage. Please take it with you tonight. Should you need me in the meantime, just push the top volume button twice and I'll come."

"The top volume button—cute. Why not use an Evan icon?"

That flash-grin again. Yes, I liked it a lot. "Too obvious. Also, that would require you to be turned on, er, turn on the phone, I mean."

"I don't mind turn-ons." *Hell, Phoebe, just shut up.*

A grin combined with those knowing eyes. Hell. "Nevertheless, this way you only need to press the button twice."

"Still, I want an Evan button. Work on that, please."

His eyes met mine. "You need to give me a little more time for an Evan button."

"Take all the time you need," I said. "I'll be waiting to press your button when necessary." This wasn't the first time we'd played these double entendres but it seemed more dangerous now somehow.

At that moment a little device on the counter began emitting feeble croaks. "Evan…"

I turned and gasped. "A baby monitor?"

"Sometimes the simplest technology does the job." He jumped up and dashed from the room.

"Can you give me a hint about the phone's other features?" I called, following after.

"Later. We will continue this at another time, Ms. Phoebe. Bear with me." I wouldn't mind "baring" with him someday.

We arrived to find Rupert sitting up in bed looking petulant. "My tea, where is my tea?" he rasped.

"Baby monitor is just the thing," I muttered.

"Sir, it is getting very late and I really should get Ms. Phoebe back to her quarters."

"Before I pumpkinize," I added sourly.

Rupert flopped back against the pillow. "Very well. Have you...told her all?"

"As much as we have time for tonight. As soon as Sloane arrives, I will disclose further."

"Very well."

I strode up to the bed and looked down at my rumpled, feverish friend. Seeing him this way made my heart ache for multiple reasons. Here was a man who couldn't bear the sight of a wrinkle on his clothing but who now lay wrapped in a heap of tangled bedsheets. That alone was enough to induce conniptions. "I hear that Sloane is coming to tend you tomorrow. He'll insist you get better so you must get right on that. Besides, we can't have you croaking all over this venerable old ruin, can we?"

"So sympathetic," he wheezed. "You will...visit again, Phoebe?" he asked, attempting to prop himself up again and failing miserably. I adjusted the pillows behind his head.

"Is that better? I'll come back as often as it's safe and when my vaporetto driver there can manage. Obviously I can't come by myself."

He grasped my hand. "You'll need a...disguise."

"Yes, but it won't be the plague doctor again, I can tell you that."

"You will...help find Maria's killer?" he rasped.

"I will. Now, rest and follow the doctor's orders so that the next time I visit you, I can see more of my sartorial friend."

Evan tapped his watch.

"Must go. See you soon." I squeezed his hand. I was halfway across the room when it hit me. "Oh, Rupert, before I forget: Would you happen to have a size five millimeter knitting needle I could borrow?"

8

_____

othing about the trip back to the Contini villa encouraged conversation. Being stuffed inside a blackout hood counting the number of right- and left-hand turns was challenging enough. Exhausted by then, I struggled just to stay awake. When we finally arrived, Evan helped me to remove my hood and mask before assisting me up to the dock. I had no idea where we were.

"You only need take the right-hand turn at the end of that bridge," he said, indicating a small *porto* directly ahead, "and then you will be on the Cannaregio. From there, proceed down the canal side until you reach the villa. I will be keeping an eye on you until you are safely inside."

"Don't worry, I'll be fine. A bit of a walk might wake me up."

Evan lightly touched my arm. "I cannot overstate the need for caution, mad—Ms. Phoebe. There is something at work here that even I fail to grasp. It concerns that villa and the Continis, for certain, but beyond that we know so little. Extreme caution is necessary."

"I will be extremely cautious." I remained standing where I was, rather enjoying the feel of his hand on my arm, the man's proximity. He removed his hand and the spell was broken. "Well, then. Take care of Rupert and hopefully I'll see you soon," I said, heading toward the bridge.

I never looked back, never looked around, but kept on heading across the bridge and onto the street that rode the canal. A few people were still about but I had no sense of being stalked or even observed except by Evan's friendly eye. As soon as I crossed the construction area with its temporary steel walkway across the canal, I arrived at Maria Contini's villa. The door flew open before I had the opportunity to touch the knob.

"Phoebe!" Nicolina stood there with Seraphina right behind her. "Where have you been? We have been so worried!"

I stepped inside. "Sorry about that but neither of you were around and I needed a walk. Where have *you* been, by the way?"

I heard the countess sigh as she followed me into the salon where I took a seat and clasped my hands across my knees. Before me sat a silver tray of vino Santo, three glasses, and a dish of small biscotti. My stomach growled ominously. I helped myself to a glass of the sweet liquid and dove into the biscuits, crunching away.

"It was necessary for us to go out. I see you found the jacket. It is lovely, yes?"

"Yes, perfect, thank you—very useful, as was the gun, but I'm afraid I disposed of the spy devices. I hope that doesn't make me appear too ungrateful," I said mildly while pulling out the gun to ensure I'd disengaged the safety—check. I immediately turned my attention back to the wine and munchies.

"Spy devices?" Nicolina asked.

"The ones secreted in the lining of my jacket—surely you knew?" I stole a glance toward her. Apparently she didn't. Nicolina was staring at Seraphina, who uttered something in Italian. A brief exchange followed at which point Seraphina left the room.

"I apologize, Phoebe. Seraphina only seeks to protect you," Nicolina began once she'd left.

"Why does everybody say that?" I said while dusting crumbs from my lap. "I get the gun part but spying on me, too? That sounds more like someone hoped I'd lead them to Rupert."

"Phoebe!" To her credit, she appeared genuinely shocked, but I wasn't buying it for a second.

"Being the suspicious creature that I've become, it occurs to me that getting to Rupert might even be the real reason why you've invited me to Venice in the first place. You knew he'd contact me, so having me tracked served a dual purpose."

"I assure you that I did not realize Seraphina had you tracked. I apologize. Please believe me. She only wanted to ensure your safety. The gun, the jacket, are all to that purpose. Oh, and the jacket, it comes with a secret pocket inside. May I show you?"

"Yes, of course." I removed the jacket and passed it over, which prompted

Nicolina to stand, shake off the crumbs, don the jacket (which looked so much better on her model frame), and reveal the leather sling secreted inside.

"A hidden holster?" I said, slapping my hand over my chewing mouth in the interests of decorum.

"Yes, specially designed. I have had several made and thought you could use one, too."

"Oh, I can. Thanks. Once I removed the tracking devices, I just loved it."

Nicolina returned the jacket and took her seat beside me. "Phoebe, be truthful: Where did you go tonight?"

"Thanks for asking. Truthfulness is always the preferred state between friends, don't you think? But if I have reason to suspect someone is less than truthful with me, I'm going to be less than forthcoming myself." That statement, by the way, contains more syllables than I usually manage after a glass of wine. I bit into another biscuit. "Forgot to eat," I mumbled.

"But you left the villa without telling me. You could have texted," she said.

"You could have also texted," I pointed out. "I'm supposed to be here to help you. You were out looking for Rupert, weren't you?"

"Yes. We have had word that he has been in Venice since the day that Maria was killed but we have yet to find him. There, you see, I have been honest."

I nodded. "Good start, so I will admit that I have seen Rupert tonight." I caught her sharp inhalation. I brushed crumbs off my lap. Really, I didn't belong in a villa with a countess. "But I can't tell you where he is because I simply don't know—I was blindfolded. But I can tell you this: he is not responsible for Maria's death. Absolutely not. He received a call from Maria to come to Venice, and when he had landed, they spoke briefly about where to meet. When he arrived at the designated location, Maria didn't show up. He is being framed."

"And you believe this?" Nicolina said, turning to me with that hard glint in her eyes.

"I absolutely do and I intend to prove it somehow, but try not to assassinate him in the meantime, will you? Look, Nicolina, you don't execute a man before you have proof that he is guilty."

"But I know in my heart that he is guilty."

"When it comes to men, your heart is an unreliable measure. Besides, how can you try to harm a friend? You are basing your suspicions on circumstantial evidence. Don't judge Rupert until you have all the facts, which, I assure you, I'm going to help you get."

"Then at least let him face me and explain his innocence himself, then perhaps I will believe him."

I downed the last of my wine. "That's not possible at the moment. Can't you just take my word for it for now?"

"But, Phoebe, how can you ask that if you have no more proof that he is innocent than I do that he is guilty?"

"Because we are—*were*—all friends, that's why. He's helped you in the past, remember? Doesn't that count for something? Why all of a sudden do you want to execute him for a crime you have no proof he committed? I'm asking that you stay your hand in the name of our friendship—yours and mine—if nothing else. Tomorrow we'll discuss this in more detail and you can tell me everything you haven't yet disclosed about Maria, the paintings—the whole backstory. Because I know there's plenty you haven't told me. Anyway, right now, I'm exhausted." And possibly a little wine-soaked. I stood up and strode toward the door. "So, off to bed I go."

"Phoebe, wait."

I turned.

"Tomorrow, it will be a very busy day and we may not get an opportunity to speak."

"But I'll continue my investigations, regardless. I said that I'd help you find Maria's killer and I will but I'll need full access to the house and Maria's vault in the meantime."

Nicolina stood up. "That will not be possible. The warehouse is a crime scene and the police will not allow access. Besides, this is not my house."

"Actually, it is now, more or less, since you are the beneficiary. Get me a set of keys, which I'll take as a gesture of goodwill. 'Night."

* * *

THERE'S a reason why I avoid vino. The next morning I slept late—too late— oblivious to the stirrings around the house until at least 11:00 a.m. My eyes opened on the new iPhone Evan had given me that I'd left stacked on top of the old one on the inlaid side table. I jolted up. What if Seraphina or Nicolina —anybody, for that matter—had entered the bedroom while I slept and tampered with the phone?

Picking it up, I studied it, puzzled by the green light that flashed across the screen's surface when touched, illuminating bright blue fingerprints. What did that mean? Green meant *go* so that had to be a good thing. Blue probably not so much. Maybe Evan had worked it so that if a stranger touches the phone, the thing displayed the fingerprints? Oh, hell: I needed a phone lesson and fast.

I turned off the old phone and secreted it in my carpetbag's hidden compartment and pocketed the new. Next, I chose a fresh pair of jeans, a black turtleneck, and a multicolored scarf that was bound to dispel any notion that I was into the minimalist look. By the time I poked my head out the door minutes later with my arms full of toiletries and clothing, I could hear the cadence of new voices filling the downstairs space—male voices. The villa had company.

After quick ablutions in a bathroom—I had a sink and a toilet in my room but neither a tub nor a shower—where the pipes whined painfully and the water took forever to warm, I dressed and crept downstairs, pausing outside the salon door where two dark-suited men were speaking to Zara and Nicolina while a uniformed man looked on. The *polizia* already?

"*Signora*," one of the suited men said, catching sight of me and stepping forward. Nicolina smoothly intercepted, speaking to him in Italian, which caused him to nod curtly at me and turn away.

"We are being interviewed," she said, stepping into the hall. "I have told them that you have nothing to offer since you did not know of Maria until yesterday and are here only as my friend. There is no need for you to be involved in this tedious affair. First, I give my statement, then I must visit the lawyers and the funeral people. It is all very distressing. This may take many hours, Phoebe."

"Have they released the body or determined cause of death yet?"

"Not yet." She lowered her voice. "It's best not to ask such things when the police are around. Please, take breakfast on the patio upstairs without me. I have asked Zara to prepare something."

"Did you ask for a set of keys, too?"

"Yes, you will find them next to the coffee flask but you will find nothing here. We have combed the villa already, as the police are doing now."

I nodded. "But an extra set of eyes always comes in handy. Don't worry about me. I can take care of myself."

Nicolina touched my arm. "Yes, of course you can, but we must talk later. About Rupert, I mean. It is not good that we keep secrets from one another."

"Sure."

She retreated into the salon, clicking the door shut softly behind her, leaving me in the hall, trying to disentangle all the things bothering me, which were plenty. Not for the first time, I desperately wished I could speak Italian, at least enough to know what was being said behind those doors. Yes, I was willing to eavesdrop and, if possible, use one of those surveillance devices on my new phone, providing that I knew how. One way or another, I was being maneuvered by Nicolina, used for some purpose I had yet to discern. It wouldn't be the first time. But I had to get ahead of the game because, as it stood, I was way behind.

However, nothing is possible first thing in the morning without coffee.

I returned to the stairs and climbed three flights, continuing on until reaching a narrow marble stairwell washed in daylight. Moments later, I found myself on a small square rooftop patio with a pair of high trumpet-shaped Renaissance chimneys in one corner and a barricade of stone and canvas screening the drop. The morning breeze was bracing and surprisingly warm. I stepped out, breathed deeply, and looked around.

A Venetian rooftop loggia. I'd glimpsed them from the water countless times, always wondering about those lofty spaces where residents captured a slice of private outdoors in a city where exterior space was at a premium. This one looked as though it had been well-used for alfresco dining over the centuries with its vine-covered pergola overhanging the little table that now bore three glass-covered platters and a thermos. Beside the thermos sat a ring of keys, which I quickly pocketed, but the view momentarily banished all thoughts of food and coffee. I gazed out at a vista centuries old, a scene of canals dancing in sunshine with boats of commerce and pleasure plying the waterways.

For a moment, I just soaked in the scene, checking out the gondolas transporting tourists down the canal below along with vaporettos and private motorboats. I broke my reverie only long enough to grab a roll, a piece a cheese, a slice of salami, and a mug of strong coffee before returning to the vista. So, Maria Contini's villa stood at the beginning stretch of the Cannaregio close to the Grand Canal? A prime viewing spot with the crossways of the two canals converging.

I had just bitten into the roll and gulped back some coffee when I saw her —or, at least, I thought it was a her—the figure of a dark-haired woman standing on a roof patio much like mine only on the opposite side of the canal. A pair of binoculars was focused on my person. For a moment I thought it must be a tourist gawking at the villas in her line of sight but her position never wavered.

For a second, I tried to appear as though I was studying the view, looking slightly to the left while keeping her in my peripheral vision. She remained fixed to the spot before turning abruptly away. I tossed my half-eaten roll onto the table and scrambled around looking for something that had to be there: a pair of binoculars. Nobody has a roof vista without them and, sure enough, Maria Contini's mother-of-pearl version sat tucked under a shelf of glasses. I grabbed them and ran back to the balcony only to find that of course by then my spectator had disappeared.

So, now I needed to find out about the building across the canal. Maybe she was just a casual viewer but I thought not. I took my roll and a mug of coffee and descended the steps.

On the way down, I bumped into Seraphina heading up.

"*Buongiorno*, Phoebe. The countess asked for me to accompany you to keep you company. Everyone will be very busy today. Ah, good, you have found breakfast."

"Thanks for the offer, Seraphina, but I don't need a tour guide or a companion. I have work to do and I'm sure you do, too."

"The police, they do not have questions for me, only the countess. I am just a servant, you see? I keep you company."

Going solo was not an option, in other words. I wondered how long it would take for the police to learn the extent of Seraphina's services. We carried on to the next landing, the top-most bedroom floor. Turning, I faced her with my back to my door. "I just saw somebody staring at me through binoculars from a roof across the canal."

"Perhaps it was Evan. He is watching you, no?"

"This was a woman."

"Many people are curious about Signora Contini's death, so perhaps it is the press. Either way, it must be stopped. I will go with you."

Like I wanted that. "Fine. I'll meet you downstairs after I brush my teeth." In a second I was back in my room, resolved to shake Seraphina's company as soon as I could without causing suspicion. I'd just have to lose myself, which should be easy enough in Venice. Of course, she hoped I'd lead her to Rupert at some point, which had to be avoided at all costs. But there was another pressing matter that had to be attended to immediately—two, really.

First, I pressed the bottom volume button on my new phone and strolled around the room, ridiculously delighted when the screen flashed red, intensifying as I drew the phone closer to a little knob fastened onto a skeleton clock on the mantel. I plucked off the knob, studied a thing the size of a watch battery, and continued until I found two more. Minutes later I whacked the disks on the floor with the heel of my sneaker and dropped the broken pieces into my pocket. Only when the phone no longer flashed red did I stop.

That done, I fished out my old phone and called Max, who had yet to answer my text from the night before. The call rang and rang. Next, I tried his house phone and even the gallery with the same result. A ping of alarm hit. I was just about to hang up when suddenly a voice answered. "Yo, Peaches here."

"Peaches, hi. Where's Max? I keep trying his numbers but he's not picking up."

"Phoebe? How are you doin', girl?" Something pounded in the background. "Just me and da contractors here at da moment. How's Venice? Always wanted to go to Venice."

I lowered my voice. "Venice is fine, I think, but there's lots going on here and I could use a confab with Max."

"So confab with me. Max and Serena took off for a long weekend in da country. I'm thinking it's a bone-jumping weekend but dey're being plenty zip-lipped about it. Acted like they were looking for antiques—yeah, right."

For a moment I couldn't speak. "A bone-jumping weekend?"

"Yes, you know what I mean by dat: man and woman dig each other, man and woman decide to take off for a little one-on-one—read dat literally—time together, and—"

"I know what you meant, Peaches, but I'm just stunned that we're talking about Max and Serena. Since when did romance bloom between those two?"

"You mean, how'd dat bloom without you knowing? It's been right under your nose da whole time but you've been pretty absorbed with da breakup of you and your hottie, not to mention your brother and all. I get that totally. My bro's in jail, too."

"I know." Why was she repeating all this?

"I knew my bro was a sicko. You found out in one blow. And then your hottie turns out to be involved—gutting."

I was about to protest the use of *hottie* applied to Noel but gave up. I was picking up on signs that Peaches was upset about something—too much time alone, who knows? "How I missed that between Serena and Max is baffling but they've gone away for the weekend together, seriously? Well, that's great and I'm happy that Max finally recognized the good woman right under his nose but surely they don't plan to leave their devices off the whole time?" Knowing Max, maybe he did.

"Why not? Some people do dat. They're crazy."

"Peaches, are you okay? I haven't heard you slip into Jamaicanese since you arrived in London. What's going on back there?"

"Oh, crap. Can't keep Jamaica off my tongue when I get stewed up. It's just that the dudes we hired to do the upstairs floor called to say that they can't start on Monday like they promised. I mean, you kidding me? I said You were contracted to perform a service on a certain date and now you say you're behind on another contract so you can't start ours? It's like they're working on island time and that just doesn't go down here. That's not going to happen, I said. The whole reno gets held up until those floor guys get the job done, see? Think I'm going to let that happen? Hell, no. I told them they better get their butts over here next week or else."

"Or else what, what did you tell them?" Sometimes I forgot that the first time I met Dr. Peaches, she was slinging a machine gun at a bunch of drug runners. Though she was doing a phenomenal job of acclimatizing to her new life, it is a process, as they say.

"Or else there could be violence, I said."

"No, no, no, Peaches, please curb your kick-ass tendencies. You've scared off half the contractors already. If these guys bolt, we'll have to find yet another and that will take ages. Just chill. We can wait a week or two for the floor. We're in no real hurry, right? Who's there now?"

"Just the wall guys. I made them work Saturday to finish the drywalling 'cause we were going to get way behind. They'll bugger off after today while we wait for the floor contractors. Okay, I promise not to threaten them with bodily harm. Not yet, anyway." She inserted a string of colorful curses. "So… are you really okay there in Venice? Sure you don't need a bodyguard or a helping hand or something? Soon there won't be anything for me to do here with the worker dudes gone."

"I'm fine at the moment but I'll let you know if that changes. Please stay put until Serena and Max return on Monday. Don't go off threatening anybody just yet, okay? Take a few days off. Get reacquainted with London, maybe. I have to go now but I'll check in later." I clicked off, my pleasure over Max and Serena's liaison muddied by an anxiety that was building by the minute. Yet, I had more immediate things to worry about just then.

I quickly brushed my teeth and donned my new jacket before slipping from the room. Seconds later, I bounded downstairs to where Seraphina awaited in the hall, her petite form compacted into a buttery brown leather pantsuit and a pair of high-heeled ankle boots. She stood, arms folded, watching me descend, the salon doors still firmly shut behind her and her mouth pulled into a tight little line. I had kept her waiting. "So, you come at last."

I stood looking down at her, grateful for my two-inch height advantage. "For now, but I require much more information if I am to assist Nicolina with her investigation."

"I will assist the countess with her investigation," she stated.

So, it was like that, was it? Could Seraphina be jealous of my involvement or simply frustrated to have me underfoot? "And so will I in my own way. I presume we can cooperate with one another?"

"But of course."

I broke the standoff and indicated the closed door. "So, the interview continues. This is going to be one exhausting day for Nicolina." I was only making neutral conversation.

"The countess is a strong woman," her assistant said with a nod.

"As are we all—a good thing, considering. Oh, and before I forget, Seraphina, I have something for you." I scraped up the surveillance bits from my pocket and held them out to her. "You might want these back. Maybe you can glue them together and use them again on someone else. By the way, I consider this kind of thing very uncooperative considering I was asked to come but I won't mention this latest violation of my privacy to Nicolina unless you do."

She fixed me with a penetrating gaze best served for staring down pickpockets.

"No hard feelings," I said as I emptied them into her hand. "I'm getting used to spy paraphernalia but that doesn't mean I want it in my face. Why did you put this in my room?"

Her pert, sharp-eyed gaze intensified. "You are in touch with Sir Rupert Fox. I must assure the countess's interests."

"And I must assure *all* my friends' interests, including my own. Do we understand one another?"

"Perfectly," she said between her teeth.

"Excellent. Let's get going."

I had thought that we would walk down the canal to the closest bridge and simply stroll over to the building in question but Seraphina insisted we take the boat. That involved bounding down the basement stairs and helping her place the vessel onto its rails so that we could slide it into the water. That done, I studied the canalscape as she puttered through the narrow tributaries at the helm, transversing the main canal to a dock close by the building. There was no rush—I knew the woman would be long gone—but I could have walked there much sooner. Seraphina must have known that, too.

Moments later, we were on the street opposite the canal standing beside one of the countless little restaurant bars that lined the water, the only defining feature to this one being that it sat almost directly opposite the Continis' villa.

As restaurants go, it was a relatively humble affair with an outside eating area of a few metal tables that hugged the blue-and-white painted front with a sun-bleached striped awning over all. An aproned waiter beckoned us over, pointing to a daily special sign fixed on a sandwich board. Seraphina shook her head and began bantering (or I assumed that was bantering) as I backed up far enough to see past the awning to the upper stories—three floors with presumably a roof patio at the very top.

Seconds later, Seraphina was at my elbow. "Luigi says that this is an apartment building—three flats. He says that he does not personally know those who live there except one old man who has lived on the bottom floor for years and a young man who moved in months ago—an art student, he thinks. But the top flat had been empty until a few weeks ago. He says has seen many different people come and go over the last few days. A woman, she just arrived earlier this morning and left a half an hour ago. Very suspicious."

"Suspicious, why?"

"He has never seen any of them before last week—three men and a lady. None of them appear to stay overnight. Foreigners, he thinks."

Foreigners. I knew locals can always tell a visitor from myriad telltale signs. "Is there any way we can get up there?"

"Of course. You distract, I pick."

It is a testament to my new lifestyle that I immediately went up to Luigi and requested to use the facilities with what I hoped was a desperate look on my face. He frowned as if to say *no buy, no pee* so I ordered an espresso. As he dashed inside to fetch it, I watched Seraphina go to the door to the right of the restaurant, unfold a little wallet of tools, and open the door in seconds. I tossed down a euro on the nearest table and followed her in.

A tall narrow flight of stairs led upward with three metal mailboxes affixed on the wall nearby, each with a grimy doorbell button. The first two floors had names neatly typed in the plastic sleeves but the topmost one remained empty. Seraphina pressed the upper one repeatedly. No answer.

Without a word, we climbed the steep stairway, passing a blue-painted door on the first landing, one with a bike locked outside on the second, and a plain wooden one on the top floor upon which Seraphina knocked imperiously. I'd have loved to know what she would have said had anyone responded since I was too out of breath to do much more than pant at that point.

My companion had the lock picked in seconds and we stepped into a dusty, unfurnished flat smelling faintly of garlic with a single front window overlooking the canal and two smaller back ones facing the rear of another building. We both strolled around, me stepping into the tiny back bedroom and Seraphina into the galley kitchen. My Foxy phone tingled in my pocket.

Turning my back, I slipped the phone from my pocket and read: *Sloane has arrived. Can we meet? E*

I typed back: *With Seraphina now. Where?*

Push lower volume button twice and hold. I'll find you.

I heard Seraphina's footsteps marching in my direction. I dropped the phone back into my pocket.

"No one has lived here for weeks but in Venice flats do not stay vacant for so long."

"I doubt this one is vacant, either. I'm betting that someone's rented it for the sole purpose of surveillance. You'll need to search immediately for the lessee," I said, turning around. "You have amazing skill with that kind of thing, right?"

Seraphina shot me a quick look, possibly surprised that I had made a statement that sounded suspiciously directive. Clearly I needed to go head-to-head in a power struggle with Nicolina's indomitable assistant. "I will do this, yes, and you must not jump to conclusions," she said. "This is probably the press staking out the countess for the next big story. In Italy, we love our big stories."

I narrowed my eyes at her. Why was Seraphina downplaying this? Someone was watching the villa. That couldn't be good, no matter the circumstances. Turning, I strolled to the front window and pointed to the Styrofoam coffee cup loaded with cigarette butts. "It is a stakeout, for sure. Look at this. Someone has been watching the villa for days, if not weeks. Is the Italian press really so bent on a story that they'd put four people on the job? I always pictured news hunts to be the domain of some lone-wolf paparazzi stalking the unlikely victim. Come, let's check out the roof. I saw the little door to the left of the landing."

I bounded out of the flat and stopped by the door—locked, of course. Seraphina jiggled her little tool into the keyhole and it sprung open in seconds. Moments later we were on top of a shabby little rooftop with a single plastic table and four matching chairs, two of them knocked over. The bottom of the concrete banister was littered with stacked cups of ashes and cigarette butts. "Hmm, messy, and signs of a long, protracted stakeout," I remarked as I stepped up to the railing. "Now why would anyone be that interested in Maria's villa, Seraphina?"

"As I say, probably the press."

I didn't believe that and I bet neither did she but I played along. "So why not plant one of your little surveillance devices up here so we can at least identify the reporters who are violating our privacy? Surely there must be laws against that kind of thing in Italy? You can send the paper responsible a cease and desist order or the Italian equivalent."

I turned to find Seraphina seeming to consider this for a moment, though I guessed she was more likely trying to think up a reason why to counter my suggestion. After a moment, she nodded. "Yes, this I will do."

"Excellent. So while you're doing that, maybe I'll to do a bit of research and you can report back to me later." I made for the exit.

"But there does not need to be such a hurry," she said, dashing after me. "I can do these things later."

"Nonsense," I said, waving my hand dismissively as we descended the stairs. "This must be dealt with now. There's no time to waste."

When we emerged outside, I turned to her and waved goodbye. "See you later."

In moments I was striding down the street, leaving her standing there watching me with her mouth pursed in annoyance. Check one for Phoebe. But, I thought as I clambered over a little bridge, Seraphina did not give up so easily. She had to have another plan.

9

_____

*I*t occurred to me as I turned a corner to march down a narrow street edging the water that Seraphina probably expected to track my whereabouts using my tampered phone. No doubt that those blue fingerprints belonged to her. Now what? I pulled out my superphone and tapped out a message to Evan: *I'm free now but I'm sure Seraphina is tracking me.*

The response came back immediately: *She is but to no avail. Don't worry, I have you covered. Keep walking.*

He had me covered—an interesting thought. I strode past churches and other intriguing old buildings until I reached a smaller canal where I took a left-hand turn and continued deeper into the heart of Venice. Somehow I ended up across from the International Gallery of Modern Art, but as tempting as it was to drop in for an eye-feast, I kept on going. I'd look over my shoulder every thousand feet or so expecting to see Evan emerge from behind a building, but nothing—nothing, that is, until a motorboat suddenly came into view zipping toward me.

When the boat slowed and I looked down at Evan at the same time that he looked up at me, our eyes held for seconds too long. I ignored his hand and climbed into the boat without assistance. "Good morning, Ms. Phoebe."

That greeting nearly spoiled the moment. "So," I said in my jauntiest tone, "I see you've ditched the *Phantom of the Opera* meets the *Lone Ranger* look." Today he dressed like himself in a turtleneck under a chocolate-colored leather jacket with jeans and a version of those peaked hats he preferred. The man was very good-looking, if you liked that square-jawed brawny type. Not me, of course. I preferred them lean, swarthy, and perpetually missing in action apparently.

He smiled. "Most conflicting interests already know that Sir Rupert and I are in town and that you and I are colleagues of a sort. Doubtless we have attracted attention, not all of it friendly."

Was that what we were—colleagues? Well, I suppose we were. "I'm beginning to think we may have attracted *significant* interest."

His mouth formed a grim line when I told him about the surveillance on the roof. "Things may have intensified sooner than I anticipated," he remarked.

"What if we're tracked to Rupert's hideout?"

"Sir Rupert is thoroughly fortified in his current location and I have sentries watching from all possible directions. I've also taken precautions regarding Seraphina's tracking devices. The enhanced phone I provided detects interference and records fingerprints."

"I figured out the fingerprints."

He pulled down the throttle and began a slow putter down the canal with a self-satisfied smile on his fine lips. "Please open it now, Ms. Phoebe. I sent you another message explaining the details."

I did exactly that, grimacing at him for the "Ms. Phoebe" bit before skimming the message quickly. I looked over at him. "You sent her to St. Mark's Square?"

"That's where she thinks you've gone. Whether or not she follows you there is left to be seen. Just know that she will be unable to track you using her rudimentary tracking devices and thus you are free to move around Venice at your leisure, at least to roam without her particular scrutiny. Obviously you may have attracted other interests."

I cocked my head at him. "Do I detect a note of pride?"

His lips quirked. "A smidgen, admittedly. Since Seraphina has long been in competition with me so naturally there is a touch of rivalry between us."

"I know that you are former MI6 but is Seraphina a former agent, too?"

"She did belong to the equivalent of the Italian secret service once, out of Rome, I believe."

"I haven't been keeping up with my who's-who of ex-intelligence agents apparently."

And Seraphina seemed as devoted to Nicolina as Evan was to Rupert. The things that money can buy. I wanted to ask him what his life was like in Rupert's employ but now wasn't the time and maybe that time would never come. Evan had always been a very private man, and though the barriers between us were lowering, I didn't want to presume too much. Our colleagueship was only at the beginning, after all. "Are we off to see Rupert now?"

"Not until tonight, mada—Ms. Phoebe—after Sloane has finished attacking the building with his bleach and mousetraps. Every dust bunny appears to him like a dragon lurking in the corners so it's best we don't annoy him further by our presence."

I laughed. "How's Rupert doing, anyway?"

"Much better now that a steady stream of tea and scones have been directed to his bedside. His mood, at least, has improved. I'm afraid I've been much too busy with security duty to attend him in the manner to which he's become accustomed."

Why was he opening up to me like this? He had never shared so much delightful detail or commentary before. He had always acted as a mouthpiece for Rupert with a wall of tedious formality raised like a force field between us. Now he was revealing himself as a person. "What do you have in mind today, then?"

"I suggest we put our heads together to compare the facts we have gathered so far and see if we can work out next steps."

"Sounds good. We'll need a quiet spot for that, preferably one where dust bunnies have already been banished and I can have a decent breakfast."

He grinned. "I have just the place."

And so we zoomed down the waterways under blue sky with me feeling more relaxed than I had in days. I didn't care where we were going at first, content to let him take me there. Still, when we suddenly jetted off across the lagoon, I was intrigued. "Where *are* we going?" I called above the slap of waves against the bow.

"Torcello."

Torcello. I had never heard of it. I knew of Murano and I knew of Burano, where I had gone as part of a tour group long ago. I sat back and waited for Torcello to come into view, which it did twenty minutes later by way of a central tower stabbing the blue sky.

As Evan slowed the boat at our approach, he said: "This island was one of the first to be populated after the Veneti fled the invaders, and in 638, Torcello became the bishop's seat; hence the building of the Cathedral of Santa Maria Assunta and the central tower you see ahead. Impressive Byzantine mosaics are in there and I do wish we had time for a tour. In any case, in the tenth century, it was more important than Venice as a trading center."

"What happened to cause its demise?"

"The plague, malaria, and marshes that eventually devoured the harbor is the short story. Today it's mostly ruins, which has left it with kind of a haunting quality like a dismembered saint—"

And the man had a poetic turn...*a dismembered saint.* "I always find saintly relics sad—the toe, the knuckle, the supposed skull of Saint So-and-so separated from its body to be stared at and revered forevermore. Whole mummified bodies under glass are particularly gruesome."

"And yet, as you know, it is part of Italian Catholic culture and revered as a result. Catholicism leaves a deep, lasting mark on its citizens even among the disbelievers, especially in Italy."

So perhaps he had been raised Catholic? Whatever the case, he appeared to have some strange affinity to this little island. Stranger and stranger.

"For Torcello, sadder still is the way in which the Venetians plundered this island by absconding the stone with which to build their own structures yonder. The island has been picked apart."

We entered a short canal with a wharf at one end and boats tied up along the bank. We secured the boat among others of varying shapes and sizes and strolled down a bush-lined lane as quiet as any country path. Though a few people ambled around, the sense of space was remarkable compared to the press of bodies across the lagoon.

The buildings here were mostly shabby and crumbled with paint-scabbed shutters and mottled terra-cotta walls. Of course, this being Italy, every deteriorating inch was artlessly beautiful. I gazed down at the ground beneath our feet—primarily gravel and beaten earth—making me think that the Venetians had plundered even the cobblestones.

Soon I was gaping at a white granite stone seat positioned like a throne along one of the paths that wandered through the remains of the town when Evan stopped. "They call it Atilla's Throne but it was more likely where the bishop held court and preformed judiciary functions. Pardon me." He took out his phone and tapped a quick message. "Excellent. She is ready for us."

"She?"

"Sophia, my friend. She has agreed to provide us a quiet place to talk and breakfast also. Come, Ms. Phoebe."

Ms. Phoebe followed him to a lovely salmon-colored stucco house with green shutters hanging on by rusting hinges. I'd love to knit or paint that one day but my attention was diverted to the open door. We stepped into a kitchen as humble and charming as anything I have ever seen with an open shutter blowing a warm breeze through lace curtains and an Italian breakfast waiting at a linen-covered table.

An extraordinarily pretty woman greeted us dressed in a sweater and a full patterned skirt. I estimated her to be in her thirties, her face free of makeup and her smile wide and welcoming. "Evan, you have brought your friend. I am Sophia and you must be Phoebe." She grasped both my hands and pulled me toward her for a brief air kiss.

"Hi, Sophia. Thank you for the welcome and the breakfast. I haven't eaten properly in days."

"Oh, that is not good." I caught the look that passed between Evan and Sophia—swift and warm. "Let me take care of that right now. Please sit at the table and I will get the coffee—espresso, Americano?"

Her accent was as musical as a concerto. Everything about her was engaging, in fact. Why couldn't Evan's friend be a rotund middle-aged woman who answered to "Mama" and made heaping pots of spaghetti sauce? What was she to this enigma of a man, anyway, and why should I care?

I took a seat across from Evan and did as I was bid—helped myself to sliced meats, ham, cheese, fruit, and crusty bread. Sophia poured coffee into each of our cups and left a flask. "I will leave you now. Take as much time as you need. I will work in the shop today so no hurry. Giani is keeping watch."

Evan met her eyes again. "Thank you again, Sophia."

"My pleasure." The woman dashed out the door.

"Who is Giani?"

"Sophia's son."

A silence fell across the table while I ate and Evan sipped his coffee reflectively. Had he been anyone else I would have asked about his relationship with Sophia but I could feel the barricade rising around the subject so reined myself in. It wasn't any of my damned business, anyway.

I stirred sugar into my coffee and looked over at him. "Do you have any idea who is watching the villa? They seem to be engaged in a protracted stakeout and one or more smoke too much. Otherwise, I haven't a clue about their identity—a couple of men and a woman. I suspect Seraphina may know who they are but she's not talking. She wants me to think they are the press but I don't believe that for a second."

He leaned forward. "There's evidence that you are under watch by a group of some unknown identity, which she may suspect. Several individuals have been seen lurking about, watching the villa, watching you, Seraphina, and the countess also. I have reason to believe that they may be connected to the murder and the theft."

"But why me? What do I have to do with it?"

"My theory is that they believe that the countess brought you in as an expert to unlock the painting's secrets and thus they require you for that purpose also."

"What? I mean, that's ludicrous. I'm no expert!"

"Consider this from an outside perspective—" he began counting off on those long fingers of his "—you have been involved in several successful antiquities and art operations in conjunction with Interpol over the years; you manage a large textile and ethnographic gallery in London, which is now rumored to be emerging into a lab of some kind; and finally, of equal importance, you are connected to several antiquities elements worldwide. You can, Ms. Phoebe, easily be considered an expert."

I sighed. "I've always said that an expert is only someone who knows slightly more on a given subject than the person naming her as one." I shoved my hair behind one ear. "But I'm really no expert on Renaissance art other than what I learned in university. It's been an interest of mine, certainly, but not in the thorough sense when there are countless true experts out there that could be called in."

"Maybe they have been and found nothing?"

"Then how can I?"

He leaned toward me again. "You underestimate yourself, madam—my apologies, *Ms. Phoebe*. What have you gleaned from the paintings to date? You have seen photographs, I presume?"

I wasn't playing that game without quid quo pro. "You presume correctly, but you show me yours and I'll show you mine. You go first."

His quirked a smile.

"Rupert's seen those works in person and, knowing him, he is not without a theory, not to mention firsthand information," I continued. "Collaborate, Evan, and in the interest of partnership, the first piece of information must come from your side."

That little smile again—partly appreciation, partly amused chagrin. "Very well, though I preface this with the knowledge that Rupert had hoped to share this with you personally. "He and Maria Contini were once engaged—"

"I know all about the broken promises, including the fact that Maria had offered that painting to Rupert as a kind of consolation prize but later withdrew the offer."

"Did you know that part of the reason she wanted Sir Rupert to have those paintings was because he is Jewish?" He could tell by my expression that I did not know that. "She withdrew the offer on the night she told her mother her intent. A great argument ensued, at which point her mother disclosed the fact that the paintings held a valuable secret. Generations of Continis shielded that painting without ever knowing why. Whatever happened, Maria could not give it away, a fact that finally hit home."

"Maria must have known something about their importance prior to that."

"Only that it was essentially hidden in the house for as long as she could remember. The Continis did not want it to be seen; something Ms. Contini hinted had to do with their great value and possibly a religious element."

"Because the bride and groom were from two different religions? But surely that wouldn't have been an issue now?"

Evan grimaced. "Signore Contini was a staunch Catholic and saw marrying into another religion to be a blemish to the family line. He bristled against the possibility of Jewish blood in the Contini veins."

"So he was anti-Semitic as well as a foolish, blindsided pig."

Evan's brows arched at my vehemence but he nodded in agreement. "Aptly put. You don't appear surprised about anything I've disclosed."

This time I leaned forward. "I'm not. You've only confirmed something I've suspected—not about Rupert, of course—I didn't know he was Jewish, but about the Bartolo."

"An exquisite and valuable piece of Renaissance art. I didn't have the opportunity to see it in person, unfortunately—Sir Rupert's affiliation with the Continis being far before my time—but I have seen the photos he keeps."

I plucked out my phone to display the pictures I took of the painting, focusing in on the minute detail of the Bartolo's wedding scene in particular. "The carpets are particularly interesting. Do you see the one beneath their feet?" I pinched open a close-up.

"A prayer rug, correct?"

"Possibly but not one like I've ever seen before. It was probably presented as Anatolian by the look of some of the motifs but those large geometrics are totally out of character. The lantern design is shown upside down for one thing, and though it's not unusual for a Muslim prayer rug to be shown in a church in Renaissance art, there's something off about the whole composition. And the actual knotting of the rug looks Berber. Do you see this twisted key motif right here?" I tapped the phone with my finger as Evan pushed aside the plates to lean forward.

"It looks Chinese."

"It is based on a Chinese phoenix-and-dragon motif and yet those knots linking them form hexagrams, part of a larger one is partially hidden below the bride's feet. That could be the Star of David."

He nodded. "Quite possibly."

"Regardless, that's a mishmash of cultural symbols and has to be significant. Add to that, that the border feature is pure unabashedly Berber."

"Berber as in Morocco?"

"Exactly. I have only ever seen that composition of geometric design in Berber rugs. So why has Bartolo taken the time to visually weave together such diverse elements? The Renaissance embedded layers of messages and symbols into their art, as you know, and this carpet reads like a Renaissance encryption."

Did I see something like appreciation warming his gaze? "Now I see exactly why Nicolina called you into this."

"She asked me to come as a friend for moral support and to help solve Maria's murder. Never once did I think that interpreting Renaissance art might be part of the picture. Frankly, it isn't even my specialty and I'm hardly a cryptographer."

"But you are a carpet expert and evidently those carpets are key. Perhaps the contessa doesn't choose to involve too many outside experts. Perhaps you are the one she hopes will unlock the answers? You do have a certain reputation among the art trade."

"Which would be so nice if she'd deigned to mention it."

"In any case, she did show you the photo. What else have you gleaned?"

I pulled back and sighed. "I'm sure what I see has been seen by others. For instance, if you look carefully at the wedding picture, it appears to take place in a church or cathedral and yet you will see in the background a cluster of people who seem to be raising their hands in dance—odd for a wedding inside a church, don't you think? Also, if you look at the arches over the wedding party they actually form more of an umbrella shape than a true arch, which is just another subtle nod to another culture, probably Eastern. This painting is more than the usual Renaissance contract between two families."

"One that links two religions."

"Yes, Jewish and Christian—something almost unheard of at the time."

"I'll see if I can find out more about this marriage, if there are even records, but there should be something." He said that as mildly as if he would do a quick Google search.

I looked at him. "How? The records would be minimal that far back, wouldn't they?"

"Not in Venice, which is a city that took to recording its every breath long before the fifteenth century. And where there are churches, there will be records, and I suspect this ceremony took place in a church under the guise of a Catholic ceremony, no matter how well-disguised the event. For some unknown reason, the Contini ancestors accepted a Jewish bride into their midst, one who would have been forced to convert and the truth of their union hidden by everyone."

"And a very dangerous thing to do in the 1400s. It would be considered heresy by the Catholic church."

"Indeed, especially as Venice was moving toward segregation. In 1516, Venice would officially segregate its Jewish citizens into a *getti*, the first ghetto in history," he said.

"Oh, my God, what would have compelled a wealthy Venetian family like the Continis to support, even celebrate, such a union?"

He tapped a finger on the table. "That is the question, my dear Watson."

I smiled slowly and said: "Look, I'm Sherlock, you're Watson, and don't you forget it."

He smiled back and beautifully, by the way, but I've said this already. Some things bear repeating. I'd been known to flirt with this man and have him flirt back but that was in the days when my heart belonged to another—safe-distance flirtation, in other words. Now nothing felt safe.

"Let's get back to business, my dear Watson," I said. "It could be love that brought the bride and groom together, though I realize that such emotions hardly served as wedding material back in the day."

He was about to answer when suddenly the door flew open and Sophia rushed in. "I am sorry to disturb but a boat comes! You said to alert you of something suspicious. It is not a tourist boat but carries four people. One appears to have a gun!"

Evan and I exchanged glances and jumped to our feet. "A gun openly displayed?"

"What is this—America?" I exclaimed.

"Giani sees it with his glass thing from the tower. He saw one man open his jacket and the gun was strapped across his body. He just texted."

"Surely they wouldn't try anything here in broad daylight, and what are they after, anyway?" I cried.

"You," Evan said.

"This is crazy. I told you that I'm no expert. I just dust off old things and classify a lot." This wasn't false modesty; I really didn't see myself as being particularly gifted.

"It's not what you know but what they think you know that matters." He grabbed my hand. "Besides, you know more than you give yourself credit for, madam. Come, we'll escape into the church and wait until we can safely bolt for the boat."

Which meant a quick-paced stride across central Torcello straight toward the Cathedral of Santa Maria Assunta, which turned out to be an amazing Byzantine structure with two majestic end walls covered in gilded mosaics. The two flanking walls were whitewashed to enhance the beauty of the two ends. All of this I took in as we race-walked down the aisle.

"Slow down and walk as if you're a devotee," Evan whispered.

I slowed my pace while pulling my wrap up over my head, which probably made me look like some bizarre runaway mushroom. And I did feel a sense of deep respect inside of any religious house, but my presence here felt like an imposition of the worst kind.

The usual mill of tourists wandered around taking pictures of the mosaics, whispering their appreciation, while a handful of those I presumed to be locals lit candles and prayed quietly in the pews or before the image of a golden Christ.

I tugged on Evan's arm to pull his ear down to my level. "They'll be methodical; they'll spread out and comb every inch of this island and are bound to come in here, too."

"I realize that," he whispered back. "Follow me."

So I followed him past the altar and behind a column to where a stone bench sat in shadows against the wall. There we were holding a Bible between us, our heads together as if reading the text together. It was probably one of the strangest moments of my life, to be hiding out in plain sight in that ancient cathedral with Evan, the former MI6 guy. We barely moved as the minutes ticked by and Evan periodically shot cautious glances toward the door.

Eventually a solitary man entered, his eyes darting around the space as if looking for something or someone, neither tourist nor supplicant but a man on a mission. Our heads remained bowed as we waited tensely until he left.

Finally Evan straightened. "They won't leave this island until they find us. We'll have to risk dashing for the boat," he whispered.

"Can the boat outrun them?"

"No. Our best hope is to get a head start."

"But what do they hope to gain?"

"Perhaps to kidnap you. The paintings themselves did not tell the thieves what they wanted to know but they think maybe you can. That may mean that they don't mean to shoot you, at least not at the moment."

"Comforting. They'll just torture me first. And we thought we'd be safe here on this island."

"Torcello was a poor decision on my part for which I deeply regret. I believed it perfect for our meeting, which it was, but it is simultaneously wide open and exposed the way Venice is not. Are you ready to run?"

"Sure."

But before we ran, we walked, casually and hopefully unobtrusively, out the door and across the earthen square. Evan was a big enough man to attract attention for anyone looking for him and I stood out with my red hair and art wrap. Neither one of us wore T-shirts and baseball caps like many of the other day-trippers. Evan removed his peaked hat and tucked it under his jacket, letting his light brown hair blow in the breeze while he gazed about the square as if fascinated by every detail.

When we were halfway down the path heading to the dock, we bolted. In seconds we were untying the boat, but as soon as we jumped in, we saw a man standing three speedboats down talking urgently on his phone.

"We've been seen," Evan said, opening up the throttle. "Hold on."

As if holding on was even necessary. I just sat there, all the way across the marsh toward the open lagoon, the boat racing as fast as it could, which in speedboat terms was like a Smart car struggling to be a Lamborghini.

"I thought you love speed, Evan?"

"I believed this would putter under the radar but, trust me, I have another one more impressive."

It only took minutes to see a speedboat pull away from the island behind us and zoom at our puny wake at a much faster clip. "Do you want me to drive while you shoot?" I called.

"You watch too many spy movies, mada—Ms. Phoebe. Shooting is not wise under the circumstances," Evan called back.

"What circumstance—being chased by a boatload of armed criminals? Sounds like a few shots over the bow as a deterrent just might be the thing."

"Not if they shoot back, which they inevitably will," he shouted over the slap of waves and the putter of the engine.

I gripped the sides, thinking that we could row faster than this. Meanwhile, our pursuers were gaining on us, making me wonder what exactly they had in mind. If it was true that they wanted me, which I still considered ridiculous, then Evan would be seen as an obstacle worth killing in their eyes. And who would see a kidnapping in the middle of the lagoon where boats zip by all the time and a shout or a cry— maybe even a gunshot—probably couldn't be heard? Suddenly I felt frightened.

Evan was talking into his phone between quick glances at the gaining speedboat. Venice was growing closer but not close enough. I imagined scenes where James Bond raced down the canals in his superboat but I doubted we'd even reach the canals let alone zip anywhere in this one.

Our pursuers were so close now that I could make out their features—three tanned men and one woman, all wearing sunglasses, leather, and stony expressions straight out of some thriller movie. They looked like carbon copies of one another. And then Evan was slowing down and another boat was pulling up from the opposite direction—shiny, new, and, I suspected, jet-propelled.

"Quick, jump!" Evan called.

Leaping from one rocking boat to another is not easy even when stopped, especially when carrying a carpetbag. The chop alone set the thing to swaying like crazy even while the driver tried holding the two boats together but I still managed to leap over the side into the other boat.

A little guy with a leathery face and a cigarette between his teeth grinned at me. Evan jumped in behind me, yelled something in Italian, and took the helm while the little man sat back and bared his tobacco-stained teeth in the direction of the approaching speedboat. Our little boat was left to float away by itself.

That left our pursuers arriving just in time to grabble with our wake, the new speedboat being far faster than even theirs as we whipped the water toward Venice. This may have been the fastest boat I'd ever been in, fast enough to leave the bad guys far behind while yelling at our backs.

After that, it took mere minutes to reach Venice, Evan taking diversionary maneuvers by diving into different canals snaking through the city—left, right, left again. Our pursuers disappeared from sight. Once we were slipping down a quiet narrow canal between two buildings, Evan cut the engine. "Do you see that archway to the right, madam?"

"Yes, Evan, I do." I needed some smart-ass name for him.

"Take that alleyway through the buildings, cut across the street to the left, cross a bridge, and within a block you'll come to Cannaregio and the villa down the canal. It's the safest place for you right now as Ricki here informs me that the Contini residence is crawling with police. Go inside and stay there until I contact you. We are going to divert our friends and ensure that they are not on your heels."

"I need to speak to Rupert."

"You will."

I watched the arch draw closer with its time-worn steps leading into the water and in seconds I had jumped out. "Be careful," I called as they pulled away, and within ten minutes I was striding up to the door of the Contini villa without further mishap. My temper, however, was on the boil.

A uniformed carabiniere stood by the door, his back straight but his gaze shifting in all direction. "I am staying here," I said as he moved to block my way.

"Your name, *signora?*"

"Phoebe McCabe."

With that he opened the door to let me pass and I moved directly across the hall to the salon, combing my matted hair with my fingers and fortifying myself for what had to be done.

Inside the room, Nicolina could be seen sitting in tense silence, her hands in her lap, while across from her sat the same suited detective I had seen earlier plus another. On the other side of the room, a white coveralled man was dusting for prints. Everyone stood when I entered.

"Phoebe!" Nicolina cried in a mix of welcome and desperation.

I shoved a lock of fuzzy windblown hair from my brow. "Afternoon, Nicolina, Detective. Excuse me for interrupting but I've just been chased across the lagoon by a boatload of armed thugs who may or may not have been after me because they think me more important than I am. Mind if I join the conversation?"

10

_____

Detective Guido Peroni from the Venetian Questura was a thorough man. He had already been stationed at the villa for six hours interviewing every member of the household and returning again and again to grill the weary countess, who assured him that she was doing everything to cooperate. To Nicolina's credit, she did not pull arrogance as a shield in the kind of imperativeness that a countess might well deploy under the circumstances.

I had, however, thrown a proverbial spanner in the works. After I had disclosed to Peroni everything I knew or thought I knew about the painting, it became apparent that Nicolina had not.

"And you believe this painting may be a kind of cipher, Ms. McCabe, and that may be why you are of such interest to your pursuers today?" the detective asked as he sat there with the photo portfolio open on the table before him. He was a thick-set man in a well-tailored suit with a receding hairline and shrewd eyes that glinted in the light washing through the tall windows. Beside him on the couch sat another suited policeman, younger and leaner, taking notes while listening to every word with the diligence of a human lint-catcher. Occasionally he'd interrupt me for clarification of a word or an idea. Though both men's English was excellent, he obviously was ensuring that nothing was lost in translation.

"Possibly," I said, "though I can't imagine why anyone who knows even a little about Renaissance symbology couldn't see the same things. I'm not a Renaissance scholar by any means. I studied art history as a generalist."

Peroni was peering at the Bartolo with a magnifying glass. "Yes, but you are a textile expert, are you not, from a big London gallery? And with affiliations with Interpol and a recent history of involvement with several key finds?"

So he did his homework. I hurried on. "My reputation is exaggerated, but back to the carpets: please understand that my assessments are only guesses and need a lot of research to back them up."

Peroni turned to Nicolina. "Did you request the help of Ms. McCabe because if her expertise?"

"No," Nicolina replied evenly. "I asked her to accompany me for moral support as a friend."

"How fortunate for the countess that you have such an experienced friend." He turned back to me. "Please tell me your assessment of these carpets to the best of your knowledge."

Taking a deep breath, I attempted to pull it all together. "The paintings have an odd combination of cultural motifs that can't be accidental. You know, of course, that Renaissance art often used portraits and paintings to capture a moment of significance, kind of like a pictorial contract," I told him. "This one shows a wedding between two families, two very different families, I might add." I waited for Nicolina to explain more but she appeared locked in some fortress of her own choosing. I sighed and continued, a shield of my own in place by way of my most scholarly tone even though I was in way over my head. "Though Bartolo was not known for embedding secrets in his work the way da Vinci was, I think it's reasonable to assume that he may have been commissioned by one or both of the families to do exactly that."

"Interesting." Peroni was focusing on a detail of the nave. "I am not an art expert," the detective said, looking up at last, "but one does not live in Venice without some knowledge of the subject. Bartolo was from the Sienese School, am I correct?"

I nodded.

"So these families are Sienese?"

"Not necessarily. Renaissance artists often traveled all over Italy on commissions from wealthy patrons. If the families wanted to put a little distance from this contract and their hometown, they might choose a painter from another city. Still, I believe that the motif in the bride's robes are actually from the Continis' own weaving mills, which could mean that one of the parties is from Venice, maybe even from this family. I can't confirm that, though."

Peroni turned to Nicolina. "Is that true, Contessa, that these fabrics may be from a Contini mill, which I understand has stood down the street for at least that many centuries?"

Nicolina's face remained unmoved. "It is true that Maria Contini has many motifs stored in the vault's library and that this may be among them."

The detective did not acknowledge that comment but placed the photo upon the table and drew back. "I see with my humble and unschooled eye a beautifully painted scene of a wedding party, which appears to be taking place inside a church of some wealth and majesty. I know nothing of carpets and motifs but I do know most of the churches and basilicas in this city and this one is not known to me."

"I believe that's because it's actually a composite of two houses of worship —a church and a synagogue—and it's supposed to be a symbolic location rather than a real one." I shot a quick glance at Nicolina, who refused to meet my eye. "The altar and the nave seen to the left are clearly Christian but the dancers behind the bridal party appear to be forming a chuppah with their hands and, if I'm not mistaken, the design under the bride's feet could be the Star of David. That's just a guess, of course, but it does explain a few things. Even the arches in the wall to the right appear to be a blend of two architectural styles—half Gothic arch, half Eastern, which doesn't mean anything by itself but could when combined with the other elements. It is my guess that this painting is the Renaissance equivalent of a contract between two wealthy families—one Christian and one Jewish, an incredibly risky and startling partnership given the age in which it occurred."

Peroni looked at me in surprise while Nicolina's eyes widened with something like fear.

"The clues are recognizable but I doubt they'd be evident to any casual viewer in the past. The painting is probably for the owners' eyes only but a contract nonetheless." I turned toward Nicolina again. "The paintings have never been cataloged or appeared in any exhibitions. The family has kept them private for centuries."

"The Continis have always been very private people," Nicolina said evenly, "and naturally one does not wish to advertise their priceless art."

"And yet someone obviously discovered that they existed and hence it is gone," Peroni said.

"Yes. Anyway, as I said, it would be extremely dangerous for a Jewish girl or boy to marry into a Christian family or vice versa," I continued. "The marriage would have to be hidden, and the reasons for those two families coming together in the first place significant. The wealthy rarely married for love but as an alliance between two families in order to bring together fortunes or titles. In this case, one must have been significant enough to be worth the risk."

The detective was watching me carefully. "What do you think may have prompted this partnership?"

"Since Jews have been persecuted across the ages, that's what puzzles me, too. I don't want to eliminate the possibility of love—the bride and groom do seem happy, it's true. Maybe they wanted to hide themselves under the cover of another family, but why would the Continis agree to such a thing when it would mean risking their lives?"

"And so a secret locked into the carpet, perhaps, something worth killing for?"

I met his deep-set brown eyes. "My guess is a dowry. The bride is standing on the Star of David and the groom is on the edge of the motif. She brought a valuable dowry to a wealthy Christian family, one that for whatever reason was worth the risk both families took to secure it. It had to be protected at all costs."

11

ommissario Peroni and his team exited shortly after that, insisting that a guard be placed on the house despite Nicolina's pleas that she didn't need one. Nevertheless, a guard was assigned to the patrol outside the building and Peroni assured us that he would return within the day. I had no doubt they would.

That left Nicolina and me sitting soberly in the salon with so much unsaid between us that I swear it darkened the air. Or maybe that was just dusk.

It was me who broke the silence. "Why didn't you tell me what you knew about that painting, Nicolina?"

"Because I did not know how important it was!" It was as if I'd flipped her switch. She threw up her hands. "I did not know that this family's history was in any way related to the theft! I should have, perhaps, but it is a priceless work of art in its own right, yes? Also, I would have told what I did know once we had time. When have we had time? First the police came and the funeral arrangements had to be made on top of the horror of losing Maria under such circumstances!" She covered her face and wept. She was exhausted, overwrought even, and I knew I was being an insensitive pig.

And she had a point: there hadn't been much time and, admittedly, she had a lot on her shoulders. But I wasn't quite ready to let the matter drop. "Of course, it's been terrible for you. I understand that, but to leave me in the dark while putting Seraphina on to me, too—that I'm having trouble swallowing."

"I was looking out for you," Seraphina said, appearing like a stealth missile into the room.

Like I believed that. "Really? More like you were looking for Rupert."

Seraphina's little face was so pinched it might have been one of those apple dolls. "Yes, we wish to speak with Sir Fox, this is true, but when I saw we were being watched across the way, I knew I must protect you, too."

I got to my feet. "Without telling me, by saying it must be a paparazzi stakeout? Do you think I'm stupid?"

"No!" Seraphina and Nicolina said at once.

I crossed my arms. "Well, something's got to give. I'm not putting up with this. I was asked here to help solve a murder, not be lead around by a leash like a puppy." That's exactly how I felt.

Nicolina had crossed the room to take me by the shoulders. "Forgive me, Phoebe. I am sorry for keeping such secrets. I come from a family of secrets and promised Maria that I would not talk of her family, but now I see I was wrong. Too many things are burying us alive. They killed Maria, whoever they are—Rupert, somebody. It must end; we must find the truth! I will try harder from now on, I promise."

I pulled gently away. "Then let's start with this family history and you can tell me everything you know, but please let's eat first. I haven't had a proper dinner since we arrived. There seem to be a few good restaurants around." It was a peace offering, a chance to regain neutral ground.

Nicolina's swollen eyes widened. "This is terrible! I will rectify this as soon as possible but no restaurant."

Apparently you can tell an Italian that she's been a misguided person but never imply that she hasn't fed you properly. The country's citizens had standards. The countess rang the bell for Zara, and uttered a string of the imperious Italian sentences to the housekeeper, who shot me a hostile glance before exiting the room.

"Zara will prepare dinner for us," Nicolina said. "I have requested fish and local dishes. I have not eaten properly since we arrived, either. I have been a very poor host."

"Thank you. In the meantime, I'll head to my room and freshen up. My hair must look like I've wrestled a Gorgon and lost. We can have that long talk of ours after supper."

Escaping to my room gave me time to think and to truly fix my disheveled self, which revealed near-mythic proportions in the mirror. Medusa had nothing on me, snaky tresses aside. After something like a shower under a sad little trickle of water, I changed into my only non-jeans pants—leather—

donned a silk blouse Nicolina had given me the year before, and fastened on a pair of gold hoop earrings. Really, that's about all I could manage in the elegance department but at least I felt moderately presentable.

While I showered, someone had delivered a tray of sweets, bread, and cheese along with wine and water. It was all I could do to keep from devouring the whole lot but, as it was, I ignored the wine and took the edge off my hunger with a bit of cheese and sweets. The Italians ate so late—9:00 p.m. in this case—but that gave me plenty of opportunity to study the painting further.

I also checked my phone—no word from Max but an update from Peaches arrived assuring me that she hadn't threatened any of the construction dudes yet. Then I sent a quick message to Evan to see if I could visit Rupert that night.

The response came back minutes later. *Sir Rupert is finally sleeping soundly. Perhaps I could come to the villa and speak with the contessa and Seraphina tonight instead?*

I'll run it by Nicolina, I answered back. *Somehow you have to enter without being seen by the police guard.*

I left my carpetbag on the chair, shoved my phone into my pocket, and readied myself for dinner with the countess. By the time I descended the stairs, Nicolina was sipping an aperitif in the salon dressed in a long burnt-orange Fortuny gown. She stood when I entered the room, the woman and the gown heart-stoppingly beautiful as she twirled in the candlelight, the silken Delphos folds glimmering in the light. "I wear this in your honor, Phoebe. Maria gave it to me as a gift long ago and I brought it here to wear for her also."

"Lovely." I touched her silken sleeve reverently.

"She was wearing a stenciled velvet Fortuny coat when she died," Nicolina said, "which says to me that her appointment that night was very important to her. She rarely wore her Fortunies out as they are now too fragile."

I met her eyes. I needed to tell her sometime. "She was going to meet Rupert. She had called him in London and asked him to meet her here in Venice on some important matter. He came as soon as he could but she failed to appear at the appointed time. They were to meet near the warehouse. I believe him, Nicolina."

She turned away to face the fire. "And you did not mention this to either me or the *commissario*?"

I rubbed my neck. "Peroni only asked me about the paintings—that's my excuse. Anyway, Rupert is in hiding—from you, from who knows else—and he's sick besides. What would happen if I added the police to his many Venetian interests? I agree that he needs to step forward and speak to the police himself, which I'm sure he'll do as soon as he is able." Weak, so weak. Why did I defend him? "But, in the meantime, will you raise the white flag long enough for Evan to come and meet with us here? If we're truly going to find Maria's murderer, we need to work together for once."

"Oh, Phoebe," Nicolina said, swinging to face me. "You are so trusting!"

"And you are so trigger-happy!" I said. "Don't we need to at least gather the necessary evidence before reaching conclusions?"

"Ah, that is the lawyer in you talking. Rupert above anyone knows about the painting and that it may hold a secret. Maria's mama had revealed their importance to her during that last horrible argument and Maria went to Rupert in distress to share all before Papa Contini chased him out of town. He should be on the suspect list."

"And he could say the same about you. You are the sole beneficiary, after all."

She froze. "Me, a suspect? But I would never...and I was not in Venice when Maria died."

"You could have hired somebody—Seraphina, maybe—and you can believe that Peroni will have you checked out as a matter of course."

"Yes, you are right," she said finally, rubbing her temples with a manicured hand. "How foolish how that never occurred to me. I have been so preoccupied." She turned back toward the fireplace, her gaze fixed toward the empty place over the mantel.

"So," I said, stepping forward. "Why don't we approach this collaboratively? Let's assume that everybody is innocent until proven guilty and discuss what we know together. Let me see if I can arrange for you to talk to Evan at least, since Rupert is unwell. Maybe tonight?"

"What is wrong with Rupert?" she asked, swinging around.

"Pneumonia. He looks awful, burning up with fever and the whole nine yards. I'm convinced that he's innocent, Nicolina. Whoever murdered Maria and stole that painting is probably connected to those bastards that chased us today, not Rupert. Evan was with me when they chased us out of Torcello, remember."

"Torcello?"

"Evan thought it the safest place for us to have our meeting today."

"Ah." She smiled, nodding. "Perhaps also to give him an opportunity to see his ex and son again."

For a moment I couldn't speak. "Evan has a son?" *Giani.* That explained a lot. In fact, it explained everything except why it bothered me so much.

"You didn't know?"

"No, of course not. I don't know any personal details concerning Rupert's right-hand man. Why would I?" That came out unintentionally cross.

"Seraphina had him checked out years ago. This liaison occurred before MI6, before he even met Rupert. In any case, I agree to speak with him but it must be later tonight since Seraphina and I must go to the warehouse and retrieve some documents immediately following dinner. The police finished with the crime scene only today. Now I am allowed to enter again and there are sensitive documents I must collect immediately."

I nodded, only half listening. "I'll go with you."

"Excellent. We can use the help since I do not want to involve anyone else for the time being."

"Why?" I asked, suddenly paying attention.

"Because I do not trust anyone except maybe you." She stepped up to me and took my hands in hers. "You I see as my friend, though I know I have not behaved as a friend to you. Still, you I trust. But I must ask you to consider that perhaps Rupert did meet Maria as planned and killed her to obtain the keys to the vault."

"The keys?" I asked.

She squeezed my hands. "Just think, Phoebe: if she was meeting Rupert to take him to the vault, Maria would have had the keys with her. She always took them everywhere. She showed them to me once—on an ornate key chain from Murano. The studio's outside door wasn't broken into but the security code was penetrated and only the door to the safe was blown. Someone used the keys to enter the building and they are now missing, taken by Rupert that very night, perhaps."

"No," I said, pulling my hands from hers. "I absolutely don't believe that Rupert had anything to do with this. Promise not to try to assassinate either him or Evan. We need the chance to clear his name, to clear both your names, and find the truth."

"You trust him in everything?" the countess asked me while studying my face intently.

"Of course not! It's pure foolishness to trust Rupert carte blanche but I don't believe him capable of this particular crime. Besides, we still have this gang chasing us. They're the main suspects now."

Nicolina gave a rueful smile. "I would not have killed him, anyway, not like that, and Evan is a formidable opponent, in any case. No, I was just very angry and—what do you say?—venting. I was venting."

I lowered my voice. "What about Zara?"

"Thoroughly investigated by both Seraphina and the police. Her alibi is clear and she has worked for this family forever. She was with her family that night and Seraphina says she is heartbroken by Maria's death."

"That doesn't mean she couldn't have hired somebody."

"But why?" she asked. "And why now?"

"Maybe somebody got to her."

A bell rang down the hall and Nicolina sighed. "We will leave this for now. Let us regain our friendship over dinner."

I wasn't certain how much of our friendship existed but I really did want to trust her eventually. For the time being, I followed her into a spacious formal dining room where a sea-blue damask tablecloth had been spread over the long table set with silver and sparkling crystal. Silk velvet jacquard the hue of deep burnished bronze hung on the windows.

Seraphina did not dine with us, and other than to deliver dishes, Zara stayed out of sight, too.

"They eat together in the kitchen," my hostess remarked. "It is a long-standing custom in Italy that the servants do not eat with the owners of the house, even in this day and age. Of course, Seraphina and I don't follow such rules at home but here, and since we wish to talk, I thought it best. Also, Zara and Seraphina have been friends for many years and prefer to be by them-selves also."

"I understand. Besides, I don't think Zara likes me, either," I whispered to her over the basket of rolls. I said it as a joke but it was true.

"I don't think she likes anybody after Maria's passing, except Seraphina, perhaps. Certainly she resents me becoming the new mistress here. She is very angry, it seems. I have shared with her the sum Maria wished to leave her in her will but it brought no consolation. That blouse looks lovely on you— Gucci, correct, the summer 2017 collection?"

"I think so, and thank you for the gift. I keep these pieces for special occa-sions, which aren't all that frequent." Nicolina loved to shower me with designer clothing, which I both appreciated and treasured but left me feeling as though I was receiving a subtle nudge to dress more appropriately for the world we intersected together—hang out with an Italian countess, dress like a countess, or at least like an Italian. I took a sip of water from a crystal goblet and smiled. "Tell me what you know about the family history, please."

She gazed at me from across the table, a diamond earring catching the light. "I do not know as much as you think, and what I do know I didn't believe important at first. The Continis were wealthy textile merchants in the fifteenth century, exporting silks and woven cloths all over Europe and beyond. It was in the family stories that they had joined with a Jewish family sometime in that same century and that the painting recorded that event. That's all I know."

"Maria didn't mention a cipher?"

"She told me that she believed there may be a secret hidden in the painting but had no idea what."

"Where did the Jewish family come from?"

"It is not known—possibly from someplace East. The Jews were being persecuted all over the world and were constantly on the move so they could have come from anywhere."

"But this family must have amassed great wealth to have a sanctioned union with a wealthy Venetian family despite religious barriers. The bride must have been expected to renounce her faith, or to hide it, at the very least. How common was it for Jews to renounce their faith in order to marry, anyway?"

"No more common than it was for a Catholic to marry a Jew with the blessings of the family, I would think. In Italy, if one marries a Catholic, it is the other religion that must convert. For me even twenty years ago, to be born Catholic in this country was to ban me from marrying a Protestant unless he converted, so imagine a union between a Catholic and a Jew five centuries earlier? But this much I can say: Signore Contini was very anti-Semitic. He became so enraged when Maria wanted to study the Kabbalah that I thought she would leave the house."

"Maria wanted to study the Kabbalah?"

"It interested her greatly. In fact, she had been studying it for several years in secret. She was proud to have Jewish blood in her ancestry."

I sat back. The pieces were falling together but still with enough spaces between them to keep the picture far from my reach. For a while, I focused on eating, especially when the fish arrived to stare me in the face. I covered the head with a bit of risotto while carefully removing the bones. "What about this cousin," I asked at last. "Does she know anything?"

"She is Maria's father's younger deceased brother's daughter and she has never shown the least bit of interest in this family or its history. Maria had only met her once, to the best of my knowledge. She lives in Milan."

"And if she changes her mind and contests the will?"

"She assured me she would not. I explained about Maria's desire for the museum and that I will sell this crumbling villa in order to finance the reno-vation. She can have all the art inside these walls but for the textiles and the missing painting, should it be located. What need have I for a villa in Venice, anyway? Now that Maria is gone, I will have no desire to visit much except to oversee the museum. As for the other properties—there are two, I believe—a farm in Tuscany and a vacation property somewhere. Those I will sell to finance the warehouse restoration, as well."

Nodding my approval, I dove into the rest of my dinner while trying not to speak with my mouth full. Zara had created a feast of risotto with red wine, fried sardines, pasta, and polenta with not a speck of anything green in sight. It was delicious but I couldn't do it justice.

Nicolina poured a little wine into her glass while I waved away the offer. "As soon as the body—" she hesitated, fortified herself with a sip, and continued "—as soon as we can, the funeral will take place. I have been assured that this can happen within the next few days. I have provided you with something to wear."

I shook my head. "Whenever the funeral is, I'll use that time to explore and research since everyone's attention will be elsewhere."

"I had hoped you would keep me company."

"You won't need my company, Nicolina. You have Seraphina, and I would be very out of place at the funeral of someone I didn't know, despite my feel-ings of affinity with Maria." Besides which, I couldn't get images of *Don't Look Now* out of my head—the funereal black gondola sailing down the canal. "But thank you for the outfit. I'll return it."

She waved away the thought. "You must keep them."

"Well, thank you again and for ordering this magnificent feast." What I would do with that dramatic black outfit, I had no idea.

Nicolina appeared relieved that I'd accepted her peace offering as she toasted me over the table. "To friendship! *Salute!*" My water goblet and her wineglass clinked over the candles.

Through dessert of gelato and coffee, we spoke of more neutral subjects until the table was cleared.

"So," I began, "are we going to just stroll down the street to enter the ware-house tonight?"

That brought a smile. "No, certainly not. It is best that our activities remain private. I have another way." She rang the little bell on the table and in strode Zara, to whom Nicolina said something directive that caused the housekeeper to scamper away. Seconds later, in came Seraphina.

"Seraphina, tonight we go to the warehouse to collect those files we spoke about and Phoebe will accompany us. Following that, Sir Rupert's man, Evan, will visit us here at the villa to discuss possible suspects." Nicolina waved one hand by way of aborting protests. "We are attempting collaboration."

"Collaboration." Seraphina appeared to ponder the word. "Very well. In that case, I suggest that we take the secret passage to the warehouse so as not to draw attention and that Sir Rupert's man enter the villa through the canal door."

"Good idea." Nicolina nodded.

"Secret passage?" I asked.

"At one time, the Continis owned all the buildings in this block," Nicolina explained, turning to me. "A private passageway—probably no longer in good condition—runs at the back of the buildings at the canal level. Centuries ago it was built to assure the Continis didn't muddy their shoes when traveling back and forth to their place of business. Maria took me through it a couple of times when we were younger, all in fun. Girlish games, you know," she added with a sigh.

"Good. I'll just text Evan and tell him to meet us at the back canal entrance, shall I? What time do you think?"

Nicolina and Seraphina exchanged glances. "Perhaps 10:30?" Nicolina suggested.

"Ten-thirty, it is. I'll just go upstairs and change." Which I proceeded to do, texting Evan along the way: *Success. Come to the villa at 10:30 by boat via the back canal door.*

After I had received *Confirmed* in response, I climbed the stairs, pondering the idea of Evan with a son and an ex, the lovely Sophia. It bothered me at some level but I didn't want to prod too deeply as to why. Maybe because I'd always thought of the mysterious Evan as monkish—probably even preferred to think of him as the attractive unobtainable man, perfectly safe for flirting purposes. After all, didn't he live in a kind of cell of Rupert's choosing waiting on his every need? Now I had to broaden my image of him as a man with the same needs as any other. Well, of course I knew he had *that* need. Our playful flirting had told me that much. Luckily I didn't have time to think too long on the subject.

Since my hands would be full carrying files back and forth through this mysterious tunnel, it made sense to leave my carpetbag behind. To that end I changed into jeans, sneakers, and sweater and shoved my cell phone into my pocket. After donning my new jacket, complete with gun, I was ready for the evening.

When I met Nicolina and Seraphina downstairs minutes later, both had changed into leather jackets and pants complete with sleek little high-heeled booties that left me totally baffled. High heels for stealth missions through mysterious tunnels? Badassed chic totally escaped me. My sneakers, on the other hand, made me feel like a Clydesdale draft horse set off to plod with a pair cantering thoroughbreds. We each carried a plastic carrier bag to add to the effect.

Still, I was thankful for those treads when we stomped down to the cantina moments later, wove through the damp shrouded shapes, and watched as Seraphina pried open a low decrepit-looking door at the end of the cavernous room. The hinges shrieked in protest but eventually cooperated enough to reveal a dark, foul-smelling corridor. All three of us stepped back.

"It is in much worse condition than I thought," Nicolina remarked, holding a tissue to her nose. "Many floods over the decades."

"Mold," Seraphina said ominously. "We will need protection and perhaps to cover our noses. There are coats over there by the door. I will put something together against the mold."

Nicolina and I waited while Seraphina rummaged against the far wall by the boat door.

"Smells moldy, all right." Seemed like a bad time to mention my mold allergy so I just coughed for effect.

"Mold and spiders and all manner of unpleasant things," Nicolina agreed as she lifted a tarp covering a long shape beside us and poked her flashlight underneath. "The family's ceremonial gondola. I wonder whether it will ever sail again? I suppose I must auction it off."

Before I could comment, Seraphina had returned carrying three full carnival masks plus three yellow well-used hooded raincoats. "With the hood and the masks over our faces, this is the best possible protection for in there." Seraphina indicated the corridor with a jerk of the head. "I will go first."

She donned the slicker, pulled up the hood, and slipped a glittery, feather-plumed mask over her face. For a moment she reminded me of some jaunty bank robber with a thing for bling. Nicolina, on the other hand, being a taller and more striking figure all around, appeared utterly bizarre in an old ill-fitting raincoat and a grimace mask straight out of Greek tragedy. As for me, I was just grateful not to be wearing a plague doctor beak for once and thought my silver and golden sequin-encrusted sun/moon mask rather spectacular. Whether it offered much protection for penetrating slick, mold-slimed corridors was left to be seen.

Thus decked out like actors from some Carnevale Meets Freddy Krueger B-movie, we entered the yawning corridor. We had to hunch as our backs scraped against the fungi-encrusted ceiling while trying not to breathe in the stench of mold and whatever dead things putrefied the air. Rats, I thought. Seraphina was ahead, me behind her, and Nicolina bringing up the rear, each of us grasping flashlights along with our bags, and yet it was impossible to see much of anything. It was dark, and we were in full face masks trying not to breathe in too deeply but gasping for breath all the same time. Touching the walls even with the gloves I had the foresight to bring was to be avoided but it was impossible since balancing myself on uneven surfaces was part of the territory.

Our scout wasn't wasting time and seemed intent to traverse this disgusting corridor as quickly as possible. That wasn't the problem so much as my inability to keep up while slipping on the greasy cobbles. The ever sure-footed Nicolina behind me asked: "Phoebe, are you all right?"

"Fine," I croaked, and scrambled on.

Once, a few inches of wall to our right opened to briefly reveal the canal and briny air. The disintegrating brick must have toppled into the canal months or even years before, indicating the fragility of this passageway. Yet, that single lungful of semifresh air kept me going awhile longer.

The corridor was not only dark and slippery but refused to follow a straight line. It formed a torturous route through a closed-in passageway snaking behind the buildings, including steps in some places. By the time we reached a steep set of stairs rising straight up, Nicolina shone her flashlight over Seraphina's head and claimed: "We are almost there."

Seraphina bounded up the steps and called: "Stay back. I will fight the door." The sound of wood wrestling against stone penetrated the gloom. Splintering noises followed and soon Seraphina called: "It is free."

We climbed up and up, my breath struggling inside the condensation-slicked mask, which I couldn't wait to tear off my face, while my hands braced against the slick walls. In moments we had burst into another dark room, this one as dry and dusty as an abandoned cathedral.

I removed my mask, shrugged off the raincoat, and found myself standing in a huge space, one so expansive I couldn't see the opposite wall from where I stood. More tarps shrouded tall mounds everywhere our flashlights landed.

"This is the main studio, second floor. The first floor is storage, the top the offices. Look, Phoebe." Nicolina flung away a tent-like covering over one of the mounds to reveal an old loom possibly six feet long and still threaded with warps as if the weaver had aborted a project before it began.

"See how many kinds there are?" Nicolina said while removing the covers from several different varieties. "There are looms for silk, looms for velvet, looms for special robes for maybe a queen, yes? This one made golden thread into brocades, Maria said." She stood lost in thought before an old upright loom that still wore the remnants of fraying cloth caught between the silken warp.

"How old?" I asked.

"These are mostly reproductions of much older looms but some have been repaired and still contain the original parts maybe five centuries old. This one, for instance," she said, indicating a long frame loom with a wooden wheel attached to one side. "I think Maria said this was the oldest. The studio wove its last textile in the late 1800s, a bishop's mantle, I believe."

"Nicolina, this place is a treasure," I gasped. "I mean, really!"

"And yet so many see no value in historic textiles."

"Fools!" I said with vehemence. "Textiles clothe us, reveal who we are or who we want to be, and are quite possibly the result of some of the first of humanity's technologies." Okay, so soapbox time but that's how passionately textiles speak to me.

"Yes," she said sadly, "I knew you would understand and now it is my task to preserve it all somehow. Come, let us go upstairs to the vault."

We carried on up another flight of stairs to the third floor, Seraphina leading the way. She switched on the light, presumably because this being an interior room, cracks in the shutters had less chance of giving us away. She then proceeded to check every corner as if expecting a thief to be still lurking there.

I focused on the vault, a large walk-in structure with a blackened gaping door dominating the space. Nicolina shook her head and muttered in Italian over the debris, the damage to the floor, the papers strewn everywhere, the fingerprint powder dusting every surface.

"Plastic explosives," Seraphina remarked, poking her head in moments later. "It could have been worse."

"But what if the blast damaged the paintings? It is still an explosion," Nicolina fumed.

Seraphina pointed to the interior of the vault where no signs of damage could be seen other than a bulging impression on the inside of the door and the apparent rifling of the papers and files inside. "The blast damaged only the locking mechanism."

Nicolina strode forward. "But they did not take the jewelry box, did not take the cash in the strongbox, just the painting and what else?"

"Maybe they were interrupted," I suggested from the doorway. "The painting was presumably easy to spot but maybe other items not so much.

They wouldn't have had much time. Didn't you say that this studio may have once woven the same textile as in the bride's gown?"

"So Maria believed."

"Where might sample fabrics be, do you think?"

"In the library," she remarked, staring at a wad of papers scattered on the floor. "They were looking for something," she remarked. "Peroni thought so, too. We must find the deeds to the properties and any earlier copies of the wills plus a list of possible holdings."

"I'll visit the library in the meantime."

"Yes, do. For now, Seraphina and I must sort through what is left and compare it with the will, a copy if which I have. I doubt that everything in the vault was recorded but I'm thinking jewelry, the properties…"

"What were these properties exactly?" I asked.

Nicolina bent to pick up a leather-bound portfolio. "The Continis owned an olive orchard in Tuscany, I think, and a vacation property somewhere."

"Morocco," Seraphina said, stepping into the vault. "Zara mentioned that the family used to go to Marrakech years ago for sun during the gloomy months. It was where she first met the family decades ago."

"Oh, yes," Nicolina mused as she passed the leather portfolio to her assistant. "I had forgotten that—the riad. Maria never went by herself after her parents died. She said the intense sun did not suit her."

"I believe it's been leased out as an Airbnb now," Seraphina commented as she began collecting the documents and folders. "Maybe we will go sometime."

"More likely I will sell it." Nicolina turned to me. "Phoebe, the library, which you will find interesting, is in the room down the hall if you wish to take a look. Once we collect all these documents, we will come to retrieve you."

I checked my watch: 10:10. Still plenty of time. I turned the corner and strode down the hall to the next room. I just stood in the doorway for a moment flashing my light around. It was a small library with a single wall of tall fat books housed behind glass in what looked to be a humidity-controlled environment.

I stepped forward. A tiny round sensor measured the percentage of moisture inside the shelves and a table stood nearby. I ran my phone light over the dusty table with its study lamp before moving on to the shelves, staring at the books that were unusually thick, like scrapbooks or journals.

The writing on the spines was Italian, of course, but the thickest and the oldest-looking of the leather-bound volumes sat way back at the far end of the shelf with Roman numerals imprinted in gold onto their spines. The first volume caught my attention immediately: *MDXV-MDC.* 1515 to 1600?

My hands were trembling so much when I slid open the glass and lifted the oldest volume onto the table that I thought I'd drop it. Of course I shouldn't be handling such a treasure without gloves in the first place, but since my gloves were so disgusting, I didn't have a choice.

I flashed a quick glance up to the windows. Too long arched windows shuttered against the light and, if my orientation was correct, they looked out over the back canal and not the Cannaregio. That settled it: I risked turning on the lamp. With excruciating care, I opened the cover, letting it fall open on a compendium of line drawings of motifs and patterns. My mouth went dry. I couldn't believe what I was seeing. Could it be that every pattern produced by the house since the establishment began was recorded in these books? Why hadn't anyone mentioned it—had it been forgotten, overlooked, or what?

Nicolina appeared at the door. "Phoebe, we have collected all that is valuable. We must get back if we are to meet with Evan. Are you ready?"

"Nicolina, these are important. If they are what I think they are, they could be a repository for every fabric pattern the Contini house ever produced. It's amazing that such a thing even survived these centuries. Imagine a recording of every bolt of fabric, including who they went to—whether to market, to specific customers—since the studio first began?"

Of course a weaving house like this would record such things. They were like recipes, and other volumes might contain records of dyes and maybe weaving "cartoons," which the weavers used to set their looms. Thousands of patterns are recorded in the safekeeping by the Victoria and Albert Museum alone, but this house has remained in the same Italian family for centuries. One single family. It's incredible.

"Yes, Maria wanted them preserved. This I will do when all is settled."

"But they are at least as valuable as the jewelry and deeds."

"To some, perhaps."

"Maybe we could take a couple of these volumes with us?"

Nicolina shook her head. "They are too heavy and awkward, Phoebe, and they could be damaged in the tunnel, yes? All our bags are full. Tomorrow we will return to retrieve them, but for now, I must study what is needed for the will."

I couldn't refute her logic: dragging those precious volumes through the corridor without protection hardly made sense. "Right. Tomorrow, then." Reluctantly, I returned the one volume to the shelf, closed the glass door, and prepared to make the journey back. With my hood up and the mask secured, I gathered up the bundles, now stuffed into the carrier bags—one per hand—and followed Seraphina down the stairs.

But I could not get those books out of my head.

They stayed on my mind all the way back through the corridor, which was just as unpleasant as expected—worse actually, since my hands were full and I almost dropped my load onto the slimy surface more than once. Luckily, Nicolina was bringing up the rear and her impressive reflexes always seemed to catch me before I fell headfirst into the slime.

Ten minutes later, we broke into the dimly lit cantina and not a second too soon from my perspective. I dropped the bags and ripped off the mask before leaning against the tarp-covered gondola, gasping for breath. Meanwhile, my companions made their way through the shrouded forms toward the stairs, masks still in place.

Suddenly I heard a crash and a man shout something in Italian followed by, "Or I'll shoot!"

1 2

*S*eraphina was pointing her gun and shouting when I dashed from the shadows, my hands in the air: "Evan, it's me, Phoebe! That's Seraphina and Nicolina. Put down the damn gun!"

The man crouching behind a mound of boxes stood up and lowered his pistol. "Ms. Phoebe? Are you unharmed?"

Nicolina yanked off her sequined mask and flipped back her hood and spoke in her most imperious tone. "What are you doing here? You were asked to come to the back canal door, not break it down!"

I turned. The door to the canal hung open on its hinges, part of it shattered as if hit with a battering ram. And the boat was gone.

"This is how I found it minutes ago," Evan explained, his tone measured. "I called out but there was no answer. Naturally, I was afraid you'd been robbed or worse, and was about to head upstairs when you appeared."

"You are lucky I didn't shoot you," Seraphina muttered, glancing at the ruined door. "Someone has broken into the house."

"More likely I would have shot you," he remarked. "I've given this level a cursory check. They must have escaped with your boat."

"Upstairs immediately!" Nicolina ordered, heading for the steps with her own pistol drawn.

"No, wait, Countess! I will go first," Seraphina cried, dashing after her, but her employer's sleek booties were already up to the kitchen. Evan and I bounded after them, me pulling out my pistol along the way.

Once on the main level, everyone fanned out as if by some unspoken stealth investigation code. I took the main salon and dining area, keeping to the corners and swinging my gun around 360 degrees when entering a new room the way I'd seen television cops do. I'd have felt ridiculous if not for the overwhelming sense of threat. Either intruders were currently in the house or had been recently.

Seraphina could be heard calling to Zara. There was pounding on a door, an answering cry followed by a tense exchange in Italian before everything went silent. I continued with my downstairs investigation, poking into cabinets, peering into closets. Every room was empty but I couldn't tell if anything was missing, once I discounted the obvious, that is.

Minutes later, I met Evan in the hall. "All clear," he told me, "at least in terms of active intruders."

"Same here but what about the police outside?"

Before he could reply, my phone pinged in my pocket. I pulled it out and read a text from Nicolina: *Nothing missing up here. Do not speak of anything important aloud. Come upstairs.*

I turned the phone for Evan to read. He nodded and we proceeded upstairs in silence. Nicolina was waiting at the second-floor landing, one finger to her lips. Behind her down the hall, Zara sat in a chair with one hand over her mouth while Seraphina stood on a chair nearby taking apart a lamp sconce. Nicolina opened her palm to show us a tiny surveillance device that had obviously just been retrieved.

"Common as ants," I muttered until Nicolina shushed me.

Evan picked the thing up between his thumb and index finger, bringing it under a table lamp to study. Though I was no expert in these things, it certainly didn't look like the ones I'd smashed this morning. When he straightened moments later, he shook his head, expression tense. *Don't recognize it*, he mouthed, and pulled out his phone to help Seraphina scan the premises for more.

Nicolina and I stood together watching as her assistant glowered at him when, seconds later, his phone flashed red while passing it over a picture frame she had just investigated. "He is very good," Nicolina said barely audibly. She touched my arm and our eyes met.

"What about the police officer outside?" I whispered.

She whispered back. "Leave him. Come, we must talk." And with that she beckoned me to follow her up the stairs to the roof.

Only when we were standing under the pergola, buffeted by a cool damp breeze, did she speak. "Do not trust anybody."

"But—"

"Phoebe, listen: there has been a spy in this house, someone who has placed those devices. It could be the police when they were here today. There were at least six special agents all over the house. Dirty police happen in Italy, too, yes? Commissario Peroni may not know about it or perhaps he is on— what do you say? *On the take.* Until we know, we cannot take chances."

"But why break down the canal door and steal the boat?"

"I do not know. They were seeking something, maybe they found it. Upstairs in Maria's room, the mannequins are fallen over, the library books tumbled on the floor—all very messy, as if they were in a hurry. They knew when we left the house this evening."

"But nothing is missing?"

"Nothing I can see but I do not know every single item. When Zara recovers, we will have her go through the house to check everything. She is very upset."

"And what about Zara?"

"She can hear nothing without her aid and goes to bed early. They must have known that, too."

"And they probably bugged the salon where I shared my theories with Peroni. They must know everything I suspect by now. They've stolen my ideas!" Such a travesty. My ideas, at least, were mine, *mine*!

I cast a glance across the canal to where I had first seen the watcher in what seemed like years ago. "So they stole the painting thinking that it would lead them to something even more valuable only to discover that they needed additional information, information they may have gotten from me." A sudden chill hit my spine. "But they still need more. Nicolina, I've got to get back to my room."

"We will scan there, too."

"Now," I said, and with that I practically ran downstairs. When I reached my door, I froze. Evan stood in the center of the room with two shattered devices in his hand. His eyes said it all.

"Where?"

He pointed to the bedpost and side table.

"Seriously? But I'm sure I passed your detection device over both of those."

He frowned. "Unless you hold the phone no farther away than three inches from the surface, the sensor may miss the device. This one was tucked inside the lady's mouth." He indicated the carved nymph on the bed who appeared to be blowing kisses.

"That's no lady, that's a nymph," I remarked.

He studied the carving more closely and smiled. "Correct. In any case, I will need to work on improving the device's distance capabilities. The other one I found under the table placed in the back corner."

"And my bag?"

"Other than Seraphina's tracker that I located yesterday, it appears clear."

I relaxed. "Thank God. That thing comes with me everywhere."

"Nevertheless, my device requires more work apparently. I've tested on five kinds of trackers to date but there are more, like these, for example—cheap enough to purchase by the handful."

"Online?"

"Chinese mail-order, yes."

It was disconcerting to think that surveillance devices could be purchased as easily as printer cartridges. "But when would they have found the time to secrete them all over the house?" Despite the reputation of corruption, I didn't believe the police had hidden these. I doubted they used Chinese technology, for one thing.

"That's the question."

"Is the room clear now?"

"I certainly hope so."

I launched myself into a pacing trip around the bedroom, fuming with frustration and angst all the way. Nicolina stepped into the room and indicated for us to follow her back up to the roof. Minutes later, the three of us crowded to the back of the pergola.

"Seraphina has returned to the basement to secure the canal door and then will return to the house to continue the sweep. I will go through the house with Zara to see what may be missing before returning to the task of studying the will against the contents of the vault. The clues may lay there. You may assist me," she said magnanimously, waving a hand to include both Evan and myself.

"Whatever you need," Evan said. "I am here to prove the sincerity of Sir Rupert's efforts to work with you."

"And I no longer hold Rupert responsible for these thefts and Maria's death. Too many things do not add up."

But I was barely paying attention. Something like a collision of seemingly random thoughts was hitting me just then. "If they placed these devices here, they may have done the same thing in the warehouse," I mumbled.

Nicolina shot me a quick look. "But why?"

"They are looking for something and hoping we'll lead them to it." I said nothing more, my mind too busy running over the fact that what could be the most critical clue may yet remain safe. For now. "I have to go back to the warehouse tonight."

I heard Nicolina's breath catch. "Why?"

"I don't want to say. Everything I've said to date has been recorded apparently. How do we know that we're not being eavesdropped on still? I'll go, collect what we need, and come right back. How long would it take—maybe twenty minutes at the most? I know the way. I'll be right back."

"I'll come with you," Evan said.

"You won't fit. It was challenging enough for the three if us to squeeze through that corridor," I said.

"This is true," Nicolina said. "A big man would find it very difficult."

"I will manage. I said," Evan enunciated between his teeth, "I will come with you. It's too dangerous for you go there alone." He was towering over me, using the intimidation of his six foot two of height to hammer home his point.

That was new. I stepped back. "Don't do that, Evan, don't use that male thing on me." I was looking him straight in the eye—not that that was easy in the shadowy light, and being over a foot shorter didn't help. Actually, it was bloody awkward. "If you want to protect me, stay near the tunnel entrance and watch my back. Seraphina kicked that tunnel door open earlier tonight, leaving it compromised, and the canal door gaping, too. I'd feel much safer knowing those two entrances were protected."

He said nothing but I could feel him working it out from all angles.

"That is a very good idea," Nicolina said. "It will be some time before Seraphina can fix the door."

For an instant, it was just Evan and me locked in a moment of tense struggle—powerful, a little sexy—but I was determined to emerge as the woman on top. That was my thing. I tipped the scales by adding what I hoped as just a touch of wry humor: "And I'm Ms. Phoebe to you and don't you forget it."

13

*T*he last thing I wanted was to return to that tunnel under any circumstance but I was so focused on retrieving what I needed, I would have tried walking over hot coals. Evan agreed to play guard dog only on the condition that I remained in contact with him every step of the way.

"If I detect any issues, anything at all, I'll be through there in a shot," he whispered as he fastened the flashlight he'd jiggered together onto my hood, "Ms. Phoebe."

"Right," I said, shrugging the strap of my plastic-wrapped carpetbag into a better position over my shoulder. "And you'd probably get wedged in somewhere along the way. It's a tight squeeze, I said. I'll be fine." I turned to study the opening, which, now that I had a high-powered lamp to penetrate its gloom, looked a lot like a gaping wound.

The phone in my hand vibrated. I swung back to him. He was standing in there thumbing me a text: *What are you after? Tell me.*

He looked up and mouthed, *Ms. Phoebe.*

I put a finger to my lips and mouthed my reply: *Be back soon.* Next, I pocketed the phone and headed for the tunnel, pulling up my mask along the way. Evan had found a rubberized clown mask, which he'd lined with tissue and widened the nose and eyeholes. Though it was no less uncomfortable, I could certainly see and breathe better.

Taking a deep breath, I bent over and dove into the corridor. Having done this twice, I was better prepared. I knew where the most troublesome parts were, where I almost tripped twice, where the mold and rat droppings had slimed the floor to the point of making a gooey mess. By keeping one gloved hand on either side of my body, I could steady myself while proceeding in a bent-over run.

Surprisingly, not having Seraphina ahead of me made it easier. For one thing, I could see better and, if not exactly feeling more confident, at least I knew the path ahead. Sort of. Whatever the case, I managed to scramble to the warehouse steps without a single tumble.

Inside the building minutes later, I removed my mask and raincoat, hanging both on the corner of a loom that jutted out from under a tarp. My text to Evan was brief: *I'm in the warehouse.*

All clear back here, he responded.

I admit that knowing he was watching my back was fortifying. Forget that it was unlikely he could get to me quickly, anyway. Right then, I was focused on being inside a weaving studio alone. It was like standing inside a cathedral, hushed and hallowed with all that I revered. But I had to get to work.

So I hoisted my carpetbag farther up my shoulder, pulled a flashlight from its depths, and strode across the weaving floor to the next set of stairs. My single light didn't provide enough illumination so I used my phone light, too —anything to dispel those shadows crowding in around me. The feel of that empty, abandoned place was something I was determined not to dwell on. I'd return in daylight and take a proper look at those looms, as Nicolina promised.

I traipsed back up the squeaky staircase to the office floor, past the vault room, and around the corner into the library. I couldn't wait to switch on the desk lamp. Crazy, I know, but feeling those shadows crowding in behind me spooked me to no end. "Just an empty building," I whispered, relieved when the little lamp sent a pool of soft light around the small room. Placing my carpetbag on the table, I shot Evan a quick text: *In the library. Not long now.*

Removing the earliest two volumes from the shelves, I wanted desperately to take both but I couldn't carry two. Each volume was nearly two feet by two feet—even taking one wasn't going to be easy—but what if I missed something? I'd take the earliest volume for sure, I decided, since it would more likely hold the clues I wanted, but I'd photograph the second.

With that in mind, I hastily began taking photos of the foxed yellowed pages with my phone, careful not to damage the brittle parchment. This time I wore proper plastic gloves that Evan had conjured—too big but workable— and yet my heart pained at the possibility of tearing a single page.

Totally absorbed in my work, brittle page after brittle page passed by while

I took photos and attempted to read the cramped script—a mix of Italian and Latin: forget that—pausing to gape at this magnificent compendium of Renaissance textile design.

The phone pinged a text in my hand: *Taking too long. Are you all right?*

I texted back: *Lost all sense of time. Coming now.*

Damn. Reluctantly, I replaced the second book on the shelf—there was always tomorrow—before carefully wrapping the first in plastic and tucking it under my arm. Any archivist would have a conniption seeing me handle these priceless works that way but hopefully, someday soon, care would be taken with the entire collection. They badly needed a conservation doctor. Switching off the light, I stepped into the hall.

How is it we know something is wrong before our senses provide the evidence? I stood still as death listening to the empty building. The creaks and skittery noises I recognized as settling wood and rodents but something was off. Only when I crept to the top of the stairs did I hear the whispering clearly. I froze. There was no way in hell anybody should be in this building. Evan, maybe? No way. He'd call out or text. I pulled out my gun and released the safety.

When I took my first step down the stairs, I caught a whiff of something noxious like lighter fluid. At the same time a plume of smoke began billowing around the base of the stairs illuminated by my light like a roiling snake. A stab of fear shot through me. The only way out was down. I risked taking several more steps until I was nearly at the bottom, feeling heat on my skin and fear in my gut.

"Who's—" My cry died in my throat. A rolling billow of flame was moving toward me from the end of the room, licking at old wood, devouring scraps of fabric, consuming the entire tinderbox of a studio. I could not see signs of a single human being, just an aggressive expanding fire. Turning, I dashed up the stairs, feeling heat on my back and legs as if the flames were chasing me up. One glimpse behind me filled me with terror.

I panicked. Where could I go, how could I escape? With fumbling fingers, I called Evan, yelling, "Help! Fire!" before dropping the phone back into my bag. Shit! Maybe I could go inside the vault and shut the door? Iron and steel withstood fire, didn't they? How stupid that was, I realized. I'd suffocate or roast long before ever getting rescued. Maybe I heard an alarm, maybe I didn't. I didn't care, I had to escape.

Running back into the library with the flashlight in hand, I slammed the door shut and shoved the table under the windows, dropped my bag and book on top, and climbed up to flick the shutter catch. The shutters released immediately but the casement's mullioned glass frame had a lever so rusted that I doubted it had been opened for decades. Nothing I did made it budge even when I banged it with the butt of my gun. Next, I tried grabbing a knitting needle to lever the thing open. No luck. In pure desperation, I released the safety, aimed the gun, and fired at the catch. It blew apart instantly, allowing the casements to fly open with a shatter of broken glass.

The blast of cool night air that followed was like the kiss of life. By then, fire was lapping at the wood behind me and thick smoke was snaking tentacles under the door. But air also feeds fire. I fumbled with my phone and called Evan again. "At the rear canal window!" I cried before shoving the thing deep into my bag again. No more time for calls.

Flames crawled up the wall and licked at the sill. I balanced on the window ledge with hands grasping the frame until I felt a searing burn on my left hand. Snatching it away, I grasped the edge of broken glass, ignoring the sharp bite into my palm, intent only on what lay below. A straight drop into the canal three stories down. It was nothing. Hadn't I dived from promontories higher than this, and what was the cool depths of a fusty canal next to the churning sea? That didn't bother me. What bothered me was losing my carpetbag and relinquishing my hold on that treasured volume of Renaissance design. It was crazy but since my imminent death by roasting was delayed, all I could think about was what to save. But what could be rescued by tossing those disintegrating pages into the canal? The inks would run, the paper would pulp, everything of value would be ruined by water as readily as by fire. And now it was too late to save them all, anyway.

Soon the whole room would go up in flames and all the volumes with it. What could I do? And yet I wavered, reluctant to let go. Then I saw the boat zipping toward me down the narrow back canal.

"Jump!" Evan called out. A surge of relief hit me so strongly I could have kissed the man had he been close enough. As it was, he pulled his speedboat under the windows and called for me to jump again. I knew he didn't mean to jump into the boat itself. From this height, I could break a leg or damage the boat or both. He meant for me to jump into the canal.

I pulled inside to grab my carpetbag and the single precious volume, the smoke so thick by now I could barely see. I heard rather than saw the flames devour the other volumes as the glass shattered across the room. Fumbling for the objects while holding my breath, I returned to the window.

"Items coming down. Catch!" I cried. I tossed the priceless volume out the window, which he caught with ease. Such a good catch. Next, I tossed out my carpetbag, which he also caught, and then my jacket and my sneakers one after the other.

"For God's sake, Phoebe, will you just jump!"

Another boat could be heard echoing against the ancient walls. Sirens pealed in the night. With flames making a grab for my legs and the room succumbed by smoke, I held my breath and jumped.

14

$\mathcal{T}$he canal was that brutally cold after the heat of the fire that I thought my blood would ice in my veins—punishing cold, colder than time. For a moment I had the uncanny sense that I had plunged straight into Venice's frigid heart and that I'd freeze there until the breath left my body. But the water wasn't that deep because my feet briefly touched bottom.

Still, seconds feel like years in terror-time as I kicked my way up. Breaking the surface, all I saw was black churning water with the roar of boat engines and sirens over all. Waves of water engulfed my mouth and eyes as I gasped for air while spinning around and around trying to orientate myself. There were two boats, I realized, and shouting, lots of shouting, and then a gunshot. Suddenly hands grabbed me from behind and lifted me backward into a boat where I kicked away like some furious tuna. "Damn you!" I cried as I struggled to wipe the water from my eyes.

"It's me! Lie still," Evan called. So I lay still for seconds, coughing up water while the boat pealed down the canal. A bullet pinged somewhere to the right.

"Stay down! The bastards are shooting!"

Like I couldn't tell that. Flipping onto my stomach, I struggled to my knees. "Give me your gun!" I called. I could see it sticking out of his jacket holster as he stood manning the steering wheel, his back exposed to bullets.

"No!" he called back. "I'll outrun them!"

Hell, why didn't men ever listen to me? I assessed the situation in a flash:

our boat racing away with the pursuers gaining on us in what appeared to be their own superboat. Evan had whipped us into a main canal while performing various diversionary maneuvers by making one sharp turn after another. But that wouldn't be enough. We had a zero head start and they'd soon be right on top of us.

I was thrown against the side a couple of times before I could reach into my jacket to remove my own gun, safety catch still unreleased, and turn to face our pursuers. They were gaining fast.

Nicolina had provided me with a gun that was more than adequate for what I intended but that hardly mattered when my hands where shaking so badly that I couldn't grip the handle and my left palm hurt like hell. I must have burned it or cut it or something but damn if that would stop me.

"Don't try it! You could get shot!" Evan cried.

Oh, please. A treasure of art and design was burning and I might get shot? I was so furious just then I could take on a boatload of thugs and more. I held the gun with both hands, propped it on the back of the stern seat, and fired at the prow of the approaching boat. And missed. I turned to Evan and called. "Slow down, will you? I need a second to hit the hull full-on."

Understanding crossed his face. He let the boat drift. We ducked, both of us keeping down as the other boat approached. They had cut back on the throttle, too, and now puttered toward us cautiously. I estimated the distance —six, five, four yards until I could read the model name on the prow. I totally ignored the two figures standing behind the water-splashed windshield as I took the first shot below the waterline. Evan did the same thing, firing twice into the hull, but he had the idea to fire a flare at the boat's windshield, too.

"Brilliant!" I cried while the night blazed neon pink. Literally.

"Happy you approve!" he called back as he returned to the wheel to rev into the boat equivalent of warp speed.

I gazed back at the pandemonium. The flare had temporarily blinded our pursuers and, with a little luck, their boat would start taking on water. Meanwhile, we were zooming down one of the side canals. Just before we turned the corner, I caught a glimpse of the reddened skyline far across the city. The studio in flames! I began shaking so badly I could barely contain myself. Evan leaned over and dropped his jacket over my shoulders, warm with his body heat. I turned my back to him and shrugged off my soaked turtleneck and wrapped myself in his jacket.

"Does Nicolina know the building's on fire?" I called out to him as I poked my arms into his sleeves. He could see my bra—big deal.

"I called. They alerted the authorities," he said, looking over his shoulder at me, one hand on the wheel.

I fumbled into my bag to retrieve my phone. Three messages from Nicolina topped the list. I speed-dialed her.

"Phoebe! Thank God you're all right!" she rasped. I could hear sirens in the background, people shouting. "Phoebe, the studio is gone, Maria's legacy gone!" Nicolina was crying.

"They knew I was going there tonight. They burned the place down, all that history!" I coughed.

"Phoebe, forget that. You could have been killed!"

My hands were numb, my heart number. The phone slipped and fell to the floor. I picked it up again. "Got to go," I said. "Talk later."

"No, Phoebe, wait—"

But I turned the phone off and dropped it into my bag. My hand throbbed, my heart too numb to feel a thing. The boat was proceeding at a nearly sedate pace now but I barely noticed, barely noticed which direction we were taking, either, only that it was circuitous with a lot of turns down dark little canals.

The studio was gone. Centuries worth of priceless design information and weaving artifacts gone. Old looms that had withstood the ages with loving care had been slaughtered, burned alive as their brittle bones went up in flames. Only the ignorant would do such a thing, the kind of ignorance that had once burned witches at the stake, turning their magic and wisdom to ash. I buried my head in my hands and sobbed.

I wasn't sure when we arrived or even where exactly. Evan put his arms around me and lifted me out of the boat. There was somebody else there, too —Sloane, I realized—and lots of instructions being bandied about for the care of this soaked, half-naked woman.

"She needs a hot bath, man!" That was Evan.

"But we don't have working plumbing in this infernal hellhole, Evan, you know that. You will need to rig something up." That was Sloane.

"Then rig it up I will."

"We can use that dreadful marble death chamber upstairs. Sir Rupert refuses to go inside the place."

Marble death chamber?

"Phoebe! Dearest Phoebe! What happened?" croaked Rupert as he shuffled down a long dark hall toward me in furry bedroom slippers and one of his satin robes. He attempted to grab my icy hands in his but I only let him have the good one. "Oh, my dear, what a disaster!"

Evan answered him over my head while still holding me tight. "The bastards set fire to the building, sir. Ms. Phoebe narrowly escaped with her life."

Back to *Ms. Phoebe.* I dimly remember him using my name. "What kind of monsters set fire to centuries of history, let flames ravish priceless information that will be lost to civilization forever?" I wailed. "What kind of bastards do that?"

Rupert gripped my one hand tighter. "The same kind who set fire to a building with you inside, Phoebe. Monsters indeed! Sloane, tea, immediately!"

"Coming up," the butler called back as he dashed down the hall.

"I'm going to fix you a shower, Ms. Phoebe," Evan whispered in my ear, releasing my shoulders and passing me over to Rupert—reluctantly, I thought.

Rupert nodded at him and led me by the arm into the shadowy ballroom. "Come, come, my dear. We shall have tea and place you beside the space heater until you thaw. You are shaking like a leaf! You fell into the canal, I understand. How dreadful!"

"I jumped into the canal," I told him.

"Yes, well, I am missing part of the story, it seems."

"You still sound terrible," I told him, and then I started crying again. Really, I was a mess.

"It's shock, dear Phoebe. All very understandable." He patted my back. "Here, do sit right down."

I was guided into a big blanket-covered chair in front of a modern heating device that looked like a sleek revolving doughnut but which gave off considerable heat. Rupert fussed a bit by tucking a blanket around me until finally he collapsed onto a stool nearby and tried to take my injured hand. I winced and pulled it back inside the oversized sleeve. "Dear Phoebe, I would despair if anything had happened to you. I just don't understand who these bastards are."

"But we know what they want." It wasn't a question.

"That blasted painting! I didn't believe Maria when she told me her suspicions about it long ago—I thought it some fanciful *Indiana Jones* imaginings—" He paused to cough, recovered, and went on. "But the dear woman was apparently right all along."

"But you knew it was valuable." It came out like an accusation. Tea had arrived. With my one good hand, I took the mug Sloane proffered and sipped gratefully.

"Of course I knew it was valuable," Rupert croaked, waving the hovering

Sloane away. "It was by Domenico di Bartolo so how could it not be valuable? But to murder and burn to obtain it? It was not *that* valuable, Phoebe, not Raphael or da Vinci valuable. No, it's not, and yet somebody behaves as if it is worth millions of pounds, which must mean that Maria may have been correct all along—" he stopped to steady his breath "—when she told me that the painting held...some kind of secret."

"But she was going to give both paintings to you as a wedding present once—"

"More to keep them with her when she left the family bosom than to give them to me specifically. We were eloping, after all."

"You were eloping?"

"Well, yes, old Father Contini—a male supremest if I ever met one and an anti-Semitic nasty piece of work besides—would never allow his daughter to marry a penniless Jew—not that I was penniless exactly but I was still a little young to have yet amassed my own fortune at twenty-five, wasn't I?"

"I didn't know you were Jewish until recently."

"Yes, I am Jewish, Phoebe—not a practicing Jew but Jewish nonetheless. Does it matter?"

"Of course not but I didn't know."

"Why should you? But that's rather beside the point, isn't it?"

"No, it isn't, considering that the Bartolo commemorates an extraordinary marriage between a Christian and a Jewish family at a time when such high-profile unions could be deadly."

"Well, yes, of course. Maria was very proud of her family's Jewish roots, as thin as the bloodline was after all these centuries. Her papa, however, preferred to keep it under wraps. It was her desire for me to have the Bartolo for that very reason as well as to assuage her guilt, I suppose. I was very bitter following the broken engagement, I admit. She was my first love, you see." More coughing chased down by deep sips of tea. "Ah, yes, what was I saying?"

"You were very bitter and Maria was going to give you the paintings, anyway."

"Yes, until her mother suffered a massive heart attack and died in protest, which ended that idea rather dramatically, don't you think? Her mama wasn't...against our marriage so much as she was against Maria taking those paintings with her. They have been...oh, dear. Give me a minute, please." He breathed quietly for a moment before continuing. "They have been tradition-ally willed to the female heir of the family, you see...but should a generation pass without progeny, their fate hung in limbo. Maria didn't have children—"

he sighed "—so it's all rather tragic, really. Though she assured me…that she would will me the paintings, it didn't matter to me by then. I wanted nothing more to do with them or her…and told her as much after which…I proceeded to leave Venice. I thought—I thought—"

Another coughing fit consumed him, this one bad enough to send Sloane scurrying in with admonishments to stop talking immediately. Rupert was ordered to his bed and me upstairs.

"Evan has rigged up a shower in the master bathroom, Sir Rupert. I will lead her there now."

"That place?" Rupert wheezed from the camp bed. "You cannot allow her to go in unattended, Sloane, not after what happened. It's ghastly."

"That was a long time ago, sir. Besides which, the plumbing is far more ghastly than any sordid tale. The room itself is perfectly usable despite the intolerable cold, which I believe we have somewhat remediated. Regardless, we really must get her out of those wet clothes."

So, I was to be spoken about in the third person. I shrugged off the blanket and got to my feet. "And the book she rescued from the fire, where is that?"

"In the kitchen, madam, and it is quite unharmed after tonight's adventure, I must say."

"That's because Evan is such a good catch," I pointed out.

"So he says, though no woman has managed to catch him yet." Sloane chuckled at his own joke but suddenly sobered at the sight of my hand. "You've suffered a burn, madam, or is that a cut?"

"What, where?" Rupert croaked, sitting up.

"On the left hand, sir. We will steer her into the shower and then attend to it properly." Sloane held my carpetbag in one hand and took my arm with the other.

"I'm quite able to walk, Sloane, thank you," I said, shaking him off. "Now where exactly is this marble death chamber?"

"That is rather a dramatic term for a perfectly lovely marble bathroom on the second floor. Installed in the early nineteenth century," he said, leading me into a long dark hallway, his lamp held high. Once a butler, always a butler apparently. He was a slight middle-aged man who I had only ever seen wearing his tidy green uniform, which he wore even here. "With exquisite detailing, I must say. I'm sure you'll be impressed, at least with the finishing, if not the plumbing."

"And the 'death chamber' part?"

"Apparently a man was shot by his lover there decades ago. Old news, as they say, but Sir Rupert is rather fixated by the lurid tale, that and all the other fates that have befallen the palazzo's previous owners."

I climbed the stairs, my gaze glancing over damp-splotched flocked wallpaper and resting briefly on a chandelier whose crystal droplets glinted like frost in the flashlight. I thought of the ruined warehouse and the light that had burned out in this city tonight.

A glow was coming from an open door halfway down the hall. Evan stepped out. "It's ready for you, Ms. Phoebe."

With the two men following at my heels, I stepped into a large bathroom completely tiled in rosy marble but for a single mirrored wall. Brass fittings gleamed in the lamplight and a large marble-tiled double tub sat between four pillars in the middle of the room. It was both ostentatious and gorgeous all at the same time, yet felt massive with the shadowy light.

"I guess it's as good a place to murder someone as any," I said.

"Easier to tidy up afterward," Sloane remarked. Obviously butlers think on the practical aspects.

Had it been another time, another place, I might have laughed, but as it was, I just wanted to get this done. "So, this is the makeshift shower?" I gazed up at a contraption I took to be of Evan's devising: a large plastic water container suspended over the tub with a cord dangling down.

"Yes, a bit primitive, I'm afraid," Evan explained.

"Not up to your usual standards, you mean?" I remarked.

"Definitely not but hopefully it will function. All you need do is step in and give the cord a tug to release the flow. The water is still hot but I'm afraid it's not likely to stay that way for long."

Sloane peered into the tub. "I scraped away as much as the grime as I could but it's best not to dally, madam. Who knows what's down there. Evan, what is the story on the pipes?"

"I decided to abstain from investigating further after the snake encountered an obstruction. Hopefully the thing will drain of its own accord, which is the best we can hope for."

"Very well, then," Sloane said, stepping back. "Let us permit the lady to get on with it. I've set your bag on the counter, madam, and left a clean towel for your use. Please do take care to wash that hand thoroughly so I can tend to it when you emerge."

"We must tend to that hand" Evan said suddenly.

"It's just a bit of a cut and a burn," I told him, holding my wounded member away from his gaze. "Now, leave me, please. I'm not in the mood for a communal shower."

He almost looked embarrassed as he backed out. "Of course, ma—Ms. Phoebe, but I'll wait outside in case you need me."

Need him, why would I need him? Of course, I could use a little help taking my clothes off but this was hardly the time. I shut the door, stifling a brief bittersweet jolt thinking of Noel as I began the one-handed business of peeling off my damp jeans—trickier than I'd expected. That my hand throbbed seemed irrelevant. All that mattered was the carnage I'd just witnessed and the expanse of despair that had opened up inside me as a result. It was as if the loss of Noel, the imprisonment of my brother, and all the trauma that followed had suddenly hit me anew. And here I thought I'd managed to shove it all to the back of my mind. The heart is not so resilient, after all.

Leaving my jeans, panties, and bra on the floor and clutching my toiletries with my one good hand, I climbed shivering into the tub, cringing at the cold marble beneath my feet. In a minute, I'd pulled the cord to release a trickle of warm water, blessedly welcome after the dank canal. I tried to whip up a bit of lather from my shampoo but the most I got was a few halfhearted suds while my wounded paw burned.

As the water poured down over me, I closed my eyes and vowed to catch the bastards who killed Maria and sent her legacy up in smoke. I didn't care who they were, they'd pay. I doubted I could trust anyone anymore, not that I ever could. The world was peopled with self-serving, ruthless monsters who counted human life and history as worth nothing if it stood in the way of some kind of monetary gain. Damn them all to hell.

Minutes later, the water stopped trickling and I stood in the lamp-lit bathtub shivering. It had grown unaccountably cold despite the space heater. The one long shuttered window was covered with plastic so there were no drafts coming from that direction and yet I felt a definite breeze.

One glance to the right glimpsed my own naked image reflected palely in the floor-length mirror like a freckled ghost. Damn these Venetians and their creepy mirrors. Something was rumbling beneath my feet. I looked down to find brackish water regurgitating at my feet. Quickly, I climbed out and snatched the towel from the counter.

And it was freezing in there.

Luckily, my carpetbag carried a change of clothes—my carry-on emergency kit. I dressed as quickly as a one-handed woman could, hauling on fresh panties, yanking on a pair of dry jeans, a sweater, and topping it all with one of my art knit cardigans. My bra was damp so I'd go without. Stuffing my damp things into my bag, I tried to fling open the door but it wouldn't budge.

I shook the knob and pounded with no success. It was crazy after what I'd been through to feel panic over a stuck door and yet I did.

Hell, was Evan out there? I desperately wanted him to be out there. "Help, I can't get out!"

He was. "Madam, are you turning the knob?"

"Of course I'm turning the knob," I called back. "I didn't lock the door, I only shut it." But apparently it had locked itself. More likely the wood had swollen shut in the frame, meaning I'd just have to try harder, so I rattled the door with even more vigor. Still the thing wouldn't open. I turned back to the room, freezing now as if I stood in a refrigerator instead of two yards away from a space heater. And the atmosphere had turned as thick as sludge.

Did I believe in ghosts? Sure, I did. Centuries of people can't have got that wrong. But was I afraid of ghosts? Naturally, but right then I was too angry to be frightened of vapors. "Back off!" I yelled into the gloom. "The dead don't have any teeth next to the murderous living! Go to hell!"

And then the door flew open and Evan fell into the room, knocking me against the wall. For a moment he stared down at me, stunned. I stood crushed against his person inches away from the heating element. "Who were you talking to," he whispered.

"The dead," I told him, pushing him gently back. "Let's get out of this place." I grabbed my carpetbag and got out of there as soon as possible.

Minutes later, I was sitting in the kitchen—now spotlessly tidy with all of Evan's paraphernalia apparently banished elsewhere—while the two men inspected my hand under a large spotlight.

"Second degree burn, by the looks of things, plus a rather nasty cut. I suggest a loose bandage to let it breathe." That was Evan speaking.

"Plus the addition of basic antiseptic as we cannot count on it actually remaining sufficiently clean given the countless sources of pestilence seething around this moldering pile," added Sloane.

I looked up. "Gentlemen, thanks for your concern but I'll take both the antiseptic and the bandage for now. Could we get on with it?" Anything to stop a debate. That prompted a small smile from Evan, who quickly tended to my hand with a gentle efficiency while Sloane scuttled off, presumably in pursuit of either germs or tea.

Once I had been bandaged, I returned to the ballroom to where Rupert sat bundled in his chair beside a small table, waiting. "Feel better now, I trust?" he asked, indicating for me to join him where another chair that had been pulled up beside his. Evan disappeared for a moment and returned with a stool for himself.

"I am, and you?"

"Reasonably, though I must take care apparently. Phoebe, we really must talk."

My gaze landed on my rescued book and the two photographs sitting side by side on the table, one of the Bartolo, the other the Civelli. "I agree." I sat down and reached for the Contini pattern compendium, relieved to find that it had held up to the recent adventure better than I. "This is the only one I managed to save," I said. "The others are all gone now."

Rupert leaned over and patted my knee. "There, there—a tragedy, I agree— but I've been thinking of what possible motive these—" he paused to take a deep shaky breath before continuing "—brigands could have for attempting to burn the place down?"

"Are you certain it was arson?" Evan asked.

I looked over at him. "I smelled what I realize now must have been lighter fluid or something similar. Whoever the arsonists were, they entered the building somehow and spread a ring of something highly inflammable around the weaving level before igniting it. They meant to burn me alive apparently. Who knew I was there except Nicolina, Seraphina, and you?"

"That's what I've been asking myself. I've run your phones and all your belongings through my devices as a precaution and found no sign of tampering. I must have missed one back in the Contini home."

"What about the roof? That's the only place we spoke freely."

"Possibly," he said. "I should have checked more thoroughly." The man seemed to have a thing bearing responsibility but he'd had zero time to check every inch of that villa.

"Nicolina suspects the police," I remarked.

"Indeed, but perhaps it is she who is behind all this," Rupert remarked.

"But why? Why burn the warehouse and steal what will become her own painting?" I asked.

"To cover her tracks, perhaps, to set loose a school of virtual red herrings to throw the authorities off her trail...in order to get Maria out of the way. I'm only playing devil's advocate here, you understand, and I don't truly believe... that the Nicolina I once knew to be involved...with such a heinous crime as murdering one friend and attempting to burn...another but people do change."

"Maybe," I agreed, "but surely not that much. I don't believe Nicolina did this. No, something or someone else is behind these crimes and it all leads back to that painting." My gaze rested on the two glossy photos sitting on the table before us. "How long have you had these?"

"For ages." Rupert leaned back in his chair, eyes closed. "They have been enlarged from a very poor photo I took eons ago. The detail is very fuzzy, as you can see."

And it was. I peered over at them. "I have clearer images on my phone. So —" I pulled back "—why did the thieves send the studio up in smoke tonight?"

"I postulate that they needed to eliminate anything that might lead to the secret location," Evan replied.

He postulates. Taking a deep breath, I turned to meet his steady gaze, that lovely gray-green almost the color of smoke in the lamplight. "So, you believe the arsonists were trying to burn clues that might lead us to it?"

"Perhaps burn the clues along with the one person who may be able to decipher them," Evan said quietly.

"But if they've taken to burning clues, they must now have a pretty good idea where or what that secret is," I pointed out.

"That's what I'm afraid of."

Rupert was looking from one of us to the other. "Do you mean that these bastards already have the answers and may be trying to eliminate anything or anyone who might stand in their way?"

I didn't answer him. Instead, I wrapped my arms around myself to try to stave off a new wave of shivering. "But why wouldn't they have taken these clues on the same night they stole the painting and murdered Maria?"

"Because they didn't know what they were looking for," Evan said. "Now they do, or at least believe they do. They may have left devices around the place the night they stole the painting."

I nodded. "So they knew when I was there tonight, heard me in the library pouring over that pattern book, even heard Nicolina describe what she planned to do with those files. The whole time we were sending them every possible detail to help them send everything up in smoke." I swung around to Evan. "And now they know where you are holed out, too."

"Yes. We will have to move," he agreed, turning to Rupert. "We have already begun seeking out alternatives, sir. Sloane is on it now. I'd best give him a hand. We may have to leave tonight."

"Really, so soon? Where shall we go?" Rupert croaked.

"Still working on the details, sir. I'll let you know as soon as it's sorted." And with that, he strode from the room.

"I can't say I'm sorry to finally leave this abysmal place but I'd far rather be sitting snug in my country house about now," Rupert commented once Evan had left, "feet up by the fire, maybe a good book in hand. Meanwhile, Phoebe, what else do you remember saying?"

But I wasn't listening. I was thinking, my eyes cast down on the shadowy floor. I got to my feet, picked up the design volume along with the two pictures, and headed out the door. "I'll be right back."

"What? Wait! Where are you going?"

To the kitchen, with its superior light source, oblivious to anything else but chasing a hunch. When I entered, Sloane was across the room speaking on a phone and Evan could be seen sitting in an adjoining room busy on a laptop.

Setting the book on the kitchen table with the painting photos on either side, I fished out my phone and opened up my photos to the close-ups I'd taken. Then I orientated the spotlight so that it blazed over all and began turning the pages to study the earliest entries.

Bartolo had painted the wedding scene in approximately 1441 and the Continis had begun keeping records of their textile designs about a decade earlier. The earliest design recorded was a simple vine and floral motif set against red velvet with a gold embossed ground—all recorded in the journal with paint over ink, illuminated-manuscript-style. A few threads of the original fabric clung to a space next to the illustration. Other samples from the same period showed variations of similar designs in colors predominantly red, gold, and blue, all faded, all lovely, but not particularly extraordinary.

However, when I slipped over several pages to the later mid-1500s, the designs showed a subtle shift. The motifs became more complex—flowers inside of flowers, layers of detail so rich that the thick curving vines had sprouted curlicues with filigreed centers and extraordinary birds cavorting amid the branches. I pulled away to use my phone as a magnifying app and returned to study one particularly detailed motif: a silk cut voided velvet with what looked to be three pile warps and gold brocaded wefts depicting pomegranates and peacocks, the vines forming a knotted design like interlacing stars. A border ran along one side of the illustration depicting blues vivid enough to glow after all these years. The sample piece had apparently been removed. I opened my photos and stared at the Bartolo carpet.

"Where was that place in Morocco that the Continis owned?" I asked no one in particular.

"Why, in Marrakech."

Turning, I found that Rupert had shuffled into the kitchen and plonked himself into a chair.

"Do you know anything about it, like where exactly in Marrakech or how long the family owned it?" I asked.

"Of course," Rupert puffed. "Maria and I were going to bolt there for our honeymoon, since it was virtually uninhabited at the time...but for a couple of caretakers Papa Contini left in situ. We thought we could buy some time...at least until we could decide exactly where we would live for the rest of our lives."

"How long has it been in the family?"

"Oh, forever, I believe. It was very old and tucked away in the medieval part of the medina...and apparently had been in the family for...centuries. The Continis never parted with a thing, you see—not daughters, not paintings, not properties—"

"Do you remember what it was called?" I interrupted.

"Well, no, not exactly. Phoebe, what are you thinking?"

I pointed to the design journal. "At approximately the same time as the Bartolo wedding commemorative was painted, the designs in the Contini factory began to change with the work becoming more complex, the dyes more varied, and with certain reoccurring motifs appearing with interlacing designs, including a few geometric features that have echoes of Berber combined with extraordinary florals such as that one." I tapped the painting of the bride's dress.

Rupert leaned over and peered at my phone. "My word, are you saying what I believe I'm hearing?"

Evan stepped out from the side room. "So, the bride's family came from Marrakech!"

I swung toward him. "And it makes perfect sense. Morocco has a rich textile tradition dating back thousands of years with influences from all over Africa and the East and the Jews were moving all over the continent at the time. That must have included Morocco."

"And aspects of the Moroccan flag actually form a star," Evan pointed out, bringing up the country's flag on his phone.

"Does it?" I marveled. "So supposing that a family living in Marrakech was making exquisite textiles for the sultans at the time but because of religious persecution felt compelled to leave the area?"

"And supposing they managed to strike up a friendship with an Italian merchant trader in the same business as they, one whom, for the exchange of some secret—" Evan added, picking up the story.

"Like the recipes for special dyes or weaving techniques—" I chimed in excitedly.

"—decided to form an extraordinary contract to bind their two houses and businesses?"

"But," I said, striding up to him, "what if the Jewish Moroccan family needed to further seal the deal in the tradition of a dowry, an incredibly rich dowry, considering the risks to the groom's family?"

"Possibly one too valuable to transport by horseback along with the bride, at least not immediately. Morocco was fraught with war at the time, I believe, with factious elements in a power struggle. So if traveling across Europe wasn't dangerous enough, carrying a fortune in some kind of unknown wealth within a country at civil war would be." Evan was at least as caught up with the story as I was.

"So," I said, tapping him on the chest with my one good hand because I couldn't help myself, "the wealthy Moroccan family wrapped the location of this dowry in a cipher and had Bartolo paint it into the commemorative painting to keep it safe until it could be transported to Venice. Both parties knew of the location at the time but agreed not to retrieve it until times were safer."

"But time and life intervened. Perhaps the parties died or for whatever reason it became impossible to retrieve the dowry."

"Maybe because of the plague or smallpox or something?" I suggested.

He grabbed my hand and held it tight. "Or some other calamity befell the parties until all the individuals who could unlock the cipher were dead and the secret lost forever."

"Until now," I whispered, pulling my hand away not because it didn't feel good but because it felt too good. "It's got to be in Morocco, which explains this."

Returning to the table, I picked up Crivelli's *Annunciation*. "All this time I couldn't figure out what the first painting had to do with the Bartolo but now I think I understand: it was meant to be added as another clue but not necessarily related to the marriage painting. If you look in the background to where the landscape rises to meet the blue sky, you'll see something very strange for Italian Renaissance art—palm trees. It's not that they didn't exist in Italy at the time—I think they did—but they rarely appear in ecclesiastical art."

"Also, there is very little else that is green amid the foliage, also atypical for the period since we know how the Renaissance artists loved to ground their work with local flora and fauna," Rupert added, donning a pair of glasses from his pajama pocket. "Look at this and tell me if this doesn't rather look like an abundance of sand?"

I'd already reached the same conclusion. "Sand, yes, and that light seems very desert-like to me, though at first I thought it Tuscan."

"So what else does this tell us besides that this Jewish bride may have come from Morocco?" Rupert peered up at me, his spectacles slipping down his nose.

"That I need to go to Marrakech immediately, obviously," I said.

* * *

THE USUAL FLURRY of protests erupted from my self-appointed male protection squad. I waited until they subsided before restating my position, even hearing out each of the supposedly logical points that Rupert and Evan posed as if I seriously considered them. Finally. Foxy wheezed himself into a coughing fit.

After he recovered, I began: "Thank you for your concern, gentlemen—really, I mean it—but as you've already pointed out, nobody here is able to go with me. Rupert's too ill; Evan must protect Rupert; and we can't even alert Nicolina and Seraphina to my plans in case it tips off the mole. So, who's left?"

"Ms. Phoebe," Evan began, "I—"

I held up my hand. "Enough. Look, somebody has to go to Marrakech and trace these clues to the source and there's nobody able to do it but me apparently. Who else is there?"

"But it is exceedingly dangerous!" Rupert spewed. "You can't—" (deep shaky breath) "—go alone!"

"I'm not planning on going alone exactly. Is it possible to get me on a flight out of Venice to Marrakech before dawn?" I asked Evan.

"If not before dawn, then possibly first thing in the morning," he said, frowning. "I would suggest you travel under an assumed name, which takes some time to organize—"

"Evan!" Rupert croaked, shooting him a baleful glance.

"What's the riad called?" I asked him. "Seraphina said it was now an Airbnb."

"I don't recall," Rupert gasped, hastily downing an inch of cold tea while Sloane poured him a glass of water from a bottle.

"More like you don't want to tell me," I said. "Do I have to call Nicolina to find out?"

"That wouldn't be wise," Evan said. "We have no idea if we've located all the bugs yet."

"So it would be much safer if Rupert just told me, wouldn't it, Rupert?"

Rupert glowered at me from over his glass. "Phoebe, we will not be there to protect you but if you insist—"

"I do."

"Very well." Rupert sighed. "The riad is called—"

"La Maison Oasis Bleu," Evan intercepted. "I took the liberty of checking it out some days ago. You must try to limit speaking, sir."

"A French name?" I asked.

But Rupert was not a man easily silenced. "I believe that Signore Contini thought a French name more fitting…for the tourist trade considering…that most of the visitors are either British or French, Morocco having…"

"Morocco having once been a French protectorate," Evan finished for him, "but I believe the riad has gone through many manifestations over the centuries."

"Makes sense." I nodded, eager just to get going before I changed my mind.

"I will make your bookings under an assumed name, madam—er, Ms. Phoebe—"

"Try 'Phoebe.' It escaped your lips at least once tonight."

He chose not to acknowledge that remark. "—and arrange your travel documents accordingly. Meanwhile, there is much to do. Excuse me." With that Evan dashed back into his anteroom, which, I had decided, must have been some sort of pantry.

Sloane stepped forward. "Sir, I suggest that you return to your bed immediately. In fact, I must insist. Indeed, you will need to recoup your strength for the long night ahead. I will return to assist you to dress once the arrangements are made."

"Shall I help Rupert back to his bed so you can get to work?" I asked, offering Rupert one arm while tucking the design compendium under the other.

Sloane rewarded me with a slight incline of the head. "Very much appreciated indeed, Ms. Phoebe."

"Come along, Rupe. Your staff have their hands full so it's best to keep out of the way."

Rupert bristled but allowed me to lead him back into the ballroom. "This is so unsettling…so upsetting," he wheezed.

"Yes, I know—to be sick when there's so much going on."

"I was not…referring to that, but yes, I'm usually…more in control than this."

"Of course you are," I soothed, "and you will be again once you've recovered. Everybody gets sick once in a while, Rupert. Why are you so shocked that it happened to you?"

"Poor timing," he sighed. "Just very, very poor timing. I feel that this is—"

"Right. Stop talking."

"—part of my history, my story, perhaps." He took a deep breath. "Maria and I...it was very long ago but it is...part of who I am...yet here I am, too weak to do much."

"Sometimes you just have to allow others to tell parts of our stories for you. Maybe it will be a slightly different perspective, but it's still part of the tale. In the meantime, try to just sit back and let the rest of us take up the reins, all right?"

Once I had him sitting on the edge of the bed, he gazed up at me. "Since when did you become so...*bossy?*"

I wanted to laugh but I couldn't quite pull it off. "It's part of my personal growth continuum. Everybody changes, Rupert. Besides, if we don't change, we may as well be dead."

"Don't say the 'D' word around here, please." He shot a quick glance around the shadows while taking a deep breath through a gurgling chest. "What about Noel? You haven't even...mentioned the lad." He kicked off his slippers and lay back while I covered him with a blanket.

"And I don't intend to except to say that's over," I said briskly.

"You can't...mean that."

"Yes, I can, and I do mean it absolutely. It took a long time for me to figure out what I want in life and to realize that he can't be part of it. You haven't been in contact with him, have you?" I studied his face.

"No, of course not. Since Jamaica, he's disappeared from the radar but..." He closed his eyes. "He used to always...look out for you and...he may be doing so now. You must watch for him."

"I hope he doesn't show, but if he does, I'll be ready for him. Besides, he'd be better off looking after himself. Once Interpol catches up with him, they'll be putting him away for a long, long time. Sparks flew between us, I admit. It wasn't a relationship so much as a string of steamy events under heightened circumstances. That's not what I want."

"I hope you mean that," he rasped.

"I do. Now get some rest."

Wait, there is...something I need to tell you. Should have...told you sooner..."

"Just stop. Rest. You can tell me later."

I left him dozing while I plucked my phone from my bag and in seconds had fired off a couple of quick emails. That didn't mean that I had time to answer any, though I noticed three from Max and two from Serena.

Minutes later, I was sitting across the kitchen table from Evan, listening intently to the details of my emerging escape plan. He had the preliminaries mapped out and now all that was needed was confirmation from a couple of his contacts. I was given a prepaid Visa card and told that someone would meet me at the airport with a package of credentials for my new identity—Penelope Martin, fiction writer, researching for my new book.

"Fiction authors have unlimited scope for investigating unusual and arcane matters," Evan explained. "By the time you arrive in Marrakech, Penelope will have two books in a series for a genre known as romantic historical suspense available on Amazon. The books are bogus, of course, but since they aren't advertised, no one will ever purchase them before they are taken down. They are there only to bolster your disguise in Marrakech."

Ask why this surprised me. "Is that legal?" Stupid question, I know, but it just came out.

His restrained smile was strangely regretful, maybe a little sad that two people who believed they stood for the forces of good—at least one of them did, anyway—now resorted to the tools of the enemy. But that's just my interpretation. He was probably thinking something totally different. "Nothing we are doing here is strictly legal, madam—"

"Phoebe."

"*Ms. Phoebe*, but we employ whatever strategies and tools are available as a means to an end in a world seething in crime and violence."

I couldn't let it go. "But you used to be MI6. Your entire modus operandi was to defend Britain, presumably working as an agent on the right side of the law, and now you work for Rupert, who is…less than honest," I finished limply. For some reason I could not openly call the man before me a crook, not when I saw him as so solidly dependable, incredibly talented, and worthy of a better descriptor.

He studied me in the half-light of the lamp, the little quirk quirking away. What was he thinking, what was he restraining himself from saying? "Perhaps there is more going on here than you know."

"What a shock that would be."

And then he stood up. "Now perhaps we had best return to our preparations. Excuse me. Oh, one more thing: I have written out a set of instructions for working the features on your phone. Please put them safely into your bag."

"Sure," I said. I took the wad of paper from the table and mindlessly stuffed it into my carpetbag. That left me sitting at the table awash in a knot of feelings I couldn't begin to untangle. Meanwhile, I could see Sloane busy making reservations across the room. Apparently they were putting Rupert up at the Cipriani since they believed the danger to his health more of a threat than any assassination attempt, especially now that Nicolina and Seraphina had called off the hunt. Or had they? At least nobody had attempted to follow us here—yet, anyway.

A boat was to pick me up for a ride to the airport at 5:00 a.m., a bit earlier than necessary considering that my flight left at 7:00, but the household was exiting for the hotel at the same time.

Clearly, I needed rest. At last, I tucked myself into a shadowy corner and pulled on my still-damp bra, gathered all my things together in one spot, and took up Sloane's offer to catch a few z's on a foldout cot. The next thing I knew, the butler was shaking me awake, dosing me with strong coffee, and urging me toward a waiting vaporetto for a flight on Air France to Paris de Gaulle and then on to Marrakech. I agreed that the roundabout route made for a good diversionary tactic in case anyone followed but it also made for a long day. And I was traveling ridiculously light, even for me, and even for what was supposed to be a three-day trip. I tried to take the design compendium along but Evan suggested that I leave that with him, which I reluctantly did.

Rupert, now dressed in one of his dapper traveling suits that hung off him alarmingly, shuffled out to say goodbye. "Do take care, Phoebe. We have no idea whether this gang is on the trail in Marrakech at this very moment, and they appear to be a ruthless lot. I think you going by yourself is a very bad idea, very bad indeed. You could…be walking right into—" A coughing attack hit again.

"It's all right, Rupert. I'll be fine," I said, giving him a hug. "Just take care of yourself and get better, will you?"

"The boat is here, mada—Ms. Phoebe," Evan said. "I will try to come as soon as I am able," he whispered at the villa door after loading my luggage. "I regret to say that we never did have time to go over your phone's capabilities but please study my cursory cheat sheet. I've also taken the liberty of packing a few supplies for your voyage in one of Sir Rupert's spare roller bags." In other words, my gun. "And please keep us updated on what you discover using only the phone provided. My plan is to track down our mysterious interested parties or at least keep them occupied while you're gone."

I nodded and made for the dock, suddenly aware that no effort had been made to keep the villa's location a secret from me this time, which made perfect sense since everyone was leaving. That gave me the opportunity to gaze up at the mysterious palazzo as the boat pulled away, surprised to find it beautiful despite the interior decay and the deep wrap of gloom that shrouded the shuttered windows. Positioned on the edge of two merging canals—I had no idea where since I didn't feel like locating it on my phone just in case—it must have once been a luxurious palace on a quiet but prime location.

Turning my face to the wind, I settled in for the ride across the lagoon, clutching my carpetbag like it was my last friend on earth. Maybe I could have used a little friendly company just then as I watched the dawn struggle to crack light into the darkness. The boat driver nodded at me once but otherwise kept his eyes glued on the water, no doubt struggling to stay awake for such an early-morning trip.

15

———

$\mathcal{T}$he rest of my voyage played out like a blurry rerun of an old spy movie. While sipping coffee in the Venetian airport, a man brushed by me and dropped an envelope into my bag. Inside a washroom stall minutes later, I removed an American passport featuring my face with a false name—Penelope Martin, writer. It was sobering to witness how easily that kind of fraud could be arranged and even more so my willingness to participate in it. All for a worthy cause, I told myself. Regardless, if they ever discovered the gun or my bogus passport, I could be in jail for a long time, despite my Interpol affiliations.

Passing through customs was still a breeze and my basic French helped smooth the way through de Gaulle where I had enough of a layover to purchase a few warm weather tourist-worthy clothes. Otherwise, I slept through the flight to Marrakech, arriving at around two o'clock in the afternoon. Strolling into the airport's arrival area minutes later, I was on my way out the revolving glass doors looking for a cab when someone touched my shoulder.

"Miss Martin?"

I turned to stare blankly at the young man in the long white robe and round blue skull cap holding a sign and grinning at me. "You are Miss Martin, yes? I am Hassan, your driver. I have description." He read from his phone: "Very nice-looking red-haired lady. Not expecting ride so must approach."

Crud. Right. "Yes, yes. I'm Penelope Martin but I wasn't expecting to be picked up, like you said." I might have been had I read all the papers Evan had packed in my bag, which I only did much later. And I might have been had I practiced thinking like Penelope instead of like Phoebe—Penelope the writer, that is. And then it hit me that Evan had described me as "a very nice-looking red-haired lady." That part I liked.

"Sorry, I was just imagining the plot for my next book, which will be set right here in Marrakech," I said, shaking myself from my reverie. Weak, very weak.

"You are a writer. Very exciting. First time here?"

"Yes, first time."

If possible, the young man's grin grew even broader. "I take you to your hotel and give tour along way."

"No tour, thanks. Straight to my hotel."

It was as if he'd never heard me as he took my bags and led me across a parking lot to a plush taxi van. Soon it became clear that I was getting a tour whether I wanted it or not but I decided to relax and enjoy the ride. Being sealed inside a plush air-conditioned vehicle while driving through a panorama of color and image wasn't a bad introduction to a new land. I applied my sunglasses and wondered if I'd brought adequate sunblock.

Wide modern boulevards with sports cars easing up beside camels was only one of the many baffling sights that whizzed by. Impressions of color, sand-colored buildings, old pinkish brick walls, and glimpses down narrow, medieval streets added to the other-worldly sense. For a moment, I forgot to be exhausted.

"Very beautiful mosque," Hassan was saying. "The Koutoubia Mosque built in 1150."

"That early?" I said, staring up at the amazing minaret. So Marrakech had been an established city long before the Italian Renaissance began. "Were there many Jewish families living there back then?"

Hassan seemed taken aback. "Morocco Muslim country, Miss Martin. That is a mosque."

"Yes, of course." *So, skip that line of inquiry, Phoebe.* Suddenly I was exhausted and my hand burned relentlessly. By that time, I had my phone out and was tracking our progress to La Maison Oasis Bleu on Google Maps and realizing just how much farther we seemed to be getting from the destination. "Look, Hassan, thank you for the tour but I'm tired. Could you just take me to my riad now?"

"Yes, lady. Right away."

But *right away* did not mean directly. The taxi parked outside the arched gate of an ancient pink stone wall that rose far overhead and looked as though it dated from the beginnings of the city.

"We walk," he said cheerfully. "Follow me."

Hassan took my roller in hand while I hoisted my carpetbag over my shoulder and together we strode through the arch into a jumble of centuries. The souk, I realized as we passed stalls crammed with tiles, painted plates, copper and brass lamps, and lengths of gorgeous textiles of every imaginable fabric, many draped over walls. I could be in Istanbul and the Grand Bazaar, only a more chaotic, rougher, and less pristine version, though no less magical.

Narrow alleyways crowded with people in both Western clothing and the traditional djellabas jostled with motorcars and donkeys while the sound of ringing cell phones and the calls of the waterman filled the dusty air. Once we pressed against a wall to allow a donkey burdened with carpets to trot past us in a narrow lane, while the donkey man rang his bell and called for us to move please in three languages. I caught glimpses of carpet shops, some hanging their wares outside their doors in a kaleidoscope of pattern and color. It was all I could do not to stop, feeling as I did as though I had fallen back into time and landed in a pile of pattern and design.

I'd return to savor it all, I told myself as I followed Hassan deeper into the medina, not that I had a clue how to return anywhere in this warren of ancient streets. We passed several places that appeared to be hotels and even more restaurants, but every time I'd hoped we'd reached our riad, Hassan kept going.

"Not far now, lady," Hassan called to me as we entered a tiny malodorous square. No more than a rough gathering of dusty stone buildings with dark little alleys branching off in three directions, the place seemed populated only by skinny mewing cats—starving cats, I realized. I stopped to gaze at one particularly pathetic little white kitten while fighting the overwhelming urge to bring it food. I'd return to feed it as soon as I could.

"This chicken stall," Hassan said, catching my interest and pointing to a shelf set deep into one of the stone walls that appeared to be the source of the smell. "Chickens sold here Wednesday and Friday." He grinned. "Very busy then. Cats like."

So, a merchant would bring live chickens to this stinky little square and slaughter them right here for the waiting customers? That explained the stray feathers I saw embedded into the gravel below my feet. Got it. What we take for granted in our pristine supermarket world, I thought. Welcome to how the rest of the world lives, Phoebe. I mean, *Penelope.*

On the other hand, talk about fresh chicken…

"Please follow, lady. Riad just here."

The riad was nearby? Maybe this was part of the old Jewish quarter years ago, that is if Marrakech even had a Jewish quarter. Admittedly by then, I only longed for something simple and predictable like a chain hotel with clean white sheets, not whatever lay at the end of the short alley that Hassan was leading me down.

At the end of the narrow corridor stood a tall carved door leaning against a deep blushing terra-cotta wall. Since a potted palm sat in a puddle of sun directly before the magnificent portal, I knew it wasn't a working door, yet still I walked toward it, probably on some kind of color-induced autopilot.

"Here, lady."

I turned. Hassan had stopped about halfway down the short alley. Back-tracking, I found myself standing before another carved door, this one so low I had to duck to enter as Hassan beckoned me forward. And so I stepped straight into an oasis of calm and beauty so intense it struck me dumb.

"I am Shada," said a young woman in jeans and a silk blouse standing before me. A shy beauty in her late twenties with wide brown eyes and an up-to-the-minute dress sense (shirt half-tucked into her jeans and strappy high-heeled sandals). "Welcome."

"Thank you, Shada," I said, gazing around. "Wow, this is magnificent." Did Maria have a hand in its decoration? I wondered.

A tiled courtyard featuring a gleaming blue pool fringed with lush sun-filtering greenery drew my eye immediately, but soon my gaze skimmed past the gleaming brass lanterns, ornate tiles, textiles on the walls, and chairs gathered around the pool in gestures of comfort. I was led to one of these seats and offered mint tea, water, plus an assortment of little pastries. Only after I had sipped the tea poured by a fez-capped young man named Mohammed did I notice the copper floor lanterns, the filigreed white plasterwork, and the fact that Hassan stood beside me waiting patiently. I looked up.

"Lady, I go now but I arrange tour for you anytime. My cousin, he has van and we could go to Atlas Mountains."

"Thanks, but my research is right here in Marrakech," I said, shaking off my stupor. Actually, I wouldn't mind going to the Atlas Mountains but this wasn't a vacation. Then I realized he was probably waiting for a tip. I didn't have any dirhams, only pounds and euros, but reached into my pocket to offer him a ten-euro note, which he took with a quick bow and disappeared out the door.

Shada stepped forward. "Your room is ready, Ms. Martin. Your bag awaits you," she said in impeccable English. Though gracious and lovely, her demeanor almost seemed apologetic but I couldn't decide why. Soon, I was too busy taking in my environment to care.

The riad was built on three balconied floors that wrapped around an open courtyard with a pool embedded into its bottom floor like a faceted sapphire. Shada lead me to a narrow staircase in the corner that twisted around the stories in white marble and colored tiles. I climbed the stairs behind her, my eyes glomming on to the textiles, mostly Berber with traditional motifs, every one rich and vibrant. Some time I'd study each one but right then I was too tired to pause.

All but one guest room was situated on the two upper balconied levels with a library and lounge leading off the main floor below, Shada told me. And since the doors to every room but one were wide open, I glimpsed cozy interiors, each one unique, luxurious, and intriguing. Arched windows along the hall echoed so much of Venice's Renaissance buildings that it was impossible not to note the connection. That the trade between Venice and the East had been brisk was undeniable. The creative mingling of cultures proved it.

"I'm actually here to research my new novel—I'm a writer. Is there much information about the history of the riad? It looks very old."

"It is very old," Shada said, turning to me. "My brother studies architecture in Paris and he says the building has '*bons os*,' good bones, as they say in French. Do you speak French?"

"A little." Actually, I could read French but my accent was too rusty to mention.

It didn't help when she slipped into French, leaving me struggling to keep up. "You will find whatever we have on the building in the library but most of it will be in Arabic or French," I think she said.

I spoke in English. "Do you sleep here, Shada?"

Taking my cue, she responded in my mother tongue. "No, I live with my parents. Myself and Ingram manage the riad but we don't stay overnight."

"Ingram?"

"You will meet him tomorrow. He does not work this afternoon. This is your room here. You'll find it perfect for writing, I think, but the rooftop is equally good. Very quiet."

"Do you mean that the guests are alone here after 7:00 p.m.?" That alarmed me.

"You will be perfectly safe. The tourist police patrol the medina and the riad is very secure."

Except that the roof was wide open to the elements as well as to anyone who might decide to drop in, plus the tourist police didn't know I was being dogged by murdering thieves. Naturally, Shada didn't run in the same circles I did or know what's possible for the enterprising criminal types. I peered over the balcony at the pool glowing turquoise through the fringing palms. Sky above, pool below, and the chaos of the medina plus the world itself seemed light-years away.

"And do the owners live in Morocco?" I asked, pulling back. I knew the answer but I wanted to see if she did.

"No, the owner lives in Italy." A shadow crossed her lovely features—I guessed that she might have heard about Maria's death—but she recovered quickly. "Breakfast is served on the rooftop terrace from 8:00 to 10:00 every morning," she continued with her customary shy smile. "There is a night number to call for emergencies in your room. Everything is very safe here. No need to worry," she said.

If only she knew. "I'm sure it's very safe. Are there other guests staying?"

"Two others—a couple from America one level down and another lady arrives tomorrow. You will find it very peaceful. Would you like supper tonight?"

Of course I was hungry but staying awake until dinner seemed an unimaginable feat. "What about something light that I could eat in my room? I'm so tired right now that I just want to sleep."

"I will have a cold supper prepared for you and placed in your room's refrigerator," Shada said.

"Just leave it outside the door, please." That way if I did wake up ravenous, I'd have something to gnaw on. "I plan to take a long nap."

After that, I stepped into my room and a narrow, richly decorated space opened up around me like the inside of a jewel box—painted deep ochre with a tiled fireplace, a rug across the tiled floor, brass platters and jugs on the mantel and inlaid tables, deep chairs for reading under colored glass lamps, and a bed tucked into the far end covered in a silken patchwork coverlet. If I were a genie, I'd live right there.

After Shada slipped away, I opened the borrowed roller bag, dug through the clothing Evan had packed as a decoy—a men's silk dressing robe plus a white dress shirt still in its laundry package—sorted through my recently purchased clothes, and removed the gun secreted in the bottom level. That thing would go with me everywhere, as would my phone and anything else I needed. I wasn't taking chances, not here, not anywhere.

In fact, I took the roller, carpetbag complete with phones, and jacket into the bathroom with me, leaning the roller against the door, jiggered in such a way that if anyone tried to enter, the clatter of a brass soap dish would give warning. All the knots loosened in my neck and shoulders when minutes later I stepped into the tiled shower and let hot water pour down over me for as long as I needed. As for my hand, I gingerly unsealed the bandage, cursing softly all the way. I'd leave that open to the elements now to help it heal but the water felt like torture on my wounded flesh.

About forty minutes later, wrapped in a towel and refreshed, I stepped into the room and realized that someone had entered long enough to turn down the bed, sprinkle pink rose petals over the covers, and leave a chocolate on my pillow. Lovely. Unsettling. There was even a covered plate in the small fridge along with several varieties of juice and bottled water. Excellent service though it was, easy access to my room did not feel like a good thing.

I sipped a bottle of orange juice while checking the door—flimsy ornamental wood latched by a simple bolt. That wouldn't do. After hanging a Do Not Disturb sign on the knob outside, I dragged the roller bag into active duty again, this time balancing a brass platter from over the mantel against the door. If it fell to the tiled floor, it should wake the whole riad.

Next, I scanned my phone messages. Evan's received the first response: *Here now. Weather's fine.*

He came back immediately: *Same here. All settled. BTW: code is not necessary on this phone. It is secure.*

Really?

Seriously.

Right. Leaving that thread, I finally responded to Max's frantic demands for updates by explaining in code that it wasn't safe to describe anything right now. *They speak French and Arabic here*, I wrote. Referring to other languages was our way of saying that we couldn't write or speak freely. I added that the weather was fine since weather references indicated the safety factor and I didn't want him worrying.

He must have been waiting for a message from me and responded right away by letting me know that *The weather is clear in London but sunshine will be moving out that day.* Got it: reinforcement was heading my way. And I badly needed it. Forget this business of Phoebe rushing off to single-handedly rescue some unknown treasure on foreign soil. I knew I couldn't do this alone and, right then, I didn't want to try. I'd lost all the adrenaline that had propelled me to Marrakech. Now, all I felt was the chill of fear.

There were messages from Nicolina, too, but I'd let Evan keep her informed on my behalf. Presumably he could better figure out how to communicate with her without alerting the spy network.

Relieved, I shoved the gun and phone under my pillow, left the bathroom light on, and dropped over the velvet cliff into a deep sleep.

And awoke with a start, leaping from the bed with no idea where I was, my heart pounding. It took a few seconds to orientate myself. My watch said 12:33 a.m. Once my brain activated, I retrieved my gun and phone in seconds. Flicking on a lamp, I saw that nothing had disturbed my brass platter security system, yet something had obviously disturbed me—a loud noise, maybe. In my dream I recalled what could have been tapping sounds but now everything was quiet.

I grabbed the closest clothing on hand—my jeans, T-shirt, and jacket still draped over one of the chairs where they'd been tossed. With my bare feet shoved into sneakers, the gun in my bag slung over my shoulder, I carefully disengaged my alarm system and cracked open the door.

Outside it was surprisingly cool, the desert air descending in a frigid pall over the balcony. I crept to the railing and peered over. Below, the pool and the night-lights glowed but otherwise everything appeared deceptively peaceful.

As I crept down the tiled corridor, the full impact of being alone in a foreign land in an unsecured building hit. It's one thing to know this by the preternaturally bright desert light of day and quite another to have it settle around you in the dead of an Arabian night. Yet, by the time I'd padded down-stairs to the bottom level, the seductive lighting and hushed beauty of the place calmed most of my fears. Almost. So what if a sound woke me up? Abrupt noises startled me from sleep in London all the time so why not in Marrakech? Anyway, there was another couple staying here somewhere so it's not like I was alone. Maybe they just returned from a late dinner out.

My hand was throbbing and there was no way I could get back to sleep right away. Instead, I dashed back up to my room, retrieved the plated food, and returned to the bottom level, leaving my bedroom door locked with its useless ornate iron key. Seconds later, I had tucked myself into a back table slightly hidden behind a pillar facing the pool to devour my supper—a cold meat pie that looked vaguely like a Cornish pastie wrapped in phyllo with a side of fresh fruit. The whole thing was gone in minutes, finished off with a bottle of guava juice.

As I ate, I mused: What was I hoping to find in this building that hundreds of others before me may have sought and left empty-handed? There were only so many materials that consistently held value in centuries past and they were the same items that held value now: gold and jewels. What else would a wealthy family consider to be a worthy dowry, anyway?

On the other hand, how could any family hide something of such value for centuries in what may have once been the family home? But then again, where else would they hide it, considering that they lived in a world constantly threatening to annihilate them? If not their home, where? I couldn't imagine this long-ago Jewish family, obviously wealthy and maybe now catching the notice of a less tolerant sultan, risking burying it any place else. And *bury* had to be the operative word.

And it had remained in the Contini family for centuries and been transferred through the generations. That, too, was unusual. A Christian family owning property during uprisings in Morocco was almost as strange as Jews owning property under those same circumstances. On the other hand, Morocco had a history of being a tolerant Muslim country, a reputation of acceptance and coexistence, with the exception of occasional blips of religious persecution. Was it so far a stretch to believe that somehow alliances forged either through business or friendship had somehow helped to preserve this property and its secrets through the centuries intact?

That was the question. My gut said the story unfolded this way and that was all I had to go on at the moment. Following the union of the two families —the two religions—the Continis had been unable to return to Morocco to claim the dowry and had eventually forgotten the codes to finding it. If they'd tried in the last few centuries, they'd obviously been unsuccessful. Maria had tried, I was sure of that.

A chill ran over me. Supposing the ruthless gang knew about the riad and suspected that it may be here all along? What if they'd been here and tried to find it, were trying still? What if they thought they needed me? My throbbing hand testified to the lengths they'd go to retrieve it.

One way or the other, somewhere in this filigreed building, one that must have been renovated countless times before, lay a long-lost fortune that nobody had a clue where to find.

Leaving my plate on the table and with my phone in hand as a flashlight, I took myself on a reconnaissance mission around the lower floor. The little night-lights tucked under little brass wall sconces and in the alcoves everywhere made the extra light unnecessary but I didn't care. My phone was my security blanket even if it might track me and probably knew my very thoughts. Had Evan managed that trick yet?

Stepping into the first room off the courtyard brought me to the library. Well, now... I flashed my phone across the shelves of books, the paintings of desert scenes with the camels and sunsets, the smoldering fireplace, and realized that it would take hours to study this room alone.

Since there was no adjoining room, I stepped back into the courtyard and around the corner into another, this one with leather chairs and etched brass platter tables everywhere—the lounge? Back out again, I padded down the tiles to a door labeled Office— locked—and then through a pair of double spring doors beside it that led to a kitchen, all in a mix of marble and stainless complete with microwave and bake oven. Backing out, I next followed the entire perimeter of the pool, discovering that the rooms were only on one side of the building with the other consisting of a long wall decorated by textiles and panels of carved wood.

At the very back wall, an open door beckoned me on, a door that lead into a smaller roofed courtyard with a basin-sized marble fountain set into the center of an elaborate mosaic-tiled zellige of triangles and starbursts. I stepped up to the basin floating with rose petals and noticed two bowls sitting side by side on the blue tiles with a fat white cat busy lapping from one. The diner left its dish immediately to brush across my legs in a plume of soft fur. I sat down on the edge of the fountain and allowed myself a cat moment, indulging in the purring friendliness, oblivious to anything else except to vaguely note another room in front of me—door open, the final guest room.

Sometimes cats are better than men, I thought, deep in the comfort zone. "What's hidden here, kitty?" I mumbled into its fur. And then I heard a sharp crack that jolted me to my feet and the cat to the floor with an indignant mew. The sound came from overhead. Yes, definitely overhead because now I heard a deliberate chink-chink somewhere far above.

I bolted into the pool courtyard and all the way up the stairs. When I reached the top level of what I presumed to be the roof, the door was locked. Maybe I would have tried picking it if I knew how. On the other hand, if some unauthorized person was up there chipping away at something, did I really want to surprise them? My hand fell from the knob. No, I didn't, even if armed. I was still feeling the heat after being nearly roasted alive.

Moments later, I was back in my room, tucked into bed with my clang-activated alarm in place, my gun under my pillow, and my phone on charge. I'd have pulled the covers over my head if I wouldn't have felt like a kid.

For some reason, I couldn't distinguish the line between brave and stupid just then.

16

The next morning I read my texts while huddled under the shade of one of the roof's potted palms.

Nicolina had sent the first:

Phoebe, I know where you are. You should not be there alone but we cannot help right now. The warehouse has burned, maybe too much to be restored, and tomorrow the funeral for Maria goes forward. All so devastating! And for you very dangerous. These people are monsters! Be careful, my friend. Evan says it is safe to text you. Please respond. I worry. XXX. N

I typed back a quick response: *So sorry, Nicolina. Too many losses!*

Then I went on to read Evan's: *No sign of bad weather. I'm hoping it hasn't all blown your way.*

Shit. I looked up from my screen and gazed out across the medina. Was the gang keeping a low profile after the arson stint or had they followed me here? I had the sickening feeling that they knew exactly where I was and why.

"Yoohoo! You know what they say about those people who spend all their vacays stuck to their phones."

I looked up at the bright blur of orange waving at me from the other side of the roof. Pocketing my phone, I applied a smile to my face along with my sunglasses and strode over to join her by the railing. June and Joe Meredith from Vancouver were apparently thrilled to have someone to talk to since the riad had been mostly empty for days. They wanted to adopt me, it seems. "But I'm not on 'vacay,' June. Like I said, I'm working."

"Working? You're a writer, aren't you? It's not like a real job with a boss or something. Look, we're thinking of taking one of those camel trains into the desert tomorrow and staying overnight in a tent—" June was gazing out toward the Sahara "—and we'd love you to come with us as our guest. Joe could nab us the tickets."

"Sure thing, honey," Joe called. The paunchy middle-aged man with the air of perpetual resignation toasted us with a tiny cup of Arabic coffee from a mound of pillows.

"Joe thinks he's a sultan." June laughed. "Look at him there. Sit up, darling. You'll dribble all over your Ralph Lauren," she called.

"Thanks but no thanks." I smiled. "I mean, I appreciate the offer but I have research to do right here."

"Oh, come on. Wouldn't a voyage on an authentic camel train to meet with a genuine Berber tribe be just the thing? You could write a book about that."

A tourist camel ride to a Berber camp set up especially for show—how thrillingly authentic. "Actually, I'm well into my book now and what I really need is to settle down and do the research right here. My novel is set in a riad, you see. It's historic verisimilitude I'm after."

"Historic verisimilitude?" she said, verging on but not quite hitting a note of derision. Her smile was wide, her earrings—some kind of etched silver and dark wood dangles that I couldn't take my eyes from—shone below her short blond bob. The bright pink and orange of her silken pantsuit struck me as perfect for the climate but hard on the eyes. Attractive, probably in her early fifties, I almost liked her but at the same time couldn't wait for her to leave. "Look, Penny, there's the fascinating medina out there, you know? Surely you're not going to stay cooped up here all day and let it pass you by? At least come with us to the square this morning and take a look around."

"No, really," I said, my fixed smile making my cheeks ache. "I'm here to research and that's what I'll do. Thanks, though, really, but I'll be working."

Blowing a gusty sigh, she swung around. "Okay, Joe, I can't talk sense into this one. Let's get going."

"Let me finish my coffee first." Mohammed, the lean young man who slipped ghost-like around the riad taking care of our every need, was just refreshing Joe's cup.

"It's, like, your third dose already. Leave it and let's go."

Yes, please do. Returning to my chair, I picked up my teacup—a glass set into a filigreed brass holder—and returned to skimming *The Complete History of Marrakech* written by Pierre M. Maison in 1826. Only a writer of that age could believe that history could be complete instead of a single perspective frozen within the amber of time, understanding, and circumstances. What made Pierre's perspective interesting, however, was his line sketches of the city almost two centuries earlier. And, I thought, comparing his map of the medina with the modern tourist version, it didn't look as though it had changed all that much in some quarters.

Keeping my head down fixed on the book seemed to seal the deal with the Merediths. A reading person must seem so dull to them. In any case, they finally left, after which I got up and prowled the roof looking for signs of whatever had awoken me the night before. Something like chipped tiles or a pile of crumbled stucco shoved into a corner would do nicely but nothing appeared amiss. No obvious signs of chiseling or hammering anywhere, either. If someone had been up here banging away last night, they'd tidied up after themselves.

"Miss Martin?"

I looked up from inspecting the grout around one of the beautiful blue tiles to see Shada standing nearby. "Call me Penny. I just love these tiles," I said, getting to my feet. "Are they very old?"

"I don't believe so, maybe a few decades."

"When was the riad last renovated?"

"I am not certain but not since I've been here. Penny, forgive me but I noticed your hand." She stepped forward, pointing to my wounded member, which I had laid bare to the elements the night before.

Looking down at my reddened flesh, I realized that the swelling had increased. "I cut myself—careless, really."

"Pardon me for interfering but I think you need to have that tended. Wounds like that can easily get infected here. Perhaps a salve and to keep it wrapped would be better? There are pharmacies in the medina or I could ask someone to come here. It is no trouble."

She seemed genuinely concerned. "Thank you, Shada. I promise that if it's not better by this afternoon, I'll take you up on your offer." She nodded and slipped away.

Meanwhile, I studied the wound in the sunlight, noticing a bit of festering around the edges. Not good.

But I chose to shove it out of my mind for the rest of the morning and part of the afternoon in order to dive into the library's resources, most of which didn't exceed a couple of centuries old but which still made fascinating reading. Besides, it was comfortable in the library with its plush chairs, shelves of books, and endless supply of mint tea. The noticeable absence of bad guys wanting to roast me alive was a definite plus.

After plenty of tea sipped from filigreed cups and a perfect lunch of soup and salad served in the pool area, my hand gave up on throbbing and launched a brutal stabbing campaign. I checked my watch: 2:25. Where was my reinforcement?

Meanwhile, I met Ingram, a bearded young man with merry eyes and an obvious appreciation of pastry who bowed slightly when Shada introduced us and said he would be happy to take me to the medina along with some version of my every wish being his command.

"I'll wait, thanks."

Ingram and Shada exchanged worried glances. And then, at 3:10, my waiting was over. A bell rang and soon a very tall black woman dressed in a startling bright turquoise belted robe with a backpack slung over her shoulder stepped into the riad.

It was all I could do not to shout my delight, but through some unspoken agreement, we pretended not to know one another. She grinned in my direction. "Hi ya."

"This is Miss Penelope Martin," Ingram introduced us, "an author, and this is Miss Peaches Williams." There was no way I wanted to correct him for the "Miss" thing.

Peaches eyebrows arched. "An author, wow, just wow. I've never met a real author before."

"Hi, call me Penny."

"So call me Peaches. My real name is Penelope, too. What a coincidence, hey? Peaches is the nickname my daddy gave me."

"Cute." I wasn't certain whether she was playing wide-eyed innocent or what, but Shada, obviously overwhelmed by the sight of a six-foot-tall black woman dressed in a caftan, seemed eager to take her new guest on the tour even before the welcoming tea had been served.

"I will show you the riad. Please follow me."

"Right on," Peaches said agreeably.

Remaining at pool level, I listened to Peaches's enthusiastic and knowledgeable commentary all along the route, her melodious voice echoing over the balconies and from even inside the library and lounges. "Wow, like, the *moucharabieh* screens are just out of this world—so intricate! And the gebs are, like, fantastic!" Well, buildings were her thing.

"Yes, thank you. The owners put every care into the details," I heard Shada say. "I'm afraid I don't recognize the word *geb*, though."

"That's the trim—all that gingerbread in the corners."

"Gingerbread?"

"Stuff they make in England with spices, a sweet bread, you know? I'm from Jamaica myself, though you wouldn't know it to see me. Thought I was from Sweden—ha, ha. We love gingerbread, too. I can make it for you sometime." A deep laugh followed, one that seemed to provoke a giggle from Shada.

They were moving up to the next levels now. "And here is your room," Shada said. Once they stepped inside, the conversation grew muffled.

"Nice but I prefer the one opposite the fountain in the little courtyard," Peaches said, emerging minutes later. "That okay? I'm shy, see, and like my privacy."

Yeah, right.

"Certainly. You may stay in any unoccupied room you want," I heard Shada say.

"Fantabulous. I'm just going to settle in, you know?"

"Certainly. We want you to be as comfortable as if this was your own home."

It was like listening to a radio play, ridiculously entertaining to me in part because I knew the protagonist was actually playing an enhanced version of herself.

I sent Ingram to fetch Mohammad for mint tea all around and settled down to a poolside table to wait. By the time Peaches had been registered and joined me, Shada was wrapped in a headscarf with a robe over her Western clothes ready to exit. I realized then that she had been in a hurry to leave all along. Maybe it was a cultural misstep for a man to show a lady her room so she had to stay long enough for that.

"I do not work this afternoon but Ingram and Mohammed will take care of you." And with that she bowed and left. Mohammed, in the meantime, was slipping into the kitchen to fetch us a tray of pastries while Ingram had disappeared into the office.

Peaches sat down in the chair beside me and whispered: "So what the hell is going on?"

"I'll tell you later," I said. "What took you so long? I've waited for you all day."

"What took me so long? I went shopping in the medina and its friggin' fabulous, for one thing. Have you been? Like, I get the cabdriver to drop me off—he tried to take me to his uncle's carpet shop but I wasn't having that—and found this store that sells robes of every color you can imagine. I bought five! Serena told me there was no way I should come to Morocco in my stretchies. This being a Muslim country, I get that, but I can tell you, I've seen plenty of tourists in short-shorts that would make my threads look sedate. Don't people have respect?"

Stretchies was her word for the spandex and the leather body-hugging outfits she preferred. I leaned over. "You still don't exactly blend."

She grinned. "Think you do with your screaming red locks? Besides, I never blend, sister. Hey," she said, looking up, "here comes tea."

As Mohammed served the steamy mint brew, Ingram appeared with a map. "I have marked the place in the medina where the pharmacy is located, Miss Martin. Not very far. I have called to say you are coming. Ask for Shadiz. He will take care of your hand."

"Hand? What's wrong with your hand?" Peaches asked, whipping her attention from Mohammed's adroit tea-pouring techniques to my wounded member resting now out of sight on my lap.

"I burned it. On a stove," I added, bringing it into view. My injury looked far too severe for any minor household accident.

Peaches hissed. "So, like, I'll take her, Ingram. Pass me the map."

Ingram looked from one of us to the other. "I would be happy to—"

"No, no. I passed that place a short time ago—like something out of *Harry Potter*, right?"

The young man beamed. "Yes, miss, exactly!" Obviously the beloved wizard had reached even North Africa.

"Right. Come on, Penny. Let's get you some help," Peaches said, lifting from the chair by one elbow.

I insisted on at least changing from my jeans to loose trousers and a tunic top first (and to ensure my gun was packed deep in my bag) before allowing myself to be mustered out the door, through the alley, and into the malodorous courtyard. Peaches continued steering me by the elbow.

"I need a hat," I said.

"Forget the hat for now. What the hell happened?" she said the moment we were well away from the riad.

I provided my summary as briefly as possible, ending with my belief that the riad held the hidden dowry. "It's much more complex and serious than I ever anticipated. These bastards murdered Maria Contini and tried to kill me, too. Whatever it is, it must be valuable."

"Holy shit!" she exclaimed, slapping a hand over her mouth when a passerby cast her a sharp look. "You needed me before this. I told you I'd be your bodyguard, woman."

"I didn't think I'd need a bodyguard when I went to Venice," I protested as she steered me along. "Besides, I mostly have the skills to take care of myself.

I'm just no match for a gang." The last one I dealt with were the Willies, of which her own brother had been the head. That we helped put both our criminal brothers behind bars might not have been the traditional bond of sisterhood but it worked for us.

"What were you doing going into that building alone, anyway?"

We were in an alley now, treading the winding path among tourists interspersed with robed locals and plenty of zipping mopeds. I hated those things. They were the auditory equivalent of motorized flies and made it damned hard to see if we were being followed. One zipped too close to me, this one of the expensive motorcycle variety, forcing me against a wall and putting me further on edge. I could have sworn that same red T-shirted guy had passed us at least twice before and that at least one helmeted motorcyclist made a couple of drive-bys, too. "I wasn't alone. Evan was waiting for me by the entrance. We were in touch every second. How'd I know they planned to torch the place?"

"So why didn't Muscle Man go in there with you? What kind of bodyguard is he?"

"He didn't fit in the corridor," I said, "and neither would you, and he's not my 'bodyguard.' We're on the same side of this particular scenario, that's all."

"Well, I'm your bodyguard from here on in, got that? No foolin' around. Her Majesty has one, Sir Rupe has one, and now you have one." Her Majesty referred to Nicolina, not the queen.

"Sure but you are also our engineer and head contractor," I reminded her.

She snorted. "Multitasking is my game. As soon as the labor force gets their lazy butts back to work, I'll get back to the other job. I'm also part of our new enterprise so let me feel useful, will you? I don't know shit about art except that my brother traded drugs for the stuff. For now, I watch your back, sister. And maybe your hand, too." She had me by the wrist now, tugging me through the medina like a naughty child and I almost didn't mind. In these vulnerable moments, I was willing to temporarily take the back seat. "You're lucky you didn't get burned to a crisp and what's with trying to protect a book of fabric scraps—you crazy, woman?"

"It was a very valuable historic compendium of everything the Continis had produced, not 'fabric scraps.' I—"

"Wait, I think this is it." She dropped my hand and took out the map.

We both stared at the building before us, a partially open-air shop painted bright blue with jars and unidentifiable bottled things lining the front. Strange objects dangled in the breeze—gourds, calabashes, and at least one rare cat pelt. "That's a pharmacy? It looks like a Chinese medicine shop crossed with something right out of *Harry Potter*, like you said."

"Yeah," Peaches said. "The North African Harry Potter magic shop—a Berber pharmacy. I've seen different pharmacies all over Africa but I've only just heard of the Moroccan ones. How cool is that?" While Peaches had been studying engineering in London, she had taken several trips to the southern African continent in search of her roots. Her face broke into a wide grin. "Let's go."

"I think I'd prefer a Boots about now."

"You nuts? These guys are like one of the oldest pharmacies on earth. Half of the pharmaceutical stuff is based on these potions. They're like medicine men and they can certainly tend to a wounded paw like yours. Come along, Phoebe."

"Penny," I reminded her, stepping forward.

"Penelope's my real name, too, remember?"

"I didn't choose it, Evan did."

"I got to meet this Evan guy. Sounds like a piece of work."

Inside, the shop was a fascinating blend of the cosmetic, the medicinal, the magical, and everything in between. Cones of colored powders caught my attention right away and for a moment I was oblivious to the beautiful woman with the perfect skin who stepped before me describing the benefits of argan and rose oil, a jar held in each hand. "Sure, I'll take both," I mumbled, heading for the color wall.

"Penelope," Peaches called. "Bring your paw here to meet Shadiz."

I turned. Peaches was standing beside a man in a kind of turban and a white robe, one arm slung over his shoulder. Both were beaming as if they'd just encountered a long-lost friend.

"Shadiz, thank you for seeing me," I said moments later as we were ushered into a back room and to what could have been an examining table had it not been covered in some kind of dust. Shadiz spent a few moments cleaning up, Peaches assisting as if it were the most natural thing in the world. I was instructed to rest my hand on a length of clean white cloth while Shadiz inspected it, muttering to himself in Arabic all the while.

"I think he's saying it's not good," Peaches remarked.

"Not good but not deadly. Shadiz fix," the man assured me with an encouraging smile. "This happened how?"

"I burned it on the stove."

"But there is a deep cut there also," he said, studying my hand intently.

"I'm a mess in the kitchen," I said. "I cut myself with a knife, too."

"Tell him truth. We need friends here, Phoeb, and Shadiz is a friend."
Peaches was staring at me—I mean, seriously staring.

"I will do you no harm," he said, placing a hand over his heart. "It is my
pledge to Allah. Speak the truth and I will help you. Healing is in my hands."

Try arguing against that. "Fine. I have a ruthless gang of thieves following
me who have already killed one person. They think I may lead them to something important and maybe I already have—or close, anyway. Now it seems
they want me dead, too."

Shadiz straightened. "You have my protection." In a moment, he stepped
out, returning moments later with a basin of fragrant water, the lovely
cosmetics saleswoman with him carrying a tray of implements and
unguents.

"While I work, please read the wall and Fatima will translate."

I gazed up at the wall to my right, realizing for the first time that there was
writing in gold script above the shelves. Fatima began translating.

*"O mankind! There has come to you a good advice from your Lord, and a healing
for that which is in your hearts. And We send down from the Quran that which is a
healing and a mercy to those who believe."*

And while she read, Shadiz drained the infection from my wound with a
quick stab of something I hoped was sterilized—I didn't look—and bathed my
hand in a dish of warm, fragrant water. Next, he applied a pungent ointment
and wrapped my hand in a length of gauze. Yes, it hurt like hell and yet it felt
soothing at the same time. Unaccountable, I know, but there you have it.
When he was finished, my hand felt much better and I believed it would heal
at last. Magic, belief, a higher power—who knew?

"Thank you, Shadiz. What do I owe you?" I asked.

"When I do God's work, I do not take payment." Then he bowed.

Unable to thank him in any other way, I went shopping in the main store,
purchasing pots of dye powder, argan oil and rosewater bath oils, herbs, a
package of real saffron, eucalyptus rubs, and an assortment of frankincense,
jasmine flower, and musk, avoiding the dried hedgehog and chameleon bits. I
was probably overcharged for the whole lot but I didn't care. When I finished
paying for my treasures, Peaches had disappeared.

"In back room with Shadiz. Everything okay," Fatima assured me as she
turned to help the two Swedish backpackers looking for a snoring aid. That
left me to further explore the shop of wonders, marveling at some things,
wincing at others, until I stopped dead by the front door. The man leaning
against the parked moped outside was definitely the same one who'd streaked
past us on our way over—swarthy skin, a red sports shirt worn over jeans, a

skim of a beard. To me he looked exactly of the same ilk as those who had terrorized me in Venice. I ducked back into the shop.

"Fatima, where's Peaches?"

She pointed toward the back of the store. Dropping my parcels on the counter, I dashed through multiple rooms and through a beaded curtain until I found Peaches and Shadiz head-to-head in some kind of intense negotiation.

"Penny," Peaches said, obviously delighted with something. "Shadiz will get me a knife."

"A knife? What good's a knife?"

"Yeah, that's what I said but he doesn't deal in AK-47s or guns of any kind. A knife will have to do. I'm pretty good with one actually." Then she caught my look of alarm and added: "Kidding, just kidding, about the guns, anyway!"

"Forget the guns! There's a guy out front who followed us all the way from the riad. He's waiting for us to come out now. Tell me what good a knife's going to do us there? We can't go outside and stab him!" Admittedly, I was overreacting. Blame the trauma of the last few days. I turned to Shadiz. "Is there a back way out?"

"You expect us to run?" Peaches's expression had turned murderous. She spun around and strode through the curtain, Shadiz and I scrambling after her. We practically had to run to catch up, which we couldn't do until she was out the door, across the alley, and had taken some little man by the scruff of the neck. Only not the right little man, as it turned out. That one had disappeared.

"That's not him!" I cried.

The little man was squealing and crying out in Arabic at this tall Amazon who had suddenly accosted him. Peaches released him and he fell to the dust. In seconds, he was on his feet and scurrying down the alley.

"I know that man. He delivers packages for me." Shadiz shook his head sadly. "This will not be good."

"Damn," Peaches muttered. "I planned to just scare him, you know?"

"And here comes the cavalry," I said.

There were two uniformed men marching down the street toward us with the delivery man beside them pointing at Peaches. While we stood waiting for an encounter, Shadiz stepped forward, hands raised, laughing. He spoke to the officers as if it was all a big joke, a huge misunderstanding—ha, ha. The officers appeared unconvinced. Probably had the attacker been anyone but a very tall black woman, the matter would have been smoothed over more quickly. As it was, Shadiz had to do a lot if talking while apparently appeasing his delivery driver.

"Morocco is one of the few countries in Africa with serious racist issues against darker skins," Peaches said under her breath. "But not so bad here in Marrakech, I hope. And me being female and stronger than most of these guys doesn't help. That's two counts against me. A couple of dudes called out 'Obama' when I was walking by on my way over."

"That's a compliment, isn't it?"

"I doubt they meant it that way."

We fell silent when Shadiz returned with his arm over the shoulders of the trembling delivery man. "Kamal, please meet my friends, Peaches and Penny. They were attacked by a bad man earlier and you look just like him. Isn't that amusing? I am sure Peaches is sorry to have frightened you."

"Yes, I am, Kamal. Very sorry," Peaches said, bowing as if trying to shrink to the man's height. "Will you forgive me?"

Kamal squirmed in Shadiz's embrace but his employer gripped him tight. "We forgive, yes, my friend? Allah wishes us to forgive so all is forgiven."

One of the officers spoke in rapid Arabic, obviously unamused, but finally Kamal threw up his hands mumbling something in Arabic and suddenly the party was over. Shadiz ushered us back into the shop and called for tea, which was served in yet another back room. Then he left us alone.

Which suited me because I was shaken. "They know where I am."

"I thought it was a case of mistaken identity?" Peaches asked, sipping her tea. "Think I'm going to love this stuff eventually. Hell, that was close. Did you see how armed those cops were?"

"You tried to throttle the wrong man but the guy I saw earlier was definitely one of them. I never really got a good look at any of them except to notice that the three guys looked so much alike they could have been brothers. They all had the same wiry build and short hair. That was one of them, I'm sure if it."

"Yet he took off."

"Probably saw me from the window. Look, let's get back to the riad. We have work to do."

"We have to come back later and pick up the knife. Shadiz has to have it brought in tonight after dark but he's open until 9:00."

"What do you need a knife for?"

"Protection obviously."

"But I have a gun."

"Good for you but that still leaves your bodyguard defenseless. No, I'm getting me a knife."

We thanked Shadiz, gathered our bundles, and left. This time my bodyguard kept surveying every passerby our entire way back through the medina but neither cyclist made another appearance. Still, any little thing made me uneasy now. They were in Marrakech, I was sure of it, and every robed man, every veiled woman, could be one of them. What would they do next?

"They must know where we're staying," I whispered as we crossed the stinky chicken courtyard heading for the riad. "That may be one of them I heard chinking away last night."

"Yeah, maybe. From what you've told me, they must know you're here if your stuff was bugged and everything. We just have to make sure they don't get to the booty before us."

Which wasn't going to be easy. Back at the riad, Ingram met us at the door, relieved to see my bandaged hand and that we'd had such a good shopping episode. Though we insisted that we were just going to relax indoors for the rest of the afternoon, he and Mohammed were so attentive that it was challenging getting down to serious investigation without being observed. And then there was the housekeeping staff busy mopping the tiles and cleaning the rooms.

Finally, we resolved on a room-by-room assessment with at least one of us posted at the door at all times. "We'll make like we're playing chess together or something, you know, new best buds," Peaches said. "Let me go have a shower and change into my stretchies. Then we can get down to work."

"We should start upstairs and work down," I whispered.

"I know you heard chipping up there last night but nobody in their right mind is going to hide something for seven hundred years on a roof," Peaches pointed out. "That thing would have been repaired and then repaired some more, as in multiple times. Whatever's hidden here has to be on the floor level. That's why I chose the lower bedroom."

I saw her logic. "Fine, we'll start in the library." I held my phone before her eyes. "See this? No ordinary phone, this. Evan provided a cheat sheet for all its special features and I'm sure he mentioned something about an X-ray app."

"Are you kidding me?" she said, plucking it from my hands. "Never saw an X-ray app on iTunes."

"And you won't. The man's a genius. He invents all these fabulous effects in his spare time, when he's not protecting Rupert and reading, that is. Anyway, meet me back in the library once you've freshened up."

I retrieved my phone and took off to my bedroom to read the cheat sheet. I stared at the pages and pages of tiny print script, totally befuddled. Where I expected bullets and point form, there were paragraphs and diagrams. I shook my head, stuffing the pages back into my bag until later. Next, I started to unpack my treasures and was applying an argan cream to my parched skin when my phone pinged. Nicolina. *I found something important in the documents. Having it couriered to the riad today.*

Found what? I texted back. When the answer didn't come immediately, I dashed downstairs, meeting Ingram on his way up. "Would you like to have supper prepared here, Miss Martin?"

"Yes, sure. Ingram, how often do couriers come to the riad?"

"As often as necessary, miss. Are you expecting something?"

"A parcel from Venice but it's already almost 5:00 p.m. How late will they deliver?"

"That depends on the sender, miss. I've known them to come very late at night."

"But what if you're not here and the riad is locked up for the evening?"

"Then the courier will ring the bell. Maybe he delivers it tomorrow." He spread his hands.

"That won't do. I need it tonight. It could be very important."

"I will leave a sign on the door if it is after 7:00 and say to ring bell. Excuse me, I will go tell the kitchen to prepare supper now. Maybe a chicken tagine, miss?"

"Sure, sure—anything is fine." I was too stirred up to worry about mere food. Moments later I was knocking on Peaches's door. For a moment, I inhaled the rose fragrance wafting up from the tinkling fountain and tried to just breathe. Empty bowls sat nearby but the cat had disappeared.

The door opened and there stood Peaches enveloped in a white bathrobe with her face smeared in cream and a cat in her arms. "Meet Fadwa, the house cat. I'm giving this argan stuff a try. Apparently it's made from the undigested nut droppings of tree-climbing goats. Can't beat that for a selling point, hey? What's up?"

I stepped inside a room much like mine only wider and, if possible, even more luxurious, the Moroccan version of the presidential suite. "Nicolina texted me to say that she's couriering me something from Venice. It's supposed to arrive tonight."

"Well, that's good, isn't it? Let me wash this stuff off. Here, you take Fadwa. Keep talking. I can hear you from the bathroom."

"It's good that she found something, yes, but what if the courier's intercepted?" I leaned against the bathroom door stroking the cat. "I mean, that guy tailed us this morning, which must mean they're watching the riad. Supposing the courier comes to deliver the parcel and the thugs jump him and steal whatever it is?"

"Wow, you're, like, one step ahead of me and halfway down the road." She stepped out of the bathroom wiping her face. "So, like, we'll have to watch for him, won't we? Give me a sec to change and we'll get to work."

Peaches didn't do secs, she did ages.

Fadwa took off and I spent the time studying the paperbacks Peaches had left scattered on her bedspread—three of them, each with a bare-chested man on the cover. From there I went on to answering Max's latest weather-related text, assuring him that the sky was still clear—how often would that change in Morocco?—and that a high had blown in just today. If he were to suspect even half of what had happened, he'd hop a plane in a shot, which would only complicate things. As far as my texts to him were concerned, the weather would remain grand. Finally, I pulled out Evan's sheets and strained my eyes looking for descriptions of an X-ray app.

"Apparently it's activated by pressing on an eye icon," I told Peaches when she finally emerged from the bathroom.

"Cool."

Minutes later, I watched as she strolled around the little courtyard, studying the foundations intently in her black bodysuit with a loose silk overblouse, no doubt in courtesy to Muslim modesty. "This part of the riad's original," she remarked just seconds before the five o'clock call to prayer sounded.

"How do you know?" I said after the call had finished.

"There's no indication that the foundations have been significantly disturbed in centuries, see? Before I came, I dug up this article on traditional riad construction and they all had a big central courtyard where the pool is now and often smaller ones of washing or housing animals like this. Also, take a look at those timbers up there."

Craning my neck, I gazed overhead. "Old."

"Very. These desert climates can preserve wood for centuries. Looks like parts have been repaired like that strut over there but basically she's the same."

"Ladies, supper will be served at 7:00 by the pool."

We turned to find Ingram standing there smiling. So far the man seemed oblivious to any undercurrents between his guests, probably just delighted that we were getting along so swimmingly.

"We'll be ready," I told him. He nodded and backed out.

That left us almost two hours to search, beginning with the lounge, which came up solid with no false walls. Next, we moved to the library where Peaches paced out the perimeters with my X-ray app in hand while I tapped on the walls behind the books.

"I'm seeing nothing suspicious, either. How sensitive is dis thing, anyway?" Peaches asked.

"I have no idea." I unfolded Evan's cheat sheet to study the instructions again. "He says it will detect metal in stone and concrete within a distance of three feet."

"So, not all that ground-penetrating." Peaches was running my phone up and down every wall in a kind of grid pattern. "Dis man must be some kind of wonder."

"You're lapsing into dialect again."

She straightened, shook back her cornrows, and grinned. "Yeah, I am. Tell me about this Evan."

"There's nothing to say. He's been Rupert's bodyguard and right-hand man for as long as I've known him—ex-MI6. Ridiculously talented."

"Single?"

"I guess."

"Good-looking."

"I suppose."

"And a genius, too, you said." Then Peaches slapped her thigh and roared with laughter, waving the phone in the air with her other hand. "Nothing to say about him, right? Woman, you crack me up!"

"Why?" Truly, I didn't get it. I was just stating facts.

"Well, what's going on here? Did we miss a party?"

We turned, stunned to find June and Joe standing in the doorway, the library looking as though it had been hit by an investigation squad. Whole shelves of books sat on the chairs while I stood in the center of the room holding the cheat sheet.

Peaches flipped a wave at them from the fireplace. "Hi ya. I'm Peaches Williams. You must be the Merediths."

"Yes, June and Joe." June stepped forward, looking around.

"What have you girls been up to in here?" Joe asked.

"Waiting to grow into women, I guess," Peaches quipped.

"Checking the structure," I said quickly. "Peaches is an engineer and we got to talking about authentic riad construction and decided to check it out." I hated feeling defensive but crud.

"Seriously?" June was gazing at Peaches with undisguised suspicion. "You're an engineer? Where do you work?"

"London. Where do you work?" Peaches pocketed the phone and strode toward her, still smiling but wearing an undeniable look of challenge.

June backed up, applying a grin brighter than her lipstick. "I'm retired.

Sorry if I sounded confrontational. You just startled us, that's all. We were just coming in for a rest before going to dinner tonight. Maybe you'd both like to join us? We're going to a restaurant right off the Djamaa el Fna. Be our guests, why don't you?"

"We can't," I said, entering the fray. "We've already arranged for supper here at the riad. Some other time, perhaps."

Peaches swung around and began replacing the books, Joe helping. "Yeah, some other time."

After the Merediths had taken off for the evening and we'd devoured the chicken tagine with warm flatbread served with an orange almond salad, we began investigating the rest of the lower rooms. The staff were cleaning up after supper in the kitchen, which left us more freedom to work.

"I don't think we can find anything this way," I said, frustrated after we had run the X-ray app over the lounge and nearly the whole parameter of the lower floor. "Maybe it isn't hidden behind the walls, after all?"

"Where else would it be?" Peaches said, looking up from where she crouched on the floor. "It has to be somewhere near the foundations or in the floor itself. No place else makes sense."

"We need that envelope Nicolina sent. Where's that courier?"

"Did Her Majesty say anything more on what's coming?"

"No, except to say it was an envelope and very important."

I stepped out into the pool courtyard, now lit in candlelight and filigreed lanterns, and strode to the door as I had at least five times over the past couple of hours. Now that dark had fallen, it was less likely that a courier could reach the riad safely. Cracking open the door, I peered outside. Quiet, the overhead motion lights briefly flicking on to illuminate the narrow alley. Damn.

When I returned to the courtyard moments later, Ingram was waiting for me dressed in his jacket. "Miss, will you be needing anything else?"

"Just that courier."

"I will check the main roads on my way home but I am certain it will come tomorrow morning for sure. Do not worry."

And I was equally sure that it would not come in the morning and that I should damn well worry. If it didn't arrive that night, it meant someone had intercepted it. "Thank you, Ingram."

Moments later, Peaches and I were alone in the riad. She bounded into the courtyard with her arm draped in fabric.

"I'm going to make a dash for Shadiz's and get me that knife. Are you coming?" She was shrugging on her long robe and wrapping a scarf around her head, fastening part of the fabric over her mouth like a veil. "A guy in the

souk showed me this. I'll show you, too. I bought you one on the way here."
Out came a scarf a lovely shade of green shot with iridescence—not my style
but gorgeous. "Cactus silk, they called it, if you can believe that. Hold still
while I wrap it on your head. There."

"You look very mysterious," I said through my veil.

"You, too. That's the idea. These Muslim women are on to something.
Come with me tonight."

"No way. I've got to wait here for that courier. Do you need my gun?" I
asked, lowering the mouth covering.

"Keep it. I'll scare the bejesus out of any of these mini dudes that might try
to jump me. Would you jump me dressed like this?"

"A six-foot veiled Wonder Woman? No way."

"Right on. Be back within the hour."

I couldn't talk her out of leaving but watched her stride down the alley
with a pit of nails in my gut. "Be careful!" I hissed.

"You be careful!" she called back.

But I wasn't the one stepping outside the safety of the riad. Back inside, it
was just me alone inside the building. I returned to my room, admired my
scarfed self in the mirror, and decided to wear it for now. I changed into jeans
and my jacket complete with the gun loaded with a fresh round of bullets,
pocketed my phone, and returned to the courtyard to wait and work. At least
my hand had stopped throbbing, my stomach was full, and I almost felt
fortified.

The desert night had chilled so much that unless I stood beside a heating
pillar or remained inside one of the rooms, it was freezing. The staff had lit
the fireplaces in the library and lounge areas but I continued to stride the
perimeters of the central pool, now glittering like a jewel with its candlelit
reflected water, using my phone app as a detecting device. Nothing but earth
and maybe the occasional lost coin or buried earring revealed itself in ghost
outlines under the tiles but maybe I'd missed something. I was distracted.
Twice I went to the door to check the alley. Twice I saw nothing.

I was midway along my second round when I heard a cry. My head jerked
up and I listened, fear prickling my spine. It came from outside the riad—not
a cat sound this time but definitely human. Drawing my gun, I ran to the door
and poked my head out. At the end if the alley a motorcycle lay with its back
wheel spinning up the dust.

With the safety off and my gun raised, I crept to the end of the alley,
peering out from behind the wall at what looked to be a deserted courtyard lit
by one streetlamp and a moon far above. No humans in sight but that had to

be the courier's motorcycle with the saddlebag carriers lying there. The locals drove mopeds, not that expensive bit of machinery abandoned in the dust. Then I heard a thump followed by a mew of pain.

I took a step farther into the courtyard. Only then did I see the second motorcycle on its kickstand and a man sprawled facedown in the dirt. Another man stood over him, a knife gleaming in one hand and a large brown envelope in the other—my envelope!

He caught sight of me and sprung forward, the knife raised. I caught a flash of a dark scar across his face and an angry twisted mouth.

"Like hell!" I aimed the gun and fired at his leg, the impact causing him to spin around in a wail of shock and pain, dropping the knife in the process. "Give me that envelope, you murderous bastard!" I said, lunging forward, but he recovered enough to spring at me, giving my face such a wallop that it sent me sprawling onto the ground.

Seconds later, he had retrieved the knife and was hopping on his bike, zooming down the road as I stumbled over to the fallen driver. I didn't need to feel a pulse to know that sightless stare meant death. Damned if I was going to let that brute get away with that!

17

$\mathcal{N}$othing infuriates me more than violence inflicted on the innocent —that courier, Maria, me—let alone murdering, thieving bastards in general. And I damn well wanted that envelope back! I was too angry to sit quaking like a leaf inside the riad. When my temper detonates, I'm all in.

Only I wasn't some hotshot bike rider. I knew enough to get around on open roads but driving down a winding medina congested by stalls and people while following a moving target? Not in my skill set. I didn't even know where the headlight was at first. And the medina was alive with foot traffic, at least as busy in the evening as during the daylight hours with clusters of pedestrians clogging every path. Luckily, this pursuit wasn't about speed so much as keeping that bastard in sight. Which wasn't easy. I'd pulled up my mouth veil so at least the wild woman driving through the streets was somewhat incognito.

My bullet must have done plenty of damage because he seemed slower than I expected and unnecessarily reckless. Blood splattered the dirt as I wound through the paths, a trickle I could follow Gretel-style in some conditions. Pedestrians congesting the lanes meant I could never get close. Once, I saw him wobble into a stall of dates far ahead, sending mounds of dried fruit into the path and people screaming in all directions. I was blocked by a donkey hauling barrels and could only scream for the people ahead to be careful, that the man was dangerous. Whether they heard or not, I have no idea, but soon he was back on the bike, yelling at the stall owner and shooting a quick vicious glance over his shoulder before zipping off.

When I lost sight of him again, I panicked. Straddling the bike in a crossroads, I peered up the shadowy paths one by one, struggling to see a moving bike among the surge of evening shoppers. The stall lights illuminated only the faces of bystanders directly facing the shops. Everything else seemed like a heaving mass of shapes. To add to my distress, my jaw began to ache and my hand throb and I realized he'd hit me hard enough to cut my cheek.

For a moment, I struggled with uncertainty, a few seconds of dark night of the soul. Maybe I wasn't cut out for this badass stuff? Maybe I should just crawl back to the riad and call the cops? Who the hell did I think I was?

Then I heard a man shouting in Arabic with a group of elderly women in hijabs waving their hands in one of the lanes ahead. The women screamed, one of them swinging her shopping bag around as I zoomed up the lane in that direction. Forget uncertainty: I was going to get that bastard.

By the time I maneuvered through the shoppers, he was already well ahead and the press of buildings had opened into a huge square alive with flames, lights, and crowds—the Djamaa el Fna square, the original night circus in all its glory. Never in a million years did I expect to find myself hurling on a motorcycle in that crowded arena of wonders, glimpses of fire eaters and snake charmers whizzing past as I maneuvered around stalls and performers. He was trying to shake me by weaving in and out of the wagons and it was all I could do to stay upright in this raucous milling space. And people were shouting at me. "Slow down, lady!"—the only call I understood. Slow down? I was trying to speed up!

If it weren't for the women on the blankets, I would have lost him completely. I was just maneuvering between a snake charmer and a stall of candied oranges when I saw him far across the square being pulled from his bike by three women. I was too busy keeping one eye on the cobra rising from the basket on my right side to see exactly what was going on at first. It looked like the women, all in veils and hijabs, were trying to help him. No, wait, maybe not because the killer began shouting and trying to push them away —brute.

By the time I'd zoomed closer, I could see them pointing at his bloody leg and saw him kicking at the collection of little pots on their blankets. Henna artists! The struggle reached a pitch by the time I was within yards of them but by then the churlish idiot had seen me and was pushing the women away so fiercely that one stumbled back on her blanket. The others, now enraged, began screaming and pounding him with their fists. *Yeah, you give it to him, sisters.*

I eased closer, moving the bike with my feet. If I could only get them to hold him down while I grabbed the envelope... But suddenly he flung them off and pulled out that still-bloodied knife. The women backed up, circling around him as he climbed back on his bike, the knife still glinting in his hand, and his fierce gaze fixed on me.

By now we'd drawn a crowd.

I pulled down the mouth veil and yelled: "That man's a killer! He just murdered a man and he tried to kill me! Stop him, somebody!"

But the circle was widening, leaving the killer all the space he needed to take off, scattering the bystanders like bowling pins. Shit. That meant I had to chase him again. This time we wove around the last of the square traffic and burst onto an open rode.

An open road was preferable, maybe. At least I knew the basic rules of paved roads with cars and traffic, not that we followed any rules. The killer was swerving onto sidewalks or sandy shoulders any time the traffic backed up, which meant I had to do the same. I would have loved to blow out his back tire but who says you can shoot a gun while riding a bike?

At some point, he took off across a park along paved paths lined with rose borders and tall palms before diving back onto the road. He traveled at a good clip now, me following close behind, but his driving was crazy—nearly hitting a bench and ramming into a tree later. Once we dove through a date grove, which almost unseated me as we bumped along. He knew where he was going, I didn't, but the streetlights helped. I was so intent on keeping up that I was barely paying attention to anything else until we broke out onto a highway again.

We must have traveled straight for another ten minutes, which gave me plenty of time to figure out what I'd do if I caught him. He was failing, I could tell that much by his erratic driving. How long would it take for him to pass out? Maybe I'd wait until he was forced to stop and then take the envelope. Really, that's all I had, which didn't seem like much.

Now the traffic, the boulevards, the groves of oranges and dates, all looked the same until suddenly I realized that they had fallen away except for the occasional orchard. We were zipping on a highway straight into the desert. Don't ask me why that scared me. Hell, I was chasing a brutal killer so what was a little sand and nothingness? Maybe it had something to do with the fact that my fuel gauge had settled on empty. I was literally running out of gas.

Now what? Though there were occasional cars on the highway, a grove or two, I saw no gas stations and I could hardly pull over for a fill, and to make matters worse, I realized I'd picked up a tail. Another motorcyclist, this one in a helmet, was rapidly picking up speed. Maybe it was one of them and I was like a victim sandwich wedged between two killers. Shit!

Meanwhile, bastard number one had veered off the road into an orange grove, this one of the unlit variety. Determined not to lose him, I followed him in. It was dark and the ground uneven and soon I realized that I could no longer see his taillights, which meant he was probably off his bike and trying to trap me. Either that or had finally bitten the dust. And now the light of that other bike was bouncing through the grove right for me.

I came to a screeching halt, my heart stomping wildly as I jumped off the bike and dashed toward the trees, pulling out my gun along the way. I knew that the first guy would be waiting for me somewhere ahead, if he was still alert, while the second probably planned to block my escape. I had no intention of falling into either trap. Turning slowly around, I tried listening for the first bastard but that damn second motorcyclist was making too much racket. Slipping behind the shadowy trees, I crouched and waited.

Cyclist number two zoomed in behind my bike, jumped off his own, and made his way into the grove. That's when the shadow of the first guy staggered out from behind the palms and stumbled down the path toward him. If the first guy saw the second, he didn't show it, but then he was so bent over he could barely stand. How hard would it be to kick that bastard to the ground and retrieve my envelope? Only now I had to contend with the second biker, who had pulled out a gun. So I'd wait until the armed cyclist got close enough for me to shoot him in the knee, wait until he was disabled, and then retrieve my envelope from the first guy.

Or that was the plan. My attention fixed on the second cyclist, I watched as he strode closer to the stumbling man. The wounded guy spied him at last and lurched to a halt. I fully expected the two to greet one another other but instead the guy in the helmet lifted his gun and shot. I watched in horror as the wounded guy crumpled to the ground. The killer flung off his helmet and called out my name.

Damn, damn, damn! I jumped up and cried, "What the hell did you do that for, Noel?"

"Phoebe, are you hurt?"

"No, I'm not hurt, damn you! Did you kill him?" I ran up to the fallen man sprawled in the dust and felt his neck for a pulse. Dead. "Of course you killed him. You always do. Why do you always kill people?" I turned on him, waving my bandaged hand in his direction. "Why couldn't you have just wounded him like I did? You don't need to kill them dead every time, Noel."

He stared at me, stunned. "Hell, I should have invited him out for a beer, then—my bad. You kill them dead the first time, Phoebe. How many times have I told you that? If you just wound them, they'll come back for you, madder than ever, like this one did. Are you responsible for that mess of his leg?"

"I'm a crack shot now, and yeah, I nailed him in the leg, but you got him right between the eyes, I see." A clean shot. Hardly any blood. I wanted to upchuck into the bushes but kept it together.

"Always shoot to kill, Phoebe," he said between his teeth.

"Never!" I cried. "That's where we differ, on that and a million other things apparently. I will never shoot to kill unless I have to, got that? Even if they're murdering, brutal bottom-feeders trying to roast me alive like this one did."

"He tried to roast you alive? In that case, I'd kill him all over again, if I could." He spoke softly now. "Okay, so this isn't quite the welcome I'd expected from you. Good to see you again, too, Phoebe. What the hell is going on?"

"What's going on?" Okay, so I admit I wasn't exactly keeping it together just then. "You're supposed to be thousands of miles away on the run, as usual, not here stalking me, messing with my plans, not to mention my head. I had this under control, Noel. Who invited you to the party?"

He tossed down his helmet. "Are you kidding me? That guy had a knife in his hand. I probably saved your life."

"Look at him." I pointed to the corpse. "Does he seriously look like he could have done me any harm? He was maybe five minutes away from collapsing. Now I can't even question him, damn you. Did Rupert tell you where I was?"

"Rupert hasn't made contact with me since Jamaica. I always keep an eye on you, Phoebe. I told you I would."

"A tail on me, you mean. That has to end, Noel. I don't want you or some hireling stalking me."

He'd stopped, searching my face. "What's wrong? Look, Phoebe, I forgive you for setting Interpol after me, okay? I knew you had to do something about Toby and I accept that it meant I'd get snarled up as collateral damage."

"You weren't just collateral damage. I told you in Jamaica that either you turned yourself in and let me cut you a deal or they'd drag you to prison with my blessings."

173

His brows arched. "You seriously thought I'd agree to go to jail just so we could live some boring life together in the future?"

A knife couldn't stab deeper. "That was the choice, yes: live on the run or spend a dreary future with me."

"I didn't mean it that way."

"Yeah, you did. So you made your choice and I made mine."

"Look, woman, I've risked my bloody neck for you again and again but I will never willingly be caged up like some goddamn animal!"

"Got it. I also get that you've fallen way beyond the Robin Hood of the Art World crap and landed squarely in the midden heap of cheapo-sleazo art thieves."

"Cheapo-sleazo?" He swore with vehemence. "Haven't improved the adjectives, I see."

"It fits. Do you think I haven't figured out that you made off with the most valuable pieces in Jamaica, including the genuine Raphael? Do you think I don't know that you've become a crook of the worst kind, maybe *the* worst kind?"

"Since when did you become so damn self-righteous?"

"Since I realized what I really stood for and what I won't stand for any longer."

"Well, hell, aren't you the fierce little Pollyanna? I heard you were working with Interpol now. What are you doing for them, anyway—some kind of elite Barbie Doll agent chasing killers into the desert by yourself? I mean, seriously, are you kidding me? How dumb-ass is that? And what happened to your cheek?"

I swallowed hard, fighting back tears. There he was, my first real love, standing before me with his sharp-boned face tight with emotion and his eyes roiling pain, hurling insults at me. Even so, I knew it came from hurt and anger so I vowed to take the punches. "Forget the cheek. I want you to go away and never see me again. It's over, do you understand? We're not on the same side anymore. Don't come tracking me down unless you want me to call Interpol on you all over again."

"Whoa!" He lifted his hands. How I loved those hands once. Still did, maybe. Had to get over it. "Since when were we ever on the same side? We were just lovers caught in the line of fire, that's all, but in the big picture, I'll always be on your side, no matter what you say. Furthermore, we're kind of related, remember, my father being your godfather? I'll never be out of your life, so live with it."

Now the tears were rolling down my face in earnest. "If you ever see Max again when I'm anywhere near, we'll make like distant relatives. Otherwise, it's over, believe me, though how can it be over when we never really started? You'd just drop into my life long enough for us to fall into one another's arms —the once a year passion extravaganza—and then be gone. Talk about messing with my head. I'd stay longing for you for months afterward, hanging on for a postcard or a tip that you were off stealing something somewhere or at least still alive. That's a relationship? That's hell! When I said it was over, I meant it." And then because I couldn't just stand there blubbering, I added: "I was managing this by myself, by the way. Barbie's learned to handle a gun, defend herself in martial arts, and kick ass when she needs to, starting with yours. Get with the times, bozo."

He laughed, if you can call it that. "Bozo—got to love it. And how many degrees do you have, Miss Word Virtuoso?"

We stood facing each other, a dead man and a thousand light-years between us, while orange blossoms punched fragrance into the air and two motorcycles beamed light into the darkness. He looked haggard and pained. I felt broken and bruised. Emotion was draining from me faster than the dead man's blood, leaving me cold and brutally alone.

I wiped my eyes on my sleeve. "I need to get something off him. He knifed a courier and stole it from me. That's why I chased him."

Crouching, I felt under the dead guy's shirt where I could see the outline of an envelope. Pulling it out, I stuffed it under my own shirt. "Thank God it's intact."

"What is it?"

"I'm not sure. Nicolina couriered it from Venice."

"Ah, yes, the killer countess. Do you want to go back to my place and check it out?"

"Your place? Do you have a flat around here or something?" My arms encompassed the desert, the grove.

He grinned. "Not exactly, but I do have a tent strapped to the back of the bike. That's where I've been staying while here, which is why I look so ungroomed, in case you haven't noticed. Haven't had a shower in days."

I was trying not to notice anything more about him than I had to. "I'm not going into a tent with you, Noel. I have to get back to the riad as soon as possible. Peaches will be frantic. Oh, hell, I've got to text her that I'm okay."

I dug my phone out of my pocket and stared at the screen's upper right-hand corner in dismay. "No signal!"

"We're in a desert, remember?"

"This should be a satellite phone!"

"So maybe the satellite's busy or something."

I looked over at him as he wiped down my bike. "What are you doing?"

"Eliminating your fingerprints with bleach. I carry it everywhere in desert climes. That knife of his is probably covered in the courier's blood, right?"

I nodded.

"So, I'll leave that and wipe the courier's bike clean, leave the killer's. How many people saw you riding tonight?"

"Probably half of the Djamaa el Fna square but I had my scarf up." Or part of the time.

"Clever. They'll never clue in that a Westerner with a strand of flaming red hair sticking out might be you. At least they won't find the bikes or the body until morning. Let them figure out what happened. With luck, you'll be gone by then. Do you know who these guys are?"

"No, only that they've been tracking me since Venice—four of them, three men and a woman, now two men and a woman. I'm positive they killed Maria Contini."

"I found some things out for you that you might find useful: turns out they're all part of the same family with close ties here in Marrakech. Whatever they're after, they've been hunting it for decades and, make no mistake, they think it's rightfully theirs."

"How much do you about this, anyway?"

"Enough. Where's the courier's body?"

"Outside the riad. If Peaches comes back and finds it, there will be trouble. She was going back into the medina to buy a knife and they already think she's an anomaly."

"If they find her with that knife, they'll probably throw her in jail."

"You were the second cyclist tailing me today."

"Just watching your back, Phoebe. Come, we'd better get you to the riad. Climb on."

Like I wanted to be that close to him after all that was said but I was beyond arguing. Instead, I fastened on his spare helmet and climbed on behind him, half sitting on the mound of his tent duffel, and wrapped my arms around his waist.

"I knew I'd get your arms around me tonight somehow," he said as we zoomed off toward the highway.

18

---

*I*t was a good thing that he couldn't see my tears as we zipped toward Marrakech. If hearts were weighted, mine would have dragged that damned bike to a halt. And the man I wrapped my arms around was a lot thinner than I remembered. What had he been through during these months since he broke with his partner in crime—my brother—and escaped from Jamaica leaving all possibility of a decent life and the woman he supposedly loved behind? Whatever, he'd made his choice. Now all that was left for me was to heal the gaping wound after I'd made mine.

Twenty minutes later, the bike slowed as we approached the chicken courtyard. It was nearly eleven o'clock and at last the traffic was thinning around the city, leaving an unnerving quiet. I expected to see police cars hemming the lanes around the riad, anything except this deadly stillness.

At the end of the lane, deep in the shadows, he cut the engine and I dismounted.

"No body," I whispered.

"Did you think they'd just leave it in the dust for people to walk around?" He climbed off and wheeled the bike behind a broken wall.

"Of course not." I watched him unfasten his duffel and toss it over his shoulder. "I expected to see crime tape or something but there's no indication that there was ever a murder here. What are you planning to do—pitch your tent in the courtyard?"

He grinned that devilish grin of his. "Of course not. I intend to go around

177

to the back streets and scale the walls to your riad's roof like I've been doing for the last two nights. It's a four-foot climb from a tassel shop and then over a few tiled houses to the riad's wall—damn simple. It's worked out rather well as long as I go to roost after the staff closes up for the night."

"That was you I heard up there?"

"I was trying to open a can of beans. Look, let me into your room long enough to take a shower tonight, will you? I promise not to threaten your virtue. Like you say, it's over. No worries."

"No worries—seriously? What if somebody sees you?"

"So? Is the place crawling with morality police or something? Tell them you picked up a local for a night of fun. I don't care. I can pass as Moroccan. Doesn't matter since I'll be gone by dawn."

I thought over all the possible reasons not to oblige him but anything I came up with didn't work. I'd really rather not have his tempting freshly steamed body anywhere near mine but all he wanted was a shower.

"Besides," he added, "I'm there to keep an eye on you, and if you think you've beaten these guys because one's down, you're kidding yourself. They're out there still and I'm guessing mad as hell. They want whatever's hidden inside this place and obviously whatever's up your shirt—I wouldn't mind having some of that myself, but hands off, I get it. Trouble's just begun."

He did have a point. "Wait for me on the roof and I'll come up as soon as the coast is clear. Can you unlock the door from the outside?"

He grinned. "Of course I can. I can pick anything open except maybe your rusted heart."

So that was how it was going to be now—sniping quips? Well, fine. I pushed past him, relieved that he kept watching me right up until I had inserted the key and tapped in the code. Minutes later, I was inside the courtyard facing Peaches and the Merediths.

"Where were you, Ms. Martin? We've been worried to distraction!" June rounded on me and all I could see were those pink nails sailing through the air as if to squeeze my shoulder or pat my cheeks or stab my eyes out, take your pick. I stepped back. "We almost called the police." She stopped. "What happened to your face?"

Peaches stepped between us. "We were worried. You hadn't mentioned going out anywhere." Her eyes were searching mine and I was trying to say that I'd explain all when I could. What must I look like—the tears, the filthy face, the bruised cheek?

I looked up at her. "I decided to take off on a bit of research."

"Alone?" Joe said from behind her.

"Yes, alone." I stepped away, heading for the stairs. "I'm not a kid. Anyway, I got mugged on my way back from the square. I'm fine, though." I touched my cheek gingerly.

"Mugged!" June squealed. "And you are not fine! Look at that cheek. Come with me and I'll clean you up."

"I'm perfectly able to wash my own face. Sorry for worrying you but I'm fine, I said. Just a bruise but I gave as good as I took, I can tell you."

"Did he steal anything from you?" June called.

"No, because I didn't take anything of value with me. Now, please, all of you, go to bed." And with that, I dashed up the stairs to my room, latching the door behind me. Sanctuary at last. All I wanted to do was bawl my eyes out but I didn't have the luxury of that at the moment.

The first thing I did was pull out my phone and scan my messages. Evan's came up first. *About to board the plane to Marrakech. Should be there by 11:30.* That info sent a flurry of mixed emotions through me, the most bizarre of which was thoughts of Evan encountering Noel. That wouldn't be a love-fest but he'd be gone by then, I reminded myself.

Next came Nicolina's text: *Did the envelope arrive? The police want to know where you are. Investigation on the fire continues. Stay safe. N*

And one from Max: *Hope you have lots of sunshine. Come back refreshed. Love, Max*

And one from Serena: *Hope you're having a wonderful time. Have something to tell you when you get home. Rena*

I didn't have time to answer any of them but I posted a quick text to Interpol in London with my coordinates. If the answer didn't come back within the hour, maybe I'd place a call, but Agent Walker always reacted to my texts even if he didn't send a reply. He'd come and to hell with the consequences of that one.

I tossed the phone to the bed and I tugged out the envelope to spread the contents. Vellum, no less, and very creased and very old, too. My fingers trembled. A map, no a diagram, maybe, but the strangest one I'd ever seen. It was like miniature weaver's cartoons for multiple carpets, one on top of the other, with overlaying symbols and designs so closely packed that it was almost impossible to distinguish anything.

Somebody knocked on the door. I carefully refolded the diagram and slipped it under my pillow. "Give me a minute." Only after I had splashed water on my face did I answer it, finding Peaches, arms crossed, standing outside.

"Took you long enough," she whispered, and then more loudly: "Hi, Penny.

Thought I just check to see if you were okay."

"I'm fine. Come in." I shut the door behind her.

"What the hell really happened?" she whispered once I'd dragged her into the bathroom to ensure privacy.

I gave her the short version, ending with my showdown with Noel in the orange grove. "So I told him that it was over," I finished.

She whistled. "So, he's here and you ended it with him. Hell. How'd Lover Boy take it?" Peaches technically used to work for Noel and my brother when they were fighting her brother's rival gang back in Jamaica. She probably knew him better than I did. Yeah, it's that complicated.

"Badly but there's no gentle way to break up with a man like that. He's a born renegade and I was too blind to see it before. Life as a criminal seems to be his manifesto and life as a fool seems to be mine."

"Don't be so hard on yourself. You loved him, didn't you? We all do dumb-assed things for love. Anyway, I could have told you what he was really like long ago, woman. There were plenty of times I wasn't sure who was running the Jamaican operation—your brother or him. Finally, I decided it had to be him. Seemed that Toby had lost his marbles and Noel was taking full advantage of the situation."

I stared at her. "Why didn't you say something?"

"Hell, honey, do you think you were ready to hear that from me? Besides, it didn't matter since we blew up the whole operation and put our two master-minding bros in jail. Too bad we let the worst one get away."

I rubbed my eyes. "Anyway, now he's been hiding on the riad roof."

Her eyes widened. "Holy shit. He's up there now?"

"Apparently." I put my finger to my lips. "Keep it down."

"But why is he even here?" she hissed.

"He swears he's taking care of me, my self-appointed guard dog or some-thing. He's pulled this trick before, ghosting my heels whenever I'm in danger. I'm trying to sever the leash but it's not happening fast enough."

"You buying that?"

"It fits his pattern. He always seems to show up at critical moments. I'm going to let him in to take a shower like he requested once the Merediths go to bed. Then maybe he'll leave. Where are they now, anyway?"

"In the lounge 'calming their nerves—'" she inserted air commas "—with a bottle of Scotch they dug up somewhere. What a pair. Damn near drove me nuts."

I clutched her arm. "What happened to the body?"

"What body?"

"The courier's. When I left, he was sprawled in the dust after that guy knifed him."

Peaches held her breath, eyes fixed on mine. "I came back, like, maybe forty minutes after I'd left and there was no body outside, no blood, nothing."

"But a body can't just up and disappear. When did the Merediths return?"

"At about 9:30, long after I did."

We stared at one another. "They're watching this place, whoever they are. Noel thinks it's a family matter," I told her, "a family that believes whatever's here belongs to them. Maybe they were the ones who cleaned up the evidence so as not to draw the police?"

"Makes sense," Peaches said, "but if that's the case, they know you've got the diagram and will be wanting it back, like soon." And then she added, "And maybe revenge their brother or cousin or whoever while they're at it."

"Thanks for reminding me. They were vicious enough before one of their own got killed. Anyway, Evan's on his way, thank God. He says that a storm's coming in from Venice."

"Muscle Man's coming here with Hottie on the roof?"

"Will you stop calling him that? He doesn't feel hot to me when he shoots a guy point-blank in the head. Anyway, we could use the extra manpower if the gang breaks in tonight."

"Shit, do you really think they'll do that?"

"How else will they get to the diagram or what it's hiding? There's one more thing: I've alerted Interpol."

"Well, hell." I watched her thinking out the complications. "Yeah, we're supposed to be working with them, aren't we, but what about him?" She stabbed a finger at the ceiling.

I shrugged. "I'm going to tell him that I called them. That way, if he wants to escape sooner, he can leave."

"And if he stays?"

"His choice. Maybe Interpol will get him this time. Either way, they have to be involved since anything buried on Moroccan soil over a few centuries old belongs to Morocco and now there's a vested interest through Italy with Nicolina. That means a long drawn-out court battle and it's not our problem. We work with Interpol now so all we get to worry about is keeping on the right side of international law."

"Still getting used to new loyalties but yeah. Think I'll go downstairs and check on the Merediths."

Once she'd left, I pulled out the folded vellum again, spread it out under the table lamp, and tried to study it but everything from the labeling to the images were too cramped to distinguish with its jumble of geometrics and Latin. Using my phone, I pinched open the camera screen to enlarge aspects but nothing I saw in that scramble made any sense. It was as if some long-ago designer had taken multiple drawings of carpets or geometric shapes and applied them onto the surface, one on top of the other. I pulled away to gaze at it from a distance but that perspective improved nothing. Eventually, I just took a few pictures.

Carefully refolding the vellum, I tucked it into my bag and crept out to the balcony. Everything was so still out there, all the open bedrooms within my line of vision gaping dark. In moments I had dashed downstairs to find Peaches leaning against a pillar with her arms folded.

"They just went up," she whispered. "It took everything I had short of threatening her to keep Mrs. Busybody from knocking on your door to see if you were all right. Nosy beast. Mom has a word for those that test her Christian values. I'd give it a few more minutes before they get to sleep."

"I can't wait," I said. "I've got to let Noel know about Interpol."

"I'll keep watch in case she comes out." She stepped over to the other side of the pool and fixed her gaze on the second-story end unit, and for the first time I noticed a hilt of something sticking under her belt.

"Is that the knife? Subtle, very subtle."

She grinned. "Yeah, I told June that it was an ornamental dagger that I use as a toothpick. Hard to hide, though. They used to wear them either attached to their belts or strapped to their legs. This one's handle is real silver and sharp enough to slice a hair."

"Wonderful," I said, gazing at the thing uneasily. "See you in a few minutes." With that, I made for the stairs.

Seconds later I was tapping on the roof door. It flew open in an instant.

"What took you so long?" he asked.

"If one more person asks me that… Look, I've called my Interpol contact in London so I'd advise you to skip the ablutions and get out of here."

"Seriously, Phoebe? You've called the cops on me already?" He stood there grinning at me, all shadows and wolfishness, as if my calling Interpol was some kind of joke.

"It's not about you, Noel. I called Interpol because I work with them now. It's too bad if you're on their most wanted list, but, oh, well. Still, I wouldn't stick around here if I were you."

"They probably won't be here until dawn. I'll still take that shower, if you don't mind."

"You can take your shower but then I want you to go, and if you plan on hanging around to steal something, forget it."

"Ouch."

The door clicked shut behind him and we crept down the stairs to my floor where I indicated for him to enter my room. "I'll come back in thirty minutes, which should give you a chance to shower or shave or whatever," I whispered. "Make sure you're gone by then."

"You're crazy, woman. Before this night's over, all hell is going to break loose. You need my help. Ask me to stay, why don't you?"

"Not this time, Noel. Never again." I turned to leave.

"Answer me one thing." He was taking off his clothes right in the doorway, tossing his jacket aside and pulling his shirt up over his torso. "Is there another man?"

I looked away. "Does it matter?"

"Probably not. Want to come in and scrub my back for old times' sake? I promise I can make a clean dirty woman out of you yet."

But I turned on my heels and bounded back down the stairs without comment.

Peaches was waiting for me. "The light's gone off in the Merediths' room finally. Is he leaving?"

"At the moment he's taking a shower. You know how he likes to play close to the edge. Forget about him. Let's try to figure out this diagram or whatever it is."

"Let's use my room."

So we retreated to her back room, shut the door, and stared down at the vellum sheet together. For a few moments neither of us said a word.

"So, what is that?" she said finally. "Looks like one of those stencil drawings where the outline of, like, twenty others have been printed on top," she said.

"That's what I thought, too. Vellum was often scraped off so that new writing could be applied but usually the previous script was pretty much erased first. This looks like layer upon layer was deliberately applied. Vellum, by the way, is an expensive surface and had pretty much given way to the cheaper parchment after the 1100s."

"If you say so."

"The point is, somebody wanted this to last. It's meant to be a cipher."

Peaches strode to the other side of the bed and stood back again. "There doesn't appear to be any right-side-up."

"That's what I thought."

"I was hoping for a blueprint. Blueprints I can read. This looks more like—"

"A mandala, maybe?"

"But that's Buddhist or Hindu, not Christian or Jewish, right?" she asked.

"I'm beginning to think that maybe that painting contains every religious element for a reason. It celebrates God and love, regardless of dogma. It's a brave manifest for all that's right in the world instead of everything that isn't by celebrating an unusual marriage inside a house of worship."

She gazed at me and whistled through her teeth. "What are you getting at?"

I straightened and faced her. "This is my gut talking so take it or leave it."

"I respect your gut so maybe I'll take it."

"All right, then. I believe that the bride and groom in the Bartolo married for love in a dangerous time and that their families supported the extraordinary union for their own reasons. Yes, wealth was involved but something else besides. It's as if two families from two great religions chose to come together in the name of the similarities between their religions rather than all the differences. After all, Judaism is the foundation of Christianity—their roots are the same and love reigns true in both."

"So does plenty of negative aspects, like the horrors of religious persecution and the narrow-minded adherence to religious norms."

"All interpreted by man—and I mean that in the general sense—who in my opinion has never proved himself to be an unbiased translator."

She nodded. "Yeah, that's true enough. Blame all the religious wars regardless of the denomination on man using religion for his own purposes. No religion is exempt from that travesty."

"But what if two enlightened families saw beyond all that and that whatever we're seeking is symbolic of a religion beyond dogma? A religion truly based on love, on what connects us not divides us?"

Peaches shook her head. "Yeah, well, wow. Talk about an incredible find. Something like that is a message for the world and the timing couldn't be better. The answer has to be here somewhere."

"Yes, but where do we look?" I pulled out my phone and thumbed through until I reached the Bartolo painting and passed it over. "Do you see any similarities in the painting to anything you see in the diagram?"

Peaches peered down at the screen, pinching it here and there. "Maybe. I mean, there's lots of triangles and elements that could be easily shifted about to form iconology but it doesn't look anything like that." She indicated the vellum with a nod of her head.

I touched my cheek. Ouch. "Let's leave it for now and come back to it. I'd better check on Noel. I'll catch up with you in a few minutes."

She folded up the vellum and passed it over with my phone, which I shoved deep into my pocket. "I'm going to take a walk around, see if I get any bright ideas."

The riad was filled with a hushed quiet when I retraced my steps back to my room moments later. The Merediths' door was still shut and the night-lights had come on—some kind of automatic timer, I guess.

I knocked on my bedroom door. When nobody answered, I opened it a crack and peered in. Damp towels tangled on the floor but there was no sign of Noel. I stepped inside. So he'd used every one of my towels unnecessarily, really?

I gazed around at the mess he'd made, more determined than ever to end whatever had been between us. He might be gone from my room but I needed him gone from my heart and head, too, and everything he had done that night was helping. I'd just check out the roof to hurry him along.

Backing out of the room, I swung my carpetbag over my shoulder and strode for the stairs. If nothing else, I had to ensure that the roof door was locked. Noel had picked it open so maybe now it wouldn't lock properly. We couldn't leave that door unsecured when the gang might be on their way—three of them left, not including Noel.

I reached the top of the stairs and froze. The door hung wide open. I stood staring as a chill breeze cooled my cheeks. Surely not even Noel would do that? He might be behaving spitefully but would he deliberately endanger all of us? Besides, I'd watched him pull that shut behind him before we went to my room. Did he go back up but leave it open? Pulling my gun from its holster, I released the safety and stepped out.

Above, the stars spangled the sky, visible even here amid the medina's illumination. With gun in hand, I swung around 360 degrees. The terrace was still, night-lights illuminating enough to see that there were no pitched tents, duffels, or any other sign of obvious habitation. At the same time, it was impossible to see behind every deck lounger, table, or pile of pillows.

"Noel, are you here?" I whispered.

No response. I crept forward, keeping close to the stairhousing wall and heading toward the potted palm at the terrace's far perimeter. The air was cool. I was trembling but my hand gripped the pistol as if it were the handlebar of a bike hurling down a mountainside. Every nerve tingled.

Ducking into the shadow of the palm with my back to the wall, I stared out. Here I felt less exposed but I was picking up on something beyond my senses, something on this roof that didn't feel friendly, somebody hiding, somebody waiting.

I heard what sounded like a door clicking shut. What? Stepping out with my gun raised, I could see the stair door now closed on the other side. Maybe the wind had blown it shut. Maybe it was spring-loaded and I'd somehow tripped the mechanism. Maybe I didn't know what had closed it but I sure as hell didn't want to be locked up on that roof.

I sprung for the door—locked! I gripped the handle and shook it but it refused to budge. I'd call Peaches to let me out. I'd— Then something metal-sounding flicked behind my back, sending me spinning around. I couldn't see anything at first, only the mounds of furniture and pillows. Then something moved on my right as a shadow leaped out on me, knocking the gun from my hand and throwing me to the ground.

Deep-set eyes drilled into my skull as I lay on my back, a man on top, straddling me with his hands around my throat. "You will do as I say," he hissed, pressing on my windpipe. "Or I kill you."

I tried to nod, struggling to speak. He loosened his grip. Now there was a woman standing over us who picked up my gun and spoke to her companion in Arabic, maybe. The man climbed off me and together they hoisted me to my feet.

"You will do what we say," she said, pointing my gun on me. Great—two armed people. Where was the third? "Give me the bag," she demanded.

"My carpetbag? You want the diagram, don't you? Well, good luck with that. It's inscrutable," I said.

I could tell they didn't grasp my meaning. "Inscrutable: unreadable, useless!" I clarified.

"You will tell us meaning or we kill you," the man snarled. He stepped forward as if to strike me but the woman stayed his hand.

"No. We want her to think, Omar," she warned. "The bag!" She wrenched it off my shoulder and I could do nothing but watch as she dumped the contents onto the tiles. In a moment she had the vellum unfolded and was staring at it in the half-light. "What is the meaning?"

"Who are you?" I asked.

"Shut up. What is the meaning?"

"I don't know, I said."

"But you know." She was fixing me with her drilled-deep eyes. They looked so much alike, the two of them, like flip sides of a gender coin. Same tanned skin, same bony faces and thick black curly hair.

"No, I don't," I said. "I can't figure it out."

"You will tell us or you die," she said, waving the pistol at me.

"Where is our brother? What did you do with Yousef?" the man demanded, threatening me with every inch of his wiry frame.

"Yousef? Is that the guy who killed the courier? He's your brother? I don't know where he is. I shot him in the leg but he got away on his bike."

"You lie. He called, said he got diagram," Omar said, poking the air before my nose with his finger. "You chased him! You got diagram back!" He so wanted to hit me, I could tell.

Three could play at this. "Okay, so I did chase him, straight into an orange grove off the highway. He was losing a lot of blood and fell off his bike so I took the diagram back. That's where I left him. You'd better go make sure he's okay instead of wasting time with me."

Not a good idea mentioning the blood part. The two of them exchanged glances, which was all the time I needed to knock the gun out of the woman's hand with a sharp uplift while shoving Omar against the door with my shoulder. His shot rang wild, aiming for the stars, as I scrambled off.

Five seconds or less was all I had as I snatched up the diagram. No time to wrestle a gun, too. Seconds only to get myself out of the range of fire and away, which meant only one thing: I had to jump, this time right over the edge of the terrace roof.

19

I bolted to the side of the stairwell housing to where the air-conditioning unit hugged a low wall and flung myself over it as full of prayer as I ever had been in my life and I mean multidenominational prayer. I had no idea what was on the other side except that it wasn't the street. And like an idiot I closed my eyes and held my breath as if I were diving, the diagram gripped between my fingers.

But I ended landing on my feet no more than four feet down. And took off in a mad scrabble across the tiles, tucking the vellum into my shirt on the run. Noel had mentioned his route from the street to the roof but all I cared about was the reverse path. Since the riad backed up against a maze of buildings crammed together, I knew this one had to be the route he'd taken.

All I wanted was to get away from the killer duo and warn Peaches as soon as I could risk pulling out my phone. That meant I had to get off the roofs to a safe place but had no idea which direction to take. Noel hadn't exactly drawn me a map. Twice I tripped over a cable and pitched flat on a corrugated surface and once I banged into one of the satellite dishes that sprouted out from the roofs like slanted mushrooms. It was a crazy, uneven surface and the moonlight and starshine only baffled me with shadows.

Once, out of breath and dizzy after a stumble, I turned to see the figure of a man balancing with a gun in hand silhouetted against the deep azure sky maybe fifty feet away. I hauled myself to my feet and launched in a crouching run beside a low wall, keeping deep in the shadows. My best hope was to lose him in this maze of broken concrete and misshapen mounds. If I arrived at a drop too deep to jump, I'd scuttle off in another direction, maybe duck behind a chimney, or under a tent, or up a low promontory. People used these roofs, I realized. Signs of daytime occupation were evident in the laundry lines, the chairs pulled up inside little concrete terraces, the rooftop grills.

I kept going like this for maybe fifteen minutes until I noticed that the roofscape had changed from rough-scrabble to newer, more decorative and upscale materials. Now I appeared to be on some sprawling multilevel roof complex with white decorative trim. This must be the air-conditioning and ventilation area for some big building. With no signs of Omar, I figured I must have shaken him at last so I took a moment to slump behind an ornate chimney and speed-dial Peaches.

"Where the hell are you!" she hissed.

"Somewhere over the medina being chased by one of the killers," I whispered. "They attacked me on the roof. Have you seen them? One, maybe both, must still be at the riad. The important thing is that I escaped with the diagram."

"Well, shit, woman, don't you have all the fun? All I get to do is babysit the Merediths. Evan just arrived and the doorbell woke them up. He's calming them down now with more charm than I've seen from a man. Hell, and I thought my daddy could lay it on. He's telling him he's your boyfriend."

"Seriously?"

"Yeah, seriously. Speaking of boyfriends, is Noel with you?"

I peeked out from behind the chimney, quickly pulling myself back. "Noel's gone somewhere. Where is he when he might actually be useful? So far I'm fine, thanks for asking. The others have to be somewhere in the riad. Watch out. There's two left out there that we know of, remember, not counting the one chasing me. Got to go."

"Wait, Evan wants to talk to you."

There was a muffle and then: "Phoebe? Where are you exactly?"

He said my name. Crazy what a little thing like that will do. "I don't know," I said. "I just took off across the roofs after they tackled me."

"Text me the coordinates from your phone and I'll find you."

"No!" I whispered. "Don't leave Peaches and the Merediths alone."

"The killers are only interested in you. Text me the coordinates, I said. Never mind, I'll track you." Then he clicked off.

He'll track me, shit. Shoving the phone back into my pocket, I crept up to the wall. I needed to find my way down to the street somehow. I peered down three stories seeing nothing but handfuls of people strolling along a well-lit boulevard. There was a guy in a fez wearing some kind of uniform directly underneath me, maybe the doorman of this establishment. No way down that way.

I turned. Behind me stood a small square building that I was beginning to recognize as an enclosure for the top of a stairwell. They were all over the roofs of the medina. Some led to sunning terraces, others to technical equipment like air-conditioning and ventilation units. Each one had a door and every door I'd tried that night had been locked. This one was no exception.

Now what? I'd arrived at a dead end of sorts, and unless I felt like climbing up and balancing along a partition that separated the business end of the building from whatever lay on the other side, I'd have to retrace my steps. Hoisting myself up onto a ventilation housing, I peered over the wall that ran deep across the complex. It was like gazing down on a fantasy palace straight out of *Ali Baba*. This must be a hotel designed like a monstrous riad, all the varying terraces lit like some magical playground for the very rich.

Below was a small pool set in what seemed to be a cozy terrace area with a little bar tucked into a copse of flowering trees. To my left, a filigreed border of arches separated a much larger pool dropped into the center of a spacious balconied courtyard. Yet another small raised terrace sat under an awning in the corner to my right. The whole place wafted money along with the scent of jasmine and orange blossoms but nobody stirred that I could see. Music played from speakers tucked out of sight. Gorgeous or not, there was no easy way down and I had no doubt that security would be tight. Nothing obvious like barbed wire but alarms had to be everywhere.

A sound behind me made me turn. Light-blinded, I couldn't see anything at first but I could hear heavy breathing and something like a curse in another language. I'd been found.

I watched as the shadow man approached while I considered my options. Tackling him in armed combat could only be a last resort. I wasn't good enough to risk it unless I had to. Escaping was preferable. I swung back to the wall—a long lantern-lit crenellated border of concrete with drops to various levels, none I wanted to think about jumping. My best chance was to head to the right where the raised dais with its cushions and awning promised a soft landing. At least it was a ten-foot drop there instead of a thirty to fifty one— my best chance to keep limbs intact.

Omar lunged forward while I sprung for the wall. It was easy to hoist myself up but hellishly hard to stay upright once I got there. Maybe a foot wide with the lantern crenellations positioned every two feet, balancing on that surface would be fine if I didn't need to lift one leg periodically to cross a lamp. As for speed, forget it. Omar, on the other hand, was damn good at this while I got hit by vertigo within seconds.

I had no choice but to try stoop-crawling next, which worked long enough for me to scramble across the steepest part of the drop. Completely focused on maneuvering the obstacles, I didn't pay attention to anything else until I heard Omar speak only a few yards away. "Stop, Phoebe McCabe, or I shoot," he hissed.

"No, you won't," I called back. "You need me alive."

"Alive, yes, not whole. You hurt brother, I hurt you."

A quick look over my shoulder saw him watching me with a calculating look, his gun pointed right at me. Shit! I jumped up and made a running leap over the next few lanterns, propelled more by fear than sense. A shot cracked out and hit a lantern near my left foot. Somebody screamed as I jumped down into the awning.

And kept falling deeper into folds of some kind of striped silk that completely covered me as the tent ripped off its tethers and sent me falling into a mound of pillows. I heard cries and shouts as I struggled to release myself from my silken cocoon. It took me seconds to realize I was the one doing the screaming.

Somebody arrived to me to help me unwrap. After the last fold of silk had been pulled away, I saw a startled-looking woman standing there with a bougainvillea flower tucked behind her ear. "Are you okay?" American accent. "My boyfriend and I were at the bar and then I heard you scream," she said while untangling the rest of the fabric from my feet.

"I'm okay, just shaken up, thanks. He tried to rob me." I turned to see Omar struggling with two fez-hatted men—waiters, maybe. "Him!" I pointed. "He attacked me! I was sitting here and he jumped on me and wanted to steal my cash!"

"She lies!" Omar cried, but the gun that had fallen to the tiles didn't add to his credibility. Suddenly two security guards came dashing onto the terrace, one speaking into his walkie-talkie, the other rushing to pick up the gun. A man in a suit arrived, brass name tag fastened to his shiny blue bolero chest.

I went into wronged damsel mode. "What's the meaning of this? I come up here to relax and suddenly this...this creature attacks me! What kind of hotel is this where security is so lax?"

"Madam, madam, we are very sorry," the suited man said, hands open. He spoke rapidly to the security team in Arabic and they tackled the protesting Omar to the ground. "We endeavor to keep our guests safe. This is very unusual, very rare. We are so very sorry. What can we do to make it up to you?"

"I'm going to my room. You can talk to me later."

"Wait, lady, the police are on their way. You must tell them what happened," the manager called.

I was halfway to the door. "You can see what happened," I said over my shoulder. "An armed man broke into your hotel and tried to rob a guest. Now, I need to rest. I'll talk to the police when they come."

Which was soon by the sounds of the sirens pealing from somewhere outside. The last thing I needed was for someone to figure out that the tent had encompassed me from the outside in, not the other way around or that I wasn't even registered at the hotel. No, I needed to get away and fast.

The lobby was akin to a long carpeted portico with the oasis-like pool area gleaming through the arches. I bounded downstairs but soon forced myself into a nonchalant stride. Guests were standing around talking excitedly about something that had happened on the roof. News travels fast.

I sailed straight past them all, through the whispering automatic doors, and onto the street. In seconds I was striding away from the sirens and pulling out my phone to figure out where I was exactly.

A man strode up behind me. "Just keep walking, Phoebe," he said, linking my arm with his.

20

"*M*ake like we're a couple," Evan whispered, pulling me close as we strode rapidly down the street arm-in-arm. "The police will be all over here in a minute. Are you hurt?"

"I'm fine," I said, "but Omar is going to jail."

"Omar is one of the gang, I take it. How did you escape this time?"

I gave my summary, assuring him that much was pure luck.

"Did you use the phone's taser feature?" he asked, looking down at me at last.

"What taser feature?"

"The one where you hold down the home button and the volume button simultaneously, which signals the phone to temporarily emit a taser-like shock—very handy for disabling attackers. It's hot off the desk, so to speak. I've yet to see it tried out on a living thing."

"You don't test on animals, do you?"

He looked shocked. "Absolutely not! I only test on deserving humans."

"Good, but no, I did not use the taser feature since I didn't know about it," I hissed.

"The directions are very clear on the cheat sheet," he said with mock chagrin.

"Do you mean that lengthy tome you printed up? That is not a cheat sheet, Evan, that is an instruction booklet minus an index. I suggest that you master the point form."

He grinned. "My apologies, madam. I note that I must deploy brief teaching videos in the future."

"Yeah, you do that. Put it right up there with the Evan call button."

He smiled as we continued rapidly along, him steering me into a little path between the crush of buildings. "This way. So, I understand that Halloren arrived," he said, his tone suddenly serious.

"Unfortunately, yes. He claims that he's been keeping an eye out for me. Apparently he's been camped out on the riad roof since we arrived. He's gone now."

"Don't believe it. He's here for a reason and it's not about you, no matter what he claims."

I pulled my arm from his. "Forget Noel. He's the least of our problems considering that, whoever this gang is, there are two more left out there—a woman and another brother we have yet to see. Both have to be nearby. Two down, two to go, in other words. How are we supposed to decipher this diagram with them waiting to pounce?"

"I doubt that they'll pounce until we've uncovered the hidden dowry. Why not let us do all the work? But we'll be ready for them by then. If my hunch is correct, they've been anticipating that moment since you arrived and are probably growing a bit impatient about now. That's probably why that guy accosted you tonight."

"Only, Omar was also itching for payback because I shot his brother. Forget that Yousef killed a courier and snatched away that diagram in the first place. If the sister hadn't intervened, I'd have more than a bruised cheek."

"You killed him?" he asked sharply.

"No, I didn't kill him. I shoot to disable, never to kill, contrary to the assassins' creed or whatever. Noel killed him."

"Just his style. Is the diagram still in good condition? I saw it before the contessa packed it away to the courier service."

"As safe as a seven-hundred-year-old piece of lambskin can be after a few wild dashes onto the desert air." I stopped and looked around. "I recognize this lane."

"The riad is just ahead."

"And Noel's motorcycle was parked right over here." I strode up to the broken wall and peeked over. "And it's gone."

"And the man with it, I trust."

Somehow I doubted that. A part of me still hoped he'd be waiting in the wings ready to help at the last minute.

We crossed the courtyard and dashed down the alley, Evan watching our backs as I inserted the key card and pushed open the door.

"There you are!" June was on me as soon as I stepped into the courtyard. "What is the meaning of this, Penny, waking us up with your gentlemen callers and causing a commotion in general? Have you no consideration for your fellow guests?"

Peaches rolled her eyes behind her.

"June, sorry for the disruptions. I—"

"Disruptions? Is that what you call it when someone spends a fortune to ensure a delightful Moroccan holiday only to have a single disrespectful guest disturb her peace again and again?" She was standing in front of me with her arms crossed over her magenta bathrobe, eyes flaming indignation. For some reason, I noticed her earrings. She slept wearing dangles? "First thing in the morning, you can be sure I will be lodging my complaint. What kind of guest goes out at all times of the night and requires a man to fly in and bring her home? Disgusting." She turned on her gold-tooled Moroccan slippers and marched toward the stairs. "Come along, Joe."

Joe had been staring at Evan as if he'd just manifested out of a genie bottle but now scurried after her like an obedient puppy.

"Well, that was strange." I looked from Peaches to Evan once the couple had retreated. "Fly in to bring her home—really?"

Peaches swore. "You'd think you had been out prowling the streets picking up stray men or something. What were you doing?"

"I'll tell you later. Is everything clear around here?" I asked her.

"If you mean did I find anyone lurking in the shadows, no. I did my rounds floor-by-floor while you were gone and the roof is latched from the inside now. Nothing looked out of place up there besides your stuff all over the terrace," she told me. "I gathered it up and put it back in your carpetbag, by the way. It's on your bed."

"Oh, thanks. And nobody tried to jump you?"

"Hell, no. I'd hoped they would so I'd get my swinging arm back in use but I'm not interesting enough apparently."

"So, no signs of anyone else besides the Merediths?" Evan asked, stepping forward, his bag in hand, and gazing around at the balconied levels.

"Nada," Peaches said. "I gave all the rooms a cursory check but they looked empty."

"But I'm sure they're here. I'm working on a device that will pick up body heat signatures in rooms of a limited size but I didn't have the right equipment with me in Venice," Evan told her.

She looked at him in amazement. "Seriously, you can do that?"

"That and more," I said, "but don't let it go to his head. Maybe we should check all the rooms again just in case." I was looking up at the balconies, every room but mine and the Merediths' wide open. Each were dark, which made for perfect hiding places unless thoroughly checked. "There still could be somebody hiding up there."

"Smoking them out would take too long and require more person power than we can spare at the moment, given our time restraints," Evan said. "We need to find this thing before the staff returns in the morning. We'll deal with problems when the time comes. Let's get right to work. Where can we go that has a blank white wall?" he asked.

Blank white anything was notably absent in this pattern upon pattern environment but we led him into the smaller courtyard where the back wall had managed to remain undecorated. Following his directions, we busied helping him set up his laptop on a table dragged from Peaches's room while he fiddled with his equipment. I had no idea what he was up to.

"You didn't mention he was gorgeous in his list of attributes," Peaches whispered when we were inside her room bringing out chairs for the evening's operations.

"Will you stop," I said, my exasperation playful but my point firm. "He's Rupert's assistant, remember, not one of your man-chest heroes."

"But I bet he's got one just like that." She pointed to one of her paperbacks tossed on the bed—a bare muscled chest holding a puppy dog. She went through those things like vitamin pills.

"He's here to help us prove that neither Rupert nor Nicolina are responsible for Maria Contini's death because she was killed to get to whatever's buried here. We find whatever it is and hopefully put that and the killers where they belong. Forget the romantic fiction."

"I'm only interested for aesthetic reasons."

"He's not my type," I hissed, grabbing a chair by the rail back.

"Oh, yeah, what type is that—short, fat, and bald?" She grinned.

"Lean, murderous, and wolfish apparently. Look at Noel. Anyway, I'm just exorcising one man from my heart so the last thing I need is another, chest or no."

"That's exactly what you need, sister, and that guy's got the goods, that's all I'm saying."

We differed on the fundamentals of romance. "Let's get to work. Anyway, what's wrong with short, fat, and bald? I've met guys like that who would melt your socks off."

"Wouldn't know. I've only just started seriously wearing socks."

Back in the courtyard the two of us stood gazing in wonder as an image projected onto the wall. Hovering as if in midair, the lines and angles took a second to focus.

"Is that the diagram up there?" Peaches gazed from the laptop to the projected image.

"That's the diagram Nicolina sent, yes," I said.

I stepped forward. Evan, standing in a white shirt with his sleeves rolled up over his substantial biceps, turned and explained. "Before Nicolina sent the diagram, I photographed it in sections using a program that has the capacity to break down levels of any geometrical design, enabling one to study it from multiple angles in 3-D. Watch."

He touched the keyboard and sections of the diagram fell apart into separate areas like a folding screen. Touching the keyboard again raised the images up as if we were gazing at them sideways. Each time he tapped, the triangles, rectangles, and spheres realigned to create a new design, each as incredibly complex and beautiful as the last, like kaleidoscope mosaics.

"Like sacred geometry?" I whispered.

He smiled. "'There is geometry in the humming of the strings, there is music spacing of the spheres.'"

"And he quotes Pythagoras, too," Peaches marveled. She reached out a hand as if to touch the image. "Cathedrals were built on the principles of sacred geometry. It's everywhere in ancient architecture hidden in such plain sight. The universe is engineered on geometry."

"It is," Evan agreed.

"Can you spread the sections apart on a flat level?" I asked.

He tapped the keyboard. "Done."

As the sections rearranged themselves, Peaches stepped closer. "Bring the top square over here and move that rectangle there."

"Here, you do it." Evan stepped aside. "Move the sections around with your fingers. The screen is touch-enabled, all drag and drop." She did as he asked, moving each section around with her fingers until they formed a series of connected rectangles, large and small. Now we were looking at a schematic that looked surprisingly like a blueprint with triangles littering the top of the screen as if waiting to be placed. "This is the riad," Peaches said. "See, the central courtyard is this large rectangle here and this smaller courtyard is where we stand. If I rearrange these blocks around, it forms the other rooms, only I don't get what to do with those triangles up there."

My mouth had gone dry. "Triangles combine to make stars. Look." I dragged each of the triangles down, squeezing the images to reduce them in size and placing two overlapping equilateral triangles in the center. "A hexagram." I brought out my phone and thumbed to the Bartolo picture. "And the bride is standing on a hexagram. If we can find this geometric configuration somewhere in this riad, we might find the dowry."

"Even though the hexagram wasn't claimed as the Star of David until two hundred years later?" Evan asked.

"It wasn't acknowledged as such until the seventeenth century but it appeared all over the ancient world long before then. The star has always been a symbol of power and hope." My eyes met his.

"It must be hidden in the mosaics," Peaches said, "but the original tile work must have been replaced long ago."

"Or covered over," Evan suggested, turning away to stride across the courtyard. "It's far less expensive to tile over something than to dig it up and start fresh."

Together we gazed at the tiled floor. "It must be beneath these tiles somewhere. But we ran the detector app across every inch of tile and found nothing," I said.

"So it must be buried someplace the scan can't reach," Evan pointed out.

"The center of the riad." Peaches turned to the door, her excitement mounting. "These buildings were always built around a central courtyard from which everything else radiated outward. So where's the center of this one? The pool!"

We followed her out into the central courtyard where the three of us stood gazing deep into the blue water. "Impossible," she whispered. "They wouldn't have built a pool this deep back in the 1500s. Water was scarce—*is* scarce—in the desert. If there was anything buried here, it would have been found when they excavated for the pool in the last couple of decades."

"Water has always been sacred to desert communities and seen as cleansing, purifying, and ultimately preparing the faithful for worship," I pointed out.

"And there are two courtyards here," Evan said quietly, "one much less public than this but no less important to a family centuries ago. It is where they would have washed and prayed before meals."

Turning, we dashed back into the smaller courtyard and stood by the fountain, staring. It was a small fountain set in a basin no bigger than a birdbath. "So, it must be underneath here," I said. "A fountain of one form or another probably existed in this spot centuries ago and the latest electrical addition could have been installed without significantly disturbing anything below it. I'm betting that if we dug here, we'd uncover an old mosaic featuring a hexagram much like what we see in the Bartolo."

"Underneath which lays our missing dowry," Evan added. "Let's start. First, I'll disengage the fountain by lifting it up—no need to damage anything. The electricians would have rigged it for easy repair. Then I'll start removing the top layer of tiles. The biggest issue will be draining the basin but I think I've got that worked out."

"I bet you have." Peaches nodded.

"We'll help," I said.

"It's better if I do the digging while you two search the riad for stowaways. Now's the time," Evan said without looking up from the fountain. He seemed deep into calculation mode. "The sound of digging will draw them out so we'd better be ready for interruptions."

That made sense.

"Do you even have a shovel?" Peaches asked, always the practical one.

Now he was lifting up a long narrow bag strapped to his valise and zipping back the cover. "Of course. I always come prepared." Out came a fold-out shovel. "If I change the head, it turns into a rudimentary pickax but I doubt I'll need that." He looked up. "Do either of you have a gun?"

"I have a knife." Peaches pulled out her gleaming blade.

"The wicked sister took mine," I told him, spreading my hands, "but apparently I have a taser."

"Take mine." He pulled a pistol from his holster and passed it over, butt-first. I took it, finding it heavy, made for bigger hands. Still, I nodded and thanked him. "But while you're digging, you'll be exposed to anyone sneaking up behind you if Peaches and I are in another part of the riad," I pointed out.

He quirked a smile, holding up his phone. "A motion detector. If I activate that feature and place it in the floor behind me, it will pick up movement coming through the door up to a distance of ten yards. That's enough to send a warning."

Peaches whistled between her teeth. "Let's get to it, then," she said, turning to me. "Any suggestions on where to start?"

"At the top floor. You guard the stairs while I check each of the rooms. Between the two of us, we should be able to catch a rat if it bolts."

"Sounds perfect except that we have a bathroom issue and I don't mean that kind. While you check each bathroom, you'll be out of my sight for seconds and your back exposed to being jumped from behind." She had more commando experience than I did and it showed.

"Yeah, I see. Let me figure that one out," I told her.

We left Evan straddling the fountain while twisting it from its pedestal, his phone pulsing a blue light in the center of the floor.

I wasn't nervous about checking each of the rooms, though I probably should have been. With Peaches watching from the top of the stairs with her phone light beaming down the corridor (we still hadn't located the master light switch) and her knife at the ready, she had my back. That left me to grip the gun in one hand and my phone in the other, theoretically. Practically, the gun was too heavy for me to manage comfortably while holding the phone in my wounded hand but that's exactly what I tried to do.

First, I worked out a sequence. I approached the first room with confidence, flicking on the bedroom light and striding forward like I knew what I was doing. Slipping my hand in around the darkened bathroom wall, I switched on the light with the back of my hand while still holding the phone. Satisfied that the bright jolt of patterned color jumping out at my eyes was totally of the tile variety, I next gave the shower stall a sweep before backing out. On my way out of the room, I checked under the bed but it turned out that the mattresses sat on platforms with no space beneath. Next, I opened the wardrobe. Every room had a carved wood variety requiring me to swing open the door and wave my gun inside at anybody who might be lurking within. After the first sequence, I vowed that checking the wardrobe first made more sense.

All the empty rooms on that floor received the same treatment, my own getting extra care seeing as Noel had recently been there. It's like I felt his presence imprinted in the space he'd left behind and the thought stabbed me in the heart. A quick glance in the bathroom mirror at my own reflection was enough to bring me back down to earth. I looked like parboiled hell with a bruised cheek and hollow eyes. Wincing, I turned away and returned to my task, following the same sequence three times more on the top level. Tiptoeing past the Merediths' room, I was relieved to see the lights out under the door and that all seemed peaceful.

"All clear. On to the next level," I whispered when I met Peaches at the stairs minutes later.

She held up her hand. "Listen."

All I could hear at first was the deep chunk-chunk of Evan digging before a second sound came through, something like a chair scraping across the floor on the main level. Then we heard a clatter on the level directly beneath us. "That's deliberate," I whispered. "They're trying to separate us."

"Well, it's going to work, isn't it? We can't leave them to run all over this place. You get the one below and leave the one on the bottom floor to me." She made it sound like we were sharing treats. I watched as she bounded downstairs with her knife in hand, leaving me with no choice but to continue down to the second floor without her.

None of the rooms were booked on this level and now I had no one to watch my back, either. Why did that bother me? Maybe because my gun arm was tiring and my other hand had begun to throb. Had I the choice, I'd wimp out in a nanosecond but choice was not optional. Shoving my phone into my pocket, I gripped the pistol with both hands and prowled the floor. This time I flicked on each of the lights closest to the doors but made no move to go inside. If my hunch was right, someone was waiting for me and my task was to stay out of their clutches.

I was halfway down the row when a clang came from the room at the end of the hall—brass banging against brass. Someone wanted me to know where they were or think that. All right, then, I'd just go as far as the door and maybe shoot a warning shot to the ceiling, see if I could flush them out. Or that was the plan. By the time I'd heard the footfalls behind me, it was too late to even turn around.

I was pushed to the ground face-first, the force hard enough to throw me but not heavy enough to keep me down. The gun fell from my grasp. I bucked, which shifted my attacker to the left, giving me time to shove her off, regain the gun while scrambling to my knees. She was just as fast but no trained fighter and now we were facing each other on our knees, both of our guns pointed at the other's chest.

Petite with dark curly hair with a fierce yet delicate face, she stared at me with angry eyes. Maybe forty years old, she looked as though she'd been dragged through life by the scruff of the neck. "You think you escape us, Phoebe McCabe," she said, "but you don't escape. We are here now and will claim what is ours." I had the sense that she wanted to sound fiercer than she was. Her hand trembled.

"Who are you? What do you want?" I asked.

"You know what we want," she said.

"No, I don't. Tell me." I had to get that gun away from her without getting shot. She must know that we were close to locating the dowry so she'd have no reason to keep me alive. "Why did you burn that building down while I was in it? Why did you kill Maria Contini?"

"That was accident! We did not want to kill! My brothers, they struggled to get key and she fell, hit her head."

"Wow—what, four of you against one woman?"

Pain crossed her eyes. Not the first time, I guessed. "So you struggled to get the key to the warehouse, and when she wouldn't just let you have it, you killed her."

"By accident, I said."

"Oh, really? Killing must have been your intention all along; if not yours, then your brothers'. They have anger management issues written all over them."

"Not me!" she protested. So I was correct.

"Your brothers, then. And was trying to burn me alive an accident, too?"

"We thought building deserted! We wanted only to find old deed and burn any secrets to take back what is ours. This riad is ours."

That surprised me. "But it's belonged to the Continis continuously for centuries."

"Not true!" She practically spat the words. "It was sold to our family in 1986 and then stolen back six months later because of secret buried. All their money, they used to bribe. Now we have nothing."

I stared at her, dumbfounded. "What?"

"My aunt Zara came to work for Continis when young girl. She worked here in riad first and she went to Italy with them—like all big family. Many years pass. Signora Contini likes my aunt, wants to give her good life because her family—us—very poor, so she sell riad to her for family here at low price. Every dirham we had, we put to buy house. My aunt, she had savings. There was deed, all legal, and then—" she snapped her fingers "—gone."

Both our pistols were lowering now. Weird as it was, we were kneeling there having a conversation. "Gone? But how can that happen if you'd legally bought the riad?"

"Signore Contini made deals." She jerked her head toward the medina as if crooks were lurking behind every wall. "He discovered secret, wanted riad back to find treasure because his money now gone. Papers were signed. Said our deed illegal. My brothers were given money but it was nothing, a cheat!"

"These are the elder Continis you're talking about, not Maria," I protested, slowly climbing to my feet. She did the same.

"Not Maria, no, but she knew. Her parents die but still she not give riad back to my aunt. She promised money in will. We don't want money, we want what is ours!"

There was a sound below us in the courtyard. We stilled, listening, but continued after a few seconds. I wet my lips. "So you thought you could find it by stealing the painting?"

She nodded. "Maria Contini would not will riad to Aunt Zara. She told her this. Many times we hear Continis say that secret must lie in painting but we could see nothing even after we steal it."

"So your aunt was behind this from the very beginning?"

"No!" she said, cutting the air with her free hand. "She knows nothing! We bug her things, the house. We hear everything. She is just old woman—very sad, my aunt. Do not blame her. I moved to Venice and visit Aunt Zara with my brothers many times when Maria Contini left house. We placed the devices."

Theirs must have been the rudimentary ones Seraphina scoffed at. "And you made the call to Maria that night?"

"On burner phone, yes. I said I must talk about my aunt. She agreed. She said she had meeting with someone after but would meet with me first."

"But you and your brothers were waiting instead."

"Yes. My brothers very angry. She would not give us the key. It was accident."

I saw it all play out in my imagination. "No, it wasn't. You don't just meet with someone at night to politely ask them to pass over property possibly hiding a family fortune and expect it to all go smoothly. Of course she didn't agree; of course there was a struggle, and you and your brothers are responsible for what happened next."

Though her expression remained defiant, I caught the pain running there. Still, though she may have participated, she was not the orchestrator of this tragedy. And Zara had inadvertently been providing access to her niece and nephews spying all along. I knew she had to have factored in this somewhere. "But you still didn't know exactly where the secret lay until you heard me discussing it with Nicolina? That's why you wanted me because you think I'm an expert, which I'm not."

A smile touched her lips. "You have led us back to here. You read the symbols in the painting. Now your man digs for treasure."

"Look—what's your name, anyway?"

"Amira."

"Look, Amira, first of all, he's not 'my man,' and secondly, I have no vested interest in whatever might be hidden here, do you understand? I like the puzzle part, I like the challenge, but neither I nor any of my friends are here to steal anything from anyone."

"But you work for her, that Nicolina who now owns all."

"I don't work for her. She asked me to help find out who killed Maria Contini and now I know—you apparently."

She stepped toward me, gun still pointed at my chest. "Not me, my brothers—very dangerous men. I want only what is right and to give my aunt the life she deserves."

"What's hidden here may not only be valuable but a symbolic message to all the warring religions worldwide—Islam, Judaism, Christianity, even Hindu."

She spat. "Allah only true god. Where is Omar and Youssef? What have you done with my brothers?"

"Omar got arrested for chasing me through a hotel and Youssef—" I hesitated. Telling her that one brother was dead might enrage her.

"And Youssef?" she pressed.

But a noise drew our attention to the courtyard again. This time the sounds of a scuffle were unmistakable. Those few seconds of inattention were all I needed to knock the gun from her hand and retrieve the thing in a flash. Now I held both guns.

"You would not shoot me," she said.

"Not to kill, no, but I wouldn't let you shoot me, either. Come on, Amira, there's been enough bloodshed already. You can't help your aunt if you are all in jail or dead. Let's go down and meet my friends."

She seemed to agree with that much.

We were almost on the bottom level when a cry ripped the air. "Phoebe!"

21

$\mathcal{I}$ couldn't tell where the sounds were coming from at first.

"There." Amira pointed, running to the other side of the pool to where two figures struggled in the half-light.

Peaches had a man facedown on the floor behind a table with his hands wrenched behind his back. "Quick, give me something to tie him up with!" she called.

"Can't, got my hands full at the moment." I lifted the two guns to prove it. "Let him up and take my other gun. Amira, stand against the wall."

Amira did as I said, shouting Arabic at the man straining to break Peaches's hold.

"Does he speak English?" I asked her.

"No English," she said. "Don't hurt him."

"Then tell him to stop fighting or I'll shoot him in the leg like I did Youssef," I said.

"Abdul does not listen to me." But she said something that made him still at once. Peaches pulled him to his feet by the scruff of the neck and he—almost a carbon copy of the other two guys—threw me a vicious look as he regained his footing.

"They're all siblings," I told Peaches, "here to take what they see as their property and to compensate for their aunt's hard work, broken promises, and a swindled deal. That's the story in a nutshell, anyway."

"Lost property?"

I leaned forward to pass Peaches the other gun. "The family bought the riad years ago from the Continis, sold to them at a bargain price in thanks to their employee's—Zara's—work apparently. She'd been employed by the family for nearly forty years. Then the elder Contini swindled it back from the family when he finally started believing that a treasure was buried here."

"That explains almost everything." Evan was striding across the tiles toward us. "Here, let's tie them up. I've brought the rope."

He wrenched Abdul around and bound his hands together while speaking to him in Arabic as I held the gun.

"What did you say to him?" I asked.

"I said that it was over, that the police will arrive by morning to arrest them all."

Abdul spat something back.

"What did he say?"

"He quoted the Quran, something about wealth being like a poisonous snake unless you take care of your family, or something to that effect."

"This riad is ours," Amira cried while Peaches bound her hands. "Anything you find belongs to my family!"

"That might have been true had you told the authorities and let the court handle your property complaint." But the words stuck in my throat. I knew damned well how the poor fared against the wealthy in situations like this but that didn't justify murder and destruction.

Once bound, the siblings were marched back into the smaller courtyard where Peaches forced them to the floor against a wall and proceeded to tie their feet.

"How close are you to finding it, do you think?" I asked Evan after he'd assisted with the roping and returned to the digging site.

"Close, hopefully. I've chipped down at least a foot to the original flooring," he said, gazing down at the pile of broken tiles scattering the floor. A ragged hole now gaped where the basin had been while the fountain itself sat a few feet away with its electrical cord snaking away across the floor.

I leaned over and peered down, seeing the outline of much older mosaic revealing itself beneath the rubble. In a minute, I was on my knees prying up the top layer of loosened tiles with my fingers. The first piece—blue against white with inlays of deep carnelian red—had not faded across the centuries and seemed to form part of a triangle. I brushed away more to reveal almost a foot of beautiful, intricate mosaic.

I looked up at Evan as he leaned on his pickax. "It's the Bartolo carpet in mosaic."

"Yes," he said quietly.

"But we can't just destroy it." Tears stung my eyes. I couldn't believe I was willingly participating in the destruction of ancient art.

"We must if we are going to retrieve the dowry. I'm hoping to preserve enough that it can be reconstructed."

"These tiles are inlaid with lapis, carnelian, and other precious materials. It's a work of art in itself. How could anyone just cover it up in the first place?"

"Either politics or religion," he remarked, "the two most destructive forces in history."

"Yes, but this mosaic may say something even more explosive, especially if it celebrates all religions, which could be seen as heresy to all. And the fact that it's not a Moroccan design in itself could have compelled the renovators to bury it." I stood up.

"Do you truly believe this mosaic celebrates omnism?"

"Yes, the same way the Bartolo carpet does. It's a message, a powerful message. Is there any way to preserve it?"

"Sadly not. This should be an archaeological site and protected accordingly, I admit, but if we want to preserve what's hidden here, we need to work quickly."

"It's a travesty."

"Agreed."

I wiped my eyes on my arm. "So, how can we help?"

"Stand back and let me get back to it, if you don't mind. I'm afraid that extra help will only get in my way. I'm trying to preserve what I can."

"Right." I stepped away. I couldn't bear to watch those tiles be destroyed, in any case. I checked my phone, finding that Agent Walker hadn't responded to my midnight text and that all my other contacts in London were obviously asleep. I strolled over to Peaches, who stood staring at the siblings where they sat bound on the floor.

"How long do you think those ropes will hold them?" I asked.

"As long as necessary," Peaches said. "I can tie a mean knot and Evan a better one apparently. "Where did you find him again?"

"In London, sort of. Anyway, that's the last of the siblings," I said, gazing at Amira. Her brother leaned against the wall with his eyes closed but her gaze remained fixed on every move I made.

"You killed him," she said at last. "My brother is dead?"

"Yes, he is gone. I'm sorry, Amira, but I did not kill him," I told her truthfully. "Somebody else pulled the trigger."

"Noel?" Peaches asked.

"Of course Noel," I whispered.

"Who is this Noel? Why did he kill my brother?" Amira cried, straining against the ropes.

"He thought he was protecting me. Your brother shouldn't have stolen that document or knifed the courier trying to deliver it to me."

But Amira had begun wailing a high-pitched keen, a sound so much like pure pain that it nearly broke my heart.

Peaches covered her ears. "Will you stop?"

Evan paused his digging. "I think I've hit something," he called.

Peaches and I were at the dig in seconds, staring down past the shattered tiles at a square shape just visible under a crumble of earth. "A chest?" I asked.

"I believe so," Evan said. "Who wants to do the honors?"

"You go." Peaches nudged me. "You're why we're here in the first place."

Evan chunked away a bit of earth around either side of the box—rusted iron, at first glance—and let me try to lift it out. It wouldn't budge.

"Here, allow me." In seconds he had hoisted a small chest of about two feet wide and a foot deep from the earth and carried it over to the table.

For a moment, all we could do was stare at the badly damaged metal box that hadn't seen the light of day for over seven hundred years. Encrusted with earth, it appeared as though the fountain may have been slowly leaking onto the metal for decades, maybe centuries. Most of the outer casing had nearly rusted away and the padlock securing it hung from the ring like a broken jaw.

"I hope what's inside isn't damaged, too," I said.

"Go on, open it." Peaches nudged me again.

Evan gave the lock a final whack with his ax handle and the rest of the lock crumbled to the floor. I stepped forward, touching the lid, trembling with anticipation for that moment in time when a person from one age gazes into another…

"What is the meaning of this?" a shrill voice demanded.

I swung around, my arm still outstretched toward the chest. June was striding through the door, Joe scampering at her heels. For a second, I viewed the scene through her eyes—a ruined floor, three people obviously involved in a search, and two more bound up against the wall. If you could paint a scene for nefarious, we'd nailed it.

"Pardon?" I said, scrambling for an explanation and finding none.

"I said, what is the meaning of this?" June's gaze swung from the siblings to the three of us and back again.

It was such a stereotypical question that I countered with a stereotypical answer. "I can explain everything." My arm dropped to my side.

"Oh, really?" She was pulling a phone from the pocket of her pink robe. "It's time I called the police, something I should have done long ago. There!" She held the phone up as she pressed a number in her contacts, too far away for anyone to see the details. She had the Moroccan police on speed dial? She said something I couldn't catch into the cell followed by a loud: "Come at once!"

"This isn't what it appears," Evan whispered beside me, and then: "Mrs. Meredith, don't do this," he said. "It won't unfold how you expect it to, I promise you that. Don't interfere." He stepped forward as if to intercept her while Peaches slid in front of the chest to hide it from view. "Just leave the room now."

"Are you kidding me—three people demolishing private property? Are you going to tell me that you're just repairing the fountain or something? Come now, Mr. Ashton, do you take me for a fool? What is that on the table?"

"We work with Interpol," I said, stepping forward, "and we're here on official business investigating a murder that has led back to here." That wasn't quite true, and if Walker didn't contact the Moroccan branch soon, we were going to end up in the local jail, regardless. "Obviously, we couldn't inform the staff or guests what we were up to."

"I bet," June said, inching forward. "So you're going to tell me you're detectives now, are you?"

"More like agents for the ancient lost and found. That's what we call ourselves." I was willing to say anything at that point. "My friend actually owns this riad." That wasn't quite true since the ownership of the riad may not have been officially passed into Nicolina's hands yet.

"Though we are not actual detectives," Evan said, striking his most officious tone, "we are indeed working with the authorities to locate buried or hidden artworks. I assure you our actions are quite legitimate, despite the appearance."

If he was trying to distract her with assurances, she wasn't buying it, not that I blamed her. Her look of self-righteous alarm had shifted to something more smug. "Real Indiana Joneses, are you? Why don't you just open the box before the curtain falls?" She met my eyes. "Well, go on."

I turned, reluctant to pollute this treasured moment with June Meredith and her cowed husband looking on but seeing no choice. While everyone watched, I lifted the badly rusted lid and gazed down at what looked to be a bundle of dark red rags that might once have been velvet. As I lifted the bundle from the box and set it on the table, the disintegrating fabric fell away. All we could do was gasp.

Green fire shot from the surface as Evan ran his phone light across the four sides of the box.

"Oh, my sweet Jesus!" Peaches exclaimed. "Is that what I think it is?"

I touched the surface reverently. "A box made of sheets of carved solid emerald? Yes, it totally is." Staring at the ornate, jewel-and pearl-encrusted lid with its omnistic symbols, I fought the urge to cry—so much beauty with such a powerful message. "And it celebrates the god in all religions, a universal symbol of religious unity."

"Open it."

That was June's voice but I didn't look up, couldn't tear my gaze away from that casket for a single moment—none of us could. I lifted the lid while Evan beamed light into the interior, illuminating the gem surface from the inside out like some surreal jungle mystery. "It's filled with jewels," I whispered, scooping a fistful of precious gems into my hand—sapphires, diamonds, rubies, all sparkling like crazy.

"Holy shit," Peaches whispered, gazing down at a palm full of gems. "I never really got why people would kill for a bundle of shiny rocks but, like, I'm changing my mind."

"This is worth a fortune in any century and is a simply magnificent find," Evan said, while holding a faceted diamond up to the light. "Flawless."

My tears released, blurring in the light of so much beauty. After a few moments of reverent gaping, I shook away the spell. "What's taking Interpol so long? This is going to need an armed guard to safely transport it anywhere."

"Step away now." June again but I ignored her, so intent was I on this amazing discovery.

Amira was shouting from behind me.

"I said step away or I'll shoot."

That caught my attention. I turned to June, who now held a gun pointed right at me.

22

$\mathcal{I}$ should have seen it coming. Maybe at some level I had but refused to pay attention.

"Don't looked so shocked, Phoebe. Do you think you're the only one who can make a booking under an assumed name?"

June stood with a gun trained on us, Joe behind her holding a pistol of his own. The three of us were unarmed. I'd left the two guns I'd been carrying near the fountain, and since one of them was Evan's, that left him defenseless, too. Peaches's knife was firmly shoved into her scabbard but that didn't do much good under the circumstances. One move and she'd be shot.

"Who are you?" Evan asked, pitching his voice over Amira's keening. He, at least, did not seem surprised.

"Let's just say we're an interested party. Joe, shut her up."

Joe marched to the wall where our prisoners sat and whacked Amira across the face with the back of his hand. When her brother started shouting at him, he was slugged on the head with the butt of his gun—some distorted sense of chivalry. The brother slumped against the wall unconscious while Amira fell silent.

"There, much better," June remarked.

Now we knew what we were up against. "Who *are* you?" I demanded.

"Call me June—that part is correct. Otherwise, we work for someone with vested interests—not them obviously," she said, indicating the siblings. "You—

Peaches or whatever the hell your name is—bring us the box. Joe, get the bag ready."

Joe strode over and I realized that he had a backpack slung over his shoulders. Keeping his gun on Peaches while June leveled hers on the rest of us with a kind of periodic wide-angled swing, he slipped the bag off, one shoulder at a time while still gripping the gun. Peaches cast Evan and me a quick look as she proceeded to lift the chest.

"You were ready for this, weren't you? Just waiting for us to lead you right to the treasure. How did you get to the riad before us?" I asked. I had to keep her talking, maybe distract her.

June smiled a rictus of self-satisfaction. "We've had you bugged for months, listening in to your every thought, even way back in London. We've been tracking your every move, darling. And my, oh my, you have lived a very boring life these past few months, haven't you? At least until recently. As soon as you hit Venice, things picked up but we had no idea you'd lead us to such a bounty as this—emerald and jewels, well, well."

"Bugged her how?" Evan snapped.

"Oh, yes, the gizmo whiz. My employer uses a nifty new technology that, once inserted into an item—let's say the inner seam of a carpetbag—is virtually undetectable even by you. And she carries that old thing everywhere, don't you, Phoebe?"

My traitorous bag was still in my room. How long had it been listening in on my life? At least I didn't need to ask who had put the device there. That much I'd already figured out. I felt sick. "When is he coming?" I asked.

June pulled her lips from her teeth. "Oh, you guessed—bright girl. He's on his way."

"Who's on his way?" Peaches asked standing with the chest in both hands.

"Noel Halloren," Evan said under his breath.

Peaches swore. "You work for that bastard? But how? I mean, we blew that operation up in Jamaica, and when he took off we figured he'd have nothing left."

"Halloran has been pocketing loot for months before that while building his own operation on the side," Evan said. "We've long suspected it but lacked proof."

June smiled, so obviously enjoying this. "Well, he does have a policy: follow Phoebe McCabe and she'll take you to the goods every time. He calls you his lucky charm, sweetheart."

I swore viciously.

"Everyone is being spied on these days, you just more intimately than most," June said. "What, don't tell me you thought he was smitten by your charms alone when he followed you here?"

I didn't actually, but it hardly mattered just then. It would be enough if I kept myself together when I saw him next. What I did before and after was all that mattered.

"Joe, put that thing in the bag, and you, Peaches, if you do anything stupid, I'll blow your brains out. You two, stay where you are," June ordered. She held the gun like she meant every word but even she must have known that she was outnumbered. Besides, I had the sense that she was hired more for her disposition than her skill.

Joe stepped forward with the bag open while Peaches went to meet him carrying the casket, mere seconds when Joe literally had his hands full. And seconds was all it took. Peaches tossed the casket at Joe while Evan and I both launched at June, Evan aiming for her legs, me at her gun arm. The gun went off, hitting the ceiling and sending June back against the tiles screaming, Evan on top of her. I raced to help Peaches, who was rolling around the floor with Joe trying to wrest the knife from her grasp. I lifted the casket and brought it down on his head, sending him to the floor in a heap and scattering jewels everywhere.

"Damn, we're good!" Peaches exclaimed as she pushed his limp body off her. "You'd think we orchestrated that but I would have had him in a few more seconds."

Meanwhile, Evan had June on her feet with her arm twisted behind her back. "We'll tie her up," he said.

"I should have shot you when I had the chance," June snarled as she attempted to kick out at him. "Big MI6 guy, are you? You're nothing but a well-packaged hunk of shit!"

Evan wrenched her arm a little harder. "Now, don't go hurting my feelings, June, if that's your name. We'll just put you over here with the other two."

While he and Peaches bound her up and dragged Joe over to the wall, I busied myself picking up the scattered gems. The casket was undamaged, the emerald sides impervious to even Joe's skull. Still, I was ashamed of myself for using a priceless work of art as a bludgeon. The things we do in desperation.

When I next looked up, Peaches and Evan had both Joe and June tied up beside the other two and were turning back to pick up the firearms. I had just lifted the casket from the floor and set it on the table, Joe's gun tucked into my belt, when a gunshot ripped the air. I saw Evan spin around gripping his shoulder while Peaches lunged toward the door, both stopping short at the sight of Noel's gun.

"Don't make me shoot you, Peaches—we used to be friends once—but you, Ashton, you I wouldn't hesitate to shoot again in a minute." He lifted the gun as if to do exactly that, his eyes flashing a cold light.

"No, Noel, don't!" I cried, throwing myself in front of Evan.

"Phoebe, get behind me," Evan hissed, trying to shove me back. Blood oozed between the fingers gripping his shoulder. He'd try reaching for his gun next and Noel would kill him. That couldn't happen.

"No!" I ran to within three feet of Noel and stopped. "Don't do it, Noel, don't hurt them, please."

"You know my policy on that, Phoebe. Step out of the way and you, Ashton, lay the gun on the floor—now!"

But Evan wasn't moving and I could imagine him calculating possible next steps, none of which would end well. I kept inching toward Noel, my hands in the air. "Don't do this, Noel, don't turn into one of those bastards we used to talk about, the ones who'd inflict violence on anybody for greed. Don't tell me you've turned into one of them!"

"Get the fuck out of the way!" Noel cried, lunging to the left to level another shot at Evan.

Peaches was diving for her knife and June was yelling obscenities as I rammed into Noel, sending his shot wide. But then he had me whipped around with one arm, gripping me across the chest, and the gun shoved into my temple. Everybody froze.

I watched as Evan slowly lowered the gun to the floor.

"Kick it toward me," Noel ordered.

"Don't do it, Evan! He wouldn't hurt me!" I cried.

The arm bracing me tightened. "Are you so sure about that, my love?" Noel whispered into my ear. I wasn't sure of anything anymore. Evan clearly wasn't, either, since he kicked the gun toward him.

"Back off, both of you. Peaches, take that knife of yours and cut the ropes on June here." Joe was still unconscious.

"You tink I'll do what for you, Noel? Do you tink I'm still your little worker bee or something?" Peaches snarled.

In answer, Noel lifted the gun higher on my temple. "Or I'll shoot her, I said."

She hesitated, maybe moments too long, but then picked up the knife to do as he asked. In minutes June was back on her feet holding her hand out for the knife, which Peaches reluctantly relinquished. June then leaned over and plucked my gun from inside my waistband.

"Now, this is what's going to happen," Noel said. "June, you're going to gather up those guns and then proceed to pack that casket into the backpack and then pass the bag to me. If anybody moves in the meantime, shoot them, got that? Don't hesitate. It's simple, really: if you have to shoot one of them, I'll shoot Phoebe and everybody loses."

"Don't worry," June said, picking up one of the guns. "I would gladly shoot all these pains in the asses without hesitation."

"What in the hell happened to you, Noel?" I whispered as June went about her work. "The man I knew would never do anything this maniacally devious." Maybe I was crying, maybe not.

"Oh, really? How well did you know me really, Phoebe, baby? I'm the same man I've always been only you wanted me to be something better. I never pretended to be anything else."

"Oh, yeah? What about that Robin Hood of the black market crap you sold me on?" I asked.

"That was all Toby. Your dear brother really thought he could rescue stolen art and return it to the original owners beneath the legal radar—that is, until he spun out on drugs and got lost in his own madness. I never bought into that shit."

"Halloren has been skimming the goods for years, Phoebe," Evan added, watching him closely. "He's been the real villain all along."

"Why didn't you say something?" I asked him, straining against Noel's hold. Noel just held me tighter.

"I couldn't," Evan said, pain clouding his eyes.

"He couldn't because he's undercover Interpol, Phoebe—haven't you figured that out yet?" Noel said. "He and Foxy have been tracking you to get to me for years. It took the Jamaica heist for me to figure that out, too."

"Is that true?" I demanded.

Evan met my eyes without flinching. "Phoebe, I deeply regret all of that, believe me."

"And the chauffeuring and bodyguarding bit with Foxy?" I asked.

"All part of our cover."

"*Our* cover? You mean you and Foxy have been playing me for a fool all along?" I swore.

"Not a fool," he said earnestly, "but a valuable connection to a crime family who has been stealing art for years. Rupert and I are both very fond of you. Nothing there was a lie. You must believe me."

"Want me to shoot him for you, Phoebe?" Noel said. "My pleasure, believe me. June, what's taking so long—hurry up, will you?" Noel called.

June scurried back with the bag in her hand, the gun still trained on

Peaches. "Here you go, boss. I took two diamonds as part of our payment. It's not like you pay us enough or anything."

But I couldn't take my eyes off Evan.

"Yeah, sure, sure. You do this right and I'll wire you a bonus. Put it on my shoulder and watch the rest of them while we take off."

"Even her?" She indicated me with a flick of the gun.

"No, not her. She's coming with me. As for the others: if Peaches moves, shoot her."

That snapped my attention back. "Me coming with you? Are you crazy? I'm not going to be your hostage."

But then everything happened so fast. Noel fired his gun and Evan collapsed to the floor. Peaches screamed and June yelled at her to be quiet while I was being steered out the door by Noel. And I went, anger and panic burning so deep that all I could think of was how to get this bastard. Play along.

"Okay, Noel, I'm coming with you," I told him as he marched me out the front door of the riad and down the narrow street. "I'm not fighting you so stop twisting my arm."

He released me but kept the gun pressed into my back as he hurried me along. Dawn was just pushing a sharp band of light into the sky over the medina and the air felt heartbreakingly chill. We carried on without speaking until we turned another corner to a narrow street where one of the parked cars winked its lights in greeting.

I didn't know what to expect but not this. "A getaway car? Are you serious?"

"Just get in, Phoebe," he said.

He opened the door and shoved me into the passenger seat, dropping the bag on my lap. "If you don't do as I say, June will shoot Peaches—that's the deal. It's you or her." He pitched his voice louder. "June, you hear me?"

"Coming in loud and clear, boss," June's voice crackled from somewhere under his jacket. A wire.

"Keep the gun on Peaches. If I say shoot her, shoot."

"Got it, boss."

I looked up at his shadowed face. "Bastard! I'll come with you, I said."

"Good, so no attempts to jump out or try anything more creative. I know how creative you can be."

"Ask her how Evan's doing," I asked.

"How's Evan doing, June?"

Crackle. Crackle. "Losing a lot of blood. Should bleed out soon."

216

"Why did you have to shoot him?" I cried.

"Why do you think, Phoebe?" he said while climbing into the driver's seat and pealing us down the street, narrowly missing a mule piled with carpets. "Shoot them while you have the chance or they'll come after you every time. Once I found out he was undercover Interpol, I wished I'd shot him sooner. Foxy will be next. You should thank me. They've been using you to get to Toby and me for years."

"Damn you all to hell!"

"That's my girl. Fasten your seat belt now. We have a long ride ahead of us."

All I could do was swear at him at first while churning away inside. Admittedly, my brain was not functioning optimally.

"Oh, come on now, Phoebe, not that tired old expletive. You can do better than that."

The thought of Evan dying when all I wanted was to scream at the man for hoodwinking me for so long was one thing, but being in the company of Noel again was something else. My heart was a mess, my mind worse. "You goddamn hunk of stinking twisted assholean chicken shit!"

"Assholean chicken shit—almost has an Oxfordian flare. Better, but not up to your usual standards. Just so you know, you were absolutely right back there: I would never harm a hair on your head. Never have, never will. I don't care if you believe it or not but I love you."

"You call kidnapping me, shooting my friends, stealing a treasure you know I went to a lot of trauma to retrieve all while spying on me...*love?*"

"Oh, Phoebe, come on. Your friends are all working against my enterprise —fair's fair. You are, too, but you my heart puts in protective custody. Come on, admit you still love me just a little. I'm still the lovable rogue you fell for years ago."

"I hate you," I spat.

"Flip side of the love/hate continuum—better than ambivalence any day. I'll take it."

More expletives followed on my part. It seemed as though my ability to communicate in full sentences had gone. It took several miles of driving into a brilliant desert sunrise before I calmed down. "Where are you taking me and why in hell do you expect to get away with this?" I said as I sat slumped back in the seat, numb with pain. "Do you really think I'm going to play your mol and go dashing off on the run with you?"

He squinted into the rising sun and flipped down the visor. "Forgot my bloody sunnies. No, I'm not going to try dragging you on the run with me, don't worry. You'd only slow me down, and cause me a piss-load of trouble besides. No, Phoebe, my love, I'm taking you only as far as I need to get away from Interpol before the troops come flying in this morning. You were my ticket out of the riad without having to shoot Peaches. I've got my getaway all planned, don't worry. My organization is far more extensive than anything I had established with Toby. Even you'd be impressed, methinks. Also, I don't want it to end like this between us. Cutting me loose has left me gutted. I'd hoped we could end things on a brighter note."

"What do you mean I cut you loose? You've been loose from the day we met. I've been your lead to the next heist all along, you (insert colorful expletive) butt-licking bastard!"

He whistled between his teeth. "Now, that was an interesting one, but for the record, I did follow you as much to keep you safe as anything else. That's how it began, honestly. I wanted to see you again, hold you in my arms, kiss you and more—always more. Our mores were something else, weren't they? We've had some—hell, makes me hot just thinking about it—wild times. Remember that night on the roof in Cappadocia? Anyway, I was late grappling on to the value of what you were after. When I saw the Moroccan family tailing you in Venice, I realized the stakes must be higher than I thought so I began to dig around."

"And you discovered that there was a valuable hoard buried inside the riad."

"Thanks to you, yes, exactly. The Moroccan family got in my way once or twice, but shit, they were such amateurs that you and Peaches easily took care of them—nice work, by the way. And then I spent a few days digging around Marrakech and discovered that a sultan, Abu Abd Allah al-Burtuquali Muhammad, ruler of the Wattasid dynasty, struck up some kind of an alliance with a wealthy Jewish Berber family back in the day, the details of which are obscured by time."

"It may even have been an enlightened union of individuals from three religions."

"You always were a romanticist, Phoebe; it's one of the many things I love about you. Whatever the case, something empowered the Jews to the secrete the sultan's riches against political upheaval—who knows? Those guys had enemies like you wouldn't believe. It's all wrapped up in folklore locally and well worth listening to if you ever get the chance. Anyway, how exactly a sultan's hoard gets buried under the floor of a Jewish family's home may never be fully known, but thanks to you, the treasure itself has been retrieved."

I gazed down at the backpack. "And is about to be lost to the world again. This is significant, Noel, important far beyond the monetary value of its contents. This casket is embedded with symbols celebrating unity among religions instead of the bloody divisions. Doesn't that mean anything to you? It needs protecting! The world needs to see treasures like this for what they are —humanity's attempt to rise above the bloodshed and worship universal good!" Okay, so I was crying again.

"You really care about that stuff, don't you?"

"I thought you did, too. I thought we understood one another, fought for the same things! What about the archaeologist's creed?"

He grinned. "You don't seriously think there is such a thing, do you? Besides, I haven't worked as an archaeologist in over a decade. No, the only creed I follow is my own, and though it pains me to see something with so much history and passion behind it fade into the woodwork, in the end that casket will fetch a fortune on the underground market and those jewels will keep me going for a long time."

"You're contemptible. What is your creed now: take what you want and screw everybody else?" Ahead a ragged bite of mountain cut a sharp silhouette against the horizon and sliced my wounded heart all over again.

"Pardon me for being crude but I'd love to screw you one more time."

"Very funny. You're taking us to the Atlas Mountains?"

"Mountains are a great place to hide. I only need a few days before the dust dies down with a lot of places to hole up in the meantime. Morocco isn't a rich country. They don't have the resources to chase me for long."

A few cars passed us on the highway, a few saddled mules and camels plodding along on the sandy shoulders, too, but otherwise the road was empty. I thought about trying to jump out but he had the child minder lock on. I considered trying to wrest the steering wheel from him but I didn't see how that would end well. For one thing, his gun was in his other pocket and I doubted I'd be fast enough to get it from him. Instead, I sat still, scheming and furious, feeling the press of my phone in my pants pocket. Would anyone track me and who was left standing to do it, anyway?

Recrimination burned deeply. Why was I so trusting? Did love make me blind and stupid, too? I should have never let him into the riad, not that that made a difference in the end. If I was being brutally honest with myself, I still gave Noel too many ins—ins to my heart, ins the riad, ins to my life. Always had. Love was like a squatter: once it set up house, it was hell getting it evicted. My mind said one thing, my heart another. I was so done with this. I needed to change my tact.

"I can't bear to think we're going to end this way, Noel, not after all the years we've sort of been together," I said softly.

The sun had broken through the mountains to pour bloodred light down on us both. "Yeah, Phoebe. It hurts me, too. It's always been you and me, no matter what you think, despite all our differences. What we had together was real but I couldn't just turn myself in and go to jail."

"I could have negotiated a lighter sentence if you had." Having been an almost lawyer, I had connections.

"I'd have died in there, you know that, and besides, do you really see me as living some kind of ordinary life? What would that look like, anyway? Me coming home from work at six every night and watching TV while you knit?"

I snorted. "As if that spells out everything worth living in an ordinary life, and by the way, that sounds pretty damn appealing to me. Life isn't all adrenaline and breathless moments, Noel. There's comfort in having someone you care about nearby on cold nights, someone to hold you when you're hurt and afraid, someone to make supper with on a Friday night plus all those little moments in between. Love breathes life into the ordinary things."

"Sounds like you want a puppy, not a man."

I clenched my teeth after that. We drove for another five minutes until we were at the foot of the mountains with nothing but expanses of scrabbled earth and spotty palm trees all around. He pulled off the road and bumped over the earth to a copse of palms with a flat sandy area nearby and cut the engine.

"This is my rendezvous point and where we part. You can take the car and drive back to Marrakech once my ride arrives. No hard feelings, all right?"

He was gazing at me, one brown arm on the steering wheel, his dark eyes warm and that mouth of his exactly as I remembered so fondly. I leaned over and kissed him. He hesitated only seconds before kissing me back, one hand grabbing mine in case I lunged for his gun. All the passion between us ignited as if all the years and pain didn't exist. He pulled away, breathless. "One more time for old times' sake, my love?" he asked.

"One more time," I whispered.

We were out of the car in seconds, he tossing his gun in the back seat in case I tried to grab it and then locking the door. No one was around but the car shielded us from the road just in case. He furled his jacket on the sand, Sir Walter Raleigh–style, and beckoned me to lie down.

I smiled and shook my head. "You first."

"You always were my woman-on-top kinda girl," he murmured into my hair as he embraced me.

"And don't you forget it." My hands were under his shirt and exploring, a familiar electricity hitting my vitals as I touched him in all those secret places. In moments he was on the ground with me on top of him, our kisses wild and fevered, nothing forced, nothing feigned. I had his pants down and mine half-off when I pulled my phone from my pocket, held the home button down along with the volume button, and pressed the phone against his bare skin. I whispered into his ear: "Thank you for making this so easy for me."

A jolt of real electricity zapped beneath my fingers as the man beneath me flopped still.

23

 all, dark and tasered was a good look on him. Lying there bare-chested with a rectangular burn below his heart, he'd never looked so fetching or so dead. For a moment, I thought I'd killed him, but no, he still had a weak pulse. I dropped the blistered chunk of phone into the dust beside him. The taser app worked fine but destroyed the phone, seared my good palm, and nearly killed the victim, too. I had to remind Evan to tweak that feature. If there even was an Evan. Shit! *If there even was an Evan!*

I buttoned my shirt and snatched the keys from Noel's pocket, ripping off the wire from inside his jacket while I was at it. I took his phone and wallet, too, and then started up the car before returning to try dragging the limp man into the back seat. Though lean, he was still heavy, and with both hands injured, I lacked my usual leverage. And then I heard the unmistakable sound of a helicopter far in the distance.

Shielding my eyes, a speck like a faraway bug could clearly be seen heading my way. I had expected a car for the rendezvous, not a bloody helicopter! In seconds, I was behind the wheel, forced to leave Noel and take off while I could. I doubted I could outrun a car, but I knew I couldn't outrun a heli-copter. And then there was the little matter of the loot in the front seat. Once they found Noel dishabille and the bag missing, presumably they'd come gunning after me. I also had to factor in the fact that by taking Noel's phone, I may have made it easier for them to track.

I pushed down the window and reluctantly tossed the phone. Damn. I'd hoped to use it to call the police. If lucky, maybe I'd get a half hour head start before Noel's team realized what had happen.

Turns out, I got less. Fifteen minutes after I'd started zipping down the highway, that helicopter was trailing behind me. The traffic had picked up. What would they do, shoot the car full of holes like they do in the movies and not care what collateral damage they caused along the way? Maybe they'd try to run me off the road, then drop down and pick the loot out of the wreckage. What did I know? There were plenty of places for a helicopter to land in this desert flatland.

Quick decision time. I whipped off the highway into the parking lot of a gas station complex. The possibility that the car was identifiable or trackable was too high a risk. I dashed into the adjoining leather shop and bought a tooled and beaded camel-skin bag from the money in Noel's wallet. Moments later I had the casket transferred into the bag and left Joe's backpack in the bathroom.

In the truck stop minutes later, first I tried to use the phone. No problem except I had no idea of local area codes or even who to call exactly and my efforts to communicate with the attendant too fraught. What if I called the regular police, then what? Imagining the questions I'd answer while carrying a fortune in my bag and leaving a tasered man by the side of the road didn't bear thinking about. Next, I tried negotiating a ride to Marrakech with a tractor-trailer driver. Whether the language barrier was to blame or some company policy, none of the guys smoking cigarettes and drinking coffee would give me a lift at first, at least until I flashed a few American dollars. Then I was overwhelmed with offers. I finally settled on a delivery guy packing a trailer load of dates to the city.

By the time I'd hurried Salim out the door, the helicopter was in the distance heading back toward us with two more far in the distance. If Salim thought it odd that I leaped into the truck's cab without so much as a hoist up or an official invitation, he didn't say. Besides, he didn't speak English and I didn't speak Arabic. That left a long ride back to Marrakech in a cab full of smoke and Moroccan pop music. I kept the window down, so tense I thought I'd snap in two. Forty-five minutes later, I thanked Salim as he dropped me off near the square and I jogged my way through the medina to the riad.

This time, armed uniformed men packing machine guns surrounded the riad. When I identified myself and held up the bag to prove I was who I said, the bag was whipped from my hands and I was promptly marched inside at gunpoint. All that mattered was Peaches and Evan. By then I didn't care about anything else, not the treasure, nothing.

"Phoebe!" Peaches cried when she laid eyes on me. "My God! I thought he'd dragged you off somewhere!"

"He did. We managed one last tender moment before I tasered him." We hugged, her squeezing the breath out of me. "Thank God, you're okay. What about Evan?"

Agent Walker stepped out from the tangle of uniformed men. "Phoebe McCabe, you never cease to amaze me."

"What about Evan?" I repeated.

Sam Walker gazed at me with his cool blue eyes. "He's been taken to the hospital with two bullet holes and a lot of blood loss. I'm waiting for an update but the last I heard he was still alive, that's the main thing. Otherwise, there's one woman down, two men with a head injury, and another two on their way into headquarters for questioning."

Over his shoulder I saw Mohammed and one of the other riad helpers mopping up the tiles.

"And Noel Halloren is by the side of the highway unconscious, I hope half-dead," I said.

"We've got helicopters out there now. If he's there, we'll get the bastard. Peaches filled me in on what happened."

"I shot June," Peaches said, "and Amira helped by tripping the bitch. Didn't kill her, though. My bad."

I nodded, part of me too numb to take any more in.

* * *

BACK IN VENICE DAYS LATER, the world had taken on a different cast. It had become a noticeably colder universe for me, slightly less infused with the exuberance in which I had previously viewed it. The colors were still clear in my retina but how I saw them had shifted—darker, deeper, richer. But no, just for the record, I was nowhere near depressed, just sadder and wiser.

"Phoebe, thank you again for all you have done," Nicolina was saying. "If it were not for you, we may never have known why Maria was killed or by whom," she continued.

We were sitting in the Contini villa salon with the Bartolo hanging in pride of place over the mantel. The police had located the missing painting tucked into a closet at Amira Alaoui's shabby apartment and now it hung triumphant and undamaged. I could not take my eyes off it, specifically at the hexagram outlined in what must have been knotted gold silk beneath the bride's feet.

"If it were not for you, we may never have known many things," Nicolina continued, looking up at the painting. Those things were too numerous to outline yet again, thankfully—Evan Ashton and Sir Rupert Fox's true roles, Noel Halloren's modus operandi, Zara's unwitting duplicity, and it went on and on. All of it was more than I could process right then. All I wanted to do was crawl inside some quiet place and pull the covers over my head but I had the feeling that the world would always find me anywhere I went.

"I will give the Bartolo to a museum here in Venice, possibly the Galleria dell'Accademia. It memorializes a marriage in Venice and should return to Venice," Nicolina said, but I was hardly paying attention.

"There are lots of things we might never have known without my Phoebe," Max said from the couch beside me. He had flown in the day before and our conversations had been intense ever since. Try telling a man that you tasered his son in a moment of passion. The fact that the son was a bastard was borderline irrelevant; the fact that he still managed to get away with his crimes may have been a comfort to Max but not to me. Noel's helicopter team must have picked him up and whisked him off to safety. My only consolation was that he'd bear a phone-sized brand below his heart for life, a permanent reminder of just how hot Phoebe McCabe can get.

"Look," I said, getting to my feet. "I just have to get out for a walk, do you mind?"

Nicolina and Max erupted at once. "Phoebe, are you all right?" "Shall we come with you?" I don't know who said what.

"No, thank you. I just need to be alone for a bit. Stay here, both of you. Please."

After all, it had been three full days of interrogation, first with the Moroccan authorities and then with Peroni, plus all the endless, convoluted discussions with Sam Walker and my friends in between. And then there was the treasure, a hotly contested item that would be tied up in international courts for a long time—found on Moroccan soil on property owned by an Italian estate. Untangle that one, if you can. At least it was in "public" hands, whatever its ultimate destination, and I had my photos and my convictions. There was a story there that needed to be released to the world, not that I believed for a moment that it alone could change the world. Still, every story of hope counted.

I just needed to leave it all behind and blow some fresh air into my thinking.

"Sure, darlin'," Max said, rising. Nicolina stood, too, both of them casting worried looks at me with the two bandaged hands and what they believed to be my broken heart. If they could see through my shirt, they'd discover that the heart in question hadn't broken so much as hardened to a tensile strength.

I left them standing there and strode into the hall, snatching up my carpetbag where I'd dropped it by the door. The thing was in rough shape, its seams slit and the battered Ottoman kilim textile carefully cut away to reveal the leather interior. There was a metaphor to be had there. Carrying it under the arm was the only possibility now that the handle had been sliced off.

I passed Seraphina in the hall but barely acknowledged her presence. Her friend Zara might yet be charged as there were unanswered questions about how much the family retainer had suspected about her niece and nephews' actions. By default, Seraphina herself might have in some way obstructed justice by not disclosing her own suspicions earlier. She'd had them, I was sure of that. Not my problem either way. Let somebody else figure it out.

In the spring sunshine, moments later, I inhaled deeply and took a left-hand turn outside the villa to avoid again seeing the smoldering and heart-breaking remains of the warehouse in the other direction. Thinking too long on everything that had been lost was more than I could bear.

"Phoebe, wait up!" I turned. Peaches was striding down the street toward me carrying a package. She had taken off on a shopping expedition that morning, determined to update her look, Italian-style. "I've commissioned a leather pantsuit like you wouldn't believe—made to measure, since that's the only way I'd ever get something to fit my booty. What, is everybody size two in this country? They'll even ship it to London for me. Whoa! What's wrong?"

Did my face reveal that much? "I decided to get out of the villa for a while. Max and Nicolina are still there chewing things over but I'd had enough." I continued walking.

"Don't blame you. Would you rather be alone?"

"No, join me if you want. Just don't talk about what happened. I'm done."

"Yeah, okay." She fell into pace beside me, which meant shortening her steps considerably. "May I ask where we're going?"

"I'm not sure exactly but I'll know when I get there."

"Yeah, sure."

We carried along aimlessly, enjoying the warmth and sunshine, the brilliant sense that a fresh new season could override all the pain of the months before. We paused by shop windows to admire a piece of Murano glass or maybe an interesting hat or just anything that caught our eye. Eventually we stopped at a café to order cappuccinos even though the Italians didn't believe in drinking milky coffee that late in the morning.

Sitting there gazing out at the Grand Canal, Peaches tapped my hand. "Mind if I ask one question?"

I caught her eye. "I know what it is."

"No, you don't."

"Yes, I do. It's about Evan, right?"

She sat back and frowned. "Yeah, right. So when are you going to talk to him?"

I sighed, looking away. "I haven't decided. So far, I've just sent him an email to say 'get well soon,' which I thought suitably banal."

"Yes, really. If he knows you at all, he'll know that you reserve such heart-felt messages for houseplants or something."

I laughed. "I'm hoping he'll translate it to mean that I need time to think things through. As for Foxy—can I even call him that now that I know he's been acting in the interests of the law? Anyway, *Sir Rupert Fox* has sent me endless texts with updates, even though I have yet to respond to a single one. It seems that Evan has been recovering reasonably well in a London hospital where they airlifted him a couple of days ago. That's all I know."

"You're not really mad at him, are you? I mean, seriously, if he was under-cover he couldn't exactly tell you what he was up to."

"I thought we weren't going to talk about this? But no, I understand perfectly why he did what he did. It all makes sense."

"And yet? Why do I hear a 'yet'?"

And then my phone rang. Pulling it from my pocket I stared down at the call identifier. "Sir Rupert Fox. Again."

"Are you going to answer it this time?" Peaches asked.

I pushed the end button. "I think not. When we get back to London tomorrow I'll have that conversation. Today I'm not ready and right now I have something left to do." Getting to my feet, I shoved the phone back into my pocket.

Peaches moved to stand but I waved her back. "Finish your cappuccino, my friend. I'll just be a minute."

I had caught sight of what I needed while passing along the canal a few minutes earlier and now it was time to do the deed.

The big steel box piled with garbage bags was positioned beside the canal waiting for pickup and, like any malodorous trash heap, worth avoiding. However, I walked straight toward it. If there really was such a thing as an agency for the ancient lost and found, it most certainly needed a virtual dumpster for the letting go part. We all needed one and it didn't matter where.

Pulling my mangled carpetbag from under my arm, I silently thanked it for keeping me company through so many adventures. It had been my amulet, my comfort through all my travels, as much a physical bolster as an imaginary friend. *Release what no longer serves you* applies equally to people or objects. Both can hold you back when you need to move forward. Without a backward glance, I tossed my battered companion of a decade into the dumpster and walked away, strains of *Time to Say Goodbye* streaming on autorewind in my head.

I was halfway down the street when my phone buzzed again.

Pulling it from my pocket, I read Foxy's text:

Phoebe, this silence on your part is extremely distressing (angry emoji). We must talk in person. Please come to see me at once when you arrive in London. We have work to do, and do it together we must. Already I have been presented with a lead for our efforts in the ancient lost and found department. This cannot wait.

Your colleague and, I trust, friend still, Rupert

I smiled and turned off my phone.

THE END

AFTERWORD

Like many works of fiction, this novel names real historical personages without recounting actual historical facts. The painter Domenico di Bartolo was a Sienese painter most noted for his fresco *The Marriage of the Foundlings* upon which the painting described in this book is based. However, I took license with the details of the painting as well as with the backstory described.

One thing that is verifiably true, however, is that both Bartolo and the celebrated artist Carlo Crivelli painted detailed carpets into some of their works and it is this point that inspired *The Carpet Cipher*. Everything else is unapologetically fiction.

THE CROWN THAT LOST ITS HEAD

THE AGENCY OF THE ANCIENT LOST & FOUND 2

Agency of the Ancient Lost & Found

Book Two

THE
CROWN
THAT
LOST
ITS
HEAD

JANE THORNLEY

PROLOGUE

*A*révalo Castle, Spain
   12:45 a.m., July 24, 1568

IT WAS an unholy night when the man in the black velvet cloak, accompanied by a pair of soldiers and two priests, approached the tower. Despite the warm evening, a gusty wind blew across the plains, forcing the men to duck their heads as they approached the fortress walls.

The gatekeeper recognized the man in black at once and bid the group to enter without a word. This was not the first visit the king's secretary had paid to their special prisoner but he prayed it would be the last. Still, the presence of the two priests puzzled him. Surely it was still too soon to administer the last rites?

The five men trod the torchlit halls without speaking, focused on the task ahead. One priest held a velvet pillow upon which rested a priceless object covered in a silken cloth while the other gripped a Bible as if the holy book was all that kept him on this side of the earth. Meanwhile, the soldiers kept their eyes fixed straight ahead, their faces expressionless as they left the corridor and trudged up the stone stairs to the very topmost floor of the tower. Only one prisoner was held here.

The guard, dozing on his stool by the door, awoke with a start and leaped to his feet. Seeing the king's secretary, he bowed deeply. "My lord, our prisoner d-does not rest this n-night," he stuttered. "He flings himself against the window attempting to take flight and still refuses to eat or drink." Straightening, he shot a nervous glance at the priests and bowed again.

"Have you administered the draught as I have bid?" the man inquired.

"Yes, my lord, though the prisoner drank but a small amount before throwing the goblet at the wall. He will not drink more. Says that he has been abandoned and desires only to die."

At that moment, a wail escaped the room, such a heart-wrenching reverberation of voice on stone that it was as if some poor creature had been dragged to hell while clinging by his nails to the walls. The sound echoed for a second longer before petering to a pitiful whimper.

The king's secretary closed his eyes briefly. When he opened them again, his handsome face was pained. "In the king's name, I demand that you pay no heed to any sound that issues from this room this night. Should you disobey my orders and an alarm be called, you will pay with your life."

"Yes, my lord, of course, my lord. I hear nothing, nothing. The prisoner, he screams and cries most every hour. We hear nothing, nothing."

"Pass the keys and go," the man commanded.

The guard, daring not to raise his gaze another time, took the ring from his belt and made to insert the iron key but one of the soldiers intercepted—a cue for him to make his escape while he still could. The iron bar clanged overhead as he bolted down the steps.

At last the wooden door flew open and the king's secretary stepped into the room accompanied by the priests. He was accosted by a sight pitiful enough to give him pause even for one unused to pity. The well-appointed room, fitting for the status of its charge, lay in shambles. The red brocade bed curtains hung in shreds, the furniture tumbled over, food smeared on the floor. The crucifix that had been bolted to the wall now lay upside down on the floor, and the air reeked with excrement. The secretary forced himself not to visibly recoil. "Your Highness?"

The heap of torn clothes in the middle of the soiled floor twitched and lifted its ravaged head. "Why has he forsaken me?" he whispered.

The secretary fell to one knee. "You are not forsaken, my prince, but soon will be honored in the manner to which you were born. Your veins flow with royal blood and it is time to meet your destiny. Your Highness, your coronation day has arrived."

"My coronation?" The man stirred, for he was a man, after all, though one deformed by nature and left broken by those who knew not how to give him love.

"Your Highness." The secretary rose, bowed again, and smiled. "We have brought your crown." He flicked his fingers and the two priests stepped forward, one unfurling a silk ermine-lined cloak, the other revealing a jeweled crown glimmering in the torchlight as it rested on the velvet pillow.

The man stumbled to his feet. "Mine?"

"Yours," the secretary said with a nod.

"Fine as my father's, yes?"

"More so—more beautiful, more sacred," the secretary assured him.

"Sacred?"

"Sacred, yes. We shall crown you, my prince, and you will become Holy Roman Emperor of all that lies above and all that lies beyond—king of the realms. Your power will extend far beyond your father's as you will be rendered immortal and rule forever more."

"Immortal?" the broken man asked. "But I have wished...only to die. My father has...forsaken me," and he began to cry.

One priest draped the ermine robe over the man's shaking shoulders and stepped quickly away while the other held the crown aloft and began chanting in Latin. The king's secretary retrieved an upended chair and set it in the center of the room. "Sit, my prince. You will live anew and we shall worship you forever more."

"The day has come?" the man asked, gazing at the man with his one good eye, the other now so infected it looked like a bloodied egg.

"It has," the king's secretary stated. "And I have brought you wine to celebrate and to help us anoint you in this holy moment. Drink, Your Highness." He passed the broken man a goblet into which he had poured a liquid from a silver vial. "Drink deeply this night so you will live again."

"Live again?" The man tried to smile as he took the goblet with his filthy hand and began to drink, the red liquid dribbling down his beard and onto the ermine robe.

The priest holding the crown stepped before him and bowed. "Your Highness. I crown you King of the Holy Forever."

"Yes, yes, I will be king...king," the broken man said, rocking back and forth as the crown was placed on his deformed head. "King...king...king!"

The men watched in silence until the crowned man began to still, the priests crossing themselves and praying while the draught took hold. Moments later, the broken man's eyes glazed over and his ruined head fell back against the chair. A priest rushed to brace him before he toppled, one hand keeping the crown in place. "Call the soldiers, my lord. It is time," he whispered.

The king's secretary snapped his fingers and the soldiers entered, both holding mallets and fists full of bolts.

"What we do tonight, we do in Your name," one priest whispered, averting his gaze as a soldier took the first blow.

1

One evening early in September, I reluctantly agreed to take my first social foray outside my flat for a private function at the British Museum. The idea was to present my electronic business card for the Agency of the Ancient Lost and Found while pumping up the volume on my previous exploits like some TV host pushing season two—from six feet away.

In case I lost my gumption, I brought along my extroverted friend and colleague Penelope Williams, aka Peaches, for moral support. Peaches didn't do introversion. She just got on with things.

A small cluster of guests and dignitaries had been brought in after hours to commemorate the repatriation of a beautifully preserved Roman slipper that our agency had located many months before. Since the slipper still bore its decorative leather tooling and was perhaps one of the earliest examples of fine Italian shoe design found in Britain, it had attracted lots of interest. I half expected Ferragamo to drop by, as if "dropping by" actually happened anymore.

The museum gave the slipper prominence in Room 49: Roman Britain, where we now stood properly distanced in a semicircle around Dr. Wong. The director of Roman Antiquities was speaking on how the importance of the find helped to understand life in Roman-occupied Britain. The topic would normally interest me but I was edgy and fearing contagion everywhere.

"Is that Sir Rupe I see standing on the other side?" Peaches leaned down to whisper, looking magnificent in a tailored rust Italian pantsuit with a matching patterned face covering. Somehow she even made virus avoidance look fashionable. My mask, on the other hand, was of the surgical variety and probably looked more like a diaper. It was testament to my state of mind that I didn't yet care about the optics.

I couldn't see over the glass display case but Peaches, being taller than most humans, commanded the view. "Probably. He'd finagle a way into an event like this," I said.

"He looks thinner," she whispered.

"Thinner, as in sick?" I asked, stifling my concern. I might be annoyed with him but I'd always cared about the guy.

"Maybe, but I presume he used lockdown to recover."

I nodded. He'd been under a doctor's care for pneumonia the last I'd heard but admittedly we were out of touch. "Is he alone?"

"Evan's not with him, if that's what you're asking."

That's exactly what I was asking. I hadn't seen either Sir Rupert or his supposed right-hand man since our last mission, which was followed by the global quarantine. Actually, I almost relished the distance since I had put my heart into self-isolation. I needed time to adjust to the new reality there, too. "Look, as soon as Dr. Wong stops talking, I'm bolting. I'll leave you to do the promotion, if you don't mind. I still don't feel up to socializing."

"You've got to meet with him sometime, Phoebe. May as well get it over with."

Dr. Collins, the stunningly photogenic professor of British History at Oxford, shot us a visual *hush* from her position across from me. A reporter stood equally spaced on her other side recording on his phone, while six feet to my left a masked Interpol agent was looking pleased with himself. I nodded at the man, who I'd worked with before. Interpol hadn't had much of a role to play in this particular acquisition but somehow managed to take most of the credit. I didn't care about that, either.

At last, a chorus of polite clapping erupted in which I quickly joined while saying to Peaches, "Sorry to leave you holding the virtual cards but I'm out of here. You stay and do the well-spaced networking thing, if you want. I'll see you back at the fort."

I successfully worked my way through the gathering without breaching the spacing protocols while easing my way toward the gallery door, thinking only of a speedy escape. I'd miscalculated: this was a museum of treasures. There were guards and rules, most taken seriously.

"Sorry, madam," said the uniformed masked man blocking the gallery door. "We ask that all guests remain in the designated area until such time as the event is over and we can escort you to the main entrance—for security reasons, you understand."

"Of course. You can never be too careful." Trapped, then. I smiled as graciously as I could before remembering that I wore a mask. So how was I to communicate acquiescence now? I turned on my heels and walked straight into Rupert.

"Really, Phoebe, you did not think you could avoid me forever, did you?" he asked, lifting his paisley silk mask.

I stepped back. "Rupert. What a surprise. Put your mask back on right now. You of all people need to protect your health."

"I'm very well now, thank you. Actually, I was diagnosed with the dreaded pestilence almost six weeks ago but am recovering, albeit slowly, thank you. I consider myself among the lucky and, furthermore, feel quite secure in present company knowing that you have not left your facility for months."

"I hadn't heard. I'm so sorry."

"Never mind. Let us not dwell. This blasted virus has devoured enough of our energy. My point is that we can now share a bubble together with impunity." Definitely thinner but no less dapper in his Savile Row suit in a fashionably late-summer linen-and-silk weave the color of burnt sugar, he stepped toward me as I took another step back.

"You knew I'd be here, as I did you," he continued. "Indeed, I expressly inquired whether the Agency of the Ancient Lost and Found had received an invitation, seeing as you are responsible for this particular find. Isn't it time that you emerged from the shadows? The Covid restrictions have loosened, which is our signal to rejoin the world, I say. May we speak in private?"

I looked around. "We *are* speaking in private, Rupert. No one is paying us the least bit of attention." In fact, they were still circling Dr. Wong to admire the new acquisition.

He took my arm, leading me back into the gallery toward a far wall where a golden ceremonial helmet held center court in halogen-lit splendor.

"Whatever happened to social distancing?" I muttered.

"Phoebe, this cannot continue. We are colleagues now—not under usual circumstances, I realize, but colleagues nevertheless. Everything I hid from you in the past was absolutely necessary."

"Of course." I moved back until I again stood six feet away. "I understand completely. I can't deny how endlessly useful I've been to all concerned, thief and Interpol alike." The fact that I had been leading my possibly deceased thieving ex-boyfriend to various priceless artifacts for years was beside the point. My only saving grace there was that I had finally nailed the bastard.

"Phoebe, my friendship toward you has never been feigned—well, maybe in the beginning but not afterward. You do understand that, don't you?"

I was staring over his shoulder, straight into the glass case where the glided helmet gleamed coldly in the light. "Of course."

"I have tried to express myself in my letters and emails but I fear my attempts have been clumsy at best," he continued.

I sighed. "Rupert, please just get to the point." He was never known for brevity.

"Very well. Let us forge a new beginning. I have a case for us to crack."

New beginnings were fraught with possible failure, in my view. I found it easier to hide out on the tail end of a minor triumph. "Fine. Of course, we will proceed as colleagues, just not right away. Give it a few more months, maybe until the vaccine has been vetted." I turned, hoping to make another bolt for the exit. "How do I get out of here?"

Rupert snapped his fingers and a guard came dashing over. "Tell Dr. Wong that I must escort our esteemed guest from the gallery immediately as she feels unwell."

"Yes, sir, right away."

Taking my arm again, Rupert steered me into one of the adjoining galleries.

"What, you can just command your way through the British Museum now?"

"I am well known around here, Phoebe. Several pieces on display are here because of my efforts, too, so naturally they know I won't be pilfering anything. If you weren't so modest, they would also recognize you as an asset," Rupert continued.

"I prefer to keep my assets to myself, thank you. Besides, I'm grieving, remember? Lockdown just allowed me to bury myself a little deeper."

"Well, do dig yourself out, Phoebe. If the Agency of the Ancient Lost and Found is to continue its success, you must get back in the game. I know this Noel business has delivered you a terrible blow but we must get on with it and all that."

"Is that the British stiff upper lip thing talking?"

"Even delightful Canadians like yourself know the truth of that old saw. Get back to work, Phoebe, and let the healing begin."

We were now in Room 85, where bust after bust of Roman heads watched us proceed down the aisle.

"Besides, it is not fame I wish for you so much as respect," Rupert continued. "You deserve to be credited for your work in preserving history for posterity, which leads me to the matter at hand. Indeed, I have our first joint assignment, if you'll agree to accept. In fact, it could be a paid assignment, hopefully the first of many to come."

I should have been more enthusiastic regarding the monetary part. Instead, I shook my head at a Roman glowering at me from the shelf. "I'm not ready to go back into the field. Maybe later." I moved on down the row.

"This is a matter of some importance, Phoebe, and time-sensitive. It must be handled speedily and with some delicacy."

"Sounds like a job for Interpol."

"But we are affiliated with Interpol. This is a job for us."

"What could possibly be that important?" I asked, stopping beside a terra-cotta woman from the late Roman Republic missing both hands and not looking too pleased about it.

"A great deal more time is required than we have now to explain the details, but let it suffice to say that it concerns a client who has lost his head, quite literally."

He knew that would get my attention.

"Oh, come on, a headless client?"

"Truly. Please meet me at my gallery tomorrow afternoon at 1:00 p.m. and I will explain further."

He almost had me.

* * *

"You didn't need to wait," I said to Peaches when I emerged from the museum to find her standing near the wrought-iron gates. "But I'm glad you did. Shall we take the tube?" I adjusted my mask, relieved to be back outside with enough fresh air to oxygenate myself.

"Sure. Anyway, by the time I finished chatting and doing the electronic card transfer thing to every museum bigwig in there, I figured I may as well hang around. I was everybody's token woman of color. They practically fell over themselves to introduce me to doctor this and director that and then waited around for me to spew my qualifications."

"And what did you say?"

"I said I was a Jamaican gunslinging engineer who brings art thieves to their knees."

I laughed. "So modest."

"Modesty doesn't cut it when you want to be remembered. I told them that if they needed an ancient item retrieved, we were the ones to do it."

"And then what?"

"And then I grilled a few board members over what they intended to do about the museum's looting in its colonial past. A significant number of objects in that collection were stolen in the name of imperialism, I said. I named a few from Africa. The Oduduwa helmet mask in particular gets my blood boiling. Did anyone even ask if Nigeria wanted it back? It's not like it was taken with their permission. It belongs there, not in England."

"And you watched them squirm."

"Yeah, with pleasure. They all looked hemorrhoidal but that's not going to stop me. This is a conversation we've got to keep on having. If Black Lives Matter, so does black culture. So what did Rupert say?"

"He offered us a job that involves travel, money, and a headless client," I told her as we strolled down Great Russell Street.

"Headless? Fantastic—much less backtalk. I was wondering how long it was going to take before something interesting happened. When do we start?"

"I said I'd have to think about it."

She stopped dead. "What's there to think about, woman? We've been buried alive for months. Let's do something that doesn't involve a computer."

"There's a pandemic in progress, remember? Do you really want to get on a plane right now? Besides, we have too much work to do," I pointed out. "We're only halfway through cataloging our brothers' hoard." Both of them had been art-heisting drug dealers, which had certainly helped us bond.

"So? You'd choose cataloging over travel, funds, and a headless client—are you crazy? Cataloging can wait, headless clients can't. As for the pandemic, we'll take precautions. We are now free to move around the cabin, remember? I hear that plane travel is perfectly safe with precautions. Besides, you and Max need a break from one another."

Initially I didn't see that last point. I'd become good at avoiding my partner/godfather, Max Baker, since our relationship had grown fraught. Our new facility provided lots of room and I tried to remain well-spaced until matters improved.

"Focus, focus, Peaches. Let's finish what we've started," I said while marching on.

At first Max had handled the fallout of the Morocco and Venice adventure rather well, considering. We continued to emotionally support one another through the weeks that followed. Then came Covid, which provided too much time for each of us to mull. After the third FaceTime session, things began to change.

We both had wounds that needed healing. For me, the man I loved turned out to have been using me as a lost-art sniffer dog for years, but since he also happened to be Max's biological son, matters were complicated. I guess we had both underestimated the toll the event had taken on us. Now we were back to working, socially distanced, side by side.

* * *

"I HAVE to ask you again, Phoebe: did you mean to kill him?"

I looked up from where I had been scrolling through my emails. It was the morning after the museum event and we had all been busy at our computers cross-referencing artifacts and emailing experts.

Max stood in the doorway of my temporary office wearing his checkered mask and gazing at me with what had become a familiar pained expression. We were about to have the discussion that had been playing over and over again between us for weeks. None of them had ended any better than I knew this one would.

I lowered my phone. "Max, I know we're both still trying to process what happened so I'm going to try to explain again: I didn't deliberately set out to kill Noel but I wasn't about to let him escape with the treasure, either. What I did, I did out of desperation—"

"And anger."

"And anger, yes, and why not?" I was trying to keep the emotion from my voice. And failing. "Hadn't I just watched him kill one man and attempt to assassinate another, not to mention threaten Peaches and steal a fortune of cultural significance? And that's not even mentioning the way he used me. Yes, I was angry, damn angry, but that doesn't mean I deliberately set out to kill him. That's not who I am. Besides, we don't know I even did kill him, remember? He was unconscious when I left him."

"You tasered him right over the heart and left him by the side of the road for dead!" Max rasped, the pain in his eyes fierce enough to twist my gut. "A man you said you loved, my *son*."

"The taser tool was all I had." Taking a deep breath, I closed my eyes. "I used it to disable him only. The thing was faulty so maybe it zapped too high a charge." It was actually a super-smartphone with a taser app but that was beside the point. This wasn't the first time he'd heard all this.

"He was my *son*."

Here we go again. "And your son, the man we both thought we knew and loved, turned out to be a murderous, thieving, underground vulture. He's not the man you thought he was, Max. He's a man who has been using me for bait for years. Face it: life on the run has turned him into something else."

"He's still my flesh and blood."

I swallowed hard, trying not to cry. I'd done enough crying in the past months to swamp a galleon. "I know, Max, and I'm sorry—sorry that the dream we shared of Noel didn't come true, sorry that he left us both broken. But I absolutely am not sorry I tasered him. I did what I had to do and now all that's left is for us is get past it."

"I just can't, Phoebe, just can't—not yet, anyway." And he turned and walked away. Talk about the walking wounded.

I grabbed a used surgical mask crumpled on the desk and blotted my eyes. Bad idea, I know.

Minutes later, I walked up to Peaches as she stood inspecting the renovated lab and instructing workers to fix some detail. "I'm meeting Rupert this afternoon to discuss our next case. Do you want to come?"

2

I didn't expect this visit to Sir Rupert Fox's gallery to be easy. For one thing, there was Evan, whom I formerly believed to be Rupert's assistant only to discover that both worked undercover for Interpol more or less as equals. That meant that the whole time I thought Rupert an unscrupulous but lovable art dealer accompanied by his bodyguard-cum-driver, he was actually operating undercover with a colleague. My brain needed time to recalibrate.

As we rang the bell to Carpe Diem, Rupert's Knightsbridge by-appointment-only gallery, that afternoon, I was fortifying my backbone with the starch of professionalism. "I'll just remain friendly and courteous and shut down any effort either one of them makes to discuss their duplicity," I said. "To avoid awkwardness, you understand."

"Sure," Peaches remarked. "Why not shake hands while you're at it?"

I was going to say that shaking hands was not recommended given the pandemic but the door flew open before I had a chance. There stood Evan, former MI6 agent, devastatingly handsome man of a million attributes, the least of which was the ability to look at me as if he had more than business on his mind. How a man can look sexy wearing a black face mask was beyond me.

"Phoebe," he said, his eyes alight. "I'm so happy to see you again at last. It's been—"

I extended my hand briefly before pulling it back. How soon we forget. "Too long, I know. Evan, what a pleasure. I trust you've been well?"

I sensed he was smiling behind the mask. "Yes, I've been well. All bullet wounds are healing nicely, thank you."

"Excellent, and you received the Get Well Soon card I sent?"

"A few months back, the one with the red balloons? Yes, duly received." Amusement was definitely twinkling in those fine gray-green eyes. You may find me mentioning those eyes repeatedly.

"The cards were all picked over," I said in my defense.

"Hey, Ev," Peaches said behind me. "Nice to see you again. I read that book you recommended to me, by the way, the one about Renaissance architecture —great read."

She gently moved me aside and enveloped Evan in a big hug, which he returned with gusto. I stood staring, mildly offended by this open display of affection in the age of Covid, yet feeling strangely bereft. But I quickly got over it. Soon we were all strolling into the inner sanctum of the antique haven known as Carpe Diem.

"Excuse me for one minute," Evan said. "Must check on a few details, but Sir Rupert will be along directly." Then he had disappeared.

"'Ev'? And I didn't know you two were in touch," I said.

"So? Every time I brought up his name, you shut me down. By the way, I was only joking about the hand-shaking thing—are you kidding me? That man took a bullet for you."

"What else am I supposed to do—kiss him?"

She would have had a comeback for that but luckily we had arrived at the salon door. Rupert was stepping out to greet us, complete with another interesting face accessory made of pleated silk. "Phoebe and Penelope, I'm so delighted you came. I was momentarily afraid you might decline."

"Thank Peaches," I said. "She convinced me that a headless client was too good an opportunity to miss."

"And a very wise conclusion indeed," he said with a nod. "Please come in. Dr. Collins will explain the details."

"Dr. Collins?" I gazed past him at the illustrious doctor of British Studies at Oxford waving at me from across the room in a red suit and a lovely patterned mask that could be genuine Jacobean.

Rupert stepped aside to let me walk across the Persian carpet to meet her halfway. "Dr. Collins. Great to see you again even if the last time was only yesterday." Her mask, I noted, was fashioned from a scrap of genuine Jacobean vintage fabric, probably dyed in woad that perfectly matched her blue eyes. This prompted my first serious twinge of mask envy.

"Connie, please. Twice in one week—lucky us." She was about to grasp my hands before pulling away and clapping with a delighted grin. "Oh, Phoebe, I'm such a fan. I'd wanted to tell you that but never had the opportunity. Rupert is always describing your exploits so I live in awe thinking how fabulous it would be to chase art criminals around the world and wrest treasures from their gnarly grasps." She plucked the air as if snagging a bad guy midflight.

I could only gape. The esteemed academic television personality was my fan? "I'm flattered," I said. "Make that stunned." I saw no need to mention that most of the bad guys I'd snagged had been either relatives or my ex. A woman needs to embrace kudos where she can.

"You are such an inspiration. All I get to do is babble on about my passions, but you get to go out there and live them. I'd love it if someday you could make a guest appearance on the show, when things become more normal, of course."

Articulate and academic but never stuffy, Dr. Constance Collins was a media personality for a reason. Her popular British history television series delivered the past with doses of style and wit while she held down an esteemed Oxford seat and looked amazingly fetching while doing it. How she managed, I'll never know, but I was as much a fan of her as she of me. "I can't imagine being on TV but thanks, anyway." I grinned back at her. "So what do you have to do with my headless client?"

She slapped a hand to her blond bobbed head. "Oh, it's such a mess, Phoebe. Come, ladies, and I'll explain." Taking Peaches by one arm and me by the other, she steered us over to one of Rupert's clubby leather couches and bid us to sit.

The spacing protocol had suddenly evaporated and I felt this crazy need for a hug, but of course I restrained myself. "Peaches, I champion you on tackling Dr. Wong and crew with your colonial looting statements yesterday. Time to shake up those stodgy male enclaves, right? Tea, anyone?"

And she poured, leaving Rupert and Evan—esteemed members of the stodgy male enclaves—to twiddle their thumbs once deprived of their hosting roles. Both took seats at the opposite ends of a couch across from ours and looked on while Dr. Connie ran the show. Since we were about to take tea, we removed our masks with relief.

"So, let me begin with my qualifier: nothing I disclose here has anything to do with Oxford University, my area of study, my television show, the museum, or even Britain, perish the thought. By necessity, I'm remaining very much behind the scenes."

"In other words, you're not even here," I said.

Connie smiled and nodded her glossy golden head. "Exactly, but when Rupert suggested that you could help, I leaped at the chance. With you being on the covert side of Interpol, perhaps only you can." She waved her phone, which was opened on our website. "He is truly looking for something ancient and lost here."

"He?"

"Your prospective client."

We had a prospective client already? "We're not actually a part of Interpol, only affiliated." I always felt obliged to stress that point. The Agency of the Ancient Lost and Found was funded totally from my brother's ill-gotten gains: I spent his thieving profits in the name of repatriation while he spent time in prison. Seemed a fair exchange given the damage he'd wreaked. Yes, you can love someone and still watch them suffer punishment, one of the unbearable truths I'd come to learn. Even so, that money couldn't last forever.

Connie slipped her phone back into her pocket. "That's why you're perfect for the mission. You can fly under the proverbial radar, the preferred approach right now."

"Okay, now that you've got our attention," I said, "what's going on?"

"It concerns the client I referred to—my brother, as it happens," Connie said.

"Your brother?" Peaches asked.

"Yes—"she clasped her hands "—my brother is the famed British forensic archaeologist Markus Collins. Perhaps you've heard of him?"

Neither Peaches nor I had.

"Well, famed in other circles, then. In any case, his services were requested by an archaeological team in Lisbon recently to help process multiple remains found in an old crypt flooded by torrential rains. The crypt is part of a small chapel built in 1147 but last used for interments in the late fifteenth century. Still, that's no less hallowed ground, you understand. The original church was destroyed in the Great Lisbon Earthquake of 1755 and rebuilt in 1784, but the crypt remained more or less intact until recent flooding. Even after all this time, it's no small matter to disturb the dead."

I nodded sagely. I tried never to do it myself.

"Considerable controversy surrounds the whole thing—disinterment, a forensic autopsy," Connie continued. "The Catholic church doesn't approve such things lightly. The remains had to be removed to an unused morgue for temporary safekeeping, so why not do a few tests while they were at it? They finally received approval to begin the disinterment. Perhaps you caught some of that on the news?" One look at our faces prompted her to hurry on. "Anyway, DNA samples were to be taken to look for general health of the occupants, prevalent diseases during the years of the European Renaissance, and to trace the whole ancestry tangle."

"There is even DNA left after so long?" Peaches asked.

"Oh, yes, where there are bones there is usually DNA." Connie seemed unable to contain her enthusiasm. Death became her. "In 2012, archaeologists found the remains of an adult male under a car park in Leicester that turned out to be King Richard III. You might say he'd been missing in action for a while, seeing as he met his end at the Battle of Bosworth. His identity was only determined through DNA testing. Seems we've been driving over the poor man's bones for decades."

"And he was just left there by his contemporaries?" I said. "I always wondered about that. I mean, a king is a king, right? Were they getting him back for the whole princes in the tower scandal?"

"Which was never proven," Evan said quietly. "What is ever proven to be true that far back in time? Everything is filtered through a combination of current prejudices combined with a contemporary rival's viewpoint, not to mention hundreds of years of supposition." He didn't quite sound like the Evan I knew but more like a man in a suit with a big degree wearing a mask, all of which looked good on him, by the way.

"Yes, exactly," Connie said, sending a beatific smile in his direction. "But back to Markus and this particular situation. An X-ray revealed two skulls in one coffin and that captured everyone's interest from the beginning." We waited as the television host paused for perfect timing. "He—and it was presumed to be a he, by the way—was missing the rest of his skeleton. The other fellow was intact."

Peaches snapped her fingers. "I knew it! Our headless client reveals himself at last."

"Do we know who he is—was?" I asked, itching for the details.

"Ah, there's the rub," our scholar added. "Markus has not yet had the opportunity to take DNA samples, but he's since done enough research to present a working theory identifying the owner. The skull had certain contusions and abnormalities that made it somewhat easy to identify after a little preliminary research. If his assumption is correct, the bodiless skull may be related to the Spanish royal family at the time."

"And the time was?" Peaches asked.

"We're thinking 1568."

"And who does Markus believe this royal skull belongs to?" I asked.

"I have been instructed not to say. He will give you the rest of the story if you agree to help," Connie said.

"Fine but answer me this if you can: does this skull belong to a king, or a prince, or something?" I was leaning forward at this point.

"Probably the minor prince kind of something since the final resting places of all the Portuguese and Spanish kings of the time have been accounted for—to our knowledge at least," Connie said. "This chapel had never been associated with monarchy. And, to heap mystery on top of mystery, the skull of our possible royal chap was found wedged beside an ordinary citizen's remains in the same coffin, almost as if it had been dropped in or stuffed in, perhaps."

I pulled back. "Someone beheaded a crown prince and dropped his skull into another person's tomb and nobody noticed?"

Connie frowned. "Those were dark times, Phoebe. Recorded history only knows half of what went on and leaves us to guess the rest. Now an anonymous party badly wants to find the missing skeleton and unite the bones so that the remains can be buried where they belong," she added.

"And does this anonymous party know where that location is?" I asked.

Connie spread her hands. "Markus is working on that. He has a lead but would rather discuss the details in person. I don't know the complete information myself. There is a certain sensitivity to the whole matter. This may be a piece of Portuguese and Spanish history, after all."

Peaches shook her head. "I still don't get why Interpol wouldn't get involved in finding the remains of royalty."

"Because, Penelope," Rupert said quietly, "and pardon me for being crass, but unless there is clearly something of monetary value involved, Interpol remains officially uninterested."

"Yes, indeed," Evan added. "Interpol has no time to chase skeletons, so to speak, when they are far too busy tracking down stolen art and antiquities pilfered for drug money and arms deals. No, such a plum job as this has fallen to us."

"And you will receive monetary assistance for your efforts apparently," Connie continued. "Markus is willing to fund your efforts to begin with and presumably the anonymous party will fund the rest."

"And if we don't find the skull?" I asked.

"Then at the very least your expenses will be covered before we decide next steps," she said.

"But why even do this?" I asked. "Granted, retrieving an intact royal personage to place in their final resting place is important, but why fund four people to help do it?"

Connie wrinkled her pert little nose. "Well, because, Phoebe—and this is unknown to all but a few—Markus tells me that the missing skull may have been wearing a crown."

3

$\mathcal{T}$racking down a crowned skull that had been missing for over five hundred years wasn't exactly in my skill set. I was more of an art historian with a specialty in textiles and trauma, the latter mine. Apparently, I had the uncanny ability to locate lost artifacts while barely escaping with my neck intact, a tendency that kept me too busy to formally diversify. But I am insatiably curious.

This is a long way around saying that we took the job.

"Besides, we need the money," Peaches remarked as she attempted to sip water with her mask half-off while sitting beside me on the plane, the seat empty between us. She had resolved to poke the bottle up under the mask and toss her head back. As a result, water dribbled down her chin.

I watched in fascination. "Try the straw," I suggested.

Flying post-lockdown was even less enjoyable than I imagined. No in-flight service. Masked crew members. No in-flight service. Hand sanitizer coming out of your ears. No in-flight service. Luckily, London to Lisbon was a reasonably short flight and was frequented enough to ensure that we weren't canceled at the last minute.

As we rode a taxi from the airport into the city later, our faces indented from being masked for hours, it suddenly occurred to me that I was finally back in the wide world. It felt good and a little unnerving, too.

Though it was still only 6:45 p.m., dusk fell early in September and all I could see through the cab windows was a surprisingly modern city with plenty of concrete and spacious boulevards. That changed the moment we headed up one of the nearly vertical streets where the buildings became older, more crowded together, and intriguing all at the same time.

The driver pulled into a narrow side street halfway up a hill and assured us that we had arrived. A tall white balconied building stretched far overhead.

"This is it?" I asked.

"Entrance around corner," the driver said, stirring the air with his finger. "One-way street."

I nodded and hastily paid our fare—by credit card only—and the driver helped us haul our two bags onto the sidewalk before dashing back to his seat to dose his hands like we were plague bearers. At first I felt totally disorientated as masked people squeezed past us on the narrow sidewalk.

"This way," Peaches called, heading up an even narrower road leading off the main street. Slinging my backpack over my shoulder, I followed, glad that the two of us had decided to travel lightly.

We were to stay at one of Lisbon's Airbnbs, which Rupert insisted made the perfect cover for our under-the-radar operation. Let me just say that I would never have put the name Sir Rupert Fox and Airbnb in the same sentence otherwise. Rupert owned a house in Belgravia and a country estate. Rupert did not do tourist class. However, given that he had been playing an act for all the years I'd known him, who knew the real Rupert in action?

I had agreed to let the Evan and Rupert duo make the accommodation reservations but insisted on flying by ourselves, as if that small measure of independence meant anything. Whether I liked it or not, our working lives were inextricably connected to Sir Fox and Evan Barrows.

"This is the place, all right," Peaches announced once we crammed ourselves onto a strip of sidewalk outside a large door, "and according to Ev, we have maybe forty-five minutes to check in, change, and get our tails off to supper somewhere up there." She had her phone in one hand while thumbing over her shoulder toward the mostly vertical streets. Meanwhile, I rang the buzzer.

"Are we meeting Dr. Collins there?" I asked.

"I think so—over supper. Ev didn't say who was on the guest list."

After being checked in by an amiable young woman with excellent English who plied us with maps to all of the local sites, we quickly showered and changed inside our spacious two-bedroom apartment.

"Wow, look at this place," Peaches enthused while gazing over the terracotta rooftops of our balcony as the last of the sun bled away over the horizon. "You take the bathroom first. I'm just going to stand here and admire the view."

I opened my backpack travel bag and stared down into my clothes. Since I'd exchanged roller bags for an adaptable satchel-cum-backpack that I could run with if necessary, my options had become more limited. My one nod to style was that this backpack was created from an old Turkish carpet—a carpet backpack.

Lifting out a blouse and pair of black corduroy pants to wear with my jacket, I strode to the bathroom. The jacket, a gift from an Italian friend, had multiple pockets, secret receptacles, and a built-in gun holster, currently empty.

Minutes later I emerged, trading places with Peaches, and twenty minutes after that, Peaches left the bathroom smelling like a piña colada. She had changed into a bright pink printed dress under a Chanel-style jacket with her long brown legs ending in a pair of booties. There'd be a mask to match the outfit, I knew. Once she'd traded the island vibe for high street fashion, she embraced style with gusto. On the other hand, I was more of an arty disaster dresser, more Bohemian than anything. However, now that we were on the move, I had managed to pick up a few dozen nice masks at Heathrow.

Turning my gaze away, I scanned the living area, only vaguely taking in the open plan and tastefully neutral decorating scheme. "I thought maybe they'd leave us a message or something."

Peaches stepped back into the room. "Who?"

"Rupert and Evan."

"You set the terms for how we work together, remember?"

"All I did was keep up the courteous and formal thing."

"Maybe warm and friendly would be a good start. Aren't we establishing relationships here? That's what you always tell me when I'm yelling at the contractors."

"Right, so do I look presentable?" I studied my reflection in the mirror, carefully adjusting my knitted pre-Raphaelite-inspired Melancholy wrap, admiring the multiple shades of green and mahogany that played nicely in the lamplight. It went so well with my black jacket and millefleurs shirt, with the black face mask adding to the look.

"You could use some color. How about I lend you a scarf in a lighter shade of gloomy?"

"Thanks but I'm just not into bright."

"Stop thinking depressed is a color group. Besides, you're seeing Evan tonight and Evan is a good-looking male who adores you." She studied me carefully, her hair pulled up in a classy topknot in comparison to my free-form curly mass. "You could do with a dose of good-looking male after the Noel shitstorm."

I shook my head. "No, thanks. I'm on the rebound from a broken heart, remember? The last thing I want is another relationship."

"Oh, stop. You took a hit in the heart like most women do at one time or another. Get over it. Sure, your hit was more like a nuclear explosion but so what? The wrong man sucker-punched you. Now it's time to notice the right man and give him a chance to show you how love is done."

"Are you speaking from experience? From your own admission, you haven't found your 'right man,' either."

"Which doesn't stop me from looking. As soon as I find someone man enough to be with a woman like me, I'll let him in. Until then, I'll keep my door ajar. Besides, your right man is right under your nose. Tall, handsome, makes breakfast, takes bullets for you, adores you—or haven't you noticed?"

Whether I'd noticed or not was irrelevant. Yes, Evan and I had always flirted, but after the Noel fiasco I was done with romance. My fault lines ran too deep. Besides, it was humiliating being played the fool by one man under the knowing scrutiny of another. "I'm not interested."

"Like hell you're not. Do you think those looks you two exchange are fooling anybody? Besides, my mom used to say to always get back on the horse that threw you, and Ev looks like a horse worth riding no matter how hard he bucks. In fact, the harder, the better!" She belted out a dirty howl.

I sighed and tapped my watch. "Let's get going. We only have fifteen minutes to find this place."

Armed with a tourist map, we stepped out the main door of our building and started striding upward, our phones in our hands. *Upward* alternating with *downward* were the operable words for Lisbon, I was to discover. Occasionally we had to weave into the street or against a wall to avoid oncoming foot traffic.

My thighs groaned as we trudged up the steep hill beside tile-walled buildings and narrow streets with treed boulevards opening up at adjacent corners. Everything seemed a jumble of old and new, of intensely vertical with pockets of spaciousness here and there. It was charming. Sometimes I'd pause long enough to stare into a shop window or admire the tile work paving a building, but mostly I kept on climbing.

Twenty minutes later, we paused. "Are we lost?" I panted.

Peaches may have made a face. "Probably." She flagged down a passerby and pointed to the address on her phone. Somehow the man managed to provide directions from six feet away.

"Ever notice how here people don't look at me like I'm black? I'm just a person among many," she said minutes later.

"Didn't notice—sorry." Peaches made a point of teaching me about the black experience, and no matter how difficult it sometimes became from my position of white privilege, I resolved to take it on the chin. That evening she wasn't inclined to be too forceful with her punches.

We crossed the street, ambled through a tiny square, and began climbing again, this time up a narrow cobbled street that curved away from the main artery. The streetlights beamed down on little shops and residences forming a wall of illuminated windows. I was appreciating Lisbon more and more.

"This is the place," Peaches announced as we stood outside a tiny restaurant. "But it looks pretty squeezy in there."

I peered through the window. Several tables had been spaced around the room but many seemed to contain whole extended families. "This is the address. Let's go," I said, stepping to the door.

Inside, privacy was impossible even with the table spacing. I thought that we must have the wrong spot until I glimpsed Evan waving at us from the back of the long narrow space. I interrupted the hostess and pointed. She smiled and waved us through.

Somehow Evan had found us a room tucked way in the back of the eatery. Granted, the space was the size of a walk-in closet with seating for ten now reduced to six, but at least it was private. Besides, the walls were plastered with photos of old Lisbon and the scent of food along the way so tantalizing that I felt immediately happy—correction: *happier.*

Both Rupert and Evan appeared delighted to see us.

"First things first," Evan announced before we took our seats. "We can dispense with the masks as we are now officially in a business bubble."

I didn't know there was such a thing as a business bubble but it made sense. I watched as Evan removed his manly black face covering, prompting Peaches and me to remove ours.

"Please place your phones in the box provided along with any smart devices you may have on your person." He pointed to a long narrow receptacle he must have brought with him. "That container will block your signals and protect our conversations against eavesdroppers. The room has already been scanned."

We dropped our phones into the box.

"I suppose you've brought us new devices to replace these?" I asked. I knew he had.

He smiled, an altogether pleasant gesture, trust me. "I did." He passed Peaches and me each one of his modified smartphones. Evan's technological mastery was only one area of his considerable genius.

"I've been lusting after one of these of my very own since Morocco," Peaches said, waving hers in the air. "What does it do—X-ray scanning, bug removal, zapping murderous thieves with a jolt big enough to leave them toast like Phoebe did Noel?"

An uncomfortable pause followed.

"Sorry," she said, looking at me.

"The last device was faulty, Evan," I said after a moment. "It melted in my hand and may have killed Noel, not that that's necessarily a bad thing." I held up my palm to show the square-shaped scar.

He reached out to take my hand but I snatched it away. "Phoebe, I deeply regret causing you even a moment's harm, but as for Noel Halloran, he got exactly what he deserved. The only thing I regret is not being there to witness it."

"Don't worry about it. I just wanted to mention the defect in the interests of quality control."

He held up one of his modified better-than-smart phones. "I have improved the taser feature considerably, including the addition of a smaller charge designed to merely incapacitate the quarry. I've also added a few new killer apps besides. I do hope they are to your liking. A list of features is waiting in your in-box but allow me to provide a brief overview."

Rupert held up his hand. "Another time, old chap. Come sit, ladies. The food here is excellent so we chose this as our rendezvous of choice. May I say that I am most delighted to see you both. Allow me to treat you to supper in honor of our new endeavors. We all must eat, mustn't we?"

Peaches and I took our seats opposite one another while Rupert carried on talking. "Evan has a way of finding the best locales, don't you, dear man?" He sat down himself, unfurling a napkin over his knife-pressed jeans, and smiled. "Wine, anybody? It is a quite delectable red. I must say that Portuguese wines are the unsung heroes of European vintages and this one is yet another of Evan's discoveries."

I risked glancing at Evan—brown hair curling around the collar of the green shirt straining over his biceps, gray-green eyes on me, the warm smile, the way he remained standing until we were seated in some old-fashion notion of etiquette.

"Still acting as the world's best concierge?" I asked him.

He plucked the wine bottle from the table and readied to pour me a glass. "Research is just something I'm good at," he remarked, holding my gaze. "I have other things I'm good at, too. Perhaps you'll permit me to demonstrate someday?"

"Such as pretending to be the loyal servant, which you're clearly not? Were you and Rupert equal colleagues the whole time?" I held up my glass and watched it fill with red liquid, keeping my eyes on the wine not the man. Actually, both had practically the same effect.

"We were undercover, Phoebe," he said with a note of pique.

Right, so he'd always called me "madam" before and now I had to get used to hearing my name massaged on his lips like some sonata in A minor.

Meanwhile Peaches was asking Rupert where Markus Collins was.

"He will be along directly," Rupert said, checking his no-doubt-über smart-watch. "I have yet to meet the gent but spoke to him earlier and found him sounding most distressed. I am certain he will disclose all upon arrival. I trust you found the accommodation suitable?"

Rupert was wearing a yellow polo shirt underneath a tweed sports jacket with a lime-green silk ascot tied at his neck. This had to be his Englishman Does Tourist look circa 1970, but his unusual pallor dampened the effect. I was used to seeing him ruddy and brimming with health the way a man in his fifties should look.

"Fine, thanks," I responded, taking a deep gulp of wine. "Which floor are you two on?"

"Top-floor penthouse." Rupert smiled. "My apologies for commandeering the best view."

I laughed. "I'd expect nothing less. Were all the Airbnb castles taken?"

Evan chuckled. "They were. I couldn't find him a room with a pool, either, so we had to make do. Try the pastries," he urged, offering me a plate of delicious-looking appetizers. Typically, I was ravenous and wondered if it would be rude to take one of each. As if sensing my thoughts, Evan forked over a selection and passed me a plate.

After more bantering, more wine, and enough pleasantries for me to believe this arrangement might actually work, the door flew open and a man slipped inside. In his thirties, bearded, with longish blond hair and spectacles, wearing a mask like a sagging diaper, he looked like he could have been chased by a rabid dog. Closing the door behind him, he tore off the mask and stared at us while trying to catch his breath.

We froze, staring.

"Dr. Markus Collins, I presume?" Evan asked after a few seconds.

"Yes, I am Markus Collins," the man said between gasps. "I recognize all of you...from Connie's descriptions and...thank you for agreeing to help me. I do hope I haven't...dragged you into the maelstrom. Mind if I sit?"

Evan slid out a chair into which the bearded archaeologist collapsed, shooting us all a brief smile before propping his elbows on the table and burying his head in his hands.

"Pass over your phone, please," Evan requested.

Markus looked surprised but plucked the mobile from his pocket without comment.

"Dear man, are you all right?" Rupert asked, leaning forward.

Markus studied us, one by one. The blue eyes magnified behind the wire-rimmed glasses seemed so deeply barricaded into their sockets they could be in hiding. I could see the resemblance in the siblings in the coloring if nothing else.

"I'm still alive, which is saying something." He sat back and dabbed his forehead with a napkin. "How long I can stay that way is left to be seen. I'm sure I was followed here. Mind if I have a glass of wine?"

Peaches leaped into action to fill the man's glass. "Drink up. You look like you need it."

"Let's order our dinners and get down to business," Evan suggested before retrieving menus along with our server and providing translations where needed. Of course Evan spoke some version of Portuguese. Minutes later, we placed our orders, each choosing a dish for sharing before settling in to listen.

"Now tell us what happened, dear man," Rupert began. "I understand that you and your team have come across a rather notable skull."

Markus sighed and shook his head. He was still perspiring heavily but appeared to be trying to pull himself together. After taking several sips of wine, he began. "If only it was that simple, but on the surface, yes, we found a skull missing its skeleton."

"So, only the skull?" I asked.

"Yes. There were two skulls in the coffin that belongs to the original occupant, a Pedro Alavares Fidalgo, who was complete. Initial X-rays indicate that this second skull has strange cranial markings and growth abnormalities."

Markus set down his glass. I had many questions but he quickly continued. "We—we being my colleague, Jose, another archaeologist, and I—needed to remove the coffin lid to investigate further, of course, but as scientists we follow a rigorous methodical system to ensure the contents were not contaminated."

"What about these cranial markings?" I interrupted.

He swallowed and gripped his glass. "The skull had cranial abnormalities indicating that the man must have suffered a severe head injury during his lifetime. However, the most alarming feature was the regular holes encircling the top part of the skull as though something was bolted onto the bone. That it was a crown is only conjecture. From what we could determine, whatever that object was, it was removed some time ago."

"As a result of some long-ago tomb robber?" Rupert said, dabbing his lips.

"Or maybe someone removed the object and hid it for safekeeping," Markus said.

We all looked at Markus dumbfounded. "Seriously?" I said.

"Perhaps. Consider this: presume that initially the skeleton was buried with a possible crown. Later, for reasons we have yet to determine, the skeleton was removed and buried elsewhere, and whether the crown was removed at that time or not, we don't know. All we know for certain is that a skull with cranial deformities and holes indicating the application of a possible permanent headpiece was buried with Senhor Fidalgo minus his skeleton. Otherwise, we have no way of knowing when the headpiece was removed or why or even where the rest of the skeleton lies."

"And you haven't opened the coffin to take DNA samples or whatever you guys do?" I asked.

He turned to me. "No, of course not. We might damage or possibly destroy the contents. There are protocols in any forensic investigation. We are scientists first and always," he said testily. "Oh, Lord, that sounded pompous—apologies. Anyway, we were waiting for more sensitive and modern equipment to arrive from another facility and only used the lab's ancient X-ray in the interim."

"Okay…" I said. Like that would have stopped me.

"Nevertheless, that inferior machine still revealed this extraordinary find," Markus continued. "There were ten coffins in total, all found within Capela de Soa Maria Baptista's tiny crypt, untouched since they were first laid to rest, or so we believed. Once we saw one coffin with two skulls, one with severe skull contusions, we knew special precautions were in order. We knew that we may have found the remains of some minor royal or, at the very least, somebody with some incredible mystery surrounding his remains."

"Indeed," Rupert remarked, looking as if he had just swallowed a bug. "And what precautions did you take exactly?"

Markus sighed. "For one thing, we agreed not to breathe a word to anyone until after we had alerted the proper authorities—standard procedure, you understand—and secondly, we knew we must guard the find until said authorities arrived. Jose and I agreed to spell one another off in shifts. Is there more wine?"

Evan topped up his glass before Markus continued. "Try the appetizers," Evan suggested, passing him a plate.

Markus took the plate but ignored the food. "We had only two nights until the authorities were due to arrive to assess our find—things are still very slow with Covid and we were a skeleton team to begin with, no pun intended. We were taking turns watching the facility overnight while the other slept. All very straightforward, really. Though we had thought about hiring a security watch, that would be like signaling that something interesting was on-site so decided against it."

"Sounds reasonable," I said. "And?"

"And the skull went missing on the second night." Markus took another swig and coughed before gazing at me in abject misery.

"The skull is gone?" Rupert asked, sounding affronted.

"Yes, I have made a terrible mistake," Markus said miserably. "I broke my own cardinal rule and unleashed a Pandora's box."

Rupert leaned forward. "Dear man, will you please fill in the details? How did the skull disappear on your watch? Where were you when it happened? What horrendous crime could you have possibly committed?"

Markus gazed down at the pastries with unseeing eyes. When he lifted his head again, his expression had changed from distraught to bleak. "On that last night, as we were approaching the graveyard shift—no pun intended—Jose received a phone call from his wife saying there was an emergency at home and that he had to leave."

"Leave the mortuary?" Evan asked.

"Yes. We had been doing shifts in pairs with one of us sleeping and the other watching, as I said, but on that last night, he left at 12:15 a.m. Where was the harm in that? we thought. The lab was mostly unused and we had only commandeered it for our purposes under special arrangement with the morgue. Staying with the coffins was only a precaution. No one but a handful of people knew we were there and the facility is well off the beaten track. Who'd be interested in bunch of long-dead remains but a pair of forensic archaeologists?"

"So what happened?" Peaches asked.

"That's just it, I don't know, at least not for certain." His brief attempt at self-control was cracking. "It's not like we had working security cameras in the facility, but I'm assuming it had something to do with my actions between the hours of midnight and 2:00 a.m. While I was sitting around trying to stay awake, I took photographs on my phone of the X-rays for my own use and risked a little online research using the antiquated printer to make copies. In retrospect, I can't believe I did that."

I stared at him blankly. Online research had always been my go-to activity for off-hour pleasure—that and knitting, of course. Nothing he had confessed so far seemed like the crime of the century.

"In other words, I *Googled*." Markus spoke the word as if it was synonymous with "machine-gunned innocent bystanders."

"Googled?" Rupert said, as if that confession was the last thing he expected.

"Yes, but in my defense," Markus went on, "it was rather a boring stint and, thanks to Jose, I already had a few clues as to the identity of the possible interloper. I wanted to learn more. It had to do with the elongated jaw and the other cranial contusions that sent me off on the research trail."

Evan was several strides ahead. "You Googled what, exactly?"

"I Googled search terms associated with royal personages during the relevant years, along with the Capela de Soa Maria Baptista crypt and, on Jose's suggestion, the crown princes of Spain and Portugal in those same years, notably those with possible spinal or cranial deformities."

"In other words, you left a search trail for any hacker prowling the Internet," Evan said, making a steeple with his long fingers. "Either that or someone may have been electronically stalking you the whole time."

"Yes, something I now realize is ridiculously easy if one is technologically astute, which I'm not particularly," Markus said with a groan.

"And the server was not secure," Evan added, as if he saw how it all unfolded.

"I'd been using the Wi-Fi at the old morgue because I didn't want to overtax my data plan. Now that I think about it, I doubt it was secure at all since nobody used it much anymore. I didn't bother to check. Why would I? Would you?" he asked Evan directly, as if trying to shore up his self-defense.

"Always," Evan said. "Internet security is one of the first things I check anywhere I go, especially when dealing with sensitive material. It's also critical that you always tape over the webcam on your computer. The web provides the easiest way to glean every one of your personal secrets these days, almost including your very thoughts."

"So, someone was tracking Markus online?" I asked, finally cluing in, at least partly.

"Apparently," Evan said.

Markus turned to me. "Somebody must have been, right? Thus, I inadvertently revealed our exact interest in the remains, including where we found them and what the coffin contained, and even went so far as to input a few clues as to the possible royal interloper's identity. This included details as to his deformed skull, indicating that the person must have suffered a head injury even before the possible application of the crown." He turned to Evan. "But surely all that couldn't have transpired from a mere hour of searching?"

"More likely that you and your find have been the subject of somebody's interest for some time, old chap," Rupert replied. "Your sister informed us that the supposed violation of those tombs hit the media here in Lisbon a while ago."

"Well, yes. There was controversy but we thought it had died down. Certainly we didn't disclose where we were taking the coffins."

"Wait, who is the suspected interloper missing his skull?" I asked.

But Evan had the deeper, more commanding voice. "What happened next?" he demanded.

"So at 1:25, I took a sleeping bag into one of the adjacent offices and caught a bit of sleep, something I would usually do only if Jose stayed on guard. But this time I couldn't stay awake a moment longer and thought to catch a few minutes rest, only I slept for hours while leaving the lab unprotected."

"Maybe you were drugged?" I suggested.

He looked at me. "I thought of that but that would mean Jose had drugged me, which I seriously doubt."

"Not necessarily. Was the office soundproof?" I asked.

"No. It was just a regular office down the hall from the lab, but I had left the door open and, when I came to, it had been closed."

"So somebody broke in?" Peaches asked.

"It wasn't hard—the outside lock had been jimmied apparently. Sometime between the hours of three and four—my best guess—someone entered the lab and stole the skull from that coffin. Not anything else, you understand, just the skull, and no other coffins were touched. It was a very specific theft, as if the thieves knew exactly what they were looking for. The coffin had been tipped onto the floor and left in shambles. Pedro Fidalgo still had his gold rings but was left in a pile of bones."

"My word, man," Rupert erupted, "but what about this Jose fellow? Could he be a suspect?"

"Definitely not," Markus said as he buried his head in his hands. "Jose was already dead."

4

---

*I*t took several minutes and more wine to get Markus to stop trembling and keep talking.

"It seemed like an accident," he said. "The police will probably think it *was* an accident but I know it was murder. Jose rushed home, taking what I understand to be his usual route—he only lived a few blocks away from the morgue —and he tripped over a curb and hit his head on the sidewalk hard enough to break his neck? What are the chances of that happening? But I'm afraid that's what the police will deduce."

"Initially, perhaps, but they'll figure it out eventually," Evan said, patting the man on the shoulder.

"Yeah," Peaches piped in. "The police are not nearly as dense as people give them credit for."

"I agree that it was too much of a coincidence," I said. "What was the emergency that sent him home?"

"Fire. His wife, Ana, called to say that she smelled smoke in the flat."

"And was the flat on fire?" I asked.

"Apparently," Markus said miserably, reaching for more wine. I stilled his hand, pouring him a glass of water instead. "I spoke to her days ago just after it all happened. She was distraught, of course, but there had been a fire in the basement, quickly put out but real nevertheless. That, too, could have been deliberately set to draw Jose away." He clutched my arm. "Don't you see?

Somebody was already on our tail. They wanted me alone, and had I been awake when they entered the premises, I'd probably be dead, too."

At that moment there was a knock on the door. Our food had arrived, delivered by three servers, all of whom shot concerned glances at the man blotting his forehead with a napkin. Conversation stopped as the plates were delivered and the water refreshed, and Evan drew the servers away with some explanation that set them nodding with sympathy before quietly shutting the door.

"I said that your girlfriend broke off your engagement," Evan said when he took his seat again.

Markus managed a wry smile. "She did, in fact, only months ago."

"Here, eat something. It will fortify you," I suggested. "Did you say anything to the police about the robbery?" I began passing around platters of chicken, fish and baked beans.

"Yes and no." Markus sniffed, staring down at the platters without interest. "I told them there had been a robbery, of course, but didn't disclose the exact nature. They believe that somebody had broken in and tried to plunder the coffins, thinking to steal jewelry and such. Old tombs are always susceptible to looting. The police believe I interrupted the robbery and that the thieves got away with nothing."

"My word, man," Rupert exclaimed while slipping a few sardines onto his plate. These were huge sardines, by the way, and by no means the minuscule canned variety. "What about the skull?"

"I didn't mention it."

Rupert paused. "Why the devil not?"

"Because," Markus said, struggling to control himself. "Because before the police arrived that night, I received a threatening phone call."

My first forkful of chicken and mushrooms paused halfway to my mouth. "From whom?"

Markus shook his head. "It was anonymous—a man with a deep voice, Spanish accent. He said that if I was to utter one word about the skull or disclose those X-rays to anyone, I'd be dead. I didn't know that Jose was dead already but I believed him nonetheless. It's not like I'm used to being threatened. My kind of archaeology is hardly of the Indiana Jones variety. Until now." He stifled a nervous laugh.

"And?" Rupert prompted.

"And I was instructed to destroy any evidence I had, including deleting my search strings—which he named, by the way, so he definitely was hacking me —and he said not to tell a soul about what I found. Or else," he added.

For a moment we were all silent.

"And did you do that?" I asked.

Markus nodded and then shook his head. "Yes and no. I deleted the photos from my phone and cleared the cookies on my laptop but didn't destroy the actual printouts or the two X-rays. How would he even know about those? I had printed out my search results on the cruddy old printer earlier and stuffed them inside my jacket along with the X-rays. I thought, how would this person know if I did or didn't obey all his instructions, and really, why should I? Wasn't it bad enough that he plundered our forensic investigation and possibly the biggest discovery of my career? There were no cameras for the bastard to spy on me. By that time, the shock was wearing off and I was furious." Something hard and resolute burned in his eyes.

"But surely this man knew that *you knew* what you had discovered, meaning…" I trailed away when I realized where that was going.

"Meaning that he actually needs to get rid of me if he wants to erase all the pertinent evidence—I reached that same conclusion. It's either that or he needs me alive for some reason."

"Which means that we're also on the hit list because we now know what you know—cool," Peaches said with a grin. We didn't share the same views on risk management.

"But what about the police?" Rupert asked.

"I saw no one, I assured them, which I didn't. The X-ray machine was never mentioned and the plundered casket spoke for itself." Markus poked a fork at his food but made no move to eat. "I suspect that will be the end of the investigation, which, under the circumstances, is probably for the best."

"My word!" Rupert exclaimed while delicately decapitating a sardine.

"I agreed to have Connie contact you because I don't know how long I can keep this up," Markus continued. "I need your help. I need you to catch these bastards, retrieve that skull, and keep me alive in the process. I have a little money to pay you but I believe I can access more, if needed."

"How did you communicate with Connie?" I asked.

"By the hotel phone." Markus shook his head. "Another blunder, I know."

"Had we that skull, we could use DNA testing to determine if it belonged to a royal personage, I take it?" Evan inquired.

"Yes." Staring at his food, Markus nodded. "The phenotype aspects like the color of the eyes plus geographical origin and the presence of certain mutations would have confirmed what we suspected all along: that the crowned individual was a Hapsburg."

"Hapsburg?" Rupert gasped.

"Wow, a Hapsburg," Peaches exclaimed. "Those are the royals with the mega-jaw, right?"

"Among other abnormalities. This skull had a Hapsburg jaw as well as certain bone markings that indicated the subject had had primitive brain surgery," Markus commented.

"Brain surgery in those days?" Peaches asked.

"It was a rare event, but presumably a royal who could afford the best surgeons in the land might be in enough of a crisis to warrant such extreme measures."

I badly needed to brush up on my European royalty but at the moment I was fixed on separating our allies from our enemies. "Connie said something about somebody offering to help? Is this the source of the money you mentioned?" I asked.

Markus sighed. "Another anonymous contact. That particular message came to me by way of a note shoved under the door of my room. It's in my package."

"Package?" Even asked.

"I brought it with me."

Evan and Rupert exchanged glances. Peaches and I did the same because we caught them doing it.

"Right," Evan said, standing. "We're here to help protect you and track down that missing skull."

"But you must tell us everything. Who do you believe is this hapless head-less Hapsburg interloper? Where are these X-rays and printouts?" Rupert asked.

Markus tossed down his napkin and stood. "Right here. This contains everything I know. You take it. It feels radioactive to me." He reached inside his jacket and brought out a plump manilla envelope, which he held over the table. Both Evan and Peaches reached for it at the same time but Peaches, being closer, won.

"*Perfecto!*" she said, waving the envelope in triumph at Evan. "We'll start here."

Markus took his seat and picked up his fork. "I suggest you study the contents someplace else. You'll need plenty of table space. Maybe we should go back to your accommodations after dinner?"

"Excellent idea," Rupert said, "but can you tell us anything about this anonymous employer in the meantime?"

"He's Jose's friend," Markus commented between bites. "You'll have to read the note."

$\mathcal{I}$t was close to ten o'clock before we finished supper, ending our meals with a plate of the delectable custard pastries the Portuguese call *pasteis de nata* for which I was to develop an addiction. I even took a box back to the Airbnb.

Stuffed and a little buzzed after the wine, we left the restaurant with Markus beside Rupert walking in the middle of the sidewalk and Peaches and Evan taking positions front and back. We were in guard dog mode.

I was left to scan the perimeters for possible stalkers from the rear, something for which I'd had plenty of practice. But the leafy streets and roads were quiet except for the occasional car or tramway slipping by, and the shadowy doorways and narrow alleys guarded their secrets. If anyone was ghosting our heels that night, we saw no sign, making it a quick and uneventful downhill trek to our accommodations.

Less than twenty minutes later, we were settled around the table of Rupert and Evan's penthouse suite beside a pair of double doors open to the cool evening air. The only thing in our line of sight were the tops of the tile-roofed buildings.

Peaches handed me the envelope while Evan made the coffee. Everyone looked on while I placed the pages of Markus's package on the table in some kind of linear fashion. Four poor-quality black-and-white printouts taken from Wikipedia were laid out along with two prints of portraits from the same source. Two brackish, nearly indecipherable X-rays crowned the top, and I placed the plain white envelope from the anonymous contact at the very bottom.

"You can see that my research was very preliminary. I only began to Google after Jose left so I could gain a basic understanding of what our find involved."

The portraits caught my eye immediately.

"Who's this?" I asked, picking up the print of a boy standing in a doublet with an ermine cloak over his shoulders and a castle in the background. Though the copy was muddy, it was clearly of some wealthy offspring in the 1500s, ermine being reserved for only the richest and the royal-est, and doublets a gent's fashion statement of the day. Of course, the castle's curb appeal brought its own cachet.

"Crown Prince Don Carlos of Spain, who died in 1568."

"So you think he's the owner of the missing skull?" I asked, staring at the youth.

"Almost 99.9 percent certain based on the skull alone. Don Carlos had noted spinal deformities plus a serious head injury in his early twenties that resulted in an extraordinary surgery that ultimately saved his life," Markus said. "Verdi made him into the hero of an opera but the truth indicates he was anything but heroic."

"Actually, Schiller was the author of that play and Verdi put it to music," Rupert said, "and it truly was a work of fiction with little relation to the truth therein but the personages themselves."

Evan strode to the table with a tray of mugs and a coffeepot. "That's Don Carlos? By all accounts he was a mentally disturbed young man even before the fall that severely damaged his skull. He wreaked such havoc in his short lifetime that his father was forced to lock him away until his death."

"Ah, yes, Don Carlos," Rupert mused, taking the picture from my hand. "That fine opera based totally on fictional elements was the only known benefit of the poor boy's existence. By all accounts, he was a nasty piece of work who liked to whip girls and torture small animals. I deduced that it might be him. Though inbreeding of European royal families at the time—both Don Carlos's mother and grandmother were Portuguese princesses and his parents were double first cousins—caused numerous genetic issues, I cannot see why a lad such as this would end up in a Portuguese tomb. His parents were buried in Spain."

"There lies the mystery," Evan remarked as he poured a round of coffee for all.

I pointed to one of the articles. "And this Don Carlos had a deformed spine as well as the Hapsburg jaw?"

"He was described as 'hunchbacked and pigeon-breasted' with one leg considerably shorter than the other, but without the skeleton to examine we can't attest to those deformities," Markus said, accepting a mug. Much calmer now, the man simply looked haggard. "Nevertheless, from the skull alone I believe he's our boy, the heir-apparent to King Philip II of Spain."

"*That* Philip II of Spain?" I asked, picking up another portrait of a man wearing an intricately embossed suit of dark armor over white silk breeches and hose. Men knew how to dress in those days. "One of the kings of the Spanish Inquisition, the one who sent the Armada after Queen Elizabeth I?"

Peaches leaned over my shoulder. "He was big on making a statement with his clothes, I see."

"Royalty knew that clothes speak," I said. "This outfit says, 'I am mighty in battle, a born conqueror, and my daddy can beat your daddy any day.' That daddy would be the Holy Roman Emperor King Charles V. Watch out, mere mortals."

"And Protestants," Evan remarked. "King Philip would come to see himself as the defender of the Catholic church and owned lands on every continent of the then known world. He sought Catholic world domination."

"And this is one of the Titian portraits," I marveled. "For ten years Titian worked for the Spanish court, transcribing parts of Ovid's *Metamorphoses* into paintings. At one time he even served as the royal portraitist."

"Bet King Bling couldn't have been too happy at having a less than perfect eldest son," Peaches commented. "Those dudes preferred perfect progeny, didn't they?"

"Most parents prefer it, I suppose, but kings demanded it. What about his queen, the royal mother?" I asked.

Evan stroked his chin. "If I recall correctly, King Philip had four queens in total with all but one predeceasing him, including Carlos's mother, his first wife."

"Maria Manuela of Portugal." Rupert was reading from one of the Wiki printouts. "She gave birth to the prince in 1545 and died four days later, poor lady." He pointed to the portrait of a woman, her expressionless face gazing away into space as if anticipating her fate.

"It was not a good time to be a woman," I whispered, gazing down at the portrait, "or a physically and mentally challenged prince, for that matter."

My eyes slipped up to the X-rays. Both were as hard to distinguish as a puddle of shadows, but one was more promising than the other. Here, a ghostly image of a skull rose from the background with evenly spaced holes visible around the upper circumference and an alarming fissure that appeared to have fused together. "Is that where the supposed crown sat? It does look like it had been..."

"Bolted to the bone? Precisely. You can just see what looks to be holes," Markus said, following my gaze. "That's what started this mess—a skull that once had something appended to the bone, something that could have been a crown."

"Somebody actually banged a crown on this poor guy's head while he was still alive?" Peaches asked.

Markus sipped his coffee. "Possibly. Hard to tell whether the man was alive or dead at the time without the skull to investigate and even that might not reveal much after all this time. However, I think it's safe to say that whoever did this had a bone to pick with the prince—pun intended. First the deed was done—probably close to the time of the prince's death—and then, presumably sometime later, the skull was moved to the crypt of Capela de Soa Maria Baptista, perhaps with the crown intact."

"Possibly for safekeeping," Evan mused.

"Possibly," Markus agreed, "only someone either stole the crown at the time of the decapitation or at a later date. And then, for whatever reason, someone stole the skull earlier this week."

"But why?" I asked.

"That is the question." Markus nodded, looking away. "It seems as though somebody long ago believed the prince and his ill-gotten crown required protection."

"But what value is the skull without the crown?" Evan asked. "Crowns are precious commodities in themselves but skulls are not, unless..."

"Unless the skull had some reliquary-like value," I added.

"But why was he permanently wearing a crown in the first place?" Peaches asked.

"Yes, why? No royal personage that I am aware of was ever buried wearing a crown, let alone one pounded into their skull," I said.

"Because the crown belonged to the monarchy, not the monarch," Rupert pointed out.

"This one couldn't have belonged to the monarchy, at least not officially," I said. "Someone would have noticed it missing."

"Making *this* one a special crown," Evan remarked. "Special enough for the monarchies involved—Spain and Portugal, to begin with—not to miss it when the crown disappeared, presuming it did disappear and wasn't of some secret nature from the start."

"But lots of people must have known about its existence initially," I said. "I mean, if Prince Carlos was crowned under unusual circumstances, as in at the time of his death, and his crowned skull later moved for safekeeping, what does that say? Nothing about this is a one-person job."

"Indeed, it has all the making of a secret society," Rupert said, rubbing his hands together.

"Do we know if the prince's intact remains are at his place of burial in Spain?" Evan asked.

"We have yet to make those inquiries," Markus said. "Officially he was buried near Madrid at his father's El Escorial palace and monastery complex, which is where most of the kings and queens of Spain were interred after the mid-1500s."

"Those tombs are closely guarded and everyone will assume that they have remained undisturbed," Evan said.

"In any event, he was first and foremost a prince of Spain, regardless of his various royal affiliations," Rupert remarked. "Though no one has had reason to exhume the remains, at least not officially, I can't imagine his skull being shuffled off to Portugal with his father's knowledge."

Markus cradled his mug in his hands, as if he found the warmth comforting. "I can only say that there would have been no room for two intact bodies in the casket of Senhor Pedro Alavares Fidalgo. According to his stone effigy, Fidalgo was a portly man and would have filled the coffin with his own girth. From the best we can tell, the prince's skull was added later, with or without the crown."

"Skulls are easier to transport than full skeletons," Evan remarked.

That grim fact settled in around us as we stood sipping our coffees and considering the implications.

"And then last week, someone picked up the trail and stole the skull. How weird is that?" Peaches said, setting her mug down on the kitchen counter. "All righty, so who else knows about the true nature of the theft besides you, Markus, this poor Jose dude, the tomb robbers, and now all of us?"

I stared at the white envelope on the table. Rupert picked it up, unfolded the thick bond contents, and began to read aloud.

"DEAR MR. COLLINS,

. . .

"JOSE BALBOA CONTACTED me with details of your extraordinary find, knowing as he did that it would be of great interest to me. Now I have learned through my sources that he has been murdered and your discovery stolen. You are in extreme danger but know that you are not alone.

"My resources are at your disposal. Please meet me in the gardens of the Museu Nacional de Arte Antiga at 5:00 p.m. on Friday, September 12. I can be recognized as a white-haired gentleman with a cane carrying a Hieronymus Bosch carrier bag. Please make every effort to come as to do otherwise may have dire consequences.

"Arrive alone and, at all costs, exercise the greatest caution.

"A CONCERNED FRIEND"

"A CONCERNED FRIEND?" Rupert turned to Markus. "How extraordinary."

"He knew Jose. What do you think your dead colleague may have told him?" I asked, turning to Markus.

Markus frowned and put down his mug. "I'm guessing everything, at least everything we knew up to that point. We had only taken the X-rays that afternoon and Jose must have called the man shortly after that. He was always dashing off to pick up lunch or buy us coffee so he had plenty of opportunity. It wasn't until later that evening when we were keeping watch that Jose confessed that he'd told an interested party about our discovery. Naturally, I exploded. We had agreed to keep the lid on this find and there he was disclosing the details to this friend."

"What was his defense?' Evan asked.

"He explained that this was a very powerful person who could intervene if necessary in case the skull was hijacked by another interested party. By the time the call came from his wife to return home, I was almost relieved to have him go."

"And then this supposed powerful friend slips this note under your door," Evan said.

Markus rubbed a hand over his eyes. "So bloody cloak-and-dagger."

"Do you plan on keeping the appointment tomorrow?" Rupert asked, turning to him. "Because, I must say, it seems most unwise to do so given that you are clearly in some danger."

"I don't know what to do," Markus moaned. "On one hand, I want to get to the bottom of this and, naturally, I want that skull back and to continue our work—if the authorities will permit it. But I'd rather stay alive as long as possible, thank you very much, and with the thieves threatening me, I figure I'm already as good as dead. All the interested parties must know that I've told the four of you but what alternative did I have—say nothing and go this whole thing alone? I doubt I'd even be safe back in England right now."

"Fear not, my good chap, we are on your side now and will get to the bottom of this while keeping you safe. You must stay here tonight—we have a perfectly serviceable pull-out couch—and Evan will go with you to fetch your things from your hotel in the morning," Rupert said while patting Markus on the arm. "But, indeed, you should not meet this mysterious emissary tomorrow as that would be far too risky. One of us will go in your stead."

"I will," I said with all the authority I could muster. Both Rupert and Evan looked ready to protest as Peaches gave me a thumbs-up. "As a woman, I may be less threatening considering that it's Markus that Mr. Anonymous is expecting. Peaches will be my backup."

6

onvincing the team of my suitability was not easy. It was a tiresome
argument that I'd had many times with Rupert and Evan but wasn't
in the mood for that night. I pointed out that brawn, height, and even MI6
training were probably not needed when meeting a "white-haired gentleman
with a cane." I didn't even mention my own martial arts capabilities, of course
—that would have been overkill. In all respects, I was perfect for the job.

Admittedly, I've been known to be wrong.

"Look, guys. Mr. Anonymous probably does his homework. He'll know
that Markus called in assistance when things turned dicey. He'll do background checks on everyone involved. That's what I'd do, anyway," I said. "How
do you think he'll react when an ex-MI6 guy shows up instead of the scientist
he expects? Wouldn't that ring alarm bells? However, a female art historian is
considerably less threatening."

"Unless it's you," Evan said under his breath.

"You'll be watched, Phoebe, doubtlessly followed," Rupert grumbled. "A
gray-haired man carrying a Hieronymus Bosch bag does not mean that he
can't be dangerous or accompanied by a posse of hidden thugs," he said
sternly.

"I know that," I said.

"Who's Hieronymus Bosch?" Peaches asked. "Sounds like a rock band—
Hieronymus Bosch and the Bastardly Beaters."

"I'll introduce you to him tomorrow," I replied, "just before we head for the rendezvous because," I added, turning to Rupert, "Peaches will accompany me, of course, and Evan will no doubt be close by."

That probably clinched the deal or at the very least saved me a few minutes of argument.

* * *

"THERE's no way I'd let you leave me behind," Peaches said later as we readied for bed in our apartment. "As your bodyguard, I intend to follow you everywhere."

She had decided to be my bodyguard some time ago and took it very seriously. "I didn't plan on leaving you behind, but we need to keep you hidden since he's expecting Markus. Besides, he said to come alone."

"How will you approach him?"

"I'll probably walk up to him and say that Markus couldn't make it."

Peaches pondered this for a moment. "That might work but you'll have to be careful. This guy probably will have people watching him, too."

"So you'll be nearby but staying out of sight."

"No worries. We'll go separately and I'll attempt to look inconspicuous."

Making a six-foot Amazon inconspicuous is not easy but there was time to worry about the details later.

Just before heading to the bedroom, Peaches paused. "Do you seriously wear that thing to sleep?"

I gazed down at my oversize van Gogh T-shirt with the self-portrait of the artist with a bandaged ear. "I picked it up in Amsterdam a million years ago and it's comfy. I wore it all through lockdown. I consider it my Covid Couture."

"Are you kidding me? I wouldn't let the tooth fairy see me in that. What happens if you have a romantic encounter? That getup will scare even the bravest of dudes away."

"Peaches, we're in a pandemic, remember? Comfort rules, not romance, even if I wasn't on a chastity diet."

She shook her head and sashayed into her bedroom. "You have to shake that attitude, girl, if you are ever going to mend that broken heart." The door clicked shut behind her.

Meanwhile, the coffee had left me wired, and while Peaches could sleep with jet fuel in her veins, I wasn't so lucky. I spent the hours between twelve and two trawling the web on my laptop. Evan had provided me with a plug-in device that shielded my search from prying eyes, and I had no doubt that prying eyes were everywhere by now.

First up, I scrutinized the available online portraits of Prince Carlos, knowing as I did that the royal painters were not likely to reveal the man's deformities and, of course, none did. Presumably, neither king nor prince wanted anything to taint the image of the crown prince of Spain and Portugal. Portraits were the visible legacy of crown and country for all the centuries to come, the ultimate selfie. However, most portraitists had caught the sulky cruelty of the boy's demeanor right down to the willful glint in the eyes.

Prince Carlos hailed from the House of Hapsburg, notorious for the inbreeding in the royal lineage. Besides the complications Rupert had noted, his maternal grandmother and paternal grandfather were siblings, as were his maternal grandfather and paternal grandfather. The boy's gene pool was an incestuous swamp all in the name of linking Europe's ruling houses. These were marriages of alliances, a crucial component of royal marriages throughout history.

One portrait by Jooris van der Straeten revealed Carlos in his early twenties wearing rich armor over a silken doublet and white hose. The stockings were designed to display a well-turned leg and artfully hid that one shortened limb. Here the artist had captured a sense of the boy's desired potential and anticipated military prowess, which was only fitting as son to a mighty king. Entitlement nearly leaped off the page in every detail, from the extravagant ceremonial armor to the rich background. Portraiture as propaganda had always been a thing.

Still, nothing I'd read or seen so far explained why someone would crown this prince, possibly posthumously, let alone steal that crown after the fact. It was all a curious boggle. Crowns were generally costly things and belonged to the monarchy, so why bury a prince with one in the first place? Furthermore, why this prince? He was so unhinged that his father finally locked him away and metaphorically threw away the key.

Next, I moved on to a summary of the five-act play by Schiller upon which the Verdi opera was based. The plot was supposedly based on Carlos's life but bore little resemblance to the boy's real existence. The essence of the tale focused on the prince's brief betrothal to Elizabeth of Valois, a beautiful young woman who his father, King Philip, ultimately decided to marry himself. That sort of thing could make any family dysfunctional.

The play had the young betrotheds shattered over the broken engagement and mostly focused on the two thrashing around being miserable. I noted the play's plot points, paying most attention to the list of characters, all of whom must have been based on real people in the court of King Philip of Spain. It was interesting to note that one other woman played a leading role: the Princess of Eboli, Ana de Mendoza, the princess with an eye patch. I vowed to check her out at some point.

When my eyes wearied of screen time, I pulled my knitting from my satchel and cast on a row. At one level, I was brewing over the missing skull, and on another, I was trying to design something for Peaches. Knitting often helped me to work out issues while calming another part of my brain, a curious paradox that knitters understand. I'd even been known to unscramble tangled thinking with only two sticks and a ball of yarn.

That night, however, that part of me trying to design something to capture my friend's Jamaican spirit hit a wall. In order to catch the complexities of her personality, I needed her power color of choice—pink. I stared at my assembled colors—black, mahogany, chartreuse, and various shades of green. No pink. I had always considered the absence of pink to be a good thing but now reconsidered. If I was to continue this project, I needed a yarn store, which wasn't on the immediate agenda.

Leaving my needles on the table, I strolled to the window and peered out across the darkened roofs of Lisbon. Grand old buildings, winking lights across the broad sinuous river, and, below, the portico of a spot-lit church with a coat of arms above the arched central window. My gaze drew down to where a figure stood on the church steps staring up at our building. I backed away to turn off the light. Seconds later, I returned, keeping well behind the curtain. The figure had gone.

Late the next morning, I returned to the research trail on my laptop, leaving Peaches to assess the neighborhood on her own after I told her about our night visitor.

"Sure you don't want to come out with me and get some air?"

"No, because I have too much research to do. I've downloaded material that I need to cram-read," I commented, my eyes not leaving the screen. "But if you need help or see anything interesting, text me."

"Sure, and I'll also let you know if I see any interesting shops open. A little wardrobe renovation wouldn't hurt you one bit," she said on her way to the door.

"I already brought one couture outfit with me, compliments of Nicolina a couple of years ago."

For some reason, my fashionable friends always wanted to give me a makeover or at least a seasonal reboot, especially my wealthy Italian one. On the other hand, I figured that if a piece cost a few thousand dollars to begin with, it should probably last longer than a couple of years. That morning I dressed in jeans and a black turtleneck, thinking to remain as inconspicuous for the day's rendezvous. "I'm good, thanks."

Peaches may or may not have rolled her eyes. "Suit yourself. When are we leaving to meet Mr. Anonymous?"

"Let's go separately and meet at 2:00 p.m. in front of the painting entitled *The Temptation of Saint Anthony.* You're going to love Hermy. Anyway, that should give us plenty of time to scope out the museum separately afterward."

"Right. I'll be back before then, anyway. I'm heading down to the church steps to see if your guy last night left any evidence." Besides reading a diet of bare-chested romance books, Peaches had taken a liking to police procedurals.

I returned to work as she exited the apartment and a few solitary hours passed with me taking notes. By noon I had breakfasted on six Portuguese custard pastries and three mugs of coffee, scanned an ebook on Emperor Charles V of Spain and his wife, Queen Isabella, plus another on his son, Philip II, as well as brushed up on my Titian. I was revisiting online portraits of Crown Prince Carlos when a text came in from Evan on my secure phone.

Have just delivered our package and am back at our lodging. Could we meet briefly to discuss our sightseeing plans?

Secure phone or not, the man wasn't taking any chances. In moments, I was knocking on the penthouse door. Evan stepped aside to let me in.

"Phoebe, I trust you slept well?" Dressed in jeans and a T-shirt in his own version of tourist attire, he looked better than breakfast, better than coffee, just plain delicious. Sometimes it was all I could do to remind myself that men were not in my viewfinder at the moment.

"I didn't actually." My gaze landed on Markus sitting on the couch staring at the floor. "Good morning, Markus."

He lifted his puffy-eyed gaze. "It's afternoon, Phoebe."

"So soon? Are you all right?" I asked.

"Not dead yet, despite appearances," he replied.

"Death by hangover is not a thing," Evan told him sternly as he locked the door behind us.

"I'm not referring to the hangover. Since you have just dosed me with some kind of concoction that might be embalming fluid, I'm hoping the cure isn't worse than the affliction."

I caught Evan's gaze and smiled. "In that case, you'll either be back to normal within the hour or preserved for antiquity. Since you're into forensics, you should appreciate that. Did you two see anything suspicious when you went out?"

"Three men are watching our building 24/7 and one tracked us all the way to Markus's hotel and back," Evan replied. "You'll be followed to your appointment this afternoon, too, so be careful. We can't even begin to determine who's working for the anonymous friend and who is part of the thief's gang."

"Do you think it is a gang?" I asked him.

"I think it must be something of that ilk," he remarked. "How extensive the group is left to be seen. Our thieves may simply have hired mercenaries to watch us every moment."

"Good afternoon, Phoebe," Rupert greeted as he shuffled out of his room in his paisley silk dressing gown. "Has Evan offered you tea?"

"No, actually, but I'm a bit overcaffeinated at the moment. I will take a tracking device if you have any lying around."

"Ah," Evan said with a nod. "I always keep an assortment of tracking devices to serve with coffee. I have some ready for your perusal right here on the table. Come, I'll show you."

The table we had used last night was now covered with various technical bits including electronic circuitry and chips plus a selection of small disc-like tracking devices. Three laptops were set up around the room and most every other available surface was covered in books or printouts. So they brought their own printer and possibly half a library plus a workshop, too? These men never traveled light.

"Impressive as usual." I turned to Evan. "Do you intend to track me while I track Mr. Anonymous?"

"Of course. Your phone will keep me apprised of your movements. I won't be far away and Rupert will be with you virtually at the apartment."

Rupert pointed to the laptop propped on the coffee table while Evan placed a tiny wafer into my palm. "Drop this into the gentleman's pocket or even into his carrier bag so you can track his movements on your phone." He paused, studying me. "You have read the itemized list of phone features I provided, I presume?"

"Yes, I skimmed them this morning. Impressive." Evan's itemized cheat sheets were so detailed they required a good hour to peruse properly, preferably with a dictionary. I had only taken a fleeting glimpse that morning.

Evan had more preparations to share including a map of the museum grounds and possible locations in the garden where he would wait. "I will never be far away," he assured me.

By the time Peaches arrived minutes later, I was in the process of refusing the gun Evan had manifested from somewhere. "Take it, please, Phoebe. You have no idea where this day will end and it's best to be prepared," he said.

"Not yet." I hated guns on principle. Even though my principles had taken a bit of a hit lately, I still wanted to avoid the inevitable. Besides, this appointment was in broad daylight and on the museum grounds. What could go wrong?

"If she won't take it, I will," Peaches said, stepping forward with her hand extended.

* * *

Lisbon's famed museum of ancient art sits on top of a hill overlooking the Rio Tejo with views across the long wide river and beyond. It was another breathtaking vista in a city so full of them that visitors rarely get to put away their phones. Though I yearned to linger under the trees and take pictures with the handful of tourists, the museum was the bigger draw. Besides, I would be meeting Mr. Anonymous in a couple of hours in that very garden, but first I needed to connect with Peaches.

But by 2:35 I was still standing transfixed before *The Temptation of Saint Anthony* by Hieronymus Bosch. It was a triptych I'd longed to view in person since my student days, but even so I didn't expect the impact of those bizarre, almost whimsical figures dancing about a phantasmagorical world to be so intense. Bosch's perverse imagery always made me smile. Every detail, from the cross-beaked bird with the funnel hat to the snout-nosed demons riding fish in the smoky air, struck me like a drug-induced dream. A horrible dreamscape of sin and temptation, yes, but wickedly humorous, too.

I checked my watch. Peaches should have been there at 2:00 p.m. but was unusually late. An art historian in a museum of ancient art is worse than a starving kid in a candy store and I was itching to see more of the museum. Where was she? We had agreed to enter the museum separately and then go our own ways. I heard a rustle behind me and swung around.

"This is..." My words died on my lips. A masked elderly man in a gray suit holding a cane in one hand and a Hieronymus Bosch shopping bag in the other had shuffled up behind me in the otherwise empty gallery.

"Good afternoon, Ms. McCabe. My apologies for startling you but I thought it best that we meet in private." Possibly in his early eighties with longish silver hair and deep blue eyes, his voice was surprisingly energetic considering the stooped frame that contained it.

"You know who I am, sir?"

"I make it a point of researching the identity of my appointments in advance, especially if they are otherwise uninvited. I am Senhor Silvio de Carvalho," he said in well-modulated English touched faintly by a Portuguese accent. "A lawyer by profession but now semiretired with perhaps too much emphasis on the 'semi' part. You may address me as Senhor Carvalho for expediency sake."

"Well, Senhor Carvalho, you are early," I said, pointing out the obvious.

"Indeed I am, but it appears that my proposed meeting in the gardens has been garnering too much attention to be safe." He waved one hand toward the door. "I have secured a more private location for our conversation. There are many spies about and I would rather not be overheard. Please be so kind as to follow me." He began shuffling toward the door.

I hesitated. This was not going the way I had planned. Maybe I should make an excuse to use the toilet in order to shoot a quick text to Peaches and Evan.

Senhor Carvalho turned as if sensing my thoughts. "It is best that you come along immediately, Ms. McCabe. Your friend will not be able to meet you as arranged."

I stared hard. "Senhor, if you've harmed Peaches—"

"Ms. Williams is currently being detained by museum security for entering the premises carrying a firearm, but I assure you that no harm will befall her as long as you cooperate. That is not a threat but a statement of fact. She will be released as soon as it is safe to do so."

"Safe for whom? I don't understand, senhor." I pulled the phone from my pocket thinking to send Evan a quick SOS.

"And I have taken the added precaution of having your devices jammed—I do hope that is the correct term—to prevent any further communication or tracking."

I stared. No signal on my phone. That anything could disable one of Evan's super-phones was shocking in itself. I narrowed my eyes at the man leaning on his cane. "What is going on here?"

"I intend to explain all but only when it's safe. Please do try to cooperate, Ms. McCabe. Given that it isn't you that I invited to meet with me today and that your companion arrived armed, I have been very obliging."

He had a point—sort of. "Dr. Collins didn't feel safe enough to come in person," I said.

"Understandable, but the more people involved in this situation, the more perilous it becomes. Already matters are spinning out of control. We are all in great danger and I urge you to cooperate. I may be in the only position to protect you for the moment."

"Protect me how?" I asked.

"Later, Ms. McCabe. Trust me when I say that we must get away from here."

What choice did I have? I pocketed my phone. "Lead the way, senhor."

I half considered alerting security but the noticeable lack of people, let alone guards, in the hallway nixed that idea. "Where is everybody? I entered a busy gallery and now the place is deserted."

"Not deserted exactly," the man said as we approached an elevator. "The museum is under emergency closure. It happens whenever suspicious activity is detected." Was he referring to Peaches...or Evan, who must be somewhere on the grounds by now?

"And yet you are permitted to walk around freely, sir?"

"As a museum patron, I am afforded that privilege, yes."

"Where are you taking me?"

"Someplace safe," he replied.

Safe was the last thing I felt at that moment. On the other hand, I found myself believing the man. Stepping into the elevator beside him, I watched as he swiped a keycard and pushed the bottommost button.

"Did you know that this museum was once a grand residence?" he asked. "The Palácio de Alvor-Pombal was built in the seventeenth century by the first Earl of Alvor and most of the museum has been constructed around the original building."

"I didn't know that," I said, watching the buttons light up at every floor. "As a patron, do the staff here work for you?"

"We cooperate, as only proper, under the circumstances. Indeed, I do wish I could take you on a special tour, but some other time, perhaps. We would need far more than a few hours to properly experience one of the foremost museums of ancient art in the world, as I am certain you are aware." I sensed he could be smiling behind his surgical mask. "Still, I am very happy that you managed to see my old friend Hieronymus."

I was too agitated for conversation. We seemed to keep going down and down. Though I counted three floors from our original level to the supposed bottom button, we were dropping even farther. Just before my anxiety bubbled to the surface, the elevator doors flew open.

"Ah, here we are. To the right and to the very end, please."

From a long hallway I could see glass rooms stretching away in both directions. Our progress was slow due to my companion's halting gait, so I could observe the lab-coated workers in the sections in passing. Paintings propped on easels, ceramics being carefully restored, and at least one large Byzantine mosaic bathed in halogen caused me to pause. "Is that what I think it is?"

"From the reign of Justinian I—a relatively new acquisition. Pity that I cannot take you in for a closer look but we must hurry." He had pulled a phone from his pocket and was peering down at the screen. "Matters have grown more alarming by the moment."

"More alarming how?"

"Hurry, please."

At the end of the hall we were buzzed into an empty room, a combination storage room/garage with crates lining two walls and three white vans parked on the other side of a large plate-glass window. A round table sat in the center, bare except for a laptop. A flat-screen monitor with loud speakers on either side was angled toward the table from the wall ahead. Various live camera views were visible on the screen but only one interested me: the one showing Peaches pacing a small room.

"Where have you taken her?" I asked, turning to Senhor Carvalho.

"I have taken her nowhere, but museum security object to guns being brought into their facility. She is in a room down the hall where she will stay until the area has been secured and it is safe for her to leave. I have instructed the guards not to have her arrested but to contain her for now."

"Let me see her," I asked, making for the door.

"If you choose to see her now, I will be unable to share the full story of the missing skull. After today, I must stay away from Lisbon and it would be wise if you and your friends followed my example."

I swung back to him. "What's going on?" Evan must be alarmed now that my devices were dark. He'd know that something was up. "Senhor, I am just about jumping out of my skin here. You know my friends will come after me and then where will that get us?"

"Exactly, Ms. McCabe, and what will that do—get somebody harmed unnecessarily? Your man has been seen on the museum grounds and will be arrested as soon as the police arrive, providing he should live that long. Arrest by the police is perhaps the best scenario given the situation, but I am certain he would prefer neither."

"What do you mean by that?"

"I will show you. Patience, Ms. McCabe." He sat down before the laptop and removed his mask. "I cannot breathe in these blasted things." He began tapping on the keyboard several times. Apparently frustrated that he couldn't get it to do what he wanted, he barked something in Portuguese. There had to be a microphone somewhere.

"Keep doing that and the computer may seize up in a sulk," I said.

He nodded at that. "Indeed, but I am no more patient than you are, it seems. Oh, here comes Manuel. He will wrest this beast into submission."

A masked young man dressed in a white shirt with a red insignia on the left pocket had dashed into the room, greeting me with a nod before taking over the laptop while the senhor looked on.

"Regard the screen above, Ms. McCabe," my host said. "Do you see those three men and the one over there? Manuel, are you able to zoom in on that fellow by the statue?"

The screen had switched to show eight exterior views. We were staring at the garden from cameras fixed around the museum premises. Amid the swaths of flowers and the statuary, several men appeared to be lounging on the benches or snapping photos. There was nothing casually relaxed about any of them. Tourists don't furtively study everyone around them while pretending to gaze at their phones. "Who are they?"

"Our enemies—and make no mistake, they are armed and dangerous. Explosives have been detected on one and firearms on the other three. There are several such men around the grounds."

I looked at him in alarm. "Surely they wouldn't attempt to blow up the museum?"

"Not the museum, perhaps, but certainly you and your companions, and me, of course. They will stop at nothing to keep their secret safe and have little concern for who may get hurt in the process. One man has been seen waiting in a cab near the museum. I suspect he hopes to kidnap you should you hail a cab. These men are ruthless. They have killed already and will target everyone who knows about the skull, which now includes you and your companions. We are all in great danger." He turned to Manuel and spoke in Portuguese. The man nodded and left the room.

"Ms. McCabe, the police are on their way, and your Mr. Barrows, who is currently keeping out of sight, will be arrested if our enemies do not locate him first. You must tell him to leave the premises immediately. You and I will proceed to a safe location and Ms. Williams will be escorted back to your apartment once it is safe to do so. You in particular cannot risk being seen leaving the building. I have your phone unblocked long enough for you to text your friend. Do be quick about it and do not attempt anything foolish."

I didn't hesitate. In seconds, I had the phone out of my pocket and typed out my text.

Evan, leave the grounds immediately. Place is infested with men armed with explosives and the police are on their way. Peaches and I are fine. Will contact you later.

I showed the screen to Senhor Carvalho, who nodded before I hit send.

"Now we must leave," he said, adding something in Portuguese as he pushed himself to his feet and grabbed his cane.

"But to where?"

He hobbled to the door to the garage. "I will explain on the way. Hurry, please."

Ask me if I thought that jumping into a vehicle with a strange man to drive to some undisclosed location was a good idea. On the other hand, leaving with no further information about this confounding situation seemed a worse one. Besides, I trusted Senhor Carvalho for reasons I couldn't explain and could see no good reason why he would be making this stuff up.

So I climbed into the back of a white panel van marked by the museum's red MNAA insignia with Carvalho. Manuel helped the older man up until the two of us squeezed together on flip-down seats facing the van's back door. The vehicle still bore the remains of packing-tape bits and straw so was clearly designed for transporting cargo not people. Manuel took the driver's seat and soon we were winding through the cars and empty parking spaces on an upward curve.

"Manuel says we must keep our heads down the moment…we reach street level," Carvalho said a little breathlessly. "It is doubtful that we can be seen back here but just in case."

"Tell me where we are going now, senhor. No more excuses," I said.

"I am taking you to my quinta where I hope we will be safer than here in the city, at least for a time. Your friends will be given instructions to follow us when the confusion dies down. I simply cannot risk transporting more than one of you at this time. Let us hope that the police can restore order quickly." He stared straight ahead as he spoke, both hands grasping the cane he clutched between his legs. I had the sense that the unfolding events were taking a toll on his health.

The van began zooming through the underground garage, picking up speed as the tires peeled around the corners. Senhor Carvalho and I continually slid into one another, each one trying to brace against the centrifugal force.

Manuel, clearly not trained in speeding through enclosed spaces in a panel van, muttered to himself and occasionally swore in two languages. Twice the van scraped against the wall in a screech of metal against concrete and once I feared we might smash into a parked car.

Senhor Carvalho gripped the handhold, his gaze fixed ahead, while I tried to brace myself against sliding into him every two seconds. The lack of seat belts didn't help.

I turned and saw a garage door opening ahead at last—the proverbial light at the end of the tunnel—but before I could exclaim my relief, the van shook as if the ground beneath our wheels was shattering into a thousand pieces and then something heavy struck the roof. Both of us tumbled to the floor.

7

---

*E*arthquake, it had to be an earthquake! Lisbon had suffered many catastrophic shake-ups. Was this the next big one? I imagined crumbled buildings, devastating fires, massive tsunamis…

"Stay down!" Senhor Carvalho cried as the two of us tumbled around against the back of the van. Manuel was shouting; we kept moving; and I could see sunshine blazing through the windshield.

Manuel was talking to somebody on his car phone.

"Manuel…says part of the garage was…blown up. He says stay…out of sight," the senhor said.

"The garage?" I asked, raising my head an inch off the floor. "Not an earthquake?"

"Explosão! Explosão!" Manuel cried.

Got it. I raised my head. Between the two front seats, I could see that we were now beetling down a busy street. I ducked back down. Several minutes of bumping along followed before I realized that my companion lay on his back breathing heavily.

"Are you hurt, senhor?" I crawled over to him. Even in the shadowy light, I could see his pallor.

"Do not worry," he panted. "Just my…old bones. I will just lie here for a… few moments to catch my breath."

Without thinking, I squeezed his hand as if he were my father since he reminded me of my own dad long passed. "Is there something I can do? Here."

I took my jacket off and folded it under his head. "Manuel," I cried. "Senhor Carvalho is injured!"

Manuel called back. "Must stay down. Call for help!"

The senhor spoke to him in Portuguese, something that sounded like instructions.

"What did you just tell him to do?"

"To keep on driving…not to stop…until we reach our destination."

"But, senhor…"

He patted my arm. "No, Ms. McCabe, we are in…too much danger…but thank you for caring. My assumptions…as to your character…were correct."

And mine about him apparently. I settled my back against the wall, remaining near him while the van rolled on. "Senhor, what if my friends were hurt in the explosion? I must use my phone."

"Your phone is…free…now that we are away from the building. I confess… I tricked you. No service…on that floor. But—" he paused to catch his breath "—using it…is still…not wise."

Of course, he was afraid that we'd be tracked through my phone's GPS. Could I be absolutely certain we wouldn't once I switched it on? Evan's anti-tracking devices had always worked but this enemy was clearly more technologically advanced than previous versions.

"Please keep it…turned off just in case. Manuel says that…it appears Mr. Barrows escaped…safely but so…did most of the…Divinios."

"The Divinios?"

"This group of hoodlums that insist…upon wreaking such havoc…on the modern…and ancient world." He was practically gasping now. "Help me sit up, Ms. McCabe, please."

I helped him lean back against the wall, the two of us wedged side by side as the van continued rumbling along. After a few minutes, he appeared to have recovered somewhat, though his breathing remained ragged. "Emphysema," he panted. "Neglected to bring…my puffer."

Several minutes passed before I asked the questions crowding onto my tongue. "Could you explain these Divinios?"

"They call themselves…*Los Divinios* after…*derecho divino de los reyes.*"

I recognized enough root syllables to figure that one out. "Oh, my God— the Divine Right of Kings? Surely that concept is dead?"

"It should be. Indeed, few royal houses…would ever abide by such a thing today…and yet a small group of men—a brotherhood, if you will—have borne…its standard for centuries. It's actually…a religious sect."

Manuel shouted something and I could feel the van slowing down. We were now bumping along what felt like a dirt road. "But these men can't seriously intend to restore a monarchy?"

"They seriously intend to restore their own power. It's always about power. We must stop now…and change vehicles," my companion said.

The door slid back. Two men in green uniforms with matching masks stood outside with Manuel behind them, his ear pressed to his phone. One man helped me and the senhor out, giving me mere seconds to squint around at the surroundings. Nothing but bare rock and rough scrabble with Lisbon just visible over a bend far below. A narrow road wound through a hilly forest ahead. I turned back to see Senhor Carvalho shaking Manuel's hand beside the battered museum van while the other men waited by the glossy truck.

"Good luck, senhorita." Manuel waved to me.

"Thanks, Manuel. If you see my friends, please tell them I'm all right."

"Yes, I will."

Moments later, we were helped up a loading platform and into the back of a waiting truck, this one a deep forest green with flourishing gold signage to match the men's uniforms.

Now Senhor Carvalho and I sat opposite one another on the truck floor amid packaged laundry with racks of clear-plastic-covered clothes dangling from overhead. Between the cab and cargo area, a row of suits hung from a rack, letting in very little light and no opportunity for me to talk to the men even if I wanted to. Getaway by laundry truck.

"Our enemies will…soon pick up our trail." My companion sighed and rested his head against the wall as the vehicle rumbled forward. "They know where I live—have always known. The explosion caused more disruption… than they must have anticipated…but I have no doubt they will…come for us."

"And then?" I asked.

"And then we will have to…work out another plan, Ms. McCabe," he said grimly, closing his eyes.

"Please call me Phoebe. After all, we are sharing the back of a laundry truck."

He smiled at that. "Phoebe, then." He did not offer to have me call him by his first name and doing so would have seemed all wrong to me somehow.

But he was fading fast. Rather than press him further about the Divinios, I swallowed my questions and focused on the clothes swaying above me on padded hangers.

Even in the half-light I could see deep jewel-toned velvets, shimmering silks in every hue, and gentlemen's suits in various textures and fibers. I longed to run my hand over those naps and silken folds, me being a shameless textile hedonist. In times of anxiety, I took comfort in soft wear. I snaked a hand up inside the plastic wrap and flipped a jacket label—Armani. All righty, then.

We bumped along for several minutes before the wheels hit smooth pavement. Now I found myself sliding inches toward the rear door. Senhor Carvalho with his head lolling to one side was listing, too. I braced myself against the door to prevent him toppling over. I desperately hoped that he was only dozing and hadn't lost consciousness.

I so wanted to use my phone to ensure that everyone was all right back in Lisbon, but the phone remained shoved deep into my pocket. It felt like treason not to trust Evan's technical prowess enough to fear tracking.

I wasn't certain how long we traveled but it seemed far too long on a road too steep, especially with Senhor Carvalho's alarming pallor and shallow breathing. Finally the truck lurched to a halt. I heard shouting and the back doors flew open followed by a blast of crisp cool air. I squinted against the shards of sudden light. "Help me, please. Senhor Carvalho is not well," I cried.

Two men and one woman appeared from somewhere, calling in Portuguese, and soon I was standing in a tiny graveled courtyard watching as the men helped Senhor Carvalho toward an arched doorway, the woman dashing beside them murmuring something.

We had arrived in a deep forested area with a grand turreted structure rising overhead, a mini yellow castle with balconies hanging over arched windows and an abundance of ornate rococo details. I gaped. This was the quinta—with turrets?

The doors of the laundry truck slammed shut. Soon the vehicle's tires spat up the gravel as it zoomed down the drive. Out of sight, a gate clanged shut, leaving me alone.

It felt as though I'd just been dropped into the midst of a Walt Disney special minus the remote control. Nothing about this mini castle looked old or worn or otherwise real. The whole experience struck me as more akin to somebody's idea of a fairy tale.

A brilliant sunset blazed over top of the trees, gilding the surrounding gardens as my feet crunched across the gravel toward the doorway. I tried the brass knob—locked. I knocked. No answer. Probably in the trauma of the ailing senhor, I had simply been forgotten. Visions of Alice in Wonderland crowded into my head.

Fine, so I'd just try the front door. So says a woman completely unaware of how large a country estate can be, let alone exactly which end was which.

I trod along what I took to be a side path beside a wall-like hedge heading in the direction from which we had arrived. At least, I could just see the lane the truck had taken before disappearing into the woods and that had to mean something. Besides, I caught glimpses of lights through the trees. Was that toward the front?

Obviously not, because soon I was surrounded by foliage so thick I could hardly make out anything in the fading light. Totally turned around, I found myself wandering into the garden, or one of them. Banks of flowers swayed in the golden light and a fountain tinkled somewhere out of sight.

I needed to stick to a path because paths are supposed to lead somewhere good, or that was the theory. But there were paths branching in every direction. Do I choose the one going down or the one heading up, to the left or to the right?

Choosing left for no other reason than I liked the look of the marble bench marking the fork, I ended descending into a wooded grove where mist snaked low against the ground. A moss-covered well tangled in ivy added to the atmospheric interlude, perfect for something out of the Brothers Grimm. Backtracking, I arrived more or less where I started, only nothing looked the same.

Alarmed, I wandered into a circular rose garden and inhaled the fragrant blooms as a kind of consolation prize for the hopelessly lost. Seconds later, I emerged beside a huge stepped fountain with a bronze dragon spewing water into a bowl big enough for a small swimming party. In desperation, I climbed the fountain steps to get a lay of the land. There, several feet aboveground, I could finally see the house glowing in a mass of lights to my right—not too far away actually, if I could only figure out how to get there.

But I wasn't expecting the fountain behind me to burst into a sudden foam-spitting light show. I may have yelped as the dragon above turned from green to orange while spewing colored water from his jaws, splashing into the pool and onto me. The entire garden blazed with artful light shows like Vegas crossed with the Tivoli fountain. Okay, so maybe I was getting cranky. The hell with dragons, anyway.

Moving away from the spray, I pulled out my phone, thinking to activate my geo-positioning device, but gazing at the blank screen sobered me. Did I really want these Divinios or whoever the hell they were to track me into fairyland? I shoved the phone back into my pocket just as I heard shouting coming beyond the botanical maze.

"Over here!" I called. "By the dragon!"

The dragon kept me company in its fashion as I leaned against the marble pool watching the flashlights bob through the dusk toward me. Occasionally,

I'd gaze up at a particularly spectacular sparkly spew as the giant reptile spat colored water into the pool.

A few minutes later, two masked men and a little girl wearing a glittery pink kitten face mask arrived.

"We are most sorry, Ms. McCabe," an older man said in thickly accented English from the bottom of the steps. "We lost you. We look everywhere but gone!"

"But do not worry because we have found you now!" the little girl called up.

"It's all right," I said, stepping down. "I should have stayed where I was put."

But then one of the men pulled a gun.

"Whoa!" I said, putting up my hands.

"My apologies, senhorita," the man said. "This for temperature. Not a gun. Sorry to alarm. Please step down."

"Oh, right." I climbed down the rest of the stairs and leaned forward while he aimed the laser thermometer at my forehead. It was one of those weird Covid moments worth tucking away along with all the others. By now I had quite a collection.

"You are cleared to come into the house," he said. My welcoming party removed their masks except for the child, who still wore her kitten variety.

"Oh, good." Because I had no idea what I would do if they refused.

"Hello." A little dark-haired girl grinned up at me, her heart-shaped face and wide brown eyes beaming with delight. "I am Ana Marie Carvalho."

No older than seven or eight and dressed in perfect girlie clothes—a lovely pink crinoline skirt and matching velvet jacket—she looked ready for a birthday party. "This is Senhor Abreu and Senhor Afonso. They work for my grandpapa, and behind you is Draggy, my dragon. Grandpapa gave him to me for my seventh birthday. Mama allowed me to come welcome you."

The short-haired older fellow who had taken my temperature and his young black companion both wore identical navy shirts and trousers and seemed otherwise delighted to see me, too. Each shook my hand in turn, smiling all the while. It seemed that, in their minds at least, once my temperature had been determined as normal, so did everything else.

"Very pleased to meet you, Ms. McCabe. I hope Draggy did not wet you," Senhor Afonso, the younger man, said.

"Only a little. Hi, Ana Marie, Senhors Abreu and Afonso," I greeted. "I'm very relieved that you found me since I was completely lost. Sorry for causing you any trouble. Why don't you call me Phoebe?"

The child tugged my jacket. "I am not sure my mama will let us call you

Phoebe but please come now. We will be late for dinner. We are dining early tonight because I am allowed to join you. My bedtime is usually at eight o'clock, which is too early."

"Hush, Ana Marie—do not pester the poor lady," Senhor Alfonso scolded in a tone that implied that nothing this child did could ever shake his patience.

I grinned. "I am not pestered, believe me. In fact, I am totally charmed."

The child took my hand and tugged me down the walk toward the house, or in the opposite direction of the house actually. "But this place is so confusing."

"My grandpapa says it is supposed to confuse. It is a maze. He calls it a big adventure but I know the way. My grandpapa and all the grandpapas before him designed the grounds like a fairyland. I love it best at night because it is magical. Sometimes Mama will let me go out to see all the fountains but not so much anymore, not since… Here, we will take a shortcut."

"The grounds were once open to the public," Senhor Afonso said, trudging behind, "but now we keep the gates locked."

I assumed that was related to Covid but had no opportunity to ask because Ana Marie ran on. Soon I was being led through spotlit hedgy tunnels, beside reflecting pools that captured the twilight glow, past a topiary pruned like a rearing unicorn, and finally through another arched door that led into a flag-stone patio by the house. A flashing light panel on the wall indicated a secu-rity system, which one of the men tapped in passing. The door clanged shut behind us.

"Is this the front?" I asked.

"No, the front is waaaay over there." Ana Marie pointed roughly to the left. "Mama says I am to take you straight to your room so you can change for dinner and have a bath." She giggled. "I should have said to have a bath and then change for dinner. Do you think my English good?"

"I think your English is amazing," I told her as she took me down back hallways leading to kitchens and laundry rooms and maybe a larder. The place was a warren of rooms. "But I don't have a change of clothes."

"Mama or Auntie Leonor will find you something. She leaves tomorrow but has lots of pretty dresses. I was allowed to choose one of my own so I could wear it to dinner tonight—see?"

"It's beautiful!"

"Thank you. It is one of my favorites but I never wear it because we never have fancy dinners anymore. You will love the dresses my mama picked out for you."

If Mama had been the woman running behind Senhor Carvalho when we arrived, I doubted she'd have anything to fit. I was of the curvy persuasion whereas that woman was model lean. Still, here I was in a fairy-tale castle about to dress for a formal dinner. After months of takeout and frozen dinners in my flat, I may as well have fallen into a magic kingdom.

A woman in a navy maid's uniform smiled shyly and stepped aside as we passed. No masks worn here, I noted. This must be a house bubble.

"Mama would not be pleased that I take you this way but it is much faster!"

Ana Marie let go of my hand and bolted up a curving staircase that obviously curled up inside one of the towers. I hurried after her as we climbed around and around the stone column.

"Ana Marie, is your grandfather all right?" I puffed. "I meant to ask you sooner but I became distracted."

I heard the footsteps falter. "Mama says he needs to rest more. Hurry, three more floors!"

By the time I reached the top, I was secretly cursing every exercise video I skipped during lockdown, and there'd been plenty.

"Here we are!" Ana Marie squealed in delight. "Mama has given you a turret room just like I asked because it is designed for princesses! This room will be mine someday but for now Mama wants to keep me close to her." She spun around on her patent-leather shoes, a butterfly taking flight.

I gazed around the half-circular room with three arched windows, a grand four-poster bed, and a fire burning in the grate. Lamps glowed on the side tables and a light had been left on in the small adjoining bathroom. Had I been Ana Marie's age, I would have leapt on top of that blue velvet counterpane and spread myself out like a snow angel.

Instead, I pulled away the window curtains. As expected, the room had a commanding view, with the garden light fantasy spreading out in all directions below. Fountains, circular shapes marked out in colored spotlights, huge topiaries casting strange shadows on the lawns, and something that looked like a miniature castle outlined in flashing pink were alight. From above it looked like a cross between a wonderland and a miniature golf park.

"I used to go out and play for a half hour every night in the lighted garden but not now," a small voice said behind me. "Now I am only allowed to look through the window but it is not the same. None of the grown-ups will take me, but I miss seeing Draggy with all his sparking water breath and my own little castle playroom. I miss my daddy more. I know he is hiding out there somewhere and I would go find him, only Mama will not permit me."

My heart caught in my throat. I turned to the child. "Why do you think that your daddy is hiding?"

Big tear-filled eyes looked up at me. "Grandpapa says he disappeared. I heard the adults talking. He went into the gardens but did not return. They told me that he never would come back and that I must wait for him in heaven. That was six months and two days ago and I think heaven is too long a wait."

I knelt down before the child and brought her closer. "I'm so sorry to hear about your daddy, Ana Marie. That must make you very sad."

And then she hugged me, sobbing into my shoulder while I hugged her back, feeling all the profound sadness that comes with trying to console a child facing infinite loss.

"I know all the secret paths to everywhere…" she said through her tears. "I could find him, I could! He's hiding from the bad ones. Nobody believes me."

What do you say to a grieving child? Do you distract her? I stood up and tried to smile. "Maybe you could show me around the gardens tomorrow. Are you allowed to go out in the daytime?"

She nodded. "As long as I am with a trusted adult. You could go with me, I think, but I want to go now."

"Maybe not now." I turned back to the window. "Come, point out where all your favorite places are."

"The lights will turn off in one minute." She held up her sparkly pink phone. "Grandpapa makes them to go off at 7:30." And before my eyes the garden was doused in absolute darkness. When I turned back to Ana Marie, the child was gazing up at me with the kind of haunted expression no child should wear.

"There are evil creatures in the garden now," she whispered. "They will snatch you away, but I am not afraid." And then her phone beeped as a text lit the screen. "Mama wants to know if you like the dresses. Come, they are on your bed."

Taking my hand, she led me to a carved four-poster bed where a selection of gowns had been laid out on the deep ultramarine velvet bedspread.

"Mama says I am to leave you now but that someone will come for you in an hour for dinner—probably Suzanna or Alma." Ana Marie was reading a text on her phone. "She says that she is sorry not to greet you in person but she was with Grandpapa. Oh, here, she will tell you herself." She passed me her phone.

I gazed down at the screen at a woman of about my age. Dark hair formed a glossy bob around a long angular face graced by magnificent cheekbones, all the elements creating a singularly beautiful woman.

"Hello, Ms. McCabe. Welcome to Sintra." The accent was barely noticeable. "I am Adriana Carvalho and I apologize for leaving you wandering in the dark only to then place you in the care of my chatty daughter. My lack of hospitality was due to my concern over Papa Carvalho. He does not follow his doctor's instructions, let alone mine."

"I totally understand. Is he all right?"

"Much improved, thank you. It is his emphysema. He is not to get excited or to overexert himself but he does too much of both. For now he is resting but will see you later."

"Please don't feel the need to apologize for leaving me with this charming little princess here."

Adriana smiled. "Princess Whirling Dervish?"

Ana Marie was now investigating the clothing options on the bed but paused long enough to shoot me a grin. "Mama was going to send you up with Auntie Leonor but she cannot move as fast as me."

"Ana Marie, hush! Do not be rude. My daughter is half princess, half indomitable spirit," Adriana laughed. "We will talk more over supper soon. Goodbye for now. And, Ana Marie, leave our guest in peace. She has had a difficult day."

I returned the phone to the child.

"Did you have a difficult day?" the girl asked, looking up at me with those enormous eyes. "I am very sorry to hear that. Mama says I should never forget that others hurt, too. Today I studied history, maths, and geography and it was hard. Mama says that I am a good student but too easily distracted. Will you go into the gardens with me?"

"Of course I will. Maybe tomorrow during the day."

She nodded. "I had better go now but I will see you at supper. We eat tonight at the big table." And with that the little whirlwind ran to the door, pausing to add, "I like the maroon one best. It is the color of the chocolate cosmos in the garden—my favorite flowers because they smell so chocolatey and my daddy planted them. My tutor says I am very good with English but must improve my maths. Bye for now." The door shut, leaving me alone in fairyland once again.

* * *

MY HEART ACHED for that child. I swallowed hard and strode to the window again to pull back the curtains. So this was Sintra. We were high up in a wooded mountain with lights in the hollows along with what looked to be other grand residences and maybe even a real castle in the distance. Really, a fairyland by any other name, despite the dark ominous garden brooding below or the missing father or the Divine Right of Kings...

Turning away, I stroked the clothes on the bed, three outfits still bearing forest-green-and-gold dry-cleaning tags dangling from the labels. Would I or would I not fit into the long burgundy silk gown with the coordinating velvet jacket, Ana Marie's favorite, or the deep gold satin gown with the elaborate neckline beading, or—heaven forbid—the turquoise silk muumuu? They all looked to be roughly a size fourteen bordering on twelve, providing one is minus hips or a bodacious bust. The muumuu was more like a satin tent.

I took a pile of fluffy towels into the blue-and-white tiled bathroom and poured a tub of scented bubbles. Once soaking, I studied the intricate harbor panel of tiles above my head, entranced by the ships laced with fanciful seashells and ornate motifs that proved why Portugal was famous for its tile work.

At the same time, I wondered what I had fallen into besides hot water, and how Evan, Peaches, Rupert, and Markus were faring. It seemed so wrong that I was steeping in luxury while they were, what—fretting over me? Escaping an explosion with their necks barely kept intact? At least I had been assured that they were all fine, but they still deserved to hear from me, no matter what. For that, I'd request the use of a landline.

And the Divine Right of Kings in the twenty-first century? Most monarchies were no more than figureheads and many more had been replaced by dictators and republics of all stripes. Still, I was always struck by how little I knew about the world and how the knots I stumbled across in history and art always dumbfounded me as I tried to pick them free.

When I emerged minutes later and tried on all my clothing options, the burgundy ensemble won. Yes, it was too tight across the bust and sitting would likely provoke extreme seam stress but the kimono-style jacket hid the result of too many Covid cookies. Besides, the silk and velvet apparently matched a chocolate cosmos somewhere in the garden, which was good enough for me. Should I or should I not wear a mask? I decided to bring it just in case.

I was still scrunching my curls dry as I walked behind the young uniformed woman who had arrived to accompany me to the dining room. We descended a stairway hung with large portraits, some modern, some possibly ancestral, on a carpet runner I recognized as late-nineteenth-century Persian of at least fifty knots per inch. My fingers itched to check but that would be rude.

The house opened up around me in marble, paintings and sculptures, more lush carpets, and potted plants. An orange tree grew in a conservatory glimpsed in passing and everywhere dark carved wood furniture lined the eggshell-white walls. I could happily linger over every detail, study the art, the carpets, even the chairs, but I was led into a large domed dining room tiled in more intricate scenes that teased my eyes all over again.

Two women rose from the small sitting area next to the fire as Ana Marie ran toward me clapping her hands. "Oh, Mama, look at Phoebe! Doesn't she look like the queen of the cosmos? And, Auntie Leonor, your dress looks so beautiful with her red hair, just as you said it would!"

Oh, yes, I did adore that child.

Soon I was flanked by the women, thanking each for their hospitality while learning that they were sisters staying at the quinta off and on since the beginning of the quarantine but that Leonor was leaving early the next morning. Adriana was a teacher and Leonor a lawyer, both relieved to realize that, thanks to the pandemic, working from home was possible with today's technology.

"However, I must return to my own home in Lisbon tomorrow," Leonor said.

"Oh, please stay with us, Auntie Leonor, please, please!" Ana Marie begged. "Uncle Gaspar can come here, too."

Leonor placed her hand on the child's head. "No, my princess, I must return to my own life as I have explained many times, but I will visit again soon and we can always Skype."

"It is not the same," the child said, lowering her head.

"Nevertheless, it is how things must be." She returned her gaze to mine and smiled. "In law it is mostly research and documentation unless there is a trial," she explained. "Now that lockdown lifts, the courts have much catching up to do and I am needed in Lisbon."

Eventually they commented on their gowns, each beautifully made custom silk and velvets designed by a seamstress in Lisbon, they said. Isabella wore a column of beaded navy satin and her sister a lovely velvet skirt and tunic the color of fine claret. They didn't always dine so formally, they assured me. "This is the first time we've been out of our leggings for weeks," Adriana said. "We decided to put on the dog, as you say in English, because at last we have a guest."

"And guests are always a gift, my grandpapa says," Ana Marie piped up.

Their English was excellent, probably better than mine because they spoke with the precision often gained among those for whom English is a second language. They ran an English household in order to help Ana Marie's education now that she was being homeschooled, but Adriana assured me that this in no way undermined their passion for Portuguese. "It is a fascinating and dynamic language," Leonor agreed, "with a story behind every consonant."

"I believe it," I said. "After all, Portugal is the nation of explorers and mariners. How can your language be anything but dynamic?"

"The Portuguese are not a boastful people," Adriana said, "but we are no less proud of our heritage."

By the time we took our seats at the long polished dinner table ladened with bowls of early autumn flowers, we were on a first-name basis except for Ana Marie, whose mother insisted she address me as Ms. McCabe.

I fell into the rhythm of the conversation, chatting about the impact the virus had on our lives and what silver linings lay behind this particular toxic cloud. I forgot how much energy comes from socializing with new friends and how badly I had missed it.

"When quarantine first began, everyone withdrew to their country houses, if they were lucky to have them. We consider ourselves blessed that Papa Carvalho kindly wished that my sister and our extended families join him here. It is not as if he was crushed for space," Adriana remarked, waving a hand around at the huge room.

"We had cousins staying with us, too, but they have returned to Lisbon now," Ana Marie offered.

"Yes, your uncle and cousins have returned to the city and we miss them all, don't we, Ana Marie?" Adriana said, smiling at her daughter.

"My husband is back to traveling for business," Leonor said, "and we thought it would be lonely for Ana Marie, Adriana, and Senhor Carvalho to be rattling around this huge house by themselves so I remained here a bit longer. Now it is time I left."

An exchange of glances passed between the sisters. Still there had been no mention of Ana Marie's father and I decided not to ask questions for the moment.

Sipping a delicious pureed vegetable soup, I smiled. "And suddenly a stranger falls into your lap from the back of a laundry truck."

Lenore laughed. "Yes, exactly. You cannot trust deliveries these days."

"And then Alice stepped into a fairyland filled with dragons and mazes," I added.

"*Alice in Wonderland* is one of my favorites!" Ana Marie giggled. "I have a Mad Hatter tea party at the end of the south lawn!"

"All designed by indulgent parents based on their children's favorite stories over the generations," Leonor added. "It was Senhor Carvalho who added the lights five years ago."

"A bit over the top, as they say, but children adore it. The garden used to be called the Story Garden in English and it had been open to the public for a few weeks each year. Now we keep the gates closed always," Adriana said, eyes fixed on her plate.

"Because the evil ones came and took Daddy away. Draggy tried to protect him," Ana Marie whispered, suddenly serious. "Maybe he is keeping him safe underneath his wing?"

Adriana leaned over and patted her daughter's knee. "Hush, darling, and please take the bread to our guest."

The child complied, holding the basket in both hands as she made her way carefully to me, eyes welling.

"Thank you, Ana Marie. You are a very gracious host," I told her, taking a roll.

The child's gaze met mine. "Can you help us, Phoebe—sorry, Ms. McCabe? Will you help us?"

"Of course!" It was an automatic response but no less heartfelt.

"Ana Marie, sit back down, please," Adriana said. "Know that you are welcome here, Phoebe, but it may be best that you leave with Leonor tomorrow morning."

"Mama, no!"

"Hush, Ana Marie, and you may return to your seat and finish your supper."

The child complied and picked up her spoon.

"I'll stay, if you don't mind," I said. "My friends and I came to Portugal to help." Once I found out exactly what matter I was helping, that is. What did this family have to do with the Divine Right of Kings? What happened to Ana Marie's father?

"You will be relieved to know that plans are in place to bring your friends here tonight," Leonor told me. "They arrive and I leave but that is how it goes. There you have it."

I almost sputtered into my soup. "Really? Oh, that's wonderful—I mean about them coming! I have been so worried and was going to request the use of your landline so I could contact them."

"Which friends?" Ana Marie asked, pausing from her careful soup-sipping. "I hardly ever see my friends now."

"Ms. McCabe's friends, and you will be able to see yours soon enough, I hope. We will have more company briefly in the meantime. Won't that be fun?

They will be leaving shortly, too. Now eat your supper," her mother told her. "Your bedtime is coming soon." She turned to me. "As your friends are currently on their way, perhaps it's best to wait."

"Senhor Carvalho keeps their passage secret," Leonor remarked. "There are so many secrets here."

"Secret from who?" Ana Marie asked.

"It is from *whom*, darling, not *who*, and you are slurping again. Please concentrate on eating and not on the adults' conversation for now," her mother scolded.

Ana Marie frowned and returned to her dinner but I sensed her ears were practically vibrating.

It was difficult to know how much to say in front of the child so I decided to stick to something safe. "Is Senhor Carvalho your father, Adriana?"

"No," she said with a small smile, "but we are all family just the same."

Now I was totally confused. Adriana called Senhor Carvalho "papa" and Ana Marie referred to him as "grandpapa" but Leonor had used the formal signatory at least once. That could mean that Ana Marie's missing father was Senhor Carvalho's son.

The main dish of spicy roast chicken and vegetables arrived, after which followed a scrumptious rice pudding so creamy I felt I could sail away on a cloud of vanilla. Conversation remained on neutral ground but I was still eager to get answers, though it seemed that nobody there was prepared to give them.

"Forgive me, Phoebe," Adriana said at last, "but it is time I took Princess Dervish to bed and read her a story. Please excuse me. I will leave you in the excellent care of my sister and hope to see you later tonight or tomorrow."

I said my good-nights and watched as the mother strode hand-in-hand with her daughter toward the door, Ana Marie waving at me as they went.

"Leonor, what happened to Ana Marie's father?" I asked as soon as we were alone.

The woman set her glass down and turned to me with her large dark eyes luminous in the candlelight. "I'll put it simply: they killed him, right here on the grounds—threw him to his death at the bottom of an ancient well. We have yet to find his body as the ground is too unstable to continue the search. Still, we know he is gone. The Divinios, or whatever those monsters call themselves, may kill every last one of us before they are done. That is one of the reasons why my husband refuses to return here and why I have been called home."

8

___

When Leonor escorted me to Senhor Carvalho's quarters later, I had learned little more except that the Divinios had somehow caused her brother-in-law's death. That was only the beginning, she assured me. The rest of their diabolical affinities were far worse but she claimed that was not her story to tell.

"If I could take my sister and Ana Marie away from this accursed place, I would, but that's not to be. Adriana refuses to leave and there's some question whether they would even let her go."

"They let her? What do you mean by that?"

She shook her head. "I will leave Senhor Carvalho to give you the full history. Adriana and I must ensure that your friends' rooms are ready for their arrival and I wish to spend time with them while I can. I will say goodbye here and wish you all the best of luck. Just knock and enter. He is waiting." With that she left me standing in front of a thick rosewood-and-ivory inlaid door.

I knocked and stepped into a marble vestibule large enough to serve as a foyer of a separate residence. In fact, it was so large that I thought at first that this had to be the library only minus the books.

"Phoebe, please keep walking," I heard the senhor call.

So I continued on into a huge semicircular room hung with thick gold velvet curtains on tall windows and walled with books. For a moment all I could do was stare. It was as if I had been dropped into the library of an ancient mariner with antique maps framed about the walls, a magnificent floor-mounted celestial globe dating from at least the 1500s, various brass navigational instruments in glass cases, and even a glinting sword suspended on one wood-paneled wall. But then my gaze swerved to the right and stopped.

Maybe I even gasped. A large portrait of a magnificent woman in a red velvet gown hung on the wall to my right. I recognized it as the famous painting of Isabella of Portugal painted by Tiziano Vecellio—Titian, in other words—that supposedly hung in the Prado Museum in Madrid. So, why was it here?

I stepped closer. Though I certainly didn't have that portrait memorized in such detail that I could recognize every aspect, something about this one seemed off. The Venetian red in the gown seemed too bright, for one thing. The background's ruby velvet curtains almost competed for attention with the subject herself, and yet how many portraits of Isabella of Portugal could there be?

"I thought you would be interested," Senhor Carvalho said, gazing at me from a leather chair by the fire, "but if that one strikes you so deeply, consider the other."

He was indicating the full-length painting of the empress holding court over the fireplace. Here the queen was portrayed standing, her gaze half-turned toward the viewer. Though she wore the same deep Venetian red gold-threaded velvet gown as seen in the first, a shade that perfectly picked up the henna tones of her hair, this fabric seemed real enough to touch.

Fine washes of paint had been layered on to create the richness of the fabric and to enhance depth. Creamy satin poured down under the sleeves in a glossy ivory color with such clarity I could almost feel the fabric gliding through my fingers. In one hand she held a rosary with her index finger pointing to the floor on her right and in the other a small book, probably a Bible.

Masterfully painted not only in terms of detail but of lighting, the subject emerged from the background in a halo of magnificence as befitting her station. After all, she had been the most powerful woman of the then known world—Holy Roman Empress, Queen Consort of Spain and Portugal, Germany, and Italy, plus Duchess of Burgundy—all through her marriage to Emperor Charles V. She was known as just, wise, and hardworking as well as beautiful. She also happened to be Prince Carlos's grandmother, though she had died many years before he was born.

"But this one is by Titian," I said, unable to contain myself, "and the other one should be by Titian but isn't!"

My host chuckled. "Ah, yes. I forgot that you were an art historian, and one with an expert eye, it seems. You are correct, at least in part. The one on the left that should have been a Titian was first painted by Seisenegger in 1531, but Isabella's husband, Emperor Charles, was not happy with the results. He commissioned Titian to redo the painting in 1534, the one which hangs in the Prado today. This is the cast-off, so to speak, but nevertheless an original, though not by the master himself."

"So Titian copied and improved upon the first?"

He stifled a cough and continued. "Yes, indeed. One wouldn't think the master a copyist but a commission is a commission. The one you stand before now is by Titian, you are quite right there, and painted after her death. Very few people know of its existence as it has been in my family for centuries, hidden away here as it were. There is an old tale that to release it to the world would bring destruction onto the family. Old lineages are filled with such stories."

I turned to my host so excited that I forgot my manners. "But how did your ancestors manage to secure two royal portraits, one of them by Titian?" I asked.

"The story goes that the empress herself requested that her likeness be sent back to her family in Portugal after her death as she knew that she would never return in person. These two paintings were to be her visitation by proxy, you might say. The Seisenegger arrived in 1535 and the Titian many years after her death in 1568."

"The same year Don Carlos died," I whispered, leaning closer to the masterpiece. Because it hung too far over my head with my nose ending more or less at the queen's feet, I could see very little close-up. Still, it seemed that a small corner of the work appeared more vibrant than the rest, as if centuries of varnish and candle smoke had been carefully wiped away.

"You've recently begun restoration but stopped," I remarked, peering closer at the original depth and beauty of the master's brushstrokes hidden beneath.

A painting of this age would be nearly buried alive under grime unless properly restored. If it was this beautiful under that sludge, I could only imagine how it would glow once fully revealed.

"True. I had a conservator in residence before the pandemic but she had only just begun to work before quarantine forced her to stop. She later caught the virus and has now passed, I am sorry to say. A tragedy as she was very gifted. Perhaps I am guilty of saving the best until last but dear Senhora Belo was quite close to tears when she began to work on what she claimed was her first master artist. I am only sorry she was unable to finish it. She had a little workshop set up by the elevator."

The painting hung over the fireplace stretched a good five feet above me, a life-size portrait. I stepped back, pulling out my iPhone to magnify the surface while roaming the camera from left to right over my head. Evan's super-magnification feature was impressive but not perfect considering that I longed to investigate with intense scrutiny. No time for that now.

"Do you mind if I take pictures?"

"Not at all."

Once that was done, I turned to my host. "Senhor Carvalho, please put me out of my misery. Is your relation to this Divine Right of Kings because Isabella of Portugal is your ancestor? Is that what's going on here?"

He leaned forward on his cane, eyes twinkling. "Dear Phoebe, you remind me of my granddaughter—quick to reach conclusions, eager to find answers, and brimming with passionate interest. Unfortunately, my answer to your question is both yes and no. Yes, my family can trace our lineage back to the House of Aviz, but no, that is not why I am involved in the Divinios matter, or at least not directly."

I shook my head. "I don't understand."

He got slowly to his feet, gripped his cane, and joined me before the empress. "She is indeed my hallowed ancestor but I have no direct claim to the Portuguese throne even if such a thing still existed. We are, after all, a republic, and rightly so. No, my involvement stems from the property this quinta is built upon, the very earth under my feet, as it were."

"But this house doesn't look old," I said.

"And it isn't, having been built in the early 1800s. After the big earthquake of 1755, most of the castles and quintas in the area were left in shambles and the residences seen around here were built upon the ruins. However, the land predates all of that. Sintra has been held in reverence by the Romans, the Templars, the Moors... It was known to be the site of many religious orders as well as renowned as a mythical and mysterious area with its own unique power. Though little aboveground remains standing, it is what lies below that drew me into the crosshairs of the Divinios brotherhood."

"But..." Really, at that point I was so lost I didn't know what to say. "Please just give me the short version, senhor."

He chuckled. "Let me try. Come, Ms. McCabe, I will show you something."

I followed him over to a bookstand where he tapped his finger on a large dictionary-size book that lay open to photographic plates of King Philip of Spain opposite his firstborn son, Don Carlos. "The Divine Right of Kings is a concept as old as time itself. Emperor Charles believed in it, as did his son, King Philip, seen here, and all the rulers going back far through recorded time, including the ancient Egyptians. Believing that the king was a manifestation of God on earth is not new."

"Pardon me for interrupting but the short version, please," I urged. "I understand all that. Who are the Divinios and what do they have to do with the stolen skull that may have once worn a crown?"

"Very well, then, the story in a nutshell: the Divinios believe that a king will lead the world back to a holier earth free of dissidents and dangerous individualism unified under one God and one religion. They believe that such a king will herald the Second Coming, Christ's corporal chief-in-arms to His spiritual being, as it were, and that all sacrifices made in his name are justified."

A chill ran down my spine. "Are you saying that these Divinios hope to start another 'holy war'?" I put the term in air quotes.

"They believe they already have. The proof to them is in all the catastrophes occurring on earth at this very moment, some of which they believe themselves directly responsible for, though I suspect they are taking credit for much of what has occurred naturally."

"But that's crazy!"

"Is it? Does what we consider to be reality make more sense?" My host was studying me; grooves of fatigue dug deeply around his face, yet the eyes remained vividly alive.

"Okay," I whispered. "I get your point: one person's crazy is another person's ideology."

"Precisely so. Bred deep into the psyche by centuries of ritual, patterns of belief become accepted truth and are potent enough to drive seemingly sane individuals to do what might be otherwise considered bizarre. Religion is the proof. Catholicism, my religion, believes that a saint's bones hold powerful magic while another religion believes it sacrilege to kill a cow. Religion and ritual have nothing to do with rational thought."

"And these Divinios believe in what rituals exactly?"

"We don't know the details. They certainly consider themselves Catholic Christians. We know that the brotherhood began during the rule of Emperor Charles and continued forming during the reign of his son, Philip. The Spanish Inquisition played a part. Whether Philip knew of the cult's existence is not known but I hardly think he could remain unaware. Unfortunately, he was never at court for very long at one time. Furthermore, it seems that the cult has been holding secret ceremonies in Sintra and in other locations in Spain ever since. We also know that a crown was created for the sole purpose of anointing their chosen king, a secret crown."

"The stolen crown?"

"Yes, the stolen crown, reportedly an object of great beauty containing ancient talismanic stones and probably commissioned by King Philip's adviser, Antonio Pérez."

"And this Pérez was the original Divinio?"

"He worked to build power within Philip's court and by all accounts was most successful, so yes, I would say so. Closely tied to power and monarchy in Spain at the time was religion itself. Much as in Britain today where Queen Elizabeth is also head of the Church of England, in Spain the kings were also deeply connected to church politics."

"And Pérez was involved in crowning Don Carlos?"

"That is our belief. He had access, being King Philip's close friend and right-hand man, and would have been involved on the perimeters of the Inquisition. Much evidence exists that indicates that he both did King Philip's bidding and worked against him for his own ends."

"So he arranged to crown poor Prince Carlos."

"While presumably acting on the king's request to put an end to the unfortunate prince's life. By then Prince Carlos was locked away at Arévalo Castle, attempting to throw himself out of windows and otherwise end his own miserable life. There was ample evidence that he had attempted to commit treason against his father, though in all probability that was at Pérez's instigation. Whatever the case, he died under mysterious circumstances in 1568."

"But what good is a crown for the Divinios if the king wearing it is dead?" I was only taking a stab in the dark.

"A living king is not necessary. They only need his skull and the crown to make their king live again, symbolically speaking. It all harkens back to the intense belief in the relics of faith."

Suddenly I felt ill. "So the crowned skull becomes the symbol—the saint's bones, as it were—for the rituals this brotherhood performs. If they have the complete set, so to speak, they believe they have everything they need."

"Now you are grasping the seriousness of the situation. Yes, the Divinios believe they need both skull and crown. They have been seeking those two components for centuries. Once those elements are again united, presumably they will feel empowered to enact their final deed."

"Which is?"

"We don't know what is planned, but since they apparently claim responsibility for everything from Chernobyl to Covid, we must assume it will be something catastrophic."

"Catastrophic how?"

"We can only guess. To their way of thinking the world needs what my son, Ricardo, used to call a 'major reset.' It was he who convinced me of the gravity of this situation. Before then, it was too easy for me to believe that the brotherhood was merely an archaic and tiresome cult. His research proved otherwise." He paused for a moment. "And they killed him for it."

I swallowed hard. "I'm so very sorry. How exactly?"

"They threw him down an ancient subterranean well on this property. His body was never recovered. His lamp was located nearby along with footprints we have been unable to identify. We tried for weeks to retrieve his body but the earth is too unstable, quarantine was in full affect, and I could not risk more lives."

I swallowed. "Are you sure that this wasn't a tragic accident?"

"Positive. It was no accident, it was murder." His eyes misted but he soldiered on. "My son was a professional archaeologist and amateur historian, all studies he undertook in his drive to...learn more about Portugal and Sintra's history. Excuse me, but I must sit." He lowered himself heavily into a nearby chair.

"Senhor, if you need to rest—"

"There is no time to rest. As I was saying, it was Ricardo who uncovered an ancient site he believed still in use for ritualistic purposes on this very property—an inverted tower or a well. The two terms are used interchangeably. There are other sites, too, many as yet uncovered. Sintra is riddled with them. Some are Templar remains, others older still. It seems the Divinios will borrow anything they believe hold ancient power."

By now I had my fist pressed to my mouth and my eyes were moist—from fear or sorrow, I didn't know which.

"Ricardo would take too many chances—roaming the land around here until well into the evening, excavating, always excavating. And I would beg him to stop but he was like a dog with a bone, my boy. He had a friend, Jose Balboa, who would help, plus he trained many men on the estate."

"Markus's colleague, the one that was killed the night the skull as stolen?"

"Yes. When the Divinios killed Ricardo, Jose vowed to help bring these beasts to justice, at his peril obviously. That was a little over a year ago and Jose worked with me to trace the existence of the skull and the crown ever since...until they murdered him, too, that is."

311

"But they used him to track the skull, which he did. That's why he told you about the X-rays. He was working to find the skull and crown all along?"

"Correct, but we had no idea that Prince Carlos was in any way connected to the Divinios before that find, and Jose was following a hunch. Once he told me what those X-rays revealed, I knew we had found our king."

"And after he'd served his purpose, they killed him for it."

"As they will kill us all once we serve ours. We know too much but the crown has yet to be retrieved. I'd wanted only to warn Senhor Collins away from further investigation when I asked him to meet me today, but instead he has dragged you all into the fray."

"For the record, I don't feel dragged anywhere. We must stop these crazies but are you safe here?"

"They need us for cover. As long as the Carvalhos remain here, a mantle of normalcy shields their actions. You must leave. I would have had you escape Lisbon today but had no way of doing so and was forced to use my own escape hatch already arranged."

"I'm not leaving, I said. We're going to find that crown and stop the madness."

"At first that is what I wanted, too. Now I desire only to protect my family. Ms. McCabe, you are all in grave danger. I will attempt to help you and your friends escape the country as soon as possible."

"No. This madness affects us all worldwide, which makes it my battle, too. I don't want to escape, I want to win," I said, pulling myself straight. "As soon as my team arrives, we'll formulate a plan."

It is always a question whether one is brave or simply mad. In my case, it was probably more the latter.

"You might want to ask them first," he said wearily. "My resources are at your disposal, whatever you decide, but first understand what you are getting into."

"I am beginning to."

"I strongly advise you to leave now while you still have the opportunity, but if you refuse, let me say that I am both heartened and dismayed. I want no more deaths on my hands. The Divinios will soon regroup and strike again. I have long suspected that many are among my staff."

"Do you know who exactly?"

"Unfortunately, no. I wait and watch. For now we are safe because they need us, but finding the skull has emboldened them. I have security guards patrolling the grounds day and night and we use state-of-the-art electronic security, all of which is no help if the enemy lies within."

I shook my head as if that might dislodge what I couldn't immediately absorb. Taking a deep breath, I stared down at the portrait of Prince Carlos. "But tell me, why this poor physically and mentally challenged young man?"

"According to Ricardo's research, the brotherhood had recruited Prince Carlos under Pérez when he was in his early twenties and secretly groomed him for the role he was to play."

"Under his father's nose?"

"Philip II was never around. When you rule multiple lands on multiple continents while waging war on one nation after another, you are always in the saddle or aboard a ship."

"Okay, so Carlos was more or less alone with his entourage."

"Yes, there were those who attempted to shield him—Queen Elizabeth of Valois and her mostly female entourage, but the power circle were mostly men, many of whom worked with his father in the name of the Inquisition. Pérez and his men were a powerful group...continually strategizing for more...in a court run by a deep current of religious fanaticism. They were the...core of the Divinios' brotherhood and they included a band of renegade monks. Excuse me, it is time for my puffer." He pulled out an air chamber and inhalant from his pocket and took two deep puffs.

"Maybe you should rest, senhor?"

"Now, don't you start. One women admonishing me constantly is quite enough. As I was saying, Philip II and his father, Charles, before him believed that Catholicism was the one true religion and that all others were heretical."

"Yes, and bloodshed, martyrdom, the Inquisition, the Spanish Armada, and general persecution followed—all in the name of Jesus. Where's the irony in that? But why would this Pérez take a mentally ill young royal and crown him as this particular holy warrior?"

"Because," Senhor Carvalho said, sighing heavily, "his mental instability made him ripe for the picking, as you say in English."

"They used him, in other words."

"Just so. All they needed was a man of royal blood who would submit to their rituals and embrace the fervent belief that he would be made God on earth. Neither Charles nor his son, Philip, took that bait for they already considered themselves agents of God. Prince Carlos, on the other hand, was always being sidestepped by his father, who recognized the boy's instability at an early age. Pérez had only to wait in the wings playing the treason game."

"So it really was all about power."

"It is always all about power, Phoebe. The brotherhood formed by Pérez wanted it all. Though they believed in the Divine Right of Kings, in their view neither Charles nor Philip carried persecution far enough. For example, they wanted women even more subjugated than they historically were and would never have tolerated a queen like Isabella being made regent in her husband's absence. Philip's queen, Elizabeth of Valois, on the other hand, knew her place."

My gaze swerved to the Titian portrait. "How the beginnings of this brotherhood must have rankled during the years of Isabella's regencies."

"How they must have, that fury continuing as the group further strengthened during Philip's reign. All they needed was an agent at court like Pérez to spur it on and then Don Carlos develops into a very disturbed young man. They sought a male of royal blood to be their chosen king and there he was."

"But then Carlos died or they killed him. How could a dead prince serve them?"

"Because, Phoebe, it does not matter whether the king is alive or dead as long as he has been anointed during his lifetime. Prince Carlos was crowned while he was still alive and it is only his skull and crown that matters now."

I thought of the X-rayed skull with the rivets in the cranium and sat beside him in a nearby chair, my stomach churning. "The brutal bastards. And now they have located the skull."

"Yes, but presumably not the crown. That went missing centuries before and we must locate it before the brotherhood."

A phone jingled from my host's pocket. He pulled it out and peered at the screen. "Your friends have arrived.

9

*S*eeing Peaches, Rupert, and Evan trudging up the tower stairs at that moment rated right up there as the best thing that had happened to me all year. Senhors Abreu and Afonso and another employee I didn't recognize arrived behind them carrying some of our luggage. I waited until Peaches reached the landing before I lunged at her in a hug.

"Whoa, Phoebe! Glad to see you, too, girl! What's with the dress?"

The fact that hugging Peaches always placed my face more or less at her chest was another matter. I pulled away. "It's borrowed. Are you okay?"

"Yeah, sure, I'm okay, though I just had the most interesting transportation experience in ages—beats the jeep-with-snorkel-and-crate-of-chickens thing I had going in Jamaica."

The three employees arrived on the landing with Markus, Rupert, and Evan. Markus greeted me at the top of the stairs with a weary wave. "Nice dress," he commented as he followed the men down the hall.

Rupert arrived at the top of the stairs, puffing, and demanded: "Do I receive a hug also? I daresay I'm overdue."

I waited until he reached the hallway before I heartily embraced him. "There, there, Phoebe," he said, patting me on the back. "Not so tightly, if you don't mind. I have no breath left after that interesting train ride we just took…in a cargo carriage keeping company with canned goods and crates, if you don't mind. Nevertheless, I am very happy to see you, too."

I stepped away, practically ramming into Evan. He set down the bags he had been lugging and readied himself for his hug. Never did a man with a mask dangling from one ear and day-old stubble look so attractive. "Where's mine?" he asked.

"I'm guessing your room is that way. Follow those guys." I indicated the three employees leading Rupert down the hall.

"I wasn't referring to the room, Phoebe."

"No? But you'd better hurry before Rupert claims the only other turret."

Senhor Afonso called: "This way."

Evan cocked an eyebrow at me, quirked a smile, picked up the luggage, and followed after.

Peaches leaned down and hissed: "Coward."

But I had already launched into tour guide mode and beckoned her into the room next to mine. "Look, luxury accommodations after your harrowing day." And it was amazingly luxurious with a fire in the grate and supper awaiting on a table by the window.

She dropped her bags onto the bed and checked under the chafing dishes. "Ah, soup and a sandwich, wine and bread. You have no idea how starved I am."

Dashing into the adjoining bathroom, she washed her face and hands and emerged to nab the sandwich. "Okay, start talking while I eat. Tell me everything that happened from the time you left for the museum until now and don't leave out a thing. Security locked me up, by the way. I totally forgot about not taking a gun into a museum but they gave it back. No hard feelings. Is Covid not a thing around here? Nobody is wearing masks."

"Did you have your temperature taken?"

"Yeah, sure."

"Well, I guess we've all been cleared, then. All I can say is that it's alarming how easily I've slipped back into my pre-Covid ease. Anyway, let me fill you in." I perched on one of the chairs and recounted the day sequentially, right down to Senhor Carvalho's startling admission about the Divinios.

She paused halfway through spooning up the last of the rice pudding. "You mean we're dealing with some kind of nutsy religious sect?"

"Something like that. This has been going on for centuries with the Divinios waiting for their moment to achieve world dominion—a brotherhood of sorts."

"They are always brotherhoods. Sisterhoods have better things to do."

"And like most brotherhoods, this one is misogynistic, secretive, and fueled by fanaticism made even more dangerous now that they've found their anointed king's skull. All they need is the lost crown," I continued.

"Holy shit."

"Aptly put."

"Christians?"

"Hard to grasp but yes."

"If you had told me this a few years ago, I would have thought you had a screw loose."

"I do rattle sometimes."

"My mama is a staunch Baptist and nothing gets her goat more than people using Christianity as an excuse for violence and murder. Actually, any religion, for that matter, and most of them have."

"And it's been going on for thousands of years, as you know. This particular sect is similar to all the other fanatical groups who believe everything they do is justified in the name of their beliefs. My brain catches me thinking that surely all that's in the past but then I see the news and realize it continues on and on."

"And men keep clawing their way to power. Reality keeps playing the same old tune."

"Exactly."

"Well, shit and damn." She wiped her mouth with the napkin. "Let's get the bastards. Wait, I'm vibrating." She pulled out her phone. "Ev just texted to say that the guys are getting cleaned up, will quickly eat, and are then requested to meet Senhor Anonymous—"

"Senhor Carvalho."

"Him—in a library somewhere."

"I know where that is. I'll just change out of this gown into my own clothes before I rip something."

"And I need a shower and a change. I had to pack for you and just let me say that now I'm convinced more than ever that you need a makeover. Loved some of those rags that Nicolina gave you but the rest is just sad, Phoebe, sad."

"You just like sparkly things more than I do. Come by my room when you're ready."

Peaches got to her feet. "Hmm," she said, still studying her phone. "Doesn't look like the sisterhood is officially invited. The message reads: *Rupert, Markus, and I have been invited to take a glass of port with our host in his library.*"

I laughed. "Is this like one of those nineteenth-century gender divisions where the women retire to discuss pretty dresses while the gents retire to the boys' club to smoke cigars?"

"And chew away on meatier topics like politics and world order."

"Like they didn't make a mess of that over the centuries," I said. "I'm sure that's not the intention here but let's go bust a party."

"Right on."

With that, I went to my own room. It only took a few minutes to remove Leonor's lovely gown—luckily without rips or stress tears—and climb into my own comfortable clean pair of corduroys with a deep green vine-printed long-sleeved shirt. For a moment, I eyed the velvet spread on the bed longingly. Swanning around in velvet had always been one of my childhood fantasies, but I discovered early on that I wasn't right for the job—too many spillages. At the last minute, I added a pair of green-leaf dangle earrings and swept my unruly locks into a top knot to dial up my elegance factor.

While Peaches showered, I slipped down the hall toward the men's rooms. If I wasn't mistaken, Rupert would have claimed the turret at the end of the corridor, meaning that Evan probably took the room next to his. That left three bedrooms in between. Since two of the unoccupied bedrooms had their doors flung open, it was easy to tell that Markus had been allocated the room next to Evan's. From some quaint notion of propriety, the women were at one end of the hall, the men at the other. Otherwise, we were kept together on the same floor despite the building's multiple wings.

I knocked on the door, hoping that he wasn't indisposed. It opened immediately on Markus holding his cell phone in one hand and his shirt half-buttoned. A suitcase lay open on the bed behind him and the largest table held the remains of his meal.

A bread crumb had snagged in his beard like a shell nesting in a bed of seaweed. "Phoebe, hi. I was just about to take a shower." His round glasses magnified those pale blue eyes under that mop of lank blond hair.

"May I come in? This won't take long."

He blinked but backed away. "Sure. To what do I owe the pleasure?"

I walked into his room, noting the open laptop on the table near the window. "How long did you know about Jose's connection with Senhor Carvalho and the truth about the Divinios and when did you plan on telling us?"

He looked like I'd just smacked him. "What do you mean?"

"Oh, come on, Markus. Nothing irks me more than having my intelligence underestimated. Don't give me any more reason to distrust you than I already have. I figured out that you knew exactly what you were looking for when you and Jose began investigating that flooded crypt. The only thing you didn't know in advance was the connection to Prince Carlos, right? That part and the fact that you were being spied on is the only aspect of your story that rings true."

He swore, and turned away. "You figured it out sooner than I'd hoped."

"Once Senhor Carvalho mentioned that his son was friends with Jose and that the two of them had been helping with the excavations here in Sintra, I got the picture. He also mentioned your name, by the way. Were you involved in that, too?"

"No, Phoebe. This is my first visit to Sintra, believe me."

"And yet I have trouble believing anything you say now. I researched yesterday and discovered your name associated with Doctors Jose Balboa and Ricardo Carvalho a little over a year ago on another forensic investigation in Spain. You've been looking for the lost skull and crown for a while, haven't you?"

He turned to face me. "All right, yes, but what of it? We didn't know that Prince Carlos was the Divinios' supposed king until we found that coffin, but okay, so Jose, Ricardo, and I have been seeking the missing crown and skull for about a year. Now they are both dead. I presume you know that part, too."

"Yet you neglected to mention such critical details."

"I needed time to grasp the entire background before letting you in on the facts, didn't I? Besides, what would you have thought if I'd told you that we were really on the trail of a fanatical sect who believed that a crown and a skull held magical powers?"

"How about *informed?*"

"Yes, well, I regret not telling you sooner, all right? I was only interested in locating that skeleton with Jose and Ricardo. Besides, I was sworn to secrecy. Everything that happened this week feels like a tsunami of catastrophes. Once I discovered that I was responsible for alerting the Divinios to the connection with Prince Carlos—that I may even be inadvertently responsible for Jose's death—I panicked. Besides, I couldn't risk you refusing to help, could I? Getting involved in this is like signing your own death warrant."

"Is that supposed to pacify me? How much does Connie know?"

His hand chopped the air. "She just thinks I'm off on some kind of Indiana Jones caper. She hopes to do an episode on me when I return."

I narrowed my eyes. "And how well do you know Senhor Carvalho?"

"I don't. I know of him and he of me, that's all. I knew the note shoved under my door was from him because references to Bosch became some kind of code between him and Jose. All this was going to come out tonight, anyway. I've considered hiding up here in my room in case Evan throttles me."

"Maybe I should save him the trouble."

He shot me a startled look. "Look, I'm sorry to have kept this from you. It won't happen again. I was confused, frightened, and didn't think straight. Let's just put this behind us and move forward, shall we? God knows we're going to need to work together if we're going to find these bastards before they try to vivisect us or whatever these nutcases do."

Charming thought. "Don't give me any more reason to distrust you going forward."

"I assure you I won't."

Turning on my heels, I left the room. From the very beginning, everything about Markus's behavior had set my teeth on edge. Now more than ever I didn't trust the man.

I marched down the hall and knocked on Rupert's turret door next. The sound of running water told me that he was in the shower, so without giving it a second thought I rapped on the next door over. It swung open immediately on a freshly steamed Evan wrapped in nothing but a towel. Bare muscular chest. Damp hair combed straight back from his forehead. A little scar on the right temple. I stared.

"Phoebe. Are you all right?"

I kept my gaze fixed on his eyes—green like sun on agate. I felt my face flush, no doubt wine-induced. "I'm fine," I blurted. "I just need a minute of your time."

"Come in. You can have all the time you need."

Maybe it was telling that he said "need" instead of "want" but admittedly *want* was on my mind. While keeping my eyes averted from any part of the man below the neck, I filled him in on Markus's duplicity. He swore softly and strolled away toward the bed, which was the only time I allowed myself a moment to appreciate those long muscular legs and the way the damp towel adhered to his body. Yes, I am that weak.

I tore my gaze away. Books and papers sat stacked by his bed and a laptop was propped on the desk with the remains of his supper neatly piled on a tray by the door. He'd been deep into researching something while multitasking his way through a mental checklist was my guess.

The scent of Portuguese lemon olive soap suffused the air above a faint layer of the man's subtle spicy cologne. "I never trusted him from day one," I said, leaning over to read the top of a stack of photocopies neatly fanned on the bed. "Don't ask me why. Maybe it's because he seems so weaselly and sweats too much. Or then again, maybe I've just gone off archaeologists as a breed."

When I turned around, he was standing there wearing a little smile. And just that towel. "Perspiring—that's as good an indicator of lying or with-holding information as any but it could also be caused by fear. He did have killers chasing him at the time." The man was ex-MI6, remember. "Still, the weaselly part is pure—"

"Instinct?"

"Instinct and astute observation. Nevertheless, you know I've always appreciated your instincts, Phoebe, as well as just about everything else about you. As for the archaeologist part, I presume you're referring to Noel. I—"

"Probably shouldn't go there," I finished for him. "Sorry I brought it up. What are all these?" I indicated the printouts on the bed in an effort to change the topic.

"I had them emailed to me from a librarian friend in Barcelona and printed them up before we left Lisbon. They comprise a fascinating collection of research on Don Carlos. For instance, this one—" he leaned past me and picked up a folder "—describes the early years of the young crown prince."

"Written in Spanish?"

"I can read Spanish, Phoebe," he remarked, "though reading Portuguese still eludes me."

"Give it time."

"In any event, these letters and accounts were originally written in archaic Spanish with a smattering of Latin here and there but later translated into modern Spanish by scholars across the centuries."

"Do you mind summarizing?"

"Certainly. This particular paper elaborates upon the young prince's tendencies. Apparently, he was notoriously self-willed and obstinate, which led to outbursts of bad-tempered violence. For example, following his father's extended absence in the 1550s, Carlos went into the stable and maimed twenty of the steeds to the point where they had to be put down. One of the letters from the household advisers at the time claimed that Carlos liked to roast small animals alive."

I held up my hand. "I get the picture: Don Carlos was a dangerous and sadistic little horror. What else does the research say?"

Evan stood there with his glasses on the bridge of his nose reading from his sheaf of papers as he'd totally forgotten that he was practically nude. You've got to love a man that entranced by his interests and a woman who can appreciate it, aesthetically speaking. "Here's something else illuminating: the reports indicate that the boy was only interested in food, wine, and women. Apparently, he developed a passion for one of the servants—'passion' in this context meaning that he chased the poor maid around the castle in order to force himself upon her—which resulted in him stumbling down a dark stairwell and suffering a massive head injury. That must be the skull contusion Markus referred to that we saw in the X-rays. In any case, the injury was so severe that his brain began to swell, causing him to lose his sight in both eyes."

"Any mention of his briefly betrothed Elizabeth of Valois or any other women in his life?"

"Valois is mentioned only as being his fiancée before his father the king decided to marry her himself. There is some rumbling that the king feared his son was not suitable for marriage."

"Which he wasn't, and seemed truly unable to form bonds with any person."

He looked up. "Shall I continue?"

"Aren't you cold?"

He grinned and pushed his glasses farther up his nose. "Not in the least." I was certainly warm enough.

"Then carry on."

"Right." He returned to translating the document while passing me a sketch of three men standing around a prone man who appeared to be having his head drilled. "This is the treatment for the prince's head injury."

"Trepanning."

"Yes, you know of it. This is a medieval illustration of the procedure showing a surgeon boring a hole into the skull to relieve pressure on the cranium wall."

"It's actually the forbearer of a similar procedure still in use today." I remarked.

"Yes, indeed. This account states that the royal surgeon attempted this on Don Carlos without success and by all accounts the court believed the prince was ultimately on death's door. King Philip rushed home to the castle." He paused to gaze at me over the top of his glasses. "Here's where it gets interesting."

"It's all interesting."

"It is, isn't it?" He flashed me a grin and continued. "So, Carlos's father, the king, spent his days and nights in prayer for his poor son while calling in all the healers across the land. Nothing worked. The king grew desperate and in a last attempt to save his son allowed the Franciscan fathers to bring in the remains of the holy Fray Diego, who had died a century before. His bones reportedly bore healing properties."

"A skeleton?" I asked.

"A holy mummy that was placed in bed beside the prince, who was raging in delirium by then."

"If he wasn't before, he soon would be after. Sleeping with a corpse would do it for me."

"The account reads that Don Carlos dreamed of the blessed Diego that very night and woke the next morning cured. Remember what I've said many times about the devout Catholic's belief in the power of bones and the holy dead?"

"I remember very well. And the mummy thing really happened?"

"It's all in these accounts mentioned multiple times by various courtiers and by the king himself. This is a faith that believes in miracles, Phoebe."

"All faithful believe in miracles. I know that you were raised Catholic but I really don't get the holy bones concept."

"And yet you believe in faith in general?"

"Of course—in deep spiritual conviction, just not on bones infused with magical properties."

"Magic and faith brew from a similar fount, Phoebe," he said softly.

I was leaning over his bicep, staring down at the printouts of cursive script and typed translation. That scent of lemon and soap was so heady my head spun.

"I'd better let you finish getting dressed," I said, pulling away.

"But there's more."

"Another time." I backed away toward the door.

"In the meantime, I'll pay a quick visit to Markus on my way to the library."

"And do what?" I asked.

"I'll put him through my own internal lie detector test," he said with a smile.

"Good." I took a deep breath. "One more thing and speaking of holy bones: we are on the trail of a group called the Divinios. Have you heard of them?"

A tremor of shock crossed those chiseled features. "The Divinios? Yes, of course I've heard of them. The brotherhood has worked to undermine the European governments for centuries."

"They reportedly began in the court of Emperor Charles and grew in strength during the years of his son, Philip."

"So that's what's behind all this."

It was growing increasingly warm in there. "I have never bought into any of those conspiracy theories but I may just have to change my mind. It makes sense that events like this holy cure of Prince Carlos by this dead saint's bones further fueled the Divinios."

He was staring into space, deep in thought.

"Anyway," I said, "I'm sure we'll have lots to talk about when we get together in Senhor Carvalho's library later so I'll leave you to finish getting dressed. Bye." I practically launched myself through the door, my face flaming, my head crammed with images of holy bones, damaged princes, and a half-naked man.

I returned to my quarters just minutes before Peaches swept in wearing one of her long purple wrinkle-proof stretch numbers with the matching spandex and sequined bolero jacket.

"What's wrong with you?" she asked.

"Nothing, why?"

"Your face is red."

"It's the wine."

"Yeah, well, you'd better lay off that stuff. You know you're a lightweight in the drinks department. Okay, so how'd you get a turret room?" she exclaimed, looking around.

"I'm a princess obviously." I shrugged.

"Well, I'm a queen," she said, thumbing her ample chest. "I can trace my heritage so far back it'll make your head spin. My aunt Rosemary was the pineapple queen in Kingston for decades and my uncle Jack was king of the Port Douglas Couch Festival for five years running. Can you beat that in the royalty stakes?"

I snorted. "No way. Your lineage beats mine hands down. My dad didn't even win the Lunenburg herring festival when he tried twenty years ago. His haul was a good ten pounds too short. You absolutely deserve the turret room, not I."

"Damn right I do!"

We burst into laughter. And quickly sobered.

"With all this talk about the Divine Right of Kings, what the hell happened to the divine right of queens?" I asked.

"I wondered the same thing."

"History will say that the concept applied to both genders but unless you had steel and fire behind you, women had to fight ten times harder to keep their power. Most queens of the day remained in the background but there were famous exceptions. There are two portraits of Queen Isabella of Portugal here—that's the later queen not the medieval edition who married

Ferdinand—and one of them's by Titian. How does she play into all this, or does she?"

Peaches shrugged. "Sorry, not my field."

"No matter, let's get down to the library in case the men try to solve the world's problems without us."

"And we know how well that's worked out in the past."

I stepped into the corridor. "But seriously, here we just joked about monarchy being won according to merit, but in the Divine Right of Kings mythos it's bestowed by right of birth." I shrugged. "That never made sense to me."

"And it's not going to make sense to you now that the supposed divine king is no more than a bag of bones and a crown."

"True."

On our way downstairs—and admittedly I got lost once or twice and needed reorientation from one of the staff—I explained my suspicions about Markus.

"I thought there was something fishy with that one," Peaches remarked while studying a vaulted ceiling in one of the halls. "We'll keep an eye on him. Did you say he was just wearing a towel?"

"I said that Evan was wearing a towel. Focus on the important bits, Peach."

She grinned. "I was. Maybe it's time you did. Speaking of bits, that good-looking black guy, Lino Abreu, told me there's a child in the household who sometimes tries to go out at night when she shouldn't. He said the house locks up with a security system like you wouldn't believe but I talked him into letting me have the code. I've been locked up once today and I don't need it a second time. Here, take a picture of the numbers with your phone."

I pulled out my phone and quickly snapped a photo of the numbers she had typed out on hers. "Done. By the way, that child is Ana Marie," I whispered back. "She's our host's granddaughter and believes her daddy is still out there. He's been missing for months."

"Poor little darling. Did you ever want kids?"

"Not at the moment."

"Of course not at the moment. You haven't even set yourself up with a man yet."

"I mean, let's not talk about this now."

"Sure. Where is this place, anyway?"

A man approached us wearing what I recognized to be the house uniform and escorted us to the library. Minutes later we were comfortably ensconced with the gents, each having graciously welcomed Peaches and me into the inner sanctum as if we'd been invited all along. Based on the "pick your battles" concept, neither of us mentioned our uninvited status.

Senhor offered us a glass of port from the decanter on the other side of the room and we helped ourselves before settling down in the capacious main seating area. Across the semicircle from me, Evan sat looking somber (and clothed) while Rupert sat next to Peaches, frowning into his glass. Markus had yet to arrive.

"I was just bringing your companions up to speed on the Divinios," Senhor Carvalho said, "and requesting that they leave Portugal before this goes further." He sounded bone-weary and I couldn't help but worry about him.

"Which we absolutely refused to do," Evan remarked, glancing at me.

"We are in complete agreement there," I said, meeting his eyes, which looked nearly hazel in that light.

"Indeed, we came here to find a headless client and to return him to his rightful resting place, which is exactly what we'll do, regardless of the grandiose notions of a band of holy thugs," Rupert added, looking resplendent in his paisley silk smoking jacket. Despite his usual blue-blood attire, he was still looking unusually weary and pale. I stifled a pang of worry there, too. "Where is his final resting place?"

"In the El Escorial Royal Monastery of San Lorenzo in Madrid," Evan replied. "I checked. As far as anyone knows, he's still there—complete."

"But now we know otherwise," I said.

"Yes," Rupert agreed. "And we must endeavor to bring together the chap's missing parts."

"But the risks, Senhor Fox," our host reminded him while rubbing his temples, "are not small and affect more than just you. I admit that stopping the Divinios is no longer my focus. Now I wish only to protect my family. Those 'holy thugs' have established a considerable network, some of whom are no doubt powerful in their own right, and they will kill anyone who gets in their way."

"And yet now that we know what they intend we can't let them get away with it," Evan said.

"And yet we are hardly in the position to stop them. We don't know the half of it. I have a friend in Spain who has a vested interest in our efforts, too, and is mustering additional resources as we speak, but it may all be for nothing. Let us never underestimate the power of the Divinios. They have killed two already and God knows how many in the past. Should they find the crown before we do, we may all be doomed."

"Do you have any idea of where the crown could be located?" Evan asked.

"No," Senhor Carvalho said. "We have been searching for years but for an intact skull and crown. At times we believed it must have been hidden on Spanish soil, but then a new clue would be found that sent us back here to Portugal. Then Jose and Markus located the skull without the crown in Lisbon—that was a shock, I can tell you. The fact that the two elements must have been buried separately or separated in later years complicates things immensely. Ricardo was convinced that something was buried here on this property and focused his search here until...the end. Many archaeologists and historians have been helping him."

"Like Markus Collins?" I asked.

"Yes, including Dr. Collins. Where is he, may I ask?"

"Taking a shower, I believe," Evan responded. "I dropped by to chat with him, which no doubt caused a delay." He glanced at me. "I am certain he will be along directly."

"He didn't tell us that he knew Jose Balboa or your son, your identity, or even anything about the Divinios," I said.

"Totally unacceptable," Rupert grumbled. "To think that the man had asked us to assist without providing the full background detail is a breach of good faith, at the very least."

"I had no idea," Senhor Carvalho said. "In Collins's defense, however, I had cautioned Jose to involve as few people as possible. I would not have agreed to your involvement had I known in advance that Markus planned to engage your services."

And then as if on cue, Markus knocked and entered the room. "I apologize for being late." Crossing the space, he briefly scanned the two royal portraits without meeting anyone's eyes before proceeding directly to our host and extending his hand. "Senhor Carvalho, please don't get up. It is a pleasure to meet you at last."

"And I you, Senhor Collins," the gentleman said, grasping his hand in two of his. "We were just discussing your involvement."

"Call me Markus, please. Yes," he said, turning around slowly, "and I apologize again to my companions for not telling you about the Divinios. I was terribly conflicted—too many deaths, the threats. I didn't know what to do. I hope we can get past this."

"That will be left to be seen," Evan stated mildly while pinioning the man with an icy stare. That warm green could chill in an instant apparently. Markus abruptly looked away.

"Help yourself to a glass of port, Markus," Senhor Carvalho said, "and I shall proceed with my story. I was just about to tell your colleagues about my son, Ricardo, whom you knew, too."

"Um, yes…Ricardo…" Markus turned as if looking for an escape route and aimed for the decanter, where he proceeded to pour himself a glass with trembling hands. "Fine fellow. Sorry for your loss, Senhor Carvalho. Yes, Ricardo and I worked on a dig together in Spain." He took a swig.

"And you were hunting for the Divinios' king even then," I remarked after taking a sip from my own glass. Rich and delicious with a robust red color that was akin to the queen's red dress, the liquid slid down as smoothly as silk-lined velvet. And zapped my brain. I was struck by the sudden effect it had on me. An intense warmth reached my toes immediately, accompanied by a wave of sudden sleepiness. Good but not good. I set the crystal glass on a nearby table and kept my attention focused on the archaeologist.

Markus had begun speaking quickly. "I didn't know him well but I admit to being fired up about his quest for a crowned skeleton when he first told me. At the time we had been investigating crypts in Valencia and I thought that this sounded like a jolly good adventure—hunting for a crowned skull… why not? My work up until then had been dead boring—"

"Pun intended?" Peaches interrupted.

He stared at her uncomprehending. "Pardon? Oh, yes, pun intended." Markus coughed and carried on. "Of course, I didn't realize the extent of it—had no idea, really. Had I known, I might not have accepted the challenge. All this Divinio business was new to me, though my sister, who has more background on European history, gave me a quick education. In any case, we stopped investigating for a while due to Covid and there you have it." He shrugged and took another sip.

I leaned forward. "It seems to me that you're left out plenty, Markus, especially since a forensic archaeologist like yourself must be so methodical."

He glanced at me before focusing on his glass. "Methodical, me? On the job, yes, but otherwise no, not really."

"Let us move along, shall we?" Rupert urged. "About the Divinios, of course most of the modern world have always believed that this sect died out long ago."

Senhor Carvalho nodded. "And for a while we had hoped so, too, but there were too many signs that they may have been operating for centuries. We should have heeded our instincts then and stopped the hunt long ago, but my son could not let go. To his mind, we had come too far to stop, but if we had, he might still be alive today."

"And the Divinios knew you were on their tail?" Evan asked.

Senhor Carvalho wiped a hand over his eyes. "Not at first. To this day I have no idea how they discovered that we were researching their history. Perhaps we were more careless than we thought or there were spies, always spies. We had even engaged trusted help from the museum to shield our efforts. Regardless, Ricardo's death was a warning, one which the Divinios believed I had heeded until I intervened following José Balboa's murder."

"Perhaps José tipped them off, Senhor Carvalho?" Markus said. "They must have been hacking him, too."

"Possibly," Peaches agreed, glancing at Markus, "but that doesn't make you any less of a slimeball." She stared at the archaeologist as if she wanted to slap him silly, prompting the man to take another gulp.

"Whatever the case, they now realize that everyone in this room knows that Prince Carlos is the Divinios' crowned king. You all have been identified and will be targeted," our host stated.

"And who knows how long they have been stalking me—us. Poor Ricardo, poor José," Markus said, still standing. He took another swig of port and looked around for a seat. "We are all in this together."

Evan pulled a chair out from against a wall of books and set it down beside him, patting the seat as if inviting a small dog. "The question remains why did they not kill you, too? They had the opportunity the night they stole the skull," he remarked.

Markus half perched at the edge of the seat as if readying to bolt. "I wondered the same thing. Maybe they think I know something and will lead them to the crown."

"And do you?" Evan asked, his tone mild but the tensile strength of his warning unmistakable.

A flash of panic crossed Markus's face. "Me? No, or at least not that I know of. I keep reviewing everything Ricardo and José discussed, everything we researched as a team in Spain, but nothing comes to mind. In fact, I often thought they were keeping things from me. I'd overhear them speaking in Portuguese, of which I know only a little. In any case, we all must keep up the search."

"I suggest that you all reconsider. I cannot bear to see more people harmed." Senhor Carvalho turned to Peaches. "And do you feel the same as your fellows, senhorita?"

"'Senhorita'—I like that—but I'm with the others. We're the Agency of the Ancient Lost and Found and we've come to get a head."

"And I've already told you my position," I said, turning to our host. "Do you believe this brotherhood will really come for you here?"

"They already have," Senhor Carvalho said, setting his glass down on a side table. "The security around the property was strengthened long before Ricardo's death and we put patrols in place even then, but it was still not enough. We believe they have found one of the ancient tunnels snaking under this land and have access to the property beyond my property lines."

"And your staff?" Peaches asked.

"Most are like part of the family but I feel as though we are constantly watched," Senhor Carvalho replied.

"Nevertheless, any security can weaken over time and every detail requires constant evaluation. I saw the fence when we entered—impressive but not foolproof," Evan remarked.

"There lies the dilemma, Senhor Barrows. It is almost impossible to secure fifteen acres of property given the present circumstances, especially since the greatest security risk lies underground."

"You say that there's a network of tunnels below the property?" Peaches asked.

"An extensive one and that system extends all through Sintra. Many are impenetrable, others have been secured with gates and blockades, and many still remain undiscovered. Ricardo had been excavating one in particular that led him eventually to an underground tower—more of dry inverted well— where he met his death. It was quite a find archaeologically but we begged him not to continue, to leave it alone, to stop inviting this madness into our lives, but he could not let go."

"A dry inverted well?" Rupert asked. "That would be a find indeed."

"It is really more of a subterranean inverted tower used for long-ago ritualistic purposes. Ricardo used to tell us about it," Markus remarked. "It is a fascinating find actually, one of great historical import, but would require a huge investment to excavate properly."

"And Ricardo believed it has been in use by the Divinios for centuries and possibly even recently," Senhor Carvalho continued. "The widest part lies on top with a circular stairway leading around and down to a narrow bottom platform that was most likely an altar of some kind. One access can be gained from under the site of my granddaughter's dragon fountain, which leads to a network of tunnels, and the other entry point, which is far more direct, lies in the forest. That one we've gated."

So that's where Draggy fit in. "Where did Ricardo go missing exactly?" I asked.

Senhor Carvalho heaved himself to his feet and shuffled over to a large map cabinet, indicating for us to join him. "I will show you."

Soon we all were gazing down on a large diagram of something that almost looked like a funnel-shaped tower with an open staircase twisting around and around and ending at a dizzying drop to the platform below. Worked in pen and ink, each aspect of the drawing was rendered with precision and labeled in Portuguese.

"This is Ricardo's drawing and is, I believe, an accurate depiction of the site he was excavating at the time of his death. Most of the initial structure was intact and appears to have been repaired multiple times across the centuries by various civilizations and interests," our host explained.

"Ricardo showed me a photo he had taken of the diagram back in Spain just before he returned here to begin his own excavations." Markus leaned over and took a photo with his phone. "It will be thrilling to see it in person."

"We will arrange for a tour tomorrow," Senhor Carvalho said, "but I warn you, the area is treacherous and you cannot go in there without a guide."

Peaches whistled between her teeth. "A disaster waiting to happen, no matter how you look at it."

"And a disaster did. My son disappeared near this subterranean tower in April. There are deep fissures left over from the earthquakes all through that area and it appears as though he was thrown down one of them. Our staff searched everywhere but found no trace. A full rescue operation was not possible with lockdown in effect, but that may have made little difference. Even now the authorities believe the area too dangerous to risk a more invasive search."

"Is there a possibility that he may have fallen by accident?" Evan asked.

"Absolutely none, in my opinion. He had roped or barricaded off every exposed treacherous crevasse. Besides, he was last seen by his workmen standing by the gate about to lock up for the night."

"And were the workmen trustworthy?" Rupert asked.

"They have been in our employ for years. No, the Divinios tackled him when he was alone, dragged him back into the tunnels, and pushed him to his death. The fissures are so deep we may never retrieve his body, and with the area's instability, the authorities will not even try. I have considered launching an excavation with my own resources now that lockdown has lifted, but the risk of the whole garden collapsing is too great."

"How heartbreaking," Rupert commented. "I am so very sorry. To lose a son...well, it must be excruciating."

"Thank you," Senhor Carvalho acknowledged. Though his voice trembled, it refused to crack. "Where heartbreak is concerned, what may be the most difficult for my family is the lack of closure. My dear granddaughter still believes her daddy is alive…somewhere…and how can I convince her otherwise?"

"But are you certain he isn't still alive?" I asked.

"To be alive and not return to his family? That makes no sense at all," the gentleman insisted, "and it has been far too long to think that he may have survived…down there." As his gaze turned to me, it's as though I felt the burden of his grief.

"Do the authorities believe the Divinios were involved?" Evan inquired.

"Very few know the Divinios even still exist. One doesn't mention their name without fear of censure. It would be like saying that my granddaughter's dragon comes alive at night, so no, they have no idea. I certainly would not introduce the subject. Instead, they believe Ricardo must have fallen down one of the fissures by accident, as if Ricardo would ever be so careless. No, the Divinios killed him, pushed him down one of those shafts, killed my son as if his life was of no consequence, and now they will come after the rest of my family."

"My deepest sympathies, Senhor Carvalho," Peaches said, "but why do you think they'll come after your family?"

"Because shortly after Ricardo's death I received an anonymous phone call threatening just that if I didn't stop searching. I planned to stop—did stop for a time. How could I not when my son had gone missing and they threatened my family? Then Jose Balboa contacted me, followed by his recent murder, and here you are. Now it starts again."

We fell silent for a few seconds. I glanced at Markus and found his gaze so fixed on that diagram that it was as if he hadn't heard.

"Your condolences are appreciated. Now you must excuse me but I will retire for the night," our host said with a sigh.

"Of course, you must be exhausted, sir," Rupert said.

"It has been a longer day piled onto an even longer few months and I am too weary—weary in body, weary in soul. Besides, I must go to bed before my daughter-in-law scolds me."

Leaning heavily on his cane, Senhor Carvalho stepped away from the cabinet, paused, and turned back to us. "Please consider this library your own. It will always remain open for your use. All of the material my son gathered on the Divinios is here, plus more besides. Do not worry about awaking me because I sleep far overhead in the main tower." He pointed above, causing us all to look up at the ceiling. "Good night for now, my friends."

We watched him shuffle toward a carved wooden door at the far end of the room and said our good-nights as the door clicked shut behind him.

"I believe I will retire for the evening, as well," Rupert said wearily. "It has been a long day for all."

I checked my watch, amazed to discover it was already 11:32. I had been stifling yawns for the past hour. "Yes, it's definitely past my bedtime, too."

We all agreed that we'd had enough for one day and made our way for the door. Just before exiting, I cast one look over my shoulder at Titian's Queen Isabella. It was all I could do not to bow.

Rupert sidled up to me. "Magnificent, isn't she? But I was dumbfounded to find two such royal portraits here, one being by Titian, since so few remain in private collections."

"Apparently, both paintings have been in the family for centuries and the Aviz family will not let them go."

"I cannot blame them, in truth. Had I a queen in my family lineage, you can be certain that I would want her likeness reigning over my household for eons."

"Don't you have an earl or two in the family tree?" I asked.

"Low-hanging fruit in comparison, Phoebe. Not the same at all," he sighed.

Rupert's late wife had been the daughter of a British earl, so his affinity to royalty was much stronger than mine. Nevertheless, since his own father had been an antiques dealer, he was much closer to the common man—and me—than he preferred to acknowledge.

We continued on our way, the five of us wending toward our quarters through the hushed house. This time we took an elegant main staircase that led three floors up to our wing.

By now, I was realizing the extent of my exhaustion, and the others must have been feeling the same since we barely spoke. All the other family portraits hanging on the staircase walls passed without comment.

The stairs ended at the top landing next to Rupert's turret.

"I'm surprised there's no elevator here," Rupert huffed as he opened his door. "There is one, but it heads up the main tower from whence we came, a private one for Senhor Carvalho's convenience, but I daresay another is required."

I hid a yawn.

"Maybe we can ask for a tour of the house tomorrow?" Peaches suggested.

"As much as I'd enjoy seeing the entire castle," Evan said, opening his door, "the subterranean chambers and the inverted tower interest me more."

"You are such an on-task dude, Ev." Peaches grinned at him.

He grinned back. "I try. Don't forget to scan your rooms, friends," he reminded us. "You never know who's watching. There's a scan app on your phones."

"Oh, you mean for bugs. Right. Night, gentlemen," Peaches said. "I suppose that's his version of 'sleep tight,'" she whispered as we strode down the hall. She pulled out her phone. "I've never used the bug app before. I presume it's the feature with the green beetle icon?"

"Yes. Just tap the icon, hold down the volume button, and run your phone over every lamp and crevice. If the light remains green, you're good. If it turns red, let me know and we'll do the removal bit together. I doubt we'll find anything but it's best to be sure."

"Cool."

We passed a table with a bowl of flowers and a three-tiered painted lamp, also some small landscape paintings, and continued on to our respective rooms. I gave Peaches a little good-night wave and entered my turret.

Stepping inside, I paused. No matter how tired I was, I had an unwavering prebed ritual: first secure the door, then scan the room for surveillance bugs, next prepare a getaway outfit in case I needed to bolt. Yes, that had become my traveling life in a nutshell. All other basic nighty-night things like brushing teeth and washing my face had to wait.

Step one: I threw the antique brass bolt—rudimentary but presumably sufficient in a castle surrounded by guards, or so I hoped. Step two: I powered up my phone, skimmed the earlier text messages, and tapped the green bug app icon. In seconds, I was scanning every likely spot to plant a bug while awaiting a flashing red light alert on my phone. None came. All systems go in the surveillance department.

That done, I peeled off my clothes and pulled on my van Gogh sleep shirt, put my shoes next to the bed, and flung my jacket over the closest chair. There. My final task was to lay my phone faceup beside my bed with the detector app activated. This handy feature would alert me should it detect an intruder's body heat. That done, I brushed my teeth, washed my face, and collapsed. Once my head hit the pillow, I was out.

But I never sleep well the first night in a new bed no matter how exhausted. The first few hours are deep and restful but then something inevitably wakes me up. Sometimes it's an unfamiliar sound but mostly I end up blaming my internal anxiety meter.

That night I sprung to sitting, glanced at my phone, which detected no sign of intrusion, and sat there with my heart thumping at 3:25 a.m. Since I had turned out all the lights, the room was dark except for a thin bar of light under the door to the hall.

I flopped back against the pillows and lay with my eyes fixed on the darkness above. And tried to sleep. Twenty minutes later, I was still wide awake and feeling thirsty. I dragged myself from the bed and scouted my room for a water bottle, using my phone for a light. My own empty water thermos had been stuffed in my backpack and I wasn't sure that taking water from the taps was a good idea. Too much lead in these old pipes. Maybe I'd have to stay parched until dawn or find the kitchen.

Perching on the side of the bed, I skimmed my texts and messages again. Most were a flurry of questions about how I was getting along from Max and assorted friends, a request for a review from the Airbnb in Lisbon, plus confirmations of this and that. It was the message from Connie Collins that made me pause:

Phoebe, how goes the adventure? Be very careful over there, won't you, and let me know if you need help from this end? And don't permit my esteemed brother to drive you to distraction. He can be such a pain sometimes but his heart is always in the right place. Put me on speed dial using this number so we can stay in touch.—Connie

Connie wanted me to put her on speed dial? She knew about the Divinios, too, since Markus implied as much.

I responded with: *All fine here so far but it seems that there may have been a few critical things you neglected to mention when you hired us.*

I was just about to pocket my phone when an answer came back pronto: *Mea culpa, Phoebe. Trust that I could not share the details. Surely now you understand why given the gravity of the situation? BTW, is your phone secure?*

I trust this phone more than either of you, I answered before pocketing my phone and striding to the window.

Now I was not only wide awake but irritable as hell. Pulling back the curtains, I gazed out into the night.

A beautiful still early morning stretched before me and for a moment I savored the Moorish castle far on a hill to the right with its illuminated crenellated parapets before skimming over the village below. A quick glance and it could be an Alpine village with all those ornate roofs bathed in up-lit grander. Taking a deep breath, I attempted to still my twitching self.

I was about to raise the window to get some air when I caught a flash in the garden below. I stared. There it was again, just a burst of light quickly extinguished. Somebody in the garden with a flashlight?

Backing away, I pulled my jeans on under van Gogh, snatched my jacket and phone, shoved my feet into my sneakers, and tiptoed to the door. I simply intended a reconnaissance to see who might be up and about that early.

The lamp was on, the hall hushed and still, as I padded along heading toward the main staircase. At first I assumed that my companions were all asleep until I saw a light beaming from one door—Markus. Without hesitating, I knocked softly, expecting a moment of commiseration between the sleepless. When no one answered, I nudged the door open far enough to find the room empty.

Backing away, I picked up my pace and marched off down the hall. Could Markus be the one wandering the grounds by himself? Not likely since he hardly seemed the courageous sort, but maybe he'd seen somebody awake about the house.

In seconds, I had dashed down the four levels where the kitchen lay, where I paused. Everything was dark, not even a night-light. To my knowledge, nothing lay to the right except laundry and storage with a corridor leading to the main wing, while to my left lay the kitchens and back entrances. If Markus was in the kitchen, surely he'd turn on a light?

I was just about to head back upstairs when I heard whispering. Or at least I thought that dry scratchy hissing sound coming way back in the darkness was whispering. I listened, a chill running up my spine. Why would anyone be down in the dark whispering unless they were up to something?

I padded down the hall in the direction of the sound, using nothing to guide my steps but the memory of a wide straight corridor where I'd entered the day before. After five yards, the sound abruptly stopped. Now I couldn't tell which way to turn, left or right? Then came a shuffling sound, followed by a click, followed by silence.

Turning on my phone light, I padded in that direction but there was no way I could tell exactly from which of the warren of rooms the sounds came. I spun around, hoping for something to go on, but nothing lay ahead except a long hall of endless rooms combined with mute silence. Turning, I headed back for the stairs.

I badly wanted to track down Markus. What were the chances that that was his light I'd seen outside or that he'd been one of the night prowlers on the bottom level?

When I reached the second floor, I paused, noticing a light about midway down the hall. Had I missed that on my way down? I'm certain I hadn't. That would be the library. Taking a deep breath, I strode forward and burst through the door. There at one of the room's numerous work tables sat a bedraggled Markus, head down over a spread of documents and printouts.

"Markus?" In the lamplight he looked as though he'd been dragged head-first through a thorn bush.

He glanced up, shoving a strand of hair from his forehead. "Phoebe? Couldn't sleep, either, I take it?"

I stepped forward, noting the half-empty teacup with the damp squeezed bag on the saucer rim, the crumpled biscuit wrapper, the little pocket flashlight on the side of the table. "Have you been to the kitchen?"

"Not necessary. Our hosts have kindly set up a carafe of hot water and snacks on the buffet against the wall." He thumbed in that direction and, sure enough, an ewer of water and an electric kettle sat on the counter.

My gaze returned to the archaeologist. "I must have missed that announcement."

"One of the employees set it all up earlier last night."

"And you're sure you haven't been outside tonight?"

He laughed. "Are you serious? Do you really think I'd just walk out one of those doors and trot around that garden of earthly frights by myself?"

"Well, you *are* a forensic archaeologist, so if anyone has the stomach for 'earthly frights' it would be you."

"Let me guess: you saw a light?" Something flickered behind his eyes.

"A light in the garden moving around."

"Probably one of the night watchmen. Apparently, there are guard teams prowling the grounds. Wouldn't that make more sense than accusing me of some pointless nocturnal ramble?" He sat back and crossed his arms. "You really don't like me much, do you?"

"You haven't given me much reason to."

"I admit that I deceived you and accept all the blame and recriminations that I deserve, but I am not your enemy, Phoebe. I am not working with the Divinios to overturn life as we know it, but remain firmly on the side of the good guys attempting to prevent destruction. Look—" and he shoved a drawing toward me "—this is my latest theory."

I picked it up and studied the notations printed out by hand on a photocopy of Ricardo's tower diagram. "What's this?"

"My assessment of where the crown may lie based on what we know now."

"And what do we know now?"

"That the Divinios are likely here on this property and therefore so must be the crown. I theorize that it may be hidden below the altar at the bottom of this well that we will finally visit tomorrow."

"But wouldn't Ricardo have found it before now?" I was peering at the arrows pointing to the rectangular shape at the base of this unusual construction. Strange etchings appeared to be chiseled into the rock. "Are those hieroglyphs?"

"Roman numerals and a cross. Ricardo discovered the remains of at least two forms of ancient writing on the slab including what he hypothesized to be the Roman numeral I. The point is that multiple groups spanning many centuries have been using that altar for their purposes."

"Making it the perfect place to bury a crown?"

"Exactly."

"A bit obvious, isn't it?"

The blue eyes magnified behind those glasses held a twinge of annoyance. "That was the area he was working on before he died and possibly the reason they killed him, Phoebe. Think."

"I *am* thinking."

"It's the only thing we have to go on and the evidence speaks for itself."

I made an effort to rein in my pique. "Depends on what language you use." I cast a quick glance toward Queen Isabella standing in the shadows. I turned back to the archaeologist. "Well, thanks for sharing, Markus."

I couldn't help but reach out and pluck a leaf tangled in his hair. "Been sleeping in the woods tonight, have you?"

And with that, I poured myself a glass of water and returned to my room, more convinced than ever that Markus was up to something.

10

_____

*T*he next day after lunch we assembled in the garden under the watchful gaze of Senhors Abreu and Afonso plus two other men to whom we were not introduced. Both of the new guys kept their heads down and made no eye contact.

"Please do not stray from the path," Afonso said. "We take you by safest route. There must be no changes."

Abreu nodded. "We take you to the well, down the stairs to see altar, then quickly back. No lingering."

"Very dangerous," Afonso added. "Stay behind me. Stay on path. Senhor Abreu, he follows last. Our men help you if needed."

And so we set off through the garden, heading for the forest, traveling in single file like young children with their daycare teachers. Markus remained directly behind Afonso while Rupert, decked out in his safari jacket with a wide-brimmed hat and looking more prepared for a wildlife trek, followed behind him. Somehow I ended up dead center between Evan and Peaches with Abreu and the two men bringing up the rear.

For some reason I had pictured the entrance to the mysterious well to be closer to the castle but we left the gardens and headed for the forest instead.

It was, I realized as I gazed around, the epitome of the fairy-tale woodland. Tall trees shielded the forest floor from sunlight while a rich threading of white woodland flowers bloomed amid the ferns. The paths were wide and in places even manicured, with small pools opening up here and there to reveal swans floating in pale splendor on the calm surfaces. One such pond even had a little castle-shaped duck house on the center island.

"Even the ducks live well here," Peaches remarked. "Many of these are specimen trees."

"Pardon?"

"See that fig tree up there?" She pointed overhead.

"Yes," I said.

"Those are indigenous to South America. Somebody a long time ago introduced specimen trees here."

We continued for almost twenty minutes further until Rupert requested a rest.

"We are almost here," Afonso called. "Few steps more."

By now we had left the path and had begun climbing a steep incline. Rupert trudged valiantly upward and plopped himself down on the first mossy rock he found at the top. Behind him stood a chain-link fence so overgrown with vines and foliage that unless you knew it existed it would be nearly impossible to see.

"Rupe, are you all right?" Peaches asked while patting his shoulder.

"Fine, Penelope, fine. I just need a brief respite before we continue."

So rest we did, giving Abreu the opportunity to dispense water into paper cups as if we were on a picnic.

"Do you guys drop bread crumbs, too?" Peaches whispered to Afonso as he stood nearby.

He grinned. "If you need. Are you hungry?"

"Depends on what's on offer." She smiled back. I figured that probably got lost in translation, which was no doubt a good thing.

Ten minutes later, the men unlocked the chain-link gate and we proceeded through a narrow path to stand by a large circular opening approximately thirty feet across strung with draping fines.

"This is opening to well. Best now when sunshine beams overhead. Stairs very steep and slippery. Be very careful. Remain on left-hand side on way down. Do not go near open part," Afonso instructed.

From this vantage all I could see was moss-skimmed marble and strands of ivy hanging down. Minutes later we were carefully negotiating the stairs, bracing ourselves against the left wall as we descended around and around a circular staircase that opened on one side to a straight drop.

At one point, I leaned over and clung to one of the pillars long enough to risk glancing down. It was a dizzying view made more vertiginous because the staircase narrowed as it wound its way down. It felt like gazing at an upside-down Escher drawing from the top of the Leaning Tower of Pisa. I estimated the drop to be around 150 feet.

Finally we arrived at the bottom, which measured a considerably smaller circumference than the top—maybe twelve feet across at most. A raised table-size marble platform dominated the center and for a moment all we could do was stare at it as we shuffled around in a circle to find standing room. At our backs six doors in various states of decay, each either blocked off with stone or gated, led away into the dark earth—the tunnel system. The dark scent of earth permeated everything.

"Where do you believe Ricardo Carvalho fell?" Peaches asked.

"We think here or in one of the tunnels. Very deep holes there, the earth unstable. Senhor Carvalho Senior ordered all tunnels blocked after the search. Too dangerous," Afonso replied. He was gazing around at the doors that encircled up, seeming edgy and uncomfortable. "We not stay long."

A brief silence descended on the party, broken by Evan. "That is most certainly an altar," he said. "Possibly Roman in origin judging from those stones at its base."

It appeared as though a two-foot hunk of once-smooth marble had been placed on top of the huge hunks of carved squared stone. He crouched down to run his phone along the numerals carved into the surface. "And these are definitely Roman—MC and the other letters have been worn away. Possibly the altar was originally used for a suovitaurilia sacrifice."

"True that the ancient Romans had sacrificed pigs, sheep, or bulls to Mars as a gift to the Gods," Markus remarked.

"But it looks like a Templar cross over here," Peaches said. We followed her around to stare at the distinctive four-armed cross with the flared ends carved into the stone.

"Yes, and I'm guessing that Senhor Carvalho was correct in his belief that this altar has seen many uses over the centuries," Evan remarked.

"Including human sacrifice?" Peaches asked.

Markus leaned over to inspect the carved image more closely. "Possibly. We don't know which of the Roman mystery cults may have worshiped here or the nature of their practices. There have been indications but nothing definitive."

"The sun shining through the oculus-like opening may be significant," I said, gazing upward.

"Maybe Mithras," Markus commented as he circled the altar, taking photographs. "Mithras was a solar deity, so perhaps rites were performed when the sun was directly overhead, and the Romans would worship Mithras in caves or underground places like this."

"But that upside-down tower overhead is much later," Peaches mused, looking up. "The foundations are Roman, maybe, but those columns are medieval through and through."

"And other pagan religions may have used this site," Rupert added. "Indeed, with a full moon overhead shining directly upon the platform, what a prime time it would be to mutter incantations to conjure up the earth gods." He raised his hands and murmured something incomprehensible.

"But if that cross is Templar, which I agree it must be, then Christians had taken over this spot for their own uses." I stared at the platform. "Maybe the Divinios. Any signs of recent use?"

"Footprints would have been brushed away," Peaches said, studying the stony ground beneath her feet. "Or packed down."

"It's been an excavation site up until a few months ago and I would think it easy to eradicate all signs of recent use," Rupert remarked as he leaned against the altar.

I was gazing around at the six evenly spaced doors exiting to tunnels. "What's through there?" I asked Abreu, pointing to one at random.

"That way to dragon fountain," he said, indicating the gated opening behind Peaches. "This one to house." He pointed to another door that had been walled over with stone. "And that one Senhor Ricardo ordered closed when one man almost fell through. No idea where it goes. Very dangerous, all very dangerous. Possible to go through only if you know way."

I nodded. Turning away, I noticed that Markus had stepped back to speak to one of the two guys that had accompanied us. They stood together in the shadows making hand signals. I shuffled toward them, but by the time I'd gone counterclockwise, Markus was back taking photos of the altar.

Rupert was still leaning against the altar, fanning himself with his hat by then. "Blasted warm in here, isn't it?"

One of the men caught sight of him and barked something in Portuguese, pushing Peaches aside to advance on Rupert with his fists clenched. Peaches caught the man by his collar and pinned him to the spot while Abreu stepped in front of him, muttering something in angry tones. An argument quickly erupted, which Abreu silenced with a chop of his hand. He sent the man away before Abreu returned to apologize to Rupert.

"I am most sorry, Sir Rupert," he said. "Some employees new and not well-behaved."

"Indeed," Rupert remarked. I may have been the only one who caught the instant that Rupert had reached for the gun he always carried inside his jackets.

"No leaning on the displays," Peaches said to Rupert. "Bad boy."

"Perhaps not," he said, straightening. "Still, how excessively rude."

When Abreu announced that it was time for us to leave, nobody protested except Markus, who was on his hands and knees studying the altar's base. A few minutes later we were all trudging up the stairs.

"Stress fractures everywhere around here," Peaches said, pointing to a lightning-bolt-shaped crack nearly severing one of the marble pillars in two. "Another shake-up and this place goes."

"Yes, I can see that," I said, touching the wall. If possible, looking up is even more dizzying than looking down.

When we had stopped by the pool to let Rupert rest on the return trip, I sidled up to Markus. "So what were you saying to that guy there?"

"Senhor Craca?" he asked, turning his magnified blue eyes to me.

"You know his name?"

"I asked his name, Phoebe—not so difficult, is it? Anyway, I was just asking if I could be allowed to take a brief look down one of those tunnels."

"And?"

"And the answer was a very decisive no." He illustrated with a mini air chop. "Satisfied?"

I wasn't actually.

The remainder of the day passed with the team cloistered in the library combing Ricardo's research material. While the men focused on the court of King Philip of Spain and his son, Don Carlos, I took a slightly different tack. I studied the queens, specifically Queen Elizabeth of Valois, Philip's French queen, and Queen Isabella of Spain, his mother in the portrait.

There were two queens in Spanish history who had stood out across the ages, both named Isabella. Isabella I, known as Isabella the Catholic or Isabella of Castile, ruled jointly with her husband, King Ferdinand, until her death in 1504. She was undeniably a force to be reckoned with, a queen of the Inquisition who also held the banner for Spain's dominion over land and sea, heaven and earth.

On the other hand, the Portuguese-born queen, her namesake, Isabella of Portugal, was born the year before the other queen died and came to the Spanish throne through her marriage to the Holy Roman Emperor Charles V of Spain.

Queen Isabella, Empress of the Carnation as she was named, emerged as an able consort for the powerful ruler and the union appeared a love match, strangely enough for the times. This was the queen in the portrait I couldn't take my eyes from, a queen among queens. She assumed regency roles in her husband's absence and proved a strong and able leader.

She must have seemed the gold standard of queens of the day: pious, strong, adored by her husband, and powerful in her own right. Philip's queen during the Don Carlos years, on the other hand, may have felt overshadowed by her late mother-in-law. Elizabeth of Valois was the daughter of Henry II of France and Catherine de' Medici, so no slouch in the lineage department. By all accounts she kept a low profile and thrived on personal pursuits surrounded by female friends rather than on politics.

The female painter Sofonisba Anguissola and Princess Ana de Mendoza became her friends shortly after Elizabeth's wedding and remained in her company for the rest of her days. I could only imagine how those women relied on one another in the politically fraught male domain of the court. Elizabeth even picked up the brush herself under Sofonisba's tutelage and pursued a creative and nurturing role in the court. By all accounts, she remained fond of the disruptive Prince Carlos and was a mother to Philip's other children, illegitimate and legitimate alike. Not all queens yearned for power but saw their duty in other roles.

I lifted my eyes to the portrait of Queen Isabella. In many ways, Elizabeth of Valois was the polar opposite of her mother-in-law. One queen held the country together through politics and might while the other worked a different kind of feminine power.

* * *

EXHAUSTED AFTER SUCH A LONG DAY, I must have slept for several hours that night dreaming of queens lost in dark tunnels. And suddenly I was shaking. I bolted upright thinking, *Earthquake!* I was going to fall into a dark hole and never be seen again! And there was that alarm! Then I noticed my phone flashing red.

"Phoebe?" a small voice whispered in the dark.

I blinked down, trying to still my thumping heart. A short shadowy figure stood beside my bed, one hand on my arm. A pink light illuminated her face.

"Ana Marie?" I snatched up my phone, disengaged the app. "How did you get in?"

She pointed toward the table. I stared, not understanding. "There are double walls. I can go anywhere."

I got up and checked, flashing my phone light under the table at the small hatch-like door that hung open. Pushing it shut, I realized that it was virtually undetectable. "So you came to visit me in the middle of the night?"

She nodded. "Do not tell Mama but please help me find my daddy now."

"Now?" I straightened. "I mean, why now, honey?"

Taking my hand, she tugged me over to one of the windows and pulled back the curtains. "Look!"

I gazed far across the darkened gardens at what appeared to be three flashlights weaving in and out of the hedges.

"It's Daddy," the child whispered. "I watch for him every night. Tonight he signals me to come. He wants me to find him. Please come with me, please." She tried to tug me toward the door.

"Wait, Ana Marie," I said, holding her back. "Those are probably the guards patrolling the grounds. It's not safe to go out there at night, which is why your mommy won't let you go."

"They are not the guards! On Saturday nights, Senhors Pao and Rios patrol and they always take the same route. Senhor Pao is on the other side of the garden near my pond and Senhor Rios is near the woods. And there were *three* lights tonight. Sometimes I see even more."

I shivered. "All the more reason not to go out there."

"But I have to!" she sobbed. "I miss my daddy and I promised never to go alone!"

My heart breaking into a thousand pieces, I fell to my knees before the girl and gripped her little shoulders. "Ana Marie, your daddy wouldn't want you to go anywhere dangerous. He would want you to stay inside where it's safe."

"No! I thought you would help." She pulled away. "Daddy needs me!" And she unfastened my lock and dashed out the door.

11

_I_ ran after her. "Ana Marie, I'm coming with you," I called. I didn't care if I woke everyone—that was the idea. "Wait for me!"

I could see her phone light against the walls as she ran down the corridor. In seconds, she had darted down the turret stairs as I bolted after.

Dashing down the steps in my bare feet, all I could think of was stopping that child. I had broken every cardinal rule of emergency exits and didn't care. Around and around the curved staircase I went, hearing her footsteps pattering below. Her phone cast long shadows on the tower walls, but the moment I reached the last step everything plunged into darkness.

"Ana Marie?" I paused, flicking on my phone light. No more footsteps, no more telltale glow, and not a single sound but for the mechanical whir of a refrigerator somewhere. Then something banged at the end of a dark hall to my left that sent me scrambling after.

A speck of light followed by a clang. She had to be heading out a back exit. My bare feet padded on the tile floor until I reached a steel door, which I flung open onto a blast of chill air. One step farther and gravel was biting into my feet as the door slammed shut behind me. An alarm began screeching from the house above.

"Ana Marie!" I cried. Now I could see her light bobbing through the hedges somewhere ahead. I took after her, only I couldn't figure out exactly which way she'd gone. Every direction ended in a wall of boxwood, and back-tracking just brought more of the same. I was in a damn maze!

Guessing that this smartphone might connect to Evan instantly, I hit the speed dial and blurted into the phone as I ran: "It's Ana Marie! She's run into the garden searching for her daddy! I'm outside looking for her."

"Phoebe! Where are you exactly?"

"Damned if I know." Then I glimpsed a light weaving somewhere to my right. I switched back to the light app and bolted after.

The house alarms were pealing so loudly I doubted she could hear me over the ruckus now but that didn't stop me from trying. "Ana Marie, wait up!"

Maybe I'd hit it right with the direction gods for once because a path opened up and soon I was bounding across an open lawn slick with dew. With her light still bouncing ahead, I thought I was finally catching up. But suddenly the light stopped. Just stopped. Maybe she was waiting?

Then something dark reared up before me and flung me facedown to the ground, phone flying from my hands. Briefly winded, I rolled onto my back and kicked out but whatever it was had gone. *Disappeared!* How did a mass big enough to throw me to the ground simply disappear?

I stumbled to my feet, snatched up my phone, and ran toward the fallen light, maybe a hundred yards away. It was her phone, all right, the sparkly case lying on the path still beaming pink light into the night. But Ana Marie was nowhere to be seen.

Picking up her phone, I called her name until my throat grew raw. Spinning both lights around 360 degrees, I saw nothing but dark topiaries with tendrils of mist snaking close to the ground. Where did she go?

"If you hurt her, I swear I'll make you pay!" I croaked. He had to have kidnapped her, whoever that thing was that attacked me, and if he harmed that child... It didn't bear thinking about.

I started running, my lights beaming straight ahead, trying to catch movement or something, but all I caught were shadows smudged by that shifting mist.

And then my feet left the grass and I was plunging through ferns and bracken in a downward hurl. Ana Marie's phone slipped from my grip but I managed to hang on to mine until a branch snagged my ankle and pitched me facedown into a bed of wet ferns.

I slid on my stomach for several feet before coming to a stop, my shirt soaked, everything dark. Pushing onto my hands and knees, I felt around for my phone. The light had gone off, leaving me blind. Damn, damn, damn. Like I had time for this.

Here, the mist was thicker, the shadows darker. Somehow, I wound up in the woods with no idea how or where—one minute I was on grass and the next not. I stood listening, sensing the shapes of trunks, ferns, and mossy rocks all around me, my heart thumping hard. Every childhood fairy tale I had ever read had dropped me right in the center of the deep dark forest and left me alone with the big bad wolf.

Grow up, Phoebe. Little Red Riding Hood has martial arts training now. But there was still something uncanny about those woods. Maybe it was only my imagination, maybe it was only that shifting mist, but the atmosphere prickled my skin. I couldn't bear to think of Ana Marie lost out there even though she must know this area better than anyone. I was the lost one.

I felt for the phone with my feet. No luck. "Come here, phone," I called in a moment of folly. Amazingly, a light began pulsing, reminding me that this was a brighter-than-average smartphone.

I waded through the ferns to where an alien emerald-green glow beamed into the night. The moment I picked up the phone, it started talking in a computer-generated version of Evan's voice: "GPS activated. Proceed to left. Follow route outlined on the screen."

"Where am I going?" I asked.

"Return to house," it said.

"I'm not returning to the house without that child," I said.

"Return to house," it repeated.

Damn.

Stepping forward, I brushed through the undergrowth following the red directional arrows on the screen until I realized that there was a path there all along, overgrown, perhaps, but there. After climbing up a set of stone steps, I was back on the lawn, delirious with relief.

A light beaming far ahead sent me running. A black shape loomed against a starry sky as my light picked up gleaming scales—the dragon fountain. *Draggy!*

In seconds, I was dashing around the base, beaming my phone on the marble foundation. An entrance to the tunnels lay below this fountain so maybe they—surely that dark shadow thing was part of a *they*—had taken her that way, deep underground where her father had died months before.

And then I saw it: an opening under the fountain, just a dark rectangular door with a light glowing deep inside the tunnel's throat. Someone was definitely in there. I scrambled down the narrow steps and froze. It could be a trap. And if I did encounter the kidnappers, what was I going to fight them with—my bare hands, feet, what? Here I was barefoot, wearing nothing but a ragged sleep shirt. Even with martial arts, I needed help.

I pressed the speed dial again but the phone kept pulsing red with the mechanical Evan repeating, "Return to the house, return to house."

I held it up. "Shut up," I whispered.

The phone shut up.

"Engage taser app," I ordered.

"Taser app engaged."

"Keep flashlight on."

"Flashlight on."

"Send message to Evan that I am under the dragon fountain."

"Message sent."

Now we're talking. I took a step down, looking around for another weapon that didn't require me getting too close to the monsters. I didn't have time to scan the app menu.

A bare earthen floor and a pile of loose rocks on one side offered the only options. I picked up a stone, holding it high in my other hand. There was some kind of stationary light straight ahead, a lantern, maybe. That's what I'd follow, not that there was any place to hide, not that they wouldn't see me coming, but a child could be trapped down there.

Several yards farther and the ground dipped. The corridor widened and there was a bright yellow reflective barrier to my right, broken as if by an ax. There'd be a fissure behind that. I didn't need to see it to feel it yawning. Electric lanterns lit the way as far as I could see.

And then it was if a hunk of clotted shadow detached from the wall and came toward me in a football tackle. I brought the rock smashing down onto his back while my other hand tried to zap him with the taser but missed. He knocked my phone from my hand and spun away long enough for me to see a black-robed man in a black ski mask and hood coming back at me.

I kicked out, catching him in the gut and moving in for a second hit, when something caught me from behind. It was as if I'd been snarled in a huge net that covered my head to my shoulders and pinned my arms to my sides. Swinging around, I tried to kick out but the man at my back only laughed while the other stepped up and punched me in the stomach. I bent over gasping while the other began pushing me down a sloping tunnel, my feet scrabbling to break my pace.

The ground declined sharply. I was stumbling so quickly I couldn't brake and, with the man pushing me along, I was in a helpless trajectory. Then I saw the crevasse ahead. Or at least I assumed that's what it was—a dark cold drop to somewhere—and at that instant I feared that this might be the end game.

I fell to my knees trying to stop my fall, but with my arms useless it was easy for the men to kick me over as if I were a Russian doll. I tried to kick out again but one took me by the shoulders and dragged me to the fissure.

"*Adeus,*" one snarled as he kicked me down into the depths. Bizarrely, I thought he murmured something else in Latin before a shower of small stones rained down on my head and the lights extinguished.

Meanwhile, my legs shot out to slow my descent and, after several scraping seconds, the netting over my head snagged on a piece of rock and held. There I dangled literally by a thread supported by my aching legs hanging in the dark. I barely dared to breathe. I wondered if this was how I was going to die—alone in the dark.

But I couldn't have fallen more than six feet. Should I risk trying to climb back up? One sliding inch convinced me of the wisdom of holding still, excruciatingly still. Even the slightest movement threatened to send me skidding down. After minutes—seconds?—of wondering how long I could hang on like this, I remembered my phone. If they'd left it where it had fallen, I had a chance.

"Phone," I cried. "Start alarm!"

I waited, wondering if the thing could even hear me this far down. Seconds later, the Evan robot voice said, "Alarm set."

"Add pulsing lights!"

"Pulsing lights added."

The noise was deafening but I was too relieved to care. Minutes later a posse of men plus Peaches and Evan were calling down to me overhead. "Hang on!"

"Trying not to go anywhere," I called.

Peaches called. "We're coming to get you."

As the aching minutes passed, I could hear men shouting somewhere, heard footsteps, felt my legs splitting in two and my feet scraped raw. Someone was lowered down in a sling to fasten a harness around my waist —Peaches.

"Good timing, Peach," I whispered. "Don't know how long this butterfly net would last."

"Some butterfly net. Nylon fishing net, more like it. Hold on while I get this thing between your legs."

Once I was securely harnessed, the men above lifted me to the surface with Evan waiting to take me into his arms.

For a shocked moment, I stood trembling as his arms wrapped tightly around my shoulders. Gazing straight into his eyes, my face only inches away,

I managed to say, "Thank you, thank you to everyone, and your new phone is… great…"

"You're welcome," he whispered, holding me like he had no intention of ever letting me go. "I'll take you back to the house now."

I stiffened. "No!" I pushed him gently away. "I haven't found Ana Marie yet. No child goes missing on my watch."

He pushed a lock of hair from his eyes with a muddy hand. "She's home safe, Phoebe. She arrived back under an hour ago."

* * *

I SAT in the library with my feet bathing in a basin of warm water and floating flora. Every inch of me ached, stung, or burned, my stomach and feet especially, but Ana Marie was safe and that was all that mattered.

Those dark monks had terrified the child so badly that she had bolted back home like a frightened rabbit, her knowledge of the secret routes probably all that had saved her. As much as I wanted to talk to her then, she was cloistered with the family, so that would have to wait.

"Those bastards tried to kidnap her," I said again to no one in particular. I sat wrapped in a blanket across from Rupert, who had fixed me a soothing pot of tea and added one of his own special digestive biscuits to the saucer. Peaches was crouching at my feet, fussing with my cuts while applying Band-Aids where necessary. The Carvalho family remained upstairs and Evan and Markus were with the security team combing the grounds.

"It can only be those unholy thugs attempting to use that poor child for their devious purposes," Rupert said. "That any group could be so disconnected from their callous hearts to use a child for such a purpose is unforgivable. They must have been plotting a blackmail scheme."

"They're fanatical," I said. My voice was slowly improving thanks to Rupert's medicinal tea. "They killed Jose and Ana Marie's father, too, remember?"

"Do you really think they'd sink so low as to harm a child?" Peaches asked, looking up from dabbing my knee. "Wait—forget I said that. Of course they would. Anything to further their depraved agenda, right? The monsters. I swear I'll throttle them to within an inch of their lives for this."

"Only if I don't get there first," I said. "They must have been trying to lure Ana Marie outside all along. She thought her daddy had been signaling her and I saw the lights myself. Imagine luring a grieving child that way? Those were the same dark monks who attacked me. They were after Ana Marie all along."

Rupert leaned forward. "At least we know them to be vaguely human. Had you said that you'd been accosted by something supernatural it wouldn't have surprised me considering this extraordinary location."

I shook my head. "They were definitely part of the material world—men in a black-hooded robes. Monks in ski masks who blend into the shadows."

"So, these Divinio chaps are running around in monks' robes?" Rupert asked, widening his eyes above his bristled brows. I appreciated how he reduced these creatures with words like "chap" and "thugs," as if refusing to grant them more power than they deserved. In fact, at that moment, I appreciated that so much that I beamed at him in gratitude.

My sudden blaze of warmth must have taken him aback. He stared at me for a moment before saying, "The tea *is* rather fortifying, isn't it? It is the honey, I believe. Would you like a little top-up, Phoebe?"

"No, I'm fine, thank you. I'm just really thankful for my friends tonight—both of you, all of you," I whispered. And let's face it, tea and sugar can be very fortifying.

Rupert met my eyes and smiled. "As we are you, Phoebe." He cleared his throat.

"Yeah," Peaches added. "I don't fall at the feet of just anyone."

I smiled. "And stick just anyone's feet into a basin of watery twigs."

"Herbs," she countered. "Comfrey, bay leaves, sage, plus a dash of oregano. If that doesn't soothe your feet, at least we can make a pizza out of you."

I glanced down at the muddy water in which I steeped. She and one of Ana Marie's nannies had gone into the gardens to gather herbs under her instruction. Apparently, her Jamaican granny had taught her all there was to know about medicinal herbs.

Rupert emitted a little cough. "Meanwhile, it would appear that as Senhor Carvalho surmised, these *thugs* must be using those tunnels for their own foul purposes, possibly entering the tower chambers from multiple avenues."

Peaches remarked without looking up: "We have to block those suckers off."

"If we can determine their entry and exit points, we will have something to go on indeed," Rupert agreed. "It is quite probable that they believe the crown is buried down there in the depths, which is as good a theory as any, I surmise. Apparently, the dragon entrance had not been used since before Ricardo's death, to anyone's knowledge."

I nodded. "That's what I was thinking. This time they used it to lure a child."

Rupert paused to read his phone. "Evan informs me that they have found nothing further but have located the child's phone. Currently they are securing the area for the evening."

He leaned forward. "Phoebe, pardon the sudden change of topic, but I am alarmed to see the outfit in which you have chosen to wear in this establishment. Am I truly seeing correctly and you have donned a ragged shirt emblazoned with van Gogh's unfortunate bandaged ear?"

"Fitting under the circumstances, don't you think?" I pointed to my wounded knee before pulling back the blanket far enough to reveal the artist's bandaged head, which actually was so plastered with mud it was hardly recognizable. I pulled the blanket tight. "Well, you get the picture."

"To the detriment of my sensibilities, indeed I do. Surely you sleep in something more proper?"

Peaches raised her head. "Yeah, Rupe, you tell her. Phoebe does the comfort-over-style thing."

He paused as if considering whether to protest the amputation of his name and, deciding against it, continued. "Indeed, one does not exclude the other," he said, warming to the topic. "I always assure my well-being by packing five pairs of the finest silk pajamas so that my comfort does not preclude style for a single moment. One never knows where one might spend the night, such as in a majestic Portuguese family home owned by ancestral nobility, for example."

Peaches glanced up. "I'm with you there. I bring a selection of slinky night-gowns just in case. You never know. 'Be prepared' is my motto."

"Girl Guides?" I asked.

"Girl *Scouts*, badass division," Peaches countered. "Guides do brownies and chocolate chip cookies. As I was saying, I always sleep with a pair of leggings on under my nightie for just such emergencies as these. You should try it sometime."

I stared at her. "Seriously? Look, I usually take my nighttime excursions fully dressed but I didn't want to lose sight of that child for a minute. Good thing, too."

"Still, van Gogh T-shirts just don't cut it in our business, Phoebe. What did I tell you?"

"If I recall, you suggested I wear something slinky and weren't referring to danger management."

Any fondness I felt for my friends bristled. I adored them but I wanted to throttle them sometimes, too. Thus is the contradiction of human relations. My sharp comment died on my lips when Evan strode into the room.

"It's done," he said, his voice heavy with fatigue. If possible, he looked worse than I did in the scratched and worn department. That made him no less attractive, by the way. "We searched every inch of the gardens, secured as much as we could, and the rest will have to wait until morning. The house is finally returning to bed."

"I'm not surprised that you didn't find anything. Those brutes have some hidden route where they can leave us all in the dust," Peaches remarked while I quickly began wiping down my legs and feet with the towel she'd brought.

"How are you doing, Phoebe?" Evan asked softly.

"Much better, thanks." Without looking at him, I was now attempting to squeeze my feet into my sandals, Peaches helping by holding them still. I imagined how bad I looked. "In fact, I'm ready for bed, so whoever wants to come with me. I mean, accompany me." *Just shut up, Phoebe.*

"I'd be happy to accompany you to bed, Phoebe, but hopefully you don't expect to just walk unassisted?" Evan said.

"Of course I—"

But he strode over to me and simply picked me up as if I were two years old and proceeded toward the door before I could protest. "You're in no condition to be walking anywhere more tonight."

"This is ridiculous," I protested.

"Just stop talking, Phoebe. Your throat is sounding raw," he said with the smallest of smiles.

"I'll be up in a minute," Peaches called behind us.

"And I will be along also," Rupert added, "as soon as I gather my tea stocks."

I was gazing at Evan. "As much as I appreciate your manly manner, please don't think that helplessness is going on my résumé anytime soon."

"I wouldn't dare make such assumptions. I'm merely taking advantage of the situation while I can," he said with a grin. "By the way, I'm leaving you with a pistol to keep with you at all times."

He got no argument from me this time. And I didn't half mind throwing my arm over his neck, either, if I was being honest, though that did dredge up memories of another man at another time.

As we passed through the door, I caught Queen Isabella's eye in a moment of female understanding: the age-old conundrum of female sovereignty under the power of the male will.

12

I had a delayed start the next morning, sleeping late and rousing slowly, but after showering and attending to my scrapes, I managed to don a pair of jeans and a fresh long-sleeved shirt. My mangled van Gogh sleepwear ended in a waste bin on my way down to breakfast, deposited with regret.

"Can you walk?" Peaches asked, meeting me in the hall.

"Of course I can walk—just not comfortably."

Peaches nodded. "All righty, then."

We had received a text from Adriana saying that breakfast would be served in the library, and by the time we arrived, Rupert, Evan, and Markus were already sitting at a circular table set up in the spacious tiled foyer. It's as if the library was to be our communal sitting, dining, and convening room, removing us from the family, whether by accident or design I didn't yet know.

Everybody appeared to be reviving themselves with copious amounts of coffee poured from a silver urn. The buffet table also held a selection of bread, cheese, and fruit. Once I answered the inevitable questions about my well-being, I loaded up a plate and sat down beside Markus, noting that he at least seemed unruffled after the night's events. In fact, freshly showered with his hair combed straight back from his forehead, he looked relatively pulled together for once.

"Were you part of the scouting party last night?" I asked him.

Without looking up, he replied, "I was. I managed to find the child's phone."

Big win," Peaches remarked. "Phoebe tackled rabid monks and was tossed down a hole."

"Is this a competition?" Markus asked.

Evan looked up from his fruit and caught my eye while Rupert cleared his throat. "After last night's events," he said, "it appears that we will not be permitted to study the inverted well and the altar a second time. I took the liberty of requesting another opportunity to survey the site again today and was flatly refused."

I looked up from buttering my roll. "By whom—Senhor Carvalho?"

"Not directly, no. It would seem that following the events of last night, Senhor Carvalho has retreated to his chambers and the chatelaine of the castle has taken over. She does not wish us to further our efforts," Rupert said.

"Not at all?" I asked.

"I spoke with the gentleman's daughter-in-law at some length—"

"Adriana?" I asked.

"Adriana Carvalho, yes—Phoebe, do stop interrupting me. We are all just as alarmed as you obviously are. Allow me to continue."

"Sorry."

"So, it seems that Senhora Carvalho has quite made up her mind on the point and insists that her father-in-law feels the same. Regardless, the family went so far as to block off the forest access following last night's unfortunate events and barricaded the dragon entrance once and for all," Rupert explained. "Though I do rather understand the impetus, I admit that the news is most distressing."

I could barely swallow. "But the Divinios were down that tunnel last night," I croaked. "Now that we know they're here, we need to scour every inch."

"Regrettably that's not possible now, Phoebe," Evan said, stirring his coffee. "The work is already done. I checked earlier this morning. Between the hours of 6:00 and 9:00 a.m., a concrete barrier was erected as per Senhor Carvalho's instructions."

"Without telling us?"

"It is his property," Markus reminded me as he focused on spearing a slab of cheese. "He is under no obligation to tell us anything, let alone ask our permission."

Rupert glanced at him. "Indeed. Apparently, he claimed that he could not risk another accident such as the one that befell Phoebe and almost took his granddaughter."

"Senhora Carvalho proceeded to stress that her father-in-law refuses to offer the Divinios one more opportunity to harm yet another person in this house," Evan clarified.

"You cannot blame the poor chap. My attempt to convince the senhora otherwise fell on deaf ears, I'm afraid. We are to remain here as invited guests only." Rupert gazed down at his plate soberly.

I sat back in my seat. "But we're hardly invited guests. We're on the heels of mass murderers. Somebody attacked me and tried to kidnap a child. Are we supposed to ignore that?"

Evan nudged me under the table, startling me so much that all I could do was gape. "Yes, we must," he said solemnly. "As guests we must obey house rules."

I was about to say, *Since when?* but restrained myself. Even without my first cup of coffee, I knew something was up.

"Besides," Evan continued, "we scoured every inch of tunnel right up to the trench where you were attacked and whatever footsteps may have been evident have been packed down or deliberately eradicated. What remains is indistinguishable."

"Who's 'we'?" I asked.

"The five men who Ricardo trained as his assistants. They live here on the property and helped with the search last night," he said.

"And are they trustworthy?" Peaches asked. "I mean, they seemed like straight-up guys but that doesn't mean anything."

Rupert's gaze fixed on hers. "It matters not that they are 'straight-up guys' as you say, since they have won the family's complete trust, Penelope."

Okay, so I was cluing in by now. Either we were under surveillance or somebody in our group couldn't be trusted. "So we're unable to return to the well site from any direction?" I asked carefully.

"No," Evan insisted.

I paused, studying his eyes—green, steady, and worried as hell.

"So we just stop?" Peaches inquired.

"Yes." Evan was watching Markus, who remained engaged in making himself a kind of cheese baguette by piling several slices of cheese on a hunk of bread. His appetite had obviously improved.

"However," Markus said as if sensing Evan's eyes on him, "presumably we can continue our documentary research."

Peaches turned to him. "Have you discovered anything new, Markus, maybe something you have yet to mention?"

The man paused from his slicing and dicing. "Peaches, are you implying that I am working from my own agenda here? Perish the thought. It's true that Ricardo shared specific details of his findings with Jose and me while we were in Spain but nothing that you don't already know—that everybody doesn't already know."

"What exactly were those findings again?" Peaches asked.

"I presume you're not interested in the technical minutiae of our forensic findings," Markus said mildly. "Ricardo had already shown us that photo of the tower diagram, which was startling enough, and I have since shared with each of you my thinking as to a possible location for the crown. The nature of the altar is telling in itself. I believe that the brotherhood has reached the same conclusion."

"Brotherhood?" I asked.

"Yes, brotherhood. That's what they are, right?" He stared at me.

"That the crown must lie under the altar?" Peaches inquired at the same time.

"Where else?" he asked.

"Where indeed," Rupert remarked, brushing crumbs from the table onto a plate. "But unfortunately we are now unable to investigate further."

"All the evidence, including everything we discovered in Spain, leads back to this property and to Portugal itself." Markus waved his knife in the air. "Prince Carlos was half-Portuguese; his mother's family lived here on this land. What better place to hide the crown of her prince but in the land of his mother, especially since Spain was rife with intrigue and therefore hardly safe?"

"You believe that the crown was stolen by the prince's maternal line?" Rupert asked. "I must say, that does seem the likeliest scenario, given what we know. Certainly there must have been a group working counter to the Divinios here if the skull and crown were moved for safekeeping."

"But we don't know the identity of that counteroperative, which is surely key to the crown's location?" I said. I remained fixed on Markus. "What did you discover in Spain, Markus—specifically? And don't worry about it being too advanced for present company." I figured that whatever ruse we were playing, we needed to sound convincing. Anything less than an open discussion of possibilities wouldn't do.

Markus stopped his super-sandwich construction to reply. "Ricardo had launched a research trail using tertiary documents from King Philip's court including the somewhat rambling letters of Prince Carlos himself, but found no mention of a missing crown or a breakaway sect. I believe copies of all those documents are here in this library, by the way. Evan, Rupert, and I have been raking through some of them but doubtless there's more. The point is, Ricardo found nothing significant in the written documents and, so far, neither have we."

"Maybe because secret societies and countersocieties might consider the wisdom of not putting anything down in print?" I suggested.

"Whoever was working against the Divinios did everything in their power to remain covert obviously. A secret society requires a secret counteroperation," Evan said.

"Yes," Markus continued, "but the point is that the only thing Ricardo came away with after years of research was the certainty that both the crown and the skull are buried on Portuguese soil, which is why he returned home to dig. Unfortunately, our physical digging must now stop." That statement was so out of character that I knew Markus was also part of the smokescreen.

Peaches was tearing up a plump roll and dabbing it with marmalade. "That still doesn't mean that the missing crown is here. Wouldn't it have been located some time ago if it was?"

"Not after numerous earthquakes," Evan remarked. "Finding anything in those mangled tunnels must be extremely difficult."

"I guess," she said grudgingly.

But surely in order to understand where that crown was buried, we needed to understand the thinking of whoever hid it? It was a conviction that had slowly been growing in me but one which had to remain off the collective table until we could speak freely.

"Phoebe," Evan said suddenly. "Are you still having trouble with your phone?"

I paused my thoughts. "Oh, yes," I pulled it from my pocket. "The reception has been spotty. I thought it might have to do with the altitude. Will you take a look at it for me?"

"My pleasure." He held out his hand. "Are you having the same issues, Peaches?"

She glanced at both of us. "Yeah, sure. The thing craps out and drives me nuts. Here, see if you can make it better."

In seconds, Evan had both our phones pocketed, leaving us to eat our breakfasts in silence while Markus proceeded to sail his enormous sandwich toward his mouth like a submarine heading into port. I watched in amazement as he opened his jaws wide enough to gnaw a big chunk of bread and cheese. Rupert, who had been carefully bisecting a pear, paused to observe the spectacle before averting his gaze.

"Nice going, Markus," Peaches commented. "You have the bite of a stealth shark."

Markus chewed in apparent enjoyment, making no further comment. That left the rest of us to sip our coffees, eat our bread, cheese, and fruit, lost in our own thoughts. After a few minutes, I took my mug and limped into the main library area, making a slow steady progress toward Queen Isabella.

There I stood before the standing queen, my attention fixed on the piece of canvas that had been uncovered by the conservator, a small dark square in the lower left-hand corner that blended all the shadows together seamlessly. Yet, here the paint seemed unusually thick in that area, as if smeared with solidified grime. Too bad that the conservator hadn't tackled that part. She must have been very methodical since she worked in a kind of grid formation, uncovering the original glory inch by inch but stopping just millimeters before tackling that particularly grimy bit.

Other than that, something about the portrait niggled at me. In all obvious ways, the queen stood in the same fashion as many royal portraits of the time —beautiful, richly adorned, and surveying her domain from afar. Her aloofness was part of the symbolism of royalty perched high above the common man, gaze fixed on her duty to God and King, which were considered one and the same. That, at least, was the accepted royal PR of the time.

Behind her, an open window revealed a deeply wooded mountain that could be anywhere. Turning toward the other portrait, I studied the background there, too—another mountainous scene differing only slightly from the other. Both windows looked similar but not identical—arched stone, as if part of a castle.

"Are you thinking that perhaps those paintings might hold the clue?" Evan whispered.

I looked up at him standing beside me, coffee mug in hand. "Is it safe to talk here?" I asked, keeping my voice low.

"No place is ever safe from surveillance in our business, as you know, but for now, just stay as far away from walls and furniture as you can get and trust no one. I'm doing constant sweeps in the meantime and will recheck our phones' security."

I nodded. "We may have to resort to passing notes. As for your question, surely this family must have considered that possibility of the paintings holding clues over the years. Has anyone identified the landscape behind either painting?"

"I asked Senhor Carvalho the night we arrived and he assured me that all aspects of the paintings have been thoroughly investigated. It is his belief that the geography was designed to appear more or less like any mountainous region in the monarch's dominion, whether it be in Spain, Portugal, or beyond."

"But both portraits were probably painted in Spain."

"Or in Italy and transported."

"I'm thinking Spain and what does that tell you?" I asked, looking up at him.

His gaze met mine. "I hesitate to say."

"Because you know what I'm thinking."

"But, Phoebe—"

Before he could finish, the door flew open and in strode Adriana Carvalho. Markus and Rupert rose from their seats but she waved them down.

"No, please sit and finish your breakfast. I have come to say only that first thing tomorrow morning a van has been arranged to take you back to Lisbon. It is not possible for you to stay here one more night after this. I apologize for the inconvenience but that is the way it must be."

And then she turned and left.

"No, let me," I told my colleagues as they rushed to the door.

She was almost halfway down the hall before I caught up with her. "Adriana, wait."

"No, Phoebe. It has been decided: you must leave. I would have you go immediately but I am unable to arrange transportation sooner."

She didn't look at me and nothing broke her stride. I had to half run to keep up. "But why?" I asked. "What have we done?"

She looked at me then, her expression fierce and pained. "How can you ask that? The moment you arrived, it signaled to the Divinios that our family was against them."

"But you *are* against them!"

"Everything quieted down after Ricardo died because my father-in-law stopped searching, but then you came and it started all over again. They tried to kidnap Ana Marie!"

"I know, I'm sorry, but that didn't happen because of our arrival. The discovery of the skull has ramped up their efforts."

"Because you are here!"

"No, because now that they have the skull, they need to find the crown and will let nothing or no one stand in the way! Whether we are here or not, nothing will stop them."

"They will leave us alone once you are gone. Besides, your presence is having a bad effect on Ana Marie. She thinks that you will take her to her daddy—you! Her daddy is dead and no one or nothing can bring him back! Now leave us alone!"

Her pace quickened as she strode down the hall. She flung open a door and entered a room, me following after.

"Leave me alone, I said!" she cried, swinging around, her cheeks wet. "You will not change my mind."

We were in an elegant sitting room with brocade couches and a scattering of Persian rugs. A large arched window looked out across the forest. "I'm sorry for Ricardo, Adriana, sorry that Ana Marie thought that I would somehow help her find her daddy, and yes, they tried to lure her away last night and they will try again whether we leave or not. They are still here!"

"I know they are still here. That's why you must leave."

I threw up my hands. "That makes no sense! You banishing us will not stop the Divinios from targeting your family again and again, don't you see? It's too late for that. Your property is positioned over their sacred ground; your family is related to their supposed prince. What's more, the enemy of the Divinios probably operated here all along. How can you escape that? The only option you have is to stand and fight."

"What do you know about fighting?" she snarled, turning on me, fists bunched at her hips. I took a step back. "Do you have a daughter to protect? Have you lost the man you love and stood by while your world literally crumbles beneath your feet? Last night, those bastards tried to take my daughter, *my daughter.* They've already taken my husband. I'll do exactly what he says from now on."

I paused. "Do exactly what he says? What do you mean by you'll 'do exactly what he says'? Did someone give you instructions?"

Her back was to me again and at first she wouldn't answer. Then, without a word, she strode to a wireless phone on a small table, tapped something, and passed the phone to me.

With the receiver pressed to my ear, I listened to the deep voice speaking in Portuguese on playback. "But I don't understand a word," I said.

"Allow me to translate since I know the words by heart: *'The next time we will succeed and Ana Marie will go the way of Ricardo, deep down the earth's black jaws. You cannot escape us, Carvalho. We are everywhere. Your guests must leave or we strike again and then your Ana Marie dies and our holy king will be born.'"*

A chill hit. I pressed the replay icon and played the call again, this time listening for background sounds or some telltale signs that would identify the caller. Nothing. "It must be the same man who threatened Markus. I'd like him to validate that, if you don't mind."

"Yes, of course. As long as you leave tomorrow morning, you can validate anything you like. Be ready to leave at 5:00 a.m. Now go." She sniffed.

Still holding the phone, I tried to dial down the emotion streaming in my veins. "Yes, if that's what you want, of course," I said softly, "but that won't make this end, Adriana. Blackmailers and extortionists don't work that way, especially not cults as vicious as the Divinios. If you give them what they want, they'll still keep coming. You're standing in the way."

She swung back to me. "Go!"

I held up a hand. "Okay, okay, but please think over what I said." Turning, I froze when the door opened and there stood Ana Marie with her nanny, Alma.

"Phoebe! I mean, Ms. McCabe!" She dropped Alma's hand and ran for me, throwing her arms around my waist and burying her face in my shirt. "I am so sorry! Please forgive me for getting you into trouble! I know you tried to stop me but I am a naughty girl who will not listen to reason," she sobbed.

I dropped to my knees and held her. "You are not a naughty girl, Ana Marie. You are a brave whirling dervish princess trying to fight the monsters out there, but you must listen to your mama." I caught Adriana's eye over the child's head.

"Come, Ana Marie," Adriana said. "Say goodbye to Ms. McCabe. She will leave us tomorrow."

"But I don't want her to go," the girl murmured, holding me closer.

I got to my feet and gently unfolded the child's arms. "Go to your mama," I whispered.

"But I don't want you to leave!"

"Ana Marie, come here at once," her mother commanded.

The girl stepped back to take her mother's hand, her eyes never leaving my face.

"I'd like to say goodbye to your father-in-law, if I may," I told Adriana. "May I visit him?"

"You may not," Adriana told me. "He is resting. Last night's events have left him very fragile. Now please leave us."

I passed Alma on my way out the door, surprised that the woman appeared to be trying to catch my eye.

The whole episode had left me reeling. I had failed to convince anyone of anything and now we were being forced to leave just when the stakes had never been higher.

13

I strode down the hall thinking only that I could not let that child or her family come to harm. Yet everything was lining up for exactly that. Our exit would signal to the Divinios that they were winning, opening the way for them to charge through the doors and perhaps raze this castle to the ground, metaphorically speaking.

Hell, I may as well have fallen into a medieval historical drama, yet this was real, hideously real, with that same sense of the surreal that blew in on the winds of 2020.

Bursting into the library, I announced: "The Carvalhos received another call late last night." I held up the house phone. "A man with a deep voice threatened to kidnap Ana Marie and swore that next time he would succeed. He said he would send her down the hole where they buried her father. Who would threaten a child like that?"

Evan swore under his breath. "Bloody terrorists," he muttered.

"Here, Markus, tell me whether this is the same voice you heard the night the skull was stolen. I've brought the house phone so you can listen to the replay," I said, holding out the phone.

My colleagues had been standing around the map cabinet. Suddenly Rupert sat down on the nearest chair, his face pale, while Peaches stood nearby looking ready to throttle somebody. Markus stepped forward while I hit the replay button. For a few breathless moments we all watched while he listened.

"Yes," he whispered, his arm dropping to his side. "That's him, that's the one who threatened me. What a damn creepy voice, right? Makes me positively ill. I can't believe it belongs to a real human. He must be altering it somehow."

Evan took the phone and listened intently before passing it on to each of the others. "He's using a voice camouflage."

Peaches had a theory: "Maybe that call was placed from inside the house?"

"Were you successful in convincing the castle's chatelaine to permit us to stay?" Rupert asked from his seat.

"No," I said. "Adriana wants us gone. She believes those threats absolutely." I gazed toward the door through which our host had exited that first evening. "I have to talk to Senhor Carvalho. Maybe he'd understand that forcing us to leave is the last thing this family needs." I moved toward the back door.

"We tried that," Markus said behind me. "It leads to a locked elevator operated by a keycard. No amount of button-pushing activates the thing."

I continued, anyway, while Peaches quickly caught up. "Adriana's become like the ultimate gatekeeper but I totally get where's she's coming from. She's not thinking straight."

"I don't care if she's not thinking straight. She's risking everyone." We had entered a small marble-tiled alcove no bigger than a coat closet with a single-wide elevator door directly ahead and a smaller door to the left. I pushed the button directly beside the elevator doors, only half listening. "She's clinging to what she has left—her only child—but capitulating to blackmailers never works."

"Still, fear of losing a child can drive a woman mad," Peaches said behind me. "I mean as in grip-your-gut-and-twist-until-you-break mad. You think your whole being is collapsing from the inside out. Losing a child has got to be the most heart-wrenching thing there is and it can leave you so broken you can't hardly think straight."

I swung around to face her, surprised to find her eyes moist. "Peaches?"

"Yeah, okay? So I lost my baby when I was eighteen. I was young and stupid and her father was just as young and ten times stupider. Kenyatta died while RayBoy was taking his baby daughter on a joyride through Kingston. Can you believe the idiocy? You protect your kids, not zoom around showing them off to your buds. Drug wars. Bastards shot up the car with my baby and then-boyfriend inside it. He survived, she didn't. The drug-dealing bastard ended up in prison and good thing, too, or I would have killed him myself."

For an instant, it all played before my eyes in a surge of pain and violence that my teenage self never had to experience in rural Nova Scotia. My friend's grief felt so raw that it emanated from her in waves. "God, Peach, I'm so sorry," I mumbled. "I always thought you grew up in the tropical paradise image I have of Jamaica and your parents—father a doctor, mother a teacher, life sunny and blissful."

She laughed. "It was blissful until my teenage self grew bored and decided to strike out for the big city alone. Anyway, I'm just saying this so you'll understand Adriana. She sees how it could all end up for her when she's probably already hanging by a thread. A parent will do anything to protect her baby even if it makes no sense to anybody else. I didn't do enough to protect mine and I'll never forgive myself." She leaned past me and pushed the elevator button again.

"You were just a kid," I whispered.

"Just stop. I don't want forgiveness. I want to make every bastard that hurts or threatens a child pay."

I had the overwhelming urge to hug her but one look at her face told me this wasn't the time. Turning back to the elevator, I stared at the elevator button, my heart reeling. How little we know about even the people closest to us, when it all comes down to it. I was so stunned by Peaches's admission that I temporarily forgot what I was about to do.

"It's not going to work, Phoebe. We tried multiple times," I heard Evan say from the doorway.

I turned to walk toward him, squeezing Peaches's hand in passing and poking my head in the closet for just a second. The art conservationist supply room. Shutting the door, I made my way back to the library, Evan stepping aside to let me pass.

"We have to do something," I whispered.

"I absolutely agree," he said softly. He took my arm to stop me in my tracks. I gazed up at him, seeing something in his tone, in his eyes. "We have the beginnings of a plan," he said, leaning toward me. Then he abruptly straightened and said aloud, "But if our hosts insist we leave, then we must go."

Had he discovered a new bug and wasn't certain he had caught all the possible surveillance devices?

"Yes, of course," I said cautiously. "But we don't have to like it."

"Certainly not." He glanced back at Peaches, who still stood where I'd left her. "Is she all right?" he whispered.

"She just needs a moment." I took his arm and led him over to one of the floor-to-ceiling windows that looked out over the garden. A gray day had descended on the mountains bringing down a heavy blanket of fog and mist.

"So, as you were saying, the Divinio crown is hidden on this property?" They must all be in on the ruse, including Markus, though in his case I was convinced he might actually believe the crown was here."

"The best possible location given what we know to date, don't you agree?"

"Probably, but we can't continue Ricardo's work if we're being forced to leave." My voice sounded plaintive even to myself.

"Sadly, no."

Hopefully that little show would convince somebody, even though anyone who truly knew us would reach another conclusion.

After several minutes of flipping through the papers with Evan, I left him to study further while I excused myself and wandered back to stand by Titian's Isabella portrait. Soon Peaches was beside me.

"She looks so thin and pale in her magnificent duds," she remarked.

"Pallor was the preferred look of the day," I said. "She may have even used powdered lead to whiten her skin, though in her case, I doubt that was necessary," I replied. "According to the accounts, she worked herself to death traveling the land while her husband was away, keeping order and the economy healthy. Her pallor probably came naturally. By thirty-five when Prince Philip was still a boy, she was dead."

Peaches appraised the portrait anew. "So being a queen in those days wasn't all about wearing magnificent clothes and looking out of a turret?"

"Hardly. Being a queen in Spain was all about duty and obedience to God and King. She wouldn't have had much of a life by today's standards but she worked hard as her king's regent and was credited with keeping the land in order while he was off waging war."

"Cool lady."

"And those magnificent clothes you see were extraordinarily uncomfortable, more symbolic of her station than anything else. Her chest was constrained by a bodice designed to flatten her breasts as if negating her femininity. The men, on the other hand, got to prance around with their codpieces prominently displayed and their shapely legs revealed in silk hose. Being overtly male was celebrated, being overtly female never."

"Peacocks," she remarked. "Matron, virgin, or whore?"

"Something like that. Femininity, even of the queenly sort, was all about holding it in and stifling your true self. You never shook your tail feathers if you were a queen."

"Hell," she said, gazing up with a regal bearing all her own. "I can't imagine stifling my tail feathers for a moment."

Since her tail feathers at that moment were encased in violet stretch leggings, I laughed. I took a quick scan around us—no chairs, tables, or lamps nearby to house surveillance items and the fireplace still crackled loudly enough to mask conversation. I whispered: "How are you doing?"

"Fine. I just had a bit of a meltdown. Little Ana Marie is dredging stuff up."

"Sorry."

"Don't be. We all have our wounds. The key is to go through life without bleeding all over the place. I just dribbled a bit back there."

I gave her a quick sideways hug.

"So tell me more about this painting," she asked.

"Something's up," I whispered. "See that blob of sfumato?"

"That blob of what-o?"

"Sfumato. It means to blend like smoke, a technique the masters used to blend tones and colors together to create a realistic shading that recedes seamlessly into the background. It made their subjects shine."

Peaches leaned closer to the painting. "I thought that might be dirt, old varnish or something."

"Maybe it is."

"Excuse me for interrupting," a voice said at our backs. "Penelope, but would you mind terribly if Phoebe and I were to stroll the garden to take a spot of air?"

We turned to see Rupert looking as though he needed something— either coffee or a nap but probably not air.

"Does air even come in spots?" Peaches asked.

Rupert smiled wanly. "A figure of speech, Penelope, my dear, as well you know."

She pursed her lips, then laughed. "Just funning with you, Rupe, honey. So will taking this spot of air involve just the two of you?"

"Yes, if you don't mind terribly. We have had so little time to speak alone for many, many months."

"Sure," she said with a shrug.

"Excellent. We won't go far," Rupert assured her.

14

---

*M*oments later, Rupert and I strode into the hall. The quickest route outside would have been one floor down and out one of the many side entrances leading to the gardens.

We were just turning right toward the main stairs when a man stepped out in front of us. I recognized him from the day before—one of the men who had accompanied us to the well, the same man who'd threatened Rupert. Short, muscular with a bony forehead lunging over deep-set eyes, he flashed us an unconvincing smile. "I am Senhor Craca and I will be your escort. Where you go?"

"We were only planning to take a little stroll in the garden, if you don't mind," Rupert huffed.

Craca peeled his lips back from his teeth. "Where you go, I follow," he said. "For your safety."

"Our safety?" Rupert countered. "But we are only taking a brief walk in the garden in broad daylight, I said. Surely that won't require an escort?"

"Very dangerous now. You need escort."

I nudged Rupert, who sighed and stifled his complaints. Together we followed the man without further protest down the central staircase toward the main hall. Once on that broad tiled boulevard, Craca turned right, as if heading for the formal entrance. A maid heading toward us suddenly ducked inside a room while another ladened with a tray of tea things stopped short at the sight of us and retreated quickly down an adjacent hall. Rupert and I exchanged glances.

And so we walked the entire grand central hall and for once none of the treasures on either side caught my attention. We were just approaching the main doors when I glimpsed something small and pink flash out of the corner of my eye. I blinked. It was Ana Marie crouched in a corner behind a potted palm. She was inching forward as if planning to dash out. Rupert motioned her back. She glanced toward Craca before shrinking into the shadows and disappearing.

I paused, trying to see where she had gone, but saw nothing but the wall and a cluster of greenery. Craca ordered to us to hurry, so we quickened our pace.

"There is barely a veil of civility," Rupert muttered as we struggled to catch up. "It is most alarming."

The front garden's formal sweep of boulevards and fountains were shrouded in heavy mist when we descended the outer stairs, the damp pressing against our faces like a wet cloth. Still, I breathed in the moisture-ladened air with a strange sense of relief. It only then occurred to me how claustrophobic the interior had become.

"I fear that I may not have dressed appropriately for the day," Rupert remarked, gazing ahead. His dapper linen jacket did seem a little thin for the day. "Best we keep our walk brief."

"My feet are still a bit sore so that's fine with me. Besides, we may have little choice. The Doberman seems restless," I remarked.

As if he'd overheard, Craca stopped in his tracks and turned to wait for us to catch up. "You stay close. Easy to get lost in mist," he said.

Rupert led me toward the edge of the path. "Surely we're in no risk of becoming lost while on the main thoroughfare," he protested. "If you don't mind, senhor, I would rather not have you walking so close." He flapped his hand at the man as if shooing flies. "Do step back." The man stepped back. "More, more. There. At least three meters distance will suffice."

Craca glowered but remained a distance behind us.

"A most unpleasant guard dog," Rupert whispered as we strolled on ahead.

"Since when did we even have guard dogs?" I asked. "And the fact that he went through the main doors is meant to be a show of power—somebody's, anyway."

"As you've no doubt deduced, the Divinios have infiltrated the castle," he whispered. "That one is proof. Evan is attempting to secure our communication channels just in case we are under surveillance. Since many have no doubt been on staff all along, they have doubtless won the family's trust." He brought his lips so close to my ear I could feel his breath. "We have devised a plan."

"You have?"

"Thank you for accompanying me, Phoebe," Rupert said loudly as we continued down the path. "I merely craved some air. In truth, I have not been feeling quite up to snuff."

"No problem, Rupert," I assured him, patting his arm. We were halfway down the first broad manicured path and Craca was walking only a few feet at our heels.

Rupert spoke more loudly. "What we saw yesterday must be one of the best preserved underground archaeological sites in existence. I have never seen such a thing. I am very glad to have had the opportunity to view it before we leave tomorrow."

"Subtle," I whispered.

He paused to dab his forehead with a hanky, one of the old-fashioned accessories he refused to relinquish. "Oh, my, but all this walking is quite laborious, isn't it? I was feeling unwell in there and hoped fresh air would help."

"Rupert, stop trying to fool me or yourself," I said. "This entire trip has been too much for you given that you are still recovering."

"Nonsense. You do know that the word 'invalid' can also be pronounced with the emphasis on the middle syllable as in *in-VA-lid*. I refuse to be rendered *in-va-lid* by a microorganism. There is only so much insult a man can bear. Besides, I live for adventures such as this." Then he dropped his voice again. "We must talk. No place is safe but this is the best opportunity we have."

"Let's rest," I said loudly as I steered him over to one of the marble benches positioned between a troll-like topiary and a small leaping dolphin statue. "Senhor Craca," I called. "My friend is exhausted. We'll be along momentarily. Don't feel the need to wait."

The man's blunted features seemed even more blurred in the mist as he gave us a curt nod. For a few aching seconds I feared that he'd come stand over us and nix any chances for privacy. Instead, he abruptly turned to talk into his phone, strolling far enough away to put us out of earshot.

"He will not be leaving us unaccompanied for long, believe me," Rupert whispered. "That cur is one of them."

I stared at the man's back. "Okay, tell me what you need to say and please keep it brief."

"Yes, indeed. Senhora Carvalho is merely playing into their hands but leaving the family alone with these monsters is most unadvisable, no matter where that blasted crown may lay."

I leaned forward and lowered my voice further. "I agree that we can't leave tomorrow. And?"

"We have formulated a plan. Truly I am not feeling up to snuff, which can be used to our advantage. Wait for the sign."

"Who's 'we'? And the plan is?"

"Careful, here comes our pit bull."

Senhor Craca was marching forward, his feet crunching on the gravel. "We go now," he ordered. "Move, please."

"Tell me your plan before it's too late," I whispered.

But it was already too late. Craca arrived to stand over us, glowering. Rupert heaved an exaggerated sigh and stood, the two of us making a slow measured progress behind the guard toward the house.

Rupert was perspiring so heavily that I knew his weariness wasn't feigned. Without knowing the details of the plan, I had no idea how to play the situation from here on. Best to just follow his lead. "Rupert, you need to rest. You're in no shape to go anywhere tomorrow," I whispered.

"I don't plan to," he murmured. "We must communicate by note from here on," he whispered. "We have been attempting to line up transportation but it fell through. The coronavirus—"

"What is problem?" Craca barked.

"He can't move as quickly as we can," I snapped.

Craca turned on his heels and marched into the house.

The moment that we stepped into the castle behind him through yet another side entrance, I caught that flash of pink again, this time in the shadows to my right. Now Ana Marie was beckoning us to follow her around a dark corner. Putting a finger to my lips, I pointed ahead to Craca and shook my head. She peered around the corner and pulled quickly back while mouthing something and pointing overhead.

Rupert, leaning heavily on me, watched the exchange. "Senhor Craca, hold on, please," he called.

The man turned and waited, a flash of irritation visible on his broad features.

"I don't feel quite well enough to brave those steps to the bedrooms at the moment—quite out of the question. I would prefer to retire to the library for a spot of tea and recuperation; it's more manageable given my present state."

"I take you to room as instructed," Craca said.

"Instructed by whom?" I asked. "Senhora Carvalho? I am certain she would not want one of her guests to pass out on the stairs. Let me speak to the lady." I held out my hand for his phone.

Craca hesitated. I knew damn well that Adriana wasn't at the end of that phone.

Rupert pressed our advantage. "Do tell her that Sir Rupert Fox is not well and requests a brief respite in the room to which has been afforded for our leisure. Tell her," Rupert said more loudly, turning up the garrulous quotient like a pro, "that I really must insist unless you plan to carry me up those stairs single-handedly. I simply cannot …manage them…at the moment." Still leaning against me, he mopped his brow. "Shall I call her myself?" He removed his own phone.

Craca stepped forward as if to intervene and for a second I was afraid he might try to wrench the phone away.

"Do you want your guest to pass out on your watch, senhor? Do as he asks and take us to the library, which is much closer at hand," I insisted, though nothing was really close in that place.

Craca began talking hurriedly into his phone. After a second he jerked his head at us and led us down the long hall. His heavy footsteps masking our whispers.

"Adriana is not at the end of that phone," I said.

"I agree," Rupert said between huffs. If he was feigning his breathlessness, he was doing a damn good job.

Climbing even one set of stairs seemed truly challenging for Rupert and by now I realized his condition was more serious than I thought. Craca made no offer to assist, leaving everything up to me. After many long laborious minutes, we finally arrived at the deserted library.

Rupert stumbled to one of the velvet couches and collapsed. "Tea!" he croaked.

Craca muttered something before retreating. We heard him shouting to some hapless servant. I felt Rupert's forehead, relieved to find no signs of a fever.

"It's all right, Phoebe," he whispered. "I am merely exhausted from all this excitement and not on the brink of some nasty virus apocalypse, if that is what you are surmising."

I smiled and held his hand, my eyes swerving to Queen Isabella. "Where are the others?"

"Evan will be in his room…working on the technology. I have no idea about the others."

Minutes later, a maid entered with a tray of tea things. She set it down on the table, cast us a quick smile, and quickly left. I followed her to the door long enough to see Craca standing on guard outside.

That's it, it was official: we were prisoners. When I turned around, something pink was waving from the elevator alcove. Rupert, now propped on his elbows, waved back before sinking back against the pillows.

"I'm just going to sit by the window while you rest," I told Rupert loudly. "Whenever you're ready to go to your room, let me know."

"I shall," he murmured, closing his eyes. "No doubt the tea will fortify me sufficiently to make it up…the next flight…"

I slipped around the perimeter to the elevator alcove.

Ana Marie was waiting, finger on her lips. "Phoebe, I will take you to my grandpapa now," she whispered. She tugged me into the conservationist's closet. "I do not know why Mama will not let you see him but he wishes to see you."

She dropped my hand long enough to dart under a table packed with boxes, shove away one of the containers, and beckon me under. In seconds, her little pink leggings were disappearing as she crawled out of sight. I bent down to look at the two-foot-square opening hidden behind a flap of false wall.

"Come, Phoebe, hurry!"

I had no idea if I could even fit in there, let alone hurry doing it. But soon I was on my hands and knees squeezing through the hatch, fearing that my bottom end would wedge in the opening leaving all of us in an untenable position and me in a humiliating one. But by pushing my elbows against the floorboards, I managed to drag myself forward until I had just enough room to unfold myself into a kind of crouching stand.

The area was dark, dusty, and stuffy. I sneezed.

"Shhh!" the girl warned. Already far above me in the cramped stairwell she was out of sight. I scrambled after her in a narrow twisting stairway that appeared to curve all the way up beside the elevator shaft. Muttering to myself, I used my phone to light the way while stifling sneezes.

At last we arrived inside another closet, this one much larger and filled with gentlemen's clothing, cubicles of footwear, and the scent of cloves.

"Come. No one knows that I am gone but we must be very quick," Ana Marie told me.

"Quick," I said, brushing dust off my sweater.

"Yes, not slow."

"Ana Marie, I'm sorry about last night. I couldn't catch the bad men who tried to hurt you."

She gazed up at me in the half-light, her heart-shaped face solemn. "The monsters tried to steal me away but I escaped them. All things are dangerous now, Phoebe. Grandpapa said that we must be brave."

That shut me up. She took my hand and led me through the hanging suits, past the shelves of shirts and sweaters, and into a spacious round room where the floor-to-ceiling drapes had been drawn against the light. I blinked, trying to adjust my eyes. Around me I glimpsed a bureau, a dresser, dark wallpaper...

"Grandpapa, I have brought her!" Ana Marie dropped my hand and ran across the room toward a bed plumped high with brocade cushions where Senhor Carvalho sat, book in hand.

"Ana Marie! So you have successfully escaped poor Alma again! In truth, I believe she only pretends to sleep so you can get away," he said, setting aside his iPad and awaiting his granddaughter's landing.

The child practically flung herself at her grandfather, tumbling in among the pillows with a giggle. "And I have brought Phoebe as you requested, I mean Senhora McCabe."

"Phoebe, I am so relieved to see you. I did not know how we could manage it at first but this little girl is a brilliant strategist." Senhor Carvalho caught my gaze over top of the girl's head in the midst of giving her a hearty hug.

Ana Marie lifted her head. "What is 'strategist'?"

"It means one who is very clever like you are. Now, my dear, you must leave us and return back to poor Alma so she does not get into trouble once again."

Ana Marie sighed. "Yes, poor Alma. I will come back to see you as soon as I can, but first I must distract Senhor Craca. I like that word—distract."

"Distract? Ana Marie, what are you planning now?"

"I will go out through another way and make him follow me. He runs, I hide. It will make him very cross. Senhor Craca does not like me." She grinned.

"Be very careful, child. That man is not our friend."

"I know, so I annoy him more. Bye, Grandpapa."

Senhor Carvalho shook his head. "Be careful. Remember what I told you: this is not a game."

"Not a game," the child agreed, "but a battle between good and evil. I won't forget. Goodbye for now, Grandpapa, and goodbye, Phoebe. I hope Grandpapa helps you stay." Ana Marie blew him a kiss, tossed me a little wave, and darted back inside the closet.

Only once the child disappeared did Senhor Carvalho speak. "I apologize on behalf of my family for the manner in which you and your friends have been treated. My daughter-in-law is terrified and refuses to listen to reason. She hears only threats and gives too much credence to certain staff. We are now infiltrated by our enemies, who grow bolder by the day."

I stepped forward. "So you do know?"

"How could I not? It is as if we are surrounded by strangers wearing the masks of our friends," he continued. "Some are loyal, others do the brotherhood's bidding, either from bribery, coercion, or conviction, we know not which. Ours has become a tenuous existence."

"But they are forcing us to leave tomorrow."

"Yes, that is why I asked Ana Marie to bring you to me. Their plan is not to send you to the airport but to ensure that you come to a horrible end along the way. That's the Divinios' pattern: accidents, unfortunate events, seemingly random twists of fate. Believe me, Adriana has no idea."

"We can't let that happen and we certainly can't just leave you alone with the Divinios."

"I have been in touch with a Spanish friend to arrange your escape, but with Covid, transportation has become more difficult. He can only guarantee safe passage for three. In the meantime, Sir Rupert and I have devised a plan that keeps him here."

"You and Sir Rupert?"

"Dear Phoebe, do not look so shocked. It is the mistake of the young to believe that those older are unable to plot. Ana Marie has passed several notes between your friend and me, which has assisted us to formulate a strategy."

I laughed, sobering quickly. "I know Sir Rupert's ability to plot. I've been on the receiving end of that enough times. Rupert implied that he was up to something a few minutes ago but didn't get into the details. What exactly are you brewing?"

"The gist of it is this: tomorrow, Sir Rupert will appear too ill to travel. Let them think what they will regarding the cause but it will be necessary for him to stay behind in isolation for which he will require support. He and one other will stay while you, Senhor Collins, and Senhor Barrows are transported elsewhere. It's you the Divinios wish to destroy most. Senhor Fox and Senhora Williams will be safe enough for now."

"But for how long?"

"The Divinios will not harm them or our family as long as we appear to remain compliant. They need to retain an appearance of normality to carry out their diabolical plans. A sick man and his nurse will be of no concern. It's you three they fear the most. You they know by reputation."

"Then we will be the ones to escape to Spain. That's where we'll hunt for the crown."

He studied my face. "That was one of the theories Ricardo was chasing for years but he found nothing to confirm that theory. He returned to Portugal to continue the hunt. I hold little hope that you'll find something there."

"Sometimes we can't see what lies right under our nose."

His eyebrows rose. "Dear Phoebe, what are you thinking?"

"Just that I must get to Spain."

"But you know that Spain is at least as dangerous as remaining here, maybe more so, even with my friend's considerable assistance. There are hundreds of the Divinio brotherhood active there."

"But once that crown is safely beyond their reach, that monster loses its teeth, right?"

"So we hope."

"Then we have to try. It's the only chance we have. Please tell me more about your Spanish friend. You've been so scant on details up until now."

Senhor Carvalho closed his eyes for an instant. "And reticent I must remain at his request. He—they, actually, for there is more than one, though I know the elder best—will remain anonymous." When he opened his eyes again, his gaze held mine in a strong grip. "What assistance he'll offer will be at arm's length but he does have better access to historic places than I. I will contact him again."

"Thank you. My hunch is the best chance we have."

"And what can you tell me about your hunch?"

I smiled. "I prefer to keep my hunches under wraps. Call it superstition but if I expose them to air too early they tend to shrivel."

He smiled slightly. "And who am I to threaten something so fragile? In the meantime, you and your friends must pack for exit. It's imperative that you follow the preliminary plan that Adriana established even if it is only to deviate at the first opportunity. Leave that part to me. Once everything is arranged, I will dispatch a note tonight."

"Through one of the myriad secret passageways that snake through this house?"

He smiled. "Hidden passageways abound in large houses like this. We keep them secret so they can serve us when we need them."

"One more thing, senhor: do you have documentation regarding the exact time the Titian Isabella portrait arrived in Portugal?"

"The Aviz ledgers were destroyed in the fires. So you believe the answer lies somewhere there?"

"Maybe."

"Then good luck, my friend. God knows you'll need it." Studying me from over top of his glasses, his gaze struck me as alert and calculating. "I will communicate with you by note regarding tomorrow. In the meantime, please be safe and keep this with you at all times."

I took the object from his fingers, smiling as I tucked the little metal button down into my jacket pocket. "A tracking device."

"My Spanish friend will need it to locate you."

"I'm sure he will."

"One other thing, Phoebe."

I waited.

"You will need a password. Choose your own and I will ensure that he receives that, too."

"You are a strategist, too, I see." I thought for a moment. "Isabella."

He nodded and smiled. "Godspeed in the name of Isabella."

"You, too," I said, backing away, "and forgive me for what I am about to do."

"Pardon me?"

I grinned. "Desperate times require desperate measures, senhor."

Soon I was carefully negotiating the stairway downward, which had been bad enough going up. When I finally hauled myself out of the crawlspace, I was suppressing sneezes and covered in dust. I took a moment to beat the dirt off my clothes, replace the boxes, and study the bottles, jars, and boxes crammed into the small space. The room smelled faintly of solvents.

I then proceeded to slip into the library and inch toward the seat closest to the garden window, thinking only to pretend to study long enough for Craca to check in. Who knew how long Ana Marie could distract the bastard.

Taking a seat, I stared across the room. "Rupert?" I called. "Are you feeling any better?"

No answer. That sent me to the couch, heart in my throat. There my friend lay stretched out against the cushions, eyes closed, his face pale and shiny, the tea untouched…

"Help!" I cried, running for the door.

15

Supper that evening was a solemn affair. Rupert remained in his room complaining of illness, leaving the rest of us to hurry through our fish and soup, too anxious to enjoy the meal.

Adriana had arrived in the library earlier to deliver instructions for the morning, careful not to meet our eyes before sweeping out. If she knew that the Divinios intended to ambush us somewhere between Sintra and the airport, would she have aborted her plan? I guessed that she was simply in emotional lockdown, trying to keep the pieces together any way she could.

"We're acting like this is our last supper," Markus complained, ladling himself another serving of vegetable soup. The food had become much less bountiful in the past day but no less delicious. It was as if the entire household was operating under occupation.

"It sure feels that way," Peaches mumbled, gazing sourly at her plate.

At 5:00 a.m. a van was to arrive from Lisbon to take us to the airport where we would remain at a hotel until we could negotiate our various flights back to Britain. Or that was the official script.

"I have checked the flights leaving Lisbon for London and have only managed to secure two seats on the Porto flight at 6:00 p.m. so far," Evan remarked. "I will keep trying, of course."

In the meantime, we needed a way to pass a hardcopy of a running dialogue among us, a problem that had been preoccupying me along with everything else. Any obvious transfer of notes might be seen by the spies infil-trating the place. Subterfuge was needed.

An idea came while nibbling on a pastry. "Hey, is anybody having trouble with the mineral content in the water? At first I couldn't find a shampoo that foamed sufficiently," I said, conscious of how ludicrous the topic sounded but determined to see it through. "Nothing seems to suds up the way it should, which left my hair feeling not quite clean."

Everyone stopped eating to stare. I touched my mass of shoulder-length curls and grinned like someone out of a TV commercial. "But I just happened to find a bottle of a hotel shampoo stuffed in my bag that works like a dream. I'd be happy to share when we get back to our rooms."

Evan shot me a heart-stopping smile. "Your hair certainly looks beautiful just as it is, Phoebe, but if you think it would help my locks…" He leaned forward so I could touch his hair. I couldn't resist, tangling my fingers for mere seconds in the stray curls at his neck.

"Oh, just stop," Markus muttered, tossing his napkin down. "I'm trying to eat here."

I pulled back. Still grinning like an idiot, I added: "Oh, come on, Markus. You look like you could use something to strengthen your lank strands—maybe a fortifier? I have one of those, too." In truth, I always lugged a collec-tion of trial-size hair products everywhere since nothing ever worked consis-tently on my unruly tangle.

"My hair's fine, thank you," he grumbled. Suddenly he jerked forward, his face registering shock. I'd guessed he'd been kicked under the table, possibly by Peaches's long legs. "But of course I'll try whatever you have to offer."

"Good idea," Peaches remarked. "But I don't expect it'll do much for me. Still, if it suds up in the shower, it'll get my vote."

"Luckily I have enough for everyone." I smiled, satisfied that we'd found our communication ruse. "Conditioner, too."

With all our dependence on modern communications, here we were back to operating in longhand like captives from another century. The irony wasn't lost on me. I'd already passed one note around under the table with a brief warning that we were to await further instructions from Senhor Carvalho. I'd save the more important communication for later.

Our phones had already been passed back to us with a sticky note from Evan warning that though he believed them safe enough for normal use, we were still to exercise extreme caution. I had no idea what that meant since we couldn't risk a conversation long enough to find out. Even standing in the middle of the library to whisper as we had done earlier had become too risky apparently. It was to be pen-and-paper notes read and hastily burned in the nearest fire.

By 8:45 we were back in our respective quarters packing while waiting for details we didn't have. I planned to pass a note up and down the hall explaining who would be leaving tomorrow and who would be staying behind. Because I figured there'd be some arguments, I was waiting until we had the partial privacy of our rooms to communicate the details.

After a few minutes, I resolved to explain which three would be actually leaving for Spain in the morning and why. Using the paper found in the desk drawer, I first passed a note to Peaches taped to the travel-size shampoo bottle, saying at the door that after she took some maybe she could give the bottle to Evan next? It was such a limp ruse but the only one I could come up with at short notice. Pathetic how shackled I felt without text and email, let alone conversation.

After that, I returned to my room to sit at the little desk, waiting. It would only take one lucky glance from an enemy spy or a moment of carelessness to bring the whole thing crashing down. On the other hand, few servants came to our floor lately. Bed-making and the other niceties had been abandoned. We even made our own fires, borrowing wood from the library hearth, which was always well-stocked. It occurred to me that I'd better light mine with the one piece of wood remaining.

While I was coaxing the log to burn, Peaches knocked on my door and stepped in. "The guys say thanks for the shampoo. They've all taken a bit to use later. Not much left. I thought for a minute that Evan and Markus might squabble over the last drop."

I stood to take back the bottle, feeling the note taped to the bottom, out of sight in my palm.

"It smells good," she said while striding out the door, "but the truth will lay with the foam, won't it?"

"Isn't that always the way?"

Taking the now-empty bottle into the bathroom, I switched off the lights and peeled off the note to read by the light of my phone.

Peaches in a penciled scrawl: *As her bodyguard, I must go with Phoebe to Spain. I can speak the language, sí? Peach*

Markus using a felt-tipped-pen printed: *I must stay here. The crown is not in Spain, IMO. M*

Evan in his classical cursive hand wrote in ink: *I am the only one who is fluent in Spanish AND Latin so must go to Spain with Phoebe. Markus, you come with us. No arguments. My apologies, Peach. Evan*

And Rupert in his gorgeous almost calligraphic script wrote: *As previously decided, I will remain. The English Patient, Sir Rupert Fox*

I READ the note over and over again. Damn. Couldn't something just be simple for once? Of course Peaches would expect to go with me as my supposed bodyguard, and I had forgotten that Evan was the only one of us fluent in Spanish *and* Latin, but why was Markus so intent on remaining? He knew damn well that the place was crawling with murderers who would slit his throat in a millisecond. Unless—I stared into the half-light—unless they wouldn't for some reason. He must know something he'd been keeping from us, which I suspected all along. Shit.

Dropping the empty shampoo bottle in the trash, I returned to my room, tossed the note into the fire, took a fresh sheet of the house stationery, and returned to the bathroom. This time I penned a message solely for Peaches:

Peach, I need you here. Evan's mastery of Latin is critical for going through church documents and other accounts often written at the time of our hunt. Besides, the enemy knows his reputation but they have no idea just how dangerous you are. Plus, you're the only one I can trust to protect Rupert and the Carvalhos, especially our little princess, Ana Marie. And something's up with Markus—I just don't know what exactly. Please say you understand. Also, please be ready to watch my back at 2:00 a.m. I'll explain later.

What was I asking her to do: stay here virtually defenseless in this nest of fiends? And, more immediately, help me to commit a criminal offense against art and man? But Senhor Carvalho believed those left behind would probably be the safest and at least she had a gun and could handle a knife like nobody's business. As for Rupert: "never underestimate Rupert" was my motto. As long as he breathed, he could plot, and I had no doubt that he and Senhor Carvalho were cooking up something.

Taping the note to a tube of smoothing lotion, I knocked on her door. It flew open in an instant, the full six feet of grandeur draped in a Moroccan kaftan.

"Smoothing lotion." I waved the bottle before her eyes. "Hope it works."

She whipped it from my fingers and peered at the label, which was plastered over by the note. "Depends on the contents, doesn't it? The last shampoo had sulfates. You know I detest sulfates. Leaves the cuticles sticking straight up—like I need that."

"I didn't know that you hated sulfates."

"Now you do, and if this one has chemicals I'm not going to like it any better." She peered at the label as if reading it. "Lots of big words here: glycol distearate, isopropyl alcohol, Behentrimonium chloride—are you kidding me?"

She actually remembered that stuff? "Shea butter," I said quickly. "I'm sure I read it contains that, too."

"Fine. Just remember that black hair requires special care just like the women who grow it." The door slammed in my face.

Got it: she wasn't happy about being left behind. I waited several seconds before striding down the hall to visit Rupert.

The English patient was tucked into bed emitting occasional moans, laying it on a little too thickly, in my opinion. When I had approached his bed earlier that evening, he only winked and shooed me away with a convincing cough.

"Rupert, I'm not happy about dragging you out of here tomorrow morning. In fact, given the current restrictions, I doubt they'd even allow you on a plane," I said.

"Then I shall just have to recoup at an airport hotel, perish the thought," he said, coughing. "I trust we can locate one with room service. Where are the private jets when we need them?"

Where indeed. Our Rome branch did have access to a private jet that we'd used in the past, but when I'd texted Nicolina from London, she had informed me that the pilot, Otty, had been struck by Covid. *Things are not good in Italy,* she wrote, *but everyone strolls around as if we were back to normal. We are not in normal, Phoebe. Stay safe. Nicolina*

"Never mind, Phoebe," Rupert said, interrupting my thoughts, "I'm sure I shall be much improved tomorrow."

As if. That's when the show would really begin. "Right. I'll leave you to rest, then."

He'd managed to eat all of his soup, I noticed. Stacking his supper dishes onto a tray, I carried them from his room and left them on the hall table along with a mounting assortment of dirty dishes. I saw that Evan's door was open as he sat at his desk with his back turned, working away at some gizmo.

Edgier than ever, I headed for my room, stopping by Markus's open door along the way. "All ready to leave tomorrow?" I asked.

His head lifted from the diagram spread across the bed but he hesitated before answering. "If I must."

"You must," I said pointedly.

"Are you ready, then?"

"Ready," I said. I had the Glock Evan gave me stuffed into the hidden holster of my jacket, my phone alarm set, and my clothes ready to climb into at 4:30 sharp—actually before. What else was left to do besides wait for Senhor Carvalho's instructions?

I continued to Peaches's room but the sound of the shower running left me to wander back my turret quarters, transfer my collection of notes from my pocket into the embers, and head for the window.

The garden lights were off; in fact, they had never been switched back on following the attempted kidnapping. The house now slumbered in that tense, watchful stillness that I imagined descends upon houses during a siege. Whether that threat be in the form of a sickness or something physical, it must feel the same. I turned away into the darkened room.

The dying fire cast a low glow. For the past day, I'd only left the bathroom light on in case the room was under surveillance, doing every task in the shadows with the lights off, including packing.

I'd take a bath and pretend to get ready for bed, which would kill at least an hour. I shut my door and was heading toward the bathroom when my gaze caught something white under the desk. I would never have noticed if I didn't automatically check Ana Marie's secret hatch since discovering it existed. I swept up the paper and strode into the bathroom with my clothes in my arms.

Once inside with the lights off and using my phone, I read the note, which was scrawled in an ornate loopy hand on monogrammed stationery:

Proceed as planned. All secured for three.

The monogram above read: *Senhor Silvio de Carvalho*

While my bath ran, I slipped back into the room and burned the message in the last of the embers.

I didn't expect to get much sleep that night. The fact that I managed to squeeze even three hours before 2:00 a.m. was a bonus. My alarm pitched me out of bed at the appointed time, heart pounding like I'd been dragged from bed by my feet. Fully dressed, I only had to grab my jacket and my phone to feel ready for anything.

When I crept into the hall, Peaches was leaning against the wall, arms crossed.

"What are we doing?" she whispered.

I waited until we were farther down the corridor before answering. "Committing a crime against art."

"What the hell does that mean?"

"Shhh!"

We padded past all the bedrooms, every light off, every door closed. At the bottom of the stairs, I hesitated. The house's deep watchful silence didn't fool me. Somewhere in this acreage of a house, some faction was busy plotting, and they weren't the only ones.

Finger to my lips, I led us down the hall toward the library, keeping against the walls and checking every passageway crossing. Once we reached the library, I tried the door, startled when the brass handle didn't budge. "Locked —seriously?"

"Did you bring your pickers?" Peaches whispered.

"In my room," I said.

She nudged me aside and took out a foldout packet from her pocket, selected a pick, and got to work. "Hold the light," she ordered. I aimed my phone at the ornate lock while she expertly fiddled until it clicked. In minutes we were inside, shutting the door behind us and shoving the brass bolt home.

Why had we been locked out? Probably another sign that we were persona non grata in this occupied regime.

"Watch my back," I whispered, leading Peaches before Titian's Isabella portrait. "Wait here."

She stood stone-still, a gun in one hand, while I slipped around the perimeter of the room to the conservator's closet. What I was about to do was the single most audacious act in my art career and I didn't do it lightly.

I swept my phone light around the six-by-six-foot closet, crammed as it was by easels, jars, a standing light, what looked to be a mobile air purifier, a box of plastic gloves, goggles, and a broom and dustpan. It must have originally served as a storage area for cleaning supplies, fitting enough since its most recent use concerned cleaning of another kind. I studied the bottles and jars neatly lined on the shelf, searching for the necessary solvent.

Art conservation was a painstakingly exacting science that involved removing centuries of woodsmoke, varnish, and grime from priceless artworks without damaging the original. One mistake, one wrong stroke, and the masterpiece was ruined, sometimes irrevocably. As I learned in my student days, it was as much an art as a science and took years of specialized study.

I had but one course taken nearly a decade ago.

Using my phone light, I scanned the labels on every box. Next I pulled on a pair of vinyl gloves, took a pair of goggles, a brush, a tiny palette knife, and a pocketful of cotton swabs and peered again at the solvents.

They marched in a row on the top shelf, all carefully labeled with many jars near-empty. I selected the last one in the row, a distilled turpentine labeled in English pushed into the very corner. It had never been opened. Perhaps the strongest and the riskiest were relegated to the end of the line? I doubted a conservationist would ever want to use something so potent if it could be avoided. A conservator with time on her hands would use a gentler option but I didn't have that luxury. I took the turps.

Back in the library, Peaches watched me approach, her eyes wide.

"Solvents," I whispered, lifting the bottle.

I signaled for her to help me drag over a chair and in seconds I was standing face-to-face with Queen Isabella, my phone light roaming over the background with no time to pay proper homage to either masterpiece or queen. This close I could scrutinize every inch, yet I aimed straight for the square in the lower left-hand corner just above where the conservator's efforts had stopped.

The sfumato here was so leadened and heavy that even considering the application of varnish applied over the centuries, it looked wrong, all wrong. No master of blending would create something that muddy even after years of grime. My guess is that it had been overpainted, maybe multiple times.

Peaches beamed her phone light on the area as I dabbed the cotton tip into the turpentine and proceeded to gently stroke the wad across the canvas.

It was sacrilege. It was a wanton act of desperation prompting me to send silent apologies to Tiziano Vecellio for the crimes I was committing against him that night. If I wasn't so convinced that others had gone before me in this travesty, I would never have continued. There was evidence that the painting had already been tampered with at least once.

As it was, I swabbed the surface; it felt as though every movement raked my gut. The cotton began removing layers of smoky resin, the varnish being the revered preservation medium of almost every age.

Dropping the used swab to the hearth, I pulled out another and this time soaked up more solvent and applied it even more aggressively. My goal was to wipe off layers of actual paint, knowing as I did that I might penetrate down to the original brushwork and possibly ruin a piece of priceless art. This swab came away a sooty black. Dropping that cotton tip, I took another.

"Someone's in the hall!" Peaches hissed.

We switched off our phones and I froze, me standing still in the dark as she padded across to the door to listen, her gun cocked. Fumes from the turps were so strong I wouldn't have been surprised if it rode the air beyond that door.

Nerves strung tight, we listened to voices low and urgent outside, followed by a patter of footsteps and then total silence. I allowed myself to exhale the moment Peaches flicked on her phone light.

I got back to work, removing swab after swab of thick dark paint. Finally something began to emerge from the background: a bit of green followed by a touch of red. Moments later, a leaf came into view followed by a fallen flower, exquisitely portrayed as if someone had plucked the bloom from the queen's fingers to lay it dying at her feet. Peaches stretched up for a closer look. "It's a carnation. Why's that important enough to hide?"

"Don't know but it's symbolic of something. Isabella was known as the Empress of the Carnation but why hide it?" I whispered, staring at the flower.

It had been masterfully painted but not in the style of Titian. The artist didn't even try to emulate his brushstrokes.

I dropped that used cotton tip and took another, this time aiming my efforts on the rocky outcrop to the right of the queen's head. Here it wasn't the shadows that bothered me but the brushstrokes themselves. With Titian you barely saw signs of a brush anywhere; the artist so masterfully blended his elements that they seemed to emerge lifelike from the canvas. This paint had been applied heavily, using a technique out of sync with the rest of the work, even with the carnation. In fact, it appeared to have no technique at all.

I applied the solvent thickly, allowing it to soften the paint before scraping the green off with the knife. Layers of green sludge came off like solidified butter, revealing a slightly different shape to the mountainous terrain beneath and a peaked hexagonal watchtower.

I glanced at Peaches, who stood with her mouth open. "Where's that?"

"Dunno," I said.

"Weird," Peaches whispered.

"Isn't it?" Though I'd like nothing better than to dig deeper, those were the two main abnormalities.

"It's almost 3:30," Peaches said.

"Right." I took pictures of the two revealed areas with my phone and one of the entire painting before climbing down. While Peaches gathered the discarded swabs, I returned the tools to the closet and picked up a brush and two tubes of paint, one dark green and one smoky brown, both tubes of Winsor & Newton. I squeezed a small amount onto a palette and diluted it massively with thinner.

A conservator often repaired damaged pieces by replicating the same paints used in the original but exceptions were sometimes necessary. Necessity drove me to great depths that night.

Peaches watched aghast as I returned to my perch and blotted the areas I'd been working on before brushing paint over the cleared patches, covering the delicate plaintive carnation with a brown blemish, smudging the trees around the watchtower with a thick swirl of paint, and burying everything under an appallingly shoddy patch job. Anyone taking a closer look would see the outrage in an instant but I was betting that no one would be looking that closely short-term, especially since the painting hung far from eye level.

That done, I returned to the conservator's closet, packed away the painting supplies, and wiped the brushes on a cloth, but carried the turpentine bottle over to one of the desks, cover off. Placing it on a wad of paper, I arranged papers to look as though some careless twerp had been rubbing solvent on wads of tissue.

"What?" Peaches whispered.

"Decoy," I replied, "to explain the fumes." It might work for a moment, which could be all we needed. Besides, it was the best idea I had.

That done, we cleared up what evidence we could, and just before exiting, I led Peaches to the closet and pointed out the secret passageway. "It leads directly to Senhor Carvalho," I said.

"Fat lot of good that will do me. I'd never get my booty through there."

"It's not as tight as it looks. Besides flesh has give," I said.

"Yours might. Mine's all muscle."

Like I had time to argue that.

After checking the corridor, we exited the library, practically bolting down that hall, up the stairs, and back to our rooms, arriving in breathless triumph until we saw Markus's door wide open.

"Shit!" Peaches exclaimed.

We stepped inside and gaped. The archaeologist had vanished, taking his bags with him.

17

At 4:45 Evan was downstairs spreading the alarm about Rupert's supposed worsening condition to any person he could find. Three staff members trudged to our floor in their nightclothes, all masked and talking excitedly. None would go near Rupert's room. Minutes later, Adriana arrived with a man and woman we didn't recognize and, once we explained the situation, demanded that the wing be sectioned off.

"But you must still leave," she ordered.

"Sir Fox is not going anywhere," Evan said, standing in the center of the corridor, arms crossed, doing his most manly command pose. "He is not well and must stay put until he recovers."

"What is wrong with him?" Her eyes widened with fear.

"I don't know," he said. "Perhaps you can have a doctor visit to determine that point. I can only tell you that he has a fever and a dry cough."

"A fever! This can't be happening! We haven't had a doctor here since—well, for a while. There is one in the village that attends Papa Carvalho occasionally. Maybe he will come."

"I suggest you arrange for testing," he said.

"Testing for...?" Her look of shock made me feel as guilty as hell. This seemed so cruel. "Sir Rupert must go into quarantine," she said after a moment. "The rest of you leave as planned." She looked as though she might burst into tears.

"You can't expect us to just leave him. Somebody must stay and nurse him," I said.

"Unless one of your staff will take on the task," Evan added, "none of us will be leaving this morning." He stood tall, imposing and resolute.

Adriana's eyes looked around her above the white mask, almost as if she was seeking a place to hide. "Fine." She turned to speak urgently to the man beside her and moments later faced us again. "Choose one person to stay with him, then, but it cannot be you, Senhor Barrows, or you Senhorita McCabe. You can stay." She indicated Peaches leaning against a wall behind me.

"'You' has a name," Peaches said, straightening. "I'm Peaches Williams but you can call me Senhorita Williams, if you must. I'll stay with Rupert, under certain conditions."

I glanced at her in surprise. She was setting terms?

Adriana dropped her gaze. "Forgive me if I am rude." Her hands flew into the air. "But I am so alarmed! To have this happen to our household along with everything else."

"No problem. I'll make a list of things needed to keep Sir Rupert and me comfortable. In the meantime, if you don't mind, take your staff away and leave us to it. And we want coffee and breakfast. Eggs would be nice—boiled, not too hard."

"Yes, we will go. The rest of you come downstairs in ten minutes. Adriana turned to Evan. "Where is Senhor Collins?"

"Unfortunately, we can't answer that," Evan replied. "I had hoped you knew."

"Why would I know?" she said, glaring at him. "I want you out of here." She swung around and dashed downstairs with her staff.

"I feel sorry for them," I whispered as their footsteps died away. "To know what she's fearing…"

"Let the virus work to our benefit for once," Evan remarked, returning to his room.

By 5:00 a.m., my backpack and his were at the bottom of the stairs with the two of us standing tense and silent in the hall, waiting.

We had made no effort to find Markus, not just because we were sure that he had left on his own accord but because we didn't have time to search. Our biggest worry, mostly left unsaid but for a hastily scribbled note, was that he had been working for the Divinios all along. On the other hand, I suspected he believed he knew the location of that crown on the property and may have gone off to search on his own—unlikely considering his temperament but not impossible. God knows what archaeologists burning with a quest will try to do, at least in their minds.

But if he did work for the Divinios, it meant that every bit of our plan had been exposed—what little we knew of it, that is. Senhor Carvalho may have been short on details for a reason. The uncertainty, heaped on all the rest, made Evan and me unusually tense.

Evan passed me a piece of paper that I hastily read and shoved into my pocket. *Where in Spain are we going?*

I'm not sure, I mouthed. He lifted his brows at me, maybe not as amused as I had hoped.

Minutes later, we heard footsteps marching down the long hall as two men wearing masks appeared, only one of whom I knew—Senhor Abreu. I stifled my relief at seeing someone assumed to be an ally but nothing in the man's eyes gave any indication that he felt the same.

Abreu introduced the driver, a Senhor Magro, who was to take us to the airport. We hastily applied our face masks, picked up our bags, and followed the men outside. I turned long enough to catch Peaches waving at me from the stairs. I hated to leave her behind and yet was so grateful that she and Rupert would pull together to do whatever was needed back at the quinta.

The dawn hung damp and cool with a band of luminous ultramarine bleeding into the sky beyond the treetops and mist snaking through the grass. We piled into a long gray unmarked six-seater van, our bags at our feet, nobody saying a word. Evan and I sat stiff and watchful.

When the car pulled away down the long drive, I turned back to gaze at the castle, noting lights on at the very topmost tower but the castle otherwise dark. Turning away, I stared ahead, my arm pressing against the gun in my jacket, ready for anything. Gun, phone, and Evan—what more did I need to plunge into the unknown? Actually, I could think of plenty. Would I ever see my friends again?

The van wound down the drive, through the gates, which opened as we approached, and onto a deeply wooded road, but instead of going down toward the village we headed up.

I shot a look at Evan but he kept his gaze fixed ahead, which prompted me to do the same. I watched as the silhouette of the Moorish castle bit into the sky over our heads. We were heading up to the ancient castle? I had seen the illuminated walls from my window and knew that the Castelo dos Mouros had been built in Portugal's medieval Moorish era and destroyed by the Christian crusaders, but what did it have to do with our escape or was it part of the Divinios' murderous plan?

Floodlights beamed up at the gray stone walls when the van lurched to a stop at the foot of the rocky outcrop leading up to the ruins.

"You two go!" Abreu called. "Now. Up the stairs! He waits!"

Who waits? Why up the stairs? Heart galloping, I sprung into action, grabbing my bag and jumping out the door at the same time that Evan exited from the other side.

My heart shattered at the thought of all the things that could go wrong but I couldn't dwell on that now. The van was already zooming back down the way it had come and was soon swallowed by the mist.

"Phoebe, hurry!" Evan beckoned me up a path leading toward a set of rough-hewn stairs. Spotlights illuminating the ruin's exterior walls did nothing to light the stairs between the low parapets. Here the shadows clotted like glue and Evan turned on his phone light to guide our way raggedly upward.

We were climbing up the old castle's battlements with nothing between us and the drop but the remains of the ancient walls, the exterior versions waist-high, the interior ones knee-level. On the right, the mountain opened around us in dizzying glimpses of mist and rocky outcrops, the lights of the village dropping far away to our left, the forest to our right.

Up here the wind cut into my face and the steepness of the climb nearly took my breath away. Soon I was stuffing my mask into my pocket and transferring my bag into backpack mode as I forced my legs to keep pushing.

We climbed and climbed as the dawn bloomed pink all around. Evan was too far ahead for conversation and I didn't have the breath left to try. I knew he had to be feeling as ripped in two as I but his training kept him focused and powering on. But why anyone would wait for us here? It was all rock and bramble with a watchtower ahead and walls curving into the distance. Unless the idea was to ambush us and throw us off the wall, in which case I had to admit the location was perfect.

I paused long enough to gaze through the wind-roughened parapets to catch my breath. Then I heard a faint beating far to the right at the same time as I caught sight of lights weaving through the trees below, approaching from two directions.

Picking up my pace, I launched up the next length of dizzying stairs until I stood beside Evan on the windy battlement watching a silver speck come into view.

"We have more company!" I cried, pointing behind us.

He swore and gazed ahead. In front lay the watchtower, to the left the rocky remains of the keep edged in dawn and rimmed by thick shadow, and beyond that the battlements continued curving like a snake up the crest of the mountain.

It was at that moment that we heard the explosion. Something far down to the left burst into flames and burned in a dark smoky plume. We watched in horror as the object tumbled over and over in flames and smoke, finally dropping straight out of view.

"It's the van!" I called.

"That was supposed to be us," Evan said, voice tight. He grabbed my hand. "Keep moving."

"But—" There was no time for fear or to cry, let alone talk. We began climbing downward now just as we saw the helicopter growing closer by the moment.

We watched as the small silver helicopter came into view overhead, hovering over the ruined keep. Now we saw how the rocks on the inner side of the ruins fell away to a flat gravel space directly below. It didn't look wide enough to land a chopper but that's exactly what the pilot seemed to be doing. He began lowering the machine straight down toward the only flat area on the rock.

Evan and I pressed ourselves against the outer parapet as the blades beat overhead. I turned to avoid the spin of dust and glimpsed the lights bobbing below the lower walls. "They're on the walls!" I called.

The helicopter dropped into the narrow space with amazing finesse and in seconds we were dashing down the remaining stairs and ducking under the vortex toward the open door just as two men appeared on the battlements and started shooting.

"Get up fast!" Evan called to the pilot, repeating himself in Spanish and urging us into the seats. He swung open the door and shouted something. We climbed into the seats behind him as he slammed the door shut, giving us only seconds to strap ourselves in before the machine lurched upward.

My first time in a helicopter and here I was rising in the air from atop a mountain promontory being chased by religious fanatics while heading to parts unknown. Sometimes I'd rather be knitting.

A bullet pinged against the blades.

As I soon discovered as the machine zipped away, helicopters offer the best flight view of any aircraft thanks to that wraparound windshield. This gave me an uninterrupted view of the men scrambling over the rocks below, the sparks of their guns firing, and, as an added bonus, the flashing emergency lights far down in the valley.

Evan passed me a pair of ear protectors from the console between us. I was grateful for the instant quiet but kept my gaze fixed on the shrinking ground, my heart in my throat. He squeezed my hand as we zipped off into the dawn, me squeezing back in silent fear for those we left behind.

We were now flying over land, forests, villages, and towns visible far below. Though my knowledge of helicopters was scant, I knew enough to know that they can't travel as far or as quickly as planes. How far this one would take us was left to be seen and I could only hope that our pilot had a plan.

But despite the adrenaline, my heart began to settle and I must have dozed. It seemed like several hours had passed when a sharp sound lurched me awake. I looked out and saw us going down—quickly—and to someplace in the middle of nowhere. Nothing but sandy hills and a rocky grassland baking in the bright sun, a scruff of forest off to the left, a vineyard to the right.

I turned to Evan with a question but the sound of gunfire answered me before he could. The pilot was shouting.

"The gas tank's been hit," Evan called. "He's got to land before we lose power!"

"Where are we?" I called.

"Somewhere in Spain!"

So we landed somewhere in Spain with a bouncing crash followed by the the crunch of landing gear and the screech of something major breaking off—the tail, we discovered, as we leaped out of the helicopter.

Now we were on the run, heading toward the copse of trees, the pilot in the opposite direction. He called something back to us, Evan translating: "We're to hide. Keep away from him."

No time to ask why. Two white helicopters flew low across the field peppering the ground with machine gunfire. We were almost to the trees when I turned and saw the pilot hit. He spun in a full circle before falling to his knees. I took off after him until Evan grabbed my arm and wrenched me back. One of the helicopters was landing. We had to keep on running.

We bolted into the trees. In a few minutes, they'd be on foot coming after us. An orchard, I guessed. Here the sun filtered down in long motes, beautiful had we time to enjoy. But the cover was scant and we could hear the roar of the second helicopter overhead along with men shouting.

"They're gaining!"

And suddenly we burst out of the trees to teeter on the brink of a steep scrubby mountainside with no option but to scramble down over loose stones. Below we saw a cluster of white buildings, a little village beyond that. Yet we hesitated. Hardly any cover. Parts of the drop too steep.

Across the sky from the opposite direction, another helicopter was speeding toward us—longer, painted in camouflage, two roof propellers. When a bullet pinged against the rocks at our feet, we lunged down the hill, caught in a wild sliding scramble heading roughly for a boulder outcrop. Two men were firing at our backs now.

We leaped behind a pile of boulders as Evan pulled out his gun and fired back. I had my gun in hand as the new helicopter flew overhead.

Evan paused to study the underbelly. "They saw us. Camouflaged AS532 Cougar. Looks like it belongs to the Spanish army. Who did you say Senhor Carvalho's friend is?"

"Another Señor Anonymous. Are they on our side?"

"We can't wait around to find out."

We watched the army helicopter drop low over the gunmen, a soldier leaning out the door firing at our pursuers while the second enemy helicopter was speeding off into the distance. It certainly seemed that they were on our side and they gave us the break we needed.

Instantly we were scudding downward, grabbing on to bushes to brace ourselves as we slid. Our backpacks knocked off our balance so we sent them sliding down ahead. It was all I could do to keep my feet under me and at one point I stumbled, nearly tumbling downward face-first, but I managed to steady myself against a rock. Evan remained ahead, turning occasionally to point out obstacles or to offer me a hand.

"Just go!" I cried. Men.

By the time we reached the bottom and retrieved our bags, the sun hung low in the sky, the gunfire had stopped, and the helicopters had disappeared. We were trudging around a white-walled farm compound. A corral of white ponies whinnied away to the right. Somewhere a dog barked and barked.

"We'll hide in a barn somewhere until dark," Evan said.

We had seen a village farther down the road but who knew what the response would be if two strangers suddenly appeared in the streets? We obviously weren't tourists. We couldn't even claim that our car had broken down on some nearby highway—was there even a nearby highway? Hiding until nightfall seemed the best option.

A man raking a small field in the distance didn't catch sight of us as we scuttled into the walled enclosure. Inside, a small house lay at one end with a cluster of stucco outbuildings forming a rambling rectangle. A fountain looking as though it hadn't spewed water for years sat in the center of a cracked cement drive with a clump of yellow weeds blooming around the base.

We slipped inside a large storage building that smelled of motor oil overriding something musty and hid in a corner behind an old tractor. Sacks of veggies and an upended wheelbarrow kept us company along with a mewing cat that skittered away. Tools hung on the walls, most of them rusted and bearing signs that they'd been repaired multiple times. The last rays of sun were cutting through a high cracked window in long motes as we settled down in the shadows on mounds of sacking.

My heart only then began to settle. I leaned back and closed my eyes.

"Are you all right?" Evan asked, passing me a water bottle.

I sat up to wave away the offer and retrieve my own bottle from my backpack. "Fine, thanks. Just a bit winded. That was close."

"Too close." He rubbed his forehead on his sleeve. "This is a good time for you to tell me where we're heading. We haven't had time to talk."

"I don't know where we're heading exactly," I admitted before taking a long drink.

"Right then, we need to comb the archives in Madrid and search through all the court documents from the reign of Emperor Charles to Philip II. Maybe Ricardo overlooked something. It's a long shot, as is everything else. There's still a chance the crown lies buried beneath the altar just as Markus believes, but in the meantime, Madrid is a logical next step."

He was being so decisive, so take-charge male—endearing. "No, it isn't." That came out more absolute than I intended. "I mean, when I said I didn't know where we were headed, it wasn't because I didn't know what to look for. It's nothing related to King Philip or even Prince Carlos, at least not directly. It's subtler than that. Maybe this will lead us to Madrid or maybe not." I pulled out my phone and opened up the pictures I had taken of the overpainting.

He gazed down at the screen. "You tampered with a Titian?" There was surprise in his tone along with more than a little amusement.

"I wasn't the first, possibly not even the second. Somebody buried clues in that portrait long ago and sent it to the House of Aviz for safekeeping."

"I'm not judging."

"Don't you see? The carnation, which was not painted by Titian but by someone almost as masterful, was covered over with a layer of paint. The same thing with the tower behind the queen's head. They're messages. Whoever did this was counting on no one daring to touch a painting by the royal portraitist since Titian had reached acclaim in his own lifetime and had

King Philip's protection. It was a brilliant strategy considering that it kept the clues safe for over five hundred years."

"Until you came along."

"Until I came along, but listen, Evan, that flower means something. I just don't know what. Carnations were Isabella's symbol but why hide that? If we discover who that painter was, we'll come that much closer to understanding. There's a whole language threaded through here, the language of visual imagery and symbolism. The anti-Divinios didn't use words, they used art."

"You amaze me," he said softly.

"Is that a good thing?"

"You know it is." He was gazing at me in that intense way he had that always made me feel like I was only one in the universe for those fleeting seconds.

"Are you with me or not?" I asked softly.

"I've always been with you."

I took the phone from his fingers, which held on maybe seconds too long. "Good. Thank you. I'm thinking no Emperor Charles or even King Philip. Even Queen Isabella was a smokescreen. That they used her portrait to hide clues is significant."

"How?"

"Maybe the anti-Divinios supported the monarchy but not the sect? Maybe they were implying a connection with queens and women somehow? It was a wickedly sexist and often misogynistic age. It's bad enough today but this is nothing compared to what women endured in the fifteenth century, even those of noble blood, maybe *especially* those of noble blood. My point is, in this hunt, think like a woman."

"But I'm a man." Now he was teasing.

"And that's one of the things I love about you, Evan, but I sense a female presence working as our allies across time. For once being a man may not be the usual advantage." I paused and smiled. "But don't feel the need to change on my account."

"That's a relief. Seriously, though, we need to track down the women who surrounded Prince Carlos in those dark days before his death."

"Yes, let's start there. I've done some preliminary research but I need so much more."

"But we'll need our latest Señor Anonymous's help to get there, wherever 'there' might be. If our Spanish benefactor is in any way connected to the Spanish military, he's one powerful ally, and by now should know where we are."

"Because I'm wearing a tracking device?"

"You're wearing a tracking device?"

"Senhor Carvalho gave it to me yesterday."

"I was actually thinking that they would determine our position based on where our helicopter went down, which is a fairly definite clue. Also, the army helicopter saw us."

"Oh, yes, there's that." It was growing so dark now that I could barely see his face.

"But the Divinios have the same information and I expect they'll be on our heels soon enough." He had his phone in his hand. "Sir Rupert texted that all is well back at the castle. They're under quarantine. He says that the 'plague doctor' has been called in from Sintra and would arrive tomorrow. As soon as he tests negative for Covid, the game will be up."

I sighed. "We don't have much time. Where are we, anyway?"

"About fifty kilometers outside of Córdoba."

I skimmed the texts on my own phone—one from Peaches saying that the smoothing lotion had worked; another from Max back in London saying that he was worried about me. *Why no phone call?* he asked. Connie texted to say that she apologized for her brother's behavior but that his heart was in the right place. What did that mean? His heart might be in the right place but the rest of him wasn't. Did she know where he was?

I was about to show Evan the messages when he put a hand on his arm and indicated his own screen. Two red dots could be seen approaching the drive leading to the farm on one of his radar apps—cars, I guessed.

We turned off our phones and ducked down behind the tractor, squeezing deeper into the shadows as car doors slammed and footsteps pounded on the cement outside.

Barely breathing, we listened. Men entering the compound—three, maybe four. One speaking softly but no less definitively, and footsteps spreading out across the farm. We were being hunted. Another set of footsteps ran past from the other direction, a person shouting a question—the farmer?

An argument erupted between the farmer and someone else followed by a third man interrupting in a voice as soothing as liquid honey.

Evan left my side to climb onto the sacking and peered out the high window. In seconds, he was back, whispering: "Three men, one priest."

"A priest?" I hissed.

"It's them. We have to get out of here. They'll find us."

We waited only long enough for the footsteps to spread around the outbuildings before bolting from our cover and risking a dash for the gate. It was a long shot.

We could see the farmer speaking quietly to a man in a dark robe whose back was turned. As long as he didn't catch sight of us and raise the alarm, we could make it.

Only it didn't work out that way.

18

We hadn't counted on guards watching the compound. And now we were surrounded by four armed men wearing stark, grim expressions with matching clothes, their guns pointing at our chests. When two others joined them, we were hemmed in like stray cattle. And that's how I felt—cornered and terrified.

To my left, Evan stood tense, his hand hovering over his hidden holster, and I was afraid he might do something reckless. But we were outnumbered and surrounded. All we could do was wait for a chance to escape. I caught his eye and shook my head.

The priest strode toward us, a little smile on this plump lips. In his early fifties with short graying hair, heavy build, and an expression on his round cherubic face that was unsettlingly mild, he lifted his hands. "Welcome to Spain," he said in well-modulated English. "I am Father Don Santos and you are now in my care."

So this was a Divinio. What was I expecting? Not this. "Some care," I mumbled. "Didn't you just try to kill us and probably intend to do the same again?"

"Do not be an alarmist, Señorita McCabe. For now, we talk only. Empty your pockets of all devices and weapons, and pass them to my men with your bags. Señor Barrows, do not try one of your notorious tricks or your lady here will suffer."

He thought I was a lady and that only the ex-MI6 guy knew tricks? Already he'd given me hope.

We emptied our pockets—phones, guns—as two men stepped up to claim them along with our backpacks. I was beginning to feel ill and more than a little angry. Evan had gone into full alert mode, all senses probably scanning for an escape plan.

"Señorita, you and I will travel together in the first car, and, señor, you will follow with your guards to the second. They have been instructed to secure you by any means necessary so let us avoid further violence, if possible. We have had enough excitement for today."

"Excitement? Is that what you call shooting our helicopter down from the sky?" I asked.

It was as if he hadn't heard me. "Please be so kind as to wear your masks and we will do the same." He lifted one hand as if summoning the wind and bid *adiós* to the farmer watching by the entrance.

"It's a trick!" I bellowed to the farmer, "Call the police!" I should have taken my cue from Evan and saved my breath.

Don Santos sighed and shook his head. "Señorita, señorita…my friend does not speak English, and even if he did he would not believe you. I am a sacerdote—the bond between these people and the church is too deep for you to comprehend."

No doubt the man had also been fed a pack of lies by his dear sacerdote.

Don Santos's black-clad men ushered us toward two white cars parked in the drive—Evan into one, me into the other, accompanied by our guards as though we were off to some unholy communion.

"Where are you taking us?" I asked when I was wedged in the plush leather back seat between the two men, Don Santos sitting up front with the driver.

"Someplace safe. The two of you have given us quite a difficult time and it is necessary for this to cease. Now do sit back and enjoy the ride. This is a beautiful part of Spain."

As if sunsets over mountains and narrow winding roads through gilded orchards would soothe my heart. Trapped and helpless, I sat with my eyes fixed out the window. Evan was in the car behind but my guards refused to allow me to look out the rear window. Any time a car passed, Don Carlos would lift his hand as if bestowing a benediction on the passengers, who would wave in return. There's no way the locals would believe any story we told.

After about twenty minutes, Don Santos's phone rang a few bars of some Gregorian chant. Did the devil have a sense of humor? He answered in Spanish, speaking in that measured way of his, and when the call ended, a conversation ensued between him and his driver that seemed so relaxed and conversational they could be discussing the weather. Meanwhile, my guards—a young man and an older one both clad in black shirts and pants—sat grim and silent.

Finally, we turned off the main road onto a lane that wound farther down the valley into a little village. Glimpses of narrow cobbled streets with strings of flowers strung between the white-tile-roofed buildings rushed by as we turned a corner and drove straight up a long drive toward a church on the hill.

I stared. A church—not surprising considering our host, but this structure was unusually magnificent for the size of the village and commanded its position with absolute authority. A huge painted statue of the Virgin Mary stood in the spotlight, a garland of wilted flowers adorning her head.

The cars parked around the back where it was dark and shielded from the village by the bell tower and a tiny orchard. We were ushered in through the basement stairs, entering a corridor with a series of three little rooms off to one side that opened to a larger function hall.

I caught Evan's eye only briefly before he was shoved into one room while I was marched through the hall flanked by my two guards. Don Santos remained behind.

Glimpses of children's drawings of angels lined the stairs as the guards nudged me upward with their pistols. The sight of those sweet little crayon angels almost brought me to tears. I thought of Ana Marie, of Peaches's dead baby daughter.

The moment we had left the sacerdote's presence, it's as if my two guards eased into minor acts of cruelty. Maybe I could launch a surprise attack—kick out the way I'd been trained, use the element of shock to disarm them. With only two, it might even work, but what about Evan now bound in some tiny room with his captors? I couldn't risk it, not now, anyway.

Instead, I was shoved down the center aisle of the large, beautiful candle-lit church decorated with occasional frescoes, painted statues, and gilded carvings—not rich but still impressive—and was slammed into a wooden chair facing the altar. Before me a gilded carving of the crucified Christ gazed down at me in loving sorrow. At least He had to be on my side.

One guy bound my hands and feet with cruel efficiency while the older one stood over me murmuring what I could only guess were sexual insults. I kept my gaze fixed on the floor, doubting that they would try anything in a church, but what did I know?

A young short-haired woman in a printed skirt and top dashed in with a handful of fresh candles, caught sight of us, and gasped. The older man men yelled at her and she turned and dashed away. He ran after her. I heard a stifled scream, then silence. I pulled against my ropes until the other guard kicked me in the shins. I stopped.

He was standing over me now, holding Evan's and my phones, one in each hand. Turning them over and over, it was as if he expected them to speak. He must have heard that they were special somehow and wanted desperately to crack their secrets.

"Password," he barked. It was hard to see his features in the candlelight especially with that black mask covering his lower face, but he seemed like he'd be a good-looking kid no older than twenty-something.

"No!" I said.

He kicked me again, this time harder. Damn him. My device was voice activated but whether it could identify me through a mask was another matter. Worth a try. "Intruder alert!" I cried. "Burn!"

And just like magic, the phone screen flashed orange, turned smoking hot, and seared the kid's palm. I could smell singed skin through the mask.

He dropped the phone like the burning thing it was and kicked it under the pews. I turned to see it slide three rows down, still pulsing orange before going dark. Evan was a genius.

"There," I said, turning to the kid. "My phone says go to hell."

He might have grasped the gist of that if he hadn't been so busy nursing his hand. He plunged the wounded member into a flask of what might be holy water—no, wine, I realized as the red liquid dripped over the yellow embroidered altar cloth. Shame—it looked to be late-eighteenth-century silk.

When another guard stomped in to find his young comrade still going on about his singed palm, he exploded.

"*¡Me duele, me duele!*" the younger one wailed.

"*¡Callate!*" the man barked, slapping the kid across the side of the head.

"*¿Que esta pasando?*" Don Santos demanded, now striding down the aisle. A flurry of excuses followed that the priest cut off with a chop of his hand. Whatever he said next caused the men to scurry toward the basement door.

"You just can't get good choirboys these days," I whispered, but the priest wasn't paying attention. Glancing from the ewer to the stained altar cloth, he wrinkled his nose and attempted to blot the stains with the edge of his robe.

"You need to soak that in cold water," I said, "Soon, before the stain sets."

He turned to me. "Señorita McCabe, I regret to say that your man has not told me the information I require, which is very unfortunate. This is becoming tedious. Know that we haven't time for games. Now I must ask these same questions of you, and should I not learn the truth, I will be forced to add some painful incentive. Do not force my hand. Answer me this: what is your business in Spain?"

What painful incentive? What had they done to Evan? "We're here because we were forced to leave Portugal and abandon our ailing friend." I was guessing that he knew all this, which meant that I had to keep to the script. "There's a chance that he may be infected with Covid."

"Yet you come to Spain and not London?"

"All flights to London were either booked or canceled so we managed to secure a helicopter—at great expense, I might add. But as you know, small helicopters can't travel as far as jets and our only chance to make it home was to reach an airport in Spain and fly from there. That is before you shot us down. Was that pilot killed, by the way? Is your brotherhood satisfied with the blood they shed across the ages?"

"I will not defend my organization to you, señorita. It is well beyond your comprehension. Are you here to locate the crown?"

He considered his brotherhood an organization, not a holy order? "Hardly. I presume the thing lies in Portugal and is currently beyond our reach. Senhor Carvalho has forbidden us to look further, anyway. Now we just want to escape in one piece, deliver our friends safely back to London, and collect our fee."

He was studying me carefully, the way a man might who had served a congregation as chief confessor long enough to know when someone was lying. He knew I was lying. "What do you know of this crown?" he asked softly.

What did I have to lose? "Only that a pack of religious fanatics have kept alive a cult for five hundred years based on the belief that religious persecution is grounds for a holy war. Like thousands of years of human history has taught us nothing." Go for broke was my next strategy. "These nuts hope to force the globe under one God, one belief system. Like that's worked in the past."

He pursed his lips together, causing his round face to look disconcertingly baby-like and his marble-like eyes anything but. "The faithless do the world a great disfavor. You have so little respect for your betters, or understanding. You are like a dog that sniffs at a wall and believes you know how to design a building. Yet you believe you have the right to this, the right to say that. Your opinions do not matter, señorita. It is time that you learned to bow to a higher authority, woman, and not presume to speak of which you know nothing."

"Then teach me." I was counting on a priest's longing to convert a lost ewe to the flock. "Tell me how the skull of some poor dead prince from five hundred years ago can impart something holy on today's messed-up world."

His dark brows furrowed. "It is because this world is so 'messed up,' as you say, that our crowned king must act quickly to save us all by clearing the way for the world to be born anew. Just as Christ rose from the dead, so must humanity."

"Through a skull and a crown?"

"Dare not speak of what you fail to understand!" he roared. "Our crown contains a fragment of bone from the King of Kings—" he paused long enough to genuflect and raise a hand to the crucifix "—and the skull is merely His corporal representative on earth. Once they are united, we will hear His call and the faithful will be saved."

Oh, good: I was making him angry. "You want to resurrect an archaic notion that the world can fit into some simplistic one-size-fits-all belief system where we all must look, live, and behave the same? Are we going to pretend that the past never happened?" I'd found his button and kept pushing.

"You do not know what you say!"

But I was on a roll. "Would you burn people at the stake, and inflict even more suffering in the world in the name of Jesus, is that what you're saying? Do you really think He would want that?" My eyes had turned to the crucifix. I didn't need to be religious to be incensed. In fact, I imagined Jesus was fully on my side. I could almost hear the angels singing. "The Inquisition is dead for a reason; the world changes for a reason; and this is only one more power play in the name of your patriarchal doctrine! Don't talk to me about entitlement! Men have always demanded entitlement and hidden it under one guise or another!"

He looked as if I had struck him. God, I realized that no one had probably ever spoken to him like that for a long time, maybe never, let alone a woman.

"You dare speak to me that way," he sputtered, adding something in Spanish—either a prayer or a curse.

"If a mortal stands before me and spews nonsense about destroying the earth in the name of religion, I dare speak to you that way." In for a penny…

"The earth is already destroyed," he roared in his pulpit voice. "Look around. The seas are rising, nature is dying, men are still fighting among one another in the name of their false gods and misguided beliefs. Technology is the god of the young. The only way to save humanity is to burn it to the ground so we may be born anew in the name of Jesus Christ!"

His hands rose in the air and he waved them around, as if evoking the gilded angels on the walls to fly. For the first time I gazed into the face of madness and was terrified.

"Enough! I have wasted too much precious time on you two." Suddenly he was sweeping back down the aisle while speaking urgently into his phone, calling for reinforcements from the god of technology.

In seconds, he disappeared, leaving me alone before the altar with the bindings biting into my wrists and my heart galloping. I looked up at Jesus. "So did I mess that up?" But I had maybe seconds until they returned. How could I break free?

I strained against my bindings, kicking my bound feet over and over again trying to loosen the ropes. And then I heard a faint noise behind me. "¡Deja de retorcerse!" a female voice whispered.

Something sawed into my bindings as I stilled. After my wrists sprung free, a young woman ducked in front of me and began cutting the bindings at my feet with a penknife, the same woman who had brought the candles earlier. Now a vicious bruise blackened her cheek. In her twenties with straight dark hair styled in an almost boyish fashion, she caught my eye, beckoned, and slipped back through the altar door.

But I wasn't leaving without my phone. Instantly I was on my stomach reaching under the pew and froze in that position when two men ran down the aisle shouting. The phone just inches out of reach...unless I risked ducking between the pews and kicking it out with my feet. Damn.

The men fanned out all over the church. They'd find me for sure. Suddenly the woman's voice burst in, speaking excitedly, and the men began firing questions at her. Now the guards were dashing back toward the front of the church, the large wooden doors creaking open before slamming shut.

I sagged in relief before standing up and waving at my ally. She waved back from across the aisle. I snatched up my phone along with Evan's and followed her to the vestibule behind the altar.

* * *

It was a small room with a library of books on one side and racks of church vestments on another crowded around. Hooks held various church headgear including long white pointed hoods encased in plastic wrap that sent shivers down my spine. What, like the Ku Klux Klan or something? I remembered seeing those hats in a Goya painting without understanding its meaning.

The woman beckoned me on through a back door past two offices, down a short hall, and to a set of back stairs leading both up and down. One presumably led to the bell tower, the other to the basement and outside. I pointed down. She held up three fingers. Three men downstairs—got it.

Opening up my phone, I was relieved to find it still operable and scanned for a weapon app, something that might disarm someone from a distance. Evan's phones would never shoot bullets but a laser bolt might be a good substitute. I popped open the red bolt icon and crept down the stairs with the phone raised, indicating that the woman remain upstairs.

The steps ended at the back door. To the right lay the hall we'd entered earlier and the room where they held Evan. I heard voices in the corridor, one being Don Santos, who strode from the room talking hurriedly into a cell phone. When he was far enough away and his back turned, I crept to the door and stepped in. Two men with rolled-up sleeves were working over a bloodied Evan.

"Hello, boys."

The moment they swung around, I beamed a bolt of laser light straight into both their eyes, one after the other, blinding them on the spot. As the men screamed and spun away, I rushed up to use the same burning light to sear the ropes off Evan's hands and feet. He sagged forward into my arms just as Don Santos rushed in.

"Stop in the name of our King!" he cried.

I lifted the phone, ready to launch another bolt, when the priest collapsed to the floor. The candle woman stood over his crumpled form, a silver candlestick raised in both hands, a hard look in her eyes. She was one of us.

"Help us!" I cried.

She dropped the candlestick and was at my side in an instant, both of us lifting Evan from the chair. "What's your name? I'm Phoebe," I said, thumbing my chest.

"Phoebe. Me Ilda."

"*Gracias*, Ilda."

She nodded and shot me a brief smile.

"Not…unconscious," Evan whispered through swollen lips. "Can stand. Get the guns…on table."

Leaving him supported by my ally, I snatched up both guns and stuffed them into my pockets. Our bags were on the floor and obviously had been rummaged through. I hastily stuffed everything back into the backpacks, threw one over my shoulder, and grabbed the other.

The two guards were flailing around, screaming about the room with one stumbling into the hall. And yes, I felt pity for them but not enough to let them kill us instead. One was lurching around, arms outstretched, trying to grab somebody. He came too close to Evan, who let go of Ilda long enough to slug the guy in the jaw. The guard crumpled to his knees and stilled.

Two down, four to go. Where were the others? And then as if in answer, we heard voices upstairs. I passed Evan a gun and I cocked the other, shoving my phone into my pocket.

Two men were pounding down the stairs crying out, no doubt seeing the priest's prone form in the hall. Evan leaned out and fired, winging one guy in the arm while the other kept shooting.

"Where are the other two?" I asked.

"Santos sent...them out to pick up...supper," Evan mumbled.

I ducked out from the other side and aimed for the second guy's legs, hitting him in the kneecap. He screamed, dropping his gun and leaving the three of us to climb over the unconscious Don Santos and bolt out the door in the opposite direction.

Outside, darkness had fallen hard as we dashed toward one of two parked cars. The keys were in the ignition, typical rural-style, so we tossed in our bags and folded Evan into the back seat. I took the driver's side and beckoned Ilda to join me in the front.

She shook her head. "No."

"What do you mean 'no'? They know you helped us. They'll kill you."

"No," she repeated.

Evan leaned forward and spoke in Spanish and whatever he said convinced her to climb in. Seconds later I was easing the car down the hill with no idea where to head next except away.

"Give me my phone," Evan mumbled. I dug in my pocket and Ilda passed it back.

"Head for the village—right," he said, trying to read his phone through swollen eyes. "Head for Córdoba. Use your translation app...the one with the...lip icon."

Lip icon? Like I had time to fiddle with a lip icon and where the hell was Córdoba? We were way up in the mountains with nothing like a main highway in sight. We were on a road so narrow a car could barely turn around. Ilda was tapping something into the dashboard's GPS and up popped a map. She pointed to the screen. "Córdoba." Yes, Córdoba, which looked many miles away.

"Evan, can you translate for me?" Silence. I shot a look at Ilda, who slumped in her seat to pantomime that he'd passed out. Right.

"¡Mira!" Ilda cried, straightening.

In the rearview mirror I could see another car gaining fast. "The other two guards." With Evan out cold and Ilda and I officially incommunicado, I had no choice but to keep on driving—only faster.

Ilda was pointing at a signpost, I was putting my foot down on the gas pedal, and all of a sudden a police car was zooming toward us from the opposite direction with another car not far behind that.

"*¡Gendarméria!*" Ilda cried.

Right, but were they on our side or the Divinios'?

When the car behind us slammed on its brakes and began to reverse, we had our answer. I slowed down and the police car drove right past us, roof lights pulsing, sirens blaring.

A long black limousine pulled to a stop before us. A tall dark-haired man in a suit got out and sauntered up to our car as I lowered the window.

"*Buenas noches, señorita. ¿Eres Isabella?*"

19

"*I*sabella?" Evan mumbled as we sped along.

"My password. Are you badly hurt besides what I can see? A concussion, internal bleeding, maybe?" I longed to open his shirt to see if he had open wounds but thought it best to wait.

Instead, I began dabbing his cuts from a bottle of water found in the well-appointed back seat, using a cloth one of the suited men had passed back along with a first aid kit. Ilda had the kit open on her lap and was handing me bandages, antiseptic, gauze…

"I'll be fine," he mumbled through those swollen lips, his head resting against the seat. "They didn't want to knock me out in case…I couldn't talk but I refused to talk…regardless. How did you…escape?" he asked, fixing one half-swollen eye at me.

"I riled Don Santos up so badly by daring to challenge his beliefs—me, a mere substandard human of the weaker sex—that he stomped off in fury. Probably thought that a woman couldn't possibly slip from his grip, but two women bested him in the end. Ilda here saved my life and probably yours, too."

He turned to Ilda and flashed her one of his beautiful, currently distorted smiles. She beamed back. "*Gracias,*" he said, adding something in Spanish before turning back to me. "First time I've seen that laser bolt…in action." He sounded like a boy with a new toy. "Works…perfectly."

"It's deadly effective, if that's what you mean. I blinded those men, Evan."

"You had no choice. I would have killed them given the chance."

Noel had said something similar to me once: never let your enemies live to come after you a second time. Kill them on the spot. But I could never do it. Besides, those two men would live a long dark life as a result of my actions and that was bad enough.

"Probably…drained the battery," Evan mumbled. "Haven't found a…solution…yet."

I sat up to check my phone for messages, distressed to find that the laser feature had, in fact, completely drained the battery. A charger was handily available on the back of the front seat so I dug out my cord and began recharging. After that, I drifted off to sleep in the midst of worrying about Peaches, Rupert, and the Carvalhos. Oh, and us…

We dozed off and on as the limousine zoomed through the evening. Ilda and I sat on either side of Evan, his head occasionally lolling on either my shoulder or hers. Our rescuers up front spoke little English and either could not or would not tell us who they worked for, but we did learn their names—Salvi and Luis, first names only. Both were in their thirties, both tall and well-built, as if they had been hired based on their physique. Ilda and Luis kept exchanging shy glances in the rearview mirror.

I awoke with Ilda saying, "Córdoba!"

Sitting up, I watched as the car drove over a long lovely bridge, the lights of a cathedral, towers, and arched-windowed buildings reflected on a calm water's surface—a river.

We gazed in hushed wonder as the car navigated wide boulevards and narrow streets, winding its way under up-lit palms toward a sprawling crenellated walled structure. I recognized medieval when I saw it and this fortress with its mellowed gold stone towers had to be at least that old.

"Alcázar de los Reyes Cristianos!" Ilda exclaimed.

Alcázar de los Reyes Cristianos? What did I know about the Palace of the Christian Kings other than to translate the rudimentary Spanish? Nothing. My one trip to Madrid when on a youthful backpacking trip would not help me here.

Evan, stirring beside me, winced and sat up. "The Castle of the Christian Kings? It was actually built from Roman remains on the bones of a Visigothic fortress…before succumbing to the Umayyad Caliphate, so the origins are hardly Christian…though Alfonso of Castille began rebuilding it in the 1200s." Various pronunciations were somewhat butchered due his lip swellings but I caught his meaning.

"Glad you're feeling better," I whispered, "and obviously haven't suffered brain damage."

He mustered a kind of lopsided smile as the car stopped by a guard post and the driver spoke into an intercom. "But why are we here? It's now a national historic site."

"I have no idea," I said.

Ilda spoke beside him.

"She says it has been closed periodically...since the pandemic, and wonders what we are doing here...too," he translated.

Our drivers were the silent types, so all we could do was wait as the car slid in through the gates and wove between imposing stone walls and under arches, hoping that somebody would eventually provide an explanation. When we stopped in a small parking area, a man and a woman were awaiting us, both dressed in dark clothing.

Luis, our driver, opened the door and helped us out while Salvi tried to assist Evan. I'm assuming Evan's Spanish response said that he could walk unassisted since the man stepped aside.

The woman, her hair pulled back into a sleek chignon, wearing a white blouse, a crisp navy jacket with a matching pencil skit, and vertiginous high heels, stepped forward. The only ornamentation she wore were a pair of gold hoop earrings and a large marquee-cut diamond on her wedding finger that flashed the light. Her white mask completed the severe ensemble. "Señorita McCabe, Señor Barrows, and..." She hesitated before Ilda.

"Señorita Ilda Garcia," Ilda said, adding something in Spanish.

"Welcome to Córdoba and the Alcázar, Señorita McCabe, Señorita Garcia, and Señor Barrows. Consider yourselves our special guests. You are most welcome. I am Dr. Sofia Morales and this is my assistant, Señor Barco. We will be your contacts while you are in Spain. Please follow me."

Señor Barco nodded and smiled behind his mask, pointing to the face covering. "If you please."

We hastily applied ours while I gave Ilda one of the surgical variety I'd packed. Señor Barco offered to relieve us of our bags and reluctantly we agreed. We strode down a long white arched corridor that seemed to open up onto a garden on one side, up several flights of stairs, on through connecting hallways, and along a grand hallway paneled with red striped silk with a high ornate gilded ceiling. I couldn't stop trying to absorb every detail from the tapestries to the paintings lining the space.

"Didn't Isabella of Castile and Ferdinand of Aragon live here?" I asked as I dredged my information databanks.

Dr. Morales turned, and then stopped while the men proceeded ahead with our bags. "You are correct. The alcázar, which means 'palace' in Arabic, was home to Queen Isabella and her husband, King Ferdinand, for eight years and also became the headquarters for the Spanish Inquisition for nearly three centuries. It is indeed a fortress with a long, often bloody history."

"And why are we here?" Evan asked, determined to stand on his own two feet as if he hadn't been battered for part of the afternoon.

Dr. Morales studied him. "Señor, may we call a doctor to tend your wounds?"

"I will be fine after a good rest but thank you for the concern."

She nodded. "It is perhaps best that I take you to your quarters to rest before we talk further. Forgive us for being unable to put you up properly, but for as long as you are with us in Spain, you will be our guests inside one of our historic sites."

"We're going to sleep in palaces and castles?" I asked.

I thought I caught a slight smile behind the mask. I estimated her to be in her early fifties but she seemed almost ageless. "Perhaps this sounds more romantic than it is," she said. "They are not designed as hotels but as museums. The facilities you might come to expect are unavailable." She spread her hands, sending her mega-diamond sparkling. "However, these buildings are very secure with guards and the necessary technology to ensure your safety. This makes them our best option to protect you. I will take you to your rooms first and then you must eat."

Which reminded me that I hadn't eaten since the morning. We left the ornate palatial area and crossed a porticoed walkway into a long buff-colored stucco building that appeared almost regimental next to the royal residence.

"These were once were the soldiers slept. Today they are offices but we have set up temporary beds here. There are no furnished bedrooms at the museum sites. We have washrooms available down the hall and have brought in temporary beds. Please let me know if you need anything else. We have set up dinner five doors down and I will wait for you there."

We were shown to three rooms side by side, all furnished alike. Seeing my backpack there, I stepped into the first, a plain butter-yellow room with a crucifix on one wall and a small bookcase against the other. A foldout bed had been made up with a pile of towels stacked next to extra blankets on a chair. Our hosts had thought of everything, right down to a new toothbrush and other toiletries.

Evan arrived at my door minutes later holding an icepack to his mouth and clutching something green in his other hand. "Phoebe?" My name now came out as "Fweebe."

"Evan." I turned.

"Yours, I presume?" He held out a pair of my silk undies that I must have stuffed into his bag by mistake.

"I was in a hurry," I said, taking them from fingers that held on seconds too long.

"I don't mind." He was trying to smile.

"You're in no condition to tease." I whipped them out of his hand, trying not to notice the twinkle in his swollen eyes.

"Always in condition...to tease."

"Wait until the swelling goes down first. Are you hurt anywhere else?"

His shirt was torn and now that he'd removed his jacket I could see the beginnings of a livid bruise forming across his chest. Without thinking, I peeled back his shirt and gasped. The bastards must have punched him repeatedly. "Oh, Evan, let me bathe and bandage that!"

He clasped my wrist. "You can bathe me...any time you want but...later. We need information first."

I suppressed a smile and watched him walk away with a slight limp.

Back in my room, I hastily gathered up a change of clothes, cringing at the thought of those brutes pawing through my stuff. Using one of the washrooms to clean up and change, I returned to my quarters only long enough to scan my phone for emails and texts.

I hastily dispatched an *I'm fine* to Max, minus relevant details, and sent something similar to Peaches after reading that Rupert had been issued a Covid test by somebody in a hazmat suit. Rupert himself texted only to complain that he'd run out of his beloved tea bags so we had best return before he was forced to drink coffee. There was a message there that worried me. Connie emailed asking our location but I didn't respond.

Minutes later, I counted five doors down the hall and entered a barrel-ceilinged room where a table had been set with paper plates of food and drinks. Dr. Morales was already seated at the head of the table, her mask removed, talking with Ilda, everyone six feet apart. Don't ask me why it surprised me that she wore bright red lipstick.

"Señorita McCabe, I have just learned what a day you have had and heard that you encountered Don Santos," she said.

"You know of him? And please call me Phoebe. I am not used to such formalities."

"Phoebe, then, and you may call me Sofia. Yes, we know of Don Santos. He is one of the order of the Divinio brotherhood, one of at least twenty members spread across the world with an unknown number of followers."

"Are they all priests?"

"The ruling brotherhood, yes. 'The world is full of monsters wearing the faces of the angels'—an old Spanish saying. Please do not think that the Catholic church has been corrupted by this sect's beliefs. They do not represent the church today, though much has been done in the name of Catholicism in the past. There are many priests and sisters from various orders who work on our behalf. Please eat and then we will talk further. This is what you refer to as takeout, I'm afraid, from the restaurant nearby."

Evan stepped in behind me and held out a seat for me, which I took, catching the wry glint of humor in Sofia's eyes at this little display of gallantry. Ilda only beamed and passed us a plate of small ham sandwiches along with other platters of bite-size edibles like sausages and seafood. We all ate in silence while Sofia sat at the end of the table with her hands folded, her perfectly manicured red nails adding color to the otherwise austere room.

"Aren't you eating?" I asked.

"Thank you but I have already dined. Try the sangria. It is a local specialty."

"Not for me, thanks." Though I noted that Ilda had taken a tall glassful. "Do you live near here?"

"I live in Madrid with my husband and two daughters but I travel often for my work. I am in charge of the nation's historic properties. That is my official role."

"Are the museums funding this operation?" Evan asked as he carefully divided his tapas into even smaller pieces. He chewed carefully as if favoring one side of his mouth. "We'd appreciate an explanation of the resources you are able to command such as government helicopters and historic sites."

Sofia smiled again, a self-possessed glimmer of humor that seemed to flicker just below her otherwise severe exterior. I sensed that passions ran like an underground river beneath that surface. "My historic properties role is only a piece of my work for my employer. They are very powerful and generous. I have worked in their employ for many decades, since I was very young. They financed my education as a historian and I have devoted my career to Spanish history in order to stop this scourge that grows more powerful by the day."

"Do you work as a historian?" I asked.

"Yes, and my employer has provided me with all the resources necessary to assist you. Whatever you need, it is only necessary to ask."

"Is this room secure?" Evan asked. "Are all your devices masked against technological intrusion?"

"As much as possible, yes. My employer established a secure network solely for our use and Señor Barco is vigilant against hacking and technological intrusion. And what of you, Señor Barrows? I see your devices are active."

"I have them shielded through encryption, though I admit with the speed of technological change, I worry that our defenses could be compromised at any time."

Dr. Morales nodded. "We must remain vigilant. We understand the situation in Portugal grows dire and we have dispatched assistance. But the sect is far less disciplined there and we fear what they may do next. There is not much time."

"Our archaeologist, Dr. Collins, disappeared last night," I said. "As you probably know, he was hacked in Lisbon, which alerted the Divinios to the location of Prince Don Carlos's skull."

"Most unfortunate, yes. And now we must find the crown," she said. "Do you have an idea as to where to look? We hold great hope that you will provide a unique perspective."

I set down my fork and took out my phone, passing it to Evan to hand to Sofia. "These underpaintings were uncovered from a Titian portrait of Queen Isabella of Portugal. The first is of a watchtower behind her head. Do you recognize it?"

Her fine arched brows rose as she gazed at the paintings. "This was uncovered beside a portrait of Queen Isabella of Portugal, the Empress of the Carnation?"

"That one is by Titian and it was returned to the House of Aviz at the empress's request. It's hung there ever since. There is another, which is a copy of the Titian that hangs in the Prado, but this one interests me most."

"Those hills could be anywhere and that style of watch post is common throughout Spain. You will see it in many fortresses. There is one outside this very door."

"Can you tell me anything else?" I asked.

"I know of this painting, of course. There have been many efforts on the part of Spain to bring it back home but the flower...the empress's association with the carnation is legendary." Her dark eyes met mine. "Emperor Charles ordered seeds from a Persian flower to be planted for her, seeds which grew in abundance and pleased her enormously. The carnation became Spain's national flower as a result, but why would it be painted over?"

"That is the question," I said, tapping another photo and sliding my phone toward Sofia, "and why would this wilted carnation be painted on a Titian portrait by someone other than Titian?"

"Are you certain of that?" she asked, picking it up.

"Positive. The brushstrokes and style are very different. Though the flower is beautifully executed, it's not by Titian. No, it was deliberately painted and deliberately hidden. That means something."

Sofia sat back, her reserve temporarily disrupted. "But who would do such a thing and when?"

"The painting hung in the apartments of King Philip II for years, I understand, before it was shipped to the Aviz family in Portugal at the late empress's request. These clues have a feminine hand. What influential women were at court at the time of Prince Carlos's death besides his stepmother, Queen Elizabeth de Valois? I have gathered a few names but I'm not sure how they fit."

"Ana de Mendoza, Princess of Eboli, for certain."

"Yes, the woman featured in the Verdi opera."

"She was unique, completely revolutionary, and lived unapologetically for her time. Besides raising nine children, some of them rumored to be King Philip's, she remained a friend of the queen. If she did indeed sleep with Philip, he was probably exercising his Divine Right of Kings."

"Any woman he wanted he could have," I remarked.

"Indeed, and she was a beautiful woman despite the eye patch. After her husband's death, she became lover and ally to the king's friend, Antonio Pérez. He plotted against the crown and managed to get away with his crimes while the princess died imprisoned alone in 1592, suspected of treason. Pérez is who we believe to be behind the later manifestation of the Divinios."

"Could she have been working against Pérez all along and taken the blame for his crimes?" I asked.

Sophia stood up. "As a spy, you mean?"

"A spy for the counter-Divinios."

"Nothing would surprise me about this rebel. She was intelligent, beautiful, and daring. Antonio Pérez, on the other hand, was known as a master manipulator who was responsible for assassinating the king's uncle at the royal request and now we think he killed Prince Carlos, too."

I grew excited. "Meanwhile the princess takes the fall for his earlier crimes."

"Not so surprising, yes?" She opened a photo on her tablet, turning it around to reveal a handsome man in black velvet holding a scroll in one hand. "Pérez held great sway with King Philip. He advised him of policies that would eventually bankrupt Spain. His goal like many of the powerful men at the time was to increase his own clout using this breakaway cult to serve his needs."

I gazed at Sofia, transfixed. "And maybe Ana de Mendoza, Princess of Eboli, worked against him while pretending to be in his corner?" I was standing now, too, leaning over the table toward Sofia while Evan and Ilda watched.

"Perhaps," Sofia whispered. "But she could not have done so alone even if she was trusted by Pérez. By then, Don Carlos was locked away in 'strict confinement'—those were the king's words. Even the queen would not be allowed access."

"Did King Philip know how his son died?"

"We don't believe he knew the full details but there was evidence that Don Carlos had been plotting the death of his father so treason was already in Philip's mind. The king lost patience. He shut himself away and sat in an armchair the days before his son's death. We believe it likely that he had given the order for his son's agony to be brought to an end. By then Don Carlos had gone on hunger strikes and tried to jump from a window. To Philip, no doubt, Pérez had merely brought to an end a difficult and painful problem."

"But he didn't necessarily know how. Would he have seen his son after death?" Evan asked.

"That is not known. The matter was shrouded in mystery. Whether the crown was applied before or after the prince's death remains unclear. The moment Senhor Carvalho sent word that your archaeologist had located the skull and was able to identify it based on well-known abnormalities, the pieces fit at last."

"But supposedly the king retreated to a monastery to mourn?" Evan said.

"Yes, immediately following the funeral."

"And maybe during King Philip's absence, a woman managed to steal and hide the crown?" I asked, barely able to conceal my excitement.

"I do not see how she could have done so. This was men's work, dark deeds they were not likely to expose to women. Women were mostly shackled in the Spanish court, though these had more freedom than most and claimed far more than many dared. Still, I do not see how they could have gained entrance to the prince's prison especially after this horrible event." She retrieved the iPad, tapped it again, and slid the device toward me opened to a portrait of a strikingly beautiful woman in a starched ruff, black velvet gown, and an eyepatch.

"Yes, the princess with the eye patch rumored to be the result of a fencing match," I said, gazing down at Ana de Mendoza, Princess of Eboli, who had married the man who would later become the Prince of Eboli when she was only thirteen.

"More likely an eye disease but the more cavalier story suits her spirit," Sofia said with a decisive nod. "If any woman was deep enough into the court to counter the Divinios and work against Pérez, it would be Ana de Mendoza. She was supposedly involved with Pérez. Still, she could not have done this alone."

"Would Queen Elizabeth of Valios have helped?"

"The queen was not known for her strength of character but supposedly possessed a good heart and attempted to help Prince Carlos, to whom she was briefly betrothed. That was before she became his stepmother. She pitied him, as did Ana de Mendoza. Apparently, they were some of the few women he treated with respect."

"But there had to be others in this conspiracy." I nodded, gazing down at the portrait. "Whoever painted the empress's wilted carnation must have been in Philip's court at that time, too. It certainly wasn't Titian. I'm thinking Sofonisba."

Sofia snapped her fingers. "Sofonisba Anguissola! Slide to the right."

"She was a rare female artist of the Renaissance," I said, "talented and supported by the men in her life despite the prejudices against her gender. Though Italian, she had moved to the Spanish court at Philip's request." I had studied her in university and refreshed myself on the details in the last few days. "I believe she's part of this."

"I think you could be right. Her portrait of the princess is there, too."

Sliding through other portraits of the much-painted Ana de Mendoza, I stopped at one showing the princess wearing a dashing plumed hat. Here the princess was portrayed in a low-cut summer gown holding a tray of what looked to be roses. A pink bud was held delicately between two fingers.

The similarities to the style of painting between the flowers in this portrait and the empress's wilted carnation hit me immediately. Both had the same delicate application of paint, the same gray-green leaves, and though I couldn't be sure without viewing the actual portrait, I was willing to hazard a guess. "This is by the same artist. We have found the artist who dared hide a clue in a Titian—Sofonisba!"

"She was very much part of the court and even attended the infanta Isabella Clara Eugenia and served as a lady-in-waiting to Queen Elizabeth of Valois," Sofia exclaimed. "She gave art lessons!"

Our eyes locked. "We have found our allies in Philip's court; we have found the female counteroperatives to the Divinios."

Sofia smiled, a beam so dazzling that it transformed her face. "I believe we have!"

"However," Evan interrupted in sober tones, "and as much as I hate to disturb this euphoria, we are still no closer to discovering where the crown may be hidden."

20

Though it was true that we had yet to find the location of the crown, the story of the women in King Philip's court was a treasure of another kind. It was as though they were allies from another century trying to communicate with us using all the skills they had available—art, symbolism, and their very femininity.

For most of that evening we sat around the table with Sofia Morales combing through the research material accessed from her employer's private online archives. It seemed that most of the valuable tertiary documents existent from the court of Philip II had been transcribed into digital form for posterity's sake and that Sofia held the online keys.

"Your employer must be very powerful," Evan had commented, studying Sofia through his puffy eyes.

"Very," she acknowledged, "but not so powerful that we can see all things in all ways. A fresh perspective proves most invaluable. Consider your every wish my command."

I grinned at the illusion to the fairy tale. "You are our fairy señora, our godmother?"

"Not as old as that, I hope." She laughed and waved her hands. "My two daughters are still too young."

She ordered computers to be delivered to the room so that we could research more comfortably and even Ilda joined in with the help of the translation app left open on my phone. Anything spoken in either English or Spanish was automatically translated in Evan's mechanical voice.

"What shall we call them?" Ilda asked in Spanish, the app immediately translating. By now I knew our rescuer was twenty-three years old and had been volunteering in Don Santos's church since a teenager. In her own way, she was of the same ilk as the Princess of Eboli, bravely working to counter injustice in a world dominated by men.

The things she had seen behind the congregation's back, the many injustices Don Santos permitted in the name of his worldview, had hardened her. Now Sofia would be keeping her under her wing. Once things calmed down, Ilda would inform her grandparents that she would be moving to Madrid.

"What will we call our anti-Divinios?" I mused. "Does your employer's organization have a name?"

"No," Sofia said, "and we are not an organization but an—how do you say it?—a network. Yes, we are a network.

"What if we called them de Nuestras Damas or the Damas for short?" Ilda offered.

"'Our ladies'? I like it," I said, since all of the women we had now encountered in history were ladies of the noblest sort. We all agreed but that brought us no closer to the crown.

"The Damas must have had help," Sofia said while pondering a sixteenth-century court document she produced on her screen. "Three women: a queen, an artist, and a princess from one of Spain's ruling houses could not have stolen the crowned head from this poor prince after burial and hidden it somewhere by themselves."

"It is not a typically feminine act, for sure. Beheading is a guy thing," I said, half-jokingly.

Evan lifted his own battered head. Though the swellings had subsided, he now sported two black eyes along with those pulpy lips. It didn't make him less attractive. "What if Pérez and his men took the skull and the crown immediately following burial? The king was supposedly so grief-stricken—or guilt-stricken—that he retreated to his El Escorial monastery shortly after the funeral. That left a man with Pérez's power ample time to perform the distasteful deed."

"So you're thinking that Pérez stole away the head and the crown, maybe to Portugal?" I asked. "He would have had opportunity, especially if the priests of the Royal Monastery of El Escorial where the prince was buried were in league with the Divinios."

"Which they probably were." Evan sat back and tried to cross his arms, found the pressure on his chest too uncomfortable, and returned his hands to his lap. I had managed to convince him to take a couple of my painkillers but otherwise he soldiered on. "But I'm guessing that something happened en route. Perhaps Portugal was his ultimate destination and that Pérez planned to enact some kind of ritual at our altar in Sintra."

"But someone interceded, someone working for our Damas?" I asked.

"Exactly. They must have ambushed his party and stolen the crown somehow, possibly the skull, too. How else can we explain how the crown and the skull became separated?"

"But who would have the strength to ambush a troop of the king's guards under Pérez? Not Ana de Mendoza, not even the queen," Sofia countered. "That would have soon been communicated to the king with untold repercussions."

"Wait!" I had been skimming another biography of the Princess of Eboli. "After her husband's death, Ana retreated to the convent of the Pastrana monastery and stayed there for years before leaving and igniting the supposed affair with Pérez. Did she actually become a nun?"

"Of sorts, yes," Sofia said. "It was common for wealthy widows of the day to retire to a convent following a husband's death, especially to avoid another marriage and to grieve in peace. Ana's marriage to de Silva, her husband, was reportedly a happy one, or happy enough, and he was King Philip's chief councillor."

"So she may have formed a strong bond with the convent sisters?"

"Definitely. Both she and her husband had generously provided to the Pastrana convent and monastery."

My eyes fixed on hers. "What if the sisters of this convent were Damas' allies? What if Ana convinced them to help her retrieve this crown and skull?"

Ilda was on her feet. "The Carmen de Pastrana, founded by Saint Teresa of Jesus!" She was speaking so quickly that the translator app couldn't keep up. In fact, it garbled the last part.

"Yes, Ana de Mendoza and her husband were the duke and duchess of Pastrana in Guadalajara where Ana was born as well as great benefactors of the area," Sofia said, catching Ilda's excitement. "In 1569, the Princess of Eboli called upon Saint Teresa to found a Barefoot Carmelite convent, and Prince Carlos died in 1568—the timing is very close!"

"Saint Teresa?" I asked. Sometimes I felt like such a heathen.

"Saint Teresa!" Ilda said, quickly genuflecting. "Saint Teresa of Jesus!"

"She was a charismatic religious figure in Spain at the time and still revered today. She held that the Mother Mary must be worshipped as the Mother of God and not just as some holy receptacle," Sofia said.

"The sacred feminine again," Evan commented. "Men have long overlooked, underestimated, and undervalued the power of women."

I caught his eye and smiled. "Amen." Turning back to my comrades I said: "So are we now thinking that our Damas may have included an order of nuns?"

"Yes, it is possible! It makes sense!" Sofia was now pacing the room, her high heels abandoned for bare feet. "Saint Teresa was a powerful person in the church at the time, respected by many, including brethren, and eventual canonized. If she put her force behind the Damas to stop the Divinios, it would make a powerful obstacle."

"And nuns would have had sanctity to travel across the country dispensing assistance to the poor and needy. Travel for them would have been relatively safe in Catholic Spain and Portugal," Evan added. "They, too, would have had soldiers to guard them and reason to enter a chapel in Portugal to secretly deposit a skull, for instance. No one would question them."

"But what about the crown?" I asked. "If the sisters also took back the crown, where would they have hidden it—in Pastrana?" I scrolled through the photos on my tablet to land on the background behind Isabella's head. "That watchtower must be significant. Do they have them in Pastrana, too?"

Sofia threw up her hands. "They are everywhere. In Pastrana, yes, here, yes, everywhere, yes!"

"But with mountains behind?"

"Yes," she said, "mountains everywhere."

Sometimes history feeds you wisps of information enlivened by the shadows of those who lived long ago. At that moment, we all wanted to grab the past by the throat and demand that it give up its dead, tell us the full story, fill in all those missing pieces. But history, like time itself, speaks in code, leaving us to piece together the best picture we can with what little it offers. We had our Divinio counteroperatives and they had sent us clues but we still could not piece it together. Something was still missing.

"The hexagonal watchtower," Sofia mused, "the mountains behind. It is strange to see those arched windows below the roof."

I looked up. "Strange, how?"

She shook her head as if to clear it. "The Moorish influence is everywhere in Spain, either by the original Arabic builders or through their influence on our design, but when I first saw this, I thought maybe it was Guadalest. Still, it is too finished to be Guadalest. The Guadalest castle would have been in ruins even in the fifteenth century."

Evan summarized from his computer screen. "El Castell de Guadalest in Valencia province. It existed during the Muslim occupation until the Christian conquest of the thirteenth century when it passed through many hands until destroyed by multiple earthquakes. I see no direct link between that castle and our power women."

I gazed down at my own screen, flipping from the painting of Princess Elba by Sofonisba Anguissola to my picture of the hidden carnation. "We're allowing ourselves to be led down the wrong track," I said slowly, almost in a trance of concentration. "We're thinking like men, not women."

"How so?" Evan asked.

"Buildings, dates, rational, linear thought...that is traditionally male thinking. The princess is painted with flowers revealing her femininity at the hands of a female artist. Here she's vulnerable, unlike all the other formal black-clothed portraits of the princess encased in the armor of court fashion. Sofonisba painted a carnation on the Titian, a flower of great importance to Queen Isabella, who must have seemed like the ideal queen in their eyes—unblemished, a regent of the most powerful man of the then world who appeared to have loved her absolutely, the mother of the current king..."

"The carnation," Sofia mused, caught in the net of my thinking, "is a symbol of love, of Spain, the flower of God."

"And legend says that carnations grew at the Virgin Mary's feet when she cried at Jesus's death. And yet it is painted wilting," Ilda said, "as if it is dying, too."

I looked up. "Where would King Charles have planted carnations for his queen after her death—at their castle in Madrid?"

"The El Escorial palace complex was built by Philip, not Charles," Evan said. "I believe that a man who loved his queen and wanted to plant something meaningful in her memory would do so at a place special to them both. Charles and Isabella honeymooned in Granada, a honeymoon that lasted much longer than expected since the two were deeply attracted to one another."

"Alhambra," Sofia whispered, her face alight. "In Granada, where Charles initially buried her."

"Though Philip eventually had her body transferred to the Royal Monastery of San Lorenzo de El Escorial in 1574 to rest beside her husband after his monastery and palace compound was finished."

"The same place where Prince Carlos was buried," Evan said.

"They buried the crown at Alhambra," I whispered, turning to Evan.

Evan caught my eye. "When it comes to how a man loves a woman, it helps to think like a man."

21

*I*t was settled: the next day we would travel to Granada, a two-hour drive. We decided it was best that we travel disguised and arrive after nightfall but that meant that Sofia had to find us wigs and a change of clothes by the next morning. She sent Salvi, one of our two guards, to start searching.

"Are you not staying here for the night?" I asked.

Señor Barco, who appeared to be in charge of security and had popped in and out throughout the evening, arrived to deliver bottles of water and a box of rolls and cheese that would serve as breakfast. The other guard, Luis, stood posted outside our building.

"I stay at a hotel nearby. We do not believe the Divinios yet know we are here, but just in case, I will follow my usual pattern. I frequently travel the country to visit our museum and national staff—or did before the pandemic. My presence here would not be unusual but my staying overnight would. Before I part, we must exchange mobile numbers." Holding her phone, she brought up her contacts. "This is my secure number. Few people have access. Why can I not do an electronic contact transfer?"

"It's Evan's blocking device. Here, let's exchange the old-fashioned way." We input our details before she gathered up her purse, stepped into her shoes, and smiled. "I hope you sleep well in Alcázar tonight. There are other guards posted around the complex and the necessary technology to assure your safety. It is best that you do not wander about the property without alerting Señor Barco. He remains on-site."

It was only a little after 9:00 p.m., too early to turn in even after the day we'd had. Besides, we were at a castle in Spain. Could I really be expected to ignore that? But my brain was filled with princesses and sisters and a knot of men intent to shore up their power using the bones of a poor, deranged prince.

Evan had already retreated to his room and I wanted to check on him. After biding good night to Sofia, I dashed down the hall to find him spread out across the bed.

"Evan," I whispered, sitting on the edge of the bed. "Let me see your chest."

"How I've longed to hear those words," he whispered with a quirk on his bruised lips, "but perhaps my manly abdomen is not currently...at its best."

"Oh, stop." I unbuttoned his shirt, spreading it open to see the manly chest in question, wincing at the sight of the livid bruising spreading down his torso and beneath his trousers. There were scars, too, signs of bullet wounds, maybe even a long-ago knife injury. It looked ghastly but I guessed his impressive musculature had protected his internal organs in the end. "Do you sense any internal bleeding?" I asked. It was all I could do to stifle my shock. "Any injuries I can't see?"

He gave me another lopsided smile. "All my parts are still working, I assure you."

"I meant *internal* parts. Did they kick you in the kidneys, for example?"

"They kicked me...everywhere, but I'll be fine. You've found our Damas, Phoebe."

"*We* found them. Let me ice that bruising at least. I see that Señor Barco has delivered a cooler." I left his side long enough to fill a zip bag with cubes, wrap it in a cloth, and apply it gently to his chest.

His hand caught mine as I rested the pack on the worst of the visible swelling. "I'll be fine. Bruises heal in time. When will yours?"

It took me a moment to grasp his meaning. I chose my words carefully. "Sometimes a wounded heart takes longer. Noel kicked me in the heart, Evan. I really thought he loved me and I him, but he betrayed me again and again."

"Maybe he loved you but didn't have the fortitude to make you more important...than his cravings and greed," he whispered. "You need a man who will make you his queen, who will love you absolutely. Halloran was the wrong man, Phoebe. Can you recognize the right one even when he's been beaten...to a pulp?"

Oh, God. One hand flew to my mouth like a startled heroine, the other held fast in Evan's grip. I tugged my fingers away slowly. "It takes time, Evan. It's too soon for me to fall again." I couldn't yet admit the truth: that I had already fallen for him and had been fighting against it for a long time. I just was too cowardly to lower my defenses long enough to risk another shot. "I'm just not ready."

"When you are ready…to fall again, let me be the one to catch you," he whispered.

I left him to dash down the corridor, stopping halfway to sob into my hands. Suddenly my emotions were welling to the surface, carrying all my anguish and heartbreak with it. My feelings for Evan were in there somewhere stirring things up, tugging at me in powerful ways that I didn't have the courage to handle right then.

"*¿Que pasa?*"

I looked up to find Ilda gazing at me while the phone in my pocket said, "What's wrong?" in Evan's robot voice.

"Nothing and everything," I said, the phone translating as I pulled it out. "I'm worried about Evan, that's all, though I'm sure he'll be fine."

"You love him. I understand. He is a strong man who loves you also," she said with a little smile.

I was about to deny it but gave up. "It is more complicated than that. I am getting over my last boyfriend who was…a murderous, thieving bastard."

"I understand!" she exclaimed, throwing up her hands. "My boyfriend also. I told him about Dos Santos but he didn't believe! When the church was closed, the men would gather and then—" she shook her head "—he joined them."

"Your boyfriend joined the Divinios?" I couldn't believe that the translator app had got that right.

"Don Santos's guards, yes. Little men, big power."

"Was he one of the men I saw today?"

"Yes." She held my gaze, fierce and unwavering. "Juan hit me. I had broke up with him but still he hits me."

"And your parents and the church permit this?"

Her gaze lowered. "Both dead. I live with my grandparents. They are good people but believe the church can do no wrong. They knew that Juan hits. They complained and Don Santos visited and quoted them the Bible."

"The parts that imply that women must serve men?"

"Yes! Don Carlos said I was misbehaved. He urged me to marry Juan to be tamed. Marry the man who beats me? Never! I prayed to the Virgin Mary and she has brought me you and Señora Morales." And with that she genuflected and embraced me. I was so ready for a little personal contact that I hugged her back.

When we pulled away moments later, both our faces were wet. "I'm sorry you have suffered under men," I began.

"Many women suffer under men. Not all. Many friends are happy with good men but not me. I will join the sisters and serve God."

A statement both rebellious and traditional. I nodded and linked my arm in hers. "Let's take a walk."

We found Señor Barco working at one of the terminals back in our work room. He jumped up to accompany us on our stroll while speaking into his cell phone.

"Come, I show you the gardens," he said. "Much of the original destroyed but this they left."

He led us under arches and beside huge walls to a large square pool lined with marigolds and orange trees. Somewhere night jasmine bloomed and water tinkled from fountains running down the center of the pool.

"Very beautiful, yes?" Señor Barco asked.

"Gorgeous," I agreed, inhaling the scent of flowers under a balmy starred sky. Gazing around, I could see the deep crenellations and towers spotlit around the property. I thought I heard the faint sound of a flamenco guitar playing on a distant street beyond the walls. And this lovely place had once been the Court of the Holy Offices, the seat of the dreaded Inquisition?

Señor Barco strolled away to check his phone while Ilda and I stood arm in arm enjoying the warm night. "And here we are in the twenty-first century with a group of holy terrorists scheming to thrive again," I whispered.

"My church bears much shame, yes," Ilda said, "but it is the crime of men, not of God. God holds His hand out for the faithful to carry His word. I will work for the power of good, not evil."

"I know you will," I said.

"Why is that man on the wall?"

I followed her gaze to a figure in black dashing across the parapets. Scanning around I said: "Shit! Where is Señor Barco?"

22

---

a bullet pinged at our feet. We dashed under the trees, heading toward the portico while I speed-dialed Sofia. She picked up immediately. "There's a man on the walls shooting. Security has been breached!" I cried.

"Where is Barco?" she asked.

Ilda screamed, stopping to stare at Señor Barco facedown on the tiles. I didn't need to roll him over to see bullet hole blooming blood under his chest. I felt for a pulse at his neck.

"Dead," I said into the phone. "We are heading back." I grabbed Ilda's hand and ran.

Ilda was saying something to me in Spanish and my phone was offering a garbled translation. I thought it said that we couldn't just leave Barco.

"He is dead!" I told her. "Señor Barco is gone!"

Sofia told us to gather in the workroom and await instructions. I patted my pocket even knowing that I'd left my gun on the bed.

We burst into the hallway of our rooms scanning for infiltrators and security personal alike but how could we even tell the difference? They all work dark clothes. But then I saw one of our original drivers, Luis, running down the hall shouting while my app translated: "Gather your bags and follow me. Where is Señor Barrows?"

Where was Señor Barrows? I ran to his room and found it empty. Even his bags were gone. Damn. Dashing back to my room, I grabbed my gun and bag. He wouldn't have left without good reason and the moment I heard the first gunshot, I understood: Evan was at the far end of the hall firing at someone.

I poked my head out, saw Ilda standing in the workroom doorway, and waved her back. Luis was in the room opposite mine, firing down the hall. He caught sight of me and tried to beckon me to hide while he stepped out with his gun aimed. It was just a second, that moment when he turned toward me yelling, that at the same time I saw Evan struggling with a man while another ran down the hall. I spied a gun aimed straight for Luis and my hand cocked the trigger, aimed, and fired. Just seconds, burned into memory. I watched in shock as the man fell to his knees.

Luis cried, *"¡Buen tiro!"* and flashed me a smile before bolting down the hall to help Evan. By the time Ilda and I reached them, one man was trussed like a chicken while the other lay facedown, unmoving.

Our guard was speaking rapid Spanish, Evan responding in kind.

"Did I kill him?" I whispered, staring at the man splayed on the tiles.

Evan slowly stood up nursing his jaw. He glanced at the fallen man. "Looks that way. Luis says you saved his life and that you're a great shot."

"I killed someone!" I cried. "I don't kill people!"

But Evan wasn't listening. He'd taken my arm and was steering me down the hall behind Luis, who had Ilda by the hand. "We have to get out of here. Luis says that Sofia will get a car ready to take us to Granada. But first we have to destroy those computers. They know we're here."

I got his thinking. We entered our workroom only long enough to smash the computers with chairs.

"They could still access the hard drives, but not easily. Let's go. Put on your masks."

There was no time to talk. We wound through dark corridors and down long hallways decked with tapestries, scuttled along the sides of the old walls while keeping hidden beneath shrubbery. I thought we'd be heading for the carpark but instead Luis unlocked a small side door to the left of one tower and urged us out.

"To the street?" I whispered.

"They'd expect us to leave by car," Evan told me. "Walk slowly." He said something in Spanish and linked my arm in his. Ahead, Ilda did likewise with Luis, both of them slowing down to a stroll.

Couples passed us exclaiming at the beautiful fortress with its palm-treed fringe so glorious against the spotlit wall. One group were obviously British tourists. No one gave us a second glance as we strolled the evening like the leisure travelers we weren't.

Meanwhile, all I could think of was that I had now killed a man and blinded two others—*me*. I had crossed a line that day, something I could never undo. Somehow tasering Noel didn't seem half as bad, maybe because I knew that enemy well.

We crossed a broad boulevard with no sign of pursuers. At a street corner, Luis paused to look back at the fortress before talking into his phone.

"Salvi thinks we got away unseen," Evan said. "He's renting a car and says the coast is clear."

"But how does he know everything is safe?"

"Run," he ordered.

So we ran down cobblestone lanes and along narrow streets until we arrived by a bridge. A little red car sat double-parked on a curb with Salvi wearing a peaked cap and manning the steering wheel. We crammed in, Ilda, Evan, and me in the back, Luis with Salvi up front. Luis passed us a couple of hats.

I donned the baseball cap and Evan the broad-rimmed number. "Now I look like a battered matador," he mumbled.

"They breached security but how?" I asked as soon as we were zipping across the bridge.

"No idea. I'm afraid they either hacked those computers, we were tracked, or we have a mole."

"A mole?" I whispered.

"Perhaps. Luis and I heard gunshots," Evan said. "He tapped into the CTC system and learned the bastards had cut the wiring to the central alarm. We were too late to save Señor Barco but thank God you two are all right."

"He was a good man," I whispered. "Maybe my urge to take a walk led to his death?"

"Stop the self-recrimination, Phoebe." My name still sounded like "Fweebe." If you hadn't gone out, they would have ambushed us in our rooms."

"But I killed a man, Evan."

"Tell Luis that. He believes you saved his life."

So take a life to save a life? Why did that make me feel so depleted? Noel would be laughing at me wherever he was. Maybe I'd killed him, too, and he had really been my first.

In so many ways I was ill-suited to be a warrior. At that moment, I just wanted to crawl away somewhere and paint pretty pictures and knit for the rest of my days.

The car drove on for at least twenty minutes with me staring straight ahead, oblivious to the darkened streets zipping away around me. We'd all been sobered by the recent events, heartsick. I gathered from the conversation up front, which Evan summarized, that Señor Barco was a loved and respected member of the team and that the younger men mourned him. They also expressed bitter anger over his senseless killing and cursed the Divinios.

We wound down into a little town with white stucco houses and blooming bougainvillea. The car pulled into a deserted parking lot and stopped behind a plain white rental van and Luis called for us to move. Out we tumbled, bags slung over our shoulders, and in seconds had transferred into a van. It took a few minutes for me to catch on that Sofia was behind the wheel.

"I cannot believe this!" she cried. "How did they know you were there?"

Dressed in leggings and a brown suede jacket with her hair all but hidden under a baseball cap, she was almost unrecognizable. Luis offered to drive but she waved him into the passenger seat while we climbed into the back seat and Salvi into the very back.

"Is your phone tracked?" Evan asked.

"Who knows? It is supposed to be secure but what is secure with these bastards?"

I leaned forward. "Maybe they listened in on our discussion about the possible crown's location or hacked those computers you thought were secure? Either way, they're on to us."

Sofia swore, my app kindly translating a garble of words. "Maybe yes, maybe no. How do we tell? We must arrive ahead of them!" She slapped the steering wheel with her gloved palm. "They should never have found us! Barco was so careful!"

She was furious—I got it. Her smooth exterior had cracked under the weight of fury. "We will stop these bastards, I swear we will!" she cried as the van peeled away from the lay-by onto a small paved road, the tires screeching beneath us.

After a few minutes, she regained her composure and began speaking rapid Spanish through her hands-free phone system.

"She's calling for reinforcements in Granada and issuing directives to somebody named Raul," Evan whispered while Ilda dozed on his shoulder.

"What kind of reinforcements?" I asked.

"Possibly police or army. I'm not grasping everything. It's clear that her employer has the cavalry at his fingertips."

"Good, because nothing less will help us get that crown," I remarked.

After that we drove into the evening without speaking. No one appeared to be on our tail and the night remained dry and clear. But that meant nothing.

After about an hour and a half, Sofia pulled into a roadside lay-by. Across the parking lot a truck stop convenience store washed a cold fluorescent light across the pavement. Eighteen-wheelers sat parked amid sedans.

"We stop here. I have brought clothes for changing and wigs—bad wigs. Such a hurry! Please use the back and be quick."

We took turns changing in the back of the van, me pulling on a frilly blouse under my jacket complete with an ankle-length skirt. Fearing I looked like a reject from a masquerade, I tossed off the skirt, figuring that with the blond wig and a face mask I'd be unrecognizable. Evan, on the other hand, emerged looking like an eccentric guy from hippie past in a long gray wig and limp linen jacket. Ilda took my full skirt and just looked lovely.

"Granada is ahead," Sofia said minutes later as we zoomed down a highway. I stared through the windshield as another illuminated castle complex rose from a forested hill far in the distance. I grabbed Evan's arm. "Alhambra amid the mountains!"

"Mountains everywhere in Spain," Sofia remarked.

We wove into town minutes later, a mix of old and new with white stucco buildings and terra-cotta-tiled roofs dominating the architecture and the palace complex rising like a golden beacon far above.

"I have called ahead the chief security officer for Alhambra to say you will spend the night but I have not told him the truth. I said that you are professors from Oxford who ask to sleep in the palace. Evan and Phoebe, you are doctors of history conducting research—married—who wish to capture—how do you say the environment of the place?"

"The ambience?" I offered.

"The ambience, yes. I said you are very well connected and pulled many strings. Ilda is your daughter studying Spanish and staying with me."

"My daughter? I'd have to have given birth at thirteen years old!"

"It happens." She shrugged.

"And my daughter doesn't speak English? And, I mean, two supposedly esteemed British professors of something or other suddenly dropping into a Spanish UNESCO World Heritage Site dressed like escapees from a costume party during a pandemic? How unlikely is that?"

She laughed. "Unlikely? What is more likely—that we hunt for an ancient artifact that a fanatical brotherhood will use to destroy the world?"

She had me there. I sat back and shut up.

"However, we hardly look dressed for the part," Evan pointed out.

Sofia lifted one hand. "This does not matter," she said. "In Spain we think the British very strange."

After that, he gave up, too. So we were eccentric professors of history who had pulled strings to stay overnight in a Spanish palace. Why not?

"So, Dr. Barrows, married at last. Are you ready for this?" Evan asked, turning to me. "We can have our honeymoon in Alhambra just like Charles and Isabella."

"Yes, with our adult daughter along for the ride. And I'm Dr. McCabe, understand? I refuse to sacrifice my independence," I told him.

"And I would never ask you to." He gave me his lopsided grin.

Sofia glanced at us in the rearview mirror and shook her head.

Soon we were driving upward, the lit fortress rising overhead—two round towers at one end, a square structure at the other, and myriad golden stone buildings with arched porticoed walkways and balconies in between, all revealed in spotlit splendor. Yet it was the hexagonal spired watchtower that caught my eye immediately.

"Look!" I touched Evan's arm.

"The same one as in the painting?"

"I'm sure of it. The crown is hidden in Alhambra!"

"And all we have to do is find it."

"I need to stand in the vantage point where Queen Isabella stood in the Titian painting. Does the interior have the same layout?"

"The Christian monarchs did not completely destroy the Arabic architecture but it fell into disrepair," Sofia said. "Much has been restored and still exists, this palace the Moorish poets described as 'a pearl set among emeralds.' The architecture was appreciated by the Spanish monarchs, if not the Moorish conquerors."

"But there must have been many renovations over the centuries?" Evan asked.

Sofia sighed. "Yes, of course—a Renaissance addition, parts altered to suit tastes, everything built outward in quadrangles. This is the same site where Christopher Columbus received his royal decree from the first Isabella and King Ferdinand in 1492 but in the Renaissance addition. There were changes, always changes, and Napoleon wrecked the site when he came through. Let us hope we will find this spot. Here we are. We will park and then walk up. This way is more protected. Come."

Sofia drove the van onto a grassy patch under tall cypress trees and we tumbled out, stiff from the drive. "Up," she said, "way up."

"Sofia," I said, touching her arm. "They know we're here. I can feel it. Someone or something has been spying on us."

She frowned. "I know. I have requested reinforcements. Let us pray that they arrive in time."

Leaning back my head, my gaze scoured the walls of the imposing fortress, surprised to see that the bricks had an almost reddish cast this close. When I dragged my eyes back down, Sofia was talking to a man who seemed to have appeared from nowhere.

"Señor Raul Saratoza, meet my good friends," she began, "Dr. McCabe and Dr. Barrows, professors of history at Oxford, England, and their daughter, Ilda. Ilda has been staying with me while studying Spanish. They will be our guests overnight."

The man, balding, about sixty years of age and surprisingly fit, probably from climbing stairs all day, had obviously been dragged into duty at the last minute. It was 11:15 and the complex should have been closed to visitors. He nodded, shrewd eyes glittering above his mask as he said: "Most welcome to Alhambra. We will make you as comfortable as we can."

I could just imagine what Saratoza must be thinking. Even as eccentric academics, our attire didn't cut it, and Evan's sunglasses couldn't quite hide the fact that he'd been in a fight. Still, Saratoza gamely played along. He opened an iron gate, deactivated a security system, and then unlocked another door while speaking into his cell phone. Soon Salvi and Luis were carrying our backpacks up a long narrow flight of concrete stairs.

"I say, but I understand that it was rebuilt over Roman remains in the thirteenth century by an Arab leader who constructed one of the most beautiful royal palaces in the historic world," Evan said in his most ponderous academic tone. Under ordinary circumstances, it might have been impressive but his lisp and inability to properly pronounce words ruined the effect. "When Ferdinand and Isabella assumed responsibility after the Christian conquest thus banishing the Muslims, it became one of their royal palaces."

"Yes, very true. A favorite royal palace, a pleasure palace, you might say, but it was still neglected for many years," Sofia explained. "It's since been restored."

"How thrilling," I exclaimed, "to spend a night here!" I felt rather than saw Saratoza rolling his eyes. I nudged Evan to keep him from trying to speak again. "Don't say my name, whatever you do," I whispered.

We climbed up the narrow stairway, through an iron gate, onto a plateau surrounded by the huge stone walls. Lighting picked out pathways and shone down on the mellowed stones and up on trees. Overhead, stars sparkled and somewhere water tinkled. My skin tinged with anticipation. And fear.

"Do I hear nightingales?" Evan asked, taking our bags from the men with a nod.

"Yes, nightingales," Sofia replied, turning to us. "Señor Saratoza has turned on the lights all over the property and will have a room where you sleep—nothing fancy, no bed. Just the floor and many blankets. It will not be comfortable but I know you wish to camp out like you do in Britain." Our eyes met.

"Oh, yes, we love to camp out in Britain," I remarked while watching Saratoza march away, Salvi and Luis in tow. Had I ever camped out in Britain? There'd be no sleep for us that night, anyway.

"Is Saratoza trustworthy?" Evan whispered once the men had disappeared. He sounded like a bass-toned Bugs Bunny.

"We do not know who is trustworthy and who is not," Sofia said. "We have no choice but to trust. He is in charge of the complex and has called his men to guard the property while we wait for my employer's people. It is the best we can do until my employer sends help. Where do we begin to look? Do you need a shovel or another tool? We must hurry."

"I carry a portable shovel but something stronger may be needed—maybe even a pickax," Evan said. "Where would Queen Isabella have spent time?"

"Charles constructed his new palace over there in 1527." She was pointing to the left. "That part would have begun by then but not finished when the pair were first married."

"No," I said, gazing around at the walls, the trees, the spotlit ramparts. "We are looking for a garden where the king would have eventually planted his lady carnations. Our Damas were thinking of flowers."

"But there were many gardens in Alhambra!" Sofia threw up her hands. "One near the Puerta del Vino, another near the Square of the Cisterns, in the Generalife, in the Garden of the Ramparts, in the Court of the Sultana's Cypress Tree—everywhere gardens!"

"But which one would have been present during Charles and Isabella's time?" I asked.

"That we don't know. Many buildings have changed, and gardens, too. Gardens especially would alter according to the tastes of the time," she said.

"But surely he would have preserved some of this original beauty?"

"Yes, so I think. Charles appreciated the art of the Islamic conquerors if not their religion. He did not deface the inscriptions. There was respect."

I stood directly in front of her, fixing her dark eyes in mine. "Think, Sofia. It's 1526. The royal honeymooners are staying here. They stroll the gardens together, and Charles is eager to show his bride the most beautiful places. What would have impressed her most?"

She snapped her fingers. "Follow me."

We crossed the pavement, traversed a short hall, went down many stairs, and entered a porticoed courtyard carved of creamy filigreed stone so intricate it could have been lace. "Oh," I marveled.

"The Patio of the Lions, built during the rule of Muhammed V, 1362 to 1391," Sofia said, spreading her arms. "Emperor Charles thought this very beautiful. He would have brought his queen here."

I gazed around. But everything in this stunningly gorgeous place was tiled or of carved marble, including the round basin featuring the marble lions that gave the patio its name. All of it looked original. "But would there have been plants here?"

"Probably once but they are lost now. Come, we go to the Generalife where the rulers of Granada once took a rest from work in their gardens."

We dashed under deeply embossed ceilings with Arabic script carved into the stone and stepped through an arch into a long garden with a central water feature running its length and plumes of water tinkling into the channel every few feet.

Ilda exclaimed: "So beautiful!"

"Yes, the Patio of the Irrigation Ditch—not a very romantic name, I know. These fountains were in the Jardines Altos del Generalife here even in the fifteenth century. It is the brilliant engineering of the Arabs to feed water down from the hill to work the fountains and gardens at Alhambra. Once there would have been flowers and fruit trees but today our gardeners have planted mostly myrtle hedges to line the water."

I nodded and stepped forward, turning around until I caught sight of the hexagonal watchtower far in the distance. I positioned myself in the same manner as Isabella had stood and checked over my shoulder to see if it matched. It didn't—too far away.

Across the tiles, Evan stood near the myrtle hedge doing the same. "We can barely see the tower," he remarked.

"And no mountains," Ilda added.

"These buildings are eighteenth century in origin," Sofia said, indicating the comparatively plain white stucco buildings running on either side. "Only the arches at both ends are original."

Maybe I caught a flicker of movement in one of porticoed balconies at one of those ends but couldn't be certain. Every shadow moved in this place, a factor of the breeze and the spotlights casting patterns on the stone.

"Even if they weren't there, the angle still wouldn't have been right," Evan was saying. "The tower is shown behind her right shoulder."

"Come," Sofia beckoned, "we try another." We dashed back through the portico, up more stairs, along a walkway under trees with glimpses of the city far below, and through an arched door into another courtyard.

"Here we come to the Court of the Sultana's Cypress Tree, Patio del Ciphers de la Sultana. In Isabella's time there would be this central pond and inside that pond another. Charles marveled again at the engineering and there you see the Water Stairway at the end, the oldest stairway in these gardens. It existed in the Muslim period."

I stepped forward and stared. As enchanted as Isabella must have been to see those three flights of stone stairs rising up amid a tunnel of trees with water flowing down either side or the square pools with their treed islands, the tower was not visible in this section, either. I closed my eyes to hear the fountains tinkling, the nightingales calling.

"No," I whispered. "She is standing high up but not outside. On a balcony beneath an arch with the mountains and watchtower behind her." Spinning to face Sofia, I added: "She was pointing down to the garden with her right hand, not standing *in* the garden." I brought up my photo of the painting and showed it to her while looking back to the main courtyard where water ran in a rectangular pattern around two islands of trees and flowers.

Ilda, standing behind her, reached over and took my phone and posed exactly like Isabella. *"Alli arriba,"* she said, pointing behind her.

We all turned to gaze up at the covered porticoed walkways open on both sides, one of which overlooked the garden.

"Would that have been there in Isabella's time?" Evan asked.

"Yes, but not like that. It has been much restored," Sofia told us. "Follow me."

In minutes, we had climbed a stone staircase and stood in the open corridor scanning both sides. Opposite the garden, the illuminated guard post could be seen in the distance with the darkened mountains beyond.

Ilda, still holding my phone, posed again, her right hand pointing down toward the garden. *"¡Hir!"* she whispered.

Evan followed the direction her index finger pointed, using his phone to beam a red laser line down into the garden. It landed into a square planting of jasmine beside two cypress trees on an island surrounded by the running water. "There!" he whispered. "Perhaps once that part was filled with carnations."

Soon we were back down in the garden, kicking off our shoes to wade across the ankle-deep water to the square island. Evan waved us to stand on the marble edging while he scanned his detector app across the earth planted with trees and jasmine.

"It must be deep down," I whispered. "If it's here at all."

"This garden would be dug and dug many times," Sofia agreed.

"Still, if they wanted to preserve the original layout, they would only go deep enough to change the soil, maybe remove the roots of a dead tree," Evan pointed out. "The piping for the fountains is several feet to the left according to this, and yet..." He paused, staring at his screen.

"And yet?" Sofia prompted.

"And yet there is indication that something metal may sit much farther down...six feet down."

"But we have detected this earth many times," Sofia said.

"How long ago?" I asked.

She shook her head. "The last garden renovation was many years ago. We lined the flower beds with myrtle hedges."

"They would have run a surface detector looking for pipes and the ancient plumbing works. Look." He held up his phone, which marked out the grid in a blue light, something pale and pulsing from red to purple in the middle of the rectangle.

"What does that mean?" I asked, leaning forward.

"The blue lines are ferrous and trace the water pipes, which range between two to three feet below the surface, and the red to purple pulsing light indicates something lies much deeper between the two trees—maybe six feet down," he said. "Nonferrous," he added.

I caught his eye. "Nonferrous?" I asked.

"Not iron-based. Maybe gold or silver. The blue means something gold is encased in something ferrous—red and blue making purple," he said.

A momentary hush descended. I turned to Sofia. "Can you call the guys to help us dig?"

"Let's not risk it," Evan said as he pulled his periscopic shovel from his duffel and hung his jacket on a tree branch. "We don't know who to trust."

Sofia pulled out her phone. "But I must call my employer. Our backup should be here by now."

Sofia was talking rapidly into her phone while Evan climbed over the myrtle hedge into the center of the planting. He struck his spade into the earth and in seconds only the sound of digging broke the night.

"Evan, pass me your gun," I whispered.

He stopped long enough to pull it from his pocket. I leaned over the hedge and took it.

Sofia had put away her phone. "My contact does not answer. I left another message."

"Another?" I asked. "Do you mean that we don't know if help is coming?"

She shook her head.

"Can you fire a gun?" I asked.

"No!" she said. "That has never been my job. My job is research only."

Ilda stepped forward with her hand outstretched. *"Soy la hija de un granger,"* she said.

"She can shoot," Sofia translated. "Farm girl."

I gave Ilda Evan's gun and cocked my own and together we patrolled the edge of the courtyard, her going one direction, me the other, watching the parameters. Once Ilda thought she caught a shadow moving across the portico above but shook her head. False alarm. This continued for maybe twenty minutes while I kept thinking that I heard sounds over the walls, strange noises, cries. Were we surrounded?

Sofia paced the tiles, repeatedly leaving messages and calling her employer's agents. "Nothing!" she told me when I caught her eye. "I called Saratoza and the two boys but no answer!"

To say I didn't like the sound of that was an understatement.

Meanwhile Evan kept digging and digging. I was at the water stairs end of the courtyard the moment I heard metal hit metal. I quickly turned and splashed through the water to the island. Evan was lifting something from the earth.

We watched in rapt wonder as a rusted metal container roughly the size of an old breadbox with a peaked lid was lifted from the earth and deposited on the marble edging. I stared at it and swallowed. "It seems too big to be a crown."

"A casket," Sofia whispered, "a reliquary casket. The sisters may have placed it inside such a container or the monks transported it in one. We must open it."

"Not now," I said. "We have to get out of here."

Evan splashed into the water beside me and lifted the box. "Get my duffel."

Grabbing his bag, he laid the filthy box down on top of his clothes, shoving his spade in last as we pulled on our shoes.

"We're not going to get to just walk out of here," I said.

"I know. When they come for us, hope to God that Señor Anonymous brings the troops," Evan said.

I was about to respond when a deep voice called over a loudspeaker: *"Gracias.* Now set down the bag and step away."

443

---

*B*ut we ran.

We plunged into the fountain's rectangular canal system and waded toward the water stairs. Nobody spoke. Evan was up front, Sofia in the middle, Ilda and I bringing up the rear. We were shielded by the trees and hedges. Men were shouting from somewhere behind us. Over the wall to our left, more shouting and flashing lights.

"Do not be foolish!" bellowed the deep voice. "You are surrounded. Do not make us shoot!" He repeated everything in Spanish in case we missed anything.

We bolted up the stone steps, the trees bowing down over our heads, rivulets flowing down either side. If we just reached the top of the stairs, maybe we could head for the city below, Sofia had whispered. But the moment we reached the top, they were waiting. As we expected.

We were powerless to move.

At least twenty men stood facing us, all dressed in black, none of them wearing masks, all with guns pointed at our chests. Slowly they began to circle us like a pack of stalking lions.

"Drop your pistols and kick them toward us," the head honcho ordered. He was short, wiry, and appeared to wear a priest's collar under his shirt, though the epaulets were strangely out of sync.

We dropped the pistols, raising our hands while the men collected the weapons, every pair of eyes fixed on us. One man dragged Sofia from our group, holding a gun to her head, while another told Evan to lower his duffel and pass it over. Sofia, undaunted, spat rapid Spanish at Head Honcho until he slapped her across the face.

"If you move falsely, we shoot," Head Honcho said. "You follow now." He jerked his head toward his troops, three of whom rushed forward to bind our hands. We were told to walk so we walked, back down the water steps, across the sultan's courtyard, and along corridors we had yet to see.

The complex was huge, building after building passing while we kept our eyes peeled for help. Where the hell was the cavalry? Where was Saratoza and our two guys? Once, I glimpsed bodies sprawled on the floor while passing a doorway but couldn't identify anyone.

Soon we were back on the street, still in the Alhambra complex, heading toward a stone church. Don't ask me why it shocked me to see a church, but of course there would be at least a chapel in a complex this size. But this was no chapel and it looked to be more recent than most of the buildings, at least seventeenth century. We were marched up the steps of a plain exterior and shoved down the aisle of a stunning baroque basilica.

"The Church of Santa Mariá de la Alhambra," Sofia whispered. "Built over the site of the sultan's great mosque."

Once herded into the front pews and each assigned a guard to stand pointing rifles at us, we could do nothing but sit looking desperately for the escape we knew didn't exist. I wondered why they didn't demand our phones but figured they must have been afraid to touch them or thought we could set an explosive with the sound of our voices. Definitely they realized that as long as they remained in our pockets and with our hands bound, our devices were harmless, and they were right.

Six priests stepped into the nave from a side door, one of whom was Don Santos with a bandaged head. Nobody wore masks here, either. He caught sight of Ilda and frowned. How she must have disappointed him.

We watched in silence as the others cast us dismissive glances, if they looked in our direction at all. Their interest was fixed on the rusted iron box now sitting on the altar, which they gathered around while intoning Latin.

One of the brethren, the tallest with a head of thick silver hair and a beautifully embroidered mantle covered in a mix of pagan and Christian symbology, seemed to be the holy head honcho who could make his minions jump with a wave of his hand. He signaled for the army-type guard to lift the object from its crumbling iron case.

It was surprisingly easy since the metal practically disintegrated under his gloved hands. In moments, a glowing reliquary box was lifted from the rusted shards and laid on a red velvet cushion.

We gasped like spectators at a magic show. An intricate enameled and gold-peaked casket now reflected the candlelight on the altar, two embossed saints pointing toward the narrow crystal window through which we could just make out the contents. A hush descended over captors and captives alike. Holy Honcho prayed over the casket, his voice deep and resonant as he lifted his gaze upward amid his praying brethren. A gilded Jesus on the crucifix gazed on with an expression of profound pathos.

I felt sick. The piece was exquisitely beautiful and represented the faith of those who had hidden it. Still, I didn't want to see what lay inside, yet I couldn't tear my gaze away. My companions seemed equally rapt. Ilda was crying.

Now Holy Honcho had donned a pair of white gloves and awaited with a beatific expression as a second priest raised the casket lid. Holy Honcho lifted the contents, releasing the fastenings to raise the priceless object into the air.

Another collective gasp. A solid gold crown imbedded with twelve peaks each set with a ruby, diamond, emerald, or sapphire glittered in his hands. He rotated the coronet to reveal the central peak, which appeared to capture a shard of something in its rock crystal frame. His satisfied smile never waned.

Ilda was wailing, Sofia was praying, the priests were chanting, and all I could do was stare at this priceless wonder with loathing. It had been pounded into the head of a human being! Maybe all signs of that monstrous moment had worn away but the holes around the bottom filigreed edge were still visible.

For a sick instant I was afraid that one of the priests would manifest the skull right there but no skull arrived. A burst of hope hit: the skull wasn't here! It must be in Portugal awaiting the crown's delivery. There was still time.

At last the holy honcho lowered the crown back into its reliquary and snapped an order at a guard who stepped up to wrap the casket in velvet.

"What are you going to do with us?" I cried.

Holy Honcho turned as if he had forgotten we were there. In seconds, he was towering over me, his hair backlit in a silver halo. "You?" he spoke in his deep voice. "To you, Señorita McCabe, we owe a great debt." He brought his palms together and bowed his head. "You have found what centuries of our order could not. For you we reserve a great honor."

"I just bet," I whispered.

"You will accompany us to Portugal and to the altar where we will place the crown on our holy king on earth, King Carlos. To you we will accord the highest honor to witness this sacred moment before you join our king in heaven." The other priests began chanting.

Evan began speaking in Latin. The man turned and stared. Evan said something further and Holy Honcho answered tersely and soon the two men began conversing in that ancient language.

"What are they saying?" I asked Sofia.

"Evan asks if the order uses human sacrifices and the priest says yes, but only for special occasions and only for special sacrifices. He says you are very special and have been brought to them by God. Evan accuses the order of being more pagan than Christian and is quoting verses from the Scriptures. They are debating theology."

"Seriously?" I knew Evan was raised Catholic but his timing seemed a bit off.

Suddenly the army-type head honcho interrupted, pointing to his watch. The holy honcho nodded and folded his hands.

"They are taking us to the airport for a plane to Portugal," Evan whispered.

"That's not what he said. They are taking *Phoebe* to Portugal. Us they will kill," Sofia said.

We were ordered to our feet and separated, me dragged away into the circle of priests, the others marched down the aisle. I wanted to scream, to kick, to wail, but I forced myself into total stillness. Think, I needed to think.

I wondered if I could wait until on the plane and in the air and then order my phone to explode. Maybe it could do that. Maybe it would even be enough to down the plane and destroy the crown with it. But if it was a passenger plane, that would kill innocent people, too... However, they would all die, anyway, if this band of loonies had their way. Still, I couldn't be the one to kill the innocent.

Suddenly Evan slumped to his knees in the aisle; Sofia and Ilda quickly followed suit. As I was pushed from the nave, I realized that it was a delay tactic. One soldier moved to shoot but a command from Holy Honcho froze him to the spot. Evan took that moment to deliver a vicious kick and pandemonium followed.

I was rushed into the street by my priestly captors, Head Honcho joining us with four of his guards seconds later. A black limo sat parked by the curb, five similar cars behind it. Now I was sure I heard sirens. A helicopter was flying by overhead, someone was speaking Spanish from a loud speaker. Holy Honcho called commands in his booming voice as he and the priest holding the casket bolted for the limo. A guard tried to drag me behind. No hands, no gun, what could I do? I dropped to my knees.

One of the honcho guards tried to yank me to my feet but I kicked him away. He had his rifle aimed ready to shoot when someone slugged him on the head. As he fell to the ground, there stood a battered Luis.

"Luis!"

He grinned, helped me to my feet, and sliced off my bindings with the flick of a knife.

"Where's Salvi?" I asked.

He got the gist. In response, he ran a finger across his throat while making faces and then proceeded to air-throttle someone. Got it: Salvi had been our mole.

Meanwhile, everything was in chaos. Soldiers had appeared dressed in camo and a gun battle broke out between the two sides. Holy Honcho was now shouting from the limo as the car zoomed down the lane. More soldiers appeared from Humvees coming from the other direction.

"Don't let him get away!" I pointed to the car and held up my phone to transcribe my words into Spanish. "He has the crown!"

Luis translated, too, his voice traveling farther than mine. Next he was dashing up the stairs to the church when Evan, Sofia, and Ilda came down, along with a posse of soldiers, their hands now free.

"He's getting away with the crown! Catch the head honcho!" I cried.

Evan shouted to one of the soldiers, who in turn spoke into his head mike.

Sofia threw her arms around my shoulders. "I thought we were all going to die!"

"But your employer came through," I whispered.

The gunfire began to taper off as we watched an army helicopter land in the center of the parking area.

Evan turned to me. "They've caught them—ambushed the car and blown out their tires at the bottom of the hill."

My body nearly sagged with relief. I, in turn, threw my arm over Ilda's shoulders as the young woman stood shivering by my side. Sofia was walking toward the soldiers talking on her cell phone and Luis stood nearby with a soldier.

"Where's my backpack?" I asked no one in particular. Ilda translated and a soldier soon returned from the church with our bags. I took out a sweater and gave it to Ilda. We stood there like some kind of family unit still holding one another when we heard cars coming up the lane.

Moments later, a camo Humvee appeared with the holy honcho cuffed in the back seat. Once the vehicle braked, four soldiers piled out, nudging the priest toward us at gunpoint. One of the soldiers now carried the casket as if holding a ticking bomb.

"This is sacrilege!" Holy Honcho cried in two languages. "We are on God's mission!"

Sofia, who had been pacing in circles talking into her phone, stopped before me. "My employer, he thanks you for helping us find the crown. He commends you for your insight and bravery. We will go now someplace safe until he can take possession of it."

"Take possession of it? Sofia, that thing must be destroyed!" I cried.

She looked at me as if I had lost my mind. "Destroyed? A priceless artifact destroyed? Never! My employer will take possession of it, I said. It will go to the Prado Museum." Her eyes were alight with excitement as she returned her phone before nodding to me. "We will be transported by helicopter until a plane can take us to Madrid where my employer awaits. He will also ensure your transportation back to Portugal. Father Lorenzo and the other Divinios will go with the army to be dealt with through the law."

Father Lorenzo? The priest had never stopped praying since he'd been removed from the Humvee and dragged to the middle of the drive. Now he was lifting his bound hands toward the sky, no doubt invoking the angels to join his war. Occasionally he'd cast a particularly vicious glance in my direction.

Evan, with his arm around my shoulders, caught my eye as he stood tense beside me. "He says you're the scourge of the modern world."

"I feel the same way about him. Evan, we need to bring the holy honcho with us.

He almost managed to smile. "His name is Father Lorenzo—where's the respect?"

"Filed under serial killers in the ancient history department, subcategory religious orders," I said. "He gets no respect from me but we still need answers."

He called to Sofia. "Sofia, let's bring Father Lorenzo with us. This will be the last time we can question him about the Divinios before our efforts are absorbed by the Spanish legal system."

She considered this and nodded. "Yes, I would like to ask him many things." She turned to one of the army men and gave instructions and soon we were all being bundled into the waiting army helicopter. I had no doubt that Sofia was in command of this mission.

An expansive troop-carrying variety, the helicopter was impressive. That said, it wasn't big on amenities so all we could do was buckle up and wait.

I was in a window seat, Ilda next to me, with Evan and Luis opposite the aisle. Sofia sat in front of us with the casket in the seat next to her and the soldiers in the other seats surrounding a still-praying Father Lorenzo. Soon we were lifting off, affording me a brief view of a night-lit Granada as the chopper sped away.

I tried to relax but couldn't, not with that thing sitting only two rows in front. Pulling out my phone, I scanned my messages, zeroing in on a text from Peaches: *More smoothing lotion needed!* Followed by Rupert's demand for tea bags. I tried to catch Evan's eye but his attention remained fixed on the priest sitting one seat ahead.

Less than an hour later, we were crossing a dark expanse that could only be the ocean. I checked my GPS long enough to see that we were in the North Atlantic somewhere off the coast of either Spain or Portugal. A long lighted rectangle came into view below. Ilda pointed and cried out, my phone translating, "Airline carrier!" Why not an airport?

When the helicopter landed on the illuminated bull's-eye minutes later, all I could think of was that casket. It could not go to a museum, no matter how right that sounded in theory. This was no ordinary priceless artifact.

Everyone followed Sofia's instructions including the upper ranks as the object was carried with great care down to the next deck, us following behind. I managed to catch Sofia's attention to ask about those reinforcements that had supposedly been sent to Sintra. "My friends are in trouble," I said.

"I was ensured that the Portuguese forces were on their way."

After that, everything passed in a blur of steely gray as we were ushered into a plain room centered by a long table.

Father Lorenzo sat at the head of the table until Sofia ordered the soldiers to move him one seat down. She then took the seat of command, catching my eye in what she saw as a shared moment of triumph. I was instructed to sit opposite her at the other end, which I did.

Evan, Luis, and Ilda sat around the table along with two soldiers as a man entered wearing a snappy white jacket designating a captain's rank. He was obviously so annoyed that his place was taken that he preferred to remain standing. Introductions were kept brief after which he gave us a curt nod and exited.

One of the soldiers positioned the casket in the center of the table, opened the receptacle, and set the crown on its velvet covering. Again that collective gasp.

I averted my eyes while Sofia began firing questions at Father Lorenzo. She asked him if he was the head Divinio, where was the sect based, and to give her names and locations. When no answer came, she moved on to the historical beginnings of the sect and demanded to know if he knew the identities of the order's opposition in King Philip's court. Though he gave no direct reply, I sensed that we knew more than he did in that regard.

Evan interrupted to ask where the skull resided—was it in Sintra as we supposed? To that, Holy Honcho only cast him a little sorrowful smile.

Sofia pulled out his phone. "We have now traced your calls to your allies and sent help to Sintra where your men are being rounded up as we speak. It is over, Father Lorenzo. Accept your defeat. Your order will now be crushed like so much dust between our fingers." To illustrate she rubbed her fingers together and wiped her hands on her pants legs.

"It is not for you to ask questions of me," he said finally, "and it is for me to pray for your souls as you plunge humanity into who knows how many years of further darkness." His gaze seldom left the crown.

Eventually Sofia gave up and turned to one of the soldiers. "Take him to your brig and ensure he is guarded. And bring us food and drink," she added.

"At least we have the crown in our possession," she said to me once they had taken him away. "This priceless sacred artifact will be treasured as it deserves."

"Sofia, have you forgotten what this crown represents, where it's been, what it's done?" I asked.

"Of course not," she said. "It represents a piece of history that has had a far-reaching impact on Spain. Never has such an item been recovered with so much brilliance and insight! And look at it, Phoebe—a work of art. The gold, the jewels! I am thinking that that sapphire may actually be the famed blue diamond stolen in the thirteenth century from the Ratnashastra mines in India, and—" she genuflected "—in the crystal, a piece of the True Cross!"

I stared at her, baffled. "But, Sofia, there must be enough pieces of the True Cross around Europe to reconstruct a forest. You know that. How likely is it that this is real?"

"You are not Catholic. You do not understand," she said.

"I understand this: Pérez designed this crown to fire up a group of fanatical monks who were already riled up by the Inquisition. He pounded that thing onto the head of a deranged man unfortunate enough to have royal blood." I leaned toward her. "It was designed as a political and religious weapon and in time took a life if its own. Think, Sofia: as long as it exists, it

451

gives the Divinios the oxygen they need to rebuild and inflict more havoc in the future. It's a time bomb!"

"But we will round up and destroy the Divinios."

Evan shook his head. "More likely they will remain underground and rebuild in one form or another. Like a virus, we won't be able to catch them all, you said so yourself. They will mutate and proliferate. Phoebe's right: that crown is a global liability."

Sofia sat back, a brief flicker of panic crossing her face. She closed her eyes and crossed herself as a tear rolled down her cheeks. "It belongs to my employer; it belongs to Spain," she whispered. "I cannot be part of this. I could not live with myself."

Slowly she rose and walked around the table, taking pictures of the crown from all angles. Several minutes passed with her gazing at the thing without speaking. Finally, she whispered something in Spanish, crossed herself, and cast me a tremulous smile. "You, Phoebe, you are the brave one. You carry on the work of our las mujeres, our Damas. They were Catholic, too, and could never destroy something that had the possibility of being sacred. I must leave now and call my family. They will be worried."

Once she'd exited, Luis, Ilda, Evan, and I sat alone with the crown. I swallowed, my hands gripped together in my lap.

"Do you want me to do it, Phoebe?" Evan asked.

"Thank you but no. I have to do it—for the Damas." I gazed up at Ilda and Luis, surprised to see that they were holding hands. Ilda was crying, he was comforting her—how sweet. "You are all such good friends and I thank you. Forgive me if what I'm about to do causes you pain. It's not easy for me, either, but maybe for different reasons."

Evan translated while I photographed the object before he carefully packed the crown into his duffel. "I'll come with you," he said.

But they all came, the four of us leaving the room and heading for the upper deck. Sailors and soldiers asked us where we were going and Evan replied convincingly. "I said that we all needed air after our ordeal." One of the sailors was instructed to take us to an area of the deck believed safest for our promenade and then stood by around a corner out of sight, respecting our privacy.

I gazed around at the huge deck expanse, relieved that on this clear night the sea was calm and our progress measured in a relatively sedate level of knots. "Where are we again?"

"In the Atlantic approximately halfway between Spain and Portugal. I won't tag the coordinates just in case. Suffice to know that it's deep enough here to almost guarantee that no one will see the crown again."

"We need to video this, Evan."

"Yes—a social media moment. Just get it over with, Phoebe," Evan said. "Let's make sure the evidence of the crown's absence hits the news."

Luis and Ilda shielded us from view while Evan lowered the duffel and lifted out the crown to pass to me. He then raised his phone to video what came next.

This was no proud selfie moment for me but an act of total desperation. Here was Phoebe McCabe, the woman who had spent her life retrieving and preserving rare objects, about to throw a priceless artifact of historic and artistic importance into the sea.

The moment Evan passed me the crown it felt as if the cold metal seared my fingers. "This object is the crown of the Divinios," I said as Evan leaned forward to get a close-up. "It represents hundreds of years of pain and suffering. Now I consign this thing to the sea." A flash of pain and anguish shot through me moments before I tossed it over the railing, Evan filming every second.

Maybe I caught the glint of gold in the starlight seconds before the wash pulled the crown under or maybe that was my imagination under fire. Either way, my relief was bottomless and my anguish equally so.

In an instant, Evan had posted the clip worldwide.

24

$\mathcal{I}$t was a chilly mountain morning when Evan and I drove our rental car up to Sintra. The Portuguese police had proceeded us by days and most if not all of the known Divinios and sympathizers had been rounded up. But there had been no sign of the Carvalhos when the police swarmed the castle and we had been unable to contact Peaches or Rupert by phone.

"They must be there somewhere," Evan muttered as he drove through the forest. "They can't just disappear. I'm not even picking up Rupert's tracking device."

Neither of us would utter our deepest fear: that the Divinios had retaliated against the family and their supporters once the news of the crown's destruction hit. And it had hit—hard. The clip of me throwing the Divinios crown into the sea was all over the Internet.

After the deed was done, we had convinced Sofia to let us go directly to Lisbon rather than accompany her to Madrid. Apparently, her employer was dumbstruck once he'd seen the footage, but she had managed to convince him of the ultimate truth: that the crown could not be permitted to exist on this earth. Under water was bad enough. Had a forge been handy, I would have melted it down to bullion but, as it was, no one would find it any time soon, if ever.

Sofia had hugged me tightly before we left, the two of us crying at the loss of the crown and all the trials we had experienced these past two days. She had arranged for an army plane to deliver us from the aircraft carrier to

Lisbon, leaving her to do the explaining to her employer. We had waved goodbye to our new friends, my hug for Ilda especially tight and long.

Now anxiety clawed my gut as the car drove up the drive, through the open gates, to the dark castle. Both Evan and I were exhausted and taut with worry.

"This makes no sense," he said. "That house was a community and communities don't just evaporate."

We climbed out of the car and gazed up at the castle. "I presume it will do no good to ring the bell?" I had my phone in hand and flipped through my photos until I found the one with Peaches's code. "Let's try this."

I tapped in the code, shocked when the door clicked open. Someone had to have been around to activate the security system in the first place. That gave me hope.

We stepped inside, the dark central hall that echoed with our footsteps, the place suffused with that heavy emptiness that occupies a deserted home.

"Let's try upstairs," Evan suggested, and together we bolted up the three flights to our bedroom wing, me to Peaches's room, Evan to Rupert's.

I looked around Peaches's space, shivering. Flicking on a light, I studied everything—the unmade bed, the towels on the floor, her missing bag. Peaches never left her room a mess and there's no way a kidnap victim gets to pack her bag, either. Plucking up an empty bottle of smoothing lotion left on her pillow, I smiled.

Immediately I was back in the hall, Evan striding toward me from the opposite end. "They have to be somewhere nearby!" he said, holding up a single unused tea bag. "His main Vuitton bag is gone but he left this."

I caught his eye and held up the smoothing lotion. "But where could they be?" Then I had a thought. "Follow me."

In seconds, I was back downstairs dashing into the library, making a straight line to the conservator's closet. "I'll call you from upstairs," I told Evan as I got down on my hands and knees to pull away the boxes blocking the hatch.

"Wait, I'll come with you," he said in that manly "I exist to protect you" way of his.

I paused to look up at him, taking in his poor bruised face, healing but still discolored. "Evan, you won't fit. Could you just wait and watch my back?"

"Against what—mice?"

I smiled. "I'll call the minute I get up there."

He didn't look happy but he left me to it. And so I crawled into the dark dusty passageway and up those narrow stairs, my phone lighting the path.

Two little notes scribbled on pink paper had been dropped like bread crumbs along the way. One said *Follow me* and the other just said *Ana Marie*.

When I reached Senhor Carvalho's closet, I didn't know what I expected—to see the entire Carvalho family sitting around having breakfast, maybe—but the room was as empty as the house.

I spun around, scanning every inch. The same signs of a calm, seemingly organized exit greeted everything I saw right down to the made-up bed. Nothing seemed amiss except…the large photo of Queen Isabella now sitting on the dresser. I swear I would have noticed that before.

Picking up the ornate frame that encased it, I studied the photo—a paper photocopy, I realized. Turning it over in my hands, I noticed that one of the frame's ornate roundels centering each of the four corners seemed loose, and it fell off in my hand.

Seconds later I was on the phone to Evan: "Senhor left me sign—a signal of some sort. I just activated it. If my hunch is correct, the family is about to return."

And home they came nearly an hour later. By that time we had received calls from Rupert and Peaches, heard a rush of facts about hidden corridors and escape plans.

Senhor Carvalho and Rupert had cooked up a strategy to employ the property's secret passageways and tunnels to take the family safely from the castle to the village. There they had remained hidden in the homes of loyal employees until the police arrived to round up the Divinios and supporters. Senhor Carvalho and Rupert had only waited long enough for the infiltrators to reveal themselves before enacting their exit plan and had remained hidden until we returned to Portugal. Only then did they believe that it was safe to come home.

Evan and I were waiting on the walkway when the cars drove up the drive —five of them. In minutes, out came Senhor Carvalho, Adriana, Ana Marie, and Peaches, plus many of the staff. Rupert arrived in the last car looking pleased with himself with Senhors Abreu and Afonso.

Ana Marie burst out of a green sedan and dashed up the walk to hug me. "Phoebe, you came!"

"Of course I came," I said, hugging her back.

"They caught the evil ones! Mama, Senhorita Peaches, and I hid with Alma until the bad men went away! Grandpapa and Senhor Fox stayed with Senhor Abreu!"

Adriana, standing beside the child, nodded. "Please forgive me," she said quietly.

"There's nothing to forgive," I said over Ana Marie's head. "You were only trying to protect this little princess here."

"Indeed she was." Senhor Carvalho had arrived. "Phoebe, you are amazing. I could not believe it when I heard the details. You destroyed the crown? I swear I could never have done such a thing, though I admit that it had to end in such a manner. My Spanish friend was enraged at first but has come to see the light. We will talk more later. The staff is preparing a celebration feast for us tonight and I agree that it is time we celebrate. Until then." He raised his hand and shuffled away.

Peaches was standing by to deliver one of her enormous hugs. "So you went to Granada without me? You took on the Spanish army without me? That's going to take one pile of smoothing lotion to make better, woman. Better order up a year's supply."

I laughed and disentangled Ana Marie's little arms to ready myself for one of Peaches's mega-hugs. "I'll make it up to you somehow," I said, trying to breathe as she squeezed the breath out of me.

"Damn right you will. Are those Spanish soldier dudes as hot as I've heard?"

Ana Marie was looking up at us and asked: "What are hot dudes? Do they light up?"

"Kind of," Peaches said, finally releasing me. "They are like heating blankets for us ladies. You'll find out when you get older, honey."

Adriana took the child's hand and led her toward the house. The staff were bringing along bags and boxes of food as they wound their way into the castle, Ana Marie waving back to me. Turning, I caught Peaches's eye.

"Shit, woman, you had a hell of an adventure without me and that bodyguard of yours is looking pretty battered." She thumbed toward Evan, who was now embracing Rupert. For a moment we just stood together watching the two men hug one another. "What's up with those two?" she whispered. "Sometimes I swear that they're—"

"They're not," I assured her.

"They can't be. Evan's smitten by you."

"He asked me to let him catch me when I was ready to fall for a man again."

"And you said?"

"I said I wasn't ready and then ran away sniffling."

She slapped me on the arm. "Crap! When are you going to come to your senses?"

But luckily Rupert's arrival saved me from having to reply. "Well, Phoebe, you have done it again and with media-ready aplomb, too!" He was holding up his phone replaying the moment when I tossed the crown. "The daring triumphs of the Agency of the Ancient Lost and Found will now ring out across the globe and you will reach new levels of fame as the world watches art historian Phoebe McCabe—"

"Destroy a priceless piece of history—got it."

"But, Phoebe, you are a hero!"

"Let's go inside and have tea," I suggested before the moment became more painful. "I'm parched."

Because heroic was not how I felt—exhausted, maybe, definitely depleted, but not heroic. After a bath, a little breakfast, and a long nap, I awoke later that afternoon in much better spirits. By the time the big gala feast began, I was even ready to throw myself into the festivities, relieved that we'd all survived and that the Divinios had been bested if not eradicated. Actually, we had plenty to celebrate.

"Was Markus rounded up with all the others?" I asked Senhor Carvalho somewhere between the second course and the third, already stuffed with more food than I'd seen in days.

"We have not seen nor heard from him. I had expected the police to find him when they combed the property but there has been no sign."

"It's like the chap simply grabbed his bags and skedaddled," Rupert remarked. "He wasn't the bravest of sorts."

"It's still odd, even for him," I remarked, nabbing another piece of roast beef.

"The authorities will keep searching," Senhor Carvalho assured me.

"Phoebe!" Ana Marie interrupted. "Did you see the notes I left on the stairs?"

"I did," I laughed. "You are a princess. Maybe your mother will even let you have the turret room now?"

I caught Adriana's eye and she smiled. "Perhaps," she said.

But of all the matters I could not achieve amid my supposed successes, I could not bring the child's father back home. "You are not a miracle worker," Peaches told me later. "Ana Marie will survive and grow into the resilient, brave young woman we see in her now."

Still, it felt like a failure.

* * *

MUCH LATER, after our celebration in the main hall had wound down and most of the household had dragged themselves off to bed, Rupert, Evan,

Peaches, and I withdrew to the library to sip port and regroup. Senhor Carvalho joined us briefly before heading to bed.

Pulling our chairs close to the hearth, we settled in to wind down for the evening. Though the night wasn't cold, dampness would have chilled our bones without the fire's warmth.

"Will you forgive me for mucking up your Titian?" I asked our host as I gazed across at him. Though he looked weary, a resurgence of energy had returned and his eyes were alight with youthful enthusiasm.

"Absolutely. There is nothing to forgive and, as always, I admire your audacity." Senhor Carvalho smiled and lifted his eyes to the portrait. "The empress herself remains unblemished and that is, indeed, the important thing. Besides, you were only carrying on a long line of female tampering."

"Titian tampering," Peaches murmured to no one in particular.

"Anyway, I doubt my rushed cover-up job will cause any damage. I used a very diluted wash to cover the carnation and the watchtower." In fact, the green foliage had already begun to run.

"Never mind. All will be duly restored and the portraits given to the Portuguese Museum of Ancient Art in Lisbon. It is time, as our Isabella has served her intended purpose. As much as my friends in Spain believe otherwise, Portugal is where she belongs since the empress herself had requested that her likeness be returned to her people. And what a story this painting tells. How incredible and inspiring! To think that three women in King Philip's court, along with an order of nuns, conspired to bury clues to thwart the Divinios—"

"And succeeded," I added.

"And succeeded," Carvalho acknowledged. "And you believe that Sofonisba Anguissola painted that carnation?"

"I believe it absolutely but I'm not certain about the watchtower. To me that looks much cruder. I'm guessing that one of Sofonisba's students at court may have painted that, perhaps even Queen Elizabeth of Valois herself."

"Amazing. Dear Phoebe, what would we have done without the Agency of the Ancient Lost and Found? Please do let me see those photos you took of the reliquary and crown one more time, if you please," Senhor Carvalho requested.

"I'll send you the photos." I passed him my phone, which he peered at for several minutes.

"Or you can download them from the Internet. They're everywhere, I believe," Evan commented, catching my eye with a smile. He sat with his long legs extended before the hearth, the picture of the adorable man-spread. Every inch of him appeared to be healing nicely from what I could tell.

"Extraordinary," Senhor Carvalho announced after a moment. "The workmanship was truly exquisite. Whatever we may think of Antonio Pérez, he did not scrimp in the making of this piece."

Rupert, sitting to his left, the two men having become great friends in the past few days, agreed. "He required it to be a magnet for his diabolical brotherhood and to presumably trick the prince when Pérez and his henchmen arrived to perform the ungodly coronation," he mused. "Imagine how that would have played out."

Me, already a bit too relaxed after several sips of the rich liquor, kept my eyes fixed over the mantel on the portrait of Queen Isabella. "I can't—well, I can but it's too gruesome to dwell on for long," I said. "In many ways, I'm sorry that the crown is gone but not so much that I'd ever want to see it again. Hopefully, someday, somebody will find the skull since the Divinios aren't talking. Was it ever determined that Prince Carlos in his final resting place in Madrid is incomplete?"

"My friend has made inquiries. Unfortunately, the pandemic has delayed everything, including that investigation."

"Makes sense," I said.

"At least the reliquary still survives," Rupert remarked. "That much your Spanish friend will be able to place in one of his museums."

I took another sip of the port, not caring whether it would sail me into oblivion. Oblivion was what I craved just then.

"Indeed," our host said with a sigh.

"Senhor Carvalho," Evan began, placing his glass on a side table and leaning forward, "I realize now that your friend is a member of the Spanish royal family. I don't expect you to say who exactly, but it's clear to me that few people would have such a vested interest in the outcome of this case or the resources to commandeer the armed forces as the Spanish monarchy."

Peaches sputtered into her glass and sat up. "Seriously? The Spanish Señor Anonymous is really King Anonymous?"

"Or Queen Anonymous," I remarked.

"Did you know?" she asked me.

"I wondered," I admitted.

"I overheard Sofia speaking to her employers on the phone," Evan said. "The title 'your highness' was used at least once."

"You must tell no one," Senhor Carvalho cautioned. "We have been working with the House of Bourbon-Anjou for decades, striving to track down the Divinios to their source. The king is supportive of our efforts but it is not he who has emerged as the leader in this particular quest. I will say no more and I request that you do the same."

We all gazed at him and nodded.

"It has always been my theory that the queens lead the frontlines in this particular battle." Returning my gaze to Queen Isabella, I raised my glass. "To the Divine Right of Queens!"

"To the Divine Right of Queens!" everyone chorused.

And then the door flew open, pitching us all to our feet.

"Holy shit!" Peaches cried.

There stood Markus, looking as though he'd been dragged through the mud on his knees. His pants were embedded with grime, his face and beard filthy, and his jacket hung from his back in shreds. And yet a fever of triumph burned in his pale eyes.

Oblivious to the carpets, the tiles—anything—he tramped into our midst and dropped a moldy, lichen-covered sack to the floor. He glanced down at the bag and muttered, "Sorry, old chap," before facing us. "So, you thought I was in league with the devil, did you? Meantime, I've been working on the side of the good guys all along and it's been hell, I can tell you."

"Is that—?" Rupert began.

"The skull of Don Carlos? Yes. It's in a protective grille, don't worry."

"So you found a way to get the head, how exactly?" Peaches demanded.

"By pretending to be on the side of the brotherhood. That night in the morgue I said I'd act as their spy if they let me live. They needed an archaeologist with background knowledge of their quest with access to the Carvalhos and I needed to stay alive. Seemed like a good partnership at the time but never once did I waver in terms of whose side I was on. I did the double-agent thing."

"You bastard!" Evan stepped toward him.

Markus held up a grubby hand. "Never once did I give away anything that might cause you harm, either. In fact, I fed them lies, which they swallowed only too eagerly. If it weren't for me, they would have tracked down the Carvalhos to the village and killed them all. If it weren't for me, they would have shot that helicopter down sooner, too!"

"But where were you hiding?" Senhor Carvalho demanded.

"In the tunnels. They had a room set up there with an access route to the forest—quite undetectable unless you knew where to look. That's where they'd hidden the skull. Through them, I got to penetrate parts of the tunnels that even Ricardo didn't know about. Poor Ricardo. They really did do him in, by the way—my sympathies, senhor. I managed to find out where, but anyway, at least you can now reunite this poor bastard with the rest of his skeleton in Spain."

We all stared at the bag.

"Do you want to look at him?" Markus asked.

"No!" That was unanimous.

And then Senhor Abreu dashed into the room speaking rapid Portuguese, steering a blonde woman in head-to-toe camouflage by the arm.

"Connie?"

"What is going on?" Rupert erupted.

Connie shot us a little wave and stepped beside Markus. "Sorry I'm late but once I parked I couldn't find the entrance." She spread her hands. "Big place but luckily this nice chap helped me out. Right, so it's a bit of a long story but Markus got himself into a spot of trouble here and needed assistance. I tried to contact you but you refused to answer, Phoebe." She shot me a recriminating glance.

"I was a bit preoccupied," I countered.

"Yes, well, I took the next flight out, rented a car, and managed to pick him up before the Divinios caught up with him. Very exciting."

"Actually, they were about to toss me down a hole but I escaped," Markus explained.

"Yes, but I'm the one who picked you up on the road, Markus. Don't ruin my story." She slapped him playfully on the arm. "So I picked him up running away with part of Prince Carlos in his bag. We hid in the forest for a couple of days and now here we are. We saw that clip of you throwing the crown in the ocean—what a headline!"

"Yes, but let's wind back to the beginning for a moment, shall we? You got me into this business in the first place, sister dear," Markus accused. "Tell them."

"What do you mean by that?" Evan asked, hands on hips in full glower mode. "I thought that Markus approached you for help?"

"Mea culpa!" Connie threw up her hands. "So, I admit that I have been in league with a network of fellow historians to uncover this mystery for some time. I wanted to be more forthcoming, honestly."

"But?" I asked.

"But," she said, almost sounding a bit annoyed, "this was a *secret* initiative— we even took an oath, Phoebe. I asked my little brother to join our efforts a few years ago, which he did, and then his team discovered the skull. We couldn't disclose the whole truth, could we?" She turned her blue gaze on each of us in turn. "Sofia and others—all of us—were sworn to secrecy. But once we were certain that your reputation was well-deserved and that you truly were working on our behalf, we agreed to tell you everything. I sent you messages, Phoebe. I wanted to call but I was blocked. By then we were afraid our communication networks had been compromised, anyway. Forgive me?"

"So you were part of the counter-Divinios all along?" I asked.

"In a manner of speaking, yes, but you uncovered the originals! What a coup!" She clapped her hands together. "The art angle eluded us all, but you were just brilliant! What a story!"

"We were all brilliant," Rupert interjected. "Like any good team, we each played a part."

"Absolutely. We are a team," Peached added.

"You did! You are all simply brilliant!" Connie said. "And you'll feature on my show, won't you? This is already making international headlines!" I swear she was jumping up and down. Either that or the port had taken hold.

Of course, we forgave them both.

The moment Senhor Carvalho bid us good night, the drink began to flow in earnest. Someone brought in the wine. I have no memory of when that photo of us all standing in front of the fireplace toasting Queen Isabella was taken. Maybe Senhor Abreu snapped it, maybe not.

There we all were, me in the middle, Peaches and Evan with their arms over my shoulders, and Rupert embracing Connie on the other side. Markus stood apart—no one would touch him until he'd had a shower. Meanwhile the skull of our hapless prince sat in its bag at our feet. Someone wanted to remove him and let his skull grin away at the camera but I protested. He'd suffered enough indignities in his short life.

As it was, we were frozen in a group selfie moment of the worst kind and I admit that this was not our finest hour. As for which one of the team had the gall to plaster the picture all over social media this time, I'll never know.

THE END

COMING NEXT, *The Florentine's Secret, The Agency of the Ancient Lost & Found Book 3*

Book 3 transports you to Florence, Italy….

AFTERWORD

I always believed that history rhymes with mystery for a reason. How much do we really know for certain about the past? So much is a guessing game pieced together from the clues the dead have left behind. That means that all historical fiction is still fiction no matter how much research is involved.

Though most of the events described in this book are based on historical fact, I took many creative liberties. For instance, the unfolding mystery of what befell Prince Carlos on that fateful night in 1568 remains unknown. My version of events provides a role for women that is so often buried or overlooked.

However, just for the record, some of the strangest details in this story are actually true. Take for instance Prince Carlos sleeping with the mummy of a saint who had died a century before. Apparently that really happened. I can't "make that stuff up", as they say. Actually, I can and often do but in this case I didn't. Fact can be stranger than fiction.

As for the paintings described in this book, most of them exist and at least one was painted by Titian. However, even here I took liberties, my mission being to entertain you, dear reader, while allowing *herstory* to rule over history.

THE FLORENTINE'S SECRET

THE AGENCY OF THE ANCIENT LOST & FOUND 3

The Agency of the Ancient Lost & Found

Book Three

THE
FLORENTINE'S
SECRET

JANE THORNLEY

PROLOGUE

*F*lorence, Italy, 1497

The workroom was dark when Gabriela entered late that afternoon. After hanging up her cloak, she stepped into the long room, noting that the curtains were drawn along the courtyard-facing windows. Her father usually kept their workers sewing until the very last bit of sun had leeched from the sky, straining their eyes in the half-light to finish a seam or sew a hem or needle a few remaining pearls onto an embroidered bodice for some important client. They were far too busy to waste a single moment and yet today their workshop lay empty.

She tried to remember if Father had mentioned an appointment with an important client or some other explanation that would draw him away. By necessity, he arranged such meetings in secrecy now. Even if he had such an assignation, the workers would have remained under Jacobo's watchful eye until darkness fell. Once important visitors like the Medici would be whisked away into one of the private anterooms or met inside their homes but not now, never now.

As a very young girl she had attended the city's noblewomen in the privacy of their quarters. Women who had preferred a female to fit them were happy that her father could afford that service but now their clients were more reluctant to have her visit under any circumstances. Clarice de' Medici had once used her services exclusively but that was long ago before that lady had died and the great Medici had fallen. Fallen, yes, but not forsaken, at least not by her. Gabriela would enact the instructions of the late Lorenzo the Magnificent no matter how long it took or what the cost.

She had passed by the Medici palazzo that very afternoon, keeping her head low and her hood up so as not to attract attention in streets that did not welcome unattended women. Something was afoot in the city that day, she could feel it. Men gathered, talking excitedly. Friars called to any passerby to relinquish their luxuries and some seething energy seemed to boil up from the very dirt beneath her feet.

She shook herself from her reverie. Enough time wasted. Father would explain all once he returned, and in the meantime she could not squander this opportunity.

Gabriela scanned the massive tables where lengths of silk and velvet were spread in jewel-colored sweeps awaiting the first cut or the continuation of some fine detail upon the rich fabric. These were her paints, her tools, and she resisted the urge to stroke them in passing lest she snag a pin or worse.

Lighting a lantern, she carried it past the tables, averting her eyes from the dress forms that stood around the room in various states of undress. They always seemed to watch her reproachfully and, in the twilight, cast distorted shadows that had once frightened her as a child. Perhaps even still…

But she was no longer a child, she reminded herself. In the Florentine Republic few knew the truth: that she, Gabriela di Domenico, a mere woman, was in fact the designer of the most fabulous gowns for which her father's house had become famous. Her—not her father, not their assistant, Jacobo—but her, a woman daring to take the work of God into her own hands to create exquisite designs for the Florence nobility, designs that had gathered such fame that wealthy houses as far away as Rome had requested their artistry. Yet, in these days when such luxury was viewed as sinful, her involvement would only draw further wrath upon their heads and must remain secret, as must another, much darker confidence.

If Florence knew the truth, her father would be ruined, the great Medici might be further sullied, and Gabriela herself sent to a convent or much, much worse. She could not bear to imagine what cruel humiliation might be inflicted upon her should the secret be exposed.

Women were put on earth for but one role. How many times had she heard that? She was to bear children and to serve men and God, at times the two seeming one and the same: marry, bear children, obey, obey. But Gabriela was not born to obey but to create. Why else would she have been given this gift—to transform a bolt of cloth into something extraordinary, something that served as a tribute to God since all the glorious details were crafted in His name?

She delighted most in imagining God's creatures—the birds, the flowers, the insects, and bringing them alive on a sleeve or a hem. The craftspeople breathed life into her sketches, a great design became reality, and beauty sang its song in her art. How could this be sinful?

She strode down the long room toward the secret door, driven by her determination to see this thing through. Time was running out. The great Lorenzo de' Medici had made but one request of her before he died, a simple one on the surface, but one she knew bore unknown repercussions for all involved. He knew it might take years to bring into fruition but implored her to wait, if necessary, and wait she had. Now could not be a worse time to put his request into action. Nevertheless, a promise made must be honored, especially to the dead.

Fingering the key in her purse at her waist, she imagined the small flat object slipping into the seam in such a way as to be unnoticeable amid the velvets and silks. It would be transported as requested along with the corresponding message and her reward duly accepted, a reward she was only too eager to receive considering that there was no other way she could ever obtain the largesse otherwise. Though her father had been successful and his coffers had swelled accordingly, they would never be permitted to wear the clothes they crafted even if they could afford them, *especially* if they could afford them. The sumptuary laws made that clear: beautiful clothes were for noble citizens only and then for special occasions with the details carefully regulated—that is, before the friar Savonarola preached that all such luxuries were sin incarnate. But Gabriela would enact more than one defiance before this game was over.

The edges of the door blended seamlessly with the end wall, expertly camouflaged by the playful drawing Fili had sketched of the Florentine citizens garbed in Domenico finery. She followed the line of a full-skirted gamurra with her finger until she heard the mechanism spring loose.

Stepping into the darkened room, she latched the door behind her and set the lantern on the table. Her eyes were drawn immediately to the center of the floor. There, glowing in the lamplight stood the dress on its form just as she had left it, a vision in solitary glory on a mannequin crafted exactly to her size —and originally Clarice and Lorenzo de' Medici's eldest daughter, Lucrezia, by happenstance and ingenuity. That noble lady would never wear this piece now. If Savonarola had his way, no one would.

Here was her art, a multilayered column of the finest gold-threaded lemon-colored embroidered velvet overlaying a soft silk camicia the color of molten pearls. How her heart sang when she had first touched that fabric, enchanted by the way in which the colors changed every time she lifted the lengths this way and that—from lemon to deepest gold, a trick of the weaver's art where two colors of silk were napped to fool the light. When worn, the piece would shimmer and glow as if touched by a nymph or some other marvelous mythological creature who altered matter with a sweep of her hand.

Let Fili and Sandro work their magic on flat surfaces with their paint but her alchemy moved with the body, blew with the wind, danced in the nuances of light and shadow. Living art, she had teased them. "Can you make your creations move?" she called out to her betrothed one afternoon as he stood painting in his studio.

"I cannot, my love!" he had laughed over his shoulder, his brush held aloft, but in truth Fillipino, like Sandro, were such masters of their art that it was as though his figures breathed from the wood they were painted upon. His work caused her breath to still and her heart to flutter. Or maybe that was his doing...

Gabriela smiled at the memory as she untied her brown work dress and let it drop to the floor. Carefully lifting the lemon-gold gamurra from the mannequin, she dropped it over her head and allowed it to flow down over her cotton chemise. As always, it fit perfectly, causing her to sigh as her hands smoothed over the raised velvet pattern.

Her father would scold her if he were to catch her doing this again. To wear this gown even for a moment was like tempting the fates, he claimed. It didn't matter if she was the one to fashion it into existence. To all eyes they were supposedly made for another one gone, but even Father would agree that this garment was special. This one she prayed might even become her own wedding gown.

Gently, she picked up one of the sleeves from the pair lying on the table and slipped her left arm inside, holding it to her shoulder by the ribbon ties. Here was her true masterpiece, every motif crafted to her and the Magnificent's specifications before he had drawn his last breath. Every image told a story—her story as well as the secret the Medici requested embedded amid the creatures of garden and field. The great Lorenzo had caught the meaning when he had first studied Sandro's sketch years before but had only nodded and smiled. He had so enjoyed her little puzzles as he had told her often enough.

As long as she fulfilled her obligations, the dress and all else would be hers.

Whether she would risk wearing it was another story and one not destined to be told within the walls of the Republic. Their deal had been sealed years ago though it would take much longer for her to enact now that the Medici power had bled from the streets of Florence. Yet she prayed that there were those still able to help.

Holding the ribbon, her gaze swung toward the secret compartment where the sketch lay hidden. Sandro's promise of that painting for their wedding gift had thrilled Fili, too, even though Sandro warned that the portrait might take years to complete given his current work schedule. All that was needed was patience, apparently, patience and great care that they could play this game of intrigue in a city fraught with dangerous secrets. She could only hope that she was up to the challenge.

A sharp sound shattered her reverie. Swinging around, she stared at the front wall. It was all that she could do to keep from crying out. Was that Father? She slipped off the sleeve and picked up the lantern, holding it high as she tiptoed toward the door, keeping the gamurra raised in one hand.

She thought only to open the door a crack and check the workroom but something cautioned her to freeze. Voices calling out. Someone stifling a sharp cry while another shouted her name—her father! What was happening? And then she knew: they had been found out, their secret discovered.

She swung away, torn between helping her father and escaping with what she alone could salvage but, in truth, there was no choice to be made. All had been agreed in advance: if ever the day came and their secret exposed, she was to run, run as far as she could, escape Florence forever. She had promised, more a pact than a decision, and one to which she was bound.

Her heart galloping, she swiftly stepped out of the gamurra and bundled up every precious piece of the fabric into an old cloth before donning her own clothes. The banging shook the walls. She did not have the time to cover the dress properly. With her head bare and her identity revealed to all who would look closely, she slipped across the room to another secret door that would take her down a set of stairs to a back lane, her parcel held like a limp body in her arms. At the last minute, she snatched a scrap of fabric from the floor and threw it over her head.

As her feet scuffed down the stone steps, she could not believe what she was doing, could not believe that she might never see her father again, that she would escape her beloved city that very night. Though the price of her failure was great, the price of her success was equally so.

In the dark lane between the buildings, she gripped her bundle like a huge swaddled child before stepping into a main road. Startled, she was immediately swept into a stream of moving bodies heading in the direction of the city center. With their torches and lanterns held aloft, it was as if a seething human tide pushed her forward without a care to her distress.

They all carried something, she realized—parcels, paintings, even fistfuls of jewelry—and they were not peasants but noblemen. She struggled to break free, to turn and run towards the Porta al Prato as planned, but no, the crowd held her tight. Men, they were all men.

"What is that you carry, woman?" called the man to her right. "Do you bring a trifle of luxury to feed the flames?"

"Flames?" she cried. "I know nothing of flames! I desire only to deliver this dress to my mistress. She awaits!"

But already the man had been swallowed up by other bodies surging in from neighboring streets as the crowd pushed their heaving force into the Piazza della Signoria.

Even from a distance, she could feel the heat and smell the smoke but Gabriela was not prepared for the sight that awaited. A massive bonfire burned like the jaws of hell in the center of the piazza sending boiling smoke and licks of flame far into the night. Citizens could be seen throwing objects into the fire—paintings, dresses, books!

Somebody shoved her forward. A friar in dark robes stepped towards her. "Feed the flames in the name of God!" he cried, pointing to her bundle. She looked down, aghast. A single sleeve had loosened from her arms and hung gleaming naked in the firelight.

1

_____

$\mathcal{J}$ sat studying my computer screen, a position I'd inhabited so often lately that I often felt fused to the chair. In a mythological world, I'd probably be a chairtaur—half chair, half human. Once entranced with something, it's like it owned me body and soul so that I couldn't pull away until I dove deep into its mysteries.

The object that possessed me this time was a photo my colleague in Rome had sent by email that morning. Among all of the treasures our agency had retrieved from my criminal brother's hoard years ago, this one remained among those yet to be repatriated. I had studied it before, of course, but it had just become even more intriguing.

A sketch which looked to be worked in metalpoint and white gouache on paper, it's as if the piece had invited me to enter its world. I gazed from the image on my screen to a letter I'd received from my brother the day before. As usual, Toby wrote in brief banalities—descriptions of prison food, mention of a television show he'd watched with other inmates—and as always enlivened his descriptions with humorous drawings in the margins. I recognized the octopi and other comic characters that had once inhabited the video games he'd created years ago. But in this letter, the drawings had changed. Now I was seeing things like a little bomb attached to what looked to be a partially unfolded scroll, a baffling geometric sketch that looked nothing like his usual doodles.

Nicolina: *Are you still there?*

Nicolina and I had been bouncing texts back and forth for the last hour—the photo on my desktop screen, the texts on my phone.

Me: *Yes, sorry. You say you originally found it rolled up in a tube with part of Toby's hoard?*

Nicolina: *Yes, in a crate between two eighteenth-century landscapes.*

Me: *Would it have looked like a scroll?*

Nicolina: *Yes, I suppose.*

I peered at the screen. At first glance, the picture appeared to be of a Florentine noblewoman circa 1450-80. A profile portrait, it could have been quickly but deftly executed and perhaps served as a preliminary sketch for a painting. As far as we knew, no such painting existed, not that that was surprising. The artist may have only been studying a subject with no intention of exploring further, or if there had been a painting, it had been lost long ago.

The woman sat upright in profile in the Renaissance Florentine style, the drawing encompassing her full torso down to the hands folded in her lap. Her hair was pulled back in a simple topknot but not bejeweled, and her face, though pleasant, was not beautiful. A plain linen kerchief partially covered her hair. A real woman, then, and either this real woman or her menfolk had been intent on displaying only one aspect of her dress at the expense of all else.

Nicolina: *Still there?*

Me: *Yes. That sleeve is extraordinary.*

Nicolina: *Yes. Still.*

As a textile expert, that was the thing I had noticed first. Though an art historian by training, my expertise was textiles and my interest recently focused primarily on the Renaissance. That sleeve was fabulous in an age when fabulousness in apparel was the norm for the wealthy at the same time that such displays were closely regulated, even illegal.

Real fashion police roamed the streets of Florence during the fourteenth and fifteenth centuries apprehending citizens who broke the sumptuary laws, regardless of their station. Strict rules existed as to when and who could wear what and any infringement that might be considered excesses of fashion.

Whether this particular woman was permitted to wear that particular sleeve was another matter but it seemed as though she wore it proudly. It had several curious attributes and details that I longed to study more carefully but had never taken the opportunity until now.

Nicolina: *Are you still there?*

Me: *Still here. It's definitely from the mid-century Renaissance Florentine period.*

Nicolina: *I know it is important.*

Me: *I need to see it in person.*

I couldn't mention Toby's letter on the phone or in our texts. These days, I expected constant surveillance so took special care with when and how I communicated. Actually, that little bomb icon in the margins had to mean Toby was also employing caution. I recognized a warning when I saw one.

Nicolina: *I agree. Come to Rome and we will go to Florence and to the Uffizi. I have a friend there who might help us confirm attribution. Besides, it has been too long since we have been together.*

Florence. A brief image of that museum of treasures flashed through my mind at the exact moment that my lower back delivered such a vicious twinge that it forced me to my feet. I bent down into a curve before stretching up, arms over my head the way my physiotherapist had shown. Ah, there. If I didn't start moving more regularly, I probably would fuse to the chair.

Nicolina: *Still there?*

Me: *Sorry. Back problems. Let me see if I can pull an excursion together for Peaches and me. A dose of Italy is desperately needed. Plenty of wine and pasta, too, please. I'll text you with the details.*

Nicolina: *Wine and pasta, it is! I am excited to see you! Rupert called yesterday from Orvieto and plans a jaunt to Capri next.*

I straightened. I knew Rupert was in Italy, of course. Evan was somewhere there, too. I hadn't seen either of them for weeks but remained in touch through email and text.

Nicolina: *Evan is still in Venice visiting his son.*

I swear sometimes she read my mind. So Evan was still in Venice? I would have known had I asked him. The man was more than willing to keep me appraised of his movements. It was I who held back. I was not ready to cross the relationship threshold any time soon but we at least stayed connected.

Me: *I'll be in touch. Ciao!*

Pocketing my phone, I stretched again before seeking out Peaches. In August, the lab was quiet. Max had taken our manager, Serena, for a holiday like the rest of the city, it seemed. The moment Londoners had received their final Covid vaccinations and lockdown had lifted, anyone who could bolted for freedom about the same time that tourists began flocking to British shores. We joked that the city was running on a skeleton crew.

At our storefront, Baker and Mermaid, the ethnographic gallery was now closed to drop-in clients and we managed sales either by website or appointment. Most of the real work continued behind the scenes in the Agency of the Ancient Lost and Found's new basement facility where we still had unclaimed artifacts waiting to be repatriated. Considering all that had happened in the world lately, that bust of the Artemis staring at me from the top shelf could wait awhile longer.

I found Peaches downstairs in our showroom with her feet on Serena's desk reading on her iPad, probably devouring one of her man-chest romances, her preferred reading material when not delving into engineering tomes. She looked up as I descended the stairs. "Have you been talking to Evan lately? He's taking his son on a road trip."

My mistake: she was reading her emails.

"I know," I remarked. "Look, something's—"

"What's his ex-wife like, anyway?" She sat up and dropped her feet to the floor. "I always wondered. I asked him once and he was very complimentary about her but otherwise evasive. She sounded like a paragon of virtue."

I sighed. "Yes, she's very pleasant and gorgeous and why are you asking?"

"Just curious. He said they broke up because she wanted to live in her hometown in Venice but he was traveling all over the world. It was too much of a long-distance relationship to work out. That must have been back in his MI6 days. He said that they divorced long ago and still he never remarried. Bet you never asked him that."

"I didn't."

"Why not? Aren't you curious? And what if he finds someone else while you're keeping him at arm's length?"

I heaved an exaggerated sigh as I arrived beside her. "I'm not here to discuss my love life. I—"

"That's because you don't have a love life."

"Neither do you," I pointed out.

She grinned down at me. "Yeah, but I'm open for business, just waiting for the perfect guy to come knocking on my door and realize that I am his goddess, his queen bee in the main squeeze department. You, on the other hand, may as well have 'closed until further notice' tattooed on your forehead."

Time for a major distraction. "Want to go to Italy?" I inserted quickly.

She pulled back in mock shock. "Are you kidding me? May as well ask if I want to keep eating and breathing. Do we finally have another case?"

"Yes and no." I pulled up the sketch on my phone. "We're going to Italy to meet Nicolina and see if we can find out anything more about this. No one has reported it missing. There's nothing fitting this description in the databases, either, yet I'm certain that's the scroll-like thing Toby drew in his letter."

"The one attached to the bomb?"

"That one."

"Why would Toby even refer to any of the stolen loot? He's been in prison for years and never has before."

"That's what I wonder. Something's happening; things are on the move. I just don't know how or what. We've only been exchanging letters for a couple of months but his other illustrations were similar to his comic characters. This one's different. He's using what we used to call as kids 'doodle code' to warn me of something."

Peaches continued to stare at the picture. "Doodle code, huh? If one of our two brothers stole this, it has to be worth something—a lot, is my guess."

"It may even be from one of Noel's heists." My ex had an appetite for stealing priceless art, too, and actually leaned more toward the Renaissance variety. "Actually, Noel had the real eye for priceless art."

"Then it has to be valuable. Our thieving brothers and your ex had standards. Actually, they had no standards. Forget I said that."

"Speaking of thieving brothers, I'll be talking to Toby at 11:30 this morning," I said, glancing at my phone. "In ten minutes, in fact." My gut twisted.

"So, you managed to arrange a live call at last?"

"Yes. I don't know what finally convinced him that letters weren't enough. Maybe he relented when I said how I needed to hear his voice. Maybe now that he's been detoxed and has had time to process things, we can finally talk about all that went down in our past. I thought we could do that in letters but he never responds to anything I write."

"Won't the call be monitored by prison staff?"

"Probably but I want to discuss relationship stuff, nothing sensitive. If staff want to listen in on that, let them. Toby knows I'm affiliated with Interpol. He wouldn't say anything damning. He's using doodle code for that."

"Okay, so are you nervous?"

"I may lose my breakfast but otherwise I'm completely calm. I've been waiting for this moment a long time."

"Need me to stay around?"

"No, thanks. Some things need to be done alone and a reckoning with one's brother is one of them."

"Got you. I'll just take off down the high street to buy a toothbrush. I never travel anywhere without a new one. Going for the electric variety this time. It could give me a bit of buzz. Text if you need support."

"What about *your* brother?" I called out as she headed for the door.

"Once a slimeball, always a slimeball," she said over her shoulder. "When I saw Mom and Dad last month, they told me that he'd found Jesus. Skeptic that

I am, I figure it's more likely that he's found a ticket to early release. See you later."

The door shut behind her, leaving me alone in the capacious showroom where our priceless carpets hung in lonely splendor. I had time for my traditional once-around to greet every carpet in our collection before Toby called. He'd be ringing the gallery phone collect so I couldn't stray far from Serena's desk.

The Elgin-Middlesex Detention Center outside of London, Ontario, had been my brother's home for the past two years, ever since I helped incarcerate him and Peaches's brother for stealing a fortune in art and artifacts. In all that time, we'd exchanged letters only recently but hadn't spoken once.

Then came the email: *Be at the office tomorrow at 11:30 London time. Tobias McCabe to call collect from prison.* No signature and only an email address that seemed to be from some kind of automated scheduling program.

I waited, pacing the room in circles. I'd been warned that prison changes people, hardens them, turns them into something scarred and steely. Then I reminded myself that the drugs had changed him long before that. His letters had given little away. In fact, they had been so stilted that I was afraid he'd changed irrevocably. Only the little doodles hinted that the old jovial Toby might still be lurking somewhere.

When the call came, I nearly I pounced on the desk phone, accepting the collect charges while repeating: "Toby, are you there? Toby, are you there?"

For a moment nothing but silence swallowed up the distance between us along with sounds of people talking far in the background. Finally: "Hello, Phoebe." A voice both familiar and faraway almost brought me to tears. We had been close once. So much had happened since.

My words tumbled out in a rush. "Toby, I'm sorry. I love you. I did what was necessary to save your life and preserve art when I put you in prison. Surely you understand that? You were in such bad shape in Jamaica. I thought for sure you'd overdose and die but a day hasn't passed where I haven't thought of you. How are you doing? Tell me you're all right." I started to cry like an idiot. It was as if the sound of his voice had pressed some kind of sob button.

Again silence and then came: "How do you think I'm doing, Phoeb? I'm stuck in a wheelchair serving time in prison."

It was as if he'd slapped me. I swallowed hard, thinking how grueling, how humiliating, and how dangerous his life had to be. And that it was all my fault. I put him there, put my own *brother* in prison. Everything was all my fault. "Toby, I'm sorry—"

"Stop. You're not sorry. You'd do it all over again if I was standing between you and some priceless piece of art. You've become some kind of art warrior hotshot. Think I haven't seen the news? 'Phoebe McCabe of the Agency of the Ancient Lost and Found throws priceless Spanish artifact into the sea.' You work with Interpol. What happened to my little sister?"

"What's happened...to your...?" The question almost stuck me dumb. At the same time it snapped me straight.

"Yeah, what happened to my loyal little baby sister who used to follow her big bro around like a puppy wanting to swab Captain Toby's decks forevermore?"

I managed to laugh. "Oh, that one. Yeah, little Phoebe. She realized that she was swabbing her big brother's decks, all right—more like cleaning up his messes while he stole from one end of the globe to the other. Oh, and then she woke up to the fact that she was also playing lost-art sniffer dog to his partner in crime, too. That was the same little Phoebe who almost got killed over and over again by all those big bad men who thought she had to be working for the Toby and Noel art-heist duo. Is that the baby sister you mean? I'll tell you what happened to her: she grew the hell up!"

Wow, where did that come from? I had to be repressing more rage than I thought. I stood stone-still waiting for him to hang up in my ear but instead he boomed his barrel-chested laugh. "You really did grow up."

"Is that all you can say?" I was trying hard to steady my thumping heart. "And you're right: if I caught you stealing and dealing drugs again, I would put you back behind bars. I finally learned that loving someone does not mean that you have to love what they do or accept it, either. But I do love you, Toby. I'll just never accept what you did."

Silence and then: "I don't expect you to, and yeah, I feel like a shit for what I've done to you, especially for not warning you about Noel. That's the one thing I can't forgive myself for."

The. One. Thing. Everything else was fine. I swallowed. *Let it go, Phoebe.* I took a deep breath. "So, can we get back to something good again? I know things will never be the same between us but we're still blood."

"Yeah, we are. There were plenty of times I wanted to die in here, I'll admit that, and I blamed you, but I'm through that shit now. All trials and tribulation can be survived with the right tricks and a few allies. You find that out soon enough in places like this. Maybe you did save my life. Sure as hell Noel would have killed me had he had the chance. So, yeah, I forgive you, Phoeb— at least my head does—and now you have to forgive me. My heart still feels kicked to shit and obviously yours does, too, but we'll work on that, okay?"

"Okay," I whispered. It was a start, a big one.

"How's Max?"

Okay, so we were moving for steady ground now. "He hasn't quite forgiven me, either—for killing Noel, that is—but he's trying to get over it, too."

"You didn't kill Noel, Phoebe. Snakes are hard to nail unless you decapitate the bastards. Word travels around places like this and rumor has it that the snake's still alive and growing a few heads."

"What?"

"He's still alive. Nobody knows where he's holed up but watch your back."

"Oh, my God." I sat down on a chair with a thump. "I thought I killed him."

"You didn't kill him but you should have. He may come after you eventually. Word is that he's still recuperating somewhere. Seems like he's got a tricky ticker after you tasered him over the heart—nice touch that. Poetic justice. Look, time's almost up in my phone slot."

"Can we talk again?"

"Sure and keep writing those letters. I look forward to them. Did you get my last with the little sketch?"

"Yes."

"Heed the warning. Leave it the hell alone, Phoebe."

"Leave what alone? I'm not leaving anything alone. I—"

But he hung up.

2

---

*N*oel was still alive. That Renaissance sketch may be a bomb, whatever that meant. I didn't know which of those possibilities shook me the most. Probably both held equal weight for different reasons. Each carried implications for my life going forward but left me with no immediate way to assess the potential damage.

When Peaches came back an hour later, she found me staring at the walls in a state of semishock.

"Went that well, did it?" she said.

"Any time I think I've grown into a powerful woman, paid my dues and earned my stripes, something wallops the wind out of me and kicks me right back to zero."

"What are you talking about?" She dropped a bag on the table and came around to face me. "What happened?"

"As soon as I heard Toby's voice, I crumbled. I pulled myself together pretty quickly but that's not the point. For a minute I was back to being that little girl following my brother around and even felt guilty for putting him in jail in the first place. Can you believe it, after all the stuff he's done? I actually cried."

"Oh, hell, don't tell me you're human. I expected less of you. And all this time I thought you were an android." She was grinning. "Do you really think that family disfunction is a joyride? I still feel guilt for my useless brother, too, so I taped a list over my desk to remind me of all the hell he's caused. That soon snaps me out of it."

"That's not all." I gazed up at my tall friend in the crop top and skintight jeans. "He told me that Noel was still alive."

"Holy shit, no! What are we going to do—track him down, finish him off properly?"

"Nothing," I said. "We're going to get to work and forget about him. As long as he stays out of my way, I'm going to stay out of his. I mean it. I've spent too many years of my life chasing after that man and I refuse to do it again."

"Yeah, I get that but do you really think he's going to leave you alone?"

"He will for a while. Apparently he's still recuperating. I may have damaged his heart."

She slapped her thigh. "Damaged his heart? Got to love it! Is that poetic justice or what?" Suddenly she turned serious. "Are you going to tell Max?"

"Not right away. Let him enjoy his vacation. There's plenty of time to deliver the bad news, not that he'd see discovering his long-lost son still lives a bad thing. He'd probably drop everything and go after him. In the meantime, let's go to Italy."

So, I booked our flights to Rome the next day and then reread all of Toby's prior letters looking for more clues but saw nothing suspicious. He recounted boring tidbits about the food, the movie he watched on TV the night before —*The Dig*. The Dig? A story about the archaeological excavation of Sutton Hoo? Maybe that was significant.

By now, I was looking for clues everywhere and the doodles all along the margins of the page led me farther down the rabbit hole. He had sketched those inscrutable geometric compilations, a square with a series of rectangles and a circle at the end of a single thick line twice. Baffled, I took pictures of the doodles with my phone and began packing.

The flight was uneventful, which is a good thing in plane travel. Tourists filled the cabin ready for their first holiday away from home shores since the pandemic. The vaccination had made us feel invincible so that we could go back to worrying about the more mundane travel anxieties like losing our luggage or hotel booking foul-ups.

Luckily, we didn't have to worry about technicalities. Seraphina, Nicolina's assistant, picked us up from the airport in Rome. As usual she did nothing to encourage conversation despite the deluge of water that had crossed under the proverbial bridge since we had last met. As for her role in the Venetian affair, I had gleaned from Nicolina that she had forgiven her right-hand woman and had no doubt encouraged the law to look the other way. Countesses in Italy can pluck more strings than an orchestra.

The streets of Rome flew by in the early evening light with me gazing out the car window hungry for every detail. The Colosseum flashed past like an ancient birthday cake layered in an icing of monumental time and mystery. I saw the Roman columns rise bathed in spotlight before my glimpses were swallowed by the traffic and bustle of the city on a hot summer night. Everywhere people were out enjoying the evening, sitting in the sidewalk cafés, strolling hand in hand, some masked, others not. Laughter, conversation, enjoyment, *life*. Italy had regained her dolce vita.

We turned a corner and darted down a cobbled lane, Seraphina tooting at every pedestrian or Vespa that dared veer into her path. Finally we pulled into the Trastevere palazzo, the site of Nicolina's villa, without managing to hit anybody.

Peaches eyebrows rose. I shook my head.

"We arrive," Seraphina announced as the automatic door opened and she pulled into garage. "You take elevator up. I bring bags."

"I can carry my own bags, thanks," Peaches said as she climbed out of the car.

"I take bags. You go upstairs," Seraphina repeated, popping open the trunk and shooting a look over her shoulder.

I had neglected to warn Peaches about Seraphina's fierce relationship with luggage. At first, I had thought her need to commandeer bags was due to some exaggerated sense of courtesy but now suspected it more likely that she wanted to secrete surveillance devices at the first opportunity.

"And I said, I'll carry my own bags, thank you very much." Peaches stepped up to the trunk, slung both of our carriers over her shoulders, nabbed her own roller, and lunged for mine, which Seraphina had already lifted onto the concrete floor and now clutched.

Peaches was six-two, Seraphina under five feet. It was like watching a Great Dane face off with a rabid terrier. Smiling, I stepped between them and wrestled my bag from their grasps. "Thank you both but I'll roll my own roller. That's what the wheels are for. Easy-peasy."

My gaze turned pointedly to Seraphina in a challenge of my own. I didn't care if I won her affection but I would damn well demand her respect. She released the bag and stepped away, glowering at us both all the way up the elevator to Nicolina's apartments.

The moment the elevator whispered opened and we had stepped into the hall, Nicolina swept down on us in a waft of perfume. "Phoebe! Peaches! I am so excited to see you!" A flurry of air kisses followed that was like being greeted by a nymph air and fragrance. Of course she looked elegant and amazing in her cream-colored linen shift, the sleek dark hair framing a perfect oval face, but it was her eyes that affected me most. They sparkled with joy as if our arrival was the best thing that had happened to her for a long time.

"I missed you, too!" I said, and it was true. After a long and often challenging relationship, we were finally genuine friends. "This pandemic kept us apart for too long."

One perfectly manicured hand flew up. "The pandemic. Let us not speak of that. Too many losses, so much pain and fear, and the imprisonment in our homes for months and months! But now we celebrate, yes? We have planned a feast for you later tonight. Would you like to share wine before freshening up? Your rooms are ready."

The Italians lubricate life with wine but the thought of alcohol before a hefty late dinner had to be avoided in the name of articulate communication. The Europeans dined between eight and ten p.m. I ate at five, usually takeout at my desk. "Thanks, but I think I'll just wash up and meet you down here in a few minutes. Is that okay?"

"Okay? Yes, always okay. We have refreshments for you in your rooms also. Peaches, your room is across from Phoebe's. Will this suit? How are your parents in Jamaica? I ask because I have heard so little."

Peaches grinned. "Fine, all fine, thanks. Mom's collecting orchids now and Dad's settled into the life of the retired physician under duress."

After more catch-up, Peaches and I finally disentangled ourselves and made our way upstairs, Nicolina leading the way like the excellent hostess she was.

"You've decorated!" I exclaimed, stepping into my room. Once a luxurious but worn chamber of the antique Italianate style, the bedroom now spread out around me in a sweep of modern textiles fashioned after antique designs, everything new and lustrous.

"Yes, much time on my hands. When not working, I decorate." She smiled. "The drapes, the bedcovers—all were old so I changed. You will see some artifacts still not repatriated here and there. While we work to return these treasures to their owners, why not enjoy?"

My gaze landed on a female half-portrait, probably Flemish circa early 1500s, that perfectly caught the gold hue of the silk curtains without competing with the tiny fleur-de-lis design of the blue watered silk wallpaper. Another small still-life, probably much later but no less exquisite, hung across the room above the reupholstered daybed. I recognized them from the photos Nicolina had posted of her holdings over the months but nothing captured a painting like seeing it in the flesh. They were beautiful, masterful. And they didn't belong to Nicolina. "I suppose you've contacted the museums and galleries in the Netherlands?"

"Certainly. They will decide which facility will claim these pieces as they debate among themselves. They wish to send their experts to assess and I told them any time." She shrugged. "Still they do not come. I will leave you now and we will speak later."

I watched as she stepped across the hall to ensure that Peaches had everything she needed. Turning away, I wrested all those niggles to the ground or tried. I shut the door and leaned against the carved cedar surface to take a deep breath. At one time I didn't trust Nicolina. Now I'd resolved to accept that we did things differently. All of our art and artifacts awaiting repatriation in London remained locked in our basement lab or our offices while hers decorated her villa. Where was the harm in that? And yet it bothered the hell out of me.

Before I could do a single enjoyable thing, I pulled out my Evan-issued smartphone, pressed the bug app, and scanned the room looking for the latest caches of Seraphina's surveillance devices. As expected, I found five, each secreted in what I considered to be all the obvious places. I dropped them into a little china dish and vowed to return them to their owner at the first opportunity.

Up popped a text from Evan himself. *Why the need to debug Nicolina's villa? Is Seraphina up to her usual compulsions?*

I smiled and thumbed in a reply: *Of course. BTW, this business of stalking me through my phone is intrusive. Maybe I should turn on the privacy feature.*

Evan: *What privacy feature?*

Me: *My point exactly. So how's Giani?*

Evan: *Excellent. He's growing so fast. Soon he'll be as tall as I am. We've just been visiting Rupert in Capri.*

Visiting Rupert? The men worked together and now they vacation together, too?

Me: *Got to run.*

Evan: *Right. Stalk later.*

That made me smile. I hadn't seen him in the flesh since the Portuguese mission but rarely a day went by when we didn't exchange a text or an email. That connection provided just enough contact for us to stay in touch without moving our relationship anywhere deeper. Pocketing the phone, I prepared to indulge in the luxury of a few minutes alone. It was a relief to wash my face after hours of mask wearing and to relax.

I changed out of my jeans into moss-green linen pants and a silk Gucci hyacinth blouse Nicolina had gifted me years ago. When in Rome... That done, I sat down on one of the brocade chairs to knit.

Knitting in solitude with lovely yarns and a cup of tea was more restorative to me than a glass of wine ever could be. I noted, as I worked a row of purl, how this butter-yellow yarn caught the nuances in the Flemish painting across the room. I breathed in color, art, and light—all the things I loved—my muscles loosening at once. By the time I was on the right side row, there was a knock on my door.

"Come in."

Peaches entered resplendent in a long violet stretch sheath. "This place is something else. I could definitely get used to living in an Italian villa but what's with that greeting? They strike me as people who live life fully, and yet when they meet you, they kiss the air. Nicolina, you, and me have been through plenty of trauma together. Don't we deserve a hug?"

I laughed. "Maybe it has to do with a certain restrained elegance in Nicolina's case, I don't know. It doesn't mean that she doesn't care. Hey, I forgot to remind you to bug-check your room."

"Done. I found six. Seraphina has a problem. She's like some kind of bug-o-maniac."

"It's definitely a compulsion. The trick is to stay one step ahead of her." I checked my phone. "While it's still early, maybe we can see that sketch before supper?"

"Let's go for it."

Reluctantly I set my knitting aside and followed her downstairs.

* * *

WE STOOD in Nicolina's office and lab complex, which now occupied the basement level of her four-floor villa. Like ours, hers was newly outfitted, designed as a facility for processing lost art and artifacts. Unlike ours, hers was luxurious, if a lab furnished with spotlights, light tables, magnification devices, X-ray machines, and computer terminals could be considered luxurious. The fact that this one also showcased a range of priceless artifacts in display cases interspersed among cozy seating areas took it up several notches above ours. Everything from an ancient Gandhara bust to a 1500-year-old bodhisattva torso held court in those displays, some of which were art of

Nicolina's own collection. It was like stepping into some private museum where cocktails might be served between viewings. I always bristled when in the presence of private collections but I knew that to be the skewed thinking of the poor against the very rich.

"Would you like an aperitivo before you see the sketch?" Nicolina asked.

"No, thanks," was my reply as I wandered around the room. "You know me and alcohol. I'll wait to take wine with supper."

"I'll have some," Peaches said while tapping one of the paneled walls. "Is this on the other side of the garage?"

"It is the floor below." Nicolina swept over to a table to pour a glass from a decanter. She passed one to Peaches and took another for herself. "We built a new level with reinforced steel doors and our security, as you say in English, is state-of-the-art. Seraphina takes much pride."

I turned away to study the lab. Luckily Seraphina was nowhere in sight.

"For more details, you must ask her," Nicolina continued. "She is the expert on the technical matters."

"She'd probably bite me," Peaches remarked.

They were still discussing construction specifics as I went searching for the sketch. Not a long hunt, as it turned out. I found it under a sheet of archival glass on the room's center table. Flicking on the magnification lamp, I leaned closer. "It's not worked in metalpoint, but in pen and ink on vellum," I said, "and is remarkably well-preserved. Minimal cracking except at the edges."

"Why did you think it was in metalpoint?" Peaches asked, heading toward me.

"Because of the incredible detail. Do you have whatever container it was stored in?"

Nicolina was by my side in an instant. "In a cylinder there." She pointed to a leather tube sitting on a nearby table. It did look a bit like a scroll container only longer and distinctly Renaissance in origin.

Picking up the case, I turned the worn tooled leather with the enchased brass lid around in my hands. It felt heavy, substantial. Opening the lid, I angled the interior toward the light.

"There is nothing inside," Nicolina said. "We have X-rayed. You can see the results on the light table behind you."

But I was still fixed on the externals. "Even this is in good condition for five-century-old leather. It must have been kept someplace dry and relatively safe for all these centuries because, from what I can tell, both the case and the sketch are from the quattrocento."

"Quattrocento," Peached repeated, stepping forward. "The age when art shed the modes of the Byzantine, Christian, and Gothic to embrace classical forms of Roman and Greek—or, at least, that's what I remember my prof saying. I know it mostly from the architecture side."

"You remember right," I told her. "The Renaissance broadened the understanding of the universe that had been based primarily on religious teachings and opened up our perspective to consider the great classical philosophers of the classical age." Setting the case aside, I returned my scrutiny to the sketch.

"Is it by Leonardo?" Nicolina asked hopefully.

"No. Or at least I doubt it. Maybe from the same period, though. Look at that detail on the sleeve. It looks as though the dress was fashioned in silk and couched to make those triangular patterns and yet it's what's inside those triangles that fascinates me. Every one of those motifs must have been embroidered and each is different. Do you know how extraordinary that is?"

"Not really," Peaches said.

"It means that the intricate detail of this sleeve is not due to some silk weaver's mastery. Sleeves could be the single most valuable part of the Renaissance Florentine's wardrobe and heavily regulated. At one point citizens were only allowed to wear ornamentation on the left sleeve and even then the amount of fabric allowable was measured."

"That's crazy," Peaches said.

"In a republic built upon the fabric trade, it certainly seems that way," I agreed. "But they were always at war with the Christian values of simplicity and poverty."

"But what about this sleeve is so important?" Nicolina asked.

"It seems that someone wanted to highlight a range of special symbolic images to the viewer, each one significant, each one telling a story. Pearls and metal thread would have been used to pick out the detail, and even though this is charcoal, the artist appears to have gone over just the motifs in ink. Wait." I pulled over the magnification glass on its moving arm and peered through. "Yes, pen and ink. It's like the sleeve was more important than the sitter."

"What do all those symbols mean? There are some flowers I recognize and that wasp and bee is unmistakable but what about the rest?" Peaches asked.

I pulled back to calm myself, took a deep breath, slowly exhaled, and pointed to one of the motifs. "There." My finger landed above the sleeve's central feature.

Nicolina leaned forward. "The five balls and the trefoil crest? Yes, that is the Medici coat of arms—the palle or balls, which is believed to represent money and their status as bankers. This is why I thought the artist is perhaps Leonardo since he worked for the Medici for a time."

"Yes, the six balls peg the period probably during Lorenzo the Magnificent's time since his grandfather Cosimo's crest had seven," I said, "but the Medici were patrons of many artists and sculptors, as you know."

"So this sketch is somehow related to the Medici?" Peaches asked.

"That's my guess. The subject could be a member of the Medici family, though I don't recognize her from any of the official portraits—not the Medici sisters or wives, in any case. Then there's this motif." I pointed to an image closer to the shoulder.

Nicolina leaned forward. "The three interconnecting circles."

"I'm pretty sure those are finger rings," I said.

"If those are rings, what are those things sticking out of the top? They look like little daggers that could gouge somebody's eyes out." Peaches was leaning over the sketch, too. "With this ring, I thee stab."

"Those were probably crystal or diamonds and that type of ring was likely for ceremonial purposes," I remarked.

"But the sketch is not by Leonardo, as I had hoped," Nicolina said, disappointment in her voice.

"Probably not. This was not really Leonardo's style. Anyway, the piece is still very valuable but we'll need your Uffizi expert to assess it further."

"Which we will do in Florence," Nicolina said with a nod. "I have made the arrangements. We leave tomorrow afternoon."

I turned to face them. "Good, but, Nicolina, can you think of why my brother would call this sketch a 'time bomb' and suggest I leave it alone?"

"He said this?" Nicolina stared.

"He told me to 'leave it the hell alone.'"

"When?"

"I spoke to him the day before yesterday. He's been sketching little images in the margins of his letters, one of which was of a scroll with a comic bomb attached. That's why I asked you to post additional photos of this piece to me. He was supposedly referring to this sketch's explosive nature—metaphorically speaking, I presume. At least, I don't hear any ticking."

Nicolina shook her head. "This I do not understand. We have retrieved many priceless pieces from your brothers' hoard. Why is this one so 'explosive'?" She put the word in air quotes.

"That's what we need to know," I said. "I received this." I unfolded his latest letter and spread it on the table. "What are those supposed to mean?" I asked, pointing to the geometric tangle of squares and rectangles, interconnecting circles and lines.

Peaches leaned over. "Not his usual style, for sure."

"No, Toby's more organic than geometrical. I used to joke that he'd never drawn a straight line in his life."

Peaches straightened. "Your brother is just filled with surprises, isn't he? Toby also told her that Noel is still alive," Peaches added, turning to Nicolina.

Damn. I shot her a quick look. I had also neglected to ask her to keep that part quiet.

"Noel is alive?" Nicolina exclaimed, hands flying. "We had hoped you had killed him! But where is he? I finish him off, yes? Tell me where he is and I will do this."

That's the other thing about Nicolina: she was lethal.

"No, no—no killing," I said, holding her gaze. "No one even knows where he is, and as long as he stays out of my way, I want him out of my head, too. Forget Noel."

"Yes, but as soon as he appears—bang." She fired a finger gun.

"No, no bang. Nicolina, listen: forget Noel, I said. I spent the happiest days of my recent life believing that man was finally off my viewfinder. I want to keep that feeling. Forget him," I said.

Nicolina dropped her hands. "Yes, we forget—for now. We go upstairs and have supper."

Minutes after we returned to the main floor and Nicolina disappeared into the kitchen to check on dinner, Peaches turned to me. "Sorry about that. I had no idea you wanted to keep a lid on the Noel thing."

"I knew that as soon as she heard, she'd put a hit on him," I whispered.

Peaches shrugged. "So, where's the harm in that?"

I thought for a moment. "Good point."

* * *

SUPPER WAS THE PROMISED FEAST. Almost full by the end of the first course—bucatini all'amatriciana accompanied with crusty bread for mopping up the plate—my stomach had extended to twice its usual size by the end of the tiramisu. If it hadn't tasted so good, I might have been sensible and forgone dessert but Italy isn't about being sensible but being alive and enjoying every single moment.

"How will we get the sketch to Florence?" I asked, taking a sip of wine. Secretly I wondered how I'd get up out of my chair.

Nicolina glanced at me in surprise. "Why, Seraphina will carry it, yes?"

"Seraphina?" Peaches said while helping herself to more bread. "I'd be happy to take responsibility, me being taller."

Nicolina smiled graciously but the glint in her eye suggested that this was not negotiable. "Seraphina will take it in her carry-on luggage."

"But what if customs does a spot-check and finds us carrying a piece of priceless art?" I asked.

"Phoebe." My host smiled. "This is Italy."

I let this sink in. "Of course."

"Also," she added, "we work with Interpol and do museum business. I have certificates."

There were certificates? "Okay." I subsided into my thoughts and tried to focus on my digestion, which needed all the help it could get.

An hour or so later shortly after ten, Nicolina suggested that we all go for a stroll. By then, I was a bit buzzed from the wine so the idea of fresh air stirred with Rome was enticing.

Though we had yet to see Nicolina's assistant since our arrival, apparently she was somewhere in the villa but would not be going with us. Nicolina called her on her phone and the three of us took off on our walk.

The Trastevere area at night was a feast for the senses. Once away from the busy thoroughfares, the ancient cobbled lanes of the thirteenth rione of Rome revealed itself as if lost in time. Narrow curving paths lined with the tall faces of buildings centuries old opened up into palazzos, some grand, some cozy. Little restaurants crowded onto the cobbles with their outdoor seating areas strung with lights and climbing ivy. We crossed a bridge and traveled down an alley that opened up onto an ancient Roman ruin spotlit like a forest of marble. We gazed at it, lost in our own thoughts.

On warm nights like these, the Romans were out in droves—couples and families with young children strolled through the streets. Everyone still attempted to maintain social distancing, which had become one of the more pleasant remnants of the recent pandemic. Because of this, it came as a shock when someone bumped into me from behind. I swung around but saw nothing amiss—a couple walking arm in arm, a multigenerational group of four women farther ahead.

"We're being followed," I whispered.

Nicolina sighed. "It happens always. Sometimes Seraphina she will chase them down."

Peaches was scanning all around us. "I think it was one of those women that passed behind us. I'll go after them."

"Don't bother," I said. "Let's just head back to the villa."

Nine times out of ten these stalkers were just keeping an eye on us and nothing ever manifested, otherwise. Chasing them was a waste of energy, especially after a wine-soaked dinner. We agreed, and strolled back to the villa, relaxed and ready for bed.

Anybody can make a mistake.

3

_____

$\mathcal{F}$lorence. As much as I loved Rome, I loved Florence more. Let me count the ways: the way in which the light kisses the ancient stone; the way in which a multitude of sculpture, art, and history unfolds before your eyes without ever stepping through a single interior door; the Arno at sunset. I could go on and on. Let me say only that if you love history and art, Florence is your feast. And as usual, I was starving.

Seraphina had booked us into a luxurious villa hotel in the historic center of Florence not far from the Uffizi and overlooking a garden modeled after a sixteenth-century version. My room was the kind of light-washed expanse of sky-blue watered silk, satin, and antique textiles with a carved canopied bed that made me think that I had fallen into the pages of an historic homes magazine. It was far more luxurious than even Nicolina's villa.

Surrounded by such splendor, why leave? I could while away my day checking the thread count of the Persian carpets, date the botanical illustrations on the walls, maybe even knit. Had it been in any other city, maybe I would just sit and indulge my senses. But this was Florence and one's senses were best indulged beyond the doors.

First I spent several minutes studying the enigmatic sketches in Toby's letter. The more I studied it, the more I grew convinced that he had sent me a message. This geometric jumble was so not his style. I folded away the letter and shoved it into my bag before changing into cream linen pants, a cream-colored top, and, because I would eventually have a business meeting, I folded a printed tailored sateen cotton jacket into my backpack. Admittedly, I felt a bit awed to be meeting a fellow art historian in such a majestic location. To me, it was a bit like meeting a pope at the Vatican, not that I was Catholic or followed any specific doctrine, but awe is awe. After donning what I hoped was a jaunty straw fedora, I was ready to stroll through history.

Nobody thought twice when I said I wanted to walk the streets by myself. It was still early afternoon and our appointment with the Uffizi's Giovanni Vannucci was not until 4:30. Nicolina had decided to rest after taking a light lunch in the hotel's dining area and Seraphina would remain in an adjoining room guarding the sketch, which she clearly considered to be her job. Meanwhile, Peaches was eager to climb the steps of the Duomo, its architect-cum-engineer, Filippo Brunelleschi, being one of her all-time heroes.

"The man was a genius!" she exclaimed, waving a guidebook around. "To engineer that dome under the circumstances. Do you know that it was the first octagonal dome in history to be built without temporary wooden supports? I've always wanted to see it in person so I plan to climb right on inside the dome and study every aspect. What an opportunity! Want to come?"

"No, thanks. I'm going for a walk. The streets beyond that window—" I indicated the casements opened up to the garden "—are much less crowded with tourists than usual in August, apparently." Though many visitors had returned post-pandemic, the numbers were nowhere near the usual August swarms. "I'm going to savor the city while I can."

"Sure you don't need a bodyguard?"

"No, thanks. Go meet Brunelleschi. See you later at the Uffizi."

Did I worry about being followed again? Always. The first years of my life in England I had been constantly ghosted by crooks convinced that I knew where my brother and Noel had hidden their heisted treasures. I didn't at first but that didn't stop them. Since launching the Agency of the Ancient Lost and Found where tracking lost treasures was my business, I rarely stepped outside without being accompanied by some stalker. I just knew they were there but learned to live with their presence the way one lives with flies and stinging insects. The incident in Rome just proved that they followed us everywhere.

That afternoon in Florence, I imagined that the previous night's stalker may have accompanied us here, too. I can always sense when I'm being followed. Of course, they'd be virtually invisible in the gaggle of tourists taking selfies with the sculptures outside the Bargello. It would be almost impossible to pinpoint my stalker unless I was willing to sacrifice all of my attention to the task, which I wasn't. For the first few hours alone in Florence,

I craved time out to savor the history and atmosphere. I had given myself a two-hour holiday and planned to savor every moment.

I strolled across the fourteenth-century Piazza Della Signoria, once the political epicenter of the Florentine Republic whose well-worn pavers had been trod by nearly every famous personage during the Renaissance. A bronze plaque embedded into the stone marked the spot where the puritanical fanatic friar Savonarola had been burned at the stake in 1498, one year after he had orchestrated the Bonfire of the Vanities. In the name of evil excesses, he had torched works of art, gaming tables, and magnificent dresses while preaching that every form of pleasure and relaxation was pure wickedness.

In a state of pure wickedness myself, I stopped by a gelateria for a pistachio ice cream so delicious that I swear my toes curled as I continued my stroll down the famed Ponte Vecchio. It was the only medieval Florentine bridge to survive the bombing of World War Two, and that it had survived all the centuries up to that point was a miracle in itself.

Only a quarter of the way across, I looked around for a bit of shade in which to stand while frantically licking my rapidly melting luxury. It was a hot day and the only people on the streets were tourists. The Florentines were too smart to broil themselves alive in the summer heat.

Stepping under an awning, I studied the offerings in one of the pricey jewelry shops that lined the bridge. There had been goldsmiths here since the traditional butchers and tanners had been banished by decree in 1595 due to the bothersome stench that annoyed the citizens. The bridge was literally a cobbled lane of shops lining both sides up to the very center where arches opened onto views of the Arno before the shops continued to the other side.

My eyes slipped across the gold bracelets and necklaces on sale wondering which item would I choose had I the money and inclination to purchase. Maybe the signet ring with the tiny gold coin which could have been Roman or at least modeled after some classical emperor's profile—Hadrian, perhaps? Pseudo-buying expensive items was a game I often played during my relaxed moments but usually with luxury fashion magazines. In reality, I rarely bought costly items for myself unless they were textiles or yarn.

By chance, I caught the reflection of a woman standing behind me. Of all the shop windows on the bridge, why had she chosen this one to gaze into with such intense interest? Was there something particularly intriguing here not found in the other windows? I doubted that. Most jewelers sold similar wares.

I studied her out of the corner of my eye. Older than I was by a few years, oval face, blondish hair pulled back into an untidy ponytail, beige khakis, and a striped shirt with a crossbody bag, nothing about her carried the telltale signs of a tourist. Her stance—arms crossed, eyes above a mask calculating, confident—made me think she was studying me, too. This woman was all business.

Slowly, I turned, expecting to make eye contact, but she immediately bolted, leaving me to study her athletic form as she race-walked along the bridge. I had no intention of chasing her down but continued strolling in the same direction. Minutes later, I reached the center arched opening in time to see her striped shirt moving quickly along the street on the other side of the Arno. Puzzling but not alarming. I checked my watch: time to head for the Uffizi. I devoured the rest of my ice cream, cleaned my fingers with hand sanitizer, and turned back the way I had come.

The quickest way to this amazing museum of treasures was to hang a right-hand turn at the bottom of the Ponte Vecchio and proceed along the arched portico overlooking the Arno. Overhead, an enclosed corridor called the Vasari Corridor linked the Uffizi to the Medici's Pitti Palace across the river. Apparently Cosimo de' Medici preferred to remain safe and dry on his way to work in the morning in the mid-1400s while also avoiding the pungent bridge. Considering that the Florentine republic was also festering with intrigue and attempted assassinations, who could blame him?

The Vasari Corridor, named after its builder, had been lined with priceless art from the Medici collection from the very beginning. In fact, the Medici were such patrons of art and architecture that they were largely responsible for the explosion of artistic rebirth and learning that we call the Renaissance and still influenced Western civilization today. They encouraged, financed, and protected the incredible artistry of everyone from Michelangelo to Leonardo da Vinci. Oh, to be a guest at a Medici dinner table!

I intended to make several visits to my favorite museum in the world this trip, but today I planned only on keeping my appointment. As it was, I was instructed to proceed to the ticket kiosk and say that I had a meeting with one of the museum's art historians, Giovanni Vannucci, one of the many Renaissance specialists. By now, I had donned my jacket and attempted to look professional. After a quick phone call, the man at the desk directed me to a door where I met a security guard who, in turn, led me through the nonpublic corridors of the museum enclaves.

Twenty minutes early, I expected to be directed to wait somewhere until the appointed time but instead the guard took me down a floor and directly to an office down a bright corridor, ushering me along as if I were a visiting dignitary. A lean ,middle-aged man with intense lively eyes above a ready smile was standing just inside the door.

"Signorina McCabe, I am delighted to meet you." Perfect English with a touch of Italian cadence. "I am Giovanni Vannucci. Call me Giovanni, please. I have heard so much of you from Nicolina and, of course, I have read of your adventures in art."

Adventures in art? Wow. Not sure whether it was acceptable to shake hands these days but I offered mine, anyway, which he pumped enthusiastically. "I'm delighted to meet you, too, Giovanni, and please call me Phoebe." Not yet used to having fame in the art world, I felt my face flush but sensed that my host was far too gracious to notice.

"Nicolina has told me many things about the work of the Agency of Ancient Lost and Found and I have read the stories in the papers and journals. For this and because we have been many years friends, I help her identify pieces, no questions asked. I thank you on behalf of the Uffizi for the many allocations you have gifted us."

We had received thank-you letters, of course, but this personal thanks meant so much more. "You're very welcome. I hope to repatriate many more pieces back to Italy, perhaps even the piece we're bringing with us for you to study today. Have you seen a photo?"

"Not yet," he said. "I wait with pleasure." I think he meant "expectantly."

"Here, this will give you an idea of the item we are investigating while we wait for the others to join us. I have an idea of the artist but I'm no expert in Renaissance art." I took out my phone and passed it to Giovanni, who stared at the screen in silence for several seconds.

"Oh," he said, and then mumbled, "Perhaps," in Italian. When his gaze met mine, there was an unmistakable excitement there.

"Is it who I think it is?" I asked. "I mean, who I'd hoped."

He laughed. "I do not know what you are thinking, Phoebe, but come let us see this together."

I followed him out of his office to a staff elevator and into the main museum's halls, trying not to gasp and swoon at every Raphael or Leonardo we passed along the way. I could be such an art groupie. Giovanni moved with quick efficiency and I had to scramble to keep up but I guessed where we were heading, had suspected all along.

To art enthusiasts, a well-loved painting still strikes one anew each and every time they lay eyes on it. Love is like that, I've decided—the sight of the lover always kisses you with joy. That's how I felt when we stepped into the museum's new Botticelli room and stood before *The Birth of Venus*. By then, my heart was already full to bursting as I stared at that magnificent painting.

"I hoped so!" I whispered, aware that other viewers stood carefully spaced all around us. With the new protocols, it was as if air and light danced around us while we worshipped with the nymphs the magnificent image of Venus emerging from the waves.

"In this I see the mastery of composition, a similarity in the way in which the artist touches the cheek. Do you see?" He was still holding my phone, the picture of the sketch open on the screen.

"Even with the comparative restrictions of chalk and ink, I see it, yes. The way in which he shades the face." Botticelli had a delicate hand with shading, managing to create soft continuous shadow as if the full power of the Tuscan sun beamed upon his subjects.

"And here you see a hint of what I consider distinctly Botticelli but, of course, without any clear provenance, and my colleagues could argue otherwise…" Art historians argued everything. It was a favorite exercise among my profession unless a painting or sketch came with clear incontestable provenance. "But still, I think maybe."

Maybe worked for me.

In his rising excitement, he was speaking too loudly, displaying my phone screen with no effort to shield the image. I felt a ping of alarm. On instinct, I swung around and there she was, standing just meters behind us—Ms. Vecchio. I reached for Giovanni's arm to warn him but he was now speaking into his phone.

"Nicolina and Seraphina have arrived," he said. "Come, we will meet them in one of the labs." And he turned on his heels and zipped off across the room too quickly for me to intercept. My Ponte Vecchio stalker had already disappeared.

I said nothing about her as Giovanni and I descended to the elevator to the museum's labs. Now I realized her interest was serious and potentially disruptive. I needed to discover who she was and what she wanted and soon.

When we stepped into a lab much like Nicolina's and our own, Nicolina and Seraphina were already waiting and a guard was just delivering Peaches. I could tell that my friend was bursting to share her experiences at the Duomo but managed to contain herself as we watched Giovanni and Nicolina exchanging socially distanced air kisses. It was a peculiar sight, a bit like watching birds enacting a courtship dance midair. After the flurry of greetings, we quickly got down to business. Giovanni suggested we could now remove our masks, which we all did.

Seraphina carefully unfolded the sketch from the satchel she carried, removing the rolled item from its canister and offering it to Giovanni with gloved hands. He gently took the vellum to a table and beamed a magnifying light onto its surface while we spaced ourselves around him in breathless anticipation.

After a few moments of studying the sketch from every possible angle, he finally straightened and smiled. "I believe this sketch may be by Sandro Botticelli."

"I knew it!" said I, unable to suppress my glee.

"Yes!" Nicolina clapped her hands. "We thought a great Renaissance master, yes?"

"We will need to establish more detail, of course. I will invite my colleagues to further study this masterpiece, if I may."

"You must keep the sketch here for now," Nicolina said. "For safety."

"That's definitely the best idea since it appears we have already attracted some unfriendly interest." I caught Nicolina's eye. She lifted her brows in a question but I turned to Giovanni. "Any idea who the sitter may be?" I asked.

Giovanni stroked his chin. "Most puzzling but no. This is not unusual for the time. So many portraits remain not only unattributed but their subjects unnamed. Florence was not so large a city in the 1400 and 1500s by our standards. It is possible that the citizens knew one another well enough that attributions were not necessary. Perhaps we can find records to specify commissions. This will be researched, of course, but the sitter may always remain a mystery. We will attempt to date this to begin with. Do we know the provenance?"

I knew this would come up but, hell, surely he already knew some of the background? "Only that my brother or his business partner, Noel Halloren, or possibly Peaches's brother, acquired it illegally somehow. I'm sure you know the story. It was all over the newspapers. We found it among their loot in their Jamaican hideout. Probably stolen by Noel, who had—*has*," I stumbled, "an affinity for Renaissance art."

Giovanni was regarding me with a touch of alarm. "He still lives? We had heard that you had...incapacitated him."

I sighed. "I thought so, too, but apparently he's holed out somewhere. I don't expect him to make an appearance for a while since his health is still not robust."

Don't ask me why discussing my art-heisting brother and my ex in this temple of art was twisting my gut inside out. I felt so ashamed as if I somehow bore responsibility for their transgressions, which I did to some extent. That is to say that in the beginning I had never done enough to stop them and now held myself accountable.

"This is most disturbing," Giovanni said with a sigh. "Halloran is notorious in the art world but how would he come across a Botticelli?"

"We don't know." I was so uncomfortable by now that I felt physically ill. "No doubt heisted from some private collector. He was—*is*—ruthless where art is concerned."

"And now we know he is still alive," Nicolina stated. "Somewhere."

Peaches had sidled up to me and touched my arm. "So, moving right along, any ideas as to the date of this piece?" she inquired. I shot her a grateful glance.

"Too early to say," Giovanni said, taking the hint. "I think perhaps some time between 1482 and 1486, but this I just guess."

"But what about the Medici crest and that wasp? Wasn't the wasp an emblem of the Vespucci?" I pointed to the little stinger embroidery on the sleeve. "The Vespucci were another noble Florentine family at the time."

"Vespucci is a play on words. It means wasp in Italian," Nicolina explained for Peaches's benefit.

"And the Vespuccis were allies of the Medici, correct?" I said. "Each of those motifs are meaningful and may point to the identity of the sitter or, at least, point to whoever commissioned the sketch. Perhaps the sitter is from the Vespucci or the Medici?"

Giovanni nodded. "The emblems and symbology are interesting but what do they tell us, really? This woman does not appear to be from the Medici or the Vespucci families based on the attributed portraits of the time. She appears to be of humble origin, though her clothing says something quite different. It could have been the sketch for a painting for a wedding portrait, though even that would be odd, yes?"

"Odd how?" Peaches asked.

"Odd because the sitter is not wearing jewelry or any ornamentation, which would be uncommon for a wedding portrait where the important family must display their wealth," I replied. "All that is rich here is the sleeve."

"But Botticelli does have other portraits of women dressed in plain attire. The *Portrait of a Young Woman* comes to mind," Giovanni said. "They are diffi-cult to attribute and the best an art historian can do is take an educated guess."

"Yes, but here is a young woman dressed like a lady but apparently not one judging from her hair," Peaches said.

"And there's the *Portrait of a Young Woman*—plain clothes, undressed hair, slightly stooped posture," I pointed out. "That is perhaps the closest to this style, though there's still a huge disconnect between her clothes and her hair. The Renaissance noblewoman's coiffure was an art form in itself but this woman appears so humble in so many ways. Here she is wearing what must be a very costly dress with that magnificent sleeve and yet her hair is worn pulled back and tucked under a scarf as if she is at home or...did not have the benefit of a maid. It's almost untidy, like she was playing dress-up for an occasion she could never attend."

"Like she was doing housework," Peaches said. Catching my questioning glance, she clarified. "Back home the women always tie their hair in scarfs to keep it off their face while working. This just looks like a working woman to me. Her cheeks appear kind of ruddy...but of course it's not like I can see any color or anything." She peered down at the sketch again. "So, how valuable is it, Giovanni?"

Seraphina, who had been standing back from the table with her hands folded, issued a snort.

Giovanni seemed a bit taken aback by this familiarity but carried blithely on. "Ah, but anything by Botticelli is very valuable once attributed and benefits from clear provenance, but I cannot guess a price." He spread his hands.

"Oh, come on—give us a guess." Peaches beamed at him playfully.

No doubt startled by her brilliant smile, the historian grinned back. "Perhaps many thousands of euros."

"And what if this is the mock-up for a painting that may exist somewhere?" She asked the question I guessed we were all thinking.

"Ah," the art historian sighed, "we don't refer preliminary sketches as 'mock-ups' but 'studies.' However, if such a portrait should exist somewhere, that portrait would be a tremendous find. To discover a complete Botticelli portrait today when they are so rare? Amazing! To find anything by Botticelli is like the discovery of the century. So much has been lost."

"And Botticelli's *Portrait of a Young Man Holding a Roundel* recently sold through Sotheby's for an excess of $92.2 million dollars," I said. "They didn't know the sitter's identity there, either."

"92.2 million frickin' dollars—seriously? That's obscene!" Peaches blurted.

"Reportedly purchased by Russians," Nicolina said.

"There are only about a dozen Botticelli portraits that have survived and most belong to museums," Giovanni added. "We bid on the *Young Man* portrait, of course, but were not successful. In the art world today, it is the private collectors who possess the funds to buy such priceless pieces. Museums cannot compete. We rely on gifts. The Medici themselves indirectly gave us many of our most important pieces of Renaissance art."

"They were the ultimate collectors and benefactors," I remarked.

"Imagine an original Botticelli hanging on the wall of one's villa?" Nicolina mused wistfully.

I glanced at her while imagining the portrait of our unknown sleeve wearer gracing her walls. That made me uncomfortable.

Minutes later we bid goodbye to Giovanni with arrangements to stay in touch and to plan more meetings as the research progressed. He graciously offered to give us a private tour of the Uffizi before we left Florence and I put my request in for a guided stroll through the Vasari Corridor. Meanwhile, the museum's art historians would focus their collective knowledge on attributing the sketch and most likely we would gift it to their collection permanently.

Altogether, it was a good day's work and now it seemed that we were free to savor Florence more fully. Nicolina suggested dinner overlooking the Arno at sunset with perhaps a refreshing drink on our way back to our hotel. How could we resist?

We exited the museum, which was closing in a matter of minutes, me gazing hungrily at every passing masterpiece on our way out of the door. Admittedly, I became briefly ensorcelled by Caravaggio's *Medusa*.

"She reminds me of you," Peaches said cheerfully.

"I remind you of a monster. Thank you very much."

"Maybe not that particular painting—I mean, that's bloody terrifying—but I've seen other images of Medusa where the snakes look more like curly hair and her expression reminds me of you—I mean in the nicest possible way, of course."

I was about to protest further when Nicolina urged us out the door. The only thing that made leaving bearable was knowing that I would soon return.

Outside, the heat seemed to have intensified, the very pavers beneath our feet pulsing back hours of the Mediterranean sun's powerful rays.

We proceeded down the Uffizi's long exterior courtyard toward the Piazza Della Signoria. Nicolina was beside me, Peaches one step behind, and Seraphina bringing up the rear, her satchel slung over one shoulder.

Suddenly Seraphina cried out and Nicolina and I swung around in time to see her falling facedown on the pavers while a woman—my Ms. Vecchio—dashed away with her satchel. Peaches bolted after the attacker while Seraphina struggled to her feet.

4

"You let her escape!" Seraphina accused Peaches as we sat at an outside trattoria attempting to restore our equilibrium. Seraphina had received a blow to the head for which she refused medical attention, saying that it was nothing. There was no bleeding, only a nasty welt. Apparently Ms. Vecchio had taken her by surprise, hitting her with some unknown object before snatching her bag and making a speedy getaway.

"I didn't *let* her escape," Peaches argued, relocating the wine carafe to my side of the table as if she planned to lunge across and throttle the smaller woman. Knowing Seraphina's abilities, that wouldn't have been wise. "She disappeared, I said. That woman must know Florence like the back of her hand, and boy, can she run. One minute I thought I had her and then—poof! Gone."

"'Poof gone? What is 'poof gone'? You are no bodyguard," Seraphina said with a sneer.

Peaches leaned over the table. "But I'm not your bodyguard, am I? I protect her." She pointed to me. "You're supposed to be the big hotshot spy-trained guard dog so why can't you protect yourself?"

Seraphina launched to her feet but Nicolina put out a staying hand. "*Sedersi,*" she told her. Seraphina sat. "This does not help. This woman she has stolen an empty container, that is all. We are very lucky that the sketch is safe in the Uffizi."

"True," I agreed, "but obviously my stalker was after that sketch. So how did she even know we had it? Since she was tracking me since this morning and possibly even in Rome, she must have already known that we had something valuable."

"Looks that way." Now settled into her chair, Peaches crossed her arms and leaned back, keeping Seraphina in her sights in case the other woman launched a surprise attack.

Our waiter arrived to fill our glasses, maybe hoping that we'd empty that carafe and order another. I smiled up at him and told him to bring us another round as I took my first sip of Chianti. Distilled bliss. "Drink up, everyone. Growling at one another is not going to solve anything. We need to find this woman. My guess is that it won't be that difficult." Yes, I was breaking all my cardinal rules about drinking wine predinner. I felt the urge to celebrate possibly finding a Botticelli sketch.

"Why is that?" Nicolina asked as she picked up her own glass.

"Because she's an amateur. She came right up behind me on the bridge this morning while I was window-shopping. An experienced stalker would know that a window would reflect her image, which doesn't make her any less dangerous. If she does her homework enough to know who Seraphina is and still jumped her, she's not afraid of much, either."

"I will kill her," Seraphina said, closing her eyes.

I shook my head. "No, you won't. We need to get information from this woman. For that we'll lay a trap. My guess is that once she discovers that she's snatched an empty bag, she'll come back for the right one and this time we'll be ready for her."

It was simple, really. I figured that Ms. Vecchio might think that she had snatched the wrong bag from the wrong person. Though Nicolina and Peaches carried smaller purses, I habitually lugged my antique carpet-uphol-stered backpack everywhere. Maybe she'd think that I was the sketch bearer and not Seraphina? A logical next step, then, was for her to either attempt to steal that from me or, better yet, force me to disclose where I may have hidden the sketch. Or so my thinking went. There were so many possibilities but top of the list was to put myself in her tracks.

To that end, later that evening, I sat in the garden with my knitting. Being summer, the sun set later in the day allowing me to take advantage of the light. Nicolina had eventually insisted that Seraphina be checked out by a doctor after she began having dizzy spells during dinner so both of them were occupied elsewhere. However, Peaches lurked nearby.

The garden was a spacious walled enclosure with fruit trees, fountains, and clipped hedges set among geometric paths in the Renaissance style. I had parked myself in the center loggia, which was raised just high enough to be visible from the street. If my stalker happened to be lingering near, she could access the area through a little gate on the side with a minimum of lock fiddling.

My bag sat clearly visible while I did everything possible to look absorbed in my stitches. Actually, that wasn't difficult. Once I began knitting, time just slipped away, and considering that I'd had several glasses of wine by then, slipping of all kinds came easily. Peaches sat well out of sight near the kitchen garden in the corner. Thus, I made myself ambush bait. Yet an hour and many dropped stitches later, my attacker did not make an appearance.

"Maybe we're looking too obvious," Peaches whispered to me as I gathered up my knitting and came indoors.

"She knows that we're aware of her now," I said. "I'm going to take a stroll instead. You wait here."

Peaches laughed. "You think I'm going to leave you to wander around Florence by yourself? Not a chance. If this one doesn't get you, the pickpockets will."

"You do recall that I know self-defense."

"Yeah, but you've gotten rusty, whereas I do my practice videos every day and returned to the gym the moment they opened."

"I said I'll go alone. She'll know she's being set up if she catches sight of you anywhere near. Stay here, please. Besides, you know I can take care of myself."

"That's what Seraphina the Terrible thought before she was jumped. You of all people need a bodyguard."

"Why me of all people? Never mind. I said I'll be fine."

So I may have won that battle but whether I'd be able to corner Ms. Vecchio solo was another matter. All I could hope for was that she might take the bait.

I took off on a leisurely stroll through the winding streets away from the river this time, heading for an area where the medieval arteries grew narrower and were lined with tall stone buildings. It was like strolling through ancient urban canyons where vestibules and centuries-old niches offered multiple places to hide amid walls of stone. If I were my stalker, I wouldn't miss a chance like that. Naturally, she'd know that I wouldn't bring a Botticelli sketch along for the ride, but if she wanted to chat, here was her chance.

At dusk, most of the pedestrians had already left for home or the restaurants. Away from the main thoroughfares, a quietude descended on the cobbled streets broken only by the buzz of an occasional Vespa. Many streets were so narrow that cars were allowed through by permit only and iron posts had been installed to protect the sides of the ancient buildings. There were often no sidewalks and pedestrians had to scuttle against a wall to avoid being flattened by the occasional vehicle.

But I wasn't paying much attention to any of that. For me, it was a breathless step back into time even if those high fortress-like walls lining the streets refused to give away their secrets at first glance. Medieval and Renaissance houses were built for defensive purposes as much as for shelter. One never knew when a rival family or a band of thieves might try to scale your walls. Even though most of these stone faces had renovated exteriors, the bones of the structures remained the same.

The past absorbed me as I imagined the wealthy wool and cloth merchants that had once lived along these streets. Occasionally I glimpsed a courtyard through an iron gate and stood there for minutes picturing life in the 1400s. Still nobody tried to accost me. At one point, I became so annoyed by this total lack of opportunism that I planted myself in the middle of a quiet lane and glared back at the empty streets.

It was growing dark when I tired of the game. I resolved to return to the hotel taking a different route. This way led me down the Via San Gallo and on toward the San Marco area, a slightly convoluted route but one I anticipated because I'd be passing the famed Duomo.

I had just turned a corner off the Via San Gallo onto one of the long arteries that led to the cathedral when it happened, though I'm not sure to this day exactly *what* happened. I'm practiced at preparing myself for unwelcome encounters but no footsteps alerted me, though I'd been checking behind me every few minutes. Had I missed a flicker in the shadows?

Yet somebody grabbed me from behind, pressed a cloth over my face, and pinned my arms behind my back. Two people, I thought as I frantically struggled while inhaling a sweet pungent scent that fogged my brain. Shit! Blinded, half-shackled, I was still trying to get in a kick when my knees gave out underneath me and I dropped to the pavement.

A man's voice in Italian said, "Get her in."

I needed to call my super phone but couldn't remember the words. I was going down fast. They were dragging me somewhere.

Tires screeched to a halt followed by loud voices before I went under.

* * *

Hours later, I found myself in bed with a killer headache. For a moment I thought it had to be from the wine, though I was sure I hadn't had that much. Slowly, I opened my eyes. I could just make out Peaches pacing the room in the lamplight while Nicolina sat in a chair, hands folded in her lap.

"What happened?" I whispered.

"What happened?" Peaches snapped, swinging around. "I'll tell you what happened: you were almost kidnapped by a gang of deadly dudes!" She was at my side in seconds looking furious enough to singe the sheets. "I said you couldn't go off without me and good thing I didn't listen. If I hadn't been there, those two would have dragged you off."

"They chloroformed me," I said, struggling to prop myself on my elbows. "I remember that smell."

"Yeah, trussed you up like a chicken and tried to drag you into a car. You need me, McCabe, and don't think for a moment that you don't."

"Never said I didn't," I mumbled. "Did they take anything?"

"What, like your precious knitting or maybe your super phone? Not a bloody thing. I got there too fast—slugged one and knifed the other."

"Knifed?" I gazed up at her.

"Yeah, stabbed him just seconds before he tried to shoot me. Luckily I know a few tricks of my own."

"And then I arrived and finished them both off." Nicolina had appeared on the other side of my bed.

Finished. Them. Both. Off. *Hell.* "You followed me, too?"

"Yes, she did—separately—and together we got you into the car. You were out cold by then," Peaches added.

"What car?" I asked. Talk about befuddled.

"The taxi," Nicolina said. Misunderstanding my look of shock, she explained: "But do not worry, the driver will not talk. I tipped well."

"But unfortunately, the guy driving the other car still got away," Peaches said.

I was still getting hung up on the details. "Wait: Peaches, you knifed one guy, knocked out the other, and then Nicolina came along in a taxi and shot them both? And you just drove away leaving them on the street?"

"Where else were we supposed to put them—in a night deposit box? We couldn't just wait around for the police to arrive and start asking questions, could we? As it was, we think some teens down the road may have seen some of the action."

I flopped back against the pillow and closed my eyes. "How did you get me back into the hotel?"

"Just sort of half-walked you through the front door and up the elevator," Peaches replied. "I said you'd been hitting the Chianti too hard. Why so interested in logistics? You should be more worried that we've got some gang after us and not just that woman."

"Do we know they're not related?" I asked, opening my eyes.

"Who knows?" Peaches said.

"No. These men were too—what is the word?—*professional*. 'Professional'?" She turned to Peaches with a questioning gaze.

Peaches shrugged and said, "Yeah, 'professional' works."

"They had guns with silencers," Nicolina explained. "Very organized. I recognized the type."

I blinked. "There's a type?"

"Italian hired assassins."

"Assassins?" I shot up again.

Nicolina put a hand on my shoulder and gently pressed me back down. "Do not worry. They probably want only to torture you for information."

"Is that supposed to be comforting?"

"They think you know something," she explained.

I sighed. "Not this again. Thugs have always thought I know more than I do."

"But you always discover what you do not know originally," Nicolina pointed out. "This is your gift."

"My gift? I need a painkiller. I'd consider that a gift right now. Could you grab me one from my bag, please?"

"I will get it," Nicolina said.

"No." Peaches raised her hand. "She needs something natural to help her sleep and detoxify that chemical shit they made her inhale. Not more drugs. I found some valerian growing in the kitchen garden out back—cool collection of herbs. I'll make some tea, then we can let her rest."

Twenty minutes later, valerian tea liberally sweetened with honey eased me right back into dreamland convinced that everything could wait until morning.

But I didn't make it that long…

Hours later, I awoke befuddled and struggled to sit up in my murky room. With no idea as to time, my phone somewhere out of reach, I managed at least to recognize that I was still in my luxury Florentine bed. A soft predawn light half illuminated the space and a gentle rose-scented summer breeze wafted in through the open casements. Other than that, everything felt all wrong.

Vaguely, I recalled those casements being closed…

"Good. You're awake. I thought I'd have to toss water on you or some-thing," a woman said somewhere in the shadows to the right. "I'm Zann."

I shot upright, patting the sheets desperately hoping for my phone, a gun, something my friends might have tucked away within reach.

"Forget it. Your toys aren't nearby and both of your friends are out cold. They won't be here to rescue you until morning. I drugged their tea."

5

She was American. Don't ask me why that was such a shock. I watched as she climbed onto the end of the bed, a gun in one hand, and plumped a satin bolster at her back. She then proceeded to commandeer another pillow on which to rest her gun hand and leaned back. It was still too dark to see her clearly since she was silhouetted against the early dawn light but I recognized her just the same.

"Make yourself comfy, why don't you?" I said.

"I have."

"And your name is Zann?"

"Short for Suzanna. I'm not big on formalities."

"So, Zann, is this really necessary? Why didn't you just talk to me earlier when I gave you the chance?"

She laughed. "Think I don't know a setup when I see one? Besides, you had the boys on your heels and I know enough about them to stay out of their path. Decided to choose my own time, my own way. You, Phoebe, are supposed to be some top-notch art detective but you and your friends can be pretty damn dense at times, can't you?"

"We all have our moments."

"Would it surprise you to know that I'm staying right down the hall?"

Well, yes, it did actually, but I tried not to let it show. "Seraphina would have sussed that out eventually—if you hadn't whacked her on the head, that is. She'll probably bug every room on this floor in a few days, too."

"I'm not too impressed with that one, let me tell you—too sure of herself, maybe has a screw loose—but Peaches now, she's magnificent, isn't she? But she can be a bit spacey sometimes, too. How else can you explain how I managed to drug her and Nicolina's tea earlier? Just waited until their backs were turned and dumped some sleeping powder into their mugs in the lobby —actually a bunch of mugs. I might have knocked out a few other late-night tea drinkers while I was at it but they'll sleep well tonight."

"Can we just get on with it? What the hell do you want?"

She laughed again. "You."

I turned around and made to plump up my pillows, giving myself time to think. When I leaned back again still all I could say was: "Me?"

"You. You are going to help me make the art find of the century, *my* art find."

"You want the sketch you tried to steal today."

"What I really want is the painting that's still out there."

"Why do you think there is a painting, let alone that it's yours?"

"Because I found it, or almost found it, years ago. I was cheated and now I want what's mine."

I leaned forward. "Explain."

"Long story."

"Doesn't look like I'm going anywhere and stop pointing that gun at me, will you? I'm a captive audience."

But the gun never wavered. "Okay, so, years ago I lived in Florence. My father was a visiting professor at the Accademia di Belle Arti di Firenze, a few months that turned into a few years so I practically grew up here. Eventually I went to university and was studying archaeology in Italy when Dad pulled a few strings to get me a summer job in Florence. I was working on a dig for one of the buildings they were renovating in the Ognissanti neighborhood on a street known today as Via della Porcellana. Know it?"

"No."

"So the property was bought by a hotel chain but the original structure was known to be very old—like that's a surprise in Florence. As usual, an archaeology team was brought in to excavate first since every building in this city is built on hundreds of years of history. I was only twenty-two at the time."

"And?"

"From the very moment this place captured my imagination. I had a powerful hunch. Ever get hunches?"

"All the time."

"Oh, yeah, I remember hearing about yours—something like mystical bolts from the sky that tell you where to look for art, right?"

"You watch too much TV. It's not like that at all but more as if I have a sudden vision of connecting puzzle pieces that form an entire picture in my head. It's like a blast of inspiration. I can't explain it much more clearly than that."

"Yeah, magical bolts, like I said."

I sighed. "Continue your story."

"Yeah, so the exterior had a baroque makeover like most of the streets around here but the interior was special. There was this courtyard where we uncovered the foundations of the original floor plan. We guessed that around that central garden had once been large windows or doors opening onto the light like some kind of portico. Maybe that doesn't sound unusual now but for Renaissance Florence it would have been. I thought maybe it could have been a painting studio or a workshop."

"You thought you'd found an artist's studio?"

"I thought we'd found Botticelli's studio but we had to prove it before those developers turned the place into some glorified Holiday Inn. Nobody believed me. I was only a student assistant. The head archaeologist said he already suspected that Botticelli had his studio a couple of buildings down, that site now renovated beyond recognition, and said I was following some romantic notion. He said to think like a scientist not a dreamer. Big ego."

"Yours or his?"

She was so animated by now that she didn't catch my sarcasm or notice when I flicked on the bedside lamp. Straight dark blond hair hanging in strings to her shoulders, lean heart-shaped face, bright blue eyes, a bit haggard-looking overall. Time had not been kind to her.

"But I was driven. I began to research the streets and original maps of the area on my own. My dad had access to a secret private library of one of his friends whose family had managed to obtain part of the Medici holdings long ago—don't ask me how. Nobody asks how those things happen in Italy. Dad even helped me read the texts. He had a good handle on Latin and old Tuscan. We determined that the site could have belonged to Botticelli's father, Mariano di Vanni d'Amedeo Filipepi, who by then ran a goldsmithing business in the area. If it was not his. then it certainly belonged to an artist of some kind."

"'We' meaning you and your dad?"

"'We' meaning me and my conniving snake of a boyfriend. I haven't

mentioned him yet but he's important so listen up. He was also an archaeology student on work experience from another university. A bit younger,
sexy, really good-looking. He acted as if I were his dream girl and followed me
everywhere calling me his little 'Simonetta.'"

I almost snorted. "Simonetta as in Botticelli's supposed muse? The wife of
Vespucci, who the artist reportedly based many of his most famous works on,
including *Primavera* and *The Birth of Venus*?"

"Don't laugh. It was a while ago, okay? I had long blond hair then—light-
ened, maybe, but blond. I could have passed as Simonetta. Maybe. On a good
day. In the right light," she added. By now the gun was lying forgotten on the
bedcovers.

"Simonetta was actually already dead when those paintings supposedly
featuring her face were painted. It's doubtful Botticelli had ever met her in
person since they traveled in different social circles and even more unlikely
that she ever posed for him—damn impossible actually. He painted his image
of an ideal woman."

"Yeah, yeah. The point is, I was suckered. Forget the Simonetta part."

"Okay, so this charmer woos you by calling you after a famous Renaissance beauty and wiggles his way into your confidence while you research
possible locations for a hidden masterpiece. You did all the legwork while he
just followed you around. Am I getting the drift?"

She dropped her head and stared at me from under her brows, half
chagrin, half defiance. "I'm not the first woman to get screwed by a handsome
archaeologist, though, am I?"

Okay, so she knew my story. "You're not," I agreed. "Men like that should
come with a warning label. So, what happened next?"

But something had changed in her bearing, dulling her enthusiasm
—*shame*. It hit so hard it may as well be my own. "So this guy followed me
around, sharing my excitement every step of the way, telling me how brilliant
as well as beautiful I was."

"Bastard. I mean, you probably were beautiful—still are in all the ways that
count. Do we need a man to define us?—but he was just using you."

"And you know how that feels, don't you? So when I found what I was sure
was a false wall, he suggested that we break into the site after-hours and do
some investigating on our own. The head archaeologist wouldn't let us touch
it because the stone bit was the one authentic part the owners wanted to
preserve. Besides, student assistants don't get to make those kind of
suggestions."

"Don't tell me you actually went in after-hours and illegally knocked a hole in the wall?"

"We did."

"Probably not the best idea."

"Stupid, ill-advised, professionally suicidal, you mean? Had I done this properly, launched a scholarly case based on the documents we'd found the way my dad suggested, and convinced all the powers that be that there was something worth investigating behind that wall, I wouldn't be where I am today, which is nowhere. Instead, I followed my handsome, sexy boyfriend's lead and broke into the dig site after-hours. We poked a hole in the wall, which caused that whole interior wall to collapse, by the way, but I was right: there was a hidden alcove behind there and, better yet, I found a leather cylinder, which contained what I knew to be a genuine sketch from the Renaissance."

"Oh, my God! *You* did find it!"

"I did but fat lot of good that did because the slimy boyfriend promptly disappeared with the sketch and left me standing in the rubble—literally."

I gazed at her in outrage. "This scumball stole your find and left you with the debris?"

"And got me expelled, landed me with vandalism charges, kicked out of Italy, and my poor dad shamed forever. But what's worse, nobody believed me when I said I'd found a canister containing a possible Botticelli sketch. Nobody believed me about my boyfriend, either. I became a vandal and a liar."

"Did you actually see the sketch?"

"Briefly."

"And what about the boyfriend?"

"Gone. Took off with the sketch and left me to take the heat."

"How in hell did that happen?"

"He convinced me that he could protect it better than I could. Said that my dad might get suspicious if I brought it home but to let him guard it overnight, that he had a friend who could help attribute it. Then he bolted."

"Didn't the powers that be think his sudden absence suspicious?"

"Apparently he'd spread the word that he was flying home the next day. I was the only one who didn't know. That bastard was crafty."

"So, did you eventually catch up with him, bring him to his knees, make him pay for his deceitful use-and-abuse tactics?"

"Like you did in Morocco, you mean? I wish I had but no."

"So who the hell was this bastard, anyway?" I demanded.

She choked back a bitter laugh. "Still don't get it, do you, Phoebe? Haven't figured it out yet. No magical bolts to make it all come together, either. And you call yourself a sleuth. Let me help fill in the blanks: the archaeologist was on a work term from the University of Queensland and he went by the name of Noel. Ring any bells?"

6

---

*C*onsider that my second ambush in twenty-four hours. I stared. "You're not serious?"

"Not serious that Noel Halloren—he was going by Noel Baker then—stole my sketch and left me in that mess or not serious because we have the same bad taste in men?"

"*Had*. His type doesn't appeal to me anymore."

"What, the good-looking, sexy archaeologist type?"

"No, the criminal, conniving bastard type. And I'm not shocked that Noel did any of those things but I didn't realize he had started his criminal career so young. When was this, the `90s?"

"1996."

"That was before I knew him and I didn't realize that he had ever done a stint in Florence."

"Why would you? He was a criminal. He wasn't about to tell all the girls he screwed what he had been up to. The point is to use them to help him feed his art heist habit, right? That's what he did to you. Anyway, I want my reputation back. I want the credit I deserve for locating that sketch and more."

"Minus the wall-kicking bit?"

"I was young and easily led. Who are you to judge?"

"I'm not judging, I'm looking at this dispassionately from a legal point of view. You were still implicated for your part in the break-in. That's the equivalent of theft, any way you look at it."

"I expected more sympathy from you, Phoebe McCabe."

"Look, I'm sorry that Noel did a number on you, but even if he hadn't snatched it, that sketch still wouldn't be yours. Italy is touchy about ownership of masterpieces found on Italian soil. There would have been tribunals, legal tie-ups, and maybe still will be, should the owners of that building enter the fray."

"The building has changed hands twice since then. It now belongs to a conglomerate but I'm not after the sketch so I can hang it on my wall. I want credit for my archaeological sleuthing and to blame the real thief so I can get on with my life. I want redemption. Noel has now been outted as a notorious art thief, which works in my favor. Even dead—and thanks for that, by the way—he can be useful in clearing my name with your help."

I might have mentioned that Noel might not be as dead as she'd hoped if she hadn't kept barreling along. "I was two months away from getting my degree. I should be suitably affiliated with a university by now, taking my students out for summer digs and living comfortably on tenure. Instead, I live hand to mouth with a résumé so blotched I can't expose it to the light of day. Really, the sketch isn't the important part. I need to pick up where I left off and find that painting to redeem myself."

"What painting?"

"There's a painting based on that sketch somewhere—a Botticelli. You know it and I know it."

"But how do you know it?

"I just do."

"Not good enough."

"You're going to help me find it."

"And why would I do that? You've hardly endeared yourself to me so far."

"Because you need me. I have access to original letters and papers that could lead us to that Botticelli portrait. Well, *did* have. That friend of my dad's who obtained part of the Medici library is dead now but his son might remember me, which might not be a good thing. You, on the other hand—Phoebe McCabe, the famous art sleuth—could get in to see that collection and pick up where I left off. I'll just point you in the right direction and together we'll find that Botticelli."

"Just like that?"

"I don't expect it to be easy but since when did that bother you? I've kept up with your illustrious career and it's made me jealous as hell—just saying. Now I want some of your stardust, Phoebe McCabe. You owe me."

"How do I owe you?" I demanded.

"Because if your brother and that ass we both loved hadn't kept that sketch hidden for all these years, this whole sorry tale might be out in the open by now. Once it hit the market, its existence would prove that, first, the sketch existed like I said it did and, second, that I didn't steal it, he did, see?"

"Your reasoning is flawed and I'm not responsible for their misdeeds, in any case."

"Maybe not, but if you had tipped off Interpol when your bro and lover were stealing art, they would have been behind bars long ago."

"I thought they were stealing back stolen art to return to their owners. I was hoodwinked, too. Anyway, why all this now?"

"I'm getting to that. Do you want to find that Botticelli or not? I know things you don't; I have the inside scoop you don't. Oh, and I also know who the gang is who jumped you last night and who they work for. That might just keep you alive long enough to hit your next viral news clip—with me by your side. 'Suzanna Masters and the Agency of the Ancient Lost and Found Locates Lost Portrait of Alessandro di Mariano di Vanni Filipepi, aka Botticelli.' Get it?"

"That's too long for a headline."

"You're going to help me, I said." She was shouting now. Picking up the gun again, she aimed it at me but the door flew open and Seraphina launched into the room pointing a pistol straight at her.

"You I shoot!" she cried.

"Don't!" I flung back the covers and leaped out of bed. "We need her! Put the gun down."

"Move," Seraphina said while trying to lean past me.

Zann was on her feet, too, gun aimed at Seraphina. Had I not kept shifting back and forth trying to block one from the other, somebody might have been shot, maybe me.

And I was at the end of my last nerve. "Put the guns away, both of you," I ordered. "Seraphina, this is Zann Masters. She did not mean to hit you so hard yesterday. She was only trying to get our attention." I was winging it. "She's sorry about the concussion, aren't you, Zann?"

Zann stood legs braced, both hands on her pistol barrel, glaring.

"I said aren't you?" I demanded. "You're going to be working with us so of course you weren't intending to inflict bodily harm on one of your future colleagues."

Zann hesitated, then lowered the gun. "No, of course not. Sorry, Seraphina. I didn't mean to hit you so hard. I thought I used my plastic water bottle but grabbed my thermos by mistake. Gun's not loaded—no bullets, see?"

Seraphina didn't appear convinced and I didn't blame her but luckily Nicolina had just arrived. Holding her forehead and trying to take in the scene she asked: *"Cosa sta succedendo?"*

"Nicolina, tell Seraphina to put away the gun. Just a bit of a misunderstanding here. Meet Suzanna Masters. She's going to help us. She found the sketch originally and has valuable information we need."

Nicolina stifled a yawn and gazed from Seraphina to Zann. "You are Ms. Vecchio?"

Zann stared. "Ms. Vecchio?"

Nicolina stared back at her in a somewhat unfocused fashion.

"Yes, this is Ms. Vecchio," I said. "She has a very interesting story to tell, which you need to hear."

Nicolina lowered Seraphina's arm. "Then we must hear it. Seraphina, order breakfast for five. Add extra espresso. Meet in my rooms in an hour. Why I am so sleepy? I did not drink so much wine." Turning, she swayed toward her room at the end of the hall, her silk dressing gown flowing open.

Seraphina shot us a fierce look before traipsing after her employer, gun now safely holstered.

Facing Zann seconds later, I said: "You'd better be on your best behavior over breakfast or I can't guarantee your safety. You have a lot of convincing to do. Pass me your gun." She did as I asked. As she claimed, the thing wasn't loaded.

After Zann returned to her room, which turned out to be right next to Peaches's two doors down from mine, I quickly showered, dressed, and took off looking for an early jolt of coffee. It was only six a.m.

Our exclusive hotel had thoughtfully set up a buffet on a carved round table that centered the marble foyer. Sunlight beamed in through the garden doors as a few early risers read their papers or tablets in the seating areas. One guy peered at me from behind his tablet—middle-aged, jeans, T-shirt, thin graying hair with a bad comb-over. Too curious to be a tourist. He was on surveillance. I pretended not to notice him.

A uniformed woman darted by asking in English if I needed help. Somehow they just knew a guest's nationality.

"Coffee?" I never let on that I understood rudimentary Italian. Remaining the obtuse foreigner could be so useful sometimes.

Smiling, she led me to a round central table ladened with a towering summer flower arrangement and indicated the selection of coffees, teas, sweet buns, coronettos, and croissants. "Americano? Cappuccino?" she asked. "I make for you."

"This is fine, thanks."

Nodding, she left me to it and I circumnavigated the central bouquet until I located a silver carafe of coffee and paper cups, perfect for travelers on the go. After filling two cups, I briefly took a moment to inhale the roses, lilies, and unknown yellow sprigs, peering through the foliage at the guy who still stared in my direction. Right, so you're on a stakeout, buddy. Meanwhile, back to business.

On the way back up the elevator, it occurred to me that nothing about this hotel or Florence itself was safe despite its beguiling luxury and riches. I needed to stop acting as though stepping back into this beloved city had somehow transported me to my carefree student days. I'd never be carefree again. Somebody would always be after me for something. And as hard as it was to accept, I also had to face the truth that the previous exploits of the Noel and Toby crime duo had put my colleagues and me into the crosshairs once again.

But Toby would never knowingly risk my life now, of that I was convinced. What he did in his drug-addled days was different and, admittedly, he thought he could work me into the family business at one time. Something was going on here that he knew enough about to try and warn me away from but what? Something in his and Noel's past—again. And to think that another woman had fallen hard the way I had and suffered the consequences the way I had only helped to stir up suppressed memories. Would I ever be free of Noel's legacy?

Arriving at Peaches's door, I knocked several times with no response. Next, I called her on her smartphone, using one of the alarm features Evan had set up among the five agency members. Moments later, a befuddled Peaches arrived at the door.

I picked up the coffee I had sat on the floor. "Drink. We have a breakfast meeting."

"Huh?"

"Coffee, you need coffee, I said."

"Is it, uh, fair trade, sustainably sourced?" she mumbled.

I sighed. "You've been drugged. You need a double dose of caffeine to knock your brain back in line. Forget the bean pedigree."

She stared at the cup. "Drugged?"

I gently backed her up into her room and explained the whole Zann story while plying her with double doses of caffeine. While she showered, I went to the lobby and brought up refills. By then, she was fully cognizant.

"And we're seriously going to let that woman work with us?" she demanded, striding the room in her camisole and panties.

"She found the sketch originally," I said, thinking that, hell, she actually dresses in boudoir-style undies and that maybe I'd better up my game in the lingerie department. Not that I expected any romance anytime soon. "She's deep into this mess and has information we need. We don't have to trust her, but we still need her."

She turned to stare at me, hands on hips. "And she seriously knew Noel?"

"A younger, equally snaky version but apparently yes."

"Does that mean he's back to haunt us?"

"I doubt he's directly involved here. Remember that his health isn't the best yet. Toby said he has a bad heart—poetic justice, everyone says."

"Since you tasered him right over his ticker, that's justice all right. Don't know about the poetic bit."

"I'm just saying that we're dealing with the dregs of one of his past exploits here, that's all. I'm guessing that Noel tried to locate the painting but couldn't. Maybe he ditched Zann too soon, before he discovered that she might hold more clues. My theory is that someone found out about the sketch from Toby in prison. Either he mentioned something to an inmate who mentioned it to someone else or something of that ilk. They are all criminals in there so who knows? But that's where this started. Now we have to find out where it ends. Let's go have breakfast and grill Zann until she's crispy."

We entered Nicolina's rooms about twenty minutes later. I thought that my quarters were luxurious but Nicolina had a whole suite with a living area and adjoining room for Seraphina, plus a balcony. Breakfast had been set up by the open double French doors on a table set with a fine Italian woven tablecloth with matching summery green linen napkins. A server hovered nearby until Nicolina sent her away with no doubt a substantial gratuity.

"Explain why we should trust you?" she asked Zann as she lowered herself into a chair and smoothed a napkin over the lap of her lacy summer shift.

Meanwhile, Zann plopped into the chair opposite. "And why should I trust *you?*"

"Why? Because you are still alive, yes? Now you must explain everything. First, who are you, really?" Nicolina sipped her third minicup of espresso.

"I told you," Zann said while helping herself to boiled eggs and slices of ham and cheese.

"You are holding back," Nicolina insisted. "You say you know where we find the Botticelli?"

"I said that I know where to look."

"That is not the same," Nicolina pointed out.

"So who are those dudes that jumped Phoebe? Phoebe said you knew," Peaches interrupted while buttering her croissant. Seraphina sat across from her in wary silence.

"They belong to an arms cartel," Zann said. "As in very-bad-men arms cartel."

Nicolina froze, suddenly alert. "Arms cartel? Which one—Milan or Naples?"

"Does it matter?" I asked.

"Yes," Nicolina said. "It matters very much. One is worse."

"You mean arms dealers are measured by degree?" I asked in alarm.

"Bad ones and not as bad ones, yes," Nicolina explained. "Two main organizations operate in Italy with connections to Syria, Russia, and Yemen. Both finance operations through art theft and drugs. Italy is important in the race to finance arms with stolen art." She stared at Zann. "Which one—Naples or Milan?"

Zann's gaze remained focused on her plate. "Milan. The branch run by Alesso Baldi."

"Baldi!" Nicolina jolted in her seat. "This is very bad."

"Who's Baldi?" I asked.

But Nicolina was fixed on Zann. "What do you know of this man and how does he know about the Botticelli?"

Zann slowly lifted her gaze. "He's going on a lead coming out of Canada. He's got informants everywhere, including the prison where Phoebe's brother's held. Says that he has ears in every prison. Knows that I found a Botticelli sketch decades ago, that Halloran stole it, and that it's on the move again. Somebody alerted him that a priceless masterpiece related to that sketch may be hidden somewhere."

"How do you know this?" Seraphina demanded.

"Because I used to work for him."

"When?"

"Two days ago."

"What?" That was me but each of my colleagues issued a cry or expletive of her own.

"You worked for a bloody arms dealer?" Peaches cried.

"I didn't know he was an arms dealer when he hired me, okay?" Zann protested. "I needed a job and this guy was hiring archaeologists, didn't care if they had their degrees yet or not. Wanted us to dig around Roman remains on the edge of Turkey, on the borders of Afghanistan, places like that. The pay was great and he finagled me a visa into Italy under a false identity."

"And you weren't the least bit suspicious that these might be illegal digs?" I asked.

"Sure, I knew these were illegal digs but you wouldn't believe what goes on in different parts of the world. The tomb robbers in these places are desperate. They steal from the dead to feed the living. The lives of their kids are on the line, okay? Once you see how war savages civilians, you don't judge so easily. Baldi may be paying them pennies for these plundered treasures but those pennies keep them alive. Who are we to judge when people are that desperate? Anyway, I didn't do much of the digging myself, just oversaw the sites, verified them, that sort of thing."

"I'm not judging the tomb robbers but you! What's *your* excuse?" I was outraged.

"Get off your high horse, the lot of you. You've all done questionable things at one time or another. Think I don't know your backgrounds? Do you want to hear the details or not?"

"Continue." That was Nicolina. I sat back and simmered.

"So, like I said, I started working for him until I found my ticket out. You might say I resigned. Now I work against him."

Nicolina was on her feet now. She flung down her napkin. "You do not stop work for Baldi and you do not just resign. He kills you if you try. You lie!"

"There's more to the story," Zann said, looking up. "If you all just calm down, I'll tell you. You're right: I couldn't just hand in my resignation. He still thinks I work for him but I don't. He knows nothing about the secret letters. He hasn't a clue that I know so much about the Botticelli or that I ever did. He thinks I just found the sketch and that Noel hoodwinked me—poor, stupid wronged woman that I am. That's how I started working for him in the first place. He tracked me down based on a newspaper article years ago."

"Wait a minute." I held up my hand. "He knows that you found the sketch but thinks you know nothing about it? Oh, come on."

"He knows I believe that a painting exists somewhere but thinks I'm as clueless about the whereabouts as he is. Thinks Noel got away with the sketch, which he did, but knows that he never found the painting. Word got out somehow that your brother and ex had information about where the portrait might be but never followed it up. Maybe they had nothing to go on, is my guess. Meanwhile, Baldi's got the scoop on every one of you," she said, turning to me. "He thinks you may know something. Thinks Toby sent a clue to Phoebe. Wants me to worm my way into the agency's confidence and find out what."

It sounded so likely that I believed her. "And?"

"And it looks like I'm obeying his orders, doesn't it? Here I am infiltrating the Agency of the Ancient Lost and Found so the great Phoebe McCabe can lead Baldi to the Botticelli. Only, it's really the other way around. That's the beauty of my plan because I'll be the one leading you to the painting."

Peaches snorted. "Are you trying to say you're acting like some kind of double agent?"

"That's exactly what I'm saying. It will work, too, providing Baldi doesn't try to force you to tell him what he thinks you know like he did last night. Or kill me first, which is a distinct possibility. He's a very impatient guy."

"And you really expect us to trust you now?" Peaches asked.

"Let me just shoot her," Seraphina said.

"I'm telling the truth!" she protested. "Look, do you really think I'd tell you I was working for Baldi otherwise? And do you think I would just hand over my find—when I find it—to the likes of him?"

"How would we know what you would or would not do?" I said. "You have zero credibility with us. And keep your voices down, everybody."

Zann jumped to her feet. Now we were all standing facing one another, arguing over the breakfast table as Seraphina shut the balcony doors. "Think what you want about me, but I'm not after money or worldly goods. I want redemption. That's what this is about for me. I want my dad to see my name across the papers for something good just once before he dies." She paused as if trying to wrestle some emotion back in line.

"What does your dad have to do with anything?" Peaches asked.

Zann met her gaze. "My dad is ninety-five years old, in failing health, but still good. I want him to know that his daughter has amounted to something before he passes. I've hurt him so much—Mom, too, but she died years ago. I don't want him to die with that image of his only child, that picture the papers posted of me standing with the Italian police after the robbery." Her voiced cracked.

Seraphina slid her tablet onto the table. "This one? I look up article. There."

Peaches picked it up and peered at the photograph of an old black and white newspaper article—a lone young woman between two Italian officers looking frightened and confused.

"That's Simonetta busted, I take it?" I asked, and she did kind of look like some of those paintings—the hair caught in an artful tangle of scarves.

"That's Simonetta busted. And I want to undo all that shit that went down. If I follow those leads and find that Botticelli, I'll get acclaim for rescuing a hidden masterpiece against the likes of Baldi. That's all I want—credit—with the story hitting the media the way your Spanish crown event did last fall. If it hits CNN and the BBC, better yet. The portrait can go to a museum after that, I don't care. But I can't do this alone."

We all stood in silence for a moment trying to absorb these multiple bombs she'd dropped. It was Nicolina who spoke first. "Why would we help you? Why would we not find this portrait on our own?"

"Because you need me. You won't find it on your own. I have something no one else does."

"Prove it," Peaches demanded.

"Here." Zann reached into her laptop case but Seraphina whipped out her gun before she could move an inch farther.

"Let her show us what she has," I said, peering down into Zann's bag. "That's not a gun she's fetching."

Seraphina agreed with a jerk of her head and slowly Zann pulled out a plastic sheathed paper.

"Nobody knows about this—not Baldi, not Noel, nobody," she whispered. "It's a letter I found among my father's friend's secret Medici papers long ago. There were more but I never got back to study them before I was kicked out of Italy. I filched this, planned to bring it back but never got the chance."

Carefully she moved the basket of buns to one side and placed the letter on the table. "It's in old Tuscan. Want me to translate?"

"I read old Tuscan," Nicolina said, picking up the page and holding it carefully in long elegant fingers. Leaning over her shoulder, I could barely make out the blotchy script on the yellowed paper. Age had eaten through the parchment in places and foxed the surface everywhere else.

"It's written in Botticelli's hand, we think. My dad had it authenticated," Zann said.

"You tell them what it says and I see if you speak the truth," Nicolina ordered, and began reading.

"I know it verbatim. I'd always planned to make my way back here and finish what I've started. You are the first to see it after my dad and me," Zann said. "It was our secret. It says:

. . .

In the year of our Lord, February 7th, 1497

Dearest Gabriela,

Beauty burns *in the streets of Florence this night and even the moon cannot hide our sins against God. Was our love of beauty truly a sin? I thought not when I lifted my goddesses from the seas and set my muses to dance in the forests of the ancients but I know that you danced in God's light, too. Have we transcribed our souls to immortal ruin? The preacher says I will be forgiven because I have confessed but I fear you will perish. You say creating beauty is not a sin but a benediction of all that is love and light. I wish only happiness for you both but would that I had your courage.*

Time runs quickly through the glass. I must make haste. I will hide your painting and hope that you can follow the path to where it lays protected. Consider this my gift to you. May God forgive me but I could not send it to the flames this night, though I watched many of my paintings burn as did your much softer art. They shriveled and died before my eyes as if they were pieces of the man I once was or a soul consigned to the flames of Hell..

Tonight my very heart lay in cinders. Ash to ash, dust to dust.

Sandro

When she finished, we stood in silence.

"And you are convinced this is authentic?" I asked.

Zann nodded. "As much as one can be given that this letter is, like, over five hundred years old. We had it carbon dated and the parchment is circa late 1400s. The writing matches an authenticated piece of Botticelli's. Plus, how many Sandros lifted 'goddesses from the seas and set muses to dance in the forests of the ancients'? And the references to the Bonfire of the Vanities is pretty obvious."

The art historian side of me kicked in. "Botticelli was one of the first masters of the Renaissance to be so influenced by the renewed passion of the ancient classics that he painted his extraordinary mythological allegories like *The Birth of Venus* and *Primavera*," I said. "There were many more masterpieces either lost or burned at the instigation of Savonarola. I can't bear to think what the world has lost. But who was Gabriela?"

"We thought that he must be writing to a lover—we being Dad and me— and that Gabriela might even be the sitter of our sketch since that was hidden, too. Because of their illicit relationship, the drawing and the painting had to be kept secret."

"Yeah, that makes sense. For all we know, Botticelli may have had many lovers." Peaches took the letter out of my hands.

"He would not be the first," Nicolina remarked.

"And yet from all accounts Botticelli was not drawn to women sexually but was likely homosexual. He adored the vision of the perfect sacred feminine and it was this he was trying to capture. He's like the ideal humanist."

"But how do we know, really?" Zann asked.

"True." But I was still fixed on the context. "'Beauty burns in the streets of Florence...' That has to be a reference to the Bonfire of the Vanities. It's the same date—1497," I said. "What provenance!"

"I say Gabriela was secret lover. Why else need to hide portrait?" Seraphina pointed out, finally engaged in the mystery.

"Perhaps because she was married," Nicolina said, "though this is not usually a problem."

"It would have been a problem for a married noblewoman to be involved with a painter in Renaissance Florence," I remarked. "But the identity of this woman remains unknown and if this letter refers to the sitter of our portrait, she wore a noble dress but did not look part of the nobility."

"But there has always been this story that Botticelli and Simonetta Vespucci were lovers and this certainly isn't Simonetta," Zann said. "I always liked that tale. Simonetta was supposedly his muse and posed for all those gorgeous mythological allegory paintings. He even requested that he be buried at her feet."

I turned to her. "This was the age of courtly love, remember. Men literally acted as standard bearers to noble beauties of the day. Lorenzo de' Medici bore a standard for Simonetta during the tournament held for his wedding feast to Clarice Orsini while his bride looked on. That didn't mean that he was in a relationship with Simonetta. His brother may have been but that's another story."

"Maybe," Zann acknowledged.

"Most scholars agree that it's doubtful that the painter ever met Simonetta let alone posed for him," I pointed out. "The Ognissanti was their community church. Maybe he wanted to be buried at the feet of beauty, symbolically speaking. The Renaissance thought like that—in symbols and allegories. She died young and that almost guaranteed that a beautiful woman would be immortalized for eternity."

"Like Marilyn Monroe," Peaches remarked. "Doesn't tend to work that way for black women, though, just saying."

"I still like the Botticelli/Simonetta version best." Zann shrugged. "Where's your sense of romance, Phoebe McCabe?"

I looked over at her. "Missing in action—took a direct hit. Anyway, Botticelli would already have been in his late fifties when this was written, if indeed he wrote it at all. It's said that after Lorenzo the Magnificent died in 1492, Savonarola's religious fervor took hold in Florence. Sandro himself became caught up in the friar's fiery oration and stumbled around Florence disconsolate. He must have stood by while his patrons threw his life's work into the flames, watching his masterpieces 'shrivel and die' as he says here and also supposedly added a few to the flames himself."

"What pieces survived were either protected by powerful patrons or hidden," Nicolina said.

"Or smuggled to country estates or other cities," Zann added. "These were the days of city states, remember."

"After that, his art returned to being more devotional." I studied the plastic-encased page. "Maybe this Gabriela was a secret love or maybe she was something else. Botticelli writes that she created 'a much softer art.'"

"Lovemaking is a much softer art," Peaches pointed out.

"And there would have been courtesans and sex workers in the streets of Florence," Zann remarked.

"Maybe, but I don't think so," I mused.

"Should we ask Giovanni to check with his posse of experts for any historical references to our Gabriela and show him this letter?" Peaches asked, gazing down over my shoulder.

"No," Zann said, swinging around. "Nobody can know about this and I mean nobody. Just knowing these letters exist can get us all killed."

"How would letters get us killed?" Peaches asked.

"Think, Peaches. This letter—and there are others—are the only lead we have for the secret Botticelli portrait. I've kept this one hidden from everyone, from Noel to Baldi—my insurance policy, the key to my redemption—for nearly three decades." Zann paused to gaze up at Peaches.

"Continue," Seraphina prompted.

"So, like, I knew that the moment I let it see the light of day, it could set a chain of events going that could destroy everyone," Zann said. "But we have to keep that from happening. Baldi would literally kill to get his hands on this and others like it. He's killed for far less, believe me. We have to get to the other letters to see if they will lead us to that painting without Baldi knowing, see?"

"What other letters?" Peaches and Seraphina said in unison.

"I said there were more. Weren't you listening? I said that my father's friend had a part of Lorenzo the Magnificent's library. Kept it hidden away. Clearly obtained illegally, probably by one of his ancestors, that's my guess. I didn't get to read them all."

"And your father's friend didn't notice when you stole this one?" Peaches asked.

"We're not sure. If he did, he never said anything. Signore Corsi and Dad remained friends and wrote to one another periodically after Dad returned home to New York, right up until Signore Corsi died in 2016, in fact."

"Did Signore Corsi not have his collection, um…organized?" Nicolina asked.

"Cataloged?" Peaches suggested.

"Cataloged, yes. Did Signore Corsi not have them cataloged?"

"Of course. Look," Zann said, carefully removing the page from Peaches's fingers and replacing it into her laptop case "The Corsis have the most significant collection of Medici artifacts outside of the Laurentian Library and museums, okay? An entire room has been set up in their estate to be a close proximity to what Lorenzo de' Medici's own library must have looked like circa 1460."

"Wow," I said under my breath, imagining the wealth of knowledge such a collection must contain.

"Any idea of the value of what a collection of classical Greek manuscripts scribed from monasteries all over Europe plus letters in the Medici's own hand would be? It might rival that of a Botticelli in net worth." Zann continued. "Signore Corsi was a passionate collector. Somehow he got his hands on things that he would rather not be brought to the attention of anyone but his most trusted friends—hundreds, if not thousands, of items. Priceless items on top of those he inherited. Getting my drift?"

"Got it," Peaches said.

"Signore Corsi himself was no thief but a gentleman who loved history with a passion but anything Medici was his weakness. My point is that one missing letter was not worth the family lodging a complaint that might reveal the extent of the family secret. And certainly Corsi wasn't about to mention anything to my dad either in print or by phone, was he?"

"All right, I get the picture," I said, studying her carefully. This woman was like an onion revealing herself layer after layer. What secret would she peel away next? "So where is this priceless collection kept and is it still intact?"

"I know where it was when I last saw it—in a fourteenth-century villa in the countryside that is currently run as a vinery-cum-bed-and-breakfast. Been in the family for generations. It still belongs to the Corsi family. I checked it out. The son and his wife run it now—Piero and Alexandra Corsi, with their two young sons."

"And you think the collection may still be there?" Peaches asked.

"I doubt Piero would have sold it as long as the vineyard keeps producing the Chianti Classico for which it is known. Plus, I remembered that he shared his father's passion for all things Medici. I'm betting the collection is still locked in the tower room where I saw it decades ago, still locked behind a false wall."

"So what are we supposed to do, just ring him up and ask to see it?" Peaches asked.

Zann rolled her eyes. "If only it would be that easy. So Piero knows me— we had a fling before Noel came between us. I supposedly broke Piero's heart, or so he said. But he obviously knows what I did to get thrown out of Italy. Who knows how he'd react to seeing me now?"

"I can just imagine. I wouldn't want to see you again, if I were him. Not sure I want to see you now," Peaches remarked.

"Peaches, you hurt my feelings," Zann said with a smile. "Point is, I can't just contact him and request a viewing of his secret library, especially not in the company of the Agency of the Ancient Lost and Found. You guys are all about returning stolen items to their original owners, right? That's bound to make him edgy if these things were stolen. No, have to be a hell of a lot more strategic than that."

"I know this is going somewhere. Could we just speed it up?" I asked. Really, I wasn't the patient sort. "I presume you're saying that we can't just drop by to request a viewing? Would it help if I swore upon all the swear-worthy things to ensure him that the agency is not interested in repatriating that priceless library of his? I'll quote a grandfather clause or something." But in my heart of hearts, I'd love to restore that collection to the people of Florence, the world.

"That wouldn't help," she said. "If we go anywhere near that family, it will bring Baldi bearing down on the Corsis, because if Baldi even suspects what the Corsis own those letters, that library—"

"They come in, steal collection, kill everybody, and burn villa to ground," said Seraphina.

"Always the jolly one of the bunch, aren't you?" Peaches said, glaring at her.

"But she's right," Zann said. "That's exactly Baldi's style, being a big supporter of the scorched earth policy. Roman generals are his heroes, by the way. Runs his operation like an emperor. Wears a gold medallion of Lucius Cornelius Sulla. Even quotes Roman emperors. The point is we can't go anywhere near the Corsis." She turned a shrewd eye to me. "At least not as ourselves."

7

I knew I wouldn't like what was coming next and I was right. Zann revealed an elaborate plan to digest over breakfast, most of it hard to swallow. However, she delivered it with such aplomb that we couldn't help but be impressed.

"Like I said, we can't just drive up to the Corsi estate," she said while busily cracking another egg. We were all back to sitting by then, trying to pull our group together with this new collaborator. "And we can't all travel together, either. Baldi is watching this hotel, has eyes everywhere."

"I think I saw a pair of those eyes downstairs," I remarked, watching her. Compared to our first encounter in my room, she seemed much more animated, as if her dream was all going according to plan.

"Angelo. He's been assigned to watch you now that you decommissioned Luigi and Carlo but he's no professional—probably forced to work for Baldi. Baldi's got those as well as the lifers."

"You know these guys by name?" Peaches asked.

"Just the Florence contingent," she explained. "Big operation."

"I found bugs in our rooms," Seraphina remarked. "His?"

"Those would be Baldi's, yes," Zann told her.

"We find bugs all the time, most of them belonging to that one." Peaches thumbed toward Seraphina.

"I protect you!" Seraphina protested.

"Oh, just stop." Peaches waved her off. "Admit it, you've got issues."

Zann was gazing at me. "So, do you use one of the fabulous smartphones I heard about, one that Evan Barrows cobbles together? It sweeps for bugs, too?"

"Look," I said, my patience wearing thin, "can we get back to the topic? You were talking about the plan."

"Right, so anyway, Phoebe and I will go to the estate tomorrow afternoon."

"Why you and me?"

"Because we can stake out the place as a pair of curious guests with American accents. We'll be playing American tourists and they won't peg your accent as Canadian."

"Her accent isn't Canadian anymore. It's sort of a bastardized British Canadian hybrid," Peaches remarked.

"As if most Italians can sort that out. Unless you tell them otherwise, they'll think you're American. Anyway, today's Thursday, in case you haven't noticed," Zann remarked.

"Which is important how?" I asked.

"The Corsis' wine delivery van comes to this hotel every Friday afternoon to drop off cases of wine and collect the empties—regular as clockwork, very old school," she replied. "You and I will hide out in the van and get to the estate that way. Baldi's eyes will never see us leave. We should arrive six-ish."

"We will be in disguise, I presume?" I asked.

"Yes, but nothing too elaborate—wigs, standard tourist attire."

Her ingenuity was impressive but I didn't relish jostling to the country amid cases of clinking bottles. Still, we were letting her take the lead here so we listened as she continued to lay out the details.

"Nicolina, Seraphina, and Peaches, you have to arrive separately also in disguise," she added.

Peaches almost sputtered into her coffee. "Are you kidding me? How do you disguise a tall black Jamaican in rural Tuscany?"

Zann grinned. "I have that all worked out, too. We need to get you onto the grounds on the sly. This is the deal: every Friday night, the Corsi estate has a wine tasting event with food and entertainment. Very big-ticket item. They hold it on the grounds for guests and visitors alike—very chichi and popular among tourists. Look it up online. Anyway, I've been in touch with the caterers and musicians. Nicolina, I have you and Seraphina on as one of the servers with the Tasty Tuscan Tours catering company, and, Peaches, you're going as a backup singer with a string ensemble called Canto Cantina. They feature an opera singer but do the jazzy global fusion thing, too."

"But I can't sing!" Peaches protested.

"And I cannot serve!" said the countess. Maybe I only imagined the look of amusement on Seraphina's usually pinched expression.

"No matter," Zann said, holding Peaches's gaze. "I told them that we would double the fee charged to the Corsis if they permit this little subterfuge. I said that we know the family and that this is all just a bit of fun."

"And they believed you?" she asked.

"For a few thousand extra euros, they'd believe anything. You'll be given lots of leeway, too. Just pretend that you are part of the group and everything will be fine."

Nicolina appeared affronted but made no further protest.

"You must have been pretty sure that we'd agree," I said.

"Just hedging my bets. So, I'll provide the addresses of both companies—they are located near Montalcino—and I have ideas for getting you there unseen. Meanwhile, I'll be meeting Baldi later today with information that should send him off to Volterra tomorrow thinking that Phoebe's picked up a lead. With a little luck, his henchmen will be off on a wild-goose chase by the time we're on our way to the Corsis'."

"Why Volterra?" I asked.

"It's out of the way with plenty of long windy roads to get there. Easy to get a flat tire," she said. "Easy to keep ahead of a tail, too."

"This is nuts," Peaches said. "If Baldi finds out what you're up to, you'll be dead."

"I'll be dead, anyway, if we can't pull this off," she remarked. "It won't take him long to figure out that I'm going behind his back. We've got to get the info we need, get back to Florence, retrieve the painting—wherever it is—and hand it over to the authorities. Pictures taken, viral acclaim—done!"

"Easy!" Seraphina said, looking as if she'd love nothing better than a good brush with death.

Again, I was stuck on logistics. "So we end up on the Corsi estate and then what? Are you planning to have us jump out of a box and announce our presence?"

Zann shot me an *oh, come on* look. "No, Phoebe, we're going to pretend to stay overnight and reveal our true identities when alone with the family later that evening. The entertainment ends at eleven on the dot."

"I do not understand," said Nicolina. "This is a bed-and-breakfast, yes? There will be other guests. How will we be alone with the family?"

"Because," Zann said, turning toward her, "we will be the only guests there in the end. Six rooms are booked as of now by a family called Masters out of

New York, supposedly arriving tomorrow night. The others will cancel unexpectedly."

"And you booked all the rooms, like, how long ago?" Peaches asked.

"Okay, so I hired a hacker to bug up their booking system and to send cancellation notifications to all the legit bookers. I'll put that on your bill, too. I used Dad's card to rebook us. He'll never notice. It's under his full name, Dr. Eric D. Masters, but he always went as David back in the day. You'll have to pay for the rooms, of course."

"You're kidding?" That was Peaches again. For some reason, she was getting hung up on the money part.

"Well, you don't expect me to pay for it, do you? I can't afford that kind of thing," Zann protested. "The agency has to pay for my room here, too, since I doubt Baldi will foot the bill once he discovers he's been tricked. You'll be paying for the bonuses for the musicians and the catering group, as well—all the cost of doing business. Look, I'm working for you, get it? You have financial resources, I don't."

I just stared unfocused at a tapestry on the opposite wall—French eighteenth century—my brain racing over details, possible hitches, and all the things that could and would go wrong while I simultaneously wondered where they purchased that textile. I had trouble laying my hands on good French tapestries these days.

Meanwhile, Nicolina lifted her hand as if anointing a speck of dust. "Not important. We will pick up the tab but you must deliver," she said. "We will go and retrieve these letters and manuscripts, retrieve the Botticelli, and give them all to Florence."

"Wait," I said, snapping back to the moment. "We're not going to steal the Corsis' collection. We're only after the Botticelli. We'll take pictures of the relevant papers and that's it."

Nicolina fixed me with a cool gaze. "Phoebe, those Medici papers belong to Florence. Lorenzo the Magnificent's nephew left what remained of the library to Florence in 1523. They belong here." Nicolina knew her history, too.

"So how'd they get from Florence to Rome in the first place?" Peaches asked.

"The Medici family declined after Lorenzo's death—more like collapsed," Zann explained. "The year they were overthrown and their palace sacked, whatever survived was smuggled to Rome where it was protected by Lorenzo's son, who was pope at the time," Zann said. "The Medicis were big on family popes—good for business as well as the soul, apparently—but I agree with Phoebe. No matter how the Corsis ended up with part of the collection, that's not what we're going for. We're after the painting."

But Nicolina wasn't letting go. "The Medici library, it belongs to Florence," she insisted. "Pope Clement, Lorenzo's nephew, had Michelangelo design the building for the library next to the Duomo. They have a home. How did the Corsis obtain these manuscripts? Perhaps they are fake?"

"Not fake," Zann said. "Dad said that the family obtained most of the collection long ago, maybe even legally for the time. The Corsis are an old Tuscan family and Florence was in upheaval, remember? Looting was a thing. Otherwise, we don't know and we don't care. That's not what we're going for. Forget the Medici library. We're after the Botticelli letters."

"I agree, we're after information to lead us to the portrait, not to steal or retrieve that collection." However, it would be useful to know if the secret collection was authentic. How could I tell? "And, Nicolina, unless the agency wants to launch a long protracted court case, removing that collection without the Corsis' permission is stealing, period."

Nicolina looked away, neither agreeing or dissenting. Her lack of acceptance of what I considered to be my obvious solid reasoning was unsettling. As so often the case with repatriating priceless items, to some extent she was right but equally and legally all wrong.

But we were already moving on to working out the finer points of our next day's subterfuge. In the end, it was agreed that we would infiltrate the Corsi estate as described and convince Piero of the need to grant us access to the secret library. I had my arguments ready while Zann planned to launch a plea of her own. We could only hope that all the moving parts of this complex strategy went off without a hitch. As if that ever happened.

For the rest of the day, I was determined to remain fixed on research while Zann took off to contact Baldi with Seraphina tailing her.

"I will not take eyes off you one minute," Seraphina told her.

"Good luck with that. Baldi has a complex method for ensuring his meetings remain private."

"Does he track your phone?" Seraphina asked.

Zann hesitated. "Probably."

Seraphina held out her hand. "Give me phone."

"What will I use in the meantime?" she asked, passing over the Blackberry.

"Buy new one. Burner."

Zann turned to me. "Hear that? Expect a new phone to appear on your bill. Anyway." She turned back to Seraphina. "He anticipated that one of us would track me. May as well be you."

After breakfast, Zann paused at the door and remarked: "Oh, and I need a few hundred euros to pay off the decoys." She paused, turning. "Eight hundred ought to do it—two hundred for each decoy." She counted out the amounts on her fingers. "I'll put the car on Dad's card and we can settle up later."

"Decoys, car?" Peaches asked.

"Sure. How did you think we're going to draw Baldi out of town? I've got to locate a double for each of you in order to lure him off on a wild-goose chase to Volterra, I said. Baldi's guys will see the car and think it's you based on the tip I'll provide. Guaranteed they'll follow this decoy car tomorrow afternoon. He already knows that he can't just track your phones. He thinks Evan Barrows is a genius, by the way, but wants to knock him dead. Anyway, hopefully we'll get what we need from the Corsis and be back to Florence before Baldi figures what's up. Do you have cash?"

Nicolina left for her bedroom and returned with a bundle of crisp one-hundred-euro notes. "Here. Eight hundred euros. If more is needed, ask."

Zann folded the notes into her inside pocket. "Thanks. Pleasure doing business with you and all that. Oh, maybe you should keep this with you in case." She handed the plastic-covered letter to Nicolina. "And his guys might follow you around today but they won't try anything now that I'm supposedly a plant. Catch up with you later—say dinner at eight and we dine here for privacy's sake?"

We agreed and off she went, Seraphina in tow.

"Order me the ravioli with sage sauce and a side of insalata di mista," she called over her shoulder as she strode down the hall.

"So are we her assistants now? I don't believe this," Peaches said the moment the door shut. "It's like we've been strapped onto a roller coaster and given no power to put on the brakes until the thing crashes. Why are we trusting her?"

"We aren't," I said, "but she has the best lead to the possible missing Botticelli. How can we not go along for the ride?"

"She's a crook, hardwired at an early age, by the sounds of things. She can blame Noel all she wants but she knew what she was doing when she knocked a hole in that wall years ago," she insisted.

"True," I said, "but I believe her when she says that it's redemption she wants. That woman is twisting with guilt. Let her have a chance to regain a little self-esteem and set things right. Everybody makes mistakes. Look at me. For years I followed Noel around believing what I wanted to believe when the evidence was right before my eyes."

"But you're different," Peaches insisted.

"Am I? I was a woman blinded by love. Now I'm setting things right the same as Zann is. Let's give her a chance."

"I agree." Nicolina turned and swept back to the table to fetch her phone. "With Baldi involved, matters are very dangerous. She has the inside track. Still, we must prepare."

I watched her photograph the letter. Thinking it a good idea, I did the same. "By 'prepare' do you mean call in the boys for support? Evan tracks us on our phones so they already know we're here."

"Why don't we tell them what's going on?" Peaches said. "Now that we have an arms dealer involved, things just got a whole lot more complicated."

"We can call them the moment things go wrong. They are only hours away," Nicolina pointed out. "Let us leave them to enjoy their holidays for now."

"Yes, let's," I said. "They aren't that far away if we need them, as you said."

"Outvoted again," Peaches sighed. "So this is officially an all-woman's job, is it? So, what's a few arms dealers among friends, right?"

She had a point. We were treading into dangerous territory but, so far, I figured we could handle things without bringing in Evan and Rupert.

Nicolina excused herself and got ready to meet Giovanni at the Uffizi. "He called to say he has information," she told us.

* * *

THAT AFTERNOON, Peaches and I had an appointment at the Biblioteca Medicea Laurenziana or the Laurentian Library, as it was known. Designed by Michelangelo, the building housed the Medici holdings. Built in a cloister not far from the iconic Florence cathedral formally known as the Cathedral of Santa Maria del Fiore, I had yet to pay my respects. This would be my first visit to the Laurentian Library ever. How did I let that happen?

"You know that we're being followed," Peaches whispered as we threaded our way through the leather vendors who set up shop along the streets leading to the cathedral complex.

"Of course. Angelo?" I asked.

"Possibly. Never saw the guy myself. Short, well-dressed, thinning hair, and shifty-looking, bit of a hobbling gait?"

"Sounds like him. Which reminds me, we had no fallout from that incident last night—no police visits, nothing."

"I've heard that gangs like Baldi's have crews that can clean up a crime scene pretty fast."

That was a possibility. In any case, Angelo didn't worry me. His tail actually suited my purposes. Baldi would expect me to be researching a Botticelli painting so why not begin in an archive? After the Uffizi, a library holding contemporary Renaissance manuscripts would be a logical place to start. The key was to ensure that he didn't discover my true intentions.

Most of the priceless Medici manuscripts had now been digitized. There were approximately 11,000 in total including incunabula, papyri, and prints available for study on computer. Still, I carried this romantic notion of settling myself down in one of the booths designed by Michelangelo himself to view the venerable tomes with my own eyes. Old books held a certain magic of their own and are best served without a technological barrier, at least for my purposes. But this was the dreamer talking. In reality, I was seeking something much more concrete.

In the meantime, I had no intention of accessing the library in the company of a tour group and this wasn't the kind of place where you could just drop in. Instead, Nicolina had called ahead to request a private tour. Whether it was because of our reputations or Nicolina's string-pulling, we ended up booking with a registered guide named Francesca Abruzzi. "I hear she is very good," Nicolina said. "She will help you."

As Peaches and I approached the imposing long rectangular exterior of the library that afternoon, I marveled at what a contrast its gray stone made against the glowing white and green marble facade of the cathedral beyond. The building almost seemed unfinished by comparison, a stony break against the creamy glory of the cathedral.

We met Francesca on the steps. Short straight hair, a ready smile, crinkles at the corners of her eyes, and animated features, I liked her at once. "Come, I do not wish you to miss even a minute, Phoebe and Peaches," she said. "The next group begins in less than an hour and I must get you through the highlights before they arrive. The last group is ten minutes ahead. Let us enter through the main door."

Following her up the steps, I turned before entering to shoot a glance toward Angelo.

"He's there hiding behind a map pretending to listen in on a tour to the right," Peaches whispered.

"Maybe he'll learn something, the bastard," I said. "Do I see him wearing a sports jacket in this heat?"

"Looks that way. Let him sweat."

Scurrying after Francesca, we stepped into a tall marble vestibule and for a moment I was overcome. It was like standing at the bottom of a waterfall of smooth, flowing stone, the steps leading up to the reading room having been designed by the master to create the illusion of wonder. We could be gazing up at what looked to be the outside of an imposing classical building thousands of years ago.

"It reminds me of the library at Ephesus," Peaches whispered. "But different. Wow, I had no idea it would be so…majestic."

"Majestic, yes," Francesca said. "Michelangelo followed the classical rules. Florence was in the grip of a powerful rebirth that celebrated Greek and Roman literature and art."

"But he only followed the rules long enough to break them," Peaches said, scanning the structure with an engineer's eye.

"Yes, that is true!" Francesca laughed. "You believe you understand how it goes but then you see how he plays with the proportions. He breaks the rules." She waved her hands, her expression registering wonder, serious contemplation, and delight in quick succession. She was a woman for whom history never got old.

"Yes." Peaches nodded. "Look at those columns and pediments. It's so dramatic!"

While they enthused over the architecture, I carried on up the stairs, eager to take my first step into the ancient reading room above completely alone. Give me a few seconds to stand in this cathedral of knowledge, I thought, and feel the weight of centuries bearing down on upon my shoulders. History is best savored in the deep respect of solitude.

But the long empty reading room hit me in unexpected ways—walnut booths on either side, a high carved ceiling overhead, the mosaic floor warmed in reds and toasted golds, with tall windows illuminating all.

After the monumental drama of the vestibule, the reading room seemed almost welcoming by comparison but no less awe-inspiring. This was a holy hall of knowledge, books being one of the most valuable items you could own in Renaissance Europe—hand-scribed, illuminated with gold and precious pigments, and containing knowledge almost lost to the centuries. If it hadn't been for the Medicis, many of these ancient texts would have been lost forever. Lorenzo had such a passion for ancient Greek philosophy and knowledge that he collected with devotion.

When Francesca and Peaches stepped in seconds later, I was sitting in one of the booths, my hands palms-down on the slanted wooden reading shelves, communing with the centuries. I turned when they entered and, just moments before the door closed behind them, I caught a glimpse of a man's shadow—lean, slightly stooped.

Angelo had actually followed us inside? How did that happen with security guards everywhere? I stood up and linked my arms with Francesca's and Peaches's. "Quickly—we have been followed," I whispered.

"Followed? But that must be one of the security people. I will explain the —" Francesca began.

But I was race-walking her down the length of the long room. "He's not security. Where can I speak to a librarian, archivist, scholar, curator, or whatever they have working here?" I whispered.

Francesca cast a bewildered look over her shoulder. "But I have not described all the features of the reading room, of Michelangelo's most brilliant design—"

"It's all right," I said. "We'll come back."

Peaches was retracing our steps toward the entry door. "You go ahead. I'll track down Angelo."

"But that is not allowed," Francesca protested. "You must remain with me at all times!"

"Consider this extraordinary circumstances, Francesca. That's a criminal following us," Peaches told her.

"Then we must tell security!"

But we had already reached the opposite door. "Please, Francesca, while we have time, introduce me to an expert so I can ask a couple of quick questions. After that, you can call all the alarms you want."

Her reluctance was palpable but she agreed to take me downstairs from the reading room to another part of the building which I assumed was the working part of the library. It definitely had a scholarly air. Desks were arranged behind which sat several knowledgeable-looking people checking computer screens while talking to what I assumed were scholars in hushed voices.

"These are all scholars or archivists. Wait here," Francesca said, but no sooner had she approached the desk when a stylish silver-haired woman stepped up to her. They engaged in an intense discussion, with the silver-haired woman shooting me sharp glances from over the top of her wire-framed glasses. Shortly afterward, Francesca introduced me to Dr. Silvestri and may I just say that, in Florence, the archivist wore Prada. I recognized the design from one of the windows in the couture shops we'd passed.

Francesca and I followed the woman to an anteroom where she shut the door behind us. Silvestri spoke English but said that she preferred to converse in Italian because it was the language of the learned. Since I didn't yet trust my spoken Italian, I let Francesca translate. Silvestri studied me over the top of her couture glasses and I sensed that I did not pass muster, either academically or stylistically.

"Dr. Silvestri knows of you," Francesca told me, trying to smile away the doctor's contempt. I had picked up phrases like *pseudo scholar, an affront to art history*, etc. from Silvestri's opening comments.

I smiled. "First, thank you, Dr. Silvestri, for taking the time to speak with me. I have several quick questions. I need to understand what an authentic Medici document looks like. How can it be identified? Are their seals or telling markings? Old documents can so easily be forged but are there any distinguishing features I could look for?" Actually, it was a simplistic question but my intention was mostly to draw her out.

Francesca translated. Dr. Silvestri turned her shrewd gaze to me. "There are many features that a skilled archivist or Medici scholar such as myself can use for identification purposes. I have both doctorates in fifteenth-century Italian Renaissance history, an undergraduate degree in classical languages, and am a professional archivist."

She paused as if waiting for me to spew my qualifications in return but knew I couldn't measure up. "How wonderful," I said. Damned if I was going to play that game.

"May I ask what you are hoping to find, Signorina McCabe?" she asked after a moment. "If you locate a valuable manuscript, I presume you will contact the nearest authority in Florence. I will personally make myself available."

I wonder how the good doctor did with arms dealers? Still smiling, I replied: "As an art historian, I assure you I would take the proper measures should I encounter an authentic Medici document. However, is it possible for you to provide a brief summary of what a book belonging to the Medici family might look like?"

Now I saw something like alarm rising in her aquiline features. "You believe you have located authentic Medici manuscripts, Signorina McCabe? For this you must contact us immediately."

Hell, what have I done? "No, no," I assured her. "I have definitely not seen any such manuscripts. I am only asking how I could identify such a piece if I were to come across one. If you know anything about me at all, you'll know that my agency frequently recovers lost objects. I wish only to be prepared."

"You are seeking a logo or a label, perhaps?" So the double doctor did sarcasm, too.

I smiled. "Subtle clues are fine, thanks."

Turning, she led me to a glass case along one long wall in which many old books sat encased in what I recognized as a humidity controlled environment. "Here, you see samples of the Medici collection. This volume is from Di Lorenzo de' Medici Ode brevis. He sought out priceless classical manuscripts from the monasteries across Europe and would have then had them copied out by his scribes. He was also a poet of some note."

I peered down at the speckled vellum frontispiece with the elaborate engraving of vines, leaves, and what appeared to be frolicking angels. In the center of the page was a circle encased in a quatrefoil motif containing four balls or palle around a square design.

Angels rode horses amid waves at the bottom of the page, everything linking to everything else in a complex rhythm of vines and motifs. My gaze skimmed across the rest of the opened books, taking in illuminated letters, intricate colored pages still aglow after all these centuries, the italic script clearly legible. Lorenzo had deviated from the church-sanctioned Latin and embraced his Italian roots by using Tuscan.

Stepping back, I turned to Dr. Silvestri. "Besides the palle, are there other motifs that signal that a manuscript could be from the Medici library?"

"Many books and manuscripts were destroyed in 1497. If you should discover others, it would be a significant find," she stated. "But there are common motifs that may distinguish such a Medici volume. Here you see the cover of Lorenzo de' Medici's collection of sonnets." She was pointing several volumes down, to a closed book—deep mottled red leather with ornate gold filigree corners and a central crest featuring six gold balls. "Lorenzo in partic-ular enjoyed illuminating his collection with various and unique symbols beside the Medici crest. He was a poet as well as a collector of ancient manu-scripts."

I knew that. There was more than a touch of condescension in her tone that her native tongue did nothing to suppress. "Would wasps, rings, flowers feature?" I asked.

"I have seen many things in the pages of this collection," Silvestri said, studying my face as though she'd like nothing better than to slap me silly.

"Are letters part of the collection?"

"By letters, do you mean correspondence?" she asked.

"Yes, like letters back and forth between, let's say, the Medici and the artists they patronized."

"We have many such pieces but this is a library," she said curtly. "We carry mainly books and incunabula, even papyri dating back to the ancient Greeks and Romans. Many letters did not survive the centuries. Many books did not, either, especially after the fall of the Medici. If I knew what you seek, perhaps I could assist you better."

"Thank you. You've been most helpful. One more thing: should someone approach you regarding our discussion, I'd appreciate it if you didn't disclose my questions."

That was a misstep. She glared at me as if I'd just requested that she break her oath of allegiance to F.A.K., the god of Freely Accessible Knowledge.

"Let's go," I said to Francesca, who kept in stride with me as I beat a hasty retreat out the door.

"I am sorry that she did not appear helpful. Research is very important to Florentine scholars. Everything follows the rules. I could set up an appointment with the chief archivist for you, if this is helpful?"

"No, thanks." I didn't want to disclose that I may have already dropped too many bread crumbs for a Baldi minion to follow. I'd been careless and could kick myself.

The sound of alarms ringing through the building chased all other thoughts from my mind. We arrived at the vestibule in time to see Peaches handcuffed between two polizia.

8

―――――――――

*I*t took all of Francesca's persuasive powers to get Peaches released from the Piazza Santa Maria Novella police station hours later.

"He accused me of being a pickpocket who had been stalking him all the way from the Duomo!" Peaches sputtered in outrage as we stood in the piazza.

"I am very sorry," Francesca kept saying.

"Did you tell them the truth?" I asked.

"I am so sorry. This is not the Florentine way." That was Francesca again.

"What, like he was really the hoodlum, not me?" Peaches said. "I told them that he had been following *us* but they didn't believe me. Who are you going to believe—the white Italian male or the tall black foreign female? Note that I deliberately emphasized the black part."

"He said he was a scholar and introduced himself as Dr. Angelo Ficino," Francesca explained. "He had a very fine vocabulary and claimed he was studying the style of Attavante, a scribe hired by Lorenzo de' Medici. It seems he was very convincing, this man."

Peaches and I exchanged glances. Could it be that Baldi had scholarly thugs on the payroll? Well, why not? He had Zann, not that she was either a scholar or a thug, exactly.

"The worst part is that he just strolled away and I'm the one left in custody." Peaches thumbed her chest.

"Please forgive us. I speak on behalf of all Florentines." Francesca was now clasping her hands as if begging for absolution.

"Francesca, it's not your fault," I said, patting her shoulder. "You're just the best. Thank you so much for all your assistance but you'd better give us a wide berth from here on in. I had no idea it would go down this way, believe me."

After further protests and offers to assist us any way she could, Francesca finally took off to meet her next tour group, leaving Peaches and me to fester.

"Come on," I said. "We need to lick a gelato along with our wounds. I'm told it can cure anything."

Not long afterward, we strolled toward the Duomo licking panettone and pomegranate flavors. I chose the panettone for a sense of creamy magnificence to soothe my bruised ego. It was almost as good as milk and cookies.

"So, tell me, did you get what you came for?" Peaches asked, trailing her tongue around the circumference of her double-scooped cone.

"Yes and no. I forgot what academia can be like sometimes. Had I been a student, Dr. Silvestri probably would have bent over backward to help me. Had I a couple of doctorate degrees she might even have been courteous, possibly respectful. As it was, she treated me with undisguised distain. The agency's activities are obviously being met with disapproval in some scholarly quarters."

"So, between racism and academic snobbery, we both took a hit today. We'll survive."

"Dr. Silvestri treated me as if I was the equivalent to art history's version of a game show—all glitter and no substance," I continued, having a bit of a vent. "She wasn't going to tell me anything unless I revealed my reasons for asking, which I couldn't do. I mean, I don't blame her, really. What am I but an upstart when it comes right down to it?"

Peaches paused licking to snarl. "Knock it off, Phoebe McCabe. We don't bow down to the disapproval of others. If it weren't for us, many pieces of priceless art would be lost forever. Think this Silvestri is out there busting her snobby butt to save history against gunrunners? Leave the scholars to do their business and we'll do ours. We're about saving art, not our reputations."

She was right. I gazed around. "I don't see Angelo lurking anywhere so let's go to the Medici Chapel and check out Michelangelo's tomb while we're at it," I said.

"Yeah, a tomb is bound to cheer us up."

Though the tomb didn't cheer us up, exactly, it certainly distracted us, which was nearly as good.

"What's with those boobs? Did Michelangelo even know what a naked woman looked like?" Peaches whispered, gazing up at the marble image of the reclining *Night*. It was safe to say she had to be in a bad mood to criticize the master.

"The figure is supposed to be mythic and not based on a real woman," I replied.

"Good thing."

After an hour of studying Michelangelo's extraordinary mastery and discussing the factors that led to the explosion of artistic brilliance we call the Renaissance, we finally decided it was time to head back to the hotel. For that, I took us on another route.

It always amazed me how the streets away from Florence's city center emptied out by seven o'clock or earlier. It's as if a button had been pushed and everyone just disappeared.

We were strolling along one of the long narrow arteries leading away from the cathedral when my neck hairs prickled.

"We're being stalked again," I whispered. "Probably Angelo."

"Bastard. I've had it up to my neck with him," Peaches said.

Behind us, I saw nothing but a row of parked Vespas and a few ambling pedestrians strolling toward the Duomo.

"Tricky bugger," I said under my breath. Unlike last night's encounter, this Baldi bad boy probably only meant to keep an eye on us rather than inflict bodily harm but his presence was annoying.

"Is this bastard really a doctor?" Peaches said with a hiss.

"Let's ambush him and find out," I whispered.

We turned a corner and ducked into the alcove of a shuttered farmacia. "No knifing," I warned, "no killing, either." I waved my phone. "Leave this to me. I'm about to try Evan's stun app set on mild."

"Why not let me do it? After all, I'm the bodyguard and I've got a bone to pick with this scrawny con man."

"Okay, you do it but set the app to stun."

Peaches grinned and held her phone. "Stun app engaged—mild."

Several minutes later, Angelo rounded the corner keeping his head down and appearing like a local heading home from a long day at work. His shuffling limp was now much more evident. I almost felt sorry for him.

We watched him for mere seconds as he gazed down the street, pausing when his quarry wasn't in sight. He kept his back to us, giving Peaches time to lunge out and zap him between the shoulder blades. He half turned before sinking to his knees. In seconds, he was sprawled on the sidewalk, semiconscious.

"Feeling shocked, are we?" I muttered, leaning over him.

"How long do these micro stuns last?" Peaches asked, checking the street for pedestrians or cars. Empty.

"I have no idea but you've got to love Evan's tool," I whispered, staring down at the back of the man's balding head.

"Yeah, you might love his tool, all right, if you'd ever let things get that far."

"I'm referring to his apps, not his… Oh, just stop. Let's get out of here. Did you find his wallet?"

Peaches was patting his pockets while Angelo tried to push himself up from the pavement. She shoved him back down.

"Got it and his phone, too. *Arrivederci, bastardo.*"

"Let's go," I urged.

We left him struggling to sit as we walked rapidly down one of the adjacent streets. Halfway along, Peaches dropped his phone down a drain in case he was being tracked.

Our stalker wasn't killed, he wasn't even harmed—unless waking up with a headache and weak knees counted—but it felt good to zap the rotter. Consider that our little payback. Yes, we can be that childish.

"We should have knocked him off. You can believe he'd do the same to us if Baldi gave the word," Peaches said.

"This wasn't self-defense," I pointed out.

"You and your code of ethics."

Once we were safely near Santa Croce without alarms going off or footsteps beating the pavement behind us, we leaned against a wall in relief. Peaches fished Angelo's wallet from her bag and we stared down at his driver's license.

"His name really is Dr. Angelo Ficino?" I said in amazement, staring over her arm.

"Baldi has doctors and archaeologists on the payroll? And look, he has a card for our hotel tucked in there, too."

"And look at that wad of cash," I noted.

Peaches whistled. "Wonder what Dr. Ficino is willing to do to line his pockets with all those euros? Should we take the wallet with us?"

"Yes. I have an idea."

We arrived back to the hotel in time for a quick shower and change before our dinner meeting, but first I stepped up to the desk and passed the wallet over to the clerk.

"We found this in the street near the Duomo," I explained. "Poor man must have dropped it. The hotel card tucked inside suggested that this Dr. Ficino may be a resident here. May I leave it in your care?"

Peaches nudged me. Angelo was now stumbling through the front doors. "Must have caught a cab. See you upstairs," she whispered before bolting.

I watched as Dr. Ficino—slightly wobbly, definitely limping, and hastily smoothing strands of thin hair back across his skull—arrived at the desk. He spoke Italian to the clerk, requesting money to pay for his cab. He'd been robbed, he said. When he caught sight of me, he blanched like a ghost.

"Why, could this be the man on the driver's license? Yes, I'm sure of it. What a stunning coincidence that we're both in the same hotel," said I. "Dr. Ficino, I'm Phoebe McCabe." I pumped his hand enthusiastically. "You think you were robbed? But I found your wallet near the Duomo and had just this moment left it at the desk. Sorry for checking inside but it seems that you have both cards and money in there so it can't have been a robbery, correct? You must have dropped it." I beamed my full set of teeth at him. "Just careless-ness. It happens." I shrugged.

Dr. Ficino seemed at a loss for words. "*Sì, grazie,*" he mumbled.

"You're welcome. Aren't you glad there's a few honest people left in the world?" I headed for the elevator, waving at him as I went.

Minutes later, I was on my way up the lift, congratulating myself for a job well done. Sometimes the smallest thing delivers the biggest punch of satis-faction.

But I needed to shower and change before our dinner meeting. However, first I stood in my room checking my messages. Not surprisingly, a text from Rupert was at the top of the list.

Rupert: *You would tell me if there was any excitement afoot, wouldn't you? It wearies me to be sitting about on recliners by the pool in Capri all day. I could use a dose of excitement. RF*

I replied at once: *Dear Rupert, enjoy your vacation. We are here on the business Nicolina told you about. No need for you to rush away from your recliner just yet. PM*

And then as if they'd planned a relay between them, in came a call from Evan. Admittedly, my heart gave a bit of a leap when I saw his name on my screen, but otherwise I answered with restraint. "Hello?"

"Phoebe, I see that you engaged the stun app at 6:36 this afternoon. What are you up to?"

He could not only track the use of every application activated on one of his super smartphones but knew the exact time, too. "Just incapacitating a stalker with the stun app, Evan. Works perfectly, thank you very much."

"Good, glad you like it. What kind of stalker?" he asked.

That voice. "What kind? The one that follows behind you, of course. You know they are a dime a dozen in our business. All's good now, though. Nice to hear your voice, by the way. Are you enjoying Capri with Giani?"

"Actually, I need to return him to his mother. As soon as I drop him off at the train station tomorrow, I thought I'd meet up with you in Florence."

Yes, tempting—strolling the streets of Florence with a handsome, charming, fascinating, and adoring man. "Great idea but we'll probably be finished up by then. Oh, sorry—have to run. Talk later." I pressed End and stood there feeling as guilty as hell. He deserved better. Maybe I did, too.

Seconds later he texted: *You don't fool me.*

Damn. Pulling myself together, I headed for the shower. As much as I was strongly attracted to the man, thought him wonderful in every possible way, and teetered on the edge of desire every second of every day, I steadfastly resisted the temptation. My heart was still not open for business.

Twenty minutes later, I emerged fragrant with the complimentary bath products, donned my hydrangea print Gucci blouse, snatched my Ode to Melancholy wrap from the chair, and proceeded down the hall. It was almost eight o'clock.

Nicolina was sitting by the window swathed in a long blush-colored silk shift. Nearby, the table had been set for dinner with fresh flowers arranged in a Majorca bowl. A fragrant breeze stirred the air.

"Phoebe, I am glad to see you. That blouse does suit you. I will buy you one from this year's collection. Did you have a good day?" she asked, rising.

We exchanged summaries of our day's exploits where I learned that the Uffizi experts did, indeed, believe that our sketch was a probable Botticelli. Of course, they would not easily commit to an absolute statement since it remained unsigned but at least the possibility remained strong.

"Do they think that the sketch is a study and that there may be an existent painting somewhere?" I asked.

"No word on that. When they see the letter, they might think yes. We will leave the sketch with the Uffizi unless we find evidence that it should go elsewhere. And this Angelo is truly a doctor?" She was as surprised as we were.

"Apparently."

I checked the time on my phone. "Where are Seraphina and Zann?"

Nicolina poured us each a glass of wine. "Seraphina texted to say that she had lost sight of Zann just before three o'clock this afternoon and attempts to locate her still."

I stared at the wine glowing gold in the glass. "That's not good. On the other hand, Zann did say that Baldi wouldn't easily give away his location."

When a knock came at the door, we both turned expectantly but it was only the servers delivering dinner, Peaches sweeping in behind them.

"Howdy, gang," she greeted, now dressed in a long floral sleeveless silk dress that furled around at her ankles, all pink roses on an inky blue background. She twirled around, exposing her new strappy sandals. "Dolce and Gabbana, very midnight gardenesque." She beamed. "Saw it in a window today on sale so dashed over and got it this morning. You like?"

"I like," I said.

"It's beautiful," Nicolina agreed.

Peaches stopped mid-twirl. "Of course it's beautiful and I look like dynamite—a mirror image of Beyoncé or maybe Naomi Campbell, since she's Jamaican, too—just in case that was on the tip of your tongues. What's with the long faces?"

We waited until the servers left before answering, one of them whispering, "Bellissimo!" to Peaches on the way out.

"Seraphina and Zann are missing," I said.

"Zann is missing and Seraphina looks for her," Nicolina clarified.

"Well, damn." Peaches did not sound too concerned as she helped herself to a glass of white wine from the silver chill bucket and checked herself out in the venetian gill mirror. "Those two can take care of themselves but maybe we really should get Zann an Evan phone while on the case. That way we can track her properly. Are we doing white wine tonight?"

I did not mention the call from Evan to avoid a lecture on missed chances, a few good men, etc. However, when I had told Nicolina earlier she understood my reluctance completely.

Half an hour later, we were still sitting around the table picking at our salads, waiting. It was almost nine o'clock when the door flew open and Zann lunged into the room, Seraphina at her heels. We sprung to our feet, our questions dying on our lips as Zann collapsed on a nearby chair, refusing to meet our eyes.

"I found her," Seraphina said, sounding winded, "in back alley."

"You did not *find* me," Zann said, glaring up at her. "I was coming toward you when we collided."

"You were on ground!" Seraphina insisted.

I stared at Zann—a bruise under her eye, a cut lip, a ripped shirt. I crouched in front of her. "What the hell happened?"

"What do you think happened, Phoebe McCabe? I didn't give boss man what he wanted." She glared. "So he had me roughed up." My look of shock made her emit a strange coughing laugh. "Did you think Baldi was some kind of self-help guru? This is what happens in the world I live in: if you don't deliver, you pay."

"What were you suppose to deliver?" I asked.

She stared at me with one eye, the other nearly swollen shut. "You asked somebody at the Laurentian Library about Medici manuscripts today, apparently."

"I did." *Silvestri.*

"So Angelo informed Baldi. I was supposed to know what you were after but didn't have a clue, did I? I'm supposed to be infiltrating the agency so how come I didn't know what you were up to? he asks. Was I holding out on him? When I denied knowing anything, he slapped me around."

"Shit," I said.

"I told him nothing. He still thinks we are off to Volterra to check out a lead on the Botticelli tomorrow but now he suspects there may be a connection to Lorenzo de' Medici. After keeping the letters secret from him for years, you threw him a lead."

"Damn," I whispered, blaming Silvestri but, deep down, realizing I was the guilty party.

"I will kill him," Seraphina growled.

"Look," Zann said, gazing up at us each in turn. "This may not be the first time Baldi's hit me but I swear to God it will be the last. Tomorrow we'll find that Botticelli and leave the bastard in the dust. If you do manage to kill him along the way, I'll consider that a bonus."

9

_____

The next morning was spent preparing our various disguises and alternative identities. Typically, Zann had planned every last detail right down to wigs and clothes that had been smuggled up to our rooms. By 11:30 a.m., four people who looked vaguely like us trying not to look like us left by cab for Volterra.

"You've got to be kidding. That was a man dressed up like me," Peaches protested after peering out behind a potted olive tree on the roof garden.

"Baldi's men don't know that," Zann said as we gathered in Nicolina's room later. "Those guys are looking for a six-foot black woman with a topknot wearing purple leggings and a tunic with a matching mask—check. She's accompanied by a willowy elegant Italian woman and a short snippy-looking sidekick with cropped hair—check times two."

"Snippy-looking sidekick?" Seraphina glared.

Zann ignored her. "Baldi's men have the descriptions I gave them. They'll follow that car to Volterra, as planned. Meanwhile, the three of you will make your back-door exit."

Which they did an hour later. Nicolina, Seraphina, and Peaches left out the delivery door to sneak away in a cab to their bogus workplaces, leaving Zann and me to prepare for our own getaway.

The moment they exited, Zann turned to me. "I have FaceTime with my dad in ten minutes. I really want you to meet him."

Minutes later, I was gazing down at a man sitting under an umbrella on a patio in a large garden. Seated in a wheelchair, the man seemed alert and eager while, in the distance, I glimpsed other seniors in groups or reading in the sun.

"Hi, Dad," Zann greeted him, holding her tablet so that we could both see the gentleman with me remaining in full view. "This is Phoebe McCabe. Remember me telling you about her?"

"Phoebe, how very good it is to meet you at last." He peered at the screen to get a good look at me while Zann avoided the camera completely. "Suzanna has told me so much about you and all the wonderful things you do for the preservation of art and antiquities. Stellar work. Brava." He softly clapped his hands.

"Thank you and lovely meeting you, too."

I planned to tell him more but Zann quickly intercepted. "Have to cut this short, Dad. We have work to do. Talk soon."

"Good bye, darling!" he called as she hit End.

"Well, that was abrupt," I said as she slapped the cover of the tablet closed.

"I didn't want him to see my black eye. I'll make it up to him next time. Besides, we have to get ready."

"How much did you tell him, anyway?"

"Not much. Just that I was helping you with something."

I soon forgot about Masters senior as we went into camouflage mode.

I stared at my image in the mirror, now transformed by a straight blond shoulder-length wig, sunglasses, and a tiered pink sundress that made me feel like a birthday cake. The wide-brimmed sun hat and bright pink lipstick ensured I was almost unrecognizable even to myself. I'd always dreamed of iron-straight hair. Now I realized that might look best on an iron-straight body. The only piece of the outfit that was mine was my undies and the capri leggings I wore under the dress. "And you say we're from New York?"

"Upper New York state—no raspy New York accent necessary. If anyone asks, say you went to school in Canada. Mixed North American accents always throw the Italians off." Zann was leaning toward the hall mirror applying thick foundation over her black eye. A bit of makeup sleight of hand had all but covered the evidence of the prior night but I knew her wounds lay much deeper. Otherwise, her black bob and chic ensemble made her look like the polar opposite of her usual self—sophisticated, pampered, and rich rather than beaten, wily, and desperate.

"I don't know how you stuck with Baldi as long as you did," I remarked, studying how the woman flipped from battered to gorgeous with a few props. Maybe Noel calling her Simonetta wasn't such a stretch, after all.

"Because I had no choice, obviously. As Nicolina said, he'd kill me if he knew I was leaving him. May still. I figured that if I waited long enough, one day I'd see my escape hatch."

"And here I am."

"And here you are," she agreed, straightening.

"But there are bits that still don't make sense. For instance: supposing we manage to retrieve the hidden painting without Baldi finding out and even get it to the authorities without mishap—unlikely but possible. You then get your redemption photo and your father is happy, you're happy. What then? Baldi says 'win some, lose some,' shrugs, and goes on about his business as if nothing ever happened, leaving you to live happily ever after?"

She smiled lopsidedly. "What's your point?"

"My point is that it doesn't add up. Your impressive planning only goes so far before falling into a mess of unanswered questions."

"Obviously, I do my planning in stages. First, accomplish this task, then worry about the aftereffects."

"The aftereffects being certain death? Unless I'm totally misreading Baldi, he doesn't sound like the forgiving sort."

"He isn't."

"So you must have a plan since that's how you work. Tell me your endgame. How do you plan to escape Baldi?"

She dug her hands into her hips. "I told you my endgame: get the Botticelli and achieve redemption for my dad."

"Baldi isn't going to let you just walk away."

"What do you think of the bag and shoes?" Turning, she staged a slightly wobbly walk across the room in her red high-heeled Ferragamos, the matching bag swinging from her fingers. I inwardly cringed at the bill she'd present us with at the end of all this. "We're going as two women who can afford to shop a swath through Florence. Everything comes from a second-hand shop but they don't need to know that. And we're sisters."

"Sisters?"

"Yes, Peggy, sisters. You can call me Sandy. Oh, don't look so surprised, McCabe. We are all sisters under the skin."

I wasn't about to wade into that one. Meanwhile, I hadn't ruled out the possibility that she was still working for Baldi and that this was all a ploy. If she was working for him, that would explain her reluctance to disclose her final plan. On the other hand, if Baldi already knew about the Medici papers, why not just steal everything from the Corsis and be done with it? And surely with the experts he had on the payroll, they, too, could piece the puzzle together leading to the possible Botticelli. Where did we fit in? At the root of it, I believed she really was after redemption and some part of me was cheering her on. That didn't mean that I trusted her.

"So, are you in a relationship with Evan Barrows?" She was standing in front of me now, studying me from under her glossy bangs.

The question took me by surprise. "Why?"

"Why not? Aren't we two sisters talking about guys? Isn't that what sisters do?"

"We're not sisters," I said carefully. For an instant, I glimpsed another facet of her complex personality: loneliness. My circle of women friends must seem like an impenetrable clique in her eyes but I was determined to maintain my boundaries without being unkind. "We're tentative colleagues, at least for the duration of this case. Personal questions don't apply, but just for the record, no, I am not in a relationship with Evan Barrows. Why do you ask?"

"Just curious. Wondered if you ever recovered from the Noel debacle."

"Recovering from a bad relationship doesn't necessarily mean jumping into a new one—at least not right away. There's a certain power in remaining in my own orbit."

She smiled with difficulty. "I get that. You're kind of like my hero. After you tasered that bastard, I thought: 'Now there's a woman who doesn't let them grind her to the ground.' I've studied you, kind of like a fangirl but not in any creepy way." She was grinning now, her still puffy lip slightly destroying the effect.

"Being held at gunpoint in my bedroom fits the creepy category, just so you know," I said. "Why so interested in my love life?"

She crossed her arms, now standing with her legs spread, again completely ruining the fashion plate mode. "Even after I was over Noel, I still wanted to kill him."

"Then you weren't over him."

"I am now because you killed the bastard for me. Wish I'd seen it, wish I'd been hovering over your shoulder watching him writhe in the dust. Did he writhe in the dust, by the way?"

"He literally never knew what hit him. Look, Zann—"

"Too bad. Anyway, he's off my radar for good now—done, toast! I'm moving on with my life. Once we find the Botticelli, I'll be free."

"About Noel—"

But she was tapping her watch. "Damn! We're here gabbing away without watching the clock. We've got to get down to the delivery bay. It's almost time."

So we hastily grabbed our bags—I had briefly traded my textile backpack for a large couture Fendi bucket bag that held a night's worth of necessities in the interests of disguise—and made our discreet path down the back stairs to the basement level.

And yes, I could have forced Zann to listen to the facts about Noel's probable nondeath but I didn't have the heart. Let her live with the belief that he was gone for a while longer. Just because I had to carry the burden didn't mean she did or at least not right away.

We arrived at the basement level, a route Zann must have plotted out in advance since it involved weaving between laundry bins and sneaking behind shelves of complimentary toiletries and she performed it with practiced efficiency. We then had to wait in a storage closet until we could descend unseen yet another flight of stairs to the wine cellar. There, loading bay doors opened to the back of a panel truck, were four guys standing around talking and smoking.

"They're already here," Zann whispered.

Tugging me behind a corner, we huddled out of sight watching as the men chatted. Two I gathered from the uniforms were hotel staff, the others the Corsi delivery crew—young men in their early twenties. Though I could only hear every second word floating down the hall, I caught enough to know that the topic centered on women and sex. Apparently Nico, the driver, went out the other night with a girl named Bianca, whom all the men knew about. He took her to his grandfather's farm and they drank wine and drove around on his Vespa until... His voice dropped. His companion, Markus, howled with laughter.

I poked my head out far enough to catch a few lewd gestures and see Nico being slapped on the back.

"Same old same old," Zann whispered, pulling me back. "The 'boys will be boys' shit."

We listened for a few minutes longer until we heard bottles clinking. "Finally. They're exchanging full cases for the empties. Once that's done, Nico and Markus will go to the back room with the other two, belt back a shot of something—probably grappa—and then hit the road. This is their last stop of the day."

She'd obviously been checking these guys out for a while. I didn't have time to protest the drinking and driving bit because in seconds we were slipping across the concrete loading bay while the sounds of laughter bellowed out of a back room. Up the loading ramp we scrambled, Zann removing her heels and padding up in her bare feet. Mine weren't full heels but strappy dressy numbers but I removed them just the same. It took almost a minute to make enough space between the cases to slip through to the back.

At last we settled down on a ledge of boxes while trying to organize the surrounding cases in such a way that nothing would topple on us should the van brake suddenly.

"Won't they notice that the boxes have been scrambled?" I asked.

"Doubt it," she said. "It's Friday afternoon. They'll just want to get home after this. Nothing back here but empties, anyway."

It was stifling in there. I leaned against the back of the cab wall, fanning myself with a map I'd stuffed into my bag.

"It will cool down as soon as the van starts up and the air-conditioning kicks in."

"They air-condition the back of a wine truck?"

"Heat destroys the wine."

That made sense. Luckily, I'd had prior experience with traveling in the back of trucks so expected it to be more about endurance than comfort. I'd brought water, a sweater, a change of clothes, a pair of sneakers, a gun (Nicolina had finally convinced me), my decoy phone along with my real phone, and an assortment of overnight necessities.

"Did you buy a burner phone?" I whispered.

"No time, remember? I got beat up before I had a chance. Shh. Here they come," Zann warned.

We heard laughing. The back door slammed shut plunging us into total darkness. Then the engine rumbled up and we lurched forward while a radio blasted Italian pop music loud enough to vibrate the walls. The guys seemed to be singing along. This was going to be a long ride. According to my GPS, at least an hour and a half of back-of-truck endurance training.

With all that noise, talking was out of the question, or so I thought. Only I had that niggling sense that I had forgotten something critical. A battery charger? Check. Extra ammo. Check. I ran down my mental list confident that I had packed every necessity. So what was I missing?

"So have you given up on men?" Zann asked after maybe forty minutes of stop-start city driving followed by a stretch of smooth road accompanied by blaring music.

I had been tracking our route on my phone's GPS so knew we were somewhere between Bagno a Ripoli and San Casciano. I couldn't bear to imagine all the scenery we were missing. "Pardon?" I could see her profile in my phone's screen light.

"Men, have you given up on them after Noel?"

Back to my love life again. Why did this keep coming up? I turned away and sighed. "No, I haven't given up on anything. I'm just taking a break, I said." The next step was for me to ask the same thing of her but that would only open a proverbial can of worms. "And you?" Blame boredom.

"I don't waste my time anymore. Women are so much more interesting, don't you think?"

For a moment I didn't answer. "Interesting people exist in all genders. You already know that so I'll just add that I'm still attracted to men. That's not a judgment, just a fact."

"Okay, thanks for the honesty. What about Peaches?"

"You'll have to ask her but she seems very interested in the opposite sex, too."

"Nicolina?"

I couldn't believe she was considering us as a dating source. "I have no idea. Again, you'll have to ask her. Haven't you tried a dating app?"

"I don't do dating apps—too tricky in my business. Anyway, she probably wouldn't be interested in the likes of me. Glad that we can talk openly." She stared straight ahead. "It's hard finding partners in our business."

Our business—were we in the same line of work? We kept quiet after that, lost in our own thoughts, but I swear that the music grew so loud that even thinking became difficult.

An hour or so later, the truck jerked to a stop, the engine cut, and the back door flew open all in a matter of seconds. We sat stone-still as the guys began lifting the cases from the back, the light slicing through the stacks bright enough to make my eyes water.

This was the moment I'd worried about and I'd even rehearsed a stow-away explanation. Only twelve cases remained between us and the open doors when somebody shouted Nico's and Markus's names. Crunching gravel followed as the two guys headed off. I caught Italian for "pile of trouble."

"What's happening?" I whispered.

"I arranged for the boys to get a phone call from the cops. Don't worry, it's bogus. I hired a guy to call. Should give us enough time to get out of here."

She'd thought of everything.

In minutes, our stiff legs were taking us down the loading ramp. We donned our shoes and scrambled across a graveled drive up a pathway between tall cypress trees beside a modern building painted a butter yellow with wraparound glass windows on the upper floor. To the left, I could just see a cluster of gray stone buildings tucked behind a wall far off on a wooded hill while behind us rolling hills of vineyards could have come right out of a Tuscan tourist brochure.

"This is the wine tasting center, a new building the Corsis put up maybe ten years ago to handle bus groups and the like," Zann whispered. "Wasn't here when I knew Piero. He was always big into modernization but his father resisted. Up there is the Corsi villa and hamlet."

"The medieval walled village," I whispered, looking up. I did my homework, too.

"The Corsis renovated all the old cottages up there into B and B rooms over the years. Did you check the website?"

"Thoroughly," I assured her. "Those walls are thirteenth century and Dante is supposed to have visited the hamlet after being exiled from Florence. Can't wait to see it. The villa itself is considered a recent addition."

"Yeah, the fifteenth century is so yesterday."

"Is that medieval tower I see where the Medici holdings are hidden?"

Zann turned to peer up into the trees. "Providing the Corsis haven't moved it. It's thirteenth century, too, and looks to be a ruin but that's all a facade. We'll check it out later. Now we've got to blend in with the wine tasters and plant ourselves here for the evening."

This part of the grounds was practically deserted. The only person we saw as we wound our way toward the front of the building was a man watering flowers. We pretended to be lost and merry tourists as he pointed us farther up the path beside a march of potted olive trees.

Nodding and laughing, we followed his directions until we arrived at the front where a tour bus stood parked in a gravel parking lot amid cars and three vans. No sign of a catering or musical troupe van in sight but they probably parked below.

"Shit, we're late," Zann said while hastily reapplying her lipstick. I didn't bother.

The sound of a woman's voice projected through a microphone led us to a set of huge double wooden doors where a young man stood guard. He smiled behind his black mask as we drew near, a grin that grew wider after Zann produced her tickets for the event. I glanced down at the stubs surprised to discover that the wine tasting extravaganza cost two hundred euros each.

"Are they serving caviar with a side of gold-embossed truffles?" I whispered as we swept through the doors.

"Probably," came her answer. "Have to pay for the entertainment and food, remember."

Inside, a spacious wood and concrete facility blended a touch of old-world high beamed ceilings with gleaming stainless-steel modernity. About thirty-five people stood in six-foot intervals around two wide concentric marble and steel counters placed steps below the other, theater-style. Between these curved counters, three young uniformed women delivered wine samples to the guests while another described the offerings in both Italian and English from a raised dais at the front of the room.

Zann and I were directed to our own bit of marble real estate where we were permitted to remove our masks. Each person had a little sink for spitting the samples as well as our own little tray of snacks—bruschetta, smoked salmon, something that looked like mushrooms on top of cheese...

I leaned toward her. "Would you recognize Baldi's men if they were here?"

"Maybe, maybe not. I don't know everyone—big operation. Besides, how could they be here so soon?"

I pulled back and studied the treats. Suddenly, I was starving but tried not to shove the tidbits in my mouth without pretending to sample the wine first. I objected to spitting out beautiful wine in principle but these tastings had their protocols.

"The finest Sangiovese grapes anywhere in the world," the hostess was saying. "These grapes are Chianti's hero. I invite you to sample our 2018..." Let me just say that that vintage was particularly delicious.

I watched as a young blonde woman delivered an inch of rich red wine to my glass next. Another vintage tasted with relish—exquisite—and duly spat it into the sink before devouring my tidbit of porcini on bread. Six more wines came along with six more snacks plus a sampling of the family's own limoncello and even olive oil. I probably swallowed once or twice but I'm sure liquor is absorbed through one's tongue by osmosis. Otherwise, I couldn't explain how relaxed I suddenly felt.

By now everyone was chatting and laughing across the spacing protocols, a sure sign that some of the brew had gone down the proverbial hatch. The German family to my left were toasting me. Zann was requesting a refill of her favorite vintage. Our server complied while directing her to the shop next door to buy her very own bottle after the tasting ended.

Meanwhile, this sip and spit dance went on for almost an hour longer while I studied my fellow tasters from the corner of my eye—a mix of national and global tourists including Japanese and Kenyan, judging from their accents—a good mix, one big happy international family. Hopefully international criminals weren't among the guests.

Once all the vintages were sampled, a hush descended over the room as an attractive man probably in his early forties stepped into the circle to stand beside the hostess and welcome us all again to his family winery—Piero Corsi.

I almost choked on my last bite of bruschetta. The man was gorgeous, as in film star gorgeous, with a charming graciousness as smooth as his family's Chianti and just as intoxicating. His English was impeccable, no doubt well-practiced along with his hospitality.

"My family is delighted to have you as our guests. Consider yourself our friends this night as I invite you to proceed through those doors to our gardens where the evening's entertainment will continue under the stars. A magnificent Tuscan feast has been arranged for your dining pleasure, which I hope you will enjoy as our guests."

Paying guests, that is, but why quibble? I watched as the attractive Piero swept his elegantly dressed self—caramel-colored linen slacks, an open-neck long sleeved shirt, and woven leather loafers that hinted of money worn casually but with great style—out of a set of glass doors toward a back corridor, ushering his slightly tipsy clients along with him.

I caught Zann's eye and grinned. "You gave up on men before you tried life with that one?" For a moment I gazed at her, shocked. I couldn't believe I'd just said that. How superficial, as if I regarded men as mere objects. "That's not me talking," I said quickly. "That's a society-conditioned fossil embedded in my cranium floating up from the alcohol."

We gazed at one another in silence before she burst into laughter. "Have you been knocking back the samples?" she asked.

"No!" I think I may have, actually. Read the part above about osmosis. I took a swig of the complimentary water and followed her out the door.

Outside a huge curved patio with potted olive trees, fountains, and vine-covered pergolas looked out over the family vineyards. For a moment all I could do was stand and inhale the view—rolling hills punctuated by rows of cypress trees, an old chapel tucked away in the distance, along with other villas and wine estates amid the rolling hills. Here was quintessential Tuscany, so beautiful that one could almost believe that it had been magically staged for tourists while knowing that was impossible.

The sun was hanging low in the sky and somehow I'd ended up with another glass of vino in my hand when I set off looking for Zann. In the time it took me to inhale that scenic vista, she had disappeared.

Weaving through clusters of laughing guests, I followed the sounds of an orchestra warming up. There, under the shade of a raised pergola-cum-stage, Peaches could be seen dressed in a sleek black suit with pants far too short for her long legs, chatting with a tall bald black man who was setting up a kettle drum. Slipping into a vine-shrouded corner, I waited until I caught her eye. In seconds she was beside me.

"That's Luigi, the drummer—great guy. The man standing in the tux is Mario," she whispered. I glanced toward the barrel-chested gent in the bow tie who appeared to be spritzing his throat. "He's from Siena and tells me he's multitalented and can sing anything, including opera."

"Wow, and modest, too. Have you seen Nicolina or Seraphina?"

She grinned. "They were here when we arrived. Try the kitchen. I tell you, before the night is over, I wouldn't be surprised if Seraphina doesn't stab somebody with a fork and Nicolina may swoon from being forced to serve the minions. What are you doing with a glass of wine in your hand?"

I glanced down at the glass. "I'm not even sure how it got there."

"Well, that's not good, is it? You need to stay away from that stuff, woman. You're like a fairy who gets knocked over by mere fumes. Give that to me. Go find some coffee. Luigi's going to teach me how to play the cymbals now. Catch you later." She took the glass from my hand and strode away toward the band.

Minutes later, I followed one of the servers through a set of automatic glass doors into a spacious kitchen where Nicolina was being passed a silver tray of tiny bruschetta bites. Dressed in a navy-blue cotton uniform with a matching cap and apron, she was almost unrecognizable. Turning, she caught my eye, lifted her chin, and swept past me without a word.

"How's it going?" I whispered, following after her.

"This uniform scratches," she said. "How do they stand this? Cheap clothes! For more hours I will be scratched to death. Pink is not your color."

"Do you know where they're serving coffee?"

"Not until later. Before then we eat."

She swept off to deliver more bruschetta while I slipped up a set of stairs to a large empty dining room overlooking the vineyards. From this vantage, I could gaze down at the guests, at the view, and even glimpse the family hamlet far up on the hill. Imagine owning a thirteenth-century hamlet, even if it had been now converted into an inn?

What really interested me lay up there, not at this wine-infused Tuscan production. Still, I had more hours to play this game before we appeared at our lodgings and revealed ourselves to Piero. I was eager to do a little reconnaissance in the meantime. So far, everything appeared to be going according to plan. Presumably Zann was keeping an eye out for Baldi but now I had to keep an eye out for Zann.

I found her on the patio, circulating among the guests. "All the hired hands have been paid and I walked right by Piero and he didn't recognize me," she whispered. "Saw Seraphina in the far pergola growling at a customer who dared ask for a wine refill."

I laughed. "So we made it here without Baldi knowing. Good planning." Only, I still worried that I had forgotten some crucial detail.

"We're not out of the woods yet. Just heard from my contact that Baldi's thugs now know Volterra was a ruse and are gunning it back to Florence. Just pray that we kept our tracks well-hidden until we get what we came for tonight."

"Which is?"

"Who knows? Something about Botticelli."

I left her to stroll around the patio. By then the fairy lights strung through the pergolas were glowing, lanterns flickered around the space, and groups were claiming their tables for the Tuscan feast to follow. I found my name with Zann's—Peggy and Sandra Masters, both of us divorced and returning to our maiden names—and took my seat across from a young newlywed Dutch couple. A pair of married guys from Verona arrived just as the band struck up a medley of instrumental pieces. Soon Zann joined me to chat with our table mates while I listened in to our supposed backstory.

"So you are both divorced sisters on a trip together and your friends join you also?" Vincent from Verona asked in broken English, and flashed me a bright smile. If possible, he was even more stylishly dressed that Piero.

"Right. They'll be along later." Zann sipped the house Chianti while flinging an arm around my shoulders. "Pegs here is just the best but both of us were dragged through a wicked divorce. This trip is a promise to ourselves. Bet you have better divorce laws in Holland and Italy compared to the US."

Ria cast a shy grin at her husband. "We are just married so we don't know these things. Divorce, what is that?" Gales of laughter.

"We had to be married in Denmark," Vincent explained. "Laws not so good in Italy—very Catholic."

And on it went. I learned that I was a real estate agent and Sandy an accountant, fascinating details of a life we hadn't lived. I hoped I could remember it all if the time came.

The setting was magical, the company fun, the music superb, and the food that began arriving delicious—ribolita, pici with duck sauce, tortilla stuffed with pears and pecorino cheese with butter and sage, pappardelle with boar sauce… By the time the warm chocolate pudding arrived, I was done. One really can have too much of a good thing, even in Italy.

Zann was chatting about motorcycling through Europe when I plotted my escape. Excusing myself, I took my glass of limoncello and drifted across the flagstones, my gaze fixed on the walled hamlet above. Like all these old buildings, the stone was uplit by spotlights tucked along the base and, again, like everything in Italy, the aspect was divine.

Drifting to the edge of the patio, I gazed up through the trees just as a full moon rose above the tower and Mario burst into tenor magnificence. I followed the perimeters of the patio until I found a lit path leading up through the trees. By that time I was beyond caring about anything but that path.

Halfway up the trail, I slipped from my stacked heels into flat sandals and carried on, my limoncello still in hand. Mario, a powerful tenor, was singing a song I recognized from Andrea Bocelli—*"Sogno"*—and if I listened closely, I could just hear a cymbal reverberate at every passionate crescendo. The moon was riding high above the trees and I was a little drunk. Now you'll understand why I diverted from the plan or maybe you don't even care. At the time, I certainly didn't.

The lane took me to a smooth dirt road that carried on up the hill and, between the music and the wine, I may as well have been floating. I arrived at the ancient archway that opened onto a narrow cobbled street winding through a cluster of stone houses. Lights were embedded into the walls every few hundred feet. The buildings were rustic, many multistoried, and built of warm sandy-colored stone with red doors and window boxes spilling spotlit geraniums. Clearly the basic structures were rustic medieval, cleverly restored to both capture the ancient spirit of the place while still accommodating the modern traveler. The Corsis knew what they were doing.

I could just see the main villa ahead. A lovely fifteenth-century cream stucco building with a top-floor porticoed balcony and an ivy-covered watch-tower of its own, every second window alight. The only thing that indicated this was a hotel was the discreet bronze sign almost lost in the ivy by the front door. I presumed one entered the open arches to register inside but I kept on walking. No one seemed to be around.

Since we were to be the only guests that night, I wasn't concerned about bumping into anyone and, if I did, I was merely a resident checking out the place. Zann had emailed the desk to say that we would be along later. Of course, they would be expecting many more guests than the handful that would eventually arrive.

Mario was singing *"Canto Della Terra"* as I followed the cobbles around the villa toward the medieval tower. Passing more little houses, an ancient well, a building labeled *Olive Press* in two languages, and a little stone chapel, I finally arrived close to the tower or as close as I could get.

For a moment I gazed up at a six-foot wall. The tower was in an enclosed walled garden. That's what the map on my phone said. Unlike the rest of the hamlet, which seemed to keep every door open, the garden was not only gated but locked. Odd.

I didn't need to touch the door to recognize an electronic mechanism. I engaged my phone's X-ray app and ran it over the lock. As I suspected, it was alarmed. Next, I activated the infrared app and ran it along the wall, confirming that it was strung with the equivalent of an electronic tripwire.

Backing away, I stared up. Appearing deceptively ruined, I could just detect what looked to be signs of a plate glass inside one of the tiny arrow slits near the tower's crenellated roof. Not so ruined, after all.

I actually considered deactivating the alarm and breaking the lock, but even with my tools, it would be complicated—breaking into the gate and the tower door, trying to locate the secret room, all dressed in a sundress even though I wore stretch capris underneath. Better to wait. Besides, the moment I used that app, Evan would be notified and did I really want to draw Evan into the action? Well, honestly, under a Tuscan moon while being serenaded by a tenor, the combination of Evan and action held a certain allure but for all the wrong reasons, all the wrong action.

Something like a branch cracked behind me. I swung around, staring hard at the deserted path. Lights fixed near the corner of each building illuminated everything in sight and the doors directly in front of me were flush with the wall. No place to hide. So where did that sound come from?

Switching on my motion detector app, I strode down the lane.

1 0

$\mathcal{I}$ swept the enhanced camera feature back and forth across the cobbled lane, the radar grid forming bright green lines across the screen. No red heat signature detected. Running the app three hundred and sixty degrees around me revealed the same—no warm-blooded creatures within range, either, not even a cat. Apparently I was alone in this part of the hamlet, yet I didn't believe that. Still, I had things to do.

Keeping my phone open, I returned to scrutinizing the tower. But the sound, whatever it was, had jolted me from my stupor. I couldn't afford to be lulled by wine and Tuscany and I couldn't afford to simply break into the tower unless it was absolutely necessary. We had planned a more under-the-radar approach for a reason and I needed to return to the plan. Besides, breaking into the tower would be messy. That could wait.

I sent a text to Peaches and copied it to Nicolina: *Am up at the hamlet and will wait for you there. Doing reconnaissance. Pls let Zann know in case she goes looking for me.*

Messaging Zann directly was impossible since she hadn't picked up a burner phone. Peaches did not respond immediately, presumably because she was busy playing the cymbals with Mario, but Nicolina got back to me right away.

Nicolina: *Back in my own clothes and now a guest. What do you seek?*

Me: *Anything relevant. Will catch you later.*

That done, I scoped out the hamlet. It was small by any comparison—a cluster of ten stone buildings enclosed by a twelve-foot-high wall with one rough cobbled street curving up through the gates, past the villa to the tower garden, and down around the other side. Plenty of little lanes jutting between the buildings plus storage buildings and a garage, an overview gleaned from the Corsis' handy website map.

All of the cottages were lit as if waiting for guests to arrive so I checked every one, counting a sleeping capacity of at least twenty. Each building was different. Some had two stories with bedrooms and lounges, others were tiny with a cozy bedsit arrangement. All had kitchens and modern bathrooms but otherwise the beamed ceilings and simple country furniture kept the rustic mood alive.

I peered into the olive press with its floor-to-ceiling windows revealing a dining room with tables and counters. The map labeled it as a breakfast room. Not much of interest there. Next, I tried the chapel door, finding it locked. That surprised me. Why lock a church when all the resident rooms with their stocked amenities were left open? Of course, chapels weren't churches, exactly.

Unlike the tower, entering the chapel seemed relatively easy. After one quick check around using the intruder app, I dug inside my bag for my tools and was about to pick the lock when I realized that it wasn't as straightforward as I expected. Instead of a basic cylinder lock, this one had a sophisticated combination mechanism meant to be disengaged by both a code and a key. That usually meant an alarm, too, but why alarm a chapel?

Now I had to see inside, regardless of the consequences. Scrolling through my super phone's apps, I located a key-shaped icon. Here was a deactivating device designed to send a jolt into the system to disengage an electronic alarm.

In seconds, I had scanned the phone over the lock, which caused something to beep multiple times before going silent. Good. Next, I picked away at the lock until a satisfying click followed. Done. Then I grabbed the handle and pulled the door open, noting that the heavy oak was spring-loaded and would slam shut the moment I let go. I propped the door ajar with a loose cobble and slipped inside. Dropping my bag several pews in, I voice-commanded the flashlight feature to engage.

And gasped. This rustic thirteenth-century stone chapel with its single nave and wooden trussed ceiling held an extraordinary secret: every inch of wall had been covered in once-brilliant frescos, some of which had almost completely flaked away. Angels and saints below, Mary and Jesus above, plus a gathering of richly robed citizens making a procession along the lower walls toward the altar.

The style of the clothing, as faded as it was in places, retained enough glorious detail to peg the citizens as fifteenth-century Florentines, meaning that the entire procession must have been painted at least a century later than the chapel's construction. Though it was not unusual for exceptional frescos to dazzle the interiors of simple country chapels in Italy, I had never known one to depict wealthy Florentines so far from home. And the clothes were extraordinary.

I stepped closer, magnifying the surface of one of the ermine-lined robed men who was bearing a gift of a gilded box. Further along almost at the altar stood a woman represented in profile, her head flaked away but standing straight-backed, hands folded demurely over her waist, and wearing a magnificent gold embossed giornea or sleeveless overdress over a gown of shimmering cream silk. Most of the sleeve had disappeared but for a tiny bit by the wrist—a tantalizing glimpse of a triangular motif that could have been embroidered and accented with pearls. My eyes dropped to the tangled jeweled vine trailing along her gown's hem.

Briefly, I forgot to breathe. The clothes indicated the work of a master tailor who employed every possible guild to embellish his client's garments but it was no less a feat to depict that glory in the first place.

Along the procession, men were garbed in what must have once been brilliant red cioppas or cloaks lined in fur. Though it was difficult to tell in a painting so faded, I guessed that those crimsons were kermes dye, the most expensive dyestuff available at the time. The Florentine republic had an entire hierarchy based on the color red alone and only the wealthiest citizens were permitted to wear it, let alone afford that deep kermes dye in the first place.

More women followed behind the men, each adorned in unique ways, some young maidens with flowers in their hair and simply dressed, others probably married with their hoods thrown back to reveal stunning headdresses including the strange horned hats popular among the nobility. Most of these were citizens of wealth showing their clothes as proof of their standing, marching around the base of a tiny rural chapel in the woods dressed in as much splendor as could be seen anywhere between Florence and Rome.

Yet, as one grew closer to the altar, some of the clothing simplified. Still lovely, still intricately embroidered, but made of what appeared to be plainer fabrics—wools instead of silks, no rich damasks, and very little fur. The frescoed surface of many procession members had been so badly flaked away that only their legs showed and the man standing beside the yellow-robed lady had nothing left but a pair of red legs. Both their faces looked deliberately eradicated as if chipped away.

And then there was the background—tangled trees in a strange fantastical forest. I could see a similar landscape to what currently surrounded me—rolling hills and what could be the hamlet itself way up on a wooded hill—but what about that stack of books tucked away under rocks, branches growing out from the pages? And was that Zephyr and Flora running through a field of flowers toward the gathering with Mars swooping down from above as if late for a party? What was going on here in this amazing scene?

Stepping back, I swept the light across the walls while taking several deep breaths to still my thumping heart. I couldn't believe what I was seeing: to find a fresco by a Renaissance master disintegrating in a tiny chapel far from an urban center. Who was the artist? I had an idea, of course, but my guess made no sense.

I began taking pictures and even ran a video all around the walls until my phone began flashing a low battery warning. Bad timing but at least I had a charger with me. The phone went dark just as I'd finished photographing the nave. Behind me, the propped-open door provided enough light for me to find my way back to my bag, that is before it slammed shut. I was halfway down the aisle when it happened.

For a moment I stood stunned. I'd tested that door; there was no way it could shut by itself. And now I stood in total darkness with a dead phone. Someone had deliberately shut me in but why? Unless my stalker planned to blow up the chapel with me in it, locking me in could either be a warning or an attempt to get me out of the way. I had to alert the others.

I shot up the aisle, counting every row until I reached the third pew from the door where I'd dropped my bag. After fumbling seconds, I gripped my battery recharger. It took more fiddling before I could get the attachment into the tiny port and then all I could do was wait for the charger to do its magic. It would take at least fifteen minutes before I could get enough juice to send a text, but in the meantime, my team could be in danger.

Setting the charger on the pew, I grabbed the handle and shook the door until it rattled. My app had broken the electronic current earlier and deactivated the alarm, something that couldn't be restored without the alarm company. That meant that someone had physically barricaded me in from the outside. No amount of pushing could budge the thing.

Shit! I swung away and paced the floor, panicked over what could be going on outside. After a few moments of senseless fretting, I realized that Mario had stopped singing, that there were sirens blaring away from somewhere down the hill. I started calling for help, yelling at the top of my voice, even while knowing it would be useless. Whatever was going on at the bottom of the hill would detract from a faint wailing up here.

I stopped that and hovered over the phone waiting for the red flashing light to turn green. The moment it did, up popped a text from Peaches. *Where the hell are u? Bloody chaos down here!*

I thumbed an answer: *Up on the hill locked in the chapel. Somebody shut me in. What's going on?*

Peaches: *Lots of guests are being rushed to the hospital—suspected food poisoning. Nicolina and Seraphina are looking green around the gills but they're not as bad off as some. We're all waiting around to be questioned by the police. As soon as they finish with us, we'll be up to get you out.*

Me: *And Zann?*

Peaches: *She's sick, too, but not as bad as the rest. They think it was one of the canapés. Everyone who ate them got sick—something porky with a spicy Italian name. The band didn't get a chance to eat anything but most of the servers did and plenty of guests. They're all busy retching now. It's a mess. The Corsis are in a panic. How'd you get locked in a chapel?*

Me: *Long story. Just get here as soon as you can.*

I sat down in a pew to wait, thinking that the food poisoning event couldn't have been an accident. Someone deliberately tampered with the canapés as surely as they locked me in the chapel. But why? Because they needed to get my team out of the way. Baldi had to be on the premises because nothing else made sense.

A message from Evan came in: *I suppose you'll try to convince me that using the lock deactivator is a perfectly normal day in the life?*

I typed my reply: *Considering the business we're in, yes, but I'm currently barricaded inside a thirteenth-century chapel with a brilliant fresco possibly by Filippino Lippi to keep me company. How far away are you?*

Evan: *Approximately twenty miles to the south.*

Me: *Arrive undercover. Somebody got to us first.*

As usual, the man had perfect timing.

11

---

*P*eaches and Zann released me from captivity about an hour later. The door had been barricaded by a huge potted olive tree that must have taken two men to budge.

"Who the hell did this?" Peaches asked, gazing around. She'd just run a quick reconnaissance around the hamlet but found no human activity except inside the villa.

"The same people who poisoned the capicola, I told you," Zann said, leaning against the wall clutching her stomach. "It's Baldi. I thought for sure he'd never track us here but he must have had his dogs on our heels all along. Damn, damn, damn!"

Her wig askew, clothes rumpled, and lipstick smeared over one cheek, it was safe to say that her disguise was slipping.

"Where's Nicolina and Seraphina?" I asked.

"At the villa. Nicolina insisted they be taken to a suite inside the main house to recover. Got them run off their feet," Zann explained.

Peaches grinned. "She mentioned something about a lawsuit so Signora Corsi seemed more than willing to give her anything she wanted."

"She almost played the countess card until Peaches gave her the look. We've got to go there now to get ready for the big reveal," Zann said. "Can't waste a single moment in case Baldi—oh, crap, not again. Excuse me: got to run."

We watched as she lurched over to the opposite cottage and bolted through the open door. The retching sounds that followed made me think she might not have made it to the bathroom.

"Won't be staying at that one," Peaches muttered.

"Any idea who the poisoners might be?" I asked.

"Nicky said that a couple of kitchen helpers disappeared halfway through the evening—a man and a woman."

Minutes later, a wan-looking Zann stumbled out of the cottage. "Sorry 'bout that. Jeez, I only had one of those damn canapés." She had straightened her wig and reapplied her lipstick. A wet spot damped the front of her chic little dress. Looking down, she added: "Spillage. I tried to get it all out."

"Didn't you bring a change of clothes?" I asked.

"Just jeans and a tee." She glanced down at her dress and shrugged. "Considering what just went on down there, they probably won't even notice. Let's get to the villa."

Gripping our bags, we strolled up the lane, scanning in all directions as we went. "Baldi's crew must be lurking around here somewhere," Zann whispered. "They'll be after you, Phoebe. He's always wanted to kidnap you and force you to disclose everything you think you know about the sketch."

"Think I know? Did he say that?"

"Yeah. He's afraid you've sniffed out something he hasn't yet. Drives him nuts."

"But why didn't he take me when he had the chance? I've been locked in that chapel for over two hours."

"Probably had their hands full with the poisoning bit. That must mean that the bastard only has a skeleton crew here and isn't on-site himself yet. Must have sent his minions as a last-minute thing once he realized what I was up to. This has all the signs of a rushed job. What happened down the hill was messy and Baldi doesn't like messy."

"If Baldi's only got a handful of men here and hasn't yet arrived, we still have a chance to get what we need and bolt, even if we've already got two of the team down," Peaches said.

"That must have been the idea—-poison our crew, including me—but I blew the plan by coming up here. The poison can't be fatal, just incapacitating," I mused.

"Yeah, sounds like Baldi: knock you off your feet and then kidnap you. When he kills you, he prefers to take his time. Must have sent his minions in a tailspin when you went off script." Zann was angling her phone so she could see her face in selfie mode. "I look ghastly. Okay, ready?"

We had arrived at the villa entrance and spent a few minutes adjusting our disguises before entering. Peaches had already changed into her own pants. Straightening our various couture accessories, we stepped into the villa's foyer just as a maid dashed out, arms filled with what I guessed to be soiled linen.

Zann caught sight of the slender woman with the brown curly shoulder-length hair and frazzled expression standing in the hallway first. "Signora Corsi, hello. We are your guests for the evening—Peggy and Sandy Masters and our friend Lulu. We have reservations. We were just down at the gathering."

Signora Corsi had been turning one way and then the other as if unsure what to do next. About thirty-five and slender, she wore a sheath dress and high-heeled sandals perfect for a soiree under the stars but not so much for managing a household full of retched guests. At first, she barely glanced in our direction. The sound effects coming from upstairs explained her distraction.

"Signora Corsi?"

The woman swung toward us, hands clasped before her as if trying to hold herself together.

"I said we're your guests, the Masters from New York?" Zann repeated.

Signora Corsi looked startled but quickly pulled herself together. "You were at the Wine and Starlight event, yes? I am so very sorry. This has never before happened. My husband, he is with the police now but the caterers are the best in Tuscany. How could such a thing happen?"

"All very odd," Zann agreed, stepping forward. "You have two others from our party staying upstairs."

"The countess?"

So Nicolina had reverted to her true identity. "Yes, the countess," Zann agreed. "How's she doing? Not too good by the sounds of things. I so sympathize."

"Very bad in the stomach. We call a doctor who says what to give but he says she will be fine after she…purges."

I considered paying her a visit but, considering the noises coming from upstairs, decided to wait. Knowing Nicolina, she'd rather not be seen until after the intestinal drama was over. So far, she hadn't even answered my texts.

"Show us to our rooms so we can freshen up after our ordeal," Zann demanded. There was an urgency in her tone that made me think she may be on the verge of another digestive event herself.

"Of course. So strange. Everyone they just cancel last minute and then you book. Happy you are here, of course, though not such a good night in the end, yes? Leave your passports, please, and we will show you to your rooms." She was already turning her attention to the two young boys—ages somewhere between ten and fourteen, I guessed—who had just entered the foyer. She spoke quickly to them in Italian, the equivalent of *Go back to your rooms, please.* The boys turned and left the way they had come.

Peaches and I exchanged glances. We had forgotten that hotels in the EU are obliged to collect passport information from each guest before registration and, of course, our pseudo identities wouldn't match. Zann, however, looked as if that was the least of her worries. She was back to clutching her stomach.

"Paola?" Signora Corsi called. A young woman appeared from behind us wearing a staff name pin. "Please show our guests to the Forrestere. I hope you are comfortable there. Paola will take good care of you. Please ring us if you need anything. Now, please excuse me for I must check my husband." Signora Corsi dashed away with a phone pressed to her ear.

"We'll be back later for the cocktails," Zann called after her.

"Cocktails?" Peaches whispered.

"In the brochure," Zann explained.

The young woman standing before us smiled. "I am sorry for the problems. Please give your passports and I will register and then take to your cottage."

Zann threw up her hands. "You've got to be kidding! I've just been barfing my brains out because I've been poisoned and you want me to hand over my passport? I need a shower, and unless you want to mop up the hall next, you'd better take us to our rooms now!"

The young woman's eyes widened. "Um, yes, of course. Follow me."

In minutes we were led to one of the two-floored stone buildings just down the path from the main villa. I'd checked it out earlier—three bedrooms and a separate lounge with a huge fireplace and very rustic furniture everywhere. Paola had no sooner delivered us through the door when a cell call sent her dashing off again. Zann had already bolted upstairs for the bathroom, slamming the door behind her.

"That one's going to need some extract of wild strawberry leaves to settle her stomach. I saw some on the way up the hill," Peaches remarked. "I knew that her best-laid plans would capsize pretty fast."

I was pacing the room, my technique for thinking being motion-activated. "As soon as Piero returns, we'll gear up for act two."

"With Baldi's thugs hiding somewhere?" Peaches was digging around in her bag.

"Evan's on his way and, with a little luck, Piero may help us locate what we're looking for, especially once he hears about Baldi."

Peaches paused her rummaging. "Evan's coming?'

"Yes, he texted me."

"How far away is he, exactly?"

"I didn't have time to look but not far."

"I'll check the group map feature." Phone in hand, she opened up her own Evan super smartphone, tapped an app shaped like five little heads, and up popped a map. I gazed over her shoulder at the two green dots heading from opposite directions toward the big green dot that I figured must be our location. "He's somewhere just outside the closest town and it looks like Rupe is closer still."

"Rupert's coming? Good, we need all the help we can get."

Peaches put away her phone and pulled a pile of neatly folded clothes from her bag. "What are we looking for, exactly?"

"I still don't know." I caught her eye and stopped pacing. "Okay, so everything is a long shot but there are plenty of strange skeletons rattling around in the Corsi family closet. I think they may hold a key to the missing Botticelli, whether they know it or not. That chapel has what's left of an extraordinary fresco by Filippino Lippi, or I think that's the artist."

Peaches whistled. "Isn't that the guy who was a priest and kidnapped a nun?"

"That's probably the most audacious story in Renaissance art history. Everyone seems to know it but you're thinking of his father Fra Filippo Lippi."

"Seriously?"

"Fra Lippi did become a bit too up close and personal with a nun, one Lucrezia Buti, but thanks to Cosimo de' Medici's intervention he ended up marrying her. Filippino, their son, was also a master painter. He's the suspected artist of the frescoes I just saw and, furthermore, Filippino was once apprenticed to Botticelli. Sort that one out."

She stared at me. "Filippino and Botticelli were connected and that artist's son who was Botticelli's apprentice may have done a fresco in that teeny-weeny chapel?"

"He was a prodigy. Apparently he was painting masterfully at only twelve years old."

She gazed up the stairs. "Makes you wonder what was in the water back then. And the only thing differentiating the handles of father and son were a couple of letters? And they call Jamaican names quirky. I'm just going to place my clothes upstairs in whatever bedroom is closest to the door. Keep talking."

"Confusing, isn't it? Plus Botticelli had once been an apprentice in the father Filippo's workshop when he was young, too, so there are double, *triple* connections," I said as she ran up the stairs.

"What's it all mean?" she called down.

"That's what we need to find out. Hopefully Piero can tell us."

In seconds, Peaches was back in the lounge. "Right, so I've got to get the extract of wild strawberry to Nicolina and Seraphina before some Italiano doc pumps them full of the equivalent of intestinal cement. I'll make some for Zann, too. While it steeps, I'll do a once-around the property and keep an eye out for Evan and Rupe. Meet you at the villa later," she called on her way out the door. "I'll text when I see Piero arriving."

"Wait—do you have your phone charged? I got caught out in the chapel."

"Charged it while I was with the band—I've also got my gun and knife, too. Don't worry about me. You two watch your backs on your way to the villa. Keep your intruder app on."

I saluted her as she dashed out of the building. Now I had a few minutes to brush up on my research. Thankfully the Wi-Fi was worthy of any urban connection. By the time I'd finished, Zann had emerged from the bathroom looking considerably better than she had when she'd entered. She quickly put her wig into place, only now wore her own clothes instead of the couture props.

"I know I messed up," she said while reapplying her makeup. "Baldi must have had a tracker on one of us. Can't think of any way he'd have tailed us otherwise. I've been racking my brain trying to figure out how this happened."

And then it hit me. I jolted up from where I'd been propped on the arm of a chair. "He *was* tracking you. We forgot to debug you after you returned from Baldi last night. Peaches, Nicolina—all of us—are automatically debugged by our smartphones. Not you. Damn!"

She turned. "Had you debugged me earlier?"

"Of course. I do it every single time I'm in your presence, but after last night's excitement, I forgot." I began running my phone over her person, her bag—everything. Predictably, I found two trackers, which I ground into the terrazzo-tiled floor. "Damn. Damn. Damn."

Her shoulders slumped. "It's not my fault, then. I don't want any more blame on me, you know?'

I stared at her. "Anyway, it's done. The important thing is to get what we need and out of here before Baldi comes down on the Corsis, that is if it's not already too late. Are you ready? It's 10:15."

By the time we arrived at the villa, Peaches had texted to say that all was clear with no sign of interlopers. She also informed me that she had dosed Nicolina and Seraphina with her natural medicine and had left a cup of extract for Zann in the kitchen. *I'll take one more trip around the hamlet before joining you. Oh, and Piero is back home now*, she added. *Lots of strange bird calls around here. Do you know anything about Tuscan birds?*

Not in the ornithology mood, I texted back. *I know the Tuscans used to eat song-birds as a delicacy.*

They just dropped a notch in my books.

Zann and I entered the villa expecting more of the agitation witnessed earlier but it was as if the Corsis had mustered their resources to appear as if normalcy had been restored. I pitied them.

Paola ushered us across the vaulted hallway into the salon, a gracious butter-colored room with a modern frescoed ceiling softened by lamplight. Piero and Alexandra Corsi sat together on a brocade love seat opposite another couch and four easy chairs. A low table set with glasses and snacks sat in the midst of the seating. At the sight of us, Piero released his wife's hand and rose.

"Ladies, welcome," he said, stepping forward with a dazzling smile. "I apologize again for the unfortunate events of this evening. The police believe it to be sabotage by two servers who have since disappeared. They give chase now." He spread his hands, his expression shifting to chagrin, every nuance enhancing the man's good looks. "Our caterers believe that rivals from another event company must be the cause. It is regrettable. It is also criminal, and I assure you that those responsible will be met with the full extent of the law. Meanwhile, we ask that you allow us make this up to you. A glass of wine perhaps, a bite to eat?"

I couldn't bear the thought of more. I thanked him but helped myself to a glass of water.

"Yes, please help yourselves," Alexandra added, now radiant in a loose rose-colored silk top and skinny jeans. "I was very upset when you arrived. I hope I was not rude. It was just so distressing."

"Of course," Zann said brightly as she took a seat. "No problem." She waved away Alexandra's offer of wine and sweets with a grimace. "Water's just fine with me, too." She helped herself to a small bottle of the fizzy water provided.

"Actually, we need to speak with you, preferably in private." I looked around the large room which probably served as a guest lounge. "Could we shut those doors?" I pulled the double doors shut without waiting for permission. When I turned, Zann was sitting across from the Corsis staring at Piero.

"I don't understand," Piero said, gazing from Zann to me. "Why must we speak in private?"

"You don't recognize me, do you, Pietro?" Zann said.

No, no—this was not how I saw this unfolding. I stepped over to sit beside Zann, placing a warning hand on her arm.

"Sorry for the intrusion. We're actually undercover agents assisting a police matter," I said, not quite truthfully. "We are attempting to locate a lost Botticelli, the key to which we believe may lay in your Medici library. The only reason we entered in disguise was because there's a criminal element after the painting, too. We need your help now. It's urgent, but I promise you, we're not here for any purpose other than to retrieve information. I apologize for dropping this on you now but I'm afraid that time may be running out."

Piero had gone ghostly pale. "How do you know about the Medici library? Who are you?"

"I'm Phoebe McCabe and—"

Zann pulled off her wig. "And I'm Zann. Don't you recognize your old flame, Pietro? It's me, your little Suzanna."

The man looked stricken. "Suzanna?"

"Who is this Suzanna?" Alexandra cried, looking from one to the other. "What is going on?"

"It's complicated," I began, trying to calm her. "I'm Phoebe McCabe from the—"

"Suzanna Masters?" Piero was on his feet. "You dare come into my home after everything you have done to me and this family?"

Now that was unexpected. Apparently time does not heal all wounds.

"It's not what you think, Pietro," Zann began.

"Stop calling me that! I am not your 'Pietro.' You stole from me and now you return to take the rest, is that it?"

"I didn't intend to break your heart. It's just that Noel—"

"I do not refer to my heart but the letter you stole from my father's library. How dare you return here. You were extradited from Italy and now you return to finish the job?"

"That's not what happened or what's happening now," Zann protested. "I always meant to return the letter and now I will. We're here to track down what I started before Noel Baker—you remember Noel, don't you, the bastard who stole my sketch? There's a lost Botticelli portrait hidden somewhere and those letters of yours hold the key. I intend to clear my name for my dad's sake."

Now Zann was standing, too, the hair plastered around her head giving her a somewhat deranged appearance. Meanwhile, Piero strode toward the door and Alexandra glared at each of us in turn.

"I will call the police immediately! You will not steal from me a second time!" Piero threw open the doors.

And there stood Peaches holding a mug with Rupert Fox standing at her side.

"Good evening, dear chap," Rupert said, extending his hand. "I am Sir Rupert Fox of the Agency of the Ancient Lost and Found. Would you happen to have a spare room available tonight and possibly a pot of proper British tea for a road-weary traveler?"

12

---

*R*upert pumped Piero's limp hand like he was trying to pump air into a tire. Piero stood frozen as if in shock. "I daresay this all comes as a bit of a surprise, dear chap, but there is a bit of urgency to our presence. I have it on good authority that your premises have been infiltrated by unsavory individuals who mean you harm. Indeed, those involved in the food poisoning incident are undoubtedly from the same nefarious clutch. Now, do you mind terribly if I take a seat so we can discuss this more thoroughly?"

Piero stepped back, his mouth agape as he watched Rupert take a chair next to mine.

"Do join us, Signora Corsi. We have much to discuss," Rupert added mildly while helping himself to a plate of cheese and crackers. "Not the tainted snacks, I presume?" He smiled at Alexandra, who vehemently shook her head.

Piero walked back to the couch. "You had better explain quickly before I call the police, sir." He was still standing.

Behind him, Peaches shut the door and passed Zann a mug of brackish liquid. "Down the hatch," she whispered.

Rupert turned to Piero. "The police have already been made aware of the situation. You do know that the Agency of the Ancient Lost and Found are affiliated with Interpol, do you not? As for the explanation, it is a bit complicated and best digested with a calm disposition and a side of tea. Please do sit lest I develop a crick in my neck, there's a good chap."

Piero returned to his spot on the couch, his wife having now scooted to the opposite end as if putting as much space between them as possible. Zann leaned toward her and whispered, "It was a long time ago," but Alexandra only averted her eyes.

"Excellent, thank you," Rupert continued. "You have heard of the Agency of the Ancient Lost and Found, have you not?"

Piero hesitated. "That is a television show, yes?"

"Oh, perish the thought!" Rupert pitched his voice to his most Oxfordian sounding vowels. "We are an agency established for the retrieval of lost or stolen works of art, and quite famous, I might add. Surely you've heard of the lost crown of Prince Carlos or our recent work in Venice? We made the international headlines. Indeed, the renown Phoebe McCabe sits right before your eyes," he said while unfolding a cocktail napkin. He shot me a quick look and frowned.

That would be Phoebe McCabe in the blond wig, electric pink lipstick, and frothy candy-colored dress. My credibility factor had taken a nose-dive. "We haven't had much of a chance for introductions after Zann revealed her identity but I—"

"Providing background, that's all," Zann said after downing the last of Peaches's elixir and making a face. "Sorry for dropping a bomb on you like that, Pietro, but I promise that I'm not here to steal. I'm working with the agency to solve a mystery and we need your help. When the countess revives, she'll pass you the letter. I gave it to her for safekeeping. Forgive me for everything that went down long ago, okay?"

Alexandra sprang to her feet. "Would you like tea, Mr. Fox? I will get it."

"Oh, yes, thank you, and it's Sir Fox."

But Alexandra had already swept from the room while Zann remained fixed on Piero. "I was young and foolish but I never meant to steal from you so much as borrow that letter to help me locate the Botticelli painting."

"Is that supposed to excuse your actions?" Piero asked.

"Probably not but please hear me out. I know the portrait exists. I tracked down the sketch that creep stole from me and one thing led to another and here I am. I need to retrieve that painting so that my dad will know the truth. He didn't deserve any of that stuff that went down years ago. You know that, don't you? He is a good man." Her voice hitched.

Piero remained silent.

"He and your dad were such good friends, remember?" she pressed.

"A friendship that you betrayed," he said between his teeth.

I jumped in. "We have reason to believe that there may be more letters similar to the one Zann borrowed that may lead us to the portrait's hiding place," I said quickly. When Zann tried to interrupt, I held up my hand. "Your Medici library may hold clues, and if you know of other letters written to or by Botticelli, I'd appreciate you letting us view them. In fact, anything referencing Filippino Lippi could be of interest, too. Please trust us. We mean you no harm."

Rupert turned to me. "Filippino Lippi?"

I held Piero's gaze. "The Corsi family's private chapel appears to be decorated with an amazing fresco possibly by that artist. At least, he's the only Renaissance painter I know to have had such a unique way of capturing the clash between paganism and Christianity so rife in this period of the Renaissance. His backgrounds are animated with mysterious trees growing from books and mythological figures appearing to dash across the fields to join what looks to be a Christian procession. The fresco may have been painted between the years 1485 and 1487 when Savonarola was stirring up religious unrest in Florence in response to the wave of classical knowledge flooding the homes of the nobility. It could be an important work, though badly in need of restoration."

Piero stared. "You broke into my property and ask for my trust?"

He had a point. "I apologize but there is such a sense of urgency in this matter that I couldn't waste a single moment. The criminals Sir Rupert referred to followed us here—in fact, they chased us through Florence trying to kidnap me and abscond with the sketch Zann located long ago. Here, this is a photo of that sketch recently assessed by experts at the Uffizi who believe it may be an authentic Botticelli. It's in their hands now."

I passed over my phone and watched as Piero studied the screen.

"Since this may have been hidden during the artist's lifetime, there's a good chance that a corresponding painting may be hidden, too," I continued. "As you know, a Botticelli portrait is worth a small fortune on today's market and a ruthless bunch of art thieves would do anything to obtain it. We want to ensure it is preserved for all."

A deep anger simmered in his eyes. He passed the phone back. "And to obtain a portion of Lorenzo de' Medici's library also. How much would that be worth to these thieves or to you, Phoebe McCabe? My family have guarded this collection for centuries and you bring them to my door!" He leaped to his feet. "I want you off my premises immediately. I will take my chances with those criminals but I will not tolerate hosting your variety of crook under my roof for a single moment longer."

"Crook!" Rupert said, affronted. "Dear fellow, name calling is most unnecessary. We have only your best interests in mind, I assure you."

Piero picked up the house phone from the side table and in seconds was striding away saying, *"Polizia? Pronto polizia?"* over and over again. Halfway across the room he stopped and turned back to us. "You have cut the line?"

"Not us," Peaches answered. "Don't you have a cell connection? Landlines are so passé."

But Piero was pounding the buttons on his phone like he wanted to shake it into operation.

"Signore Corsi, do not be hasty, I implore you." Rupert was on his feet now, too. "These types are not to be trifled with and the local constabulary is ill-equipped to deal with their insidious ways. We are gathering resources as we speak. Please exercise patience."

"Patience?" Piero glared at him. "You want my library and now ask for my patience, too?"

"We don't want your library," I assured him, "just a chance to study it, honestly."

He scoffed, whether at the honestly part or my entire statement. "It has been my family's secret for decades—no, centuries—and she betrays my confidence a second time!" Piero said, pointing to Zann.

Then the doors flew open and in came Paola carrying a tray of mugs and a teapot with Alexandra following close behind. Catching sight of her husband, she stopped and hissed something in Italian. I thought I caught the words *miserable lying swine* or an Italian equivalent thereof. In seconds the couple darted from the room arguing all the way.

Peaches turned to Zann. "You just love to contribute to domestic bliss, don't you?"

Paola set the tray on the table and made a hasty exit, too, shutting the door behind her and leaving the four of us alone.

"I daresay, Phoebe, had you handled this differently we might be much better positioned to convince this family of a good intent," Rupert said, gazing down at me, his bristled eyebrows giving the impression of colliding caterpillars.

Yanking off my wig, I freed my curls from captivity. "Okay, so maybe I should have alerted you sooner but I truly thought it was straightforward… until it wasn't. Everything happened very quickly. Where's Evan?"

Peaches peered at her phone. "He's nearby, as in very nearby, but for some reason he's staying undercover. The tracker points to him somewhere beyond these walls."

"The lad will remain hidden until he can attest to the exact location of Baldi's gang," Rupert said, heading for the tea fixings. "He is using strategic maneuvering based on his extraordinary MI6 training and will guard the perimeters accordingly. Actually, he is testing a new device that creates an electronic fence around the walls. I must say, Phoebe, I cannot believe that you have run afoul of Andre Baldi, the most notorious arms dealer and drug lord in Italy, possibly the world."

Peaches caught my eye. "I filled him in on the details," she said.

I watched Rupert pour each of us tea whether we'd requested it or not. "Then I presume you know also about Suzanna Masters. Allow me to formally introduce you: Zann, this is Sir Rupert Fox, one of the members of our agency, and, Rupert, this is Suzanna Masters—"

"—one of the members of Andre Baldi's gang," Rupert said without looking up. "Yes, I know you by reputation, Ms. Masters, and admit to being alarmed when I heard that you were involved with our team."

"And she whacked Seraphina with a thermos and held Phoebe at gunpoint," Peaches added with grin. "Our kind of gal." I shot her a look but she only shrugged.

"It wasn't loaded," Zann protested.

"What, the thermos?" Peaches quipped.

"And were you not responsible for the appalling plunder of Afghanistan's Roman ruins and more recently took part in the heist of the Temple of Neptune on Corsica?" Rupert asked, eyes fixed on his mug.

Zann, who was just beginning to regain her natural color, lost it all over again. "When you are working for Baldi, you do what Baldi tells you. I was obeying orders."

"And now?" Rupert asked.

"And now I'm not. Now, I'm getting out from under the rock he's shoved me into for years. Finding this Botticelli is my only chance. I must succeed."

"You mean *we* must succeed, don't you?" I asked. Without waiting for a response, I turned to Rupert. "Did Peaches fill you in about Noel, too?"

"Indeed." Rupert took his first sip and sighed. "Never as good as English tea, of course. The Italians fail to grasp the finer nuances of brewing the proper cup and no doubt left the bags in the pot entirely too long, but to your question, yes, Peaches explained the distressing news that Ms. Masters also had an entanglement with Noel Halloren or Noel Baker. My, but that boy did get around."

So Peaches had left the critical part for me to tell.

"Entanglement—is that what you call it?" Zann began. "More like—"

I held up my hand. "I'm not just referring to the unfortunate romance but to the fact that Toby has alluded to the sketch during a recent phone call and in our letters back and forth. He called it a 'bomb,' Rupert, a *bomb*. Now I realize why."

"Indeed, it appears as though your brother may have had some inkling as to the location of the painting."

"That's what I think, too. All those years ago when Noel took off with the sketch, he must have left the portrait in its original location because he simply couldn't find it. I like that idea best. Bastard never could find the really challenging puzzles without me."

"Yes, that is what I am deducing," Rupert remarked. "Certainly the fellow had plenty of opportunities over the years to return to Florence and retrieve that painting or possibly smuggle it from Italy, but if he couldn't find it that explains why it may still exist."

"Maybe it's not even in Florence," Peaches said, "but someplace he couldn't easily access."

"Baldi thinks it's in Florence," Zann remarked.

"And how much does Baldi really know, pray tell? Rupert asked, turning to Zann. "Or could it be that he has not disclosed all his information to you, Ms. Masters?"

Zann dropped her gaze. "I have no idea what Baldi knows. He certainly didn't tell me. Bastard plays his cards close to his chest but that's not a luxury his minions get. He beats stuff out of you if he thinks you're holding back but deep down he also believes women will just crumble under him." She coughed a kind of laugh. "Blind macho stupidity or what? All the times he's slapped me around, I still never told him about that letter or the Corsi library."

"Then how did he discover it now?" Rupert asked.

"He tracked us," I said. "I found the tracker in Zann's purse but not soon enough to prevent this. He also had one of his minions ghost Peaches and me to the Laurentian Library yesterday.'"

"The point is that Baldi has people working for him who are totally cowed into doing things they wouldn't do otherwise. Some are hardened criminals, of course. Some are like me." Zann's head lifted, proud defiance flickering in her eyes.

"It's not easy being a 'Baldino', obviously," I remarked, liking Peaches term.

"It's hell," Zann agreed. "He practically beats his men senseless—cuts off their toes to make a point—but never the women. Us he just roughs up a bit. Thinks we'll capitulate that easily but I never did." A small smile crossed her face. "The whole time I've been plotting to steal him blind. I swear, he's not getting that Botticelli even if I have to die to prevent it."

We all gazed at her in silence for a few seconds. Rupert cleared his throat. "Yes, well, let us hope that no one needs to die in this situation. Now, back to Toby and Noel for a moment. Phoebe, did you mention something about sketches in your brother's letters?"

"More like cryptic doodles. I think Toby knows the approximate location of the painting, too, and has sat on the information for all these years—both of them have. If I could meet my brother in person, he'd tell me, I think, but so far he's just sending me doodles."

I handed him my phone where I'd photographed each drawing separately. Rupert stared at the images for a few minutes, turning the drawings in all directions. "How odd. Indeed, I recognize the style from his video game productions but these little rectangular creations almost look maze-like."

Peaches leaned over his shoulder. "Or like a knot garden. All those square compartments were a Renaissance thing, after all, but the rectangles within boxes baffle me. Is your brother into puzzles?"

"Definitely," I explained. "Toby's old video games were all puzzle-based but not like this. His designs were far more organic and this is more geometric. That's why I believe he's trying to send me a message."

"What about the maze idea?" Zann added, studying my phone.

"That's like no maze I've ever seen," I remarked. I pulled away and stood listening. "Anybody notice how the house has gone a little too quiet all of a sudden? We'd better fan out and check to make sure we know exactly who's here. Let's all meet back here in twenty minutes. Zann, you come with me."

I didn't want Zann's company particularly but I figured I might be the only one able to handle her, not that I'd managed that so far. Either way I considered her my responsibility.

"I'll check outside again," Peaches said.

"And I will seek out the Corsis. The last I heard, the couple appeared to be arguing in the kitchen and I heard the serving woman call out goodnight on her way out the door." Rupert patted a gun in his jacket holster. "Best to keep a firearm handy lest the villa has been infiltrated."

"Don't worry, I've got mine. Zann and I will check the upstairs. Keep in touch by text, everybody," I said.

We spread about the premises, Zann and I heading for the first landing.

"How well do you know the layout of this place?" I asked. The decor held the right balance of authentic fourteenth-century villa style and what was essentially a public place. Nothing could be easily pilfered from the huge Majorca painted vases to the occasional landscape print or decorative plaster.

"Doesn't look like they've changed much since I was here. Added a lick of paint, maybe. Looks like Alexandra may have brightened things up here and there. This is the floor with all the guest bedrooms. The top is the family quarters and the kitchens are on the bottom level with the lounge."

We crept down the hall, checking each guest bedroom, en suite bathroom, and wardrobe, all of which had their doors ajar. At the end of the hall next to a bathroom with lights blazing, we found Nicolina's and Seraphina's bedrooms side by side.

We entered Seraphina's first, finding the woman sleeping deeply in a comfortable but not luxurious bedroom. A lamp glowed on the nightstand where sat a collection of glasses and an empty sludge-lined cup. Her phone lay nearby faceup set on intruder mode, flashing "1 Intruder + Phoebe McCabe." At least her phone was active. I guessed the combination of concussion and poisoning would keep her in a deep sleep for hours longer.

Backing out, we tiptoed into Nicolina's considerably more spacious bedroom where I slipped up toward the pale figure on the bed. I only made it a few steps before the patient sat up and pulled a gun on me.

"Oh, good, you're awake," I said. "How are you feeling?"

"Phoebe?" The gun hand dropped and the other brushed away a lank lock from her forehead. "Very bad still but better. No more retching. Peaches's medicine is very effective. Never again I will tease her about those boiled leaves. What is happening?"

I filled her in. "We're going to continue checking out the villa and then try to convince Piero to let us into that library again. I don't want to have to break into that tower but I will if I must."

She leaned back against the cushions. "Maybe you should not wait. If Baldi is on his way, it is better to get the information now."

"Good point. First, we'll make sure that his honchos aren't here already and then I'll do exactly that, with or without Piero's help. Will you be all right?" I asked.

She waved her gun and smiled wanly. "Yes, for I am armed and dangerous."

"Never doubted it." I grinned and left her to rest.

A few moments later, Zann and I had checked every one of the bedrooms once again before heading up to the family's level. Rupert texted me that Alexandra and Piero were in the kitchen and that he would attempt again to urge them to cooperate. Peaches informed me that there were no signs of unusual activity—in other words, heat signatures—within the hamlet walls and that she was going to scout out the woods in the immediate vicinity. She had heard from Evan, who was still setting up his detector equipment. I needed to text Evan myself but that could wait.

On the top landing, we followed the sound of voices to the end of a corridor where we found the two Corsi boys lounging on a couch playing a video game. Zann flicked the ceiling lights and both kids leaped to their feet.

"Hi, don't be frightened," I said in very bad Italian. "We're here to help."

Zann refused to permit me to mangle another Italian sentence and translated after that. "It's important that you two be extra careful. There are some very bad men on their way here and maybe a couple on the property already. Do you have a place you can hide?"

The boys looked at one another. "We know places," the eldest said.

"Okay, great. At the first sign of trouble, run and hide, okay?" Zann held their gazes until the boys agreed, after which followed a battery of questions we didn't have time to answer.

"Are our parents all right?" one said.

"What do these men want?" his brother asked in English, which turned out to be excellent. I spoke to them directly after that.

"As soon as we can, we'll answer your questions," I said. "Right now we have to hurry to make sure these bad guys are not already hiding in the house, but yes, your parents are fine. How do we get to the lookout tower from here?"

The eldest kid, Enrico, delivered us to a staircase at the end of the corridor that was locked from the stairwell side. Apparently guests were welcome to use the stairway door from the guest level to take tea or drinks up to the tower balcony.

"There is nothing up there but chairs and a table. Shall I turn on the light?" he asked.

"No, thanks. We'll use our phones," I told him, waving mine around.

But minutes later, we climbed the narrow steps to the lookout tower finding it was just as Enrico said—empty but for chairs and a table, a lovely place for drinks on a summer evening. We spent a few seconds studying the view from every direction but saw no suspicious lights anywhere in the surrounding woods. The nearest village seemed far away.

I decided that this was the best time to text Evan. I hastily keyed in my message: *Where are you?* The response came immediately.

Evan: *In the forest behind the olive press. Just tracked down a man dressed in an apron attempting to scale the walls. He won't be poisoning anyone again.*

Me: *Dead?*

Evan: *Very. Don't worry, Phoebe, he had a painless end. I have an app for that.*

Me: *But he might have been some innocent minion obeying Baldi's orders.*

Evan: *If he's sneaking around this property armed, he's not innocent by my definition. I'm after the second one now.*

Me: *The woman?*

Evan: *Nicolina sent a description—slight build, short black hair, and female, yes. Criminals don't become less so by gender.*

Would he kill her, too? Had he ever killed a woman before and why in this age of female empowerment could I even think like that? I had to let it drop.

Me: *Meet me by the tower in fifteen. I've got to get inside that library and find those letters. The Corsis are not cooperative.*

Evan: *I'll be there.*

"I'll be there"—words that caused my heart to lurch, as if I had time for heart lurching.

"You want him to spare one of Baldi's gang because she's a woman —seriously?"

Zann was peering down over my shoulder again. I jerked away. "Stop that!"

"I just can't believe you're a bleeding heart over these assholes based on gender. I know most of the women on the payroll and they're ruthless bitches."

"Maybe some of these ruthless bitches are like you, Zann—some screwed-up woman who made one mistake too many and now can't break free. Being female can make it that much harder to escape in the power game."

That shut her up.

"Come on," I said. "We need to join the others."

The boys were waiting for us on the second floor. "We could stay guard up in the watchtower and let you know if we see danger," the youngest, Vincenzo, said. "Like in the old days, we could be the tower watch."

"Sure," I said, seeing a way to keep the boys occupied and possibly out of harm's way. "Lock the door, okay?"

"We will," Enrico said excitedly.

We air-dropped our contact information and dashed down the stairs to the lower level where Rupert was again sitting in the salon across from Alexandra and Piero. Though the couple were side by side, I could tell from their expressions that he'd made no headway with our request.

"Alexandra, Piero, your sons are in the watchtower keeping an eye out for intruders."

"The intruders are already here—you," Piero said.

I ignored that. "One of the poisoners has been captured by a team member while he was attempting to scale the walls. Another is still at large," I told them. "If you won't help me access the tower, then I'm going to do it without your help. We believe the mastermind is on his way here with reinforcements. Please reconsider. There's not much time."

Piero leaped to his feet. "You cannot possibly break your way into the tower! I have installed the most modern of security systems. You will fail but go ahead and try." He waved his hand. "I hope you are caught in the act when the police arrive."

I nodded. "I hope so, too. We could use their help. Rupert, would you keep the Corsis company? Nicolina and Seraphina are still recovering."

"Most certainly," he assured me.

"Excellent. Come on, Zann."

We left the villa but I held Zann back in the doorway. "Keep to the shadows," I whispered as I engaged my phone's detector app. Currently there was no way to run two apps simultaneously, such as activating the detector scan at the same time the laser feature was engaged or read texts at the same time as anything else. Frustrating. I made a mental note to remind Evan to keep working on that one.

The two of us crept along the edge of the villa avoiding exposure under the stark moonlight. Except for the cry of an owl and some little animal squealing in the night, all was still. We kept to the shadows until we reached the edge of the villa. At that point, we needed to dash across a narrow alley to reach the next block. Only then could we work our way down to the exposed lane that separated the buildings from the tower.

"How are you going to get inside?" Zann whispered as we paused to do a three-hundred-and-sixty-degree scan.

"Technology," I said.

"That phone of yours, you mean? I want one of those."

"Shh! We have company." The detector app had picked up movement ahead. I stared at the screen at what appeared to be a figure slinking through the shadows along the wall. My guess that it was female by the shape. Too short to be either Evan or Peaches. So where was Evan going to meet us? I switched over to the text feature and shot him a quick: *Where are u?*

Evan: *On the other side of the wall chasing some bastard with an AKA.*

Me: *An automatic rifle? Baldi must be here! I've just spotted somebody, too. I'll deal with that one.*

Evan: *My intruder circuit picked up two more. I'll get to you as soon as I can. Zap to kill.*

Zann was looking over my shoulder again. "Smart guy."

Switching over to the taser feature, I set the slider to the milder end of the spectrum. I'd knock the Baldino unconscious. "Here." I passed Zann my gun. "It's loaded. Cover me. I'm going out."

"By yourself? Are you crazy?"

"Just do it!"

I stepped under the moonlight, my eyes fixed on the deep shadows around the wall, phone held up before me. The phone was vibrating, alerting me that a text message that I had no time to read was coming in.

"Hello? Anybody there?" I spoke the inane statement deliberately: let the enemy think that you play in stereotypes so you can deal their assumptions an unexpected blow.

A figure stepped from the shadows into the silvered light. I blinked to make sure I wasn't hallucinating. A female action hero in camouflage? A leaf-patterned jumpsuit, goggles, and a single dark braid hanging down over one shoulder rounded out the effect. She could have climbed out of the pages of a video game but the assault rifle pointed at me looked deadly real.

"You are Phoebe McCabe," she said in a thick accent, possibly Eastern European.

"I am, and you are?"

"Irena. I take you now to boss."

"I am my own boss, Irena, and I have things to do. I'm not going anywhere. How many of you are there?"

She took a couple of steps forward. "You do as I say."

"I don't think so." I lined up the big red dot on my screen so that the beam would hit her mid-shoulder.

She laughed and lifted the rifle to aim straight for me. "What, you take picture now?"

Good, she didn't know about my super phone. "Is it okay if I take your picture, then? I mean, you're pretty amazing looking, like some super chick."

She grinned. "I like that—super chick. You take one more step, I shoot you but not with picture," Irena said.

"She won't shoot you," Zann called behind me. "Irena's been told to bring you in alive."

Irena's rifle swerved to the right. "Zany? You I can shoot!" But a shot blasted behind me, hitting Irena straight in the chest and knocking her over backward. The woman landed faceup on the cobbles, limbs splayed.

"What in hell did you do that for?" I cried, swinging around as Zann dashed from the shadows.

"She was going to shoot me!" Zann yelled. "You saw that. It was self-defense! You wouldn't feel so stricken if you saw what she did to that village in Afghanistan, she and her sister, Lana, who is twice as vicious."

I whipped the gun from her hand and shoved it deep into my bag. "If you'd stayed put I would have just stunned her. Goddamn it!"

"And she would have shot me eventually." Zann picked up the rifle.

"Leave it," I said.

"What, you leave assault rifles lying around now?" Zann was already holding the thing as if she knew how to use it.

Leaning over Irena, I checked for a pulse but I already knew she was dead, shot through the heart. Mental note: Zann was a crack shot.

At that moment, a gunshot blasted in the woods followed by another and another. I straightened, seared with anxiety for Peaches and Evan. No time to text them, either. Just in case I lost my bag, I shoved my phone deep into my bra, the thing still vibrating with incoming messages.

Zann held on to the rifle. "Hear that? We have to get out of here!" she hissed. "Baldi's arrived." She grabbed my arm and dragged me into the bushes.

"Head back for the villa," I whispered. No time to break into the tower now. Time for defensive maneuvers.

We were halfway along the side of the villa heading for the front door when a male voice barked behind us.

"Drop your guns!" British accent this time.

We froze and turned. Three men were marching out from the side lane, rifles trained on us.

13

_____

"*M*eet Peter Dunbar, super bastard," Zann whispered. "Baldi's praefectus castrorum, European division."

Baldi really did organize his team like a Roman army.

"Step out from the shadows, ladies," the man called. "Lay your guns and bags down and your hands up."

We did as we were told, stepping out under the moonlight. One of the three men—a thin red-haired guy—took my bag while a thickly built blonde hulk with a Viking physique complete with long braided hair whipped up the rifle. That left Peter Dunbar to study us from his position of power. It was a strange relief to see that at least he was not dressed as a Roman centurion but in jeans and a T-shirt.

He stepped forward, whistling through his teeth. "Still in your party dress, I see, Phoebe McCabe. And look at little Zany. So it's true that you've been working against us." Mid-thirties, short brown hair, boyish good looks, scar across his left cheek. "The emperor has been right all along. 'Someday Zany will be very useful,' he said in a mock Italian accent. 'She will reward us for our patience.' Right again. For the record, I didn't believe a word of it myself. I thought you were a liability from day one."

Zann spat at him. "Wrong again, Dunbar. You should start taking lessons on how to stop being such a brown-noser for once."

He smirked, but before he could respond, a woman dashed up behind him.

"They kill Irena!" she cried. "She is dead! They kill her!" She was sobbing hysterically, wailing at the moon like a runaway banshee.

I stared in disbelief. Here was a mirror image of Irena only the braid hung down her back instead of over one shoulder—same camo outfit, same everything. Twins. *Hell.*

Dunbar shot out an arm to silence her. The sobs switched off like a faucet. "Bloody tragic," he said. "Damn regrettable. Irena was a good soldier. Now pull yourself together, Lani. If you hope to have Baldi let you have your way with her murderer, turn off the waterworks. Which one of you ladies did the deed?"

Dead silence followed as the four of them stared down the two of us.

"Oh, come on," Dunbar said. "Baldi will get it out of you eventually. Much better just to 'fess up."

"Me," I piped up after a second, convinced that admitting that Zann had pulled the trigger would get her killed on the spot. Me they had to keep alive.

"Then I kill you." Lani lunged forward.

Dunbar held her back. "Discipline, girl. Now move, you two. We're off to see the boss."

Every rifle pointed at our backs as the men herded us forward like stray sheep, Dunbar whistling, *"We're off to see the wizard, the wonderful wizard of Oz..."*

I thought maybe we'd detour to one of the guest houses, but no, we headed straight for the villa. That wasn't good. In seconds we had crossed the threshold and were steered into the salon, gun muzzles shoving us along.

Inside we found Rupert sitting beside the Corsis with two men standing with combat rifles pointed at them. Two other men sat across from the hostages in armchairs, one of whom I recognized to be Angelo staring morosely at his hands. The other sat legs crossed, enjoying a glass of wine and smoking a cigarette, blowing the smoke up toward the painted ceiling. Seeing us, this one stood and raised his glass. This had to be Baldi.

"At last, here is Phoebe McCabe, who they say can find lost art like magic." The man grinned, revealing a space between his teeth. "The lost-art sniffer dog."

How did Baldi know that term? Had I ever once referred to myself as that publicly? It was my tongue-in-cheek name for myself.

"I am glad to meet you at last," Baldi continued. "You see I have your friends in my care and the two ladies upstairs rest comfortably with my men to keep them company. That leaves us to talk."

Baldi in the flesh was not what I expected. Blame word association but I thought he'd be bald. Instead, he had plenty of thick gray-streaked black hair growing in close-cropped curls against his skull. Wiry tuffs emerged from the top of his short-sleeved shirt and more crawled down his arms. About mid-height with a stocky build, I pegged him to be around fiftyish. The glint in his small dark eyes made me doubt that he had a compassionate bone in his body.

He ignored Zann as he stood sizing me up, dragging on his cigarette and blowing the smoke into my face. I coughed, trying to wave away the fumes. "Haven't heard the news yet that smoking's bad for your health, Baldi?"

"Haven't heard the news yet that crossing Baldi is very bad for yours, McCabe?" He laughed. Passing his empty glass to the skinny red-haired guy, he slowly walked around me, sizing me up like a prize cow.

"That one, Phoebe McCabe, she kill Irena, boss," I heard Lani say behind me. "Kill her dead!" she sobbed.

"Ah, too bad, so sad. Maybe I let you have her when I'm finished, my girl."

"But—"

"Silence!" Baldi continued to walk around me while Dunbar and his troop formed a line standing side by side in military formation.

"How did she make the kill, by gun or phone?" Baldi inquired.

"Glock G17 standard," Dunbar told him. "Don't worry, we disarmed her."

"If you did not take her phone, you did not disarm her. Where is the damn phone?" Baldi barked.

He was standing so close to me now that I could smell the nicotine on his breath. I stood still, hoping like hell he couldn't hear the phone vibrating in my bra. Zann was frozen to the spot beside me as if solidified in fear.

"Check her bag!" Baldi yelled.

The Viking strode past me to dump the contents of my tote onto the floor. Out tumbled my change of clothes, zippy of hair products, undies, map of Florence, and my decoy phone, which slid across the tiles to stop inches from my feet. Viking was about to pick it up when Baldi yelled, "Halt," in Italian: "Do not touch!"

Pushing past me he pulled out a gun and shot the phone to smithereens before kicking away the pieces of tile and circuitry. I noticed another mess of electronic debris in a pile under a chair across the room—Rupert's, I guessed. Was that his dummy or the real one and had they slaughtered Nicolina's and Seraphina's phones, too? I risked catching Rupert's eye. His guarded expression communicated caution. I looked dismayed.

"There," boss man said, grinning at me. "No tricks now. I hear about these phones—very dangerous. True burner phones." He laughed at his own joke. "Where are your friends—the boyfriend and the big black one?"

I stared as if unable to grasp his meaning. "Boyfriend? Big black one?"

"Don't play with me, Phoebe, for you will lose." He turned to Dunbar. "Find Barrows and the black girl. Kill them both and find those two boys. Are you an idiot that two kids escape you? And what about the road?"

"Rigged with explosives as per your command, sir," Dunbar said. "Nobody's getting in or out in one piece."

"Excellent. Take your troops back to their posts. Lars, stay."

The Viking remained in position by the door. When Baldi fixed me with those cold dark eyes, I understood Zann's fear. It was like staring into the abyss. "So, tell me, Phoebe McCabe, why are we here?"

I sensed that he'd know if I was lying, which meant I had to balance on the tightrope between fact and fiction. "I don't know exactly," I said carefully. "I had a lead that a clue to the Botticelli painting may be here. So far I've found nothing."

He assessed this statement and nodded. I could just make out the glint of a gold medallion nested in his chest thicket, a laurel-wreathed profile of an emperor clearly visible. "A clue that drew you to the Laurentian Library after you delivered the Botticelli sketch to the Uffizi. Too bad but it's the portrait I seek. What did you want at the Laurentian?"

"Anything. The library seemed like a good place to start since I didn't have time to comb the official archives."

A sharp shift in his eyes. I'd misstepped. "You know why you went there and you know exactly why you are here. You do not come to this place for wine holiday." He walked back and forth before me, his gaze never leaving my face. "There are important items here—books, manuscripts, yes? I have informants, too, and they say the Corsis hide valuable papers. So far, these fools tell me nothing but they will. You want to study these papers for clues about the Botticelli, and you, Phoebe McCabe, have a clue yourself."

"Me?" Was he referring to Zann's letter or something else? "I don't know what you're talking about."

A slow cold smile crept across his face. "Your brother gave you a clue. That is why you are here."

"My brother? I haven't seen my brother in years. How could he give me a clue?" Oh my God! He did know about Toby! Everything Zann said was true.

"I said do not play with me." Baldi lifted one hand and I watched aghast as Lars leaned over the table and dragged Alexandra to her feet by the hair, the two other gunmen leaning in with rifles pointing at Rupert and Piero. Piero made a lunge for Lars but Rupert held him back and simultaneously cracked a hand across the gunman's arm when he tried to slug Piero with a rifle barrel. The gunman swung his weapon to Rupert ready to shoot.

"Stop!" I cried.

Baldi lifted his hand. "Stay."

The men froze.

"Talk," Baldi said to me.

But Piero spoke first. "We have a Medici library here with many of the Medicis' private correspondence and other manuscripts—books, as well. You can have anything you want but don't hurt my family! Please don't hurt my family!"

Baldi jerked his head at Lars, who released Alexandra so quickly she fell back into her husband's arms. The two huddled together, Piero comforting her while saying: "Zann stole a letter from our library decades ago and that was what led them here. There are other letters, too, which they hope will lead them to a presumed lost Botticelli, but we never found any such clue among those papers. All nonsense, like my father said, another of Suzanna's crazy ideas."

"She stole a letter and did not tell me?" Baldi turned slowly to Zann, who I sensed was trying to shrink herself invisible. But not that invisible.

"So what? You expect me to tell you everything? You think you know me so well, Baldi bastard?" Zann said in a low fierce voice. Her whole body trembled.

When Baldi strode toward her, I knew what was coming. I stepped between them. "Don't touch her. I need her alive and well. If I'm going to figure out the location of the Botticelli based on the Corsi manuscripts, I need her knowledge of the Florentine streets in the fifteenth century. As an archaeologist, she's a valuable asset."

Baldi grinned, that space between his teeth annoying me for some reason. "I give her stay of execution only. She will be dead soon enough. You will find the Botticelli for me, and if you do, I let you live."

I choked back a laugh. "You won't let me live. That's not how you work. You intend to kill me once this is done."

He shrugged. "I give you a choice: you find the Botticelli, I let you work for me and then you live. If you do not find the painting, you die. If you refuse to work for me, you die. Simple."

"Yeah, so simple. And my friends?" I asked.

He shrugged. "Maybe I give them a clean death or maybe they work for me, too. Only the successful work for Baldi so you must be successful. I do not let failures live. Do you understand?"

"Of course." How could I not understand that?

"Excellent. You I see are no coward and that is good, for 'cowards die many times before their actual deaths.'"

Great, so now he was quoting Caesar. "And 'as a rule, men worry more about what they can't see than about what they can,'" I said, also quoting Caesar. I was desperately relieved that I didn't need to repeat anything in Latin or dredge up any more pithy emperor-speak.

Baldi grinned. "I like you, Phoebe McCabe. You would make good member of my legion, perhaps be my magister equitum someday. My current one weakens. I need fresh new blood."

So he had a magister equitum, too. The Roman legion counted their mounted soldiers as the highest ranking class, making the head of the cavalry a high-ranking officer—not Dunbar, in other words. He must be one of the regional commanders. I doubted they used horses, either.

"You will find what I need whatever it takes, understand? No tricks. First trick, I kill her." He pointed to Alexandra. "Second trick, I kill Fox and your two sick lady friends while you watch. I let Lani do the deed. She likes slow deaths and has ax to grind. Third trick." He fired an invisible handgun at me. "Bang but only after Lani is finished with you. Understood?"

I nodded. "Understood."

"Good." He snapped his fingers. "Corsi, you let us into library. Angelo, come here."

Angelo, who had been sitting huddled into his linen jacket, unfolded himself and shuffled over to stand by me.

"You and McCabe will be locked in tower. Zany will wait outside with Lars. The first one who finds the location of the Botticelli lives. The failure dies. With this lost-art sniffer dog and my Medici scholar, the location of that portrait will be found."

"And if we both fail?" Don't ask me why I needed to hear him say it.

"Then everyone dies." Baldi shrugged.

"And if we work together?"

"Then maybe I let you both live."

14

_____

Zann, Piero, and I were herded from the villa at gunpoint with Baldi, the Viking, and Angelo at our heels. I considered launching a disarming maneuver but it was too risky as long as armed men held the others hostage. If I only knew where Evan and Peaches were...

I stumbled over my own thoughts.

"Move!" Baldi said behind me.

We marched down through the hamlet toward the tower. As we drew close, Piero was ordered to step up and open the gate, which he did with a device as slick as any TV remote control. The thick wooden gates swung open, revealing a tidy knot garden lit with low lights embedded in the myrtle. Of course I longed to see that pattern but with a little luck I could do exactly that once on top of the tower.

Not that I longed to be locked inside a tower with Angelo, but at the same time, the thought of laying eyes on part of Lorenzo de' Medici's own library held an almost taboo-like appeal. I tingled at the thought, despite the circumstances.

The tower's exterior had the convincing appearance of a crumbling thirteenth-century watchtower with the exception of another electronic alarmed door that opened at a press of Piero's device. Inside, a curving stone stairway led upward, lights embedded into the well-maintained steps.

We climbed single file, Piero first, then Baldi, me, Zann, and Lars. The stairs were narrow and claustrophobic but a sweet breeze blew in through the lowermost arrow slit. By the time we passed three more, glass covered the openings. When we reached the top floor, puffing and panting, the interior temperature had cooled enough for me to recognize a climate-controlled environment.

Piero, Baldi, and I squeezed into the well-lit top landing, Zann and Lars still on the upper steps since there was no room for everyone at once. Again I considered launching an attack. If I could just pull out my phone and activate the stun feature, swing it around in time to nail Baldi, maybe beam over Zann's head at the Viking—but all the imagined disastrous consequences nixed that idea. All it took was one error and retrieving my phone from my bra might be hazardous enough. Instead, I watched in breathless anticipation as Piero unlocked the door and pushed it open. Lights in the ceiling illuminated a sight I could have only dreamed about.

"My father, he designed the library to the same specifications as original Medici library according to contemporary accounts."

I stepped in behind Baldi and gasped. The room couldn't have been wider than four or five meters, a compact space with a painted white, green, and deep red barrel-vaulted ceiling inset with pot lights that illuminated terracotta roundels for each month of the year. Cupboards were built into the walls, each inlaid with wood and semiprecious stones. Forward sloping shelves all around showcased books in tooled leather bindings, some jeweled, others open to reveal illuminated manuscript pages in glowing colors, and countless other tooled leather bindings embedded with semiprecious stones.

"My father believed these tiles were the original by Luca della Robbia, the master tile maker of the Renaissance."

I looked down to where Piero pointed, amazed to see that the tiles did look authentic and beautifully preserved. "But how would he have obtained them?"

"The Corsis have had a long history here. Filelfo Corsi had been a close friend of the Medici and reportedly arrived on the scene shortly after the palazzo was attacked."

Baldi whistled between his teeth. "This must be worth a fortune." He shot a quick glance at Zann. "And you kept this from me?"

"If I hadn't, it would have been destroyed by now, ruined the way you ruin everything," Zann said without looking at him. "I would have done anything to keep this from you."

Baldi tsked-tsked. "Instead, you deliver me straight to it. I should reward you for your stupidity. Enough! Where are the letters, Corsi?"

I snapped out of my awe to watch Piero remove something from a cupboard which turned out to be a thick leather-bound binder with pages encased in clear archival plastic. "Here." He set it down open on the room's single central table. "Take it and leave us alone."

Baldi chuckled. "I will not leave you now, if ever. If you are lucky and these three find what I seek, maybe I let you live but for that we must wait." He pointed to me. "You and Angelo sit. Zann, stand outside with Lars. If they need you, you come."

He then proceeded to stroll around the room, flicking open cupboards, poking through books, peering at glass-encased manuscripts while tapping something into a calculator. Bastard was doing a value assessment.

Meanwhile, I sat across from Angelo, the binder between us. His eyes never met mine once. It was as if he'd found something fascinating in the hands he folded on the inlaid table. The Viking pushed Zann back into the landing to stand against a wall beside him.

Baldi returned to the table and fired a question at Piero. "What do these letters say?"

"Nothing relevant," Piero assured him. "My father translated the Latin and old Tuscan texts and had them transcribed onto typed pages that accompany each sheet. There are accounts of family ledgers, discussions by various Medici members as to purchases like clothing, a business meeting, a thank-you letter, that sort of thing. Nothing mentions Botticelli or is in the artist's hand except for the letter Suzanna stole."

Baldi turned to Zann. "Where is that letter?"

"I gave it to the countess for safekeeping," Zann said.

"I will get it. Tell me what it says and do not try to cheat."

Zann proceeded to read it from memory, ending with the remark: "That and the sketch is what started it all."

"So," the boss man said, turning to me. "The sketch is a clue, yes?"

"It just indicates that there may be a corresponding painting somewhere. That in itself is not proof that such a painting exists." I wasn't about to tell him my thoughts about the sleeve symbology and, as far as I knew, he had never laid eyes on the actual sketch.

Something shifted in Baldi's cold dark eyes again. "So you think the sketch unimportant?"

"I didn't say that," I said, gazing up at him, deciding that his eyes were the color of an icy brown peat bog, the kind that contains the mummified remains of ancient people. I wondered how many corpses lay behind those orbs. "I just meant that the sketch gives no clue as to the possible painting's location."

Why didn't he ask to see a copy earlier? He must have realized that all agency members had copies on their phones, including Nicolina and Rupert, not that they would have showed him willingly.

In seconds, I had my answer. Baldi pulled a printout from his jacket pocket and tossed it in front of me. It was a photocopy of the Botticelli sketch. Where the hell did he get that?

"So these motifs on the sleeves mean nothing, is that what you say?"

Before I could respond, he slammed my head down on the table with enough force to scramble my vision. When he yanked me back up by the hair, it was to sneer into my face. "Do not lie to me and do not think you can outsmart me. No one outsmarts Baldi. I come, I see, I conquer. Do you understand?"

In the midst of dizziness, one thought screamed at me: *play submissive female.* Zann had implied something about Baldi's assumptions and I needed to use them.

"Sorry," I whispered. "I don't kn-know what the symbols mean yet," I stuttered. I needed to squeeze out real tears, too. That would be harder. "I mean, I recognized the symbols like flowers and fruit but don't know how they come together."

Still holding my hair, he turned to Angelo. "Angelo, say what you have found."

Angelo cleared his throat and began in a flat tone. "I have deciphered many symbols from the sleeve including the Medici crest, the oak leaf to indicate endurance, the plum for fidelity or independence, the bee for order and work, the goose for vigilance, and the sparrow indicating someone lowly. There is also the wasp, which may refer to either the Vespucci family or to trouble. It is an unusual selection of motifs on a piece of apparel of such obvious cost and workmanship. I have not yet deciphered their combined meaning."

A tear trailed down my cheek. Damn, I was good. "You forgot the lemon and the peach—marital fidelity and silence, respectively," I whispered. "Those two are located near the sleeve hem, almost invisible."

"True," Angelo stated mildly.

"Do you know the identity of the woman?" Baldi demanded.

"No," I squeaked.

Baldi released my hair and my head fell forward. I pressed a hand against my forehead where a bump would soon form. "May I ask how you came by that photocopy of the sketch?"

"No," Baldi replied. "Instead, you may ask how you can decipher the symbols on that sketch and use this library to locate the Botticelli. That is the only question important now and I suggest you work quickly to find the answer."

"We can't concentrate with you hanging over us," I said. "It's too small a space."

He dropped a phone-sized black box onto the table. "I leave you but will listen to everything you say. Do not play tricks, McCabe. Remember, the Corsi woman will pay for your first mistake."

"Please, no!" Piero cried, begging me with his eyes. "Leave my wife alone. Take me, do anything you want with me but leave her alone!"

"I will do whatever I want with you both," Baldi said with a smile. That gap between his front teeth again. "Maybe I will even let one of you live."

As if we would all just walk away from this; as if our lives depended solely on my good behavior. But I smiled encouragingly at Piero before turning to Baldi. "I'm on it." I would have added a trembling lip if I could have pulled it off. The tears had been hard enough.

Baldi seemed satisfied. He turned to Piero and said: "Move. Back to villa. My men and I need something to eat. Tell your wife to get into kitchen and fix us something." He pulled out his own phone and barked orders to somebody on the other end.

I risked a single request. "May we have coffee?"

"Stay alert, so coffee, yes!" Baldi responded. In seconds he was nudging Piero before him down the stairs and soon we heard the tower door slam shut, leaving Angelo and me sitting across from one another, the other two staring in at us from the landing.

Angelo had already taken the binder and begun to read the first of the letters.

"May I?" I asked, indicating the binder. Without looking, he shoved it toward me. I flipped over the next plastic sheet and peered down at the accompanying typed translation. "It's in Italian," I said.

"We are in Italy," he replied.

So this was how it was going to be, was it? And my translator app was tucked out of reach. I looked over to Zann. "I need your help."

Zann left Lars's side and entered the room to stand by me.

"Please translate these for me," I asked. I could read basic Italian but didn't trust my abilities on something this important. The last thing I wanted was to miss significant nuances.

"He tell you what it says," Lars said from the door pointing to Angelo.

"Angelo prefers to play solo so Zann will have to help me," I said. "Angelo doesn't buy in to the collaboration thing, apparently."

Lars shot a searing look at Angelo, who ignored him—ignored all of us—and kept his head down over the letters. Zann pulled up the only other remaining chair and proceeded to translate the documents, one by one, reading aloud and referring to the Italian transcription of the Latin where necessary.

We went through twenty-three letters in all, most of which were as Piero said, primarily domestic communication between the Medici family across many generations with various business associates and tradesmen. Some were penned on vellum, others on parchment. Several were in Lorenzo's own hand such as a thank-you letter for services rendered and a clothing order to his tailor. Others were by his father, Piero, his wife, Clarice, and another from Lorenzo's grandfather, Cosimo.

I returned to Lorenzo the Magnificent's over and over again, not just because I could stare at the handwriting of the famed maestro of the Renaissance but because one letter dated 1479 in particular intrigued me. At first glance, it was no more than an order to a tailor, a one Antonio di Domenico from whom Lorenzo requested several bolts of cloth in a particular shade of the finest red to fashion a travel tunic with embroidered sleeves and a fur-lined cloak. A travel tunic. Lorenzo was going somewhere. The date was too obscured by what appeared to be a damp stain to read but it was clear that his destination required the finest clothes.

Another was an order from the same tailor for a gamurra. Since a gamurra was a woman's over-gown, it seemed odd that the patriarch of the Florentine republic would invest time in ordering women's clothing. Why not leave the task to his wife, Clarice? I had never understood him to be a domestic micro-manager like some of the noblemen of the time. Here he made special reference to a ricamatovi and ricamatrici, who would have been the embroiderers of the day, most of whom did piecework at home, and he referenced a design of which he seemed keenly interested, one that clearly he and the tailor had discussed many times.

As always, Lorenzo wrote, *I leave this to your capable hands and artistry. Know that you will be well rewarded. I require the garment to be worked exactly as we have discussed and for the same assistant to oversee the details and attend us for the fitting.*

It had to be for Clarice and must refer to one very special dress, too. Why else would he single it out? I had read many accounts where patriarchs of wealthy Florentine families had ordered clothing for their households including one contemporary Medici ledger that I had studied for my thesis back in my art history days. That account had described clothes required for Lorenzo's own wardrobe, including an astounding amount of yardage for tunics, cippas, manitellos and cappucios, which were all standard menswear for the time, but never descriptions for women's apparel except by the women themselves. In the Medici household, the needs of most of the womenfolk landed in the lap of the wives or sisters.

This man, like all of his wealthy contemporaries, did spend a great deal on clothes and must have appreciated them as an art form like all the other masterpieces he collected. Though Lorenzo dressed down for his civic duties, when entertaining in his palazzo or appearing in public on feast days, it was important to his standing that he flaunt his riches. All Medici women did the same only their apparel was even more ornate and designed to showcase the family's wealth and standing. I had read nothing about Lorenzo being actively involved in his wife's wardrobe before this. He was, after all, a busy man— poet, statesman, art collector, banker, warrior, diplomat, patron of the arts and sciences…

"What are you thinking?" Zann asked.

"I'm thinking that perhaps we're looking at this from the wrong angle. The only item of clothing considered to be so significant as to engage the head of the family would usually be a wedding trousseau. This was the age when a noble family saw a bride's trousseau to be of the utmost importance. Many families were willing to break the bank in order to properly outfit their daughter's bridal garb. A single dress could be equivalent to half a year's income to some families. If they couldn't afford to outfit a daughter properly, they'd often send her to a convent. One scholar estimates that at least seventy-five percent of the young women in Florence's forty convents of the day were from noble families sent there because papa either couldn't or wouldn't fund their dowries."

"Seriously?" Zann said. "But why is Lorenzo's letter so important? Obviously, he could afford to outfit any daughter."

"Or sister or wife, but look at the date: 1479, one year after his brother, Giuliano, was viciously murdered in the Piazzi conspiracy. Lorenzo rallied the city, who avenged Giuliano's death by lynching the perpetuators from the walls of the signoria."

"One of the insurrectionists was the archbishop of Pisa, if I recall," Zann remarked.

"Yes, and dangling him from a window didn't endear Lorenzo to Pope Sixtus IV, regardless of the archbishop's crimes. As a result, Florence was excommunicated and the Holy Roman See seized all of the Medici assets they could lay their hands on."

"Yeah, and didn't Lorenzo end up in prison while trying to make matters right?"

"In Naples, where he was imprisoned briefly by King Ferdinand," Angelo said without looking up. "Lorenzo requested an audience with the pope and traveled to Rome where he stated his case and won."

I glanced at him. Maybe he was warming up. "In other words, Lorenzo had his hands full and here he is ordering cloth?"

"For his travels, perhaps," he said. "This is not important."

"Yeah, and Clarice was a 'good wife—'" Zann put the term into air quotes "—who even hand-sewed the family's personal linens sometimes, right? She could have handled that part if there was a marriage in the works."

"But in 1479, none of Lorenzo and Clarice's ten children were getting married. The children were still young and wouldn't marry until the next decade, but here is Lorenzo in the middle of a crucial time ordering cloth and lining up fittings?"

"You waste time on unimportant details," Angelo said. "This has nothing to do with Botticelli—too many years between the dates."

We looked over to find him glaring at us. His sharp-bone unshaven face made him look like a rabid ferret.

"We'd figure out this puzzle so much faster if we all work together," I pointed out.

"I will not work with you or be led down the wrong path. I will stay alive while you he will kill. This has nothing to do with Botticelli."

"Maybe not directly but I believe it fits in somewhere. What if Medici was using this portrait as a kind of message where each of the symbols impart some meaning?"

"If this is true, it is for another time. For now we have only to *find* the portrait. We do not need to interpret its meaning," he said.

Zann sighed. "Angelo, you're so not a fun guy. Very tunnel-visioned."

Angelo waved us away. "You distract me with your chatter. I must concentrate and suggest you do also."

I glanced at Zann, who caught my gaze and held it for seconds, or at least until the moment a man arrived with a tray of coffee, another keeping him company with his gun in hand. While the second guy chatted to Lars at the doorway, the coffee bearer set two mugs down on the table, leaving the third on the tray. Turning to Zann, he said in Italian: "The boss says you are to go back and stand with Lars and leave these two to work. Take coffee with you."

I looked over at Lars, who seemed to have scored an entire thermos filled with the brew along with a snack of some kind. Zann slid out of her chair, grabbed the mug off the tray in passing, and returned to stand beside the Viking.

"Boss says not to dribble over merchandise," the man said before making a hasty exit out the door.

That left just Angelo and me. Angelo kept his head down, rereading the correspondence and ignoring me. I kept staring down at Lorenzo's letter, almost in a trance of concentration as I sipped my coffee.

I studied the photocopy of the sketch Baldi had left. At the center of the drawing with its mix of symbols was a dress—a sleeve, actually. Lorenzo put great importance on clothing. Was this sleeve significant in some way, an intended gift to somebody with a message embedded in its symbology? But what did Botticelli and this Gabriela have to do with it? Was Gabriela Lorenzo's lover? Somehow I doubted that. Lorenzo did supposedly have a lover but she was reportedly a great beauty and her name was not Gabriela. What was going on here?

I got up and began to pace around the small space, my brain turning over ideas. There was Filippino's extraordinary fresco in the chapel with so much detail lavished on elaborate gamurras and cappucios, embroidered hems and tunics. Why? Clothing played a part in this mystery, I was sure of it, but Angelo was right about one thing: the immediate task was to locate that portrait. I thought of Toby's doodles. They had to mean something, too.

"You distract me," Angelo said.

I stared at him. He didn't bother to look. Quietly I stepped over to one of the forward sloping shelves. These were mostly holding red-bound leather books that looked very much like those in the Laurentian Library. One shelf showcased a brilliant blue velvet Book of Hours with a lapis lazuli cabochon embedded into the cover. I carefully opened the pages to gaze in wonder at the illuminated content. Then something else caught my eye on the shelf below. Not as brilliant as the illuminated pages, not as stunning as the carefully scribed manuscripts copied from rare ancient works, but arresting just the same—a map.

I peered closer. Encased in special glass, it appeared to be an original pen and ink map of Florence dated 1481, colored with a wash of tempura and carefully labeled. I stared at all the known landmarks and streets laid out exactly as they were today—the Ponte Vecchio spanning the Arno along with other ancient bridges, the roads leading up narrow streets where buildings huddled together, the Duomo appearing like a star from which radiated so many streets, and text that highlighted many other churches. Amazing how few changes there had been across the centuries. Unlike most of Europe, Hitler had not bombed Florence with his usual destructive gusto. The bones of the original city still existed and I could stare down at it as if I were a bird hovering over another century.

Lars poked his head around the corner. I must have been standing in his blindspot. "I'm working," I said. He stifled a yawn and nodded, quickly stepping back to his post.

I returned my attention to the map, keeping my back to Angelo. In seconds I had fished my phone from my bra, skimmed over the texts covering my screen, and opened up my camera app to take several quick photos of the map. I then brought up my brother's doodles in my photo library and stared hard. The telltale tremors started radiating through my body. I was on to something. I broke out into a sweat. Oh my God—brilliant! My brother was diabolically brilliant!

Quickly I tapped the crossed-out ear icon. This application would send a blocking signal within a radius of twenty-five feet where no listening device could send a signal in or out but mine and other Evan super phones. That done, I read my texts, focusing on Evan's first. Of course he knew my exact location.

Evan: *Phoebe, are you all right up there?*

I texted back: *Fine, so far. I'm finding interesting clues and have a dynamite hunch. What's the status of everyone?*

Evan: *Nicolina and Seraphina have escaped. I have no idea how. Baldi smashed their phones so we've lost contact. Baldi found both his guards upstairs dead. He's threatened everyone in the house but I understand that his men are unusually lethargic. One appears to be asleep, Rupert says. Rupert's phone is intact, BTW.*

Me: *Poison?*

Evan: *A drug. I assume Nicolina and Seraphina were never as sick as they appeared.*

I smiled. *Can you get me into Florence?*

Evan: *Your hunch is that good?*

Me: *I felt the tingle. I have a pretty good idea of the approximate vicinity where the Botticelli may be hidden but I just don't know why it was hidden there in the first place.*

Evan: *Let's focus on the where for now. Give me a few minutes and I'll get back to you.*

I texted Peaches next. Several irritable messages had come in from her ranging from *Are u okay????* to *I'm hiding out in this bloody knot garden*, and one final, *Rapunzel, let down your hair!*

Me: *Okay, okay. I have a guard watching me up here. Evan's going to arrange a ride into Florence for us.*

Peaches: *Us?*

Me: *I need your engineering and architectural knowledge. Need Zann and maybe Angelo, too. Can't go as long as the Corsis are in danger.*

Peaches: *Somebody dosed the guards' coffee, probably Nicolina. Zann sneaked a package of a drug to all three of our peeps. Don't know how many Baldinos drank it. Baldi didn't. Maybe seven or more guys still in the woods here. U need help getting out of the tower?*

Me: *I'll let you know.*

Switching the phone over to the stun app, I strolled into the middle of the room. Angelo was still at work, head down, but Zann now stood at the doorway with her arms crossed. Stepping aside, she pointed to Lars, slumped against the wall, snoring.

"You drugged him?" I asked.

"Yup. Same drug I dosed Peaches and Nicolina with days ago only stronger. Smuggled some upstairs for them to use, too. If they use it on Baldi's gang, perfecto."

I grinned. "Perfecto is right. Looks like they managed to dose at least some of the Baldinos."

"But Baldi doesn't do coffee."

"What is this!" Angelo scrambled to his feet, panic flaring in his eyes. His gaze swung from Lars to my phone. "Why you do this? Baldi will hear and shoot us all!"

"Baldi can't hear a thing at the moment, Angelo. I have my blocker on."

He raised both hands. "Don't zap me, please don't zap me!"

"I'm not going to zap you. I'm going to offer you a chance to stay alive. Work with me."

"I will not work for you! I must live!"

"I said work *with* me not *for* me."

"I have a family. Baldi will kill me and my wife if I do not do as he says. He has already…hurt me many times. I do not want to lose another toe!"

"Calm down," I said. "I have an idea where the painting may be hidden and you don't. Working with us may be the only way you can stay alive and keep the rest of your toes. Interested? If not, we'll leave you behind and then he'll probably do worse than slice off a toe. Did he do that to you already?"

The man nodded. "Twice—two middle toes." He began untying his shoes. It was then I noticed that his left shoe was stained red.

"Did he just do that?"

"On the way here," Angelo said miserably. "Here, I show you." He began untying his sneaker.

"No, no—not necessary. If it's swelling, you might not get the shoe back on. Shit—that bastard." I turned to Zann. "Can you vouch for this guy?"

Zann studied the trembling man. "Don't know him that well. Baldi only brought him on a few weeks ago, but if Baldi's chopping off his toes, he's probably okay."

"That's what I thought." I turned back to Angelo. "If you want to live, you'll come with us. Otherwise, I'll stun you and leave you to your fate. Several of Baldi's men are already out cold, thanks to Zann's drug punch. The ones that are left will have to deal with my colleagues who are out rounding them up now. The odds are in our favor—sort of. What's it going to be?"

"I come with you," he said. "I'll do whatever you say."

"Good choice. Zann, remove any devices he may have on his person. Wait, a text is coming in."

"Sure thing." While she went to work patting down Angelo, I read the message.

Rupert: *Phoebe, are you managing all right?*

Me: *Yes. Update, please.*

Rupert: *Two Baldinos dead, three drugged. Baldi tried to shoot the Corsis out of pique but I managed to knock the gun out of his hand. He ran from the building screaming into his phone for backup. I did not follow. I have alerted Interpol. It is time for higher intervention.*

Me: *Agreed.*

Then a text came in from Evan copied to all of us: *I've lined up a transportation system to get four of us into Florence. It's complicated but should work. I have an idea that will distract Baldi & Co. which will go off shortly. Phoebe, meet me at the base of the hill in twenty min. Cut through the woods. Don't take the road.*

Me: *We're bringing Angelo and Zann as well as Peaches—make that transportation for five. If Baldi knows I'm heading for Florence, he'll grab all his functioning troops and follow, leaving the Corsis alone. Somebody has to stay behind to keep them and the library safe.*

Rupert: *Nicolina, Seraphina, and I will protect the Corsis and library.*

Me: *Great! See you in twenty, Evan.*

I then proceeded to unblock the signal and spoke into Baldi's listening device. "We found the painting!" That should set him spinning. "Come on, gang!"

I paused by the window to gaze down on the illuminated knot garden.

"See any interesting patterns there?" I whispered while taking a picture that I doubted would even come out.

"Nope. Too simplistic-looking," Zann remarked.

"This is not important!" Angelo insisted. "We must hurry!"

He had a point. Without further delay, we climbed over Lars's limp form, Zann pausing to take his rifle, and crammed into the stairs. We were about halfway down when the tower shook.

15

"What the hell was that?" Zann asked.

"Evan must have ignited Baldi's explosives."

"I cannot take this! Leave me and go." Angelo sat down on the steps and buried his head in his hands.

"Move!" Zann dragged him to his feet and down the stairs.

At the bottom, I ran the de-locking device over the tower door until it beeped open. Peaches was waiting on the other side. "Evan detonated the road," she said.

"I heard," I said. "How do we get down the hill without banging into Baldi's gang?"

"Follow me. There are now Baldinos all over the place. I've picked off a few myself but they keep on coming as if he breeds them somewhere."

"Baldi has many troops," Angelo said.

"Why's this guy even coming with us?" Peaches peered over my head at Angelo.

"He's going to help," I told her.

"But he's a snake," she said. "Remember the Laurentian Library incident with me spending hours in a police station?"

"I do as Baldi says," Angelo explained. "I have no interest in doing these things. I was working on my research when he made me work for him."

"I believe him," Zann said. "Would you have a guy like this working for you otherwise?"

"We're running out of time. Evan's expecting us in fifteen minutes. Peach, lead the way pronto," I urged.

And so she did, taking us on a circumventive route to the back of the garden wall and stopping by the far corner. "This is the best place to climb because there's a shorter drop on the other side. The wall abuts a little embankment," she whispered. "Who's going first?"

I looked up, noting the stones jutting out that would make perfect footholds. "I'll go." Thus I began to climb, congratulating myself for wearing leggings under my skirt.

"I will use the gate," I heard Angelo say below.

"Are you nuts?" Peaches said. "Do you want to traipse down the main lane and offer yourself as target practice to your fellow henchmen, really? That's fine by me, by the way."

"There is problem!" Angelo cried. "I cannot climb wall and jump down other side. Not possible with my feet." He broke into rapid Italian, which Zann countered with something like, *I'll help you. Don't be such a wimp.*

"Peach, will you give this guy a leg up before he drives us crazy?" That was Zann.

"Keep your voices down," I hissed.

There was the sound of scuffling below until finally I saw Angelo's balding head rise before me as I straddled the top of the wall. He clutched the uppermost stones before hoisting himself up to hang hinge-like over the top.

"Angelo," I said. "Back up so you can go down feetfirst instead of headfirst." I could just see a fire burning through the trees—the road, I figured.

In seconds, Zann had passed the rifle up to me before climbing up herself, followed by Peaches, who quickly leaped down the other side. Luckily, overhanging trees kept us deep in the shadows as I leaned over Angelo's back and said to Zann: "How are we going to get this guy over the wall?" I was seriously regretting bringing him along. By chance, I glimpsed what looked to be lights moving in the woods farther down the hill. "They're coming!"

It was like flipping a beached tuna but within seconds we had the reluctant scholar right side up and pushed off the wall into Peaches's waiting arms. Breaking branches and muffled curses followed after which Zann and I landed in the thicket. Soon we were on our feet and stumbling downward. I kept looking over my shoulder, thinking we were being chased before realizing that the real trouble lay ahead.

Multiple lights were bobbing in and out of the forest toward us.

"Are those all Baldinos?" I asked.

"Must be," Peaches whispered back. "As far as I know, there's just Evan and us down here at the moment. The others are back at the villa."

I stared hard. "So they've encircled us. The only way we're going to get past them now is if we zap them with our lasers and hope they don't rain us a shower of bullets."

"I could machine gun them down," Zann said.

"Not possible," Angelo said, hanging on to Peaches to keep from tumbling backward. "They form triple line. You will only kill first line but the others surround us and shoot."

"Roman tactics," Zann remarked.

"We will all die," Angelo whined.

Peaches was gazing down at her phone. "Looks like there are three levels of dots approaching us from the base of the hill. I'm counting maybe thirty. Where's he getting all these guys?"

"He called in backup from Florence and other places. Baldi has big network, some even work as police," Angelo said. "We will all die."

"Stop saying that," I said. "We'll have to use our lasers, Peach."

Peaches held her phone before my eyes. "Not going to happen. See this? Failing battery alert. I've zapped too many Baldinos full charge. I don't have time to use my recharger."

"Then we'll use my phone," I said. "Let's go!"

The longer we waited, the tighter that circle would become. Our only chance lay with somehow slipping through the advancing lines and making a dash for it. I couldn't focus on the likelihood of success—too grim. Evan must have expected that blowing up the road would slow them down but hadn't counted on the sheer numbers of the infantry. We needed an advantage but damn if I knew of one.

"Down there to the right," Peaches whispered. "There's a big pile of boulders with a narrow wedge between them. Found it earlier on one of my scouts. If we can squeeze in and wait until they file past us, we might stand a chance."

I doubted any of these backup guys even knew the terrain so it was worth a try. We followed Peaches, trying our best to be silent, though Angelo was forever tripping and stumbling. The first line of lights was still ahead when we located the stony outcrop and squeezed in through the crevice that narrowed into an even leaner opening on the other side

There was only room for the three of us to fit in one at a time and Peaches had to remain in a crouch but there we waited, staying silent while I tracked the advancing line on my phone. I counted thirty-two moving red dots and one green orb much farther down the hill—Evan, who was still five hundred yards away. Once we broke free and made a run for it, the Baldinos were bound to chase us.

I texted Evan: *Holed up in a pile of boulders.*

Evan: *I'm tracking you. Head for black car at very back. I'll flash you. Hurry. More troops coming.*

I brought up my map of the property. At the bottom of the hill lay the wine depot set in the valley. A narrow drive curved down from the main road to the winery parking lot and then around the depot to the lower service entrance parking area where the road led up to the hamlet. The flashing green dot showed at the back of the lower parking area.

Me: *Where are u—behind the wine depot?*

Evan: *Correct. You'll see plenty of cars parked every which way. Those are Baldi's.*

I waited only long enough for the last line of red dots to pass us and make it about a hundred yards uphill. One straggler lagged behind but we'd deal with him when the time came.

"Okay, gang," I whispered. "Move it! Head for the last black car."

We tumbled out of the crevice and began a headlong dash down to the bottom of the hill. A bullet fired over our heads. Angelo stumbled. Zann swung around and fired into the shadows. Ahead, I saw a jumble of cars of various makes and sizes with plenty of luxury sports cars among them— Baldi's troops traveled well. I focused only on the low black beauty at the farthest point, the one that flashed its headlights. "Hurry!" I cried.

We were running hard, Zann and I up front, Peaches and Angelo behind— or so we thought—but once we reached the Ferrari, we realized that Peaches and Angelo were not on our heels.

"Get in!" Evan called, flinging the back door open. "Where are the others?"

Good question.

Zann turned, dashing back the way we'd come, rifle raised. I followed with my phone's laser feature set. Peaches came stumbling from the shadows with Angelo on her back, piggyback style, an armed guy dressed in total black chasing after. Zann fired once and the Baldino fell to the ground. I waited only long enough to see the army turn back on the hill above at the sound, thirty lights now bobbing through the trees heading our way, someone shouting—maybe Dunbar—and knew all hell was about to break loose. Turning, we ran for the car.

Peaches and Zann crammed into the back, Angelo squeezed between them, while I took the front passenger seat beside Evan. The door whispered shut and the engine revved. In seconds we were peeling away, spitting up gravel as we sped toward the upper parking lot.

I barely looked at Evan as the seat belt automatically strapped me in. "They're going to follow us."

"They're going to try," he said. "I let down their tires. There are six other vehicles identified as belonging to the Baldi boys heading here from the surrounding countryside. My informants tell me that the Baldi network has been activated. Hello, Phoebe. It's great to see you again."

That wonderful voice. I laughed. "Even in these circumstances?"

"In any circumstances."

"Okay, you two—enough of the romantic interlude. Ev, are you seriously planning to drive a Ferrari all the way into Florence?"

It was a fair question. A scurry of lights and accompanying gunfire behind us, ahead nothing but narrow dark road cluttered with indistinguishable objects. I picked out what looked to be a car door in the middle of the lane with a smoldering pile of wreckage to the right. The remains of a white van lay on its side among upended olive trees and shattered pots. The Baldinos must have blown up every car or van they could find.

"Great to see you, too, Peaches, but no. I hot-wired this one but it's probably tracked. We need to ditch it ASAP. I have a relay of assistance lined up between here and Florence that will help get us there but I won't know what my contacts have planned until we reach each point. We'll be traveling blind."

"Do you have army, too?" Angelo asked from the back seat.

Evan glanced into the rearview mirror. "Not an army but a network of contacts. And you are?" He swerved to avoid a pile of smoking debris.

"This is Dr, Angelo Ficino," Zann said, "Baldi's temporary and very disposable-to-him Medici scholar, and I'm Zann Masters, one of his ex-archaeologists. Great to meet you, Evan. Heard so much about you."

"And I you," he said.

"Yeah, but don't believe all of it, okay?"

A bullet shattered the Ferrari's taillight.

"Ev, push down the window," Peaches called, and in seconds she was leaning out firing Zann's machine gun behind us. "Where'd they all come from? Some must be posted at the winery!"

"Yes," Evan said as he maneuvered around more smoking car parts. "I tried to get every one of them but clearly missed a few. Luckily, they're all on foot for now. We need to reach the main road. Phoebe, I've plugged my phone into the GPS. Bring up the screen, please."

I tapped on the dashboard screen. Up popped a map grid on a dark background with red dots scattered on various blue lines which I took to be roads. "I take it that every red dot is a Baldino?"

"Correct."

"Then there's a car heading towards us from every possible direction."

"Let's hope they don't know every direction possible," he replied.

"Pardon?"

But he was focused on the road, specifically on the Land Rover that had just appeared over the rise ahead, heading down toward us from the highway. We were on a narrow two-lane drive designed to lead traffic from the main road to the winery. The roofless Rover was driving dead center, barreling straight for us. I could just detect two guys in the front passenger seat.

"Hang on!" Evan yelled as he gunned the accelerator while swerving the Ferrari back and forth. He planned to play chicken in some last-ditch attempt to maintain the road. I would have tried a different approach considering that a sharp drop on either side could only lead to disaster for somebody, a high probability of that somebody being us. But then, I'm not fueled by testosterone.

The Rover guys started firing. Peaches fired back, peppering the road with bullets, trying to hit a tire. Suddenly the gun went silent. "Shit! Ran out of ammo!"

While the Ferrari sped up the hill and the Rover barreled down to meet us, Angelo began reciting the Lord's Prayer in Italian. I brought up my phone's laser app and aimed for the Rover's driver's side.

"Any final words?" I asked before pushing the button.

16

It was more dramatic than I expected—the Rover swerving off the road and tumbling over and over before bursting into flames in the vineyard below. I had to tear my gaze away from the mesmerizing orange glow.

"Ev, put your headlights on," Peaches called.

"We can't risk them," he said. "They already know where we are and what direction we're heading. Phoebe, where is the enemy on the map?"

I peered at the dashboard screen. "I see one red dot maybe ten kilometers ahead and another coming from the opposite direction." I pushed down on the road lines tracking across the screen. "We're on the SP125, by the way." Which was a two-lane road winding through the hills and valleys of mostly vineyard territory, I guessed.

"What's the name of the nearest town?"

I tapped the closest white circle. "Villore."

"How far away is Vicchio?"

"Maybe ten kilometers past Villore."

He began talking to somebody and I realized that he was wearing an earpiece. I heard him say in Italian that we needed transportation for five and that there were enemy cars approaching from both directions. He checked the screen and gave our coordinates. After listening for a few minutes, he said, "Sì," and fell silent.

"So what's the plan?" I asked.

"Somewhere ahead just outside of Vicchio there's an unmarked lane on the right which we'll have to watch for. It's shortly before the sign saying Vicchio 1K. We pull over there and the next leg begins."

"Which is?"

"I have no idea."

My eyes fixed on the road. Nothing to break the darkness ahead but one set of headlights weaving toward us from the hills beyond, so far above it seemed as if they were descending from the sky. "I hope the object ahead is farther away than it appears."

"Either way, we need to disappear long before it reaches us."

"As in get to that exit before they do?"

"Exactly." The car hugged the road despite the speed as he navigated by the moonlight. Everyone in the car sat locked in a tense silence as we zoomed through the darkness. Evan was an expert driver with proverbial nerves of steel but all it took was one false move to send us to the same fate as the Rover. Angelo whimpered in the back seat. I stole a glance at Evan's chiseled profile. If one wanted to fall for the manly sort, he made an excellent candidate. I had fallen long ago, in fact.

After negotiating a switchback turn, Evan revved the car even faster. I glanced at the speedometer—eighty-five kilometers edging up to ninety, then one hundred in a fifty kilometer zone. We swerved to avoid an animal, something that looked to be a wild boar, before the car straightened out to a clear patch.

"I'm turning the headlights on to see the sign ahead. We must be close."

I caught the reflective flash immediately. "Sign ahead."

Evan slammed on the brake. "Get out and run toward that sign. I'll meet you there."

The car screeched to a halt, Evan activated the doors, and we all tumbled out.

"What are you doing?" Zann called to him, but the doors glided shut and the Ferrari slipped away.

"Watch and see." Peaches hoisted Angelo up piggyback style and we began jogging along the road, everyone's eyes fixed on the Ferrari's taillights. Several seconds later the car stopped for a moment, after which it suddenly accelerated and shot off again. We watched the Ferrari jolt off the road and plunge down an embankment to crash through the vineyard before smashing to a halt and bursting into flames.

"Decoy," I called. "Evan's fine." Which I seriously hoped was true since no silhouette appeared anywhere near the flaming mass. When we reached the sign, still no Evan, though a strange little three-wheeled truck awaited us on a narrow gravel track. A man stepped from the shadows and told us in Italian to get into the back, which consisted of a large open box-like container.

"This is a vehicle for tending the vines," Angelo explained as Peaches helped him up into the open back. "It is narrow to allow workers to go down the rows to tend the grapes."

"Thanks for that, Angelo. Could you just shove your butt back so we can all get in?" Peaches asked. Zann climbed in after her and the driver urged me to get in, too.

"Not without Evan," I said. "You go ahead and we'll catch up."

"Signore Barrows says you get in pronto!" the man said in English.

"You go," I said, "and we'll catch up." I had no idea where Evan was but had no intention of leaving without him. "Does he know where you're going?"

The man didn't grasp my mangled Italian so Zann translated, after which the guy spat out a tirade of what I presumed were curses before slamming the truck gate shut.

"He swore at you for being an obstinate woman, or at least I think that's what he was getting at."

"Children are obstinate; women have their own ideas," came my retort.

"Yeah, I hear you," Zann said, watching the guy climb into the driver's seat and start the engine. "I think we're going without you." The truck sputtered into action.

Peaches was standing now. "What the hell do you think you're doing, McCabe? Do you seriously think we're just going to leave you here?"

"Leave me here!" I called as the truck pulled away. "You need to take care of Angelo and I need to find Evan. I'll catch up!" Not that I knew exactly where I was catching up to.

I watched her hesitate, leaning on the truck gate with a snarl on her face as the truck trundled down the dark lane toward a vineyard. Once I was sure she'd stay with the others, I swung around and bolted for the main road.

The Ferrari was still burning, the flames licking the sky, illuminating a track of broken vines that led to up to the road. Away to the right, I could see headlights zipping down a hill, growing closer by the second. I scanned the area, looking for signs of life or anything human, dead or alive, but there was nothing but moonlit fields and that burning car.

"Evan?" I called.

"What the hell are you doing, Phoebe? Get off the road!"

What happened next was the equivalent of a football tackle that sent me spinning off the road to tumble down the opposite embankment, him rolling with me. When we stopped amid the grass, he was straddling me. "Damn it, woman, do you want to get yourself killed?"

Panting, I gazed up at his shadowy face. "Not particularly but I didn't want you to get killed, either."

"I can take care of myself," he said between his teeth.

"The way you took care of yourself in Spain when those bozos were beating you senseless?"

"I'm never senseless, Phoebe."

I shifted under him, trying to push him off, yet he remained immovable. "My point is, there's no time for heroics. We're part of a team out here."

"Right now I'd rather be part of a pair." And he kissed me, deeply and with his usual deliberate perfection as if we had all the time in the world, as if we weren't hiding in the grass with an army of criminals hunting us down. And I responded. Blame hormones, blame adrenaline, blame something.

Then the earth shook and fireworks lit up the sky. I mean that literally. He pulled away to gaze up. "Excellent—they tripped the explosives. Another Baldi clutch down. We'd better catch up with the others."

He stood and pulled me up by the hand. It's safe to say that recent events had left me breathless, possibly confused, and temporarily speechless. He led me by the hand through the thicket toward the lane like a child.

I forced myself from my stupor. "What just happened back there?"

"After I rigged the Ferrari to plunge into the field and combust, I set up an explosive trip wire that blew up the approaching car. The plan is to temporarily trick the rest of the gang into thinking there'd been an accident that destroyed us all."

A farm building appeared at the end of the track, gleaming ghostly in the moonlight. "I wasn't referring to the explosion and you know it. I was referring to that kiss and your questionable sense of timing."

His face remained immovable, his tone serious. "I thought my timing excellent. Consider all the special effects added to enhance the experience, not to mention the element of surprise. I trust you enjoyed it as much as I?"

"Be serious! I told you I wasn't ready for the next step."

"I *am* serious, Phoebe, as I keep reminding you, and that was not the next step but just a kiss. Carpe diem."

Of all the infuriating, machismo-fueled, self-satisfied things to say. It ignited all my triggers, all the things I both loved and hated about male-female dynamics—the powerful chemistry, the biological urges putting heart over head, heat over brain cells, and that total sense of powerlessness I always experienced in the presence of a man I cared about. "I'm too angry to speak. Let's just catch up to the others before I combust."

"We'd better hurry. These things don't go fast but they have the benefit of traveling where more powerful vehicles cannot go." He was indicating one of the parked vine scooters lined up in the barn's shadows, this one being a four-wheeler ATV-style unit with a tractor seat and a small metal tray perched on the back. "Are you angry at me?"

I made for the driver's seat. "Yes and no."

"Well, that's clear. Phoebe, unless you want me to ride in the back like a kid crammed into a shoebox, I suggest you permit me to drive while you sit on my lap. Why are you angry? It was just a kiss, I said. Were the special effects too much, is that it?"

I laughed. There was no time to argue. Besides, the corrugated aluminum tray in the back was for holding tools not tall men. He had a point.

"Let's not talk about this now. You drive. I'll sit on your lap." I stepped aside as he climbed into the tractor seat. In minutes, I had perched more or less between his thighs, gazing straight ahead while he gripped the handlebars with one arm and put the other around my waist. I kept my gaze fixed on the vine-rowed shadows ahead.

"When can we talk about this or should I just send you a text?"

"Keep your eyes on the proverbial ball, Evan. Where are we going?"

"The vineyard ends at the bottom of the hill beside a river, actually a tributary to the Arno."

"We're going to Florence by boat? Excellent idea. Baldi won't expect that, at least not right way."

"Traveling to Florence on the Arno isn't as brilliant as it sounds."

I had no idea what he meant but I was a bit distracted. It was a bumpy ride. I was seated between his legs. Because of how the seat was arranged, that meant I had to brace my feet on the foot bed while his legs straddled mine. Remember the bumpy bit. It was all I could do to focus on the narrow track ahead as we descended steadily downward.

Evan began speaking through his Bluetooth device. I gathered that the others were waiting. We had no idea whether the Baldinos had yet reached the smoldering remains behind us or how long it would take for them to realize they'd been tricked.

I pulled out my phone and checked in with the team back at the Corsis'. Rupert informed me that all the conscious Baldinos had been called away, leaving seven of their men in various states of unconsciousness who had to be bound up and locked in the wine cellar, including Lars. The two Corsi boys had been most helpful. Nicolina, Seraphina, and the Corsis were napping and the team were spelling one another in case any gang members returned. I updated him on our progress and then stored my phone. I stifled a yawn. It was 1:15 a.m.

Several minutes later, a curve of water appeared winding its way through the hills in a ribbon of moonlight. Our group waited on a rocky shoreline beside what looked to be a battered flat-bottomed speedboat designed for navigating shallow waterways.

Without a word, we waded to the craft and climbed in. Luckily, it was large enough to accommodate all of us comfortably and even came with a windshield. A brief scan with my phone light assured me that the craft was well maintained and wouldn't sink along the way.

"You think I didn't check already?" Peaches asked, catching me in the act.

"Sorry, Peach—habit. How are you doing, anyway?"

"I'm beat like everybody else. Just so you know, this thing doesn't come with life jackets so if we tip…"

I grinned at her. "Guess we'd better not tip."

Both of us had grown up on the water but I wasn't sure about Angelo or Zann.

"We're about thirty kilometers from Florence according to my phone," Peaches told me. "That's not far but I have a feeling it may as well be."

I didn't have a chance to ask what she meant because the driver was pushing the boat into deeper water and bellowing at Evan.

"That's Luigi," she said. "Zann found out that he's part of the agency's international help network that we never knew we had. Note to selves: grill Evan and Rupe on that point when we next get a chance."

"Noted."

"When he's not on standby, Luigi owns this vineyard."

"Great."

"Got to recharge my phone."

"Sure," I said, only half listening.

In minutes we were slipping downriver, Evan at the wheel, leaving Luigi far behind.

"How long until we reach Florence?" I asked Evan.

"I'm not sure exactly," he called over the putter-putter of the engine. "We have to change craft. The Arno is not an easy river to traverse. Pleasure boats are not viable until you're close to the city itself. There are places where the river is silted up or flood control measures have been constructed, which creates all manner of obstacles. I seriously questioned whether we should try this entry at all, especially at night, but going by road would be no better. Baldi will have all the roads watched."

"And it's summer so the river is at its lowest point but I read somewhere that there has been a fair amount of rain nonetheless," I remarked, gazing out at the moon-licked waterway. At the moment, the river was smooth, broad, and edged by willows, but I had a feeling that it would not remain that way.

"Exactly. Phoebe, I—"

I touched his arm. "We'll talk later." I indicated our companions with a nod of my head. Even though all three appeared to be settling in for a snooze, pitching our voices over the engine wasn't the best idea.

"Right. Why don't you get some sleep and I'll wake you when we arrive at the next point?"

I took him up on that suggestion, dropping into a deep sleep almost as soon as I leaned back on the seat boards. Peaches was already nodding off in the well of the boat with Angelo's head falling against Zann's shoulder as they both leaned against the stern. It seemed like only minutes before Evan roused us awake.

"Time to move, everyone," Evan called.

I blinked awake, totally disorientated. We were in the middle of a dark void with a light flashing off to the right. We were slipping toward the shore, the current so light that Evan switched off the engine to let us coast. Two guys waded up to pull the boat to shore, which was no more than a sliver of scrabbled beach. The moment my feet plunged into the chilly water, I became alert enough to notice the big yellow inflatable craft waiting there.

"A raft!" Peaches exclaimed. "Are you kidding me? We're going to Florence not Val di Sole."

Evan was in an intense exchange with one of the guys, both of whom were in their early twenties and eager to kit us out. I hadn't yet reached dry ground when one dropped a life jacket over my head and tossed me a helmet.

Zann was protesting. "We're going white water rafting—seriously?" She paused to listen to the men talking. "We're seriously going white water rafting," she said. "Damn if I expected that."

"Store your stuff!" Peaches cried.

I shoved my phone back deep into my bra.

Angelo was protesting vehemently as Peaches strapped him into his gear. One of the young guys, Petro, was going with us to help navigate and I could just see Florence's glow in the skyline ahead.

As the other guy held the raft, the rest of us climbed in, putting Angelo in the middle with Evan, Peaches, Zann, and I each taking an oar and Petro perching up front, Evan in the back.

"More rain than usual in July so we make it, yes?" Petro called. "If not this…" And he shrugged.

Angelo demanded a seat belt but soon even he fell silent as the raft slipped silently across the broad back of the Arno, everyone paddling. Without engine noise, all appeared still and calm under the moonlight with nothing to break the peace but the sound of our paddles. I could see occasional headlights moving along the roads on either side but hopefully nobody would look toward the dark impassible river. With the current, we soon picked up speed.

And so we went with the flow, rounding a bend where the lights of towns glowed in the dark and we could see villas and farms far in the hills above.

"First coming up!" Petro called.

First what? He urged us to steer to the left-hand side where we could hear rather than see the sound of angry water. On the right, a low barrier of stone; on the left, rapids where the stones had washed away. We slid over the edge and splashed through the churn before the river smoothed out again. That was easy. The next bit was another washed-away barricade where we needed to half hoist the raft off the rocks by our paddles. No problem there, either. We all began to relax: we could do this.

We sailed under a bridge as the houses on either side became more frequent and something that looked to be a modern housing development slid past.

"Hang on!" Petro shouted.

Hang on? I could see nothing ahead.

"What—" Peaches began, but she didn't finish her question before we went right over the edge.

17

*I*t was like a water slide in a fun park only no damn fun. We spun down a slanted water-skimmed cement wall into a second level pool only to plunge over the side of that straight onto the rocks, the raft bumping and jostling all the way. Evan, Zann, and I tumbled out, luckily incurring nothing worse than scrapes and bruises. Everyone but Angelo helped to shove the raft off the barrier toward the ribbon of smooth water flowing beyond.

"Another flood break," Petro called once we were back in the raft. "The Arno has flooded many times. Smooth sailing now."

Smooth sailing was a relative state as we sat soaked and shivering in the warm night. Two more smaller flood breaks were yet to come, both more bearable than the last because by then we were getting the hang of it. Finally the river broadened and Florence crowded in all around as we sailed under one bridge, two bridges. Another loomed ahead.

"Ponte alle Grazie," Angelo said. "We are almost there, thank God."

"This would be a good time for you to tell us where we're going, Phoebe," Evan called.

"I don't know exactly," I replied. "I know the vicinity but our collective brains will need to help find the exact spot."

"Easy." He grinned. That's why I adored that man: he'd follow me anywhere.

"You don't even know?" Zann protested. "I thought you got one of your fabulous brain farts back in the tower."

"It didn't come with specifics or signposts. As soon as we stop, I'll tell you what I have to go on."

Still in the middle of the Arno now awash with city lights and possibly Baldino lookouts watching the river everywhere, I felt compelled to wait. A deep unease descended on us as we paddled the raft along, keeping close to shore.

"We stop before Ponte Vecchio," Petro told us. "Look for flashing light."

Florence took on a different perspective from the river—more remote and even more mysterious, the dark shoreline wrapping the city margins in shadows as thick as time itself.

The flicking on-off of a flashlight appeared to our right below the Vasari colonnade that linked to the Uffizi. Deep shadow clustered under the passage but street traffic would be easy to detect on the road. So far it remained empty.

We landed on a stretch of grass below a wall that separated the portico from the river. Another guy, this one older, waited. He stepped forward to help secure the raft. A rapid exchange of instructions with Evan followed. We were to take the keys he was providing—six for the six Vespas we would find parked down the street at the back of the museum. We were to look for six blue vehicles, all rentals, all side by side, he assured us, and not easily detected. I wasn't sure what he meant by that since six people zooming around Florence at two a.m. might be noticeable by anyone who happened to be looking, regardless of paint color.

The two men were eager to help further so Evan sent them up to the street to act as lookouts while everyone gathered around me. I stood against the wall and opened my phone.

"Look," I said, holding up the photo of my brother's geometric doodle. "I thought it was a maze at first until I found this in the Corsi collection. If you imagine Toby's doodle superimposed over this section of the Florentine map you can see how the rectangles and circles line up. They're actually buildings, domed churches, and streets."

Peaches whistled. "So Toby sent you a map of a neighborhood? Wow."

Angelo leaned in to study the images. "The entire Ognissanti? There's a piazza, a church, houses—how are we going to find anything there?"

"Botticelli lived on Via Nuova, now della Porcellana, and so did the Vespuccis," Zann pointed out. "It makes sense it would be somewhere there.

That's the neighborhood where I found the sketch, too. The Vespuccis lived right down the street."

"As in Amerigo Vespucci after whom the Americas were named?" Peaches slipped my phone out of my hand to study the images more closely.

"Yeah, cousins. The family were close Medici allies and frequent patrons of Botticelli," Zann continued, "but I racked my brain to discover where Botticelli may have hidden that painting but came nowhere near there. I thought maybe at the Corsis', maybe even in that chapel with the frescos."

"The chapel plays a role but not the way you may think," I said.

"Phoebe, put us out of our misery." Evan gently removed the phone from Peaches's fingers. "Let us follow along with your thinking here. Where did Botticelli hide the painting?"

"And why not hide the painting the same place he hid the sketch?" Zann asked.

"Because he hadn't painted the portrait when the sketch was hidden and he didn't hide the sketch in the first place—Gabriela did, in the walls of her father's workroom. The painting was completed months, maybe years, later and was meant to be a wedding present, I'm guessing. Only Botticelli couldn't get it to the young couple in time. Savonarola had threatened damnation on all those who celebrated beauty for beauty's sake and Botticelli was stricken with the belief that his soul was in danger," I said. "By then he had returned to painting mostly ecclesiastical work and kept this portrait hidden until Gabriela could return and claim it. Savonarola drained the joy from Botticelli's art. This may have been his last testament to beauty for beauty's sake."

"*I am the hailstorm that shall break the heads of those who do not take shelter,*" Angelo said quoting the radical friar.

"And the hailstorm that was Savonarola was thickening so fast that the subject of the painting and sketch escaped Florence with her friend, possibly future husband, since she could no longer risk her art in the city following her father's death."

"Her art? She was an artist, too?" Evan was smiling at me. He loved it when I did this kind of gathering of diverse clues thing.

"Gabriela, the one who hid the sketch in the walls of her father's house, was also an artist, only of another medium."

"And she knew where Botticelli hid the painting, her gift?" Evan asked.

I was so excited I was nearly tripping over my words. "Botticelli must have believed she could figure it out. He would have expected her—or them—to understand whatever clues he planted. They were all in the same circle, all working as artists and artisans. He believed she would return some day to retrieve her portrait, only she never did."

"Gabriela who?" Zann asked.

"Yes, for God's sake tell us," Angelo said.

"A tailor's daughter, Gabriela di Domenico, who also happened to be a brilliant designer in her own right. I found an entry in a Lorenzo letter referencing her father's business but alluding to 'the goddess of the thread.' Lorenzo de' Medici was a great lover of art and wise enough to appreciate artistry in any guise. One of his tailors, Francisco di Domenico, had a daughter who worked with him in his studio until she disappeared sometime in the second quarter of the 1400s. I'm guessing that Gabriela's designs may be seen in many of Botticelli's paintings—the gorgeous gowns, the exquisite craftswomanship. She was a 'goddess of the thread' and Botticelli respected her as an artist in a way that was hardly common even in the great awakening that was the Renaissance."

"The great awakening that rarely included women, you mean?" Zann remarked.

"It's very possible that Lorenzo de' Medici may have used her designs for his family for years," I continued. "She designed for the Medici, the Vespucci, maybe even for him. The vision of Simonetta probably wore her creations as did most of the muses that populated Botticelli's art—the *Primavera* and the portraits. Gabriela just may have been Florence's best keep secret amid the ruling classes that circled the Medici-Vespucci orbit."

One of the guys leaned over the wall and called for us to hurry up. We scrambled toward the steps leading up the street.

"Where are we going?" Evan asked.

"The one place that all three knew well and had access to," I said as I dashed up the stairs. "The Chiesa di Ognissanti—the All Saints Church."

* * *

"Not the church!" Angelo mumbled something in Italian that sounded like *God preserve us.* "Say that you do not suggest we desecrate a tomb!"

We were scrambling down the deserted road toward the back of the Uffizi where, as the guy had said, six shiny Vespas waited for us in the shadows. Vespas! That was like riding a scooter. I eyed the two more powerful motorcycles nearby, presumably our helpers' rides.

"Of course not," I told him. "Why would Botticelli place a painting in a tomb when he expected Gabriela would need to retrieve it? Breaking into a crypt was hardly practical and would be performing a desecration."

"Because it is the safest place, these tombs. Follow me," Angelo said. "I know all back ways. The Ognissanti is on the other side of town."

"I'm taking one of the Basanti cycles and, Peaches, you take the other. Sorry, gentlemen," Evan announced, gazing at the two guys. "I presume those are supposed to be your rides." One shrugged.

I thought I should take one of the faster ones, too, but Evan went on to explain his rationale. "We'll be flanking the others, riding shotgun for the rest of you. If we get separated, we'll meet at the church," Evan said.

"How are we supposed to know where the church is?" Peaches asked.

"Facing the river," Angelo said. "Past the university."

"Oh, like I know where that is. Never mind, I'll figure it out."

"Angelo, Zann, and Phoebe, you two go first, and Peaches and I will be behind you," Evan called. "There won't be room to ride abreast in some of these lanes."

Peaches looked ready to argue but stopped when she saw a headlight approaching from far down the road. "That could be a Baldino."

"We play decoy," one of the two guys called. "You go!" The two men took off on Vespas toward the headlights while we took a hard right around a corner following Angelo.

It was nothing but a narrow lane behind the Uffizi so we had no choice but to ride single file. Since the city maintained much of its medieval footprint, I knew this would be the norm if Angelo planned on using diversion tactics.

Which he clearly did. We maneuvered in and around more narrow lanes, passing through a back parking area onto a little square where our headlights swept across empty market stalls. Angelo made a hard left onto another, broader street that stretched between the walls of buildings and here he opened up the Vespa's throttle, the engine's whine echoing against the stone.

Evan pulled up beside him, Peaches hanging back, both of them on the much faster vehicles. Now we were going full-speed down what felt like an urban canyon and it almost seemed that we could trasverse the whole of the city simply by staying on the same road.

"Not far!" Angelo called. "Straight ahead."

Or so he'd hoped, but when the buildings fell away to reveal another square overlooking the Arno, three black motorcycles were waiting near a small roundabout.

"Shit!" Peaches cried.

Evan veered away and barreled straight toward them, Peaches following. I heard gunshots but was too focused on keeping up with Angelo to look back. He was diving down another narrow road squeezed between the buildings.

Zann was shouting: "Angelo, courtyard to your right!"

Angelo zipped under an archway, Zann and I close behind. We entered a treed area that appeared to be a parking space for the surrounding flats. Zann moved ahead of Angelo, leading the way along a dirt path that wove around the cars.

We had to disembark long enough to wheel the Vespas through a gate toward an adjacent one-way street. We were far from the river now. Back on the Vespas, we sputtered down the road until we screeched to a halt.

Four headlights headed straight toward us until another swerved into their path from adjacent street. One fired at the others, causing spin-outs and return gunfire. It had to be either Peaches or Evan. Still, one cyclist managed to break away and jet toward us.

"Ditch the Vespas," I called. There was no way in hell we could outride them all, anyway, and how long Peaches and Evan could hold them off was anyone's guess. The bastards kept on coming. "We need to go on foot or we'll lead them right to the church."

"But it is still too far away," Angelo said.

"Nonsense," Zann countered. "The Ognissanti is just over those houses, not far as the crow flies."

"But we are not crows!" Angelo protested.

"I grew up not far from here. I know ways to get us over the roofs on foot. I used to do it all the time as a kid. Come on!"

She dropped her bike and tugged Angelo from his.

I glanced toward the bike buzzing toward us—still far enough away for the driver to miss three figures in the shadows. We slipped from doorway to doorway until we could duck down a side street. There we flattened ourselves against a wall when the cyclist zipped by seconds later. When we heard the Baldino pausing to inspect our fallen Vespas, revving its engine all the while, we took that moment to bolt down the sidewalk.

Zann did know this area. She was looking for gates that led into private courtyards and found one halfway along the next block.

"Open it!" she hissed.

I ran my phone over the wrought iron gate's mechanism until it beeped open. The three of us huddled around the corner inside what looked to be a cobbled parking area as the Baldino coasted by. He would hopefully comb all the nearby streets looking for us. Once it zoomed past, I turned to Zann. "Now what?"

"This is a communal area for maybe thirty or forty flats and offices," she whispered. "All the buildings link together so once we get up to the roof, we can go almost anywhere undetected. It's like flying!"

"By roof?" Angelo croaked.

I hushed him. We followed Zann as she crept through the courtyard, which turned out to be many courtyards linked by long winding back alleys leading to parking areas and private gardens. In the final opening, the tall buildings huddled together with only a patch of sky visible above.

Zann was looking for something. "A shed or a garage or anything we can climb. There—perfect."

She was pointing to a small modern addition built onto the side of one medieval building, perhaps a storage area. These were once villas, I suspected, now sectioned into flats or offices. At a glance I could see that once we reached the shed's terra-cotta-tiled roof, it would be an easy climb up the various extensions and conservatories that owners had built over the centuries. That is, if we made it that far.

We were halfway up and hoisting Angelo up from a glass conservatory toward the next extension when a security alarm began shrieking.

"Shit!" Zann hissed.

We had three more extensions to climb before reaching the top but now every occupant would likely be roused from sleep. The next leg consisted of a little glass add-on that led to a tiny balcony. By climbing onto a patio table, we could reach the glass roof and carry on up to the next level.

We were just tugging Angelo up by his belt when the light came on beneath us. I saw a flash of greenery below, saw a woman pointing up, before the three of us scuttled up and across the tiles to press back against the wall of the last extension.

"This will wake the whole neighborhood!" Zann whispered. Angelo leaned back and closed his eyes.

"And alert everyone on the street besides." I pulled out my phone to send the others a quick group message. *On roof*, I typed. *Heading for church.*

Evan responded immediately: *We'll lead the others away. Meet you there.*

No response from Peaches. I stowed my phone to assess the last leg of our upward journey but Zann beat me to it. She was peering over the next section of roof, beckoning us to follow.

I pried Angelo from his perch and nudged him toward Zann. This section was chin-height and, once we climbed on top of that, led straight to the sky. With the alarms still pealing, we had no time to waste so quickly hoisted ourselves up and scuttled across the terra-cotta terrain on our hands and knees until we reached a foot-deep drop leading to another roof. Now we had to stand and scamper across the tiles like rats, jumping down or climbing up various levels. Though dark, there was enough ambient light for navigation.

It was like traversing a shadowy domain, every connecting section a different height, some peaked, some flat, and most following a footprint unchanged for centuries. The occasional square protuberances had probably once been towers and all the buildings linked together as if a huge ancient organism had subdivided section upon section over the years.

"Look," Zann whispered. "The Ognissanti is over there."

I followed her finger past the large dark gulf to our left, a palazzo that opened before the church's stepped facade. Bizarrely, the church seemed so close and yet far away. Many roofs and at least one street lay between us and that cluster of white buildings.

We were now standing on a flat rectangular space filled with stacked tables and chairs, clearly a restaurant, far enough away from our entry building that we relaxed a bit. At least the alarms had finally stopped, though a police siren screamed down the street. That might even send the Baldinos scattering. I risked peeking over the railing.

Below, the square sat illuminated by the occasional streetlight. A single cyclist circled the piazza like a shark, keeping the engine to a low putter. Riveted, I watched as the rider slipped under a streetlight. Female shape, black leather jacket over camo pants. The black helmet gave away nothing, but the braid hanging down the back said it all. I shooed the other two back from the railing.

"It's her, Lani!" I whispered.

"Killer Lani? That's not good," Zann said.

"Call the police," Angelo urged. "Tell them to come here and protect us."

"Forget that, Angelo," I whispered. "The regular police would just throw us in jail for trespassing and who knows what else. We have a message out to Interpol. They're the only ones who can extract us from whatever crimes we're about to commit." Actually, calling Interpol meant contacting London, who then contacted the Italian division, who would then alert the Florence contingent. In the wee hours of the morning, I guaranteed that wouldn't be a speedy process even though Rupert initiated it hours ago. "All we have to do is cross these roofs without anyone seeing us and access that church unseen pronto. Any ideas?"

"The Ognissanti has many buildings attached—cloisters, rectory, court-yard. If you can climb roofs that way, maybe you enter unseen. I will wait here," Angelo said.

I laughed. "You're coming with us. Move it."

I led the way down to the adjoining roof, a two-foot drop leading to another flat rectangular area sporting an air-conditioning unit. At the end of that, I stopped and stared: a gap yawned between us and the next group of six-story buildings.

Visually I measured maybe a yard and a bit. Below, no more than a service alleyway for storing trash bins and a relatively easy jump—if one could jump. Angelo would never manage it with his dodgy feet. And assuming one made the crossing without faltering, the next challenge was to keep climbing up using momentum to reach the peak.

Zann and I looked at one another. "You go," she said. "I'll take Angelo the long way."

"The long way?" I asked.

She pointed. Far to our right, maybe a block away, as if Florence really did standard blocks, something that looked like a medieval pedway linked two buildings across a street.

"I remember it from when I was a kid. I'll take Angelo that way and meet you at the church."

I had a flash image of Zann as a curious little urchin climbing over the roofs of Florence. Maybe I actually liked her, after all. "Where at the church?"

"It's a big complex," Angelo said. "Many entrances."

"That's why I asked. We need a back entrance, Angelo, not visible from the street," I said.

"I don't know the whole place, only the interior church," he replied.

"We could just hope to find one, I suppose," Zann suggested.

Reaching down into my bra, I pulled out my phone and brought up Florence on Google Maps, tapping on the flyover version. Up popped a bird's-eye view of the city on a sunny day, every detail clear. By sweeping along the Arno, I found the Ognissanti so that we could look down on the ambling church complex from above. It was huge.

"There." Zann pointed to a back section that looked to be an enclosed garden. "That cloister should have a back entrance because that little square is a parking area. All you need to do is unlock the door at that point and let us in."

"Easy," I said because it wasn't. "Meet you there."

I watched as they climbed over the low railing to the right and onto the adjoining roof, hanging back until I could give Angelo a push up the small incline and Zann tugged him over the other side. Once they were out of sight,

I returned to figure out how best to get a run-on when a two-foot edging barricaded the way. All I had to do was trip and that would be that.

Maybe the best way was to stand on the edge and spring for the other side. I didn't much like that idea, either, but doubted I could work up much of a trajectory otherwise.

I balanced on the balls of my feet. Theory whammed into reality. Below me, a chasm of darkness; ahead, the opposite roof barely visible in the shadows. What the hell was I thinking? I should have taken the long way around, too. I needed to pitch myself forward in order to keep from toppling backward, assuming I even made it to the other side. Damn, Phoebe! Stop overthinking.

Then I heard a mechanical buzzing deep in the alley's throat below. Fear twisted in my gut. When the shot fired, so did my adrenaline, and I jumped.

18

$\mathcal{I}$ had just enough time to sense someone waiting below before hitting the other side—literally. My chin slammed against the roof as I scrambled for a grip. Corrugated tiles, bumpy ridges. I was sliding down.

Another shot rang out, shattering a tile by my left foot. A second shot, then another. The sound of two motorcycles roared below. Finally, I managed to cup the raised tiles with my hands and gain a little friction beneath my feet. The downward slide eased and I clung there listening to the ruckus below.

Somebody, maybe Evan or Peaches, was drawing the dragon lady away. I squeezed my eyes shut and sent a silent thanks before spidering up the roof inch by inch. Once I reached the top, I slid down the other side on my bottom before leaping to my feet and scrambling across the terra-cotta terrain.

This long multileveled section appeared to connect to the church complex —great—but once I was two roofs over, I realized that the only way down was via a six-foot drop. No problem, I told myself, except I had a wonky ankle from an old injury and wasn't sure I could land exactly in the crouch that provided the most protection. It's not like I practiced these things. Somehow I managed to land perfectly, anyway, congratulated myself, and continued.

Here I was dashing across the top of Florence, so far removed from the modern world I could have been transported to another century. Just me, the stars high above, and a drug gang somewhere below, risking my neck over and over again. How perfect could life be?

I leaped to the next level, this one slightly slanted but abutting against the remains of a tower. Supporting myself against its brick sides, I reached the next three-foot drop, jumped, and kept on going. I was getting closer now. The silhouette of the church's medieval bell tower loomed ahead. Three small roofs more and I'd reach the first of the church buildings.

Again, I pulled out my phone and brought up the flyover map. I pinpointed my location and plotted my path up a couple of small peaked roofs, down to the long roof of a cloister—I couldn't quite tell from the angle—and then a quick jump to the courtyard. Then I'd enter through a door and unlock a back entrance, or so I hoped. If I wasn't so positive that I'd need Angelo and Zann before the night was done, I'd head directly for the main church, but as it was, I needed to find that back door.

As it happened, I made good time and, even better, found a little shuttered window tucked away behind an alcove on a third-story section. It looked to be some kind of secondary building judging by the lack of main windows. Guessing this one must lead to a storage room or something similar, I ran my phone across seeking an alarm and finding none. A simple jiggle of the shutter pushed the rotten wood open, a further nudge on the rusty latch and I was in, climbing onto a table into a dark stuffy room.

Silently I admonished the priests or whoever maintained this place for not realizing that God worked in mysterious ways. Why not install proper security? Still, here I was, inside the church—somewhere—and I didn't even need to make too convoluted an entrance. I turned on the flashlight and ran the light across the room, illuminating boxes, folded Christmas trees, wooden angels, a nativity scene. Now, if I could just find the back entrance.

When I entered into the hall seconds later, I found myself in a long dark corridor with stuccoed walls permeating the scent of floor polish. A row of closed doors lined the hall—offices, I thought, or more storage areas. I knew from the flyover that the cloisters and living areas were mostly on the other side of the main church, making this part uninhabited. Next, find a staircase down and a back door somewhere.

All was going so well. By the time I reached the lower hallway and followed along until I found an exit, I figured I was on a roll. On one side of the corridor, broad windows opened onto a treed garden, which meant that the parking lot must be on the right.

Deactivating the alarm, I opened the side door onto a cluster of cars—bingo! Now all I needed was to see Angelo and Zann waiting for me somewhere in the shadows. But the place was deserted.

Propping the door open, I crept out as a security light flicked on above. Another narrow back lane led to this little parking space with nothing around but cars, a jumble of mostly medieval buildings, and the occasional new addition squeezed between.

Pulling out my phone, I texted Peaches and Evan. No immediate response. Understandable if they were chasing bad guys. Then something like a yelp interrupted the dark. It came from somewhere down that narrow alley.

Diving into the shadows, I peeked around the corner. Two shadowy figures were struggling in the dark, a third bent over on the ground. Pulling up my phone, I stepped out, crying: "Stop or I'll zap you where you stand."

The taller figure turned around, dragging the other in what looked to be a headlock.

"Yes, you zap Zann. I want her dead also!" She shifted Zann in front to use like a shield.

Lani, shit! I tried to beam the phone light right into her eyes but she ducked behind Zann while keeping a grip on her throat. Zann's mouth was open. She was squeezing the life out of her while Angelo moaned on the ground. No rifle, either. Where was killer girl's rifle?

I stepped out. "Let her go, Lani. You won't win this one. Release her. It's me you want."

"I want both."

"Let her go and you can have me."

She gave me a feral smile. "Drop phone. Fight like warrior."

Yeah, like I was a warrior. My last martial arts training was prepandemic and my body felt one hundred times older than that. "Sure." I laid the phone on the ground. "Let her go."

Lani flung Zann away like a sack of potatoes. For a second, I was afraid she was dead as she rolled into a heap on the ground until a feeble gasp gave me hope. I took a step forward. "Okay, come and get me."

Lani lunged, flinging me back onto the pavers with such force the breath left my body. I kicked out and missed. She kicked back and I took a direct hit in the gut. Lani laughed. I tried to perform a rolling maneuver that theoretically should have brought me back onto my feet. Instead, I ended on my knees. Lani kicked me over again, my skull whamming against the cobbles. It was safe to say I was going to lose this one.

She intended to enjoy every minute of this. Slow kill was her thing. She circled me as if deciding which nasty move to inflict next. I rolled onto my belly in an effort to protect my vitals, wondering what command I could send that would prompt my phone to intervene. But it was facing the sky, not the enemy. I gazed at the mute square of light emanating from my screen knowing that it may as well be a million miles away. My eyes blurred. I was heaving breath into my lungs. I'd soon would be a goner.

Lani's biker boots crossed my line of vision. She crouched beside me, grabbed my hair, and twisted my face toward her. "Poor little Phoebe. Do you hurt? I hurt, too. I hurt because sister is dead. Now I hurt you; I hurt you bad."

And then I caught a shadow behind her and suddenly Lani was toppling over. Choking in outrage, she tried to rise but something slammed her down again. I flipped onto my back to see Angelo standing over her holding a cast iron planter in both hands.

"Is she knocked out?" he asked.

Propping myself on my elbows, I stared at the unmoving form, at the trickle of blood at her temple. "Knocked out, yes, but still breathing." I was gasping. "Thanks, Angelo. How's Zann?"

Zann came stumbling over to us, rubbing her throat. "Bitch!" She kicked Lani in the ribs. "Why didn't you just zap her?" she rasped. Turning, she moved toward my phone.

"Don't touch it!" I warned as Angelo helped me to my feet. "It will think you're an intruder and burn your hands."

"Really?" Zann paused, watching me hobble over to retrieve my phone. "Can you make it know me?"

I tapped the screen, entered the settings, and activated the "friendly" feature. "Here, place your thumb here and here." Zann followed my directions. "Now it knows you." Remember, I was a befuddled at the time.

"Cool." She was studying the screen. "And those are all the famous features I've heard so much about? Pretty intuitive." Her breath was raspy but she appeared fine otherwise.

"Forget the tech session. Damn, my stomach hurts." Really, I wasn't paying much attention. Just happy to be alive, feeling grateful and all that, not to mention woozy.

I was bending over taking deep breaths planning to force myself back into operation when I heard the familiar sound of my phone electrocuting flesh. I straightened to see Zann tasering Lani over the heart.

"That's for that family you burned alive in Logar and those kids you shot in Herat. You'll never harm anyone again, bitch!"

To tell you the truth, I didn't care. I was just glad Lani was gone and that I didn't have to be the one responsible. I whipped my phone out of Zann's hand and made for the door. "Let's go."

644

19

The compound was huge. By the time we reached the doors to the main church and deactivated the alarm, another fifteen minutes had passed. We stood inside the darkened nave lit only by the streetlamps beaming in from the tall windows above. Even in the half-light, the shadowy frescos, marble surfaces, sculptures, and ornate niches left me totally overwhelmed. Where would we begin?

"You think he buried painting in a tomb?" Angelo was genuflecting.

"Absolutely not. I keep saying that. Can you imagine someone sneaking in here after hours to rob a crypt?"

"We do not know that it was Botticelli that hid it. We do not know there even is a painting that still survived," he pointed out.

"Such a pessimist." I frowned at him.

"Still, a tomb might be a place to start. I always find tombs rich in artifacts and full of secrets," Zann offered.

"Because you're an archaeologist, not a painter fearing for his soul," I pointed out.

"Guess I should fear for my soul, shouldn't I?" Zann asked.

I let that one drop. Hardly my area of expertise.

"I show you something." Angelo took off down the aisle and we followed as he cut through a row of pews. We didn't stop until we were gazing down at a round marble plaque embedded into the tiled floor. I beamed my light full on the inscription.

"Alessandro di Mariano di Vanni Filipepi," he read.

"Nicknamed 'Botticelli' or 'little barrel,' presumably for his portly girth," I said.

"It is in memory only," Angelo said. "His real tomb is in a side chapel and possibly his remains do not lie there, either."

"Even Simonetta's remains are supposedly no longer here—lost." Zann pointed to another round marker to our right.

"How do you lose a grave in a church?" It seemed like a reasonable question.

"By flood," she said. "When the Arno breeched its banks in 1966, the church experienced so much damage that many tombs were destroyed or, in Simonetta's case, disappeared. They think she may have floated downstream, or that's one story. No one's been given permission to search for her remains here yet."

"Oh, yes," I said. "I remember now. The world lost thousands of paintings, hundreds of sculptures, and at least 1,500 books, if I recall. All of Florence was under water. I didn't realize it destroyed tombs, too. That makes it even more important to find Botticelli's painting, but he would never have placed it in a tomb. He'd find a place he'd think would be more accessible."

"But where?" Angelo asked.

I stepped back and gazed up at the ceiling. Even without light, I could see that it was richly frescoed like the ceilings of so many other Italian churches but in a manner too late to be from the Renaissance period. "Some place Botticelli would think might be permanent and safe. Why does this church look more baroque than Renaissance classical or even medieval? Wasn't it built in the 1300s?"

"Originally, yes, but it's been altered many times," Zann remarked. "It went from simple to this."

"And passed hands to different Franciscan orders," Angelo added.

"Okay, so think: where would a Renaissance man hide a painting inside a church?"

"Behind another?" Angelo pointed to the church's side altars, which were richly decorated by frescos, statues, and even paintings.

"Too late. Those are mostly sixteenth and seventeenth century," I said.

"And as family memorials," Zann added, "they might change over the centuries."

"I have not been to this church for many years." Angelo shrugged. "I do not know it well."

I was just about to protest when the lights came on. We swung around to see three priests standing at the main doorway, each dressed in identical brown robes with bare feet clad in white slippers.

One demanded an explanation in Italian. The little man, probably in his early sixties, took a cautious step toward us saying that the church was not open. If we were in need of solace, they would be happy to help but breaking into a church of God was not acceptable. One of his brethren, a tall lean younger man, held a cell phone and looked ready to call either the police or God at the first sign of trouble. The third, a totally bald guy, simply looked worried.

Angelo stepped forward, removing his wallet and taking out his identification as he went. He proceeded to introduce himself, I realized, catching snippets here and there. He was a scholar of the Medici and his colleagues were his assistants. There was a great urgency to find the secret hiding place of a presumably lost painting by Botticelli rumored to be hidden here—not to steal, he assured them, but to preserve. Criminals were attempting to take the painting to sell on the underground market for drugs. We must secure the painting for the Uffizi or lose another great work of art forever.

The little priest looked dumbfounded and said in Italian, "What, you are like Robert Langdon?"

Zann snickered. "Straight out of a Dan Brown novel, right?"

I shushed her.

"I am Father Agosti and my Franciscan brethren are Fathers Fontana and Leoni." The two nodding priests looked bewildered. While Father Agosti studied Angelo's credentials, I stepped forward and introduced myself in beginner Italian. The friar lifted his hand after my first few words and winced. "Please continue in English."

I thanked him and introduced myself, bringing in a few of my recent exploits, assuring him that I was affiliated with Interpol. I was only halfway through when I realized how the man's eyes twinkled with excitement.

"It is possible," he said, nodding. "I have thought of hidden art many times. This was Botticelli's church. If he were to hide one of his works, why not here? But the church was completely renovated in 1627. Many pieces of art were moved, even the frescos taken from the walls, and then God brought the flood to remind us that such grandeur is not needed for the soul to reach heaven. The Ognissanti has suffered much over the centuries, much like humanity itself, but still we live on in spirit and faith, yes? God has left what remains in our hands and now we must protect it. How can we assist you?"

I smiled at my new ally, but before I could get a word in, he was leading us up toward the nave, describing his church as he went, his slippered feet shuffling on the tiles. "During the Renaissance, Botticelli and Ghirlandaio painted here, it is true, and many others. Our church still holds many great treasures but many more were lost. God be praised for preserving Giotto's cross and Ghirlandaio's *Last Supper* in the refectory. And of course Botticelli's only fresco in Florence remains here. Do you know of them?"

I did, I assured him, though I had yet to see them in person. For some reason, this gem of a church had never been on my mental map.

The little friar was animated and clearly passionate about art and the history of his church. "The *Last Supper* was contemporary with Botticelli and remains in its original location. Let us start there. The two artists were possibly rivals. Both were given commissions to paint the choir screen. Botticelli was commissioned by the Vespucci to paint a fresco of Saint Augustine and Ghirlandaio painted another of Saint Jerome but both were moved. New altars, paintings, and sculptures were installed in the seventeenth and eighteenth centuries by my Franciscan brethren, and then in 1923 one of our convents served as a barracks for the Carabinieri. You see, in such a long contorted history, where would we begin to find the remnants of our lost Botticelli?"

It was *our* Botticelli now. The man was a kindred spirit. "By reading any remaining images from the artist's time," I suggested.

"Then let us begin in the refectory."

"Thank you, but would you mind turning out the lights first? I'm afraid to alert the criminals of our location."

"But of course." The priest gave instructions to one of the brothers, who scampered off to switch off the lights.

The refectory was located between the first and second cloisters in the old convent section. We were halfway there, carrying on an animated conversation about Renaissance ecclesiastical art, all of us chatting away, when a thought struck me with so much force that I slammed on my brakes.

Father Agosti turned in surprise as Zann bumped into me.

"What?" she asked.

"Lani must wear a tracker," I said.

"Of course, all Baldi's—" And she stared at me, equally stricken. She swore, slapped a hand to her mouth, and apologized to our companions.

"What is wrong?" Father Agosti asked.

I explained about the assassin and our struggle in the church parking lot, how it forced us to kill in self-defense, but that the killer probably wore a tracker which will lead her criminal colleagues straight to us. The priest's eyes widened. "You left her body there?"

"We didn't have time to do anything else," I explained.

"She should be properly buried and her soul restored to God," he said, lifting his hands.

"You'd never be able to save that one's soul, Father," Zann told him. "The devil got her long ago."

Even in the dim light, I could see he was prepared to disagree.

"Please, we must hurry," I urged. "I'm afraid that the gang are already on their way." I did a quick check on my phone. Still no messages from either Evan or Peaches. My anxiety spiked.

"I did not realize until now the seriousness of this matter," Father Agosti said. "Alarming." I thought I heard Father Fontana mutter, "Indiana Jones," and had I time, I might even have been annoyed by all these references to popular fiction.

A couple more turns and we scrambled down darkened hallways until we arrived at double doors which the priest unlocked with a security code. In seconds we were inside a long sparsely furnished space. Father Leoni flicked on a flashlight toward the large fresco at one end.

"This would have existed in Botticelli's time," Father Agosti said as we scurried toward the other end. Of course the fresco was magnificent, a work of incredible complexity with dynamic figures engaging with the figure of Christ at the Last Supper, but I was now single-minded.

"Regard the symbols," Angelo intoned, "the evergreens, quails, doves and fruit…"

"…which were not duplicated on Gabriela's sleeve. These are are references to the Passion and the Redemption. I can't see how this masterpiece would feature in Botticelli's clues." I ran my light over the surface, shaking my head. "I know that Domenico Ghirlandaio's work spurned Botticelli on and that they collaborated on many pieces but they were said to be more rivals than friends. One was known for portraying beautiful figures, the other a master at capturing human character, but whether Botticelli would embed a clue based on his rival's work, that is the question. I doubt that he would. We need to look elsewhere. Besides, neither Gabriela nor her friend would have access to a refectory in an active monastery."

"Who is Gabriela?" Father Agosti asked. I filled him on my detective work.

"But wouldn't a refectory be perfect? The friars would only be using it during mealtimes," Zann asked.

"Our early church did not segregate men from women," Father Agosti explained. "This brought accusations of licentious behavior and eventually the order was replaced by more observant Franciscans."

"Wow, friars and sex—got to love what goes on under the hood," Zann remarked.

I was dashing back down the room, everyone scurrying to catch up. "It's not here. Father Agosti, please take us to Botticelli's fresco."

"But it has been moved," he said as he ran up to me, puffing and panting.

"I must see it." Down through the halls we went, the night-lights dimly illuminating our path as we retraced our steps back to the church. "The fresco was painted in 1480, I know, many years before he painted our missing portrait, but if I were an artist wishing to hide something, I would start there, something I had a little control over," I said.

Father Agosti led us back to the nave. "It has been restored quite recently. Originally it would have been on the screen in the choir, which was demolished in 1564. Here you see it in its new home."

We clustered around a side altar as I shone my light up on to the painting framed by curlicues of baroque trompe-l'oeil plaster made to look like marble. The fresco, damaged along the edges, the colors newly brilliant after the recent restoration, portrayed Saint Augustine sitting in his study, one hand crossing his chest to touch his shoulder, the other holding a book, his face suffused in startled wonder as if he had just received a shock.

"According to the tale, Saint Augustine is reacting to a vision of the death of Saint Jerome, but since Ghirlandaio's Saint Jerome is in the fresco opposite, maybe he was just having a premonition," Zann suggested. She was looking across the nave at the companion piece but I remained firmly fixed on Botticelli's fresco.

A clock portrayed behind the scholar was showing the hour at sunrise when Saint Jerome supposedly died. An open book propped on the shelf behind the saint bore clearly visible writing as if it were a notebook of some kind. "What does the writing say?" I asked no one in particular.

"It reads," Angelo began, "'Where is Fra' Martino? He fled. And where did he go? He is outside Porto al Prato.' No one knows what it means. It has baffled scholars for decades."

"But it means something. There are geometric drawings visible there, too," I whispered.

"Nonsensical," Angelo said. "We do not know who Fra Martino was or why he fled to the tower by the bridge known as Porto al Prato. A joke, possibly. Botticelli did enjoy jokes."

"But in a church? That seems a rather odd time to make fun of something or someone. Though it's impossible to tell after restoration, what if that message was placed in the book many years after the fresco was painted? Would anyone even notice?" I asked.

"Probably not," Angelo conceded.

"As a known artist in his neighborhood church, no one would protest if he wanted to make 'repairs.'" I put the word in air quotes. "What if Botticelli placed that message later, specifically to alert someone else, perhaps the only one who might understand its meaning?"

Angelo turned to me. "Filippino Lippi came from Prato."

"He did," I said, barely daring to breathe.

"And 'martino' means 'warrior of Mars,'" Angelo said

"And Mars features prominently in the fresco in the Corsi chapel, plus Filippino was at war with the swell of anticlassical beliefs rising in Florence at the time."

"And Filippino's father, Fra Lippi, was a friar, not of this order but a man of cloth, yes?" Father Agosti said excitedly. "We—"

But he didn't finish his sentence before a huge crash reverberated through the church.

20

"**W**hat the hell was that?" Zann asked.

"*Il porta!*" cried Father Fontana.

Father Agosti spoke to him in rapid Italian and soon both of the other friars were on their cell phones. "We must rouse the others if they are not already awake," he explained.

"Someone's trying to break in through the front door—seriously?" Zann said. "Surely the Carabinieri would have noticed something like that? Aren't they just down the street?"

We rushed up to the huge double wooden doors—thick standard-issue old-church variety, maybe made of cedar. "They will need some kind of battering device to break down those," I said. "Just a guess." Another thump shook the timbers.

My phone beeped and up popped a message from Peaches: *We're in the church somewhere. The Baldinos have surrounded us and the police are swarming the streets. Like a war zone out here. Following your signal now to find you.*

"We may as well turn the lights back on. Our location's no longer a secret", I said, barely containing my relief. "My friends are inside the complex."

When Peaches and Evan came around the corner of a side hall seconds later, I wanted to hug them both but instead managed to blurt out introductions before leading them into the nave. "Quick, where would Botticelli have hidden a painting?"

"Oh, like that's a simple answer. Did you Google it?" Peaches said. Despite the jokiness, I could see she was in rough shape—a cut on her forehead, her stretchy black outfit ripped and muddy, blood. Evan didn't look much better but he cracked a smile. Both emanated strength and determination, though, and the gaze that Evan fixed on me caused a strange internal buoyancy all its own.

"What happened?" I asked.

"The short answer: we tried to keep the bastards away but they found your location somehow," she said.

"At which point, we decided to join you before we were arrested or shot by the police," Evan added. "It appears as though the authorities are under the assumption that these fine brothers are being held hostage while you attempt to heist the church's treasures."

"But that's ludicrous!" I cried.

"Yet very Baldi-like," Zann assured me. "He has a connection with someone high up in the local police around here. Don't know who. All he has to do is string them a story and presto! fake news."

Father Agosti nodded. "Perhaps I should open the door to assure them we are not captives?"

"No!" we all said at once. "But thank you for the offer. Let's just find this painting. Have you heard from Interpol?" I asked Evan.

"Nothing yet. How far have you come with your deductive puzzling?" Evan quirked just a hint of a smile. I had the overwhelming urge to touch his face.

"We are slowly—too slowly, I admit—unpicking the knot that wraps this mystery." I turned to our companions, now staring at us expectantly. "All right, everyone, group think time: where would a Renaissance painter hide a painting in his neighborhood church? Back to the fresco and let's work this out!"

As we dashed back down the aisle, I realized that the banging had stopped but the sudden silence brought little comfort. "What were they doing out there?" I asked.

"They've surrounded the complex. My guess is that Baldi's gang will attempt to break in while the police fiddle around deciding next steps and sort out protocols," Evan replied. "A church is still considered a sanctuary, a point I doubt Baldi will let stop him. Expect an unpleasant interruption soon. My welcome maneuvers have been exhausted."

I didn't have time to ask what that meant.

"Here," Father Agosti said as we arrived before Saint Augustine. "As we were saying, this is not the original location. In the fifteenth century, it decorated the screen of the choir." He pointed to the front of the church.

"He's looking up," Peaches exclaimed, indicating Saint Augustine. "Come on, you guys. We're in a church. Look up!"

Which we did, far up to the frescoed ceiling where saints, angels, and a friar I suspected might be Saint Francis of Assisi in his brown robe cavorted on puffy clouds while Jesus looked on. With the church lights blazing, its colorful glory was fully illuminated and had the added effect of inducing vertigo.

"But Giuseppe Romei's fresco didn't exist in Botticelli's day," Evan said. "It was painted sometime around 1770."

"It doesn't matter," Peaches insisted. "Botticelli was a Renaissance dude, right? He would have known about Brunelleschi's dome and know enough architecture to understand how these places were built. The Renaissance artists were the ultimate cross-disciplinarians. They grasped architecture, right?"

"They did," Evan agreed.

I grinned at her. "You're brilliant!"

"What do I keep telling you?" she said.

"Then perhaps we should be looking at the ceiling over the altar where the choir must have been originally," Evan suggested while heading toward the front of the church.

"But the cappella maggiore was not built until 1574," Father Agosti explained, hurrying after him.

"Let's take a look, regardless," Evan said.

We stood together beside a gilded altar so ornate that the eye barely knew where to land, and gazed up past the golden candlesticks, past Jesus on the cross, past the four angels spreading their wings against a gilded background, and finally to a dome graced by a circle of saints and angels gazing down.

"Not a true structural dome," Peaches decided.

"Half trompe l'oeil," I remarked.

"This is another late addition," Father Agosti said, resting for a moment on the marble steps. "It was not here when our Ognissanti was but a simple church."

"So only the nave is structurally original?" Evan said.

"Yes, that is so," said the friar. "In Botticelli's day, it was plain."

Back toward the center of the nave we went. By now we could see flashing lights pulsing through the upper windows.

"Botticelli painted clues in his fresco that he expected his once apprentice,

Filippino Lippi, or his friend and Filippino's love, Gabriela, would understand," I said.

"Filippino and Gabriela were lovers?" Zann asked.

"I believe so. Gabriela was a designer and the brilliance behind many of the glorious clothes painted and worn during Lorenzo de' Medici's time. She dressed many of Botticelli's subjects, both real and imagined. Remember the painting of Venus and Mars—two lovers after lovemaking? That, too, is a clue and Venus's gown a Gabriela design. When Botticelli hints at 'Fra Martino' he is alluding to Mars and to that painting. Either Filippino or Gabriela would have grasped the reference if they had ever returned to this church again. This was Gabriela's parish church, too."

"All church records have been lost," Father Agosti said.

"And the reference to Prato is also a clue for Filippino, who was born there," Angelo added. "The Renaissance communicated in symbols and classical references."

"And Fra Martino, referring to Filippino, did flee," I said. "'Where is Fra' Martino? He fled.' He fled because Florence was not safe for artists and designers anymore. Lorenzo de' Medici was dead. There'd be no more protection from Florence's once powerful champions of artistic license and beauty. If you explored subjects beyond the Bible, you were a heretic, and your art became a crime against God. Too much of a show of wealth was also an insult to Christ's poverty but for an artist, 'poor' translated to a lack of color, texture, and vibrancy. Certainly for those who loved beautiful clothes. Gabriela and Filippino fled Florence the night beauty burned in the streets or maybe even before."

"I do not agree with Fra Savonarola, though I understand, of course," said Father Agosti. "Beauty is God's work no matter what the guise."

Evan touched my shoulder. "Inspired brilliance again, Phoebe, but we still don't know where the painting was hidden."

I turned toward the windows, the faint blush of dawn just visible despite the flashing lights. The sound of sirens drove me to distraction. "He wouldn't have hidden it at ground level as Peaches says. Saint Augustine is looking up."

Which Peaches never stopped doing. "Original pitched timber roof, right?" she asked Father Agosti.

"Sì," Father Leoni offered.

"We've got to get up there," Peaches said.

"How?" I asked.

Father Agosti smiled. "Our brethren wash our windows and repair the roof with a system as old as time. We use harnesses, pulleys, and slings like our ancestors. These were also used for fixing leaks. Perhaps this could bring you close to the ceiling, yes?"

I turned to him. "You don't hire professional window cleaners or roofers?"

"We prefer to do our work in-house, as you say, and the old ways bring us much closer to God, yes?" He pointed up and smiled. I returned his smile. "I will rouse my brethren to bring the harnesses," he said as he pulled out his cell phone.

"That could help us to cross the ceiling," Evan pointed out, "but if I'm not mistaken, those lights installed around the top edge of the rafters required a more recent alteration."

"But of course," Father Agosti said, turning. "There are stairways leading there, many stairways. Father Fontana will show the way while we locate the harnesses."

"You may also ask your brothers to post a watch throughout the building to alert us to the first Baldi break and entry. If I'm not mistaken, they'll try to enter from the back," Evan suggested.

"*Sì*, but remember that we are not warriors but servants of God." Father Agosti proceeded down the aisle, speaking hurriedly into his phone as he went.

Father Fontana indicated for us to follow him, which all but Angelo did. "I will sit here and assist with my broader view." He took a seat in a pew, stretched out his legs, and leaned back. I thought he might have planned to snooze but the sound of gunfire abruptly ended that idea.

21

"They come!" Angelo cried, diving under one of the side altars.

"Sounds like it's coming from the cloisters!!" Evan called as he followed Father Agosti. "The rest of you go ahead. We'll try to hold them off."

Father Fontana had led us down the left side of the church to where a stairway rose in an arched opening to reveal Giotto's cross shining in brilliance under a canopy of painted stars. For a moment, I was stunned by its beauty.

I was just about to take the first step, Zann and Father Fontana having gone ahead, when Peaches touched my arm. "Maybe I should go with Evan."

"Yes. Zann and I will try to find the painting," I said.

"Only you don't know architecture and engineering and I do. I'm staying. Besides, I can't see you swinging from a sling from the ceiling," she protested.

"Have a little faith. I can swing with the best of them. Besides, he needs you more."

Evan, the man with the finely tuned hearing, stopped at the side door and called, "Stay with Phoebe, Peaches. Find that painting. The brothers and I have this."

Peaches shot me a quick look. "You'd think he had God on his side. Come on, Phoeb, let's go."

Zann called down from the top of the stairs to hurry. Together we scrambled up to a landing beside the glowing cross, through a side door, down a long hallway, and through another door to dash up a narrow set of stairs until the four of us were standing in single file along a narrow ledge overlooking the nave. The only thing between us and the thirty-foot drop was an iron railing. Overhead, the trompe-l'oeil ceiling seemed much farther away but it still had to be at least fifteen feet overhead. More painted baroque plasterwork lined the walls where the windows now washed with red dawn light while the spotlights at our feet beamed up at the fresco.

I squeezed past the others to the far end of the ledge where I leaned over to inspect the gilded organ that commandeered at least half of the remaining wall to the left. Behind me, the friar said something I didn't grasp.

"He says the organ is a later addition, too," Zann told me.

This church was layered with visual tricks and optical sleight of hand, none of which existed during Botticelli's time. Baroque had had its way here.

More crashing and the sound of broken glass came from somewhere deep in the complex. I looked over to see four friars slipping onto the balcony opposite ours equipped with a variety of ropes. A younger one burst through the stairway to our ledge calling to Father Fontana, who urged us to back up against the wall, which we did.

Now the friars on both sides were tossing cables up to the ceiling as if fishing among the saints and angels. Whatever they were aiming for must have been expertly hidden among the clouds because I couldn't see a thing. Then a clink of metal against metal caused one friar to praise God. I gazed up. Miraculously, a rope now hung suspended from the painted sky. Within minutes, others followed until the ceiling was strung by a network of ropes and pulleys designed to transport individuals in a kind of grid formation.

Zann whistled through her teeth. "Amazing. This contraption is so ingenious it looks as if it could have come straight out of a Da Vinci notebook."

"Maybe it did," Peaches said. "They used a system like this along with scaffolding back in the day to repair and build their roofs. And we think we have all the answers. Good thing the hardware is modern."

I gazed at the carabiners the brothers had fixed onto the railing's edge, sharing her relief. Now two friars were joining us on the ledge holding slings, a toolbox, and bags.

Explaining their use in Italian, Zann translated: "You climb into the sling and then drop over the edge. The ropes support you and by pulling on them, you can crisscross the ceiling almost any place you want using the pulleys. Return to the ledge and move over to another line each time you want to move farther across more quickly. The friars ask that you to please not destroy the fresco, by the way."

Peaches held up her phone. "Tell him that we're using an X-ray app and that nothing will be smashed indiscriminately.'"

"How do you want me to translate 'indiscriminately'?" Zann asked.

But the gunshot heard from somewhere inside the building nixed the answer.

"Hurry," I urged.

Peaches and I stepped into the slings, wide canvas straps that crossed between our legs and fastened under our chests. There were only two sets.

"Damn. I wanted to fly, too," Zann muttered. "Any guesses where in that expanse of sky you're going to look?"

Peaches was already sitting on the railing, her feet dangling over the edge. "I'm going to search for a cavity within the beams. The hooks must be embedded in the support timbers so that's where I'll start."

"I'll visually scan the surface for any anomalies since my phone is out of juice," I said. "I might see something by eye, anyway. This ceiling would have been nothing but timber beams in his day."

Botticelli may have used a system something very much like this to hide the painting initially. Maybe one of the friars had even helped him. Or maybe he didn't hide it at all and I was on the wrong track. Or maybe it was discovered long ago by my bastard ex and was now in someone's private collection, possibly lost to the world forever. But then, why would Toby have sent me the clue?

I was still sitting on the railing waffling while watching Peaches slip away across the ceiling when a loudspeaker blared from the street outside.

Zann translated. "'Come out with your hands raised and you will not be harmed' but somebody doesn't know the word for *harmed* and used *slaughtered*. Then he finished with 'Release the friars at once!' Not big on original scripts obviously."

"You've got to be kidding," I said. As if our surrender wouldn't result in all of us being thrown in jail and Baldi ending up with the painting somehow. No way. And with that, I pushed myself off the ledge and flew across the church.

Yes, it was very much like flying—very much like falling, too, until the ropes caught my weight. I dangled for a moment gazing far down at the illuminated splendor below before I snapped to and began to hoist myself across the space by pulling on the ropes. It was a bit like zip-lining across a roped grid and an absolutely exhilarating way to traverse this noble landscape while bringing me closer to the magnificent fresco. Below, the church glowed in the soft light, every gilded surface shining, while above I flew with the saints and angels.

"Find anything?" I called to Peaches, who was running her phone across the surface.

"Nothing so far," she called back.

Now we heard a roll of machine-gun fire—against one man and a brethren of friars, seriously? Sudden despair hit me. We'd never scan every inch of this ceiling in time. We were doomed. How could I feel so much despair while flying so close to the angels?

Zann called from the ledge. "The friars say that the Baldinos have entered through the back cloisters. They have barricaded the doors. See anything?"

"Not yet," I called. And maybe never would. Maybe I was wild-goose-chasing a notion that could get people killed, innocent people, good people. Even me.

Another loudspeaker message, this time in English in case anything was lost in translation. "Come out with your hands up! Do not force us to break down door! We will shoot!"

Sure, shoot the wrong people, bozos. Baldi was pulling strings, all right. I was studying the surface, hoping against hope to see something that Peaches's super app might miss, something telling, something that hinted at a secret receptacle behind the plaster. I spun around, ready to hoist myself back toward the ledge in order to cross in another direction, when the sun broke through the window.

I stared, twisting slightly in my sling. The golden light poured in through the opposite window and landed on a spot just above where we had been standing. I grabbed the rope to still myself and stared. "Zann, where would Saint Augustine be looking if the fresco was still in the choir again?"

"Maybe right there!" She pointed at the sun bolt at her knees. "But the sun may have been at a different angle when the fresco was painted and we don't even know the month it was created!"

Below Angelo scuttled out from under the altar. "Saint Jerome died at dawn!" he called. "It is dawn!"

Peaches was swinging toward the sun's landing place, me following. I arrived beside her, both of us bracing our feet against the wall. The friars helped us back on the ledge and we watched expectantly as Peaches held her phone over the sunspot. Nothing registered at first but several inches to the right and she finally got a hit.

"There's a cavity behind there," she said, waving the app across the surface. "Anyone got a hammer?"

There was a flurry of activity among the friars until one removed a hammer from a toolbox.

Peaches flashed him a brilliant smile before whacking the wall below the window. Great slabs of painted plaster fell to the floor as the friars cried out. I watched as the destroyed pseudo curlicues shattered to reveal a deep rectangular cavity.

For a moment Peaches, Zann, the two friars, and I gazed in wonder before I reached into the opening to remove a twelve-by-twenty-inch leather container no deeper than an inch dusted white with plaster and a skim of mold. Holding it up in both hands so the friars on the opposite ledge could see, I cried: "Behold, Botticelli awaits!"

And then a shot fired on the ceiling overhead.

"Behold and watch your new buddy die!" someone cried below.

I looked down. There stood Baldi surrounded by six of his men and Peter Dunbar, who gripped Angelo in a neck hold with a pistol pressed against his skull. Five brothers were also held at either gun- or knifepoint with neither Evan nor Father Agosti anywhere in sight

"Toss down the container and I let them live. Disobey me and they all die," Baldi bellowed. "All of them!"

22

_____

 M y brain went into overdrive. Baldi couldn't shoot the brethren without facing consequences. There were witnesses and the police were just beyond that door. I wrestled with my conscience, my deter-mination, my anger...

But I underestimated the depth of Zann's own rage. She began flinging tools and insults over the railing at the Baldinos below—hammers, screw-drivers, an ax. "You're not getting this painting, you scourge of the Western world! Eat dirt, you scum!" And much worse.

Dunbar ducked to avoid a flying ax as Angelo broke free and scuttled back under a side altar. Baldi fired toward the ledge at the same time as the lights went out all over the church. Somebody called out in Italian, another screamed in the shadows as I secured the container under my chest strap—awkwardly, I admit—and leaped over the side. It was all that I could do to pull the ropes and hold on to the box at the same time.

Peaches was somewhere behind me as I swept across the ceiling. The nave had plunged into shadows, illuminated only by an occasional bolt of streaming sun. I caught fleeting glimpses of what was happening below—a chaotic flurry of noise and fluster, friars flowing in from every quarter, shouts and commands, gunfire, and cries.

"Baldi's left the nave on the right-hand side holding a brother at gunpoint. I think he's heading to the ledge to get a better shot at you. Head for the back balcony!" Peaches called out to me. "Over there!"

There where? I could just see a pair of small balconies on either side of the high altar, each as wide as the window above. Closed curtains bled a red rectangle of light over each. Where there were balconies, there'd be doorways, I reasoned. Destination found.

I crossed the ceiling until I was within feet of that window. There'd be another stairway up there, maybe even an escape route.

Suddenly I jerked to a halt. Shaking the rope made no difference: I couldn't budge. I looked up toward the shadowy ceiling. The rope had snagged in the hook embedded at the edge of the fresco. Way too far up for me to untangle or even see clearly. Returning the way I had come was out of the question, too, since no matter how hard I tugged and pulled, I wasn't going anywhere.

"Peaches!" I called.

But she was already halfway across the ceiling and couldn't hear. Somebody had arrived on our ledge and was slicing a flashlight beam across the ceiling until it struck me. The curtains of the window where he stood were open so I could see them bathed in sunrise—Baldi still holding the friar hostage, Dunbar by his side. Zann and the other friars had disappeared. Peaches was approaching from the left, shrouded in shadows.

"Drop the painting, Phoebe McCabe, and I will let the good brother go and all these people will live!" Baldi called.

I shielded my eyes against the light. "You have no intention of letting anyone go, bastard," I called. Then I began to rock back and forth as if on a swing hoping to either get unstuck or gain the momentum necessary to reach the balcony. Baldi fired and missed. I began praying—seemed like the right time and place. My rocking was bringing me closer and closer. Another few heaves and my feet might touch the stone. A few more shots and I might die.

Something exploded below. I turned around and looked down long enough to see the police swarming into the church. At that moment, Peaches reached the ledge and was tackling Dunbar while Baldi and the friar disappeared through the door. He had to be coming for me using that poor man as his navigational aid.

I heaved and heaved until the forward swing brought me so close to the balcony that I could almost touch it. Suddenly the rope released and sent me flying toward the balcony. I braced for impact, hit knees first, grasped the railing, and pulled myself up and over until I lay on my stomach, landing full on the container. I gave myself only seconds to thank the angels, check for damages, and spring to my feet. Then I unbuckled the ropes and dashed through a side door, still wearing the sling. No time to detach that thing when on a headlong run down the stairs.

Holding a flat box in front of you isn't easy if you need at least one hand free to hold on to a wall. The stairway was narrow and dark. I didn't see the door until I whammed into it. Seconds later, I opened up the low hatch and peered into a short corridor lined with barrels, buckets, and cleaning supplies. The minute I stepped out, footsteps and voices sounded somewhere down the hall. I hesitated. Behind me voices, ahead nothing but a blank wall.

Then Baldi appeared steering the friar. Seeing me, he flung the man aside and fired. The bullet grazed my leg while I dashed back inside the stairwell. No inside lock. Nothing to do but scramble back up the way I'd come.

A cold realization hit halfway up that stairs: by now the police must know the truth about Baldi—the friars would have set them straight. That meant that the bastard's one chance to escape was to disappear with the painting. He'd kill me and take the portrait. I'd served my purpose. He probably had it all planned, with many soldiers waiting outside and many more lined up to cover his tracks. What did he have to lose? I was as good as dead in his eyes.

But my adrenaline was pumping like a fuel injector. Back on the balcony, I shoved open the curtains, unlatched the window, and climbed through, holding the painting under one arm. I remembered from the flyover that a short roof abutted just below each of these two back windows, with the roof of the nave and altar between. All I had to do was scamper away to safety, which sounded so simple. Baldi was right behind me shooting at every opportunity and by now my scampering had turned into more of a wobble. One leg was searing with pain, both knees badly bruised.

The roof was tiny and wedged between two stone and stucco walls. I skidded onto another short slanted roof and from there scrambled up onto a long narrow tiled construction that probably topped the cloisters—didn't know, didn't care. I was running blind by then, thinking only of escape, trying to balance while holding the painting.

The sun rose over the city, the air fresh and warm, and it set me to wondering whether this would be my last sunrise on earth. I leaped up to another level, risking a quick check behind where I spied Baldi pausing long enough to aim a clean shot at me. I turned to spring away, then realized that there was no place to go, unless straight to my death. Below lay nothing but a drop to a cobbled courtyard maybe three stories below. I hesitated before slowly turning to face the monster.

He was perspiring heavily, not in such great shape, then. "There, McCabe, it is over, see?" Panting, he straightened, holding the gun in both hands with his legs bracing him on the slanted surface. Not comfortable with heights, either. "You lay down the painting and I don't shoot."

That was almost funny. He must have thought me stupid. I considered dropping the container to the courtyard below but the risk of damaging it was too great and the chance of a Baldino lurking down there even greater. Though the police must be all over this place by now, so must they.

I caught a movement on the roof behind him, just a silhouette crawling toward the edge. Impossible to tell whether it was friend or foe. Friend, I thought, or the newcomer would alert Baldi.

"Okay, Baldi. You win. I'll pass over the painting if you let me live," I said.

"Good girl, good girl." He paused to wipe his forehead on a sleeve. "Do not lay it down. You must pass it to me so it doesn't slide off."

I took a tentative step forward, suddenly aware of how much my leg hurt. I made to reach the painting forward. Baldi didn't move—afraid to lose his footing, I guessed.

"You come to me," he said.

"You'll have to meet me halfway," I said. "I've been wounded, see?" A quick glance down proved that I was bleeding, my leggings soaked in blood. It was a surface wound but he didn't know that.

He hesitated. To stress my point, I sat on my bottom. "Sorry," I said. "Guess I'm more hurt than I thought." I tried to cry. "Help me."

He took another tentative step, afraid to shoot me outright in case I rolled over the edge taking the Botticelli with me, afraid to move too quickly in case he toppled over himself. Holding up his hand, he said. "You stay. I come to you. Do not worry."

Yeah, right.

At that moment the stalker jumped. I watched stunned as the body landed on top of Baldi, both rolling toward the edge. It was Zann, enraged Zann, reckless Zann. I scrambled forward to grab the gun still clutched in Baldi's flailing hand. Several shots fired wild. He turned on his stomach trying to grasp for a handhold when I slammed my foot down on his fingers, hearing a satisfying crunch. Zann was still punching him in the head as I retrieved the gun.

"It's okay, Zann," I cried. "We've got him. Stop!"

But she wasn't stopping. "That's for enslaving me, you miserable bastard! That's for all the pain and grief you've inflicted on people worldwide! That's for every piece of history you stole and deprived us of our heritage! That's for—"

Baldi's limp body rolled to the edge and finally Zann climbed off him but seconds too late. He shot out his good hand on the way down and dragged her over the edge with him.

Zann scrabbled for a hold, clutching the eavestrough, while Baldi dangled over the edge, wrapping his arms around both legs.

"Hang on," I cried. "Don't let go!" I lay the painting on the roof and grasped her wrist.

She gazed up at me. "It's okay. Did what I set out to do. Got the painting, got Baldi. They'll lock me up, anyway. Let me go, Phoebe."

"What are you talking about? This is where you celebrate, not give up."

"Not giving up—I won, right?" She gasped for a moment, struggling for breath before continuing. "I was with Baldi for years, remember? Hardly innocent." Tears in her eyes, tears in mine.

"What about your dad? Is this how you want him to hear about your redemption? You don't even have the photo op yet! I said hold on!"

Several people appeared beside me, including Evan and Peaches. Someone rescued the painting. Someone grabbed the gun. Evan reached down to grab Zann's other wrist while Peaches leaned over and fired at Baldi. It took two shots before the bastard released her and finally fell to the pavers below. A crowd had gathered to watch his arrival.

"You're not going anywhere," I told Zann. "We still have business to do and a story to tell, which you need to hear."

2 3

$\mathcal{W}$e gathered around the long table in the church's current refectory with a light breakfast served with plentiful coffee laid before us. Evan, Peaches, Zann, Angelo, plus the Interpol agent and Father Agosti all sat together as the sunlight streamed through the windows from the courtyard garden beyond. Our phones were charging and so were we, or at least that was the idea.

We were exhausted, in some cases wounded, filthy, and trying to remain upright using nothing but jolts of caffeine and crusty bread with cheese as props. I swear, I thought I'd topple over onto my plate at any moment. A physician and nurse had entered long enough to bandage our bleeding bits and administer salve where needed. My leg was bathed and bandaged after the doctor had braced Peaches's sprained wrist, obtained from slugging one Baldino too many.

"Look what the good folks here use for ointment," Peaches announced, though most weren't listening. "Naturally derived creams from the Farmaceutica di Santa Maria Novella. None of this cheap sleazy chemical stuff."

Evan, who had more bullet scars than any human should have, escaped this time with nothing worse than a broken arm. The sling looked good on him, by the way. Zann seemed more internally than externally battered and refused all care, but it was Angelo who required the most attention. The medical team spent a great deal of time bathing the man's feet while muttering something about "barbarians." I tried not to look too hard at his injuries but could see that an infection had taken hold at the remains of one toe. He was provided with a dose of antibiotics before the medical team left. At least none of us were on the verge of any permanent collapse apparently.

Though still in the process of answering questions from the police represented by Interpol plus an officer who came in and out of the room, we were in a kind of holding pattern. The container would only be in our keeping for a short time before officially handed over to the authorities. These moments would be all we'd likely get before the painting was eventually whisked away into official care and pounced upon by conservationists and art historians worldwide. It may take years before the portrait actually appeared on the gallery walls for the public's appreciation.

Still, we had to wait before opening the receptacle. Giovanni and an Uffizi official were on their way over and, with great difficulty, we agreed to hold on until he arrived. After all, we needed to consider the possible condition of the painting since time was not usually kind to art. It was best that the museum's official art historian participate in the big reveal.

Meanwhile, there were other matters to consider. Both Baldi and Dunbar were dead, a point that could be cause for celebration had not two friars lost their lives, one shot by Dunbar and the other by Baldi. They were good men caught in the crossfire and we mourned them even though we had never met them personally.

"They died protecting our church and our legacy," Father Agosti had said with tears in his eyes. "Heaven will welcome them both." At his request, we had prayed together, regardless of our faith or beliefs.

The police had rounded up the remaining Baldinos inside the church but many more had escaped, scattering like rats in the sunlight, and now a full manhunt was in progress across Tuscany.

"There will be more, many more," Angelo said as stared down morosely at his bandaged feet. "Killing Baldi will not end this gang. Like Hydra, when the head is removed, two more grow in its place."

"Interesting analogy," I remarked, staring into space. "My brother said something similar."

Evan hadn't heard that particular exchange because he was busy providing details to the Italian Interpol agent, a one Rudi Donati, who insisted we call him by his first name. Rudi knew Evan from prior cases and listened rapt to his recounting of the Botticelli mission. Gratifyingly, the man seemed to hold our agency in great esteem despite the fact that we had torn through his city without issuing the appropriate alert. Think of it this way: they now had a known arms dealer off the map, at least temporarily, and a possible lost masterpiece returned to the city. That granted us a certain leniency.

As for how Zann would fare legally, nobody knew. So far Donati had accepted our insistence that both she and Angelo had worked counter to the Baldi operation in cooperation with our agency but further questioning was bound to follow.

I was trying to figure out how to ensure that Zann received her press release complete with a photo of her holding the portrait, at the very least. Now I realized how unlikely that was given the circumstances. The press were outside the church now and nobody but the police were permitted to make an official statement. Add to that the authorities' reluctance to make any announcements until the portrait had been thoroughly examined, which, in official terms, could take months.

I eyed the wide shallow box sitting at the end of the table with anticipation. In my heart, I knew that the portrait was inside but my head warred another battle. What if it had been ruined by leaky roofs or seeping plaster? What if Botticelli had played a joke on his young friends or somebody else had found the portrait long ago, leaving the empty receptacle?

In the midst of this musing, the refectory door flew open and in came another policeman accompanied by a silver-haired woman. I may have gasped at the sight of Dr. Silvestri diving straight toward Angelo and definitely gaped when they embraced.

"My wife," Angelo said as he wiped tears from his eyes and hugged his exquisitely dressed spouse, who was now murmuring endearments in Italian, French, and, I swear, Latin.

"You two are married?" I exclaimed, rising. Across the table, Peaches looked ready to choke.

"She is a modern woman," Angelo said with a proud smile. "She keeps her own name but to me she gives her heart."

Silvestri released her husband and swooped on me like an elegant bird of prey. In seconds I was being hugged—not bussed, not like one of Nicolina's air-infused embraces, but a full-on squeeze. "To you I owe everything. Thank you, thank you many times over for saving my Angelo. Baldi would have killed him or removed his toes or some part of his anatomy equally useful."

When she released me all I could say was: "So that's how Angelo knew what I was searching for in the Laurentian?"

"Yes, yes," Silvestri said in perfect English. "I was to intercept you and discover what you sought or Angelo would be further harmed. Baldi expected that you might arrive at the Laurentian but had also posted others to watch for you in many other places across the city."

"And then Baldi tracked Zann as we headed for the Corsis and pulled the pieces together from there. You were a real pain in the neck that day," I added, still bristling.

She nodded while beaming away, her red lipstick a brilliant foil for her silver hair and severe black suit. "Thank you. I wished once to be on the stage."

"Hey," Peaches interrupted while stepping up to the group. "I was the one who got held up at the police station for hours being interrogated like a petty thief. Who's going to hug me to make it all better?" She looked down at the police officer standing near. "You, maybe?"

The officer caught enough of the gist to shake his head and step back.

"I will embrace you, Peaches," Angelo offered, holding his arms wide. "I am the one who called you a pickpocket. Come to Angelo and he will make it all better."

But before Peaches could take up the offer, as if she ever would, another pair of officers arrived, this time accompanying Giovanni and a man I didn't recognize.

"Giovanni!" I exclaimed, rushing forward. "At last! This is the moment we've all been waiting for."

"I could not believe when I heard that you had found it! Oh, blessed day! The news claims that a notorious gang has attempted to steal the Ognissanti's treasures."

"Half true," I said as he grasped both of my hands in his and held my gaze in an instant of shared professional camaraderie.

"Phoebe McCabe, it pleases me to introduce my supervisor, Dr. Alice Alessandro." We shook hands briefly.

"How did you know where to search?" Dr. Alice asked.

"It's complicated, but besides the sketch there was a letter—a clue from my brother," I replied, "plus I used intuition, deduction, and just plain luck."

"Brain bolt is more like it," Zann muttered from somewhere behind me.

Smiling, I made a round of introductions as Evan and Rudi stepped forward.

"Let us not wait a moment longer," Father Agosti urged. "Let us see what our blessed Father has kept hidden for all these centuries."

Everyone agreed and together we walked to the end of the long refractory trestle table where the leather container lay on a white linen towel.

Donning a pair of equally white gloves, Giovanni gently lifted the container from the table. "It does not appear in good condition," he said, anxiety leaking into his voice as he turned it around, studying the mold spots, the time-chewed effect of very old leather.

"But the basic structure has not yet been corrupted," said Angelo. "The box is firm. Feel it."

"Though Italy is basically a dry climate, when the rains come, they come with fervor. Let's hope the leather gave it some measure of protection. In any case, it has endured a long enough imprisonment," Evan remarked.

"And it's time for us to release its contents at last," Peaches said. "What are we waiting for, Giovanni?"

A hush descended over our gathering as Giovanni released the little brass catch at the end of the box and gently slid the contents into one hand while passing the empty container to the first helping hand. Evan did the honors there. Giovanni then gently placed a mottled reddish-brown rectangle on the linen fabric. For a moment all we could do was stare.

"What is it?" someone asked.

"It appears to be wrapped in cloth," Giovanni said.

"Velvet," I said, peering closer. "Possibly soaked in some kind of oil or resin. It will required careful removal since it appears to have hardened to some degree but it should come away without too much trouble." I gently poked it with my finger before donning the gloves Giovanni offered. "Does anyone have tweezers?"

Peaches stepped up with her roll of lockpicks and passed me a little tool that would work perfectly. While the others watched, I leaned forward and carefully plucked a clump of fabric away. It peeled back all in one piece.

"I'm guessing it must have been painted on wood with a layer of gesso and egg tempura mixed with oil," Giovanni said as I picked up another clump, which also lifted away from the surface.

"Botticelli must have wrapped it in this fabric to protect the painting against scratches or damp," I said.

Giovanni leaned over to pluck away the last solidified folds with his fingers.

As the fabric peeled back, the painting lay revealed as if glowing from some inner light. Our breaths caught. The sunlight streaming through the windows landed on the profile of a young woman who gazed away into the future against a cloudless sky. Her cheeks weren't pale as in the beauty standard of the time but ruddy as if she had been hard at work just moments before she donned that dress.

That dress. The golden-hued sleeve exposed in all its glory was a work of art in itself, a symphony of color and pattern depicting flowers, insects, and emblems all frolicking in their tiny satin embroidered frames as if any disturbance might set them free. Touch that quilted triangle holding the wasp and hear it buzz, brush that bright little bee worked in gold and pearls and see it fly. Each detail was so finely depicted that you could almost see the stitches, almost feel the silken gloss and texture beneath your fingers. Taken together, the images told a story of great importance to both subject and artist and maybe others, as well. They were beautiful, they were powerful, the piece both exquisitely wrought and masterfully painted. Overwhelmed by beauty, I broke into tears.

I wasn't the only one. Many of us were overcome with emotion that morning. To stand before a masterpiece, to be the first ones to lay eyes on something that beautiful after it had withstood five hundred years of captivity, and to know that you may have somehow helped set it free...

"Gabriela, I'm so sorry that you never got to see your gift," I whispered while I pulled myself from my state of wonder long enough to take photos. Time was running out.

"Gabriela who?" Giovanni asked.

"I will tell you at another time," I said, leaning closer to the painting with my phone.

Seconds later, the magic moment disintegrated all around me. Giovanni's phone rang; a knock came at the door sending Father Agosti scurrying away; both Rudi and Evan were suddenly on their phones. I knew that at any moment Gabriela's painting would be enclosed in darkness once again as it became the ownership—possibly contested—of the state and then ultimately the Uffizi. Theoretically it belonged to the church, which might have the option to keep it, but since all treasures technically belonged to Italy, nothing was ever straightforward where art was concerned.

Despite the legalities of ownership, it was the story behind the painting that I most wanted to liberate, a story built on filaments of proof entangled with the glory of art and the tenacity of the human spirit.

I had just finished photographing when Evan touched my arm. "It's Rupert and Nicolina at the Corsis' on the phone." Smiling, he passed me his cell. "They need us back in Tuscany."

Pressing the phone to my ear, Rupert spoke first. "Phoebe, congratulations! Another incredible coup on behalf of art preserved for all humanity, a momentous occasion worthy of accolades! Bravo, my friend! Soon the Agency of the Ancient Lost and Found will be on everyone's lips as though we are rescuers of time itself. I—"

"Thank you, Rupert, but we'll have to keep this short. They're packing up the painting now." I knew Rupert to be loquacious to a fault and, right then, I craved only to be alone with my thoughts.

But Nicolina came on next. "Brava, dear Phoebe! This is so exciting and a big coup for Italy, yes? Please make arrangements to return to the Corsis' by tomorrow morning and do bring my luggage so I will have something suitable to wear."

"Of course, but I—"

Rupert again. "Yes, indeed, Phoebe. Had you permitted me to finish I would have added that Piero has a significant announcement to make and has arranged a press conference tomorrow afternoon for all the relevant dignitaries. You must be in attendance, of course, but of equal importance, Nicolina, Seraphina, and I have no respectable transport to Florence that evening since all of our vehicles have been destroyed. Do hire us a proper ride, something suitably large and luxurious. A stretch limo will do nicely."

It was hard to get a word in edgewise. "Rupert, forgive me but I'm going to hand you back to Evan now," I said quickly. "I'm sure he'll know exactly what kind of vehicle will suit. See you tomorrow." Returning the phone to Evan, who caught my eye and smiled, I stepped away to watch the painting exit in the care of Giovanni and the police. As inevitable as that moment was, it left me feeling bereft.

Moments later, I tracked down Zann sitting in a deflated hunch against the far wall. Part of me wondered if I looked as physically spent as she did, but of course after the last few days, we must all look a wreck.

"Tomorrow we're all going back to the Corsi estate for a press conference," I told her. "I'm not exactly certain what that's all about but I see a prime opportunity for us to steal a moment to get that photo op for your dad. Have you been in touch with him?"

She gazed up at me. "Not yet. Afraid that any announcement will soon be followed with 'By the way, Dad, going to be extradited back home to stand trial for crimes against art. Might get to see you then.'"

"Oh, stop. You know we'll put in a good word for you. I really can't imagine you going to jail at the end of this, anyway. Remember you nailed Baldi. You're as much a hero here as anybody."

Her gaze dropped. "You know, I thought that if I succeeded, I'd feel such euphoria that it would keep me going for years but it's not like that. I just feel done in. It's like now that it's over, what's left?"

I swallowed hard and touched her shoulder. "Come. We all need a good rest. Let's return to the hotel. Tomorrow everything will seem much better."

That sounded exactly like something my mother would have said, which gave it a note of truth.

As I turned away, I nearly walked into Peaches. We strolled together toward the door. "I heard that we're going to the Corsis' for some big announcement tomorrow," she said, adding in a whisper, "and you just invited Zann?"

"She played a role in this, too. She deserves to be there."

"But she's such a wild card," she pointed out.

"Look at it this way: wild cards can take a game into a whole new direction; they can turn into a trump card at the last minute and even have the potential to play the winning hand."

"Yeah, and make on like a joker sometimes, too. Since when did you become a card shark?"

I laughed. "Since I started swimming in the deep end of the pool."

24

$\mathcal{I}$ must have slept for fourteen hours straight, awaking to a day as fresh and filled with possibilities as a blank canvas. I bounded out of bed and took my leg for a test drive around the room while sipping room-service coffee until I was satisfied that my body was in working order.

A shower resulted in wrestling my curls into line without the benefit of my usual smoothers, which were stuffed in my bag back at the Corsis'. I stared at my image in the mirror, grudgingly admitting that I did have something Medusa-like going on. To up the elegance factor, I donned my hyacinth silk blouse and dress black pants. There, ready for a press conference.

I'm telling you all this because it's so ordinary and sometimes a dose of ordinary can be just what's needed. Those few stolen minutes sitting in a chair by the window knitting also fit in that category—the bliss of simple pleasures.

Propping my phone open with a picture of Gabriela's painting applied balm to my spirit as I knit in shades of butter captive in silk. Long ago this artist loved the same things I did, maybe many of the same colors, but expressed her passions in design, fabric, thread, lace, and thousands of embroidered stitches. Sometimes the distance that separates us can be measured in the length of colored threads, and though I didn't know her story, I felt it in my heart. For me, that was enough.

My calm interlude soon ended. Time for the day—the rest of my life, in fact—to truly begin. I snatched a light breakfast at the buffet in the lobby before heading for the garden to await our ride. By 9:30 that morning, I knew a stretch limo would be waiting in the hotel driveway with a professional driver hired to take us to the countryside. Our luggage, the hotel assured us, would be duly stowed.

I was halfway across the garden when I saw him standing by the pergola lost in thought—Evan. There was no one else around. He turned and caught my eye and, as corny as it sounds, I felt a tremor through to my core. As he stepped toward me, he held out his one good arm.

Dropping my knitting bag in the grass, I strode up to him and took that hand, my attention fixed on those warm green-gray eyes while our fingers interlaced. I sensed that he wanted badly to take me into his arms but having only one available at the moment...

"I have to tell you something that I should have said sooner but just couldn't," I said.

The expression in that beautiful face shifted as if bracing himself for something painful.

"It's not that." I reached up and touched his cheek, something I'd been longing to do for days. Tracing the rise of his cheekbones with one finger, I continued. "I'm not going to tell you to leave me alone or to stop ambushing me with kisses and pyrotechnics, though that exploding Ferrari was a bit much."

He quirked a smile. "I wanted our first kiss to be spectacular."

"It was, believe me." I laughed. "But seriously, Evan, I need to explain myself."

"You don't need to explain yourself to me ever, Phoebe. I know that Noel—"

"No, please." My finger moved to his lips. "Let me finish. Yes, Noel kicked the stuffing out of me but in the end I realized he wasn't worth the anguish. What shocked me most was how much I was once willing to let my fixation with the man cloud my judgment, even bury my moral compass. It's like I permitted my brain cells to be sucked away."

He began kissing my fingers one by one. "I would never let your brain cells be sucked away. I love your brain cells, every single one of them. In fact, I adore your brain cells at least as much as I do the rest of you."

I tugged my hand away and laid my palm on his chest. "Listen to me, please."

"Sorry." Dropping his arm to his side, he stood still as if forcing himself not to touch me.

"I need to take things slow, really slow. I need to feel totally confident that I've restored my bearings enough to enter a relationship fully. I'm asking for patience. You must know how I feel about you. Of course I realize that you're nothing like Noel—no need to convince me there. It's not trust in you that's holding me back but trust in myself."

"Ask anything of me and it's yours. If it's time you need, then time it is. You've always been the one for me, Phoebe. I knew it from the day we first met but the divide between us in the early days was far too deep for me to cross. Now, just knowing that we're standing together on the same side at last is enough. I also have to tell you something while I have the chance. And it's important."

"Hey, you two." I turned to see Peaches waving from the gate. "The car's here."

Evan grasped my hand. "It's about Noel."

I turned back to face him. "What about Noel?"

"He's still alive. I wanted to tell you sooner but didn't have the opportunity. Our contacts inform us that he's holed up somewhere still recuperating."

"I know," I said. "Toby told me but I don't care where he is or what he's up to as long as he stays out of my way. Let him limp along with his weakened heart for all I care. I'm done."

He squeezed my hand. "If only it was that simple. Brace yourself, Phoebe. That bastard's been acting as Baldi's praefectus praetorio for the past two years. Remember how we couldn't figure out how he could amass the resources for his escape in Morocco?"

I gaped. "You mean he's been working for Baldi the whole time?"

"For the last two years, at least. After you destroyed his depot in Jamaica, Baldi must have made him an offer he couldn't refuse. It had probably been his plan to oust Baldi from the beginning, knowing how the bastard works. Now he must be emperor or whatever Roman war games they operate under."

"Shit! You mean I just played into his hands again?"

He gripped my fingers tighter. "Killing Baldi was probably just a lucky byproduct from his perspective."

"That's how Baldi knew about my 'lost-art sniffer dog' moniker—Noel told him! And that's how the bastard found out about Toby sending me those clues and maybe even why Zann was poached for the organization in the first place. Noel couldn't have known exactly where the painting was hidden. He needed me for that! I'll kill him, I swear I will!"

I was spinning out, I admit. Evan pulled me close with his one arm. "I'll finish him, Phoebe. That will be my gift to you, I promise."

"What's the holdup, you two?" Peaches had arrived. "Oh, this is looking passionate and it's about bloody time but the gang awaits."

I snatched back my hand and turned to her while blurting out all the relevant news and watching her grin evaporate.

Peaches always could swear much better than I ever could.

* * *

THE DRIVE through Tuscany was a glorious moving postcard overlaid by my seething anger. I knew I had to shove my emotions to a back burner to get through the day, maybe even through the year, but learning that Noel had clawed his way back into my life had left me shaken.

Though Peaches boiled along with me, the rest of our group seemed jolly enough. Angelo sat with his wife, Sylvie, in the back seat and Zann, Peaches, and I occupied the other seats with so much room between us that talking was difficult. Evan kept the driver company in the front, no doubt uncomfortable with having to relinquish automotive control. Actually, I was surprised when Angelo and Sylvie appeared at the hotel but apparently arrangements had been made without my knowing. Another car followed behind with Giovanni, Alice, and other Uffizi officials. It was as if we were off to a summer picnic in the countryside.

When at last the winery appeared on our right, the full impact of the Baldi occupation became clear—scarred earth where the Rover had crashed through the vineyard, scorch marks along the road and in the parking lot where the centurion minions had burned every car they could find.

We navigated around the debris still being cleaned by troops of guys in coveralls. A uniformed policewoman flagged us down to ask what we were up to. Apparently ingoing traffic was still being carefully screened while the investigation was in progress and entry was by invitation only. Once Evan explained our identities, the officer beamed and broke into an animated monologue commending us on our efforts. It was all Evan could do to politely extricate us so that we could continue up the hill toward the hamlet.

Halfway up the drive, Zann pointed out the stage being set up on the winery patio below. Gazing behind us, it became apparent that whatever press event the Corsis had planned, they had no intention of scrimping on the details. A platform had been constructed with festoons of ribbons and banners across the front of the dais, too far away to read clearly.

"What do you think they're planning?" Peaches asked.

"I have a pretty good idea but would hate to spoil their surprise," I said.

Peaches laughed. She'd already guessed, too, of course.

There was no room for the limo to enter the hamlet's arched gate so we climbed out. Behind us the car of Uffizi officials came to a halt also. My only thought was to head for the chapel before anyone else.

While Evan left instructions with the driver and Angelo recounted his adventures at the hamlet to his wife, Zann, Peaches, and I bolted up the drive toward the chapel. My only thought was to arrive without the need for explanations or long tedious greetings and salutations along the way. Those would come soon enough. I sensed that the villa was humming with activity behind the doors and windows as we scuttled past.

"Why are we going to the chapel first?" Zann asked.

"Because part of Gabriela's story lies here and I need to let it all seep onto me before the crowd arrives."

"Is this one of your brain bolts?" she asked.

"More like a brain whisper, if you must call it anything." And of course she had to call it something—Zann was a namer—but I could never quite explain what flowed through my mind in these moments.

The chapel seemed to welcome us. The door had been propped open by the same potted olive tree that had held me captive the day before only this time it was adorned with a big blue satin bow. For a moment I was afraid there'd be people inside but luckily the tiny chapel was empty.

I stepped into the nave and gazed around, my heart thumping in my chest. Now lights beamed down on the fresco and for a moment the three of us could stand agape. Everything appeared so much more vibrant under the lights despite the signs of damage and fading.

"Wow," Zann whispered. "What happened here?" She stepped closer to study the painted procession as I watched her follow the remains of the well-garbed citizens toward the altar. "Why would somebody deliberately chip away at what must have been a magnificent fresco?"

She was pointing at the two figures at the front, a man and a woman, both of whom were missing their head and torsos. Here, the plaster revealed deep gouges as if the painting had been vandalized with a sharp object. "This wasn't an accident of time or neglect but because somebody took a chisel to them all." She swung around and studied the rest of the procession. "All of their faces have been erased and some of their clothing, too. Why?"

"I don't know," I said, strolling down the aisle. "Somebody wanted to eradicate their identities, is my guess. The procession must have portrayed real people, citizens whose involvement here would be seen as dangerous."

"Either that or somebody came along later and wanted to erase all evidence of whatever this fresco commemorates," Peaches added.

"A wedding," I whispered.

"A wedding?" Zann marveled. "Why would a wedding be dangerous?"

"Perhaps because the bride and groom and many of the wedding party were involved in some kind of dangerous intrigue and needed to conceal their identities or maybe the fresco had been embedded with a code of some kind," I said, "like embedded in the clothing, for example."

Peaches turned to me. "You think this is Gabriela's wedding, don't you?"

"I do," I said, "but I don't know the details and can't prove a thing. I'm only working from instinct."

Stepping up to the wall behind the altar, I touched the scabs of white plaster above the remains of a beautifully portrayed gold-hued gown with a trailing vine motif along the hem. "Supposing this was Gabriela wearing her own gown at her own wedding—extraordinary given the constraints of the time. On the surface she was a tailor's daughter who would not be permitted to design these clothes let alone wear them, in Florence especially. Sumptuary laws forbade even the noble citizens of the day to wear such riches unless under certain circumstances. But for some reason, Gabriela escapes Florence with a piece of her own creation and arrives here in the spirit of celebration."

"How, why?" Zann asked.

I shook my head. "I don't know but I swear that this gown is the same one as in the Botticelli portrait. Not only are the colors that same lemon gold—at least as much as I can tell after all this time—but the scroll on the hem echoes the band edging the bodice."

I took out my phone and opened it to the portrait. "I thought Botticelli may have hidden the painting to preserve it against the purist fervor that Savonarola unleashed but maybe that was only part of the story. I'm thinking now that something else was afoot here, too."

"The references to the Medici are a clue," said Angelo, limping through the door arm in arm with his wife accompanied by Evan, Giovanni, Dr. Alice, and a man and woman I didn't recognize.

"Yes," I said, turning to face them. "Maybe there was a message embedded in that sleeve symbology designed to be understood by a select few, a message sent by Lorenzo de' Medici himself by way of Gabriela's gown."

"And perhaps that message was multifaceted and contained not only the symbology but something else—a letter or key, for instance," Evan said, catching and holding my gaze.

"Yes, perhaps," I said, smiling at him. "Botticelli knew that the portrait, which was to be a wedding gift to his two young friends, also hid a dangerous secret and made certain that it did not fall into the wrong hands, which explains the effort he took to keep it hidden. This was a period of intense political intrigue among warring families and I believe that this dress, and in fact it's wearer, played a role in some perilous intrigue that involved the Medici. That it made it this far implies that the conspiracy, if that's what it was, saw some measure of success and that Gabriela may have had reason to celebrate, if only briefly."

"That is a bold statement to make without substantiation," said a woman in the Uffizi group. Her eyes sparkled and her expression was neither unkind nor confrontational, just bristling with scholarly challenge.

"It is," I agreed, "but I can't prove a thing. Bear with me for a moment further," I said, passing my phone open to the Botticelli portrait through the gathering. "Let me read what I can untangle from the clues in the sleeve. There are the crest and the ring, both recognizable Medici symbols, which indicate the family's involvement. There is the Vespucci wasp—another great family and Medici allies as well as a symbol that simultaneously means trouble—plus the plum for fidelity, the goose for vigilance, and the bee for work."

"And the sparrow, lemon, and peach denoting humility, marital fidelity, and silence in that order," Angelo added.

I smiled. "Taken together, I read that someone hardworking and lowly of birth promises her loyalty to the Medici and the Vespucci families while acknowledging the need for vigilance and silence. That the lemon indicates marriage brings us to this chapel. This is where the designer and tailor's daughter, Gabriela di Domenico, was secretly wed to the artist Filippino Lippi with a gathering of Florentine citizens in attendance either in reality or by imaginative proxy. Hard to say who really attended since obviously Mars and Venus also received an invitation and are racing through the clouds to arrive in time." Everyone turned toward the mythological figures flying to attend the ceremony.

"And of course Jesus and the saints are already here waiting over the altar. This was a Christian ceremony, after all, but not one that excluded the classical deities, which was completely in the spirit of Lorenzo de' Medici's Renaissance Florence," Evan added.

An outcry of wonder and disbelief erupted from the Uffizi audience. Somebody clapped—Giovanni, I think. "But that is quite extraordinary," said a gentleman nattily dressed in a light linen suit, "and though there is little to substantiate your theories I commend your imaginative telling, Signorina McCabe!"

"On the other hand, Signore Luffi, do gaze about you," said Giovanni. "What remains of this fresco does look very much in the style of Filippino

Lippi, in particular the manner in which the forest and books are rendered throughout the scene. I've only seen such a style in the extraordinary *Apparition of the Virgin to St. Bernard.*"

"And what we see of the clothing appears very much like Botticelli or at least influenced by him," I said. "Botticelli loved fashion, which is how his friendship with this talented designer began. Gabriela emerged as an artist in her own right and joined this esteemed circle in secret. I believe she even designed the fanciful clothing which robed Botticelli's goddesses and muses."

"But Filippino did not share Botticelli's affinity for flowing gowns and windblown hair," the Uffizi woman pointed out,

"No," I agreed, "but he did have an affinity for those who did love them and, after all, this fresco was his celebration, too. Later, Filippino's work became very mysterious and animated. It could be jarring, almost electric," I said. "If he were alive today, he'd probably be painting fantasy since so much of what we see in his more mature works unleashes a kind of energy implied in the conflict between the Christian religion and the Greek and Roman philosophy and polytheism rife at the time. I'm guessing that Filippino had little patience for the restrictions Savonarola imposed and we know that he left Florence to work elsewhere for years. Along the way, he briefly ended up here."

"In my family exists the rumor that Filippino Lippi painted this fresco under extraordinary circumstances." We turned as Piero Corsi arrived along with Rupert.

"Can you provide more detail, signore?" the Uffizi gentleman asked.

Piero smiled sadly. "That is not possible. Whatever occurred here was deliberately hidden and all evidence destroyed. My father researched the Florence archives extensively but found nothing. We know only that the Medici and the Corsi were allies and it is possible that they were involved in some kind of conspiracy, but how Filippino came to paint in our humble chapel is unknown."

"Phoebe's theory," Evan said, "one worth considering since I can testify to her incredible talent for unpicking stories silenced by time, is that the artist may have commemorated his own wedding right here in this chapel."

"But we need proof, signore," the Uffizi gentleman said.

"Indeed you do," Rupert agreed. "Nevertheless, there is proof and then there is truth and the two are not necessarily conjoined. I say that Phoebe speaks the truth, not all of which can be nailed to the wall of documented substantiation."

"What happened to Gabriela, Phoebe?" Peaches asked.

"I don't know," I said, staring at the wearer of the glorious golden gown standing at the altar with both her head and torso damaged with such deliberate finality. "I wish I did. I desperately wish I knew the end of her story. There is no indication that she traveled with Filippino to Rome or Prato or even returned to Florence ever again."

Piero clapped his hands to divert our attention. "I regret to interrupt this fascinating discussion but my other guests gather below the hill in readiness for my announcement. Come, my friends. Let us leave this for now and proceed to the winery."

* * *

SUMMER AIR ALIGHT with warmth and promise blew across the hills as we descended the drive toward the winery that afternoon. A tangle of birds flitted across the cloudless sky and the roses climbing the low stone walls along the driveway leading down to the winery punched rich fragrance straight to our senses.

This glory almost erased the scorched earth and the faint scent of petrol now covered by fresh gravel. All signs of violence and explosives had been hastily buried, and had I not known what had taken place only a few nights prior, I might have believed it had never happened.

The knots in my neck began to loosen and I began to consider the possibility of taking a vacation. Someplace remote. Maybe a beach with diving possibilities. I pictured a sailboat afloat on an azure sea. Perhaps I'd even invite somebody to join me but first I needed to tidy up loose ends.

On our way down the hill, I stepped beside a solitary Zann and laid a hand on her arm. "I agreed to get you that press release and that's exactly what I'll do before this day is over."

She nodded. "Thanks, Phoebe. After all I put you through I wouldn't blame you if you just turfed me."

"Yes, you would," I laughed, drawing her toward the wall as the others passed by.

"Yeah, I would," she agreed.

"But I have to tell you something first and it won't be any easier for you to hear than it was for me: Noel is still alive."

She stopped and stared. "What?"

"My taser damaged his heart but didn't kill him. Apparently he's hanging out somewhere recuperating."

Her face blanched whiter than a bleached ghost. "Shit, no," she gasped.

683

"Shit, yes, and he's been Baldi's top dog or whatever Roman playacting they named their second-in-command. Evan's Interpol rumor mill suggests he might replace Baldi as emperor."

Zann gaped. "We have to kill him!"

"Why does everyone keep saying that? We don't have to kill anybody," I pointed out. "As long as he stays off my radar and out of my life, we'll just leave him alone."

"How can he be off our radar when he had to have been behind this whole Botticelli thing? He must have informed Baldi that the agency had the sketch long ago and that's why Baldi hired me. He's been pulling our strings in hope of hanging us both!"

I took her by the shoulders. "Calm down. Listen carefully: I am not going after Noel Halloren. I work for the Agency of the Ancient Lost and Found and our mission is to locate lost or stolen art, not to chase down the head of arms cartels." I gave her a little shake. "I reacted the same way you have but I've put it into perspective and now you must, too. Look, we beat him, okay? This is our triumph, *your* triumph. Enjoy the moment. Come on, let's set up your press release."

Linking Zann's arm in mine, I race-walked her down the hill until we had sidled up to Piero. "Signore Corsi, as you've probably heard, we found what in all probability is a Botticelli painting by following the clues found among your Laurentian papers and elsewhere. I realize that the entire Baldi occupation must have been traumatic for your family and I'm very sorry about that but luckily no one was hurt. We're very sorry for the whole debacle, aren't we, Zann?"

"Very sorry, yes," Zann said as if shaking herself into the present.

"Right," I said. "Still, I trust you agree that finding a lost Botticelli is worth celebrating, even if it didn't unfold the way we had planned. Hopefully we are now forgiven?"

Ignoring Zann, he turned to me. "You are forgiven, yes. Besides, not all of my family found the occupation so traumatic—my wife and I, certainly, but my boys they found it thrilling. Like a television show, yes? Bad guys and gunfire. Gunfire does not thrill me but we adults see these things differently."

"We do," I acknowledged.

"So, I have heard the news about the Botticelli from your friends," he continued. "All has been explained. My father would be so excited to know this. Perhaps he does." His gaze briefly swerved upward. "Sir Rupert tells me that the discovery must be kept secret for now."

"Yes, apparently," I said, relieved that there appeared to be no hard feelings.

"It will be tied up in red tape and officiousness for a while longer. Meanwhile, I want you to know that Zann played a huge role in our discovery. If it wasn't for her, all might remain shrouded in mystery, lost to us for decades, maybe forever. That initial sketch she found helped lead us there in the end and she assisted every step of the way. Everything she said was true."

Zann unlinked our arms and stepped over to Piero's other side. "So am I forgiven, Petro?" she asked.

He flashed a tense smile. "Stop calling me that, Suzanna. I am Piero to you now, nothing else."

"Sorry. So, Piero, will you see now how this fool of a girl that was me was tricked? I swore I would make things right again and hopefully now I have."

Piero turned to the woman who had regained some measure of her old self —quick, confident step, eyes twinkling with energy. "I forgive you, Suzanna. Even the letter you removed from our collection is back where it belongs so all is in the past."

She grinned. "Fabulous! Thanks a bunch."

"But Suzanna and I have one more request," I added quickly. "We'd like to make a statement about Zann finding the sketch at the end of your press conference. Just a couple of brief statements about her locating a canister long ago that was then stolen on the spot by—"

"A cutthroat, devious bastard of a boyfriend who we will publicly name and shame," Zann interjected.

"Or not," I said quickly. "We may not be able to mention the Botticelli painting but we can make a statement about that sketch. I won't mention your library, if you'd rather I not."

"Mention it, please!" Piero exclaimed, lifting his hands upward. "By then the Corsis' Medici holdings will be public knowledge for I am donating the entire collection to the Laurentian Library in my family's name."

"You are? How wonderful and thank you!" I clapped my hands together as if in delighted surprise. "Isn't that wonderful, Zann?"

"Fantastic and long overdue," she said.

This was becoming harder than I expected. "By the way, my announcement is for the sole purpose of sending to Zann's father to let him see that his daughter has been instrumental in preserving art," I added.

"To set the matter straight," Zann added.

"Very well. I am certain Signore Masters will be relieved to see such evidence. Now please excuse me for I must assist my wife with the arrangements below."

I had the sense that he couldn't wait to escape. Soon he was dashing ahead down the hill only pausing long enough to call back: "I will invite you to the podium when the time is right."

I waved at him while saying under my breath: "I knew it. My bet was on the Corsi collection being the center of this press release all along. I wonder what changed his mind?"

"We can thank Nicolina in part for that," Rupert remarked as he and Peaches arrived beside me, arm in arm. Evan, I noted, was still behind us entertaining the Uffizi contingent. "She launched a concerted effort to convince the Corsis to donate the collection immediately, saying that it belonged to Florence and not to a single family hidden from the public eye, regardless of how they came upon it." He paused to catch his breath while Peaches patted his arm and told him to take his time. "At first, Piero stated he wished only to bequeath it upon his passing should his sons agree…but the boys were vehement that the collection be shared at once. Do you know that Enrico is already fluent in Latin and Spanish, a prodigy, much like myself at his age?"

"Were you a really a prodigy, Rupe?" Peaches asked.

"Most definitely. My mother hardly knew what to do with me I was so advanced for my years."

"I can just imagine," she said mildly. "I just had a mental flash of a younger you spouting on and on about something."

"I certainly do not 'spout.' I—" he protested.

Time to intercept. "Did Nicolina also help to pull together this press release in what can only be considered record time?" I asked before Rupert launched into a description of his youthful proclivities and the two began squabbling.

Rupert adjusted the ascot and sighed in satisfaction. "She did, indeed. Oh, to be a countess in Italy! All that was required was to place a few requests in the correct quarters, and before Piero even knew what was happening, the media were nigh on tripping over themselves to receive an invitation. I understand that all the major networks will be represented."

"Everybody?" Zann asked. "Like CNN and BBC?"

"Both and all, I understand," Rupert said. "They are all syndicated apparently."

Zann grinned. "Well, we'd better get down there, then."

Good, I thought. The Noel bomb had been forgotten and we were moving on.

As we approached the steps leading to the Corsis' extravagant patio, Evan disengaged himself from the Uffizi party and joined us while Peaches steered Zann and Rupert away.

"Did you hear the nature of the Corsi press release?" he asked, stepping beside me.

"I did," I said, smiling up at him. For a moment all we did was smile at one another, a little inanely, I admit. Temporarily all my worries evaporated in the light of his gaze.

But the sound of Piero's voice over the loudspeaker prompted us to pick up our pace and soon we were joining the others while accepting glasses of wine from the circulating servers. On a dais overlooking the vineyard, Corsi, Alexandra, and their two sons stood flanked by a radiant Nicolina and a slightly less grumpy-looking Seraphina, everyone smiling and nodding.

"Hello, my friends, I welcome you to the Corsi wine estates on this auspicious occasion," Piero began, and went on to introduce the Uffizi officials, representatives from the Laurentian Library, local dignitaries, and Nicolina and Sir Rupert Fox representing the Agency of the Ancient Lost and Found. Smartphones recorded clips for later news releases with each syndicate eagerly catching every word.

When Piero described his ancient family's connection to the famed Medici family and announced his extraordinary donation, a collective gasp was heard throughout the gathering. A buzz of hushed comments followed. Piero raised his hand and went on to tell the tale of the possible Filippino Lippi connection, inviting people to tour the chapel following the ceremony, and even held aloft a Medici Book of Hours to tease the audience with the riches they might view in the future.

I stood rapt, admiring Piero's flare for dramatics as he bowed to each of the dignitaries in turn. When his family left the stage and joined the guests, Piero opened the microphone for questions. Following that, Dr. Sylvie Silvestri took the stage accompanied by the head of the Laurentian Library to formally accept the largess. More speeches, more applause.

When I sensed that the presentation might finally be winding down, Zann tapped my arm. "I need your phone to film my moment of fame to send to my dad," she said. Beside her stood the Corsis' eldest son. "Enrico here is going to film the moment while we go onstage."

"All right," I said, taking out my phone, "but stick to my script, okay? I'm going to claim your assistance in the discovery of a probable Botticelli sketch now in the care of the Uffizi. I will state that it was stolen decades ago but that you helped us relocate it with considerable risk. I will imply that the rest of the story will be released later. In the meantime, just nod and look pleased.

No public commentary. No answering of questions. It's not like you're accepting an Academy Award or something."

"That's all you're going to say—no mention of scumbag Noel, Baldi, or the painting found in the Ognissanti?" she asked.

"Zann, you can't possibly have missed the police decree insisting that those events remain off-camera while under investigation. The retrieval of the sketch is enough. Your dad knows the backstory, anyway. Oh, look, Piero's giving us the signal." I passed my phone to Enrico. "Let's go."

Minutes later, Zann and I were invited to the stage. After introductions and applause, I leaned into the microphone, assuming my most official tone, and said: "And I'd like to acknowledge the important role Suzanna Masters played in the return of a probable Botticelli sketch of considerable importance which is now in the care of the Uffizi. I will post photos of this sketch on the Agency of the Lost and Found's website later today but in the meantime please join me in commending the archaeologist Suzanna Masters."

A chorus of exclamations and questions mingled with applause burst from the crowd. Zann stepped in front of me and grabbed the microphone from my hand. "Thank you, thank you. I dedicate this moment to my dad, Dr. David Masters, who always said I could be anything I wanted, go anywhere I wanted as long as I never lost sight of my goals. I haven't, Dad! I made it! And here I am a member of the illustrious Agency of the Ancient Lost and Found!"

I tried to wrest the mic away but she held tight.

"It's been a long time coming," Zann continued, "and began when I was just a young archaeologist hoodwinked by a ruthless bastard who has since become head of a powerful arms cartel. Noel Halloren, listen up: you have the Agency of the Ancient Lost and Found to contend with now, do you hear? There'll be no place you can hide your miserable face with us on your heels!"

Piero slipped in front of Zann while I snatched back the mic. In seconds, he was stating that the official part of the program was over and to enjoy the wine and stroll the property as his guests. Seraphina and I were leading Zann offstage when I glimpsed Peaches's stricken face, saw Rupert appearing to be on the verge of a cardiac arrest, and caught Evan retrieving my phone from Enrico's hands.

I knew without being told that the clip would soon go viral, that our collective lives had just become a whole lot more complicated.

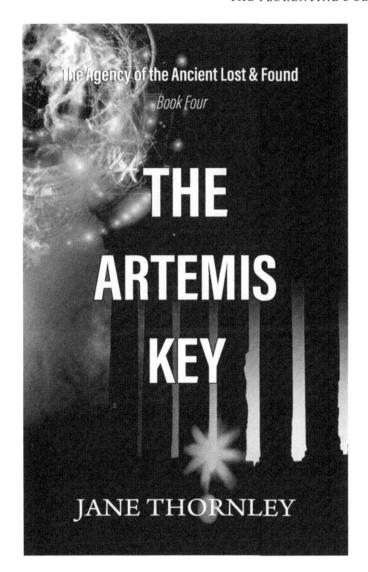

AFTERWORD

History is packed with untold stories and millions of muted voices tucked between layers of apparently ridged facts. I love nothing better than to unpack these stories while embedding them within the historical context. Fact is not always about truth. Sometimes we have to color the details in fiction in order to get at the essence of the story.

Did Gabriela di Domenico exist? No, but there are records of Lorenzo de' Medici using a tailor by the name of Domenico for many of his considerable wardrobe needs. Women were not allowed to openly design and create full clothing ensembles under any circumstances. They labored behind closed doors, piecemeal style, permitted to work their craft of embroidery or sewing as cottage work while remaining hidden behind the powerful men who ran the guilds. But how could a talented woman not bristle under such restrictions? What if she had ideas for exquisite designs but could only exercise them hidden behind a sympathetic male family member?

Florence, which had grown wealthy on the trade of rich textiles and beautiful apparel, had strict sumptuary laws that tried to curb any display of wealth and extravagance. One only has to gaze at Renaissance portraits to understand the irony there. Wealthy women who wore these exquisite designs —and there were many as the middle-class coffers grew with the textile trade —were forced to travel the streets shrouded in cloaks that hid their bodies head to toe. One eyewitness remarked that it was like watching a large moving tent cross the street. Should the fashion police catch sight of anyone, male or female, nobility or middle class, wearing excess fabric or too much of this or that, they could be fined on the spot.

Part of this curbing of luxury was based on the Christian values of poverty and simplicity. The devout Florentines worried about their souls while they grew rich on the trade of luxury items. The very same society (which included a bishop) who assassinated Lorenzo de' Medici's younger brother inside a church during the Pazzi Conspiracy, no doubt attended mass every Sunday with the rest of the devout. More irony.

The stage was thus set for Fra Girolamo Savonarola to arrive preaching the end of corrupt clergymen and the return to Jesus's teaching of simplicity and humility. He called for the end of secular art and culture that cut to the quick of the Florentine's creative soul. We will never know what beauty was burned during the Bonfire of the Vanities but there are accounts that Botticelli, himself a convert, threw his own paintings onto the flames.

Did Botticelli preserve at least one portrait for a young friend and his once apprentice, Filippino Lippi, her betrothed, as a wedding present? Here's where fiction takes over. Though the painting does not exist, the history of the Ognissanti church in Florence is true. That it was Botticelli's neighborhood church is fact and logically it could make an excellent hiding place for an artist who also painted a fresco in its nave. Which brings up the matter of that strange message written onto his fresco *Saint Augustine in his Study*. That text really does exist and was believed to read as I described until very recently when a new interpretation surfaced. Naturally, I prefer the original, as nonsensical as it first appears!

As for the friars helping Phoebe locate the painting, that, too, is pure fiction. The church is now the property of the state, though the Franciscans act as caretakers. The Corsi family is also fictive, though the location of their estate exists as half fiction, half reality, since it is based on the marvelous Tuscan hamlet B and B, the Castello di Gargonza, in Tuscany where I brought several knitting tours long ago. There exists both a chapel and a tower, though neither resemble those found in *The Florentine's Secret*.

One more thing, my reading friends: Gabriela. Sometimes a character strides through an author's head demanding to tell her story, and the more I researched Renaissance Florence, the more demanding she became. Gabriela will thus become the focus of another novel tentatively named *Spirit in the Fold*, part of the dual timeline *Time Shadows* series where the questions regarding Gabriela's secret assignation for the Medici will become revealed. I hope you will enjoy even more historical detail from the perspective of a creative woman trapped inside Renaissance Florence. I anticipate this novel's completion in 2022.

However, let's not forget that Phoebe has her hands full, too. Please join me for *The Artemis Key*, book 4 of the Agency of the Ancient Lost and Found, coming in December 2021, and if you'd like to see my research details and learn some interesting bits I discovered along the way, please join my newsletter here: The Agency f the Ancient Lost & Found newsletter .

Jane

ABOUT THE AUTHOR

JANE THORNLEY is an author of historical mystery thrillers with a humorous twist. She has been writing for as long as she can remember and when not traveling and writing, lives a very dull life—at least on the outside. Her inner world is something else.

With over twelve novels published and more on the way, she keeps up a lively dialogue with her characters and invites you to eavesdrop by reading all of her works.

To follow Jane and share her books' interesting background details, special offers, and more, please join her newsletter here:

NEWSLETTER SIGN-UP

Made in the USA
Las Vegas, NV
26 May 2025

22746571R00384